August 3, 2010

Dear Norman,

A bisl Yiddishkayt for your reading enjoyment.

Love,
Rebecca

Folktales of the Jews

Volume 2

Tales from Eastern Europe

The publication of this book is made possible
through these generous gifts:

Lloyd E. Cotsen
In honor of my great-grandparents and my grandparents,
who came out of Eastern Europe

The Maurice Amado Foundation

National Endowment for the Humanities

National Foundation for Jewish Culture

Special Gifts

Harold and Geraldine Cramer

David Lerman and Shelley Wallock, celebrating the graduate school, college, and high school graduations of their children

Mr. and Mrs. Howard S. Richmond,
in memory of Rose and Edgar Burton

Gayle and David Smith, in memory of their parents: Judge Edward and Ruth Rosenwald and Robert Smith and Evelyn Lieberman

*

Dr. D. Walter Cohen

Barry and Carol Nove

*

Rabbi Marc D. Angel · Alan J. Bloch and Nancy M. Berman · Dr. and Mrs. Edward H. Bossen
Ambassador and Mrs. Edward E. Elson · Allan R. Frank · Ellen P. Goodman · Daniel A. Harris
Phyllis M. Holtzman · Charles S. Houser · Jerome Allen Kellner
Mr. and Mrs. A. Leo Levin · Mary M. Pernicone · Rabbi Aaron M. Petuchowski · Denise H. Portner
Jerome J. Shestack · Rabbi and Mrs. Jonathan A. Stein · Dr. Harold and Phyllis Teplitz
E. Kinney Zalesne and Scott Siff

*

Emanuel M. Abrams · Mark and Michelle Abramson · Rabbi Richard F. Address · Libby R. Adelman
Mr. and Mrs. Sanford M. Autor · Ellen Barr · Larry Berkin · Stephen A. Bernard · Stephen Best
Steven A. Bleier · Eugene Borowitz · Dr. and Mrs. Jonas Brachfeld · Benjamin H. Bruckner
Rabbi Steven D. Burton · Dr. and Mrs. Norman Chassin · Nyles Cole · Wendy Fein Cooper
Rabbi Maurice S. Corson · Samuel M. Ehrenhalt · Bella Ruth Ehrenpreis
Jacqueline Koch Ellenson and David Ellenson · Melvin Fastow · Nathan B. Feinstein
Jan Fischer · Rabbi Wayne M. Franklin · The Gendler Family Foundation · Abraham J. Gittelson
Mr. and Mrs. David Goldberg · Dr. and Mrs. Kenneth B. Goldblum · Dr. and Mrs. Martin I. Goldstein
Mr. and Mrs. Alvin A. Gordon · Rabbi Daniel B. Gropper · Anne Helfgott · Rabbi Jacob Herber
Rabbi Howard and Joan Hersch · Highland Park Conservative Temple
Muriel W. Horowitz · Rabbi and Mrs. S. Robert Ichay
Institute for Jewish-Christian Understanding of Muhlenberg College
Rabbi and Mrs. Ronald Jacobs · Berton H. and Ellen B. Kaplan · Lewis S. Kapnek · Hazel B. Karp
Mr. and Mrs. Harry Kesten · Jeffrey Kichen · Sybil-Frances Kimbrig · Sam and Jessica Kimelman · Neil Kuchinsky
Joan A. Larsen · Rabbi Robert and Ruth Layman · Dr. and Mrs. Michael Leinwand · Dr. Reevan and Natalie Levine
Dr. and Mrs. Joe S. Levy · Mr. Robert and Honorable Roberta K. Levy · Herbert A. Lippitz · Bonnie Lipton
David Litan · Rabbi Joseph Mendelsohn · Cantor Claire G. Metzger · Dr. Randall and Rosebeth Miller
Captain and Mrs. Joseph R. Morgan · Hazzan Diane J. Nathanson · Irving R. Newman
Mr. and Mrs. Reynold F. Paris · Rochelle Pearl · Dr. and Mrs. David M. Pollack · Janet Greenstein Potter
Robert S. Rendell · Lawrence A. Riemer · Dr. and Mrs. Daniel S. Romm · Rabbi Richard B. and Lois S. Safran
Gideon Samet · Mr. and Mrs. Jacob L. Schachter · Mr. and Mrs. Stephen Schork · Bernice B. Schumer
Rabbi Joel M. Schwab · Martin Schwarzschild · Allen L. Shapiro · Rabbi Marion Shulevitz
Drs. Jeffrey L. and Cynthia G. Silber · Cantor Rhoda Silverman, Temple Emanuel of Baltimore
Norman and Ruth Spack · Horace A. Stern · Mark and Marsha Strauss-Cohn · Mr. and Mrs. Jerome P. Subar
Clergy Discretionary Fund of Temple Israel · Lisbet O. Temple
The Honorable David G. Trager and Ms. Roberta E. Weisbrod · Deborah and Michael Troner · Kenneth Turan
Washington Hebrew Congregation · Seth P. Waxman · Felicia P. Weber · N. William Weinstein
Arthur S. Weinstock · Alvin L. Weiss · Mrs. Simon L. Weker · Kenneth Wishnia
Rabbi Jeffrey Wohlberg · Rabbi David Wolpe

FOLKTALES of the Jews

VOLUME 2

TALES FROM EASTERN EUROPE

Edited and with Commentary by
Dan Ben-Amos

Dov Noy, Consulting Editor

Ellen Frankel, Series Editor

Tales Selected from the Israel Folktale Archives Named in Honor of Dov Noy,
The University of Haifa
and
Translated by Leonard J. Schramm

Illustrations by Ira Shander

2007 • 5768
The Jewish Publication Society
Philadelphia

JPS is a nonprofit educational association and the oldest and foremost publisher of Judaica in English in North America. The mission of JPS is to enhance Jewish culture by promoting the dissemination of religious and secular works, in the United States and abroad, to all individuals and institutions interested in past and contemporary Jewish life.

Copyright © 2007 by The Jewish Publication Society
Commentary © 2007 by Dan Ben-Amos
Illustrations © 2007 by Ira Shander

First edition. All rights reserved.

No part of this book may be reproduced or transmitted in any form or by any means, electronic or mechanical, including photocopy, recording, or any information storage or retrieval system, except for brief passages in connection with a critical review, without permission in writing from the publisher:

The Jewish Publication Society
2100 Arch Street
Philadelphia, PA 19103
www.jewishpub.org

Design and Composition by Pageworks

Manufactured in the United States of America

07 08 09 10 11 12   10 9 8 7 6 5 4 3 2 1

Library of Congress Cataloging-in-Publication Data

Folktales of the Jews / Dan Ben-Amos, editor; Dov Noy, consulting editor ; Ellen Frankel, series editor ; translated by Leonard J. Schramm ; illustrations by Ira Shander.
 — 1st ed.
   v. cm.
   "Tales selected from the Israel Folktale Archives named in honor of Dov Noy."
   Includes bibliographical references and indexes.
   Contents: 1. Tales from the Sephardic dispersion / edited and with commentary by Dan Ben-Amos.
   ISBN 978-0-8276-0829-0 (volume 1)
   ISBN 978-0-8276-0830-6 (volume 2)
   1. Jews—Folklore. 2. Legends, Jewish. 3. Tales. 4. Legends, Jewish—History and criticism. 5. Tales—History and criticism. 6. Sephardim—Folklore. I. Noy, Dov. II. Frankel, Ellen. III. Ben-Amos, Dan. IV. Arkhiyon ha-sipur ha-'amami be-Yisra'el (Haifa, Israel)
GR98.F65 2006
398.2089'924—dc22
                                                                              2006014753

JPS books are available at discounts for bulk purchases for reading groups, special sales, and fundraising purchases. Custom editions, including personalized covers, can be created in larger quantities for special needs. For more information, please contact us at marketing@jewishpub.org or at this address: 2100 Arch Street, Philadelphia, PA 19103.

Contents

Foreword	xi
Acknowledgments	xv
Introduction to Volume 2	xvii
A Note on the Commentaries	xli

Tales of the Supernatural

1. The Three-Day Fair in Balta (IFA 708)	2
2. The Kaddish (IFA 18159)	12
3. The House Vanished with All Its Inhabitants (IFA 7290)	21
4. The Rabbi Who Was Tricked (IFA 779)	26
5. The Demons and Spirits under the Fingernails (IFA 8792)	33
6. The Treasure (IFA 8256)	48
7. The Bottle of Oil from the Holy Land (IFA 4024)	53

Hasidic Tales

8. Rebbe Shmelke's Matzos (IFA 237)	58
9. The Unforgotten Melody (IFA 5794)	64
10. The Power of a Melody (IFA 5793)	70
11. The Happy Man (IFA 12214)	76
12. How Rothschild Became Wealthy (IFA 18601)	81
13. Why Rebbe Levi Yitzḥak of Berdichev Deviated from His Custom (IFA 7612)	92
14. The Blessing of Elijah the Prophet on Yom Kippur (IFA 960)	102
15. Rebbe Pinḥas'l of Korets (IFA 9797)	109
16. The Karliner Rebbe's Prescription (IFA 7912)	118
17. The Merit of the Third Sabbath Meal (IFA 5361)	123
18. The Apostate Who Made the Tenth for a Minyan (IFA 4936)	133

Holocaust Tales

19. The Fireflies on Rosh Hashanah Night in Lodz Ghetto (IFA 2361)	140
20. The Miracle of the White Doves (IFA 11165)	144

Historical Tales

21. The Exodus on Purim in the Town of Yampol (IFA 3892)	152
22. What Really Caused World War I (IFA 14026)	162

Tales between Jews and Non-Jews

23. The *Shofar* of the Messiah (IFA 6306)	168
24. The Redemption of Captives (IFA 4813)	186
25. The Long "Ḥad Gadya" (IFA 7211)	192
26. The Two Friends (IFA 3222)	202
27. The Gentile Beggar's Secret (IFA 4541)	207
28. The Boy Who Was Kidnapped and Brought to Russia (IFA 18140)	214
29. The Jew Who Returned to His People (IFA 8915)	221
30. The Boots Made from a Torah Scroll (IFA 8257)	229
31. The Gentile Who Wanted to Screw the Jew (IFA 18136)	236

Moral Tales

32. The Old Couple and Their Children (IFA 3364)	244
33. With the Rebbe's Power (IFA 19892)	250
34. Gossip Is Worse Than Profaning the Sabbath (IFA 5609)	255
35. The Tailor Who Was Content with His Lot (IFA 8255)	263
36. A Poor Man's Wisdom Is Scorned (IFA 13498)	269
37. A Change of Place Is a Change of Luck (?) (IFA 14260)	273
38. God Will Help (IFA 18130)	278
39. The Poisoned Cake (IFA 551)	282
40. There Is No Truth in the World (IFA 8004)	288
41. Everyone Prefers His Own Bundle of Troubles (IFA 14460)	306
42. Reb Zusha the Shoemaker (IFA 19949)	313
43. "As Face Answers to Face in Water" (IFA 20439)	317
44. Who Has the Right to Benefit from the Ten Commandments? (IFA 7755)	326
45. The Neighbor in Paradise (IFA 5377)	334
46. A Trial in Heaven (IFA 19585)	338
47. White Flowers, Red Flowers (IFA 18156)	342

Folktales

48. The King's Three Daughters (IFA 7202)	348
49. A Boy and Girl Who Were Destined for Each Other (IFA 18132)	356
50. The Three Young Men (IFA 6098)	363
51. The Poor Man Who Became Rich (IFA 8021)	372
52. The Stolen Ring (IFA 7812)	381
53. The Money Hidden in the Cemetery (IFA 4032)	387
54. Catch the Thief; or Don't Put Too Much Trust in a Pious Person (IFA 14962)	398

Humorous Tales

55. I Came From Mád and Returned to Mád (IFA 6814)	404
56. The Jewish Innkeeper (IFA 4815)	410
57. Little Fish, Big Fish (IFA 8889)	418
58. Three Complaints (IFA 8794)	422
59. The Elderly Cantor (IFA 6655)	427
60. What Kind of Congregants I've Got! (IFA 13908)	431
61. What Kind of Rabbi We've Got in This Town! (IFA 13909)	434
62. Half Is Mine and Half Is Yours (IFA 6976)	437
63. A Visit by Elijah the Prophet (IFA 3955)	446
64. The Emissary From the World to Come (IFA 2826)	452
65. Froyim Greidinger Revives the Dead (IFA 7127)	459
66. The Death of a Wicked Heretic (IFA 21021)	466
67. Who Had It Better? (IFA 21022)	473
68. The Shammes Who Became a Millionaire (IFA 14351)	477
69. I Have No Place to Rest (IFA 18592)	480
70. Stalin Tests His "Friends" (IFA 14263)	483
71. Communism and Religion (IFA 14264)	486

Abbreviations	489
Narrators	493
Collectors	505
Bibliography	512
Motif Indexes	589
Tale Type Indexes	608
General Index	619

Foreword

I first met Dov Noy in a book—more precisely, in an endnote.

I was putting together a collection of Jewish folktales, browsing through hundreds of stories collected in dozens of anthologies and primary sources. Early on in my research, I came across a bibliographic reference containing a baffling acronym—IFA—followed by a number. Then I encountered it again in the next endnote, and the next, and the one after that. In fact, it popped up repeatedly in most of the newer anthologies of Jewish folktales that I consulted. When I delved deeper I learned that "IFA" stood for the Israel Folktale Archives, which is the most extensive collection of Jewish oral tales in the world. I also discovered that one man was responsible for this unique treasure trove—Dov Noy.

In time I met Jewish storytellers who had mined the IFA for their books. I heard them recite these tales aloud, putting their own special "spin" on them. And I listened to their personal stories about meeting Dov Noy. It became increasingly clear to me that this Israeli professor was an unsung Jewish hero, whose efforts had contributed significantly to safeguarding a Jewish literary legacy no less precious than the holy books revered for centuries by the Jewish people. The only difference was that such oral tales rarely made it into print, so they had not caught the attention of the scholars. Until recent times, these tales had been carried around in the *pekels,* saddlebags, and aprons of *amcha*, the Jewish rank-and-file, as they *shlepped* across five continents during their 2,000-year exile. And because the transmitters of these oral texts were only simple folk, not venerated rabbis or community leaders, their tales had slipped beneath the radar of "the Tradition." They were not taught in yeshivahs or religious schools, recited around the Sabbath table or at the pulpit, not disseminated in beautifully printed *seforim,* or prayerbooks, or even in popular *haggadot*. Unlike the universal currency of normative Judaism, these tales were strictly local coinage, eagerly passed around among Jewish tradespeople, laborers, shopkeepers, and beggars, old and young, literate and unlettered, in the marketplace, at family celebrations, at home, and in coffeeshops. Remarkably, Dov Noy had understood all this when he was only a graduate student of folklore at Indiana University, and he had proceeded to devote his life to rescuing Jewish folktales before they vanished. The first step he took in accomplishing this mission was to found the Israel Folktale Archives at the University of Haifa in 1955. Today that archive bears his name.

I finally had the chance to meet Dov when I attended my first Jerusalem International Book Fair in 1991 as the newly appointed editor-in-chief of The Jewish Publication Society. Some of my storyteller friends had told me about Dov Noy's "Monday nights," weekly gatherings in his fourth-floor walk-up apartment that had been going on for decades. Anyone who was in town was welcome to come, these friends assured me, provided that they had some story to share. The night I attended there was a motley assortment of characters assembled in Dov's modest living room, some Israeli, most just passing through Jerusalem. We all sat around a low coffee table on folding chairs and worn furniture, munching on pistachios, while Dov conducted us in what can only be described as "folklore improv": one by one, we introduced ourselves, said a little about where we came from, and then shared a tale, a song, an experience, a bit of autobiography. Dov interrupted us frequently, explaining the origin of our family name or the shtetl or village our grandparents had come from, identifying the original source or a regional variant of a folksong, telling us something about how a tale had made its way across the Jewish landscape. The conversation took place in many languages: Hebrew, Yiddish, English, Russian, Rumanian. Dov comfortably negotiated all these languages, translating fluidly so we could all understand one another.

I don't remember exactly what I shared that evening or even who was there—I have now attended about 10 such gatherings and they blur together—but I do remember how I felt that night. It was as if I was in the presence of something very old and authentic, in a time machine of Jewish culture and memory, a living tradition. And Dov, with his encyclopedic knowledge of Jewish folklore and his associative intelligence, was the magician conjuring it all into being. But what a modest magician! Although he was the founder of the entire field of Jewish folklore, the teacher of every younger Jewish folklore scholar throughout the world, he was totally unpretentious, witty and coy, unabashedly delighting in all the small homespun offerings we had brought to him.

Each time over the past 15 years that I have trudged up the four flights to attend one of Dov's Monday evenings, hurrying to reach each landing before the timed lights plunged the stairwell back into darkness, I have felt that same childlike anticipation. Who will show up tonight? Where will they come from? And what will Dov reveal to us that none of us ever knew? Over the years, I have met a 90-year-old Israeli woman who first introduced the papaya to Israel, a sultry Ladino folksinger, a Jewish professor from Birobidzhan, fellow storytellers from the United States, Holocaust survivors, a Russian playwright, the founder of Mensa in Israel. Some of Dov's guests have been just ordinary tourists, sent to Dov's apartment by a friend or by Dov himself on one of his many lecture tours throughout the world.

I share all this by way of background to this JPS series. For it is only because of Dov that this project came into being. When I first learned about the IFA, I realized what a rich treasure it was—but also understood that it was a buried treasure, unknown to all but a handful of Jewish storytellers and folklore scholars. Even the descendants of the storytellers who had initially brought these tales to Israel were unaware of the IFA, ignorant about this part of their birthright. They were now Hebrew speakers and had blended into Israeli society stripped of any ethnic past. Meanwhile, thousands of orphaned tales sat silently in manila file folders in a small, crowded room at the University of Haifa, unread, untold, uncelebrated.

Enter the other hero of this saga—Dan Ben-Amos. From the very beginning of this project, it was obvious that Dov, already in his early 70s, could not possibly complete this formidable task alone. He recommended that Dan Ben-Amos, once his student, now his professional colleague, become his co-editor for the series. The JPS Editorial Committee and several scholars in the field all agreed. And so the collaboration began. For the next decade, Dan, Dov, and I would meet every year or so in the White Dog Café near the University of Pennsylvania to discuss the status of the project. During our delicious two-hour lunches, we would solve editorial problems, discuss translation issues, and debate methodology—but mostly we told each other stories. We often told them in shorthand, sharing only a fragment of a tale before we would nod to each other, by way of saying, "Yes, I know that one." Neither Dan nor I could really compete with Dov, who seemed to know every Jewish story ever told, and much more.

It's hard to believe that the series has finally appeared. It's been 15 years since I first proposed the idea to Dov. During that time, two translators in Israel have rendered the Hebrew originals into readable contemporary English. Dan has done the lion's share of researching and annotating the tales, with Dov contributing significantly from his vast storehouse of knowledge. The staff at JPS, under the tireless stewardship of publishing director Carol Hupping, has invested hundreds of hours in working with Dan during the development phase, preparing the manuscript, and shepherding it through production.

We have also benefited from generous financial support. Early on, Lloyd Cotsen, himself an enthusiastic collector of international folklore and children's literature, came forward to underwrite the Yiddish volume in the series, and subsequently gave us a major gift to support the entire project. Lloyd has been a constant cheerleader, eager to hear about progress, and infinitely patient during the project's long gestation. We are also grateful for the generous support of the National Foundation of Jewish Culture, the National Endowment for the Humanities, the Maurice Amado Foundation for Sephardic Culture, and the JPS Board of Trustees.

It is our hope that *Folktales of the Jews* will quickly find a place of honor next to another JPS story collection, Louis Ginzberg's *Legends of the Jews,* published 1909–1930. In his magisterial work, Ginzberg brought together and annotated thousands of midrashic texts, an accomplishment that has never been equaled. Dov Noy and Dan Ben-Amos have performed a parallel feat in this new work, filling in a significant gap in Jewish literary tradition.

Despite their humble origins and settings, Jewish folktales have played a vital role in transmitting the tradition known as the Oral Torah, *torah she-b'al-peh*. Within these stories can be found ethical teachings, role models, cautionary tales, and collective memory. Unlike halakhic texts, which are prescriptive, or rabbinic midrash, which is anchored by prooftexts, folktales assert their authority through the personality of the storyteller and the magic of narrative, which seize hold of our imagination and prod our conscience. With the publication of these volumes, a hidden spring has at last been uncovered for all to share. We invite you to drink deeply and be refreshed.

ELLEN FRANKEL

Tammuz 5766, July 2006

Acknowledgments

As a folktale anthology, this book presents not just the "voice of the people," but also the voices of many people—the narrators who tell the tales and thereby preserve, transmit and re-create the narratives that make up the Jewish folk tradition. Without them this book would not have come into being, and I would like to express to them my deepest gratitude and appreciation.

The transition from oral to written texts could be accomplished only through a labor of love. In transcribing these stories, the collectors have extended the narrators' audience beyond immediate family and community to readers worldwide. I am indebted to them for making these tales available, and I thank them for their conscientious effort to render the oral tales accurately. And my gratitude goes as well to Lenn Schramm, who translated them from the Hebrew.

All these tales are now on deposit at the Israel Folktale Archives Named in Honor of Dov Noy (IFA) at the University of Haifa. The archives' academic head, Haya Bar-Itzhak, and the archivists Edna Heichal and Idit Pintel-Ginsberg extended invaluable assistance to me throughout the preparation of these volumes. No question was too trivial or too complex for them, and they responded to my seemingly endless queries with patience and expediency.

The primary research required for this anthology could not have been carried out without excellent libraries and the assistance of their librarians. I was fortunate to have access to the Van Pelt-Dietrich Library and to the library of the Center for Advanced Judaic Studies, both at the University of Pennsylvania. Their extensive holdings in folklore and Jewish studies facilitated the search for books and articles, old and new alike. I would like to thank the librarians who helped me, day in and day out, in my research: Aviva Astrinsky and Arthur Kiron, the former and the current directors, respectively, of the Center for Advanced Judaic Studies' library, and the librarians Josef Gulka, Seth Jerchower, and Judith Leifer. In the Van Pelt-Dietrich library, the folklorist-librarian David Azzolina and John Pollack of the Rare Books and Manuscript Library were most helpful, and Lee Pugh, the head of the Interlibrary Loan Services, and

Ruth Rin, the cataloguer of Hebrew books, were very resourceful. I thank them all.

During the academic year 2003–2004, I was a Fellow at the Center for Advanced Judaic Studies. During this period I was able to make significant progress in my research on these tales, and I would like to thank David Ruderman, the center's director, for this fellowship year.

The Folktales of the Jews series was conceived and initiated by Ellen Frankel, the director and editor-in-chief of The Jewish Publication Society (JPS). She accompanied this project from its inception and guided it through the obstacle course that inevitably awaits any multivolume set. I thank her for her confidence in entrusting this project to me and for her unrelenting support and counsel during the many years required to accomplish it. I also thank the JPS staff, who, each according to her area of expertise, has contributed toward the successful completion of these volumes. In particular, I would like to thank Carol Hupping, the publishing director; production manager Robin Norman; and managing editor Janet Liss. Thanks as well go to Candace B. Levy for her superb copyediting, Emily Law for her edits, Christine Sweeney for her proofreading, Gilad J. Gevaryahu for his expert fact-checking. I also thank my student Linda Lee, who assisted and facilitated the editorial process.

Over many years and many tales I have incurred debts of gratitude to numerous friends who offered counsel and advice drawn from their extensive expertise. I would like thank Roger D. Abrahams, Tamar Alexander, Roger Allen, Samuel Armistead, David Assaf, Israel Bartal, Alexander Botwinik, Patricia Fann Bouteneff, Olesja Britsyna, Samuel Chalfen, Naomi Cohen, Sol Cohen, Linda Dégh, Hasan El-Shamy, Joseph Farrell, Galit Hasan-Rokem, Bill Hickman, Victoria Kirkham, Ronnie Kokhavi, Robert Kraft, Anna Kryvenko, Shuli Levinboim, Julie Lieber, Ora Limor, Victor Mair, Ulrich Marzolph, Philip Miraglia, Adrienn Mizsei, Benjamin Nathans, Arzu Ozturkmen, Gyula Paczolay, Elchanan Reiner, Uri Rubin, Shalom Sabar, Elizabeth Sachs, Ziva Shamir, Avigdor Shinan, Marcos Silber, Jonathan Steinberg, Michael Swartz, Jeffrey Tigay, Chava Turniansky, Kelly Tuttle, Michal Unger, Julia Verkholantsev, Vilmos Voigt, and Chava Weissler.

Finally, last but not least, I thank my wife, Batsheva, for her constant encouragement and support.

Dan Ben-Amos

Introduction to Volume 2

Eastern European Jewry was a relatively late Diaspora. Its communities evolved after the Jewish societies in other Diasporas such as Spain, the countries of Islam, and Western Europe had had their periods of glory and turbulence. Theories and legends abound, but evidence is slim about the origins and early days of eastern European Jewry. Even when documentation is available, its validity and interpretations are subject to challenge and scholarly controversy.

The Jewish Migration into Eastern Europe

Two major groups of hypotheses have been formulated about the arrival of Jews to Eastern Europe: The first proposes that their route was across the northern Black Sea and into southern Russia; the second suggests a eastern migration from Central Europe.

By and large, the theories in the first group assign earlier dates to the Jewish migration into Eastern Europe, suggesting that Jews arrived in southeast Europe from the Land of Israel as early as biblical times, either during the exile of the Ten Tribes (722 B.C.E.), or after the destruction of the First Temple (586 B.C.E.). Some scholars propose that the migration took place in the early medieval period, during the time of the Byzantine Empire (seventh to tenth centuries C.E.). Still others suggest that the remnants of the Khazar tribes that converted to Judaism formed the beginning of eastern European Jewry.[1]

The western route theories are less romantic, suggesting that Jews arrived in Eastern Europe either through the opening of east-west trade routes across the continent or as a result of the persecution of Jews in Western Europe. These theories date the arrival of Jews in Eastern Europe to the Middle Ages, based on documentary evidence that attests to a Jewish presence in the region from the thirteenth century.[2] Each of these theories has some tangential and some more solid evidence, and it is quite likely that Jewish communities existed in Poland and Ukraine before the thirteenth century, a period for which available evidence leaves no doubt about the Jewish presence in Eastern Europe.

The legends concerning the Jewish arrival into this territory are clearly narratives of migration. These are anachronistic tales, probably told long after the beginnings of Jewish settlement in Eastern Europe. The first of these tales recounts an event that occurred in the ninth century, upon the death of the Polish king Popiel. The council of electors could not decide on the selection of a new king and so agreed that the first person to walk into town at daybreak would be crowned king. It so happened that that person was a Jew named Abraham "Prochownik" (gunpowder merchant). He refused to ascend to the throne and secluded himself in a room. After three days, Piast, a farmer, broke into the room; Abraham then insisted that this farmer was fit for the throne. And so he became the founder of the Piast dynasty, which ruled until 1370.[3]

A second legend dates the arrival of the Jews into the preroyalty past of Poland. Jews reached Poland (at the time a desolated place) as merchants and moneylenders. The local rulers accepted them into their land but insisted that the Jews continue to wear the type of clothes they wore on their arrival. This is a legend that validates their distinctiveness in costumes and language.[4]

A third legendary tale puts the arrival in the period of King Leszek IV (ninth century), a descendent of King Piast, and involves a community delegation. The Jews of this tale all had Sephardic names, an anachronism. The legend establishes not only the distinctiveness of the Jews but also recognizes their communal self-government, freedom of worship, freedom of settlement, and royal protection.[5]

The historical trustworthiness of these legends notwithstanding, they do reflect the social, religious, and linguistic distinctiveness of the Jews, at least in the nineteenth century, when the legends appeared in print, and likely earlier, when the stories circulated orally. From their early modest beginnings up through the seventeenth century, Jews in Eastern Europe thrived, with a substantial increase in population. They spread throughout the area, all the while maintaining their social, religious, and linguistic distinctiveness; residing in their quarters; and engaging mainly in craft, trade, and commerce. The Jewish population rebounded after the pogroms of 1648–1649;[6] and by the end of the eighteenth century and throughout the nineteenth century, more Jews lived in the area known as the Pale of Settlement than in any other part of the world. This area stretched from the Baltic Sea in the north to the Black Sea in the south and from the boundaries of Prussia and the Austro-Hungarian Empire in the west to the Russian provinces in the east.

The Jews lived alongside and among the local populations of, for example, Lithuanians, Russians, Byelorussians, Poles, Ukrainians, and Moldavians; although subordinate to the local governments, they maintained a relative independence in conducting their community affairs.[7] They spoke Yiddish, a language "born and developed in the area of Loter-Ashkenaz [Alsace-Lorraine, Lotharingia]"[8] in the eleventh and twelfth centuries, which they brought with them as they migrated from the west. If there was any linguistic support for the theory of migration from the northern Black Sea, it lost credence by the emergence of Yiddish, which became the dominant spoken language and which developed with its own regional dialects.[9]

The Flowering of Old Yiddish

Even before their eastward migration, the Jews used Old Yiddish (1250–1500) as their community language and the language of their oral literature. The earliest documented literary activity in Old Yiddish dates from 1272: an illuminated prayer book from Worms. It is a rhymed blessing inscribed within the spaces of the large letters of a word at the top of a page.[10]

Another example from about a hundred years later (1382), attests to full-fledged medieval literary creativity. The work was discovered in a cache of manuscripts in Cairo known as the Cairo Genizah[11] and is now housed in the Cambridge University Library and known as the Cambridge Codex. It includes six poetic renditions of traditional Jewish, mostly biblical, themes: "The Death of Aaron," "Paradise," "Abraham the Patriarch," "Joseph the Righteous," and "A Fable of the Sick Lion."[12] The codex also includes "Dukus Horant," a German epic of which the Yiddish text is the only extant version.[13]

The Cambridge Codex includes two literary forms that also appeared in subsequent Yiddish narrative poetry: epic renditions of biblical tales and translations of medieval European epic poetry. Well known among the former are the *Shmuel Bukh* (Augsburg, Bavaria, Germany, 1544),[14] the *Melokhim* (Kings) *Bukh* (Augsburg, 1543),[15] and the *Aqedat Jishaq* (Sacrifice of Isaac) narrative poems.[16] Prominent among the latter is the Yiddish translation of the King Arthur legend.[17] Other examples of medieval European epic works are the 1507 translation of the popular romance about Buovo d'Antona by the poet and grammarian Elijah Bahur Levita (1469–1549), which was printed as the *Bove Bukh* in 1541,[18] and his probable reworking of a well-known Italian book by Pierre de la Cépède—*Paris e Vienna* (fifteenth century)[19]—as *Paris un Viene*,[20] likely composed in 1509–1513.[21]

The first recorded Yiddish folktales, found in a Cambridge manuscript, are from the German-speaking cities of Danzig (now Gdansk, Poland), Mainz, and Worms and date to the beginning of the sixteenth century. They build on themes that, though not entirely new to Jewish tradition, did not necessarily uphold the moral values the Rabbis advocated. For example, the story from Danzig is about disguise, romance, and deception. A beautiful Jewish seamstress searched for her husband, who had traveled to a distant land. She arrived in the city disguised as a young man, but there the king's daughter fell in love with her and insisted on marriage. As a solution to the conundrum, the wedding took place; but to uphold the deception, the disguised woman's husband spent the night with the princess. In the morning the Jewish couple fled the city.[22]

The story from Mainz is a tale of rivalry between two stepbrothers who compete for the love of the most beautiful maiden in town. The wicked brother blinded the other. However, after he recovered his sight he became rich, and the virtuous man returned to Mainz in time to marry the beautiful lady and expel his murderous brother.

The third is a tale of mock marriage, in which, during playtime, a youth puts his ring on a finger that is stretched out from a hollow tree. Unfortunately, by this act he unwittingly married a female demon. Later, the youth married a mortal woman, but the demon killed his bride. Then these same events happened a second time. After a third marriage, his bride pleaded with the female demon, who agreed to spare her life, provided she let the young man spend an hour with her each day. One day, at the stipulated hour, the mortal wife found her husband and the female demon in deep sleep; and the wife gently laid the demon's long hair on a bench. The demon, touched by the woman's courtesy, left the ring behind and disappeared.[23] This tale is actually a combination of two tales that appear separately in Jewish tradition: The mock marriage is known in Jewish kabbalistic tradition and is also found in earlier European narratives;[24] a story of sexual relations between a mortal man and a female demon is found in *Ma'ase Nissim*.[25] The theme has been the subject of study.[26]

Such romantic and erotic themes do occur in Jewish traditions, but only infrequently. Resonating more with the *Decameron* than with midrash, they escaped the stricture of rabbinical moral authority, particularly when told in a vernacular language. Yiddish thus expanded the thematic scope of Jewish folktales. Tales in Hebrew script and print adhered more to the ideal Jewish ethos; but narrators who used Yiddish were able to loosen the ties to Jewish tradition and explore contacts with European narrative traditions.

Folktales in Print

With the advance of print in the sixteenth century, a new era dawned in European folk literature, including Yiddish folk literature. Tales that were previously available only orally or in manuscripts found their way into various publications. Three periods in the writing and printing of Yiddish folktales are recognized. In the early period (1504–1604), from which both books and manuscripts are extant, northern Italy was considered a major printing center. The printing centers of the middle period (1660–1750) were Amsterdam and Prague, but toward the end of the period, Fürth and Frankfurt am Main became more important. During this time, numerous booklets, many of which were of known tales, were published. The final period, marked by a decline in publication and an intensification of oral storytelling (1750–1814), was a period of transition from western to eastern European printing centers. At this time, there was an increase in the publication and republication of folk narrative texts in the eastern Yiddish language.[27]

Traditional tales—mostly translations of talmudic-midrashic, medieval Hebrew, and non-Jewish tales—became available in three forms: narrative anthologies, framed narratives, and narrative booklets.

Narrative Anthologies

The earliest extant collection of tales in Yiddish was found inserted in a prayer book manuscript from northern Italy, written in 1504. The sixteen tales in the collection are translations of midrashic stories.[28] Nine other sixteenth-century manuscripts of various sizes that were written or copied in northern Italy and Germany are available.[29] In 1595, *Ku-Bukh* (The book of cows) was published in Verona; it contains thirty-five fables that draw on the Aesopian and Arabic traditions as they were represented in medieval Hebrew fable tradition.[30] A century later, the book was published as *Sefer Meshalim* in Frankfurt am Main, with some modifications by Moses ben Eliezer Wallich.[31] In 1602, just seven years later, Jacob ben Abraham, a book dealer from Mezhirich of Lithuania, had Konrad Waldkirch (of Basel) print the *Mayse Bukh* (Ma'aseh book). The book includes 257 tales, making it the largest anthology of its time. Its production represented the transition of the Yiddish-speaking community from Western to Eastern Europe. Contemporary Eastern Europe likely had the buying readership but no facilities for book production. The *Mayse Bukh* included tales from the talmudic-midrashic literature, from medieval Hebrew sources (such as narratives about Rabbi Judah ben Samuel he Ḥasid), and from sixteenth-century Hebrew books. The book enjoyed immense popularity and was reprinted in at least thirty-four editions.[32]

There were no rivals to the *Mayse Bukh* until the last decade of the seventeenth century, when three tale collections appeared. *Ma'asei Adonai*, edited by Rabbi Akiva Baer ben Joseph and published in two volumes in Frankfurt am Main (1691) and Fürth (1694), is a collection of fifty tales. The stories, mostly from kabbalistic sources and mystical books, introduced tales and concepts from the Zohar[33] to Yiddish-speaking communities. Like the *Mayse Bukh*, this collection enjoyed great popularity and was printed in multiple editions.[34] The *Eyn Sheyn Naye Mayse Bukh* (A nice new tale book), published in 1697, contained eleven tales and was edited by the Hungarian rabbi Jonathan ben Jacob.

The collection that can be considered a milestone in the history of Yiddish folktales appeared in 1696 in Amsterdam. *Ma'aseh Nissim* (Miracle works) is a slim booklet that originally included twenty-three tales. The stories were recorded by Yiftaḥ Joseph Juspa Halevy (1604–1678), who was known as Juspa the *Shammash* of Worms (Warmaisa), a city in the Rhine valley in southwest Germany that had had an important Jewish community since the eleventh century. There is only meager biographical information about Juspa Halevy. He was born in Fulda, in the state of Hesse, and arrived in Worms in 1623 when he was nineteen. Two years later, he married into a good local family and assumed the position of a *shammash* (synagogue caretaker), which he retained for over forty years. This role offered him the opportunity to observe community life, which he recorded in *Sefer Minhagim* (Book of customs),[35] and to listen to tales and legends, which he collected in *Ma'aseh Nissim* and which his son, Eliezer Liebermann, had published. The language in which Juspa wrote down the stories—Hebrew or Yiddish[36]—is the subject of debate; but the book was printed in Yiddish. The collection underwent six reprintings, until 1777, in Holland and Germany.[37]

A non-native of the town, Juspa the *Shammash* nonetheless participated in community affairs while maintaining an observant eye and an alert ear to the unique local customs and stories. Consequently, he became the first known collector to consciously record Yiddish tales from an oral tradition and prepare them for presentation to the public. *Ma'aseh Nissim* included a few tales drawn from the medieval oral and written traditions about miraculous and tragic events that involved famous rabbis; however, most of the stories are local legends about the relations between Jews and gentiles in Worms, about miracles, and about demonic figures. These are local histories of the natural and the supernatural.

In retrospect, the eighteenth century was a transitional period for the publication of narrative Yiddish-language anthologies, moving from west to east across Europe. Few original collections were printed, and the only extant compilation from that century is a 1750 manuscript prepared by Nathan Neta ben Simeon, who drew on a 1581 book, *Kaftor va-Ferah* (A bud and a flower) by Jacob ben Isaac Luzzatto, that was popular among Yiddish anthologists.[38] With the exception of Juspa's *Ma'aseh Nissim*, further underscoring the uniqueness of that book, western European narrative anthologies gathered stories from diverse Hebrew sources, a dependence that characterized the printed Yiddish folk literature of the period.[39]

Framed Narratives

During the eighteenth century, there was another transition in Yiddish folk-narrative prose: from reliance on Hebrew to a reliance on Oriental traditional sources, which became available in European languages. These books were often structured as a series of narratives framed within a compelling situation in which the hero's life depended on the telling and the content of the tales.[40] In the book *The Seven Wise Men*, a king's wife accuses the prince, who is not her son, of attempted rape. Because he took a vow of silence for a week and thus cannot explain himself, seven wise men tell stories in his defense while the wife tells accusatory stories. The book appeared in seven different translations from German and Dutch sources, but none was based on the traditional, Oriental Hebrew version of the story known as *The Tales of Sendebar*.[41] *The Arabian Nights*, the famed story in which Scheherazade fends off her own execution by telling stories, appeared in Yiddish translation in 1718, shortly after Antoine Galland's (1646–1715) publication of a French-language version. The translator and publisher of the Yiddish edition was an entrepreneur who planned to serialize the tales, printing them in small booklets. Similarly, the stories of *The Decameron* by Giovanni Boccaccio (1313–1375) and of the Dutch *Till Eulenspiegel* and *Schildburger* appeared in Yiddish translation in the eighteenth century.[42]

Narrative Booklets

The second half of the sixteenth century saw the rise in popularity of the single booklet devoted mostly to one story. During this time, fifty such publications appeared in Western Europe. These octavo booklets, published in Amsterdam and Prague, held four to sixteen pages and usually contained only a single story. Most of these tales were translations from the apocrypha, talmudic-midrashic sources, or Hebrew medieval sources, thus complementing the trends that dominated Yiddish narrative anthologies. Others were translations of similar publications in German. Zinberg[43] excludes such translated tales from the history of Jewish literature, yet they should not be because these stories became an integral part of the popular reading material within many communities. The translation of the tales into the common language of Yiddish enabled the exchange among various European communities—both Jewish and non-Jewish—and between written and oral narrative traditions. The number of translations from non-Jewish sources increased over time, while the number of translations from the Hebrew and original works declined.[44]

Tales from the Pale of Settlement

As important as it is, the evidence for Yiddish folktales in script and in print exposes only a small portion of the oral storytelling that took place in private and public spaces in the Jewish communities of Western Europe. The gap between the literary-historical evidence and the literary-social reality became more apparent during the transition from Middle to Modern Yiddish, as a consequence of the eastward Jewish migration and the consolidation of Jewish community life in the area that later became known as the Pale of Settlement.

A distinctive literary and linguistic identity of Jews who migrated from Western and Central Europe to Poland was slow to develop. Initially, some western European books were reprinted in the east. For example, *Shmuel Bukh* was published in Augsburg, Germany, in 1544 and was printed twice more in that century in Cracow.[45] Elia Bahur Levita's *Bove Bukh*, which was published in 1541, may have been reprinted in Eastern Europe in 1798.[46]

As noted earlier, Jacob ben Abraham, the book dealer from Mezhirich of Lithuania, had to travel to Basel to secure the printing of the *Mayse Bukh*. In fact, the uniqueness of eastern European Yiddish and its separation from its western European roots is illustrated by the publication history of the *Mayse Bukh*. Eliezer Paver, the editor of the 1807 edition from

Zolkiew, Poland, which was "a forerunner of folk-literature in Yiddish,"[47] stated in his introduction:

> How great is the day in which the important book the *Mayse Bukh* happened to fall into my hand. This book was published long ago in 1705 in Amsterdam and in it there are wonderful and precious tales and [stories] about events that happened to Rabbi Judah the Pious, may his memory be for blessing and for life in the world to come, and his father the great rabbi Shmuel, their soul rests in peace. . . . I said [to myself]: Indeed this book was published in the Ashkenazic [German] language that our Ashkenazic grandfather used, a language that the people in our countries now cannot understand and would not know the essence of the story. Many people appealed to me to translate this book into a clear language, and I responded to their request and translated it, as all of you can see, into a fluent language for all to understand.[48]

During the long period when the Yiddish language went through its transformation, there were few Jewish printing houses in Poland: "Since the middle of the seventeenth century [when the pogroms of 1648–1649 occurred], and throughout most of the eighteenth century, only a few books were published in Yiddish in Poland. This was a direct result of the decline of the printing profession among the Jews of Poland at that period. This was the primary cause that the East European Yiddish hardly had the opportunity to attain a direct linguistic expression in writing until the last quarter of the eighteenth century."[49]

But when the presses went silent, the people spoke. They told their tales, preached their sermons, bartered their jokes, cited their proverbs, and sang their songs—all in eastern European Yiddish. Without a recording witness and with only occasional indirect references and allusions, oral Yiddish culture flourished in conversations in the marketplace and in the tavern, in the synagogue and at the *rebbe's court*. Women sang about love and despair and told their children tales of wonder and magic; men spoke about demons and holy men, about the rewards of piety and charity, and about the punishment of sinful life. As David Roskies imagines:

> The Jews of Central and Eastern Europe are a people of storytellers. Men went off to pray three times daily; between afternoon and evening prayers, they swapped a tale or two. On the Sabbath

and holidays they returned to the study house or synagogue to hear a *maggid*, an itinerate preacher, weave stories into lengthy singsong sermons. . . . At home or in the marketplace, women drew their own repertory of stories from life and from moral tracts. . . . And just when it seemed that the winds of change blowing in from the west were about to turn these folk into philosophers, bankers, and mistresses of salons, a counter-movement called Hasidism swept in from the east and breathed new life into sacred songs and tales.

Hasidic Contributions

The formation of cult circles of Hasidim that each congregated around a particular *rebbe* became a hotbed for the growth of *shevahim* (hagiographic tales) about the Hasidic *tzaddikim* (holy people), with their piety, their miracles, their combats with demons, and their cure of the sick. Hasidic rebbes were a pilgrimage destiny for Jews seeking relief from their personal troubles, and thus these men became the subject of stories about success in combating evil and becoming even more pious. In Hasidism, an ecstatic form of Judaism, storytelling, together with singing and dancing, became an essential part of religious worship. Such practice took place informally around the courtyards of the Hasidic rebbes and more formally during the third meal of the Sabbath, when the rebbe's dinner table became a social and religious occasion designated for storytelling.[51] For almost a century, such oral narratives blossomed in Hasidic communities, while only two collections made it into print. Both of these books appeared in 1814, both combined Yiddish and Hebrew, both represented an interdependence between orality and literacy, and both later became the foundation of the Hasidic literary canon.[52]

The first of these books was *Shivhei ha-Besht* (In praise of the Baal Shem Tov), which was written down by Rabbi Dov Baer ben Samuel, the son-in-law of Rabbi Alexander the *Shohet*, who was the Baal Shem Tov's amulet and letter scribe for eight years. Rabbi Dov Baer ben Samuel wrote down the tales as he heard them from the men who belonged to the Baal Shem Tov's inner circle; to bestow authority, authenticity, and veracity on the stories, he usually attributed them to their sources. Rabbi Dov Baer ben Samuel's documentation surpassed that of his predecessor, Juspa the *Shammash* of Worms, who was not precise in citing the sources of the local tales he recorded. The manuscript of *Shivhei ha-Besht* circulated for a while in Hasidic circles and was copied by scribes[53] until the printer Israel Yofeh (of Kopys, in the province of Reissen, Poland) prepared and published the manuscript in Hebrew. Shortly thereafter, a Yiddish version was published in Ostrog; it omitted 40 percent of the tales found in the first edition but added others. Between 1815 and 1817, four Hebrew and three Yiddish translations appeared. Then, in response to the storm of controversy that the Hasidic movement had aroused, the Austrian censor banned the publication of *Shivḥei ha-Besht*. For the next fifty years only a handful of editions escaped the censor's watchful eye and made it into print.[54] The tales in *Shivḥei ha-Besht* are hagiographic and biographic, giving accounts of the Besht's magical, miraculous, and mystical activities and telling about his birth, childhood, adult life, and death.

The second book published in 1814 was a collection of tales told by the great-grandson of the Baal Shem Tov, Rabbi Nahman of Bratslav, (1772–1810) to his scribe and secretary, Nathan Sternhartz of Nemirov (1780–1845). The book, *Sefer ha-Ma'asiyyot* (A book of tales) is a bilingual edition (Hebrew and Yiddish) of thirteen tales.[55] As the term *Ma'asiyyot*, the generic designation in its title, indicates, these are not hagiographic but wonder tales, in the tradition of eastern and western European folktales, that Rabbi Nahman told in an allegorical and mystical mode. Such tales were likely known in the Yiddish narrative tradition.

The two books published in 1814 thus represent two distinct genres of Yiddish folktales told in the Jewish communities in the eighteenth century.

When Hasidic tales began to appear in print in the 1860s, they drew on an intensive storytelling tradition that spread through Hasidic communities and focused on *rebbes*, miracle workers, and saintly personalities of Hasidic leadership. Most of the stories were hagiographic tales rendered in print in Hebrew, though told aloud in Yiddish.[56] The wonder tales that the Jews told in the Pale of Settlement were not recorded or published until the twentieth century, when professional and amateur folklorists began to attend to the task of writing down the Yiddish oral narrative tradition.

Recording Yiddish Folktales

The trends of enlightenment and modernization that swept through the Pale of Settlement also motivated young people to explore, record, and study the very life and tradition from which they distanced themselves. The recording of Yiddish folktales signified their personal loss of tradition and the awareness of the ultimate change time and historical events bring to bear on social and religious life in the *shtetls* and the Jewish ghettos and quarters in the urban centers. In contrast to the research of Sephardic folktales, which was initiated by scholars (mostly linguists) who were not members of the Judeo-Spanish-speaking community,[57] the recorders of Yiddish folktales spoke the language, living between the two worlds of tradition and modernity and caught in the crucible of the transformation of Jewish life in Eastern Europe.[58]

Folklore research gathered steam during the second half of the nineteenth century. From a trickle of studies, it rose to a stream of publications that appeared as books and articles in Jewish and non-Jewish journals.[59] At first, proverbs and folk songs were written down from the oral tradition and then published. The first to record Yiddish folktales was Benjamim Wolf Segel (Benyamin Volf Segal; 1866–1931), "the old master of Yiddish ethnography," who published in Polish and German journals.[60] Awareness of and concern for folklore and folktales motivated the literary imagination and the poetic muse of prominent writers of the period, and through them folktales reached the secular Jewish reading public in eastern European communities. The twentieth century saw the development of two distinct research methods for recording Yiddish folktales: expeditionary ethnography and central text ingathering.

Expeditionary Ethnography

The primary folklorist associated with expeditionary ethnography is Shloyme-Zanvl Rappoport (1863–1920), known in Russian as Semyon Akimovich and in Yiddish literature by the pen name S. An-Sky (An-Ski, Ansky).[61] His dedication to the study of Jewish folklore in Eastern Europe is an outgrowth of his youthful involvement with the Russian Populists (*narodniki*) and the rediscovery of Jewish tradition in his later years. As a young man, he joined the Russian Populist movement and worked in the salt and coal mines; he lived briefly in St. Petersburg, where he wrote about the lives of Russian peasants and his fellow laborers. An-Sky moved to Switzerland and then to Paris, where he worked as a private secretary for Petr Lavrovich Lavrov (1823–1900), a central figure in the community of radical Russian emigrants. By the time An-Sky moved back to Russia in 1905, he was a transformed man, searching for his Jewish roots in traditional Yiddish culture. His return to Yiddish language and literature began in Paris, and his commitment to his own culture grew after he arrived in Russia. From 1912 to 1914, he headed the Baron Horace Guenzburg Ethnographic Expedition, which focused on small towns in Volhynia and Podolia. An-Sky was accompanied by a team of researchers, who took pictures, recorded folk songs, and wrote down folktales. After three summer seasons, the expedition had gathered two thousand photographs and eighteen hundred tales, now on deposit at the State Ethnographic Museum in St. Petersburg.[62] An-Sky's team developed methods, including questionnaires, which prepared the ground for the ethnographic study of Yiddish folktales. The texts recorded during those summers made up the largest collection of Jewish oral tales of the time.[63]

In his interpretations of these tales, An-Sky sought to uncover the particular Jewish spirit that shaped them and the specific cultural values that they perpetuated in Jewish society. He compared the might and violence in European folktales with the ideals of spirituality characterizing Jewish folktales and represented in the qualities of the heroes of such narratives.[64]

Shmuel Lehman (1886–1941), inspired by An-Sky but departing from his conception of Jewish folktales, was known as "the most prolific collector of Yiddish folklore between the wars"[65] and contributed to the multivolume *Ba ync Jid'n* (Among us Jews).[66] The stories in this collection are narratives told by and about the Jewish urban underworld of Warsaw and other eastern European cities. There is nothing holy or spiritual about these tales of Jewish criminals and their world. Similarly secular in nature were the legends that A. Almi (Elye-Khayem Sheps; 1892–1968) recorded, primarily from his grandmother, about the 1863 Polish insurrection against Alexander II (1818–1881) and his appointed official in Poland, Count Alexander Wielopolski. These historical legends have political overtones and purpose and are different from the pietistic and ethical tales that An-Sky assumed characterized Jewish narratives.[67]

An-Sky's scholarly tradition, but not his methods, continued with the establishment of the Vilna Jewish Historical-Ethnographic Society in 1919, which was named in honor of him a year later, after his death.[68] The leading folklorist in the society was Shloyme Bastomski (1891–1941),[69] primarily a publisher and an educator. In 1925, he was the first to publish a volume of annotated Yiddish folktales and legends.[70] Gottesman[71] notes:

> Only a few tales in the volume were collected orally. Almost all of the tales were from previously published collections; mostly from earlier Hasidic collections. . . . Some were taken from more modern works, such as Ansky's *Khurban galitsye* (Destruction of Galicia), where the tales were not "artisically reworked, but written as heard."

Central Text Ingathering

The foundation of *Der Yiddisher Visnshaftlekher Institute* (the Yiddish Scientific Institute; YIVO) in 1925 in Vilna was a major step in the development of Yiddish folktale studies. In the initial proposal for the institute, Yiddish scholarship was to develop in four sections: philology (which was soon reconceived as the linguistic-literary research section), history, social and economic concerns, and pedagogy. Within a short time after the founding of YIVO, the Folklore Commission, later named the Ethnographic (Folklore) Commission under the leadership of Max Weinreich (1894–1969), began to send instructions and questionnaires to collectors (*zamlers*), who were to gather information about different folklore genres, holiday celebrations, customs, and other aspects of traditional life in Jewish societies. The first questionnaire was related to Jewish legends; the eleventh questionnaire was about tales (*mayses*). This collecting system was a resounding success, and workers from all regions of the Pale of Settlement sent in valuable texts and information. The folklorist Yehudah Leib Cahan (1881–1937) was a driving force of the program in the 1930s. It was he who suggested that the commission change its name in 1930 to the Folklore Commission; and in that same year, YIVO brought young scholars to Vilna to train them in folklore research and the collection of texts.

The shift in method from ethnographic expedition to central text ingathering required the implementation of control over the quality and authenticity of the texts. Because there was a risk that amateur collectors could mistakenly send in fabricated or literary texts, the YIVO scholars needed to formulate criteria for text evaluation.[72] Cahan, a self-taught scholar of high standards, was familiar with the latest scholarship and comparative methods in the field of folklore. A native of Vilna, he immigrated to London in 1901 and then three years later to New York, where he made his home and conducted folklore research among Jewish immigrants. He first focused on folk songs,[73] and it was in their study and analysis that he became concerned with the questions of authenticity, purity, antiquity, and circulation in the oral tradition.[74] Later, he applied similar standards to the selection and analysis of folktales:

> We cannot even begin to discuss the problem of folktales without becoming involved in all the problems that are tied up with [comparative work], for all of our tales, the secular as well as the ethical-religious, are often tied in with the world of tales and themes.

We cannot consider one without the other. Because of this international origin of our folktales . . . it will perhaps not be exaggerating to say, that the most interesting material of all Yiddish folklore are the folktales—interesting both scientifically and artistically. . . . The further away we go from our own era and literature, the further we go into the past of our people's history, ever richer must become the various branches of our oral traditions, ever richer and varied our secular tales which were current among the people . . . which in different times were gotten from the international-chest of tales, from which other peoples also have taken their share.[75]

Cahan's strict standards were sometimes too restrictive, and they served as a deductive model, rejecting variations that might represent the oral performance of narrative with even greater adequacy than the standards of other collectors.[76] However, by and large, the YIVO folktale collection has become a major depository; it contained about twenty-six hundred folktales before World War II.[77] The first volume of *Yidishe Folkmasiyot* (Yiddish folktales), which Cahan published in 1931, includes the tales recorded from immigrants to New York; his second collection draws on folktales found in the YIVO archives.[78] Other selections of the tales published by Cahan and from the YIVO archive are available in English and in bilingual Yiddish-Hebrew editions.[79]

The An-Sky ethnographic expedition and the YIVO folktale collection project inspired other scholars to record folktales in Yiddish and from Yiddish-speaking people in Europe,[80] the United States, Canada,[81] and Israel.[82]

The Israeli Folktale Archives

When founding the Israel Folktale Archives (IFA), Dov Noy followed the model of YIVO's Folklore Commission, adapting it to Israel. The collectors (*roshmim*) in Israel recorded the tales from immigrants and descendants of immigrants. The narrators from eastern European countries who moved to the Land of Israel before World War II left behind a society in the midst of transformation. Those who came after the war left behind a destroyed life.

The transition from traditional to modern life for eastern European Jewry began in the eighteenth century, with the Enlightenment, which then vibrated ever so faintly in the Jewish streets and *shtetls*. The currents of change from the western regions of the continent challenged the notions of traditional life and ethos. Although the traditional life described in the stories offers security, comfort, and protection, the plots of the narratives do not resonate with nostalgia for the past, nor do they long for an imagined social innocence and purity. Rather, almost every tale in the collection relates the pain of a people whose lives were torn apart by the forces of modernization, which were manifested in Jewish communities as ideas of enlightenment, the notion of revolution, and the lure of migration to promised lands. Each trend has its own fragile utopian ideals, which break apart with the slightest touch of reality.

Yet, the tales present rupture in Jewish society without despair. Even the war tales—for example, tales IFA 2361 (this vol., no. 19) and IFA 11165 (this vol., no. 20)—do not convey the message of gloom and destruction that the Holocaust testimonies do. Rather, hovering between reality and the legendary, these narratives express a subdued sense of hope, offering light in the face of darkness.

The conflicting social and ideational forces of eastern European Jewish society project themselves into the supernatural world. For example, in tales of revenants, neglect is but a consequence of a change of values. In tale IFA 708 (this vol., no. 1), about a forsaken bride, the pursuit of beauty replaces parental obedience; in tale IFA 18159 (this vol., no. 2), about a forgotten father, the world of finance replaces the family tradition. Both revenants demand restitution through compensatory action or ritual. When the living do not stray from a path of traditional values, the departed can offer protection and support; in tale IFA 8256 (this vol., no. 6), a dead mother is able to provide for her living daughters.

When one is compelled to depart from the community, supernatural guardians can reward the timely recall of tradition by offering security and comfort, as in tale IFA 7290 (this vol., no. 3). In the narratives, the support of the ancestry and the world of the spirits depends on maintaining traditions. The spirits in Jewish tales prefer that the world of the living continue an existence that they themselves idealized. The tales explain the neglect of tradition and the lure of lucrative positions away from the familiar community as demonic forces that derail honest individuals, putting them in harm's way; see, for example, tale IFA 779 (this vol., no. 4) and tale IFA 8792 (this vol., no. 5).

The Hasidic Narrative Tradition

Historically, the beginning of the Enlightenment in eastern European Jewish society corresponded to the rise of Hasidism. Both occurred in the eighteenth century; and, though any causal relation between the two parallel movements is subject for discussion, from the perspective of folklore, the influences they share are evident. Whatever the motivation—be it ridicule, admiration, nostalgia, or appreciation—non-Hasidic Jews told Hasidic tales during the nineteenth and the twentieth centuries. The Hasidic narrative tradition was so pervasive it became an integral part of the folk-literary repertoire of storytellers. In non-European Jewish communities, the figure of Israel Ba'al Shem Tov (known as the Besht), the legendary founder of Hasidism, became the subject of many tales.

In the eastern European tradition, tales about *rebbes* are common. Although the Besht is one of the most popular personalities in the tales of the IFA, narrators from eastern European communities tell with equal devotion stories about other nineteenth-century Hasidic leaders and other community leaders. In some of these tales, the Hasidim appropriate prominent European Jews to their own circle, as tale IFA 18601 (this vol., no. 12), the story about the financial success of Rothschild, illustrates. Rothschild was the ultimate Jewish success story in the world beyond the Jewish community; and in the Hasidic narratives, his illustrious career is rooted in Jewish traditional values. The tale in this volume resolves the conflict between Jewish life and the lure of the glitter of urban glory by establishing a causal relation between international fame and Hasidic life. The linking of Rothschild to Hasidism accords prestige to the community and symbolic protection to Rothschild himself. Because success in the world at large—outside the protective embrace of the community—is a risky adventure, full of pitfalls and dangers, the traditional tale projects the successful hero as a member of a family, casting Rothschild as both a cultural hero and a representative of Hasidic society who enjoys divine defense in an uncertain world. The secret of success in these stories is not a manifestation of individual abilities but a demonstration of divine powers.

Tales of Comfort and Conflict, Tradition and Ethics, Love and Humor

Success, even on a small scale, exposed Jews to rampant anti-Semitism. In tale IFA 6306 (this vol., no. 23), which integrates fiction with history, traditional symbolism of redemption counters the hatred Jews encounter outside the community's folds. The relationship between Jew and non-Jew, however, cannot be described by a simple dichotomy. Revolutionary ideas promised a better world and lured Jewish youth into new political movements, exposing them to new dangers. Despite the cultural changes of the world at large, in Jewish folktales it is religious ritual that offers an escape from troubles and protection from danger, as in tale IFA 7211 (this vol., no. 25).

Historically, however, even the community could not provide protection against such eventualities as the Russian government's conscription law, described in tale IFA 18140 (this vol., no 28). At that time, Jews turned against Jews, and the lowest classes in the community became most vulnerable. Even though tradition could not separate individuals from the harsh reality of military life, it preserved their identity and enabled them to return to their families, which did not betray them, as had the local community.

The traditional culture of the Jewish community consisted of a fabric of ethical values that guided people in their daily lives. Traditional teachings, such as the Bible, the Talmud, and midrash, spelled out many of these values. Folk narratives offered another means of teaching traditional ethical values. Some of these tales are common to both Jewish society and other cultures—for example, tales IFA 3364 (this vol., no. 32) and IFA 551 (this vol., no. 39). Other stories, however, are inherent to the historical reality of eastern European Jewry and the particular conditions they lived under during the nineteenth and twentieth centuries, when some individuals succumbed to the promise of a better life, migrating to foreign lands. Tales IFA 19949 (this vol., no. 42) and IFA 18156 (this vol., no. 47) describe contrasting solutions to the dilemma of immigration, respectively resorting to ideal values. Although thematically distinct, both are tales of departure and reunion. The poor shoemaker in the first tale finds the material comfort of America to be devoid of the spiritual and social values he was used to in his old community. Disappointed, he returns home. In contrast, the girl with the broken heart described in the second story finds solace in the Land of Israel. The misunderstanding caused by unfamiliar and non-Jewish symbolism is resolved in the new country, and romance is restored.

Romantic love is a cultural value in Jewish tradition. The biblical story of Jacob and Rachel (Genesis 29:1–30) and the love that Rachel and Rabbi Akiva shared[83] emerged out of shepherd and student societies, respectively; and they continued to be narrative models in Jewish culture. Yet, within the folktales in which love motivates the action of the main character, we can find many international tale types that are hardly unique to Jewish folklore. Such tales, which could have originated in many countries, cultures, and languages, have been integrated into Jewish society to some degree. For example, tale IFA 7202 (this vol., no. 48), about the daughters of a king, retains its general European ambiance and characters. In contrast, in some of its versions, motif H592.1 "Love like salt" occurs in a narrative whose principal figures are a rabbi and his daughter, Rokhele; Elijah the Prophet functions in some variations of the story as ahelpful figure.[84]

Other tales, such as the story of predestined love in tale IFA 18132 (this vol., no. 49), cannot be understood thematically and symbolically without a knowledge of the Jewish cultural and mystical traditions in which it is rooted. The ubiquitous acceptance of the play *Der Dybbuk*, which An-Sky[85] wrote on the basis of such a tale, made it one of the classical dramas of the twentieth century, demonstrating that specific cultural tradition strengthens rather than limits the universal value of literature and, for that matter, of folktales as well.

Several of the humorous tales in this volume, like the folktales, incorporate internationally found tale types—for example, tales IFA 2826 (no. 64), IFA 7127 (no. 65), and IFA 8889 (no. 57). But within Jewish society, the humorous tales expose, more than any other genre, the social seams between professional groups and class divisions found in a small community. These are tales in which the rabbis ridicule their community (tale IFA 13908, this vol., no. 60) and the community criticizes its rabbi (tale IFA 13909, this vol., no. 61); the congregation laughs at its cantor (tale IFA 6655, this vol., no. 59) and a jester pretends to be a cantor to exploit and put down a congregation (tale IFA 6976, this vol., no. 62). Humorous tales do not portray an idealized society and do not set up ethical models of behavior (though these are implicit in the humorous social critique); rather they expose the rough edges of Jewish social life.

The distance of time and place has given eastern European Jewish society a patina of myth and nostalgia.[86] The tales in this volume bring out the longing for the past and the reality of life, the imagined warmth and the experienced pain, the integrity of ideal values and the disintegration of the community, and—above all—the memories of a cherished life that was cruelly destroyed.

---------- Notes ----------

1. See a discussion of the Khazar tribes in the commentary for tale IFA 10103 (vol. 1, no. 50).

2. Weinryb, "The Beginnings of East-European Jewry in Legend and Historiography," 455–502; Weinryb, *The Jews of Poland*, 17–32; Cygielman, *Jewish Autonomy in Poland and Lithuania*, 4–6; and Cygielman, *The Jews of Poland and Lithuania*, 25–28.

3. Bar-Itzhak, *Jewish Poland*, 89–112; Weinryb, "The Beginnings of East-European Jewry in Legend and Historiography," 453–454; and Weinryb, *The Jews of Poland*, 17.

4. Bar-Itzhak, op. cit., 46–49.

5. Ibid., 49–56.

6. For studies about these pogroms, see the commentary for tale IFA 8915 (this vol., no. 29).

7. Balaban, *A History of the Jews in Cracow and Kazimierz*; Baron, *The Jewish Community*; Cygielman, *Jewish Autonomy in Poland and Lithuania*; and Cygielman, *The Jews of Poland and Lithuania*.

8. M. Weinreich, *History of the Yiddish Language*, 47.

9. Baviskar and Herzog, *The Language and Culture Atlas of Ashkenazic Jewry*; Geller, *Warschauer Jiddisch*; D. Katz, *Dialects of the Yiddish Language*; Muir, *Yiddish in Helsinki*; and Weinreich and Weinreich, *Yiddish Language and Folklore*, 27–28 nos. 112–123.

10. Roth, "*Das Wormser Machsor*," 222; and Shmeruk, *Yiddish Literature*, 9–10.

11. Kahle, *The Cairo Geniza*.

12. Fuks, *The Oldest Known Literary Documents of Yiddish Literature (c. 1382)*; Hakkarainen, *Studien zum Cambridge Codex*; Althaus, *Die Cambridger Löwenfabel von 1382*; Sadan, "The Midrashic Background of 'The Paradise' "; Shmeruk, "Can the Cambridge Manuscript Support the Spielman Theory of Yiddish Literature?"; and Baumgarten, *Introduction à la littérature yiddish ancienne*, 167–172.

13. Galiebe, *Dukus Horant*; Ganz, *Dukus Horant*; Ganz and Schwarz, "*Zu dem Cambridger Joseph*"; Mader, *Die Dukus Horant Forschung*; and Strauch, *Dukus Horant*.

14. Falk, *Das Schemuelbuch*; Shmeruk, *Yiddish Literature*, 117–124; Zinberg, *A History of Jewish Literature*, 7:107–115; and Baumgarten, op. cit., 175–190.

15. Fuks, *Das Altjiddische Epos Melokîm-Bûk*; Zinberg, op. cit., 7:115–116; and Baumgarten, op. cit.

16. Matenko and Sloan, "*Aqedath Jishaq.*"

17. L. Landau, *Arthurian Legends;* and Zinberg, op. cit., 7:53–65. A thirteenth-century Hebrew translation preceded the Yiddish version; Leviant, *King Artus*.

18. Joffe, *Elia Bachur's Poetical Works*, vol. 1; Knaphais, *Elias Levita, Buovo d'Antona*; Baumgarten, op. cit., 216–228; Shmeruk, *Yiddish Literature*, 89–104; and J. C. Smith, "Elia Levita's Bovo Buch."

19. Babbi, *Paris et Vienne*; Leach, *Paris and Vienne*; and Baumgarten, op. cit. 228–250.

20. Baumgarten, *Paris un Viene*; Shmeruk and Timm, *Paris un'Viena*; Timm, *Paris un Wiene*; and Shmeruk, *Yiddish Literature*.

21. Zinberg, op. cit, 7:66–86, esp. 78 n. 48. See also, Knaphais, op. cit.

22. Tales of partner substitution in the conjugal bed are also found in biblical traditions—for example, when Laban substituted Leah for Rachel (Genesis 29:21–30). An ex-

ample of such a tale in the medieval tradition is of Rabbi Meir, who, being drunk, spent the night with his friend's wife, who seduced him; see Bin Gorion, *Mimekor Yisrael*, 145–148 no. 73. I was unable to find an analog to the deceived bride tale in Jewish tradition.

23. Loewe, *Catalogue of the Manuscripts in the Hebrew Character*, no 136; Erik, *Geshichte fun yiddisher literature* (The history of Yiddish literature), 343–344; M. Weinreich, *Bilder fun der yiddisher literaturgeshikhte* (Snapshots from the history of Yiddish literature), 143–144; Zinberg, op. cit. 176–177; and Zfatman, *Yiddish Narrative Prose from Its Beginnings to 'Shivhei ha-Besht (1504–1814)*, 12–13 no. 3.

24. See Bin Gorion, op. cit., 320–321 no. 176.

25. Eidelberg, *Juspa, Shammash of Warmaisa* (Worms), 85–86 no. 21.

26. Zfatman, *The Marriage of a Mortal Man and a She-Demon*.

27. Zfatman-Biller, "Yiddish Narrative Prose from Its Beginnings to 'Shivhei Habesht' (1504–1814)"; and Zfatman, *Yiddish Narrative Prose from Its Beginnings to 'Shivhei ha-Besht' (1504–1814)*.

28. Margoliouth, *Catalogue of the Hebrew and Samaritan Manuscripts in the British Museum*, no. 683; and Zfatman, *Yiddish Narrative Prose from Its Beginnings to 'Shivhei ha-Besht (1504–1814)*, 11 no. 1.

29. Zfatman, *Yiddish Narrative Prose from Its Beginnings to 'Shivhei ha-Besht (1504–1814)*, 11–22.

30. Rosenfeld, *The Book of Cows*; and Shmeruk, "Yiddish Prints in Italy," 174 no. 34.

31. E. Katz, *Book of Fables*; and E. Katz, "Das 'Kuhbukh' und das 'Sefer Mesholim.'"

32. Meitlis, *Das Ma'assebuch*; Meitlis, *The Book of Stories*; Meitlis, "Some Extant Folktales in Yiddish Mss"; Gaster, *Ma'aseh Book*; B. Pappenheim, *Allerlei Geschichten Maasse-Buch*; Sand, "A Linguistic Comparison of Five Versions of the Mayse Bukh"; Zfatman, "The Mayse-Bukh"; Zfatman, *Yiddish Narrative Prose from Its Beginnings to 'Shivhei ha-Besht' (1504–1814)*, 133–141; Zinberg, op. cit., 185–197; and Baumgarten, *Introduction à la literature Yiddish ancienne*, 365–370, 376–388.

33. The central book in the literature of Jewish mysticism, or the Kabbalah. The main part of the work was written in the last quarter of the thirteenth century in Castile, Spain, mostly composed by Moshe de Leon. A modern translation is Matt, *The Zohar*.

34. Zfatman-Biller, op. cit., 141–146.

35. Eidelberg, op. cit., 19–36 (Hebrew), 17–45 (English). This work is extant in two manuscripts in Oxford and in Worms. The first is listed in Neubauer, *Catalogue of Hebrew Manuscripts in the Bodleian Library*, Opp. 751, and reproduced in facsimile in Eidelberg, op. cit., [1a]–[115a]. The second is currently housed in the Rashi-Haus in Worms; Eidelberg, op. cit., 44; Baumgarten, *Introduction à la literature Yiddish ancienne*, 388–393; and Zinberg, op. cit., 198–203.

36. Eidelberg, op. cit., 50.

37. Eidelberg, op. cit., 49.

38. Zfatman-Biller, op. cit., 151.

39. Zfatman-Biller, op. cit., 170.

40. For a discussion of the frame narrative, see the notes to tales IFA 960 (this vol., no. 14), IFA 2634 (vol. 1, no. 22), and IFA 2644 (vol. 1, no. 23). See also Marzolph and van Leeuwen, *The Arabian Nights Encyclopedia*, 554–556.

41. Paucker, "Das Volksbuch von der Seiben Weisen Meistern in der Jüddischen

Literatur"; Zfatman, *Yiddish Narrative Prose from Its Beginnings to 'Shivhei ha-Besht (1504–1814)*, 8; M. Epstein, *Tales of Sendebar*; Runte, et al., *The Seven Sages of Rome*.

42. Paucker, "Yiddish Versions of Early German Prose Novels"; Paucker, "*Das Deutsche Volksbuch bei den Juden*"; Pauker, "The Yiddish Versions of the *Shildburger Buch*"; Zfatman-Biller, op. cit., pt. 2 , 7 n. 35; and Baumgarten, *Introduction à la literature Yiddish ancienne*, 364–365.

43. Zinberg, op. cit., 176.

44. Zfatman-Biller, op. cit., 105–121.

45. Shmeruk, *Yiddish Literature in Poland*, 83 no. 11; 91 no. 29.

46. Zfatman, *Yiddish Narrative Prose from Its Beginnings to 'Shivhei ha-Besht' (1504–1814)*, 162–163 no. 168.

47. Yaari, "R. Eliezer Paver, Life and Works," 499.

48. Quoted in Zfatman, *Yiddish Narrative Prose from Its Beginnings to 'Shivhei ha-Besht' (1504–1814)*, 167 no.175.

49. Shmeruk, *Yiddish Literature*, 176–177.

50. Roskies, *A Bridge of Longing*, 1–2.

51. For a discussion of the significance of the third meal on the Sabbath, see the commentary to tale IFA 5361 (this vol., no. 17).

52. Shmeruk, *Yiddish Literature*, 198–234; and Gries, *The Book in Early Hasidism*, 64–65.

53. One manuscript survived and was eventually published; the manuscript contains more than half the text that was later published. See Mondschein, *Shivhei Ha-Baal Shem Tov*.

54. A critical edition is by Rubinstein. *In Praise of the Ba'al shem Tov*, and an English translation is by Ben-Amos and Mintz, *In Praise of the Baal Shem Tov*; see also Rosman, "In Praise of the Ba'al Shem Tov."

55. Band, *Nahman of Bratslav*; D. Assaf, *Bratslav*; J. Dan, *The Hasidic Story*, 132–188; and Piekarz, *Studies in Bratslav Hasidism*, 83–184.

56. Dan, op. cit.; and Nigal, *The Hasidic Tale*.

57. See the introduction to vol. 1, xxxv–xxxvi.

58. There is voluminous scholarship about this period and process in Jewish history. For an introduction, see D. H. Weinberg, *Between Tradition and Modernity*.

59. See D. Noy, "Introduction," 2–3; and Kiel, "*Vox Populi Vox Dei*." U. and B. Weinreich, *Yiddish Language and Folklore*.

60. Weinig, "Necrology"; Weinig, "B. W. Segel's Folkloristic Papers"; and B. Weinreich, " Modern Yiddish Folktales," 14.

61. According to Roskies, "Introduction," xvi. An-Ski himself offered two reasons for his choice of a Russian-sounding name. At first he suggested that he wanted to incorporate his mother's name, Anna, into his literary name, adding to it a Russian suffix. According to a second account, the name was suggested by the distinguished Russian novelist Gleb Ivanovich Uspensky (1843–1902), who helped launch An-Ski's literary career in St. Petersburg.

62. Catalogs of the traveling exhibition of objects and photographs from this study are Beukers and Waale, *Tracing An-Sky*; Kantsedikas and Serheyeva, *The Jewish Artistic Heritage Album by Semyon An-Sky*; and Rechtman, *Jewish Ethnography and Folklore*.

63. D. Noy, "The Place of Sh. Ansky in Jewish Folkloristics"; Shatzki, "*S. Ansky, der Meshulaḥ fun folklore*"; Deutsch, "An-Sky and the Ethnography of Jewish Women"; Kiel,

"A Twice Lost Legacy," 401–424; Kugelmass, "The Father of Jewish Ethnography"; Roskies, "S. Ansky and the Paradigm of Return"; and D. G. Roskies, "Ansky Lives!" For biographical, bibliographical, and evaluative studies of S. An-Ski, see also Jeshurin, *Sh. An-Ski Bibliografye*; (n. 2 includes many references to biographical descriptions and memoirs related to An-Ski); Safran, "Timeline"; and Safran and Zipperstein, *The World of S. An-Sky*.

64. An-Sky, "On Jewish Folk-Creativity"; and Bar-Itzhak, "An-ski's Essay on Jewish Ethnopoetics."

65. Gottesman, *Defining the Yiddish Nation*, 11.

66. Wanwild, *Ba ync Jid'n* (Among us Jews), 59–91.

67. Almi, *1863*; and Gottesman, op. cit., 8–11.

68. Gottesman, op. cit., 75–108.

69. Gottesman, op. cit., 86–108; and Bar-El, *Under the Little Green Trees*, 273–308.

70. Bastomski, *Yidishe folkmayses un legends*.

71. Op. cit., 106. The book to which Gottesman refers appeared in Hebrew translation as *Ḥurban ha-Yehudim be-Polin, Galitsyah u-Bukovina* and a selection was published in English translation as *The Enemy at His Pleasure*.

72. For a discussion of Cahan's methodology, see Bauman, "Y. L. Cahan's Instructions on Collecting Folklore"; and Gottesman, op. cit., 145–170.

73. Cahan, *Yiddish Folksongs with Their Original Airs*.

74. Cahan, "Folksong and Popular Song."

75. Cahan, *Studies in Yiddish Folklore*, 246–248. Translation from Rubin, "Y. L. Cahan and Jewish Folklore," 41.

76. R. Biran, "L'affair Berl Verblunsky."

77. Sofer, "40 Jahre 'YIVO.' " B. Weinreich, op. cit. 15, suggests a different count of texts: "2,340 folktales, 3,807 anecdotes and 4,673 children's tales."

78. Cahan, *Jewish Folklore*, 100–215.

79. B. Weinreich, *Yiddish Folktales*; and Zfatman, *Ma'asiyyot kesem mi-pi yehudei mizraḥ Eiropa* (Yiddish wonder tales from East Europe).

80. Notable among these are the excellent collections of Olsvanger (1888–1961): *Rosinkess mit Mandlen; Röyte Pomerantsen or How to Laugh in Yiddish*; and *L'Chayim!* A more recent collection of tales, recorded mostly in Romania and Bokuvina in the 1970s and 1980s, is Stephani, *Ostjüdische Märchen*.

81. Rawnitzki, *Yidishe Witzn* (Jewish wit); and N. Gross, *Maaselech un Mesholim*. The tales of the latter volume were extensively studied by Schwarzbaum, *Studies in Jewish and World Folklore*. See also Kirshenblatt-Gimblett, "Traditional Storytelling in the Toronto Jewish Community."

82. Druyanow, *Sefer ha-Bedihah ve-ha-Ḥidud* (The book of jokes and witticisms); D. Sadan, *Ka'arat Egozim o Elef Bediḥah u-Bhdiḥah* (A bowl of nuts or a thousand and one jokes); and Sadan,. *Ka'arat Tsimmukim o Elef Bediḥah u-Bhdiḥah* (A bowl of raisins or a thousand and one jokes).

83. Goldin, "Toward a Profile of the Tanna, Aqiba ben Joseph."

84. B. Weinreich, *Yiddish Folktales*, 85–88.

85. See *The Dybbuk and Other Writings*.

86. Polonsky, "The Shtetl."

A Note on the Commentaries

When full information is available, each note consists of five sections: basic information; discussion of cultural, historical, or literary background; list of narrative analogues; folktale types; and folklore motifs.

Basic information includes the tale title, archival number, and names of its narrator and collector (recorder), as well as the time and place of its narration. The "Israel Place List (1970)" in the *Encyclopedia Judaica*, vol. 1, 169–91, serves as a spelling guide for the names of villages and towns in Israel. The spelling of names of countries and cities outside Israel follows standard English usage.

The section on cultural, historical, or literary background of the tale draws upon scholarship in relevant disciplines. Many of the texts cited are in Hebrew. However, modern Hebrew books and articles often have a title page or an overleaf in English translation. In these cases, the English or any other European language title is listed in the notes and the bibliography, with an indication in brackets that the text is in Hebrew. The book title appears in transliteration followed by translation in parenthesis when no title in a European language is available.

The next section lists narrative analogues that are available in the IFA, listing the archival number, title, and country of origin of each parallel version.

The fourth and fifth sections, on folktale types and folklore motifs, offer research tools for comparative analysis. "Tale type" is a principal concept in folktale theory and classification method. It designates narratives that have independent existence in tradition, even though storytellers may use them in combination with other tale types. Their coherent occurrence in tradition by themselves attests to their independence. Initially conceived by Johann Georg von Hahn (1811–1868) as "formula"[1] and later translated into English and considered as "story radicals" by S. Baring-Gould,[2] the concept of "tale type" was established in folktale studies in 1910 in A. Aarne's *Verzeichnis der Märchentypen* (Types of the Folktale). The second (1928) and third (1961) editions of this book, revised by Stith Thompson, and the fourth (2004) edition, revised by Hans-Jörg Uther, made it an indispensable research tool.[3] These indexes are the basic registrar of these types.

Folklorists worldwide have prepared tale type indexes of their own folk-literary repertoires, modeled upon *The Types of the Folktale* with appropriate modifications.[4] The listing in this section refers only to the published indexes of Jewish folktales, the unpublished IFA list of the modified or specific tale types unique to the Jewish narrative tradition, tale type indexes of other Near Eastern countries, and, if one is available, the tale type index of the narrator's country of origin. While the present tale collection was in preparation, a new edition of *The Types of the Folktale* appeared as H. J. Uther, *The Types of International Folktales*. This edition is listed specifically when it includes a change in title or number from the original index. But the reader is advised to consult it, even in those cases when it is not mentioned, since the new edition includes a vastly expanded list of bibliographical references for each tale type.

In contrast to the tale type, the folklore motif is the minimal narrative element that persists in tradition. The basic registrar of folklore motifs is S. Thompson's *Motif-Index of Folk-Literature*. An asterisk next to a number indicates that this motif has been identified in the present collection of tales and has not been previously numbered.[5]

──────── **Notes** ────────

1. *Griechische und albanesische Märchen*, 1:45–64.
2. "Appendix: Household Tales."
3. For selected informative and critical discussions of the concept, see Apo, "Tale Type"; Ashliman, *Folk and Fairy Tales*, 29–59; Georges, "The Universality of the Tale-Type"; Jason, "The Russian Criticism of the 'Finnish School'"; Jason, "Structural Analysis and the Concept of the 'Tale-Type.'"
4. Azzolina, D.S. *Tale Type and Motif-Indexes: An Annotated Bibliography*. Garland Folklore Bibliographies 12. New York: Garland 1987.
5. For selected studies of the concept of motif in folklore and literature, see Ben-Amos, "The Concept of Motif in Folklore," 17–36; Bremond, "A Critique of the Motif," 125–146; Christensen, *Motif et Theme*; Courtes, *Le Conte Populaire*; 15–58; Daemmrich, "Themes and Motifs in Literature: Approaches—Trends—Definition," 566–575; Dolezel, "Narrative Semantics and Motif Theory," 47–53; Dundes, "From Etic to Emic Units in the Structural Study of Folktales," 95–105; Grambo, "The Conceptions of Variant and Motif," 243–256, Handoo, "The Concept of Unit in Folk Narrative," 43–52; Levin, "Motif," 3:235–244; Meletinski, "Principes sémantiques d'un nouvel index des motifs et des sujets," 15–24; Thompson, *Narrative Motif Analysis as a Folklore Method*.

Tales of the Supernatural

1

The Three-Day Fair in Balta

Told by Dvora Fus

The court of the *Rebbe*[*] of Kozienitz[**] was overflowing with Hasidim. Everyone clustered around the *rebbe*. Among the Hasidim was a young man who was hanging about the *rebbe*'s court looking very somber and upset. He asked the *shammes*[§] to announce him to the *rebbe* because he wanted to have a private audience with him. Every time, though, the *shammes* came back with the message that the *rebbe* would not receive him and the young man should go away for the day because he could not meet the *rebbe*.

The young man decided that on Thursday he would stand right by the door and force his way into the *rebbe*'s study, throw himself at the *rebbe*'s feet, and beg him to have pity and receive him. But on Thursday the *rebbe* sent the *shammes* to tell the young man that he could be admitted. Wailing and crying loudly, he asked the *rebbe* for his blessing. He had been married for fifteen years but still didn't have any children.

The *rebbe* raised his eyes toward Heaven, furrowed his brow, and sank into thought. Suddenly he turned to the young man. "You have come to ask for my blessing, but you once committed an appalling sin. Tell me about it."

The young man proceeded to tell the *rebbe* that, fifteen years earlier, his parents had arranged a match for him. But because the bride didn't meet his fancy he had broken the engagement without his parents' knowledge.

"That was a double sin," the *rebbe* said. "You failed to show respect for your mother and father and you mortally humiliated your former fiancée. You must go find her and ask her forgiveness. After your former fiancée forgives you, you will have children who will be Torah scholars."

"But *rebbe*, I don't know where she lives, nor will I recognize her."

---

[*]Hasidic Rabbi.
[**]Yiddish for the town of Kozienice, in the Kielce district, Poland.
[§]Synagogue caretaker.

1 / *The Three-Day Fair in Balta* ✀ **3** ✀

A market fair, as one would find in Balta.

"Then," said the *rebbe*, "you must travel to Balta.* They have a three-day fair there. The fair is called 'Green Sunday.' You'll find your fiancée there, and she will recognize you."

The young man thanked the *rebbe* and traveled straight to Balta. When he reached Balta, he put up at an inn. He roamed the streets from daybreak till dusk, looking for his fiancée. He did this the first day and again the second day, and each time came back crushed and miserable because he had not found her.

On the third day, he continued his search, extremely upset because his hopes of finding her would soon be lost. At midday, though, there was a tremendous downpour. He took shelter, greatly distressed, and sank into thought. Suddenly he heard women's voices talking and laughing. One of them pointed at him and asked, "How do you like my former fiancé?" He raised his eyes, but the women had vanished. Only his fiancée was still there with him.

"I've come on account of you," he told her. "The *rebbe* told me to come here to see you. Please, I beg you, forgive me for the wrong I did you."

She said to him, "I'll forgive you if you pay my brother ten thousand ducats.** When you come back from my brother, go straight to the *rebbe*."

"Perhaps you can take the money from me?"

"No," she told him. "I cannot take it or send it with a messenger. My brother became a very rich man and made a match for his daughter. But now he is ruined, left with nothing, a poor man and heavily in debt. If the prospective father-in-law finds out, he'll break off the match at once. My brother is terrified of that. I'll give you my brother's address, and you give him the money."

"Where do you live?"

"I dwell in a place where there is no summer and no winter. For us there is perpetual peace. No one envies anyone else. And among us—no one breaks off an engagement." With this she vanished.

Exhausted and crushed, he went back to the inn. Many thoughts raced through his brain. He was going to have to make a long journey.

He stayed there overnight. In the morning, he set out to find the place and address she had given him. When he reached the town, he went up to the door of the house. He saw a man walking around inside, wringing his hands.

---

*A distance of approximately fifteen hundred miles.
**Silver or golden coins of variable value, formerly used in European countries.

He knocked on the door and entered, greeting the master of the house as if he were a relative. The brother, recognizing him as his sister's fiancé, sighed deeply and turned pale. The young man told him that his former fiancée had sent him and that he had ten thousand ducats for him. That was her condition for pardoning the wrong he had done her when he broke off their engagement.

The master of the house turned even paler and was at a loss for words: "Your one-time fiancée, my sister, is long dead. Fifteen years ago. She died from shame because you broke off the engagement."

Only now did the young man understand. . . . The Kozienitzer *rebbe* had brought him together with his dead fiancée. He gave her brother the money without further delay.

That same day, he left the town and went right back to the *rebbe*, who received him with a satisfied look. "Return, my son, to your wife and forget everything that has happened. Your fiancée has forgiven you. I add my blessing that you may have children who will be Torah scholars."

COMMENTARY FOR TALE 1 (IFA 708)

Written down in Yiddish from memory by Dvora Fus in 1958.

Cultural, Historical, and Literary Background

The Maggid of Kozienice

The Rebbe of Kozienice (or Kozienitz, in Yiddish) mentioned in the tale is Rabbi Israel ben Shabbetai Hapstein of Kozienice (1733 or 1736–1814), known as the "Maggid of Kozienice," who was a disciple of Rabbi Samuel Shmelke Horowitz of Nikolsburg (1726–1778);[1] Dov Baer, the Maggid of Mezhirech (d. 1772); Elimelech of Lyzhansk (1717–1787); and Rabbi Levi Isaac of Berdichev (c. 1740–1810). The Maggid of Kozienice was born in Apta (Opatow); he spent a few years as a teacher in Przysucha before settling in Kozienice. He is described and remembered as a thin, short, weakly, and sickly man, who was nevertheless full of spiritual energy, compassion, and great learning.

His followers attributed his poor health and small stature to a tradition that he was born when his parents were already old. He was among the rabbis whose birth was attributed to the Ba'al Shem Tov's blessing.[2] After the *maggid*'s move to Kozienice many, even non-Jews, came to seek his blessing, looking for a cure for their ailments. He was also engaged in public and political affairs of Polish Jewry, spreading, among other things, Beshtian Hasidism in Poland.[3] Analyses of his teachings and his approach to various aspects of Hasidism are available.[4]

Rubinstein[5] identified an anonymous *maggid* who is mentioned in some testimonies against the Hasidim as Rabbi Israel, the Maggid of Kozienice. The *maggid* also figures in fictional descriptions of Hasidic life[6] and is the subject of a rich cycle of legends that has appeared in both Hasidic and eastern European collections of Jewish tales.[7]

Broken Engagement to Be Married

Within the Jewish tradition, it is possible to distinguish three narrative patterns of broken marriage engagements: breach of parental agreement for their children's marriage (for example, tale IFA 18132 [in this vol., no. 49]), parental objection of a prophesied or romantic marriage (for example, tale IFA 4735 [vol. 1, no. 45], tale IFA 6591 [vol. 1, no. 44] and tale IFA 12549 [vol. 1, no. 46]), and spousal breach of a marriage promise. The present tale is an example of the latter pattern. The tale revolves around two themes: the vengeance of the neglected bride, which has a long history in Jewish folklore, and the discourse with and vanishing of the apparition, which is common to European traditions in general.

The Vengeful Bride

The theme of the vengeful bride is known in Jewish tradition as the story "The Weasel and the Pit," which is a variant of tale type 842B* "The Serpent at the

Wedding." An early cryptic allusion to this tale occurs in BT *Ta'anit* 8a, but its full narrative articulation was available in script only toward the end of the eleventh century in France and Italy. Rashi (1040–1105), in his commentary on the relevant passage in the Babylonian Talmud, explicated the enigmatic allusion with a story.[8] Around the same time, Nathan ben Jehiel of Rome (1035–c. 1110) included the tale in his talmudic lexicon, the *Arukh*, which he completed in 1101 but which was published in Rome in 1469–1472.[9]

An expanded form of the tale appears in fourteenth-century narrative collections, such as the Yemenite *Midrash ha-Gaddol* and the *Sefer ha-Ma'asiyyot* (likely of Persian provenance).[10] A fourteenth-century manuscript from Iran, which Kushelevsky[11] identified as being identical to *Sefer ha-Ma'asiyyot*, includes a version of "The Weasel and the Pit" that is truncated at the beginning and the end. In Europe, the tale appeared in print in the sixteenth century in Hebrew,[12] and at the beginning of the seventeenth century in Yiddish.[13] In the nineteenth century, this tale of romance and abandonment became popular in Jewish literature and drama; most notable is the play *Shulamis* (1880) by the Yiddish playwright Abraham Goldfaden (1840–1908).[14] In the nineteenth and twentieth centuries, the story was included in several tale collections and anthologies.[15]

In the Hasidic tradition, which the present tale represents, there are several transformations of and variations on the theme of the dead fiancée; in these stories, the forgotten bride dies and is not just in a state of severe depression. In the present tale, the groom's children do not die; they are not even born. The groom makes amends not by marrying the rejected bride (who is dead) but by financing the wedding of her niece. This version of the tale has appeared in several anthologies.[16]

Discourse with an Apparition

The appearance and manifestation of the dead has been an integral part of the human belief in magic, the supernatural, and the holy. Often, as in this story, the dead act as an intermediary between the living and God; in other cases, they have an independent will and capacity. There is a vast literature dealing with the perceptions of apparitions, ghosts, and revenants in the Middle Ages and up to the present. The examination of case studies throughout history makes it clear that the percipients, as the young man in the present tale, are experiencing a personal crisis.

Tyrrell[17] distinguished four classes of contact with apparitions: experimental cases, crisis cases, postmortem cases, and ghosts. Although these classes are not necessarily mutually exclusive, the present story illustrates a postmortem apparition in which the perceiver believes that he or she is speaking to a living being. Other studies of the subject are available.[18] In modern popular and Jewish folklore, a common figure is the "vanishing hitchhiker."[19]

In most cases, apparitions are demanding figures (for example, see tale IFA

18159 [in this vol., no. 2]), but there are different configurations of the interaction between the living and the dead. The features related in the present story are as follows:

- The dead fiancée is realistically represented.
- During the encounter, the young man does not know of the fiancée's supernatural existence.
- The restlessness of the dead is the result of an offense she suffered in her lifetime.
- There is a direct relationship between the appearance of the dead and a family crisis; the compensation for the offense of bridal neglect is bridal support.

In eastern European Jewish society, initial support for the newlyweds was the responsibility of the bride's parents. Without a dowry (Hebrew: *nedunyah*; Yiddish: nadn), engagement and marriage were next to impossible. This parental duty was a particularly heavy burden on poor families with several daughters who were close in age. In the biblical period, the monetary situation was reversed: the bridegroom, or his family, paid a bride price (*mohar*) for the wife (Genesis 24:53, Exodus 22:15–16). This was a customary rather than a canonized legal transaction.

During the talmudic period, it became the duty of the bride's family to provide the initial economic foundation of the newly married couple (BT *Ketubbot* 66a–67b). For poverty-stricken eastern European Jewry, this became a hardship, particularly for orphaned women of marriageable age. It was a patriarchal duty to provide—or if necessary, to collect—a respectable sum for the dowry; in case of orphaned young women, this task became a communal responsibility. (The common term for such a charitable act is *hakhnasat kallah*, "dowering the bride.") The theoretical significance of the use of the dowry in traditional societies has been studied;[20] but the implication of such studies to Jewish society in general and to eastern European Jewish communities in particular requires further analytical reflection. Discussions of the dowry in terms of the history of Jewish family law have been published.[21]

Following a formula in the Mishnah (*Pe'ah* 1:1; BT *Shabbat* 127a–127b), one can modify the list of "things of which a man enjoys the fruits in this world, while the stock remains for him for the world to come" from the morning prayer to include the act of "dowering the bride," canonizing such a charity in Jewish society. A modern fictive description of a father traveling through the Jewish communities of southeastern Poland to collect money for the *hakhnasat kallah* was provided by Agnon,[22] which was published in English as *Bridal Canopy* (1937). This work has been the subject of an extensive scholarship.[23] The great distance the young man in the present story traveled—from Kozienice in central eastern Poland to Balta, currently in Ukraine—was not uncommon, if Agnon's story is a testimony.

1 / *The Three-Day Fair in Balta* 9

Similarities to Other Tales
For other related tales in the IFA, see the notes to tale IFA 18159 (in this vol., no. 2).

Folklore Motifs

- D1810.0.3 "Magic knowledge of saints and holy men."
- D1817.2 "Saints magically detect crime."
- D1820.1 "Magic sight of saints."
- D1825.1 "Second sight."
- E334.3 "Ghost of a person abandoned by faithless lover."
- E363 "Ghost returns to aid living."
- E365.1 "Return from the dead to grant forgiveness."
- E425.1 "Revenant as woman."
- *E599.4.1 "Ghost asks for payment to be given to a living person (from one who does not know that asker has died)."
- F172 "No time, no birth, no death in other world."
- F403.2 "Spirits help mortal."
- *F1041.1.3.7.1 "Woman dies of broken heart when deserted by fiancé."
- F1041.1.13 "Death from shame."
- M444 "Curse of childlessness."
- Q252 "Punishment for breaking betrothal."
- Q325 "Disobedience punished."
- Q551.6 "Magic sickness as punishment."
- *Q551.6.8 "Infertility as punishment."
- Q572 "Magic sickness as punishment remitted."
- T52.4 "Dowry given at marriage of daughter."
- *T52.4.2 "Bride or bride's family does not have dowry money."
- V223 "Saints have miraculous knowledge."
- V223.1 "Saint gives advice."
- V223.3 "Saint can perceive the thoughts of another man and reveal hidden sins."
- W126 "Disobedience."

Notes

1. For more on Rabbi Shmelke, see the notes to tale IFA 237 (in this vol., no. 8).

2. See Rodkinson, *Sefer 'Adat Tsadikim* (The congregation of the holy people), 4–5; Bromberg, *Mi-gdolei ha-Ḥasidut* (Great Hasidic rabbis), Vol. 18: Beit Kozhnich (The house of Kozienice), 12–16; and M. Rabinowitz, *Ha-Maggid mi-Kozienice* (The preacher of Kozienice), 22–24. For another version about his birth, see M. Buber, *Tales of Hasidim: Early Masters*, 286.

3. M. Rabinowitz, op. cit., esp. 39–40, 83–92; H. Halberstam, *Toldot ha-Maggid of Kozienice* (Biography of the preacher of Kozienice); H. Rabinowitz, *Portraits of Jewish Preachers*, 229–234; and Raphael, *Sefer ha-Ḥasidut* (The book of Hasidism), 226–230.

4. Greis, "Israel ben Shabbethai of Kozienice"; Piekarz, *Between Ideology and Reality* (index); and Piekarz, *The Hasidic Leadership*, 179–181 (index).

5. "Notes on a Collection of Testimonies against Hasidism," and "Kozienice, Israel ben Shabbetai Hapstein."

6. M. Buber, *For the Sake of Heaven*.

7. M. Buber, *Tales of Hasidim: The Early Masters*, 286–299; Lipson, *Medor Dor* (From days of old), 1:223, 246 nos. 601, 676, 677, 2:6, 29, 104–105, 173, 219 nos. 823, 914, 1160, 1423, 3:49, 99–100, 158, 263 nos. 1891, 2034, 2209, 2558; and Zevin, *Sippurei Hasidim* (Hasidic tales), 1:9–12, 127, 173–174, 226, 232–234, 239–240, 259, 354–355, 433–434, 450, 479–480 nos. 1, 2, 126, 169, 226, 233, 242, 255, 342, 431, 457, 493, 2:82–83, 133–134, 138–141, 148–149, 225, 233–235, 305, 307, 313, 349–350, 371 nos. 84, 153, 161, 180, 256, 267, 343, 346, 356, 413, 440.

8. For an analysis of this story, see L. Landau, "Rashi's Tales in the Babylonian Talmud."

9. A. Kohut, ed., *Aruch Completum*, 3:395–396; a manuscript version is found in B. Lewin, *Otsar ha-Gaonim* (The gaonic treasure), 5:57–58.

10. Margulies, ed., *Midrash Haggadol on the Pentateuch: Genesis*, on verse 15:9; and Gaster, ed., *The Exempla of the Rabbis*, 74 (English), 59–60 (Hebrew) no. 89. On the dating of the Midrash Hagaddol of David ha-Adani, see Y. Ratzaby, ed., *R. Jehoshua Hannagid Responsa*, 15. The dating of The Exempla of the Rabbis is controversial; among the latest contributions to this debate are P. Alexander, "Gaster's Exempla of the Rabbis"; and Kushelevsky, "Some Remarks on the Date and Sources of 'Sefer ha-Ma'asiyyot'."

11. Op. cit.

12. J. Luzzatto, *Kaftor va-Ferah*, 80b–81b.

13. M. Gaster, ed., *Ma'aseh Book*, 1:173–177 no. 100 (English); and J. Maitlis, *The Book of Stories*, 63–67 no. 21 (Yiddish).

14. *Isegeklibene Shriften* (Collected writings), 33–104. For comparative and literary studies, see Kagan, *From Aggada to Modern Fiction in the Work of Berdichevsky*, 95–114; R. Meyer, "Geschichte eines orientalischen Märchenmotives in der rabbinischen Literatur"; T. Alexander, "The Weasel and the Well"; and D. Sadan, "Aggadut Ḥuldah ve-Bor" (The legend of the weasel and the well). Cf. C. Goldberg, "The Forgotten Bride."

15. For example, Farḥi, *Oseh Pele* (The miracle worker), 1:53–55; J. Eisenstein, *Ozar Midrashim* 1:161–162; and Bin Gorion [Berdyczewski], Mimekor Yisrael, 170–172 no. 87, esp. bibliographical headnote.

16. See Rodkinson, op. cit., 27a–29a; Anonymous, *Petirat Rabbenu ha-Kadosh mi-Belz* (The death of our holy rabbi from Belz), 9–12 no. 6 (reversed gender roles: the groom is neglected); Ben-Yeḥezki'el, ed., *Sefer ha-Ma'asiyyot* (A book of folktales), 3:412–418; M. Rabinowitz, op. cit., 139–141; Schram, *Stories within Stories*, 106–109 no. 14; and Schwartz, *Lilith's Cave*, 135–139 no. 31.

17. Apparitions, 33–49.

18. Caciola, "Wraiths, Revenants and Ritual in Medieval Culture"; H. Davidson and Russell, eds., *The Folklore of Ghosts*; Evans, *Visions, Apparitions, Alien Visitors*; Dierkens, ed., *Apparitions et Miracles*; Finucane, *Appearances of the Dead*; and J. Schmitt, *Ghosts in the Middle Ages*.

19. Bennett, "The Vanishing Hitchhiker at Fifty-Five"; and Shenhar, "Israelische Fassungen des Verschwundenen Anhalters."

20. Goody and Tambiah, *Bridewealth and Dowry*; and E. Samuel, "Dowry and Dowry Harassment in India."

21. L. Epstein, *The Jewish Marriage Contract*, 89–106; M. Friedman, *Jewish Marriage in Palestine*, 2:500 ("dowry"); Katzoff, "Donatio ante nuptias and Jewish Dowry Additions"; Neufeld, Ancient Hebrew Marriage Laws, 94–117; and Satlow, *Jewish Marriage in Antiquity*, 199–224.

22. Agnon, "Hakhnasat Kallah."

23. Holtz, *The Tale of Reb Yudel Hasid*; and Holtz, *Mar'ot u-Mekorot* (References and sources).

2

The Kaddish

Told by Hinda Sheinferber to Hadavah Sela

*O*nce upon a time, many years ago, there was a certain man who prayed in the synagogue every day and recited the *Kaddish*.* "Why do you say *Kaddish* every day?" people asked him. "You're only supposed to say it on the anniversary of your parents' deaths—when you have yahrzeit** for your mother or father."

"But there are souls haunting the synagogue," he replied, "waiting for someone to say *Kaddish*—not for his mother or father, but just to say it. I say *Kaddish* so that these souls will find a place in paradise."

Once when he left the synagogue, he saw a respectable-looking, well-dressed man standing there. He looked rich. "Perhaps," the man said, "you know someone who can say *Kaddish*, because I have yahrzeit."

"I say *Kaddish* every day anyway, so I'll say it. But tell me your father's name or your mother's name."

So the stranger said a name—his name was such and such—and said that he should say *Kaddish* at the evening service that day and at the afternoon service the next day. He hoped the man would come and say *Kaddish* every year. And he added, "But not for free. I'll pay you."

Now the man really needed money. He had a daughter to marry off. Whatever sum the well-dressed man gave him would be fine. The man took out a checkbook, wrote him a check, and told him to go to such and such a bank where he would get the money in cash.

The next day, the man went to the bank. He went to the teller, but the teller said, "For such a large amount, you need the manager's approval. The manager works upstairs. Go upstairs, and he'll countersign it for you."

So the man went upstairs and showed the check to the manager for his approval. The manager looked stunned. He turned white and started trembling. "Who gave you this check?" he asked with agitation.

---
*The mourner's prayer.
**The anniversary of one's death.

12

"Some man, some man told me I should say *Kaddish* in his name. But I don't know if that is the man's name or his father's name. But he gave me this check, and I want the money."

"Can you describe what he looked like?" asked the bank manager.

"He wore an expensive suit, with a white handkerchief in the breast pocket, and a hat. He looked like a respectable and wealthy man." Suddenly, looking around, he said, "In fact, that picture is just like the man."

It was a picture of the manager's father.

A third man was sitting there in the room. "You really don't say *Kaddish*?" he asked the bank manager.

"No," the manager said.

"You see," said the third man, "this fellow has to marry off a daughter, so now he has money. Sign it for him, so he can cash the check."

The manager signed and told the man to say *Kaddish* every year and come to him, with or without a check. "I'll give you the same amount every year."

COMMENTARY FOR TALE 2 (IFA 18159)

Told by Hinda Sheinferber to Hadara Sela in 1991 in Haifa.

Cultural, Historical, and Literary Background

The apparition in this tale, like the one in *The Tragedy of Hamlet, Prince of Denmark* (I.1, 4, and 5), is a demanding figure. The father's spirit in *Hamlet* demands revenge for his own murder (I.5). In the present tale, however, the dead man's son has abandoned traditional for modern life, and so the apparition asks a stranger to perform the traditional filial duty and recite the *Kaddish* prayer in his memory. Furthermore, the father in effect asks his son to pay the stranger.

The Prayer

The mourner's *Kaddish* prayer does not mention the dead; rather it is an exaltation of God, implying theodicy in a moment of personal crisis:

Yitgadal ve-yitkadash	Magnified and sanctified
Shmei rabbah	May His great Name be
Be'alma di vra	In the world that He created,
Kir'utei	As He wills,
Ve-yamlikh malkhutei	And may His Kingdom come
Be-hayekhon u-ve-yomaykhon	In your lives and in your days
U-ve-hayei de-khol beit Yisrael	And in the lives of all the house of Israel,
Be-'agala u-vi-zman kariv	Swiftly and soon.
Ve-imru amen.	And say all Amen!
Amen!	Amen!
Yehe shmei rabbah mevorakh	May His great name be blessed
Le'alam u-le'olmei almayah	Always and forever!
Yitbarakh	Blessed
Ve-yishtabakh	And praised
Ve-yitpa'ar	And glorified
Ve-yitromam	And raised
Ve-yitnaseh	And exalted
Ve-yit'hadar	And honored
Ve-yit'aleh	And uplifted
Ve-yithalal	And lauded
shmei de-kudsha berikh hu	Be the name of the Holy One
(Berikh hu)	(He is blessed)
Le-'ela min kol birkhata	Above all blessings
Ve-Shirata tushbehata ve-nehenmata	And hymns and praises and consolations
Da-amiran be-'alma	That are uttered in the world,
Ve-imru amen!	And say all Amen!

Yehe shlama rabbah min shmaya	May a great peace from heaven
Ve-ḥayyim	And life!
Aleinu ve-al kol Yisrael	Be upon us and upon all Israel,
Ve-imru amen.	And say all Amen!
Oseh shalom bi-meromav	May He who makes peace in His high places
Hu ya'aseh shalom aleinu	Make peace upon us
Ve-al kol Yisrael	and upon all Israel
Ve-imru amen.	And say all Amen![1]

The translation of the *Kaddish* is available in most American Jewish prayer books,[2] and interpretive studies of the prayer are available.[3] The *Kaddish* is a public prayer, written in Aramaic, that requires a minyan, a quorum of ten adult men, for its recitation. Within the daily service, it has only a dependent status, concluding the service or punctuating its significant segments. The recitation of the *Kaddish* also takes place at the conclusion of the Torah reading. Within the service, the *Kaddish* prayer appears with some variations, depending on when it occurs. There are five subtypes:

- The *Kaddish shalem* (the whole or complete *Kaddish*).
- The *Ḥatzi Kaddish* (the half *Kaddish*), from which the concluding verses of the complete *Kaddish* are omitted.
- The *Kaddish de-rabbanan* (the sages' *Kaddish*), in which a prayer for the teachers and their disciples substitutes for the prayer for the entire house of Israel.
- The *Kaddish yatom* (the mourner's *Kaddish*).
- The Resurrection Kaddish (includes expanded verses that express messianic expectations and the belief in the resurrection of the dead and in the world to come).

A son recites the mourner's *Kaddish* at the gravesite of his deceased parent and three times a day for eleven months on weekdays at the conclusion of the *Aleinu* (Our duty) prayer in the morning (*Shaḥarit*), afternoon (*Minḥah*), and evening (*Arvit*) prayers. On the Sabbath, he recites *Kaddish de-rabbanan* at the *Mussaf* service. After the conclusion of the year of mourning, the *Kaddish* is recited on the anniversary of the parent's death (yahrzeit).

Although the prayer is in Aramaic, its wording resonates or is a direct translation of several biblical verses. The opening phrase *Yitgadal ve-yitkadash shmei rabbah*, "Magnified and sanctified May His great Name be," resonates the verse "My greatness and My holiness, and make Myself known in the sight of many nations" (Ezekiel 38:23).

The messianic allusion to the kingdom of God—*Ve-yamlikh malkhutei* (And may His Kingdom come) can be found in several biblical verses, such as "and dominion shall be the Lord's" (Obadiah 1:21) and "His sovereign rule is overall"

(Psalms 103:19). Other references to the kingship of the Lord are found in Psalm 145:11–13 and, in messianic terms, in Daniel 2:44.

The Blessings

The eight verbs of praise found in the *Kaddish* have cognates in the biblical Hebrew, either in the same reflexive pattern of *hitpa'el* or in another verbal or nominal form. The verb *yitbarakh* (blessed) occurs in the verse "Shall bless himself by the true God" (Isaiah 65:16); in this case, as in most of the biblical texts, humankind is the object of blessing, only in the language of Psalms and few later books is it incumbent on people to bless God (Psalm 103:20,21, 134:1, 135:20; Nehemiah 9:5; 1 Chronicles 29:20).

The second verb, *ve-yishtabakh* (and praised), is a reflexive formation, which is rare for this verb in biblical Hebrew. When this form does occur, humankind rather than God is the object of praise (for example, Psalm 106:47; 1 Chronicles 16:35).

Ve-yitpa'ar (and glorified), the third verb, occurs in the verse "My handiwork in which I glory" (Isaiah 60:21; 61:3), predicated on God. The fourth and the fifth verbs—*ve-yitromam* (and raised) and *ve-yitnaseh* (and exalted)—pair in different verbal patterns in Isaiah: "I beheld my Lord seated on a high and lofty throne" (6:1), " 'Now I will arise,' says the Lord, 'Now I will exalt Myself, now raise Myself high' " (33:10), and "He who high aloft" (57:15).

The sixth verb, *ve-yit'hadar* (and honored), does not occur in the Hebrew Bible, but the noun *hadar* (splendor or honor) occurs in reference to God several times, particularly in Psalms (8:6, 21:6, 96:6, 104:1, 111:3), although it occurs in other verses and in other books. The seventh verb, *ve-yit'aleh* (and uplifted), also does not occur in the Hebrew Bible in this context. The eighth verb, *ve-yithalal* (and lauded), occurs in Proverbs 31:30 in praising a capable woman, but the verb recapitulates the honorific exclamation in Psalms, Hallelujah.

The confirmation (*Berikh hu*; "He is blessed") could have an association with Pethahiah's instruction: "Rise, bless the Lord your God who is from eternity to eternity" (Nehemiah 9:5) and the formula *le-'ela min kol birkhata* (above all blessings) resonates the biblical construction "higher and higher" (Deuteronomy 28:43).

The central blessing—*Yehe shmei rabbah mevorakh Le'alam u-le'olmei al-mayah* (May His great name be blessed Always and forever!)—is a slightly modified version of Daniel's Aramaic blessing, "Let the name of God be blessed forever and ever" (2:20), or of its Hebrew rendition in Psalms, "Let the name of the Lord be blessed now and forever" (113:2). The concluding phrase of the prayer, in Hebrew—*Oseh shalom bi-meromav* (He imposes peace in His heights)—is a direct quotation of Job 25:2.

Such intertextuality between prayers and the Hebrew Bible is not unique to the *Kaddish;* rather it is a common feature of Jewish prayers. The text of the *Kaddish* further resonates with other expressions and formulas that recur in the Aramaic translations of the Bible and in the talmudic-midrashic literature.[4]

Historical Origins

The first use of the Aramaic term *Kaddish* to designate a prayer occurs in the small and late (c. 600 C.E.) tractate *Sofrim* (10:1, 16:9, 19:1, 21:6). However, in earlier tractates there are allusions to the prayer in the phrase *Yehe shmei rabbah mevorakh* (May His great name be blessed), used as a public response. Occasionally, the phrase is in a mix of Aramaic and Hebrew (BT *Berakhot* 3a, 21b, 57a; *Shabbat* 119b). In other cases, there are variations on the opening formula of the prayer, *Yitgadal ve-yitkadash shmei rabbah* (Magnified and sanctified May His great Name be), as in JT *Berakhot* 9:2.[5] The earlier sage to whom a reference to this prayer is attributed is the second-century *tanna* Joseph ben Ḥalafta (*Sifrei* 306).[6]

Heinemann[7] considered the *Kaddish,* in style, form, and performance, as a prayer that emanated from the *beit midrash* (house of study). The features of the prayer are thematic limitation—usually giving thanks for the Torah and praying for redemption and the coming of the kingdom of God—uniformity of content, brevity, a free formula that only gradually stabilized, use of the third person to address God, use of epithets in place of the Tetragrammaton, and description of divine attributes with a sequence of present participles or relative clauses.

During the period of the *tannaim* and the *amoraim,* the *Kaddish* was not a mourner's prayer. Other prayers served that purpose, as texts and descriptions of rituals make evident. Mourners recited the following prayer in the cemetery after burial, emphasizing the belief in the resurrection of the dead: "He walks in a cemetery [and] says: Blessed be He who knows the number of all of you; He will judge you and He will revive you. Blessed be He who keeps His word and revive[s] the dead" (*Tosefta Berakhot* 7:9). In fact, the recitation of the *Kaddish* as a mourner's prayer is unknown in rabbinic sources. The only phrase in the *Kaddish* that is found in the Talmud, *yehai shmei rabba,* is part of the synagogue liturgy, and its connection at this period to the mourner's ritual cannot be determined (BT *Berakhot* 3a, 57a; *Shabbat* 119b).[8]

One talmudic description of a mourning ritual emphasizes the need for the quorum of ten men but does not refer to the *Kaddish* or any other prayer in particular: "Rab Judah said: If there are none to be comforted for a dead person, ten people go and sit in his place. A certain man died in the neighbourhood of Rab Judah. As there were none to be comforted, Rab Judah assembled ten men every day and they sat in his place. After seven days he [the dead man] appeared to him in a dream and said to him, 'Thy mind be at rest, for thou hast set my mind at rest' " (BT *Shabbat* 152a–152b). In the *amoraic* literature, the ritualistic recitation of a prayer for the dead was bound with the debate about whether the dead needed atonement or whether they had atoned for their mortal sins by their very deaths.[9]

The first time the complete text of the *Kaddish* appeared in a prayer book was in the ninth century in the prayer book of Rabbi Amram, the Ga'on of Sura (d. c. 875);[10] but at that time the prayer was not yet considered a mourner's prayer. The first clear testimony of the use of the *Kaddish* as a mourner's prayer occurs in *Or Zaru'a* (Sown light) by Isaac ben Moses of Vienna (c. 1180–c.1250), which was published in 1862 in Zhitomir, Poland (see *Or Zaru'a* 2, no. 50, 3–4).

In the thirteenth century, apparently the recitation of the mourner's *Kaddish* was not yet ubiquitous, occurring only in Bohemia and in the Rhineland but not in France. The use of the *Kaddish* for such a purpose is validated by the legend *Rabbi Akiva and the Wandering Dead Man,* which tells about a son who by his prayer atones for his father's grave sins, elevating his soul from Hell to Heaven. The same legend occurs in *Mahzor Vitry* (The Vitry prayer book), which was edited by Simḥah ben Samuel of Vitry, a small town in the Marne province of France. Simḥah ben Samuel, a student of Rashi (1040–1105), wrote his prayer book in 1108. The inclusion of the Rabbi Akiva story is likely to be a later interpolation made in the twelfth century by Rabbi Isaac ben Durbal[11] or maybe even in the thirteenth or fourteenth century; the scribe indicated he copied the legend from "*sefarim Penimiim,*" probably a term referring to mystical books.[12] If this is the case (that is, if the inclusion of the story is indeed an interpolation), the two versions of the tale are contemporaneous. Studies of this legend and its relation to the *Kaddish* prayer are available.[13]

Since the Middle Ages, the recitation of the *Kaddish* has been institutionalized as a mourners' prayer in all Jewish communities and has been studied and interpreted extensively. Analytical, descriptive, introspective, and interpretive writings about this prayer have been published.[14]

Similarities to Other IFA Tales

In the IFA the following tales have a similar theme.

- IFA 715: *The Great Kaddish* (Eretz Yisra'el, Ashkenazic).[15]
- IFA 859: *The Dead Who Was Grateful for the Recitation of the Kaddish* (Syria, Sephardic).
- IFA 2600: *The Widow Who Paid for a Kaddish for a Lonely Person* (Eastern Europe).[16]
- IFA 2611: *A Man Who Pays for the Recitation of the Kaddish for a Lonely Person Becomes Rich* (Eastern Europe).[17]
- IFA 3289: *How Valuable Is the Kaddish Recitation?* (Tunisia).[18]
- IFA 9854: *The Dead Father Gave a Promissory Note as Payment for the Kaddish Prayer* (Yemen).[19]
- IFA 11106: *The Kaddish* (Morocco).
- IFA 13234: *A Reward for Charity* (Iraqi Kurdistan).
- IFA 16561: *A Mitzvah and Its Reward* (Turkey).

Folktale Types

- cf. 2944 (Tubach) "Knight, Dead, Return of."
- 3388 (Tubach) "Monk Returns from Dead."

- 3914 (Tubach) "Prayer Asked by Dead."
- 4006 (Tubach) "Purgatory, Vision of, Seen by Monk."

Folklore Motifs

- *E286 "Souls haunt synagogue."
- E327 "Dead father's friendly return."
- *E327.6 "Dead father returns to ask someone to pray for his soul."
- *E338.4 "Non-malevolent ghosts haunt synagogue."
- E341.3 "Dead grateful for prayers."
- *E351.1 "Dead returns and writes a check."
- *E365.2 "Return from the dead to request for anniversary prayer."
- E411 "Dead cannot rest because of sin" (implicit in this tale: prayer is required as an appeal for forgiveness for a general and unintentional human sinful existence).
- E422.4.5 "Revenant in male dress."
- E425.2 "Revenant as man."
- E545 "The dead speak."
- E754 "Saved souls."
- E755.1 "Souls in Heaven."
- Q33 "Reward for saying prayers."
- V50 "Prayer."
- cf. *V56 "Kaddish: mourners prayer said after the death of a close relative."
- V112.3 "Synagogues."

Notes

1. This translation and format of presentation are from Wieseltier, *Kaddish*, where it is printed without transliteration.
2. Birnbaum, *Daily Prayer Book*, 138, 186–187, 216, 220, 280.
3. Scherman, *The Kaddish Prayer;* and Wise, *Kaddish*.
4. See Pool, *The Kaddish*.
5. Friedmann, *Seder Eliahu Rabba and Seder Eliahu Zuta,* 5, 22.
6. L. Finkelstein, *Sifre on Deuteronomy*, 342.
7. "Prayers of the Beth Midrash Origin"; and *Prayer in the Talmud*, 256–257.
8. D. Kraemer, *The Meaning of Death in Rabbinic Judaism*, 133, 158 n. 4.
9. L. Finkelstein, *"Mi-Torato Shel R. Neḥunya ben ha-Kanah"* (From the teaching of R. Neḥunya ben ha-Kanah), 352–377; and Glick, *A Light unto the Mourner*, 127–144.
10. Frumkin, *Seder Rav Amram ha-Shalem* (The complete prayer book of Rabbi Amran), 88b–89a.
11. Hurwitz, *Machsor Vitry*, 112–113 no. 144.
12. Friedmann, op. cit., 24.
13. Kushelevsky, "The *Tanna* and the Restless Dead" (1994); Kushelevsky, "The Tanna and the Restless Dead" (2004); M. Lerner, *"Ma'aseh ha-Tanna ve-ha-Met"* (The

story of the Tanna and the dead man); Obermeyer, *Modernes Judentum im Morgen- und Abendland*, 91–143; and Ta-Shema, "Some Notes on the Origins of the '*Kaddish Yatom*.'

14. Da. Assaf, *Sefer ha-Kaddish* (The Kaddish book); Berliner, *Selected Writings*, 1:85–91; Blidstein, "Kaddish and Other Accidents"; Danzig, "Two Insights from a Ninth-Century Liturgical Handbook"; Elbogen, *Jewish Liturgy*, 80–84; S. Goldberg, *Crossing the Jabbok*, 38–40; Greenwald, *Kol Bo al Avelut* (A compendium on mourning customs and laws), 365–378; Heilman, *When a Jew Dies*, 130–131, 144–146, 164–171, 183–193; Hess, "*Kaddish yatom*"; L. Hoffman, *The Canonization of the Synagogue Service*, 56–65; J. Horowitz, *The Kaddish;* Hübscher, *The Kaddish Prayer;* Karl, "*Ha-Kaddish*"; Krauss, "*Mahut ha Kaddish*" (The nature of the Kaddish); Lehnardt, "*Qaddish und Sifre Devarim 306*"; Lehnardt, *Qaddish;* Pool, op. cit.; A. Z. N. Roth, "*Azkarah, Haftarah ve-Kaddish Yatom*"; Scherman, op. cit.; Steinsaltz, *A Guide to Jewish Prayer*, 428 (index); Telsner, *The Kaddish;* Weitzman, "The Origin of the *Qaddish*"; Wise, op. cit.; and Wieseltier, op. cit.

15. Published in Ashni, *Be-Simta'ot Tzfat* (In the alleys of Safed), 122.

16. Published in Naʻanah, *Ozar ha-Maʻasiyyot* (A treasury of tales), 1:1–3.

17. Published in Naʻanah, op. cit., 1:42–47.

18. Published in D. Noy, *Jewish Folktales from Tunisia*, 109–110 no. 35.

19. Published in Caspi, *Mi-Zkenim Etbonan* (I will observe the elders), 111–113.

3

The House Vanished with All Its Inhabitants

TOLD BY LEON ALTMAN TO NATHAN MARK

My father, Yosef Ephraim, son of Ḥayyim Altman, was drafted into the Eighth Cavalry Regiment in the town of Roman. Soon after, in 1877, the war broke out—the Romanian War of Independence. My father and his entire unit were dispatched to the Dobruja front.

The captain who commanded the unit was a very fair man and took my father under his wing. The sergeant major was a Jew from Romania named Bercu. My father, who was a yeshivah[*] student in his youth, did not want to eat at the company mess. The captain let him prepare his own food.

The unit was bivouacked on a wide and barren plain, without a single house or living soul.

Passover approached. On the eve of the festival, my father reported to the captain and asked for an eight-day furlough so he could celebrate the holiday properly. The captain agreed but warned him that the nearest settlement was thirty miles away. "How will you manage that?" he asked. My father replied that his faith was firm, and he was certain that God would help him reach the town safely.

Soon after that, he left the camp and headed for the road that led to the town. He spied a small, dilapidated house in the distance. He quickened his pace. When he reached it, he saw that a dyed hunk of wool[**] was hanging above the lintel and a mezuzah[§] was nailed to the doorpost. My father entered the house and was received cordially by the couple who lived there. Even though the house gave an impression of poverty, they persuaded him to spend the entire festival with them, because the road to

---

[*]Jewish school of higher learning.
[**]In some communities it was the custom to hang a piece of wool above the mezuzah that women kissed as they entered the house.
[§]A small case containing passages from the Torah.

town was dangerous, especially now during the war. Of course, my father was glad to accept their invitation and spent the entire festival with the couple.

When he returned to the camp, the captain asked where he had spent the holiday. My father told him the whole story. The captain could not believe his ears—he knew that there was no one living anywhere in the vicinity.

A short time later, the captain informed the soldiers that anyone who paid twenty pounds could receive his discharge. You can well imagine how tempting the offer was! But where could one acquire twenty pounds? My father went back to the couple and asked them to lend him the sum. They were happy to help, and my father was discharged from active service.

On his way home, his first stop was the house where he had spent the festival and later had found the means of his deliverance. He wanted to thank them for everything they had done for him. He reached the place—but there was no skein of wool, no mezuzah, no house, no sign that there had ever been anyone there. Then he knew—Father says—that it was Elijah the Prophet.

3 / The House Vanished

A shtetl house.

COMMENTARY FOR TALE 3 (IFA 7290)

Told in 1966 in Nahariah by Leon Altman from Romania, to Nathan Mark, who recorded and translated the tale.

Cultural, Historical, and Literary Background

The narrator of the tale refers to the Russo-Turkish war of 1877, in which Romanian troops fought with the Russian Army against the forces of the Ottoman Empire. The Romanians entered into a conditional military convention with the Russians, exerting from them the recognition of Romania's territorial integrity and independence; hence the narrator refers to the conflict as the Romanian "war of independence," conflating it with a familiar historical idiom in modern Israel. Romania actually began its move toward independence a decade earlier.[1] The country's Jews had a precarious position in this conflict.[2]

In that war, hostilities began on April 24, 1877, almost a month after the beginning of the Passover holiday, which started that year on March 28. Hence the calendar does not agree with the events in the story, though it is quite possible that some troops were stationed in the area in preparation for combat.

Similarities to Other IFA Tales

The miraculous appearance of Elijah the Prophet occurs in many tales, including tales IFA 960 (in this vol., no. 14), IFA 2420 (vol. 1, no. 20), IFA 7000 (vol. 1, no. 17), and IFA 16408 (vol. 1, no. 1). The following tales in the IFA involve Elijah the Prophet's assistance on Passover night.

- IFA 846: *The Guest at the Seder* (Romania).[3]
- IFA 1113: *The Treasure That Elijah the Prophet Gave* (Poland).
- IFA 2017: *Elijah the Prophet Gives Wealth on Passover Eve* (Caucasia).
- IFA 2450: *The Poor Man Who Sold Elijah the Prophet* (Libya).
- IFA 2965: *On Passover Eve Elijah the Prophet Helps with a Magical Gift* (Eretz Yisra'el, Ashkenazic).
- IFA 3959: *Elijah the Prophet Was a Guest on Passover Eve* (Poland).
- IFA 5519: *A Letter to God* (Iran).[4]
- IFA 6042: *The Ridicule of the Poor* (Kurdistan).[5]
- IFA 7213: *Elijah the Prophet* (Hungary).
- IFA 9226: *The Miracle of Passover Eve* (Morocco).[6]
- IFA 9591: *Elijah the Prophet Helps the Fisherman's Daughter* (India).
- IFA 10321: *Good Deeds for the Holiday* (Republic of Georgia).
- IFA 10819: *The Confident Woodcutter* (Ukraine).[7]
- IFA 10852: *The Shammash Who Became a Vegetable Grocer* (Ukraine).[8]
- IFA 10953: *A Letter to God* (Poland).
- IFA 10990: *The Elijah the Prophet Synagogue* (Iran).
- IFA 11182: *Care of the Poor* (Tunisia).

- IFA 11625: *The Poor Brother and the Rich* (Morocco).
- IFA 14579: *The Miracle of Elijah the Prophet* (Morocco).⁹

Folklore Motifs

- D1133 "Magic house."
- D1133.1 "House created by magic."
- D2188 "Magic disappearance."
- *D2188.4 "House vanishes."
- F900.1.2 "Miracles on first night of Passover."
- *P165 "Poor men."
- *P165.1 "Poor women."
- P320 "Hospitality."
- P461 "Soldiers."
- P551 "Army."
- V75.1 "Passover."
- *V75.1.1 "Seder, the Passover Eve ceremonial dinner."
- *V131.5 "Mezuzah."
- *V295 "Elijah the Prophet."
- W11 "Generosity."

--- **Notes** ---

1. Hitchins, *Rumania 1866–1947*, 11–54, esp. 42–43.
2. For an analysis of the war, with an emphasis on the situation in Bulgaria, see Neuburger, "The Russo-Turkish War and the 'Eastern Jewish Question.'"
3. Published in D. Noy, "*Eliyahu ha-Navi be-Leil ha-Seder*" (Elijah the Prophet on Passover eve).
4. Published in Estin, *Contes et fêtes Juives*, 217–219 no. 51; E. Marcus, *Jewish Festivities*, 95–96 no. 51; and Rush and Marcus, *Seventy and One Tales for the Jewish Year*, 172–174 no. 41.
5. Published in Stahl, *Stories of Faith and Morals*, 21–22 no. 4.
6. Published in Rabbi, *Avoteinu Sipru* (Our fathers told), 1:55–56 no. 34.
7. Published in Warnbud, *Neḥemyah Ba'al Guf* (Nehemyah, the Heavy-Set), 40–41.
8. Published in Warnbud, op. cit., 78–79.
9. Published in Rush, *The Book of Jewish Women's Tales*, 155–156 no. 38.

4

The Rabbi Who Was Tricked

TOLD BY DVORA FUS

*I*n a small town, there lived a rabbi with his wife and children. The rabbi was a great scholar and a quiet man. The townsfolk were very fond of him. No rich men lived in the town, so the rabbi barely made a living. But he was content with his lot. He was satisfied with everything. He did not want to be a burden on the people of the town. Time passed.

Early one morning, some well-dressed men arrived in town and asked for the rabbi. When they reached his house, they greeted him and introduced themselves. They said that they came from a big city and were looking for a rabbi. They would pay him a good salary if he agreed to come with them.

The idea made the rabbi very unhappy. Because he was so content in his town he refused at once. But they coaxed him, reminding him that he had a daughter who would soon be of marriageable age and that he would never find a match for her in that small town. They pressed the rabbi until he agreed, on condition that if he didn't like the new post he could return at any time. While they were negotiating with the rabbi, they gave his wife a large sum of money so there would be plenty of good things in the house. Of course, everyone has a weakness for temptation, and a person can be easily persuaded by good things. The rabbi, too, was won over and agreed to go with them.

When it was time to leave, he called together the elders of the synagogue and the town fathers and explained the situation to them. He bade farewell to the townsfolk, with tears in his eyes, of course. "Rabbi," they begged him, "if you're not happy there, we'll take you back with open arms." The rabbi promised that, of course, he would see how he liked it.

In the rabbi's house, everyone was happy. His wife was being left a large sum of money for use while the rabbi would not be with the family to support them and until he could bring them to the city where he was going to assume the rabbinate. The rabbi told his family good-bye and set out with the men.

4 / The Rabbi Who Was Tricked

Of course, they had come with their horse and wagon. They traveled through fields and towns. On the way, they didn't speak a single word to him. The rabbi wondered about this—in the house they had been very kind and amiable. Suddenly, the rabbi felt people tying his arms and legs and throwing a bag over his head. The rabbi realized that he was being punished for abandoning the poor but honest people in the town. But the situation was hopeless. His only request of the Master of the Universe was that he might return to his wife and children.

Thus the rabbi continued his journey, tied up and with a sack over his head and, alas, his heart filled with anger at his family. He realized that he had fallen into the clutches of the devil. They traveled on like this for some time until the wagon stopped, and the men told him to get out. They led him into a dark room and pointed him to a sack filled with straw. Hungry and tired, he threw himself down without eating and let out a stifled cry. But there was no sound and no response. He prayed that God might allow him to return to his town, to his wife and children.

Every morning, they tossed him some bread and water. Soon he no longer remembered what day it was. The place where he was held was a house with many rooms. He managed to look around a little to see where he was, but all the rooms were empty. One room, though, was locked, and he could never get inside it. He decided that he simply must enter the locked room. He was afraid that if the gang of men heard him making noise, they might come and kill him. But he felt that he simply had to open the door.

When he finally opened the door, he saw a chest standing in the corner. When he touched it, he heard a human voice calling out from inside: "Don't touch me or I'll scream, and the gang will come straightaway and kill you. Keep your distance, and I'll tell you everything.

"Know, then, that you are being held by thieves and sorcerers. To work their magic they have to obtain, once every seven years, the head of a rabbi who is a third-generation rabbi. My seven years will soon be over. You can replace me because you are a third-generation rabbi. It is my duty to tell the truth. I have the power of speech because the name of impurity* lies under my tongue. You let yourself be persuaded by them and were dazzled by the idea of having a rich pulpit. Your eyes were blinded by

---

*That is, a slip of paper with the name of a demon written on it. This is an inversion of the use of a secret name of God to animate an image.

money. That is why you lost the honest Jews of your town, who were loathe to bother you with their troubles. This is what you deserve. But you prayed to the Master of the Universe and entreated him with an honest heart. So you have been saved. Your request has been accepted.

"Listen. When it gets dark, come over to the chest and take the name of impurity from under my tongue. You will immediately find yourself in an open field. The thieves will be getting together today. You must take my head and give it a Jewish burial. When you reach your house and see your wife with your children, you must not speak to them. You must turn aside and go many miles from the town. If you do as I have said, you will be saved."

The rabbi locked the door and went back to his bed, tired, hungry, and even more frightened than before. He waited until it was dark. Then he went back to the door, entered the room, and removed the name of impurity from the mouth. At once, he found himself in the open country. He took the head and ran, overcome by the terror of what had happened to him. Soon he saw a cemetery. He gave the rabbi's head a Jewish burial. When he had run farther, he no longer felt hungry. The thought that he was safe restored his strength.

When day arrived, he reached his house. Of course, his family was quite surprised. The townspeople soon discovered that their dear rabbi had come back to resume his post. He promised the dear Jews of his town that he would never leave them again.

An old Jewish cemetery.

COMMENTARY FOR TALE 4 (IFA 779)

Written down from memory in Yiddish by Dvora Fus in 1959, as heard from her mother in the shtetl of Lewdow near Vilna, Lithuania.

Cultural, Historical, and Literary Background

The tale involves supernatural agents and fictive actions in a fictive domain, but the initial episode describing the selection of a rabbi and the invitation extended to him to join a new community—thereby depriving a poorer community of its rabbi, who had achieved regional or national renown—describes a common practice. In Hasidic congregations, the rabbi was a charismatic figure, as described by Weber.[1] Accordingly, the office of the rabbi was passed from father to son, retaining the position within the family and thus creating a rabbinical dynasty. In the non-Hasidic communities in Eastern and Central Europe, however, the nomination and appointment to a rabbinical post was competitive and was awarded to the most qualified available scholar. Congregations often competed among themselves to attract prominent individuals. The history of the rabbinate in European communities has been studied.[2]

The shift in the tale from a realistic to a fictive domain occurs with the realization that the representatives of the wealthy congregation in the big city are in fact sorcerers who abducted the rabbi. Then the narrative progresses to incorporate three themes that recur in Jewish folk tradition: abduction, a speaking skull, and a proper Jewish burial for a corpse.

Abduction

Abduction narratives in Jewish tradition are known from the late Middle Ages and the Renaissance. The abductors are aliens to Jewish society—whether Christians, demons, or sorcerers. They represent the category of the religiously or existentially "other," the phenomenological negative against which Jewish society defines its own positive identity. Silberstein and Cohn[3] discussed the various categories of "the other" in modern Jewish societies, although demons and witches were not included in their analysis. In the present tale, the disguised sorcerers are the symbolic equivalent of demons.[4]

The most widely known Christian abductors story is the tale of the "Jewish pope" involving the kidnapping of an infant by his nursemaid (see tale IFA 2644 [vol. 1, no. 23], for example). See the notes to tale IFA 8792 (in this vol., no. 5) for more on demons and demonic abduction. Tale IFA 5361 (in this vol., no. 17), a narrative about an abduction by Jewish underworld robbers, has a similar conclusion to that of the present story. Compare also tale IFA 9182 (vol. 1, no. 55), which relates a voluntary visit to the land of the demons.

A Speaking Skull

It is generally necessary to distinguish between two related motifs: E783.5 "Vital head speaks" and E261.1.2 "Speaking skull tells about previous life, reveals future events." The references in S. Thompson's *Motif Index of Fold-Literature* are insufficient for differentiating the two motifs. The earliest available record of the speaking head motif appears in the first century B.C.E. in Ovid's *Metamorphoses* (11.52–53), which described Orpheus's head floating on the river with his lyre, still singing after being cruelly murdered. The image also appears in *The Narratives of Konon*.[5] In the eleventh-century collection of Welsh tales, *The Mabinogion*,[6] the story *Branwen Daughter of Llyr* describes Bendigeidfran's head as staying alive for forty-eight years after it was severed from his body. A comparative study of the motif's occurrence in Greek, Irish, Norse, and Indian sources has been published.[7]

The motif of the speaking skull has a long history in Christian legendary.[8] We surmise, but are not certain, that the occurrence of this motif in the present tale draws on its currency in European Christian tradition. An inverted cycle of tales about a skull that refused to talk occurs in several African and African American traditions, commonly titled *The Talking Skull Refuses to Talk*.[9]

In Jewish tradition, there is a talmudic passage that explains the inscription "this and yet another," found on Jehoiakim's skull.

> R. Ḥiyya b. Abuiah also said: "This and yet another" is written upon Jehoiakim's skull. R. Perida's grandfather found a skull thrown down at the gates of Jerusalem, upon which "this and yet another" was written. So he buried it, but it re-emerged; again he buried it, and again it re-emerged.
>
> Thereupon he said, This must be Jehoiakim's skull of whom it is written, *He shall be buried with the burial of an ass, drawn and cast forth beyond the gates of Jerusalem* [Jeremiah 22:19]. Yet, he reflected, he was a king, and it is not mannerly to disgrace him. So he took it, wrapped it in silk, and placed it in a chest. When his wife came home and saw it, she went and told her neighbors about it. "It must be the skull of his first wife," said they to her, "whom he cannot forget." So she fired the oven and burnt it. When he came, he said to her, "That was meant by its inscription, This and yet another" (BT *Sanhedrin* 82a).

A Proper Jewish Burial for a Corpse

The theme of a proper Jewish burial is central to the apocryphal Book of Tobit, and for its renditions in subsequent traditions, see the notes to tale IFA 4904 (vol. 1, no. 57) and compare the present tale with tale IFA 5361 (in this vol., no. 17).

Folklore Motifs

- C611 "Forbidden chamber."
- *D849.6.1 "Magic object under skull's tongue."
- D1711 "Magicians."
- *D1739.3 "Magic power maintained by holding a third-generation rabbi in captivity."
- E261.1.2 "Speaking skull tells about previous life, reveals future events."
- K310 "Thief in disguise."
- K1817.4 "Disguise as merchant."
- N819.3.1 "Helpful speaking skull."
- P150 "Rich men."
- *P165 "Poor men."
- *P426.4 "Rabbi."
- *P476 "Thief."
- *P486 "Scholar."
- R10 "Abduction."
- cf. *R11.2.3 "Abduction by sorcerers."
- R210 "Escapes."
- Z71.5 "Formulistic number: seven."

--- **Notes** ---

1. *The Theory of Social and Economic Organization*, 358–373.

2. S. Assaf, "*Le-Korot ha-Rabbanut be-Ashkenaz, Polanya, ve-Lita*" (The history of the rabbinate in Germany, Poland, and Lithuania); Baron, *A Social and Religious History of the Jews* (see indexes); Ben-Sasson, *Hagut ve-hanhaga* (Thought and leadership), 160–228.

3. *The Other in Jewish Thought and History.*

4. On the concept of symbolic equivalence in folklore, see Dundes, "The Symbolic Equivalence of Allomotifs in the Rabbit-Herd."

5. See M. Brown, *The Narratives of Konon*, 307–308 no. 45:26–31.

6. Jones and Jones, *The Mabinogion*, 34–37. Similar stories appear in other Celtic sources.

7. Nagy, "Hierarchy, Heroes, and Heads."

8. Galderisi, "*Le 'crâne qui parle.'*"

9. Frobenius and Fox, *African Genesis*, 161–162; R. Abrahams, *African Folktales*, 1–3; Bascom, "African Folktales in America"; Bascom, "The Talking Skull Refuses to Talk"; Moser, "The Talking Skull Refuses to Talk"; and Pradelles de Latour, "*'Le crâne qui parle.'*"

5

The Demons and Spirits under the Fingernails

TOLD BY AVIGDOR REEDER

In the village of Wielącza, which lies between Szczebrzeszyn and Zamosc, there lived a village Jew, a simple, hardworking, and God-fearing man. Like all village Jews, he did not sin by knowing too much Torah. When they first met him, people quickly sensed a Jew who smelled of the field and stable. He spoke with three R's—r-r-r—which sharply marked him off from the city language. In the morning, he put on his tallit[*]and tefillin[**] and spent a long time saying "Mah Tovu"—the verse recited when you enter the synagogue[§]—because he hardly knew Hebrew. The man supported himself by dealing in pig bristles, a rough commodity and, more important, one that involves animals. In fact, people called him "the animal dealer."

He had four daughters and one son. The son, as should be, was his magic ring: The man wanted his son to ensure his own portion in the world to come, too. He had him study with a teacher from Szczebrzeszyn, so he would learn what a Jew should know: to pray a little and say *Kaddish*,[§§] after 120 years,[***] for his father and to write a little Yiddish.

The village Jew took his son, Yoshke, to all the fairs to teach him to earn his own bread. Yoshke took to his apprenticeship in business well. He soon was expert at touching an animal and reckoning how much it was worth. He was more successful at business than at learning Torah.

One fine Friday, Yoshke came home to get himself ready for the Sabbath Queen. He bathed in the brook in honor of the Sabbath, cleaned his Sabbath boots and smeared them with grease, and trimmed his nails—

---

[*]Prayer shawl.
[**]Small black leather prayers boxes, wrapped around the head and arm, containing passages from the Torah.
[§]See Numbers 24:5.
[§§]The mourner's prayer.
[***]That is, after the father has lived a full life (see Genesis 6:3).

33

but, being careless, he cut his finger. In his anger and pain, he decided not to trim his nails any more. But he was to pay dearly for that vow.

What happened was that on the first night of Passover, after reciting the haggadah,* he ate heartily with the family and got tipsy from drinking the four cups of wine out of the goblet with "*Ḥag Hapesaḥ*"** embossed on it in gold. Afterward he kissed the mezuzah and went to sleep without saying *keri'at Shema*—the prayer before retiring for the night—because the custom is that people don't say *keri'at Shema* on the first night of Passover.

And that is just when all the demons and spirits run wild. They acquire great power and—may it not happen to us—hunt for victims.

In the middle of the night, when you can hear snoring a mile away, there was a loud rap on the shutters. At first Yoshke thought it must be a dream—who would be knocking like that in the middle of the night? On the first night of Passover? Perhaps Elijah the Prophet himself had come to the village? But when the knocking got more insistent, Yoshke got out of bed. Instead of Elijah the Prophet with his gray-white beard, two peasants with pointed mustaches were standing there. Yoshke was overcome by dread and terror. The peasants offered him a great bargain—good fat animals. In his dread and fear, he forgot it was Passover and went with the peasants. The demons, disguised as peasants, dragged him far away from the village. Using some magic spell and incantations they turned him into an animal and sold him to a peasant.

The peasant was delighted with the deal. He had bought the animal at a bargain, dirt cheap. That night, when the whole village was sunk in deep sleep, strange and ugly noises reached the peasant. It was the sound of a calf being led to slaughter, a sound that grated on the ears, like someone dancing and jumping in the stable. In his dread and fear, the peasant cowered with a pot over his head.

After this was repeated for several nights running, the peasant went and sold the animal precisely to our friend the animal dealer, Yoshke's father.

The animal made the same noises, dances, leaps, and muffled sounds at the Jew's house. There's something wrong with it—it's not a regular cow—the animal dealer thought, remembering the stories the peasants of the village told about witches, elves, demons, and chronic diseases.

---

*The book of liturgy, prayers, songs, and rituals used at the Passover seder.
**Hebrew for "the Passover festival."

5 / The Demons and Spirits

Yoshke's father hitched up the horse, climbed into the sleigh, dressed warmly in a lambskin, and traveled to the city to see a fine Jew, a wonder-working *rebbe*.* The village Jew told him the whole story from A to Z. The wonder worker climbed into a sleigh with a group of his Hasidim and his *shammes,* and with a hammer that could be used on Sabbath, and traveled to the stable. When the *rebbe* and his retinue came to Yoshke's father's stable, the *rebbe* rapped three times with the hammer—the way Jews are summoned to the synagogue. While he knocked with the hammer, the *rebbe* intoned, "Let whatever is good remain and whatever is bad depart in haste."

To the *rebbe*'s great astonishment, instead of an animal there appeared a man, a human being with enormous nails that had grown wild. The *rebbe* approached the fellow and immediately trimmed his long nails, so that the demons and spirits that had been hiding under them vanished. Soon the man regained consciousness and something unexpected happened.

The man fell upon his father and began to weep and cry bloody tears, "*Tatte,* don't you recognize me?" After they revived the father from his faint, he recognized his only son, the animal trader, who had vanished mysteriously on Passover night.

People in the village believed and told what had happened—such a pity—to the village Jew and his son, Yoshke. The son told his father the whole story, from beginning to end, of what had happened on the first night of Passover.

From then on, the village Jew was meticulous about trimming his nails, first of all every Friday, in honor of the Sabbath, and afterward, when the nails grew, every third day, so as not, Heaven forbid, to desecrate the Sabbath if he trimmed his nails only on Fridays.

---

*Hasidic rabbi.

Commentary for Tale 5 (IFA 8792)

Written down in Yiddish on January 21, 1968, from memory by Avigdor Reeder from Acre, who heard it from his father, Neḥemiah Reeder from Szczebrzeszyn, Poland, who told the story at the Passover seder.

Cultural, Historical, and Literary Background

The narrator opens his tale by making a few deriding remarks about the paternal figure in the story, focusing on his rural accent and religious ignorance.

When the Yiddish term *"intshfingerl"* magic (literally: wishing) ring is used to refer idiomatically and metaphorically to a person, as in this tale, it expresses the expectation of the father that his son will be the solution to all his economic troubles. Parents often hope that one of their children will provide them with reliable support in the future. The nineteenth-century Yiddish-Hebrew author Mendele Moykher-Sforim, also known as Shalom Yaacov Abramovitsh (1836–1917), titled one of his early books *Dos Vintshfingerl* (1865), alluding to the economic passivity of the Jewish population, by which many lived in poor conditions while expecting miracles and magic to be the solution to their troubles.

The phrase the father recites, *mah tovu,* opens the prayer a Jew says upon entering the synagogue to recite the morning prayer: "How fair are your tents, O Jacob (Numbers 24:5).

The pivotal narrative act in the story is the son's neglect to recite the *"keri'at Shema"* (the reading of the *Shema*) at bedtime. The *Shema* (hear) so called after the first word of Deuteronomy 6:4—"Hear, O Israel! The Lord is our God, the Lord alone"—consists of three biblical paragraphs: Deuteronomy 6:4–9 and 11:13–21 and Numbers 15:37–41. This is an early prayer recited twice a day, morning and evening.

Later, during the *amoraic* period, Jews apparently began to recite the first section of the *Shema* before bedtime. That prayer is followed by Psalms 90:17–91:16 and 3:2–9. Additional verses of an appeal for protection are also included. On Passover eve only the first section is recited because the night is *"leil shimmurim"* (a night of vigil; Exodus 12:42) and thus is already protected by definition. The term *leil shimmurim* is interpreted to mean "a guarded night" (discussed below).

Four related issues are involved in this tale: Jewish demonology, the timing of demonic activity, demonic activity associated with fingernails, and the question of exorcism.

Jewish Demonology

Jewish traditions are teeming with beliefs in demons and harmful supernatural beings. The evidence for such beliefs is sparse for some historical periods and literary forms but is available in abundance in others.

The Biblical Period

The general terms for demons are *shedim* and *se'irim,* which refer to alien, but likely indigenous to the Land of Israel, deities. The first term occurs in poetic texts, such as "They sacrificed to demons, no-gods" (Deuteronomy 32:17) and "Their own sons and daughters they sacrificed to demons" (Psalm 106:37). The second term, *se'irim,* appears in prescriptive and descriptive texts, for example, "and that they may offer their sacrifices no more to the goat-demons" (Leviticus 17:7) and "for Jeroboam . . . appointed his own priests for the shrines, goat-demons, and calves which he had made" (2 Chronicles 11:14–15). In each case, the Hebrew Bible attaches a negative value to the terms *shedim* and *se'irim.* In addition, Isaiah refers to *se'irim* in his prophecy. Describing ruins, he says, "There shall ostriches make their home, And there shall satyrs dance" (13:21) and, later, "Wildcats shall meet hyenas, Goat-demons shall greet each other; There too the lilith shall repose, And find herself a resting place" (34:14).

The term *se'irim* is borrowed from the animal world, and it refers to a goat. In a herding culture, excessive body hair, which is implied by this term, becomes a distinctive feature that separates the human not only from the animal world but also from the demonic world. Besides these general terms, the Hebrew Bible mentions individual demons, such as Lilith (Isaiah 34:14) and Azazel (Leviticus 16:8, 10, 26). Other characters may bear the names of their actions or their consequences. Hence, in some contexts, these terms are either metaphors for or actual names of supernatural forces that are agents causing diseases or disasters. Among them are the following:

- Death, *"mavet"* (Isaiah 28:15,18; Jeremiah 9:20; Hosea 13:14, Job 18:13).
- The Destroyer, *"ha-Mashhit"* (Exodus 12:23) or, more specifically, "the angel who was destroying" (2 Samuel 24:15–17) and "the destroying angel" (1 Chronicles 21:15).
- Pestilence or plague, *"dever"* (Habakkuk 3:5; Psalm 91:6) or *"qetev"* (exact meaning unclear; Deuteronomy 32:24; Isaiah 28:2; Hosea 13:14; Psalm 91:6).

The only Canaanite deity that is demonized is Resheph, the deity of plague (Deuteronomy 33:24; Habakkuk 3:5; Psalm 78:48), whose name in other contexts means "fiery flashes." The only clearly demonized animal is the snake (*nahash*), represented symbolically as a fiery serpent (Numbers 21:6–9; Isaiah 14:29, 30:6). In both cases, however, the biblical terms hover between the referential and the metaphoric, between the literal and the poetic.

Some biblical terms later acquired a demonic connotation, though in the Hebrew Bible that meaning is not necessarily apparent. For example, the description of King Saul's depression contains the phrase *"ruaḥ ra'ah"* (evil spirit; 1 Samuel 19:9), a term that subsequently has been used for a demonic force. Similarly in Psalm 78:49, the Hebrew text refers to "wrath, indignation, trouble" as *"mishlaḥat mal'akhim ra'im"* (a band of [bad angels]), a term that would refer to demonic beings in later periods. Note that this is the first textual distinction between good and bad angels, a concept that was influential in the Second Temple and later periods of Jewish tradition.[1]

The Second Temple Period

Whether suppressed by the Hebrew Bible, as Langton[2] contended, or theologically subjected to the domination of God, as Kaufmann[3] proposed, within the Hebrew Bible the references to demons and demonic forces are scant and far between. During the Second Temple period, however, after Jewish society had been exposed to Persian and Greek demonological ideals and after the control over the preservation of texts had considerably weakened, there was a flurry of references to demons in the literary and religious writings, ranging from the apocryphal and pseudepigraphical books to the Dead Sea Scrolls.[4]

Some of the names for demonic beings of the Hebrew Bible survive in the Dead Sea Scrolls,[5] albeit with the aid of considerable textual reconstruction. P. Alexander[6] identified the following terms in the Scrolls: "(1) spirits of the angels of destruction; (2) spirits of the bastards; (3) demons; (4) Lilith; (5) howlers; (6) yelpers." The last three terms are mentioned in Isaiah 34:14. Other biblical demonic names, as mentioned earlier, connote actions: "destroyer" (Exodus 12:23) and "the destroying angel" (2 Samuel 24:15–17; 1 Chronicles 21:14–17).

Around this time, new demonic forces are recorded in the apocryphal books. Most prominent is Asmodeus who, in the Book of Tobit (3:8–17), is the "evil demon" who killed Sarah's seven husbands on their nuptial nights; and in the Wisdom of Solomon, he declared: "I cause the wickedness of men to spread throughout the world. I am always hatching plots against newlyweds; I mar the beauty of virgins and cause their hearts to grow cold" (5:7; see 1–13). Later he would be known in Jewish tradition as the king of the demons (BT *Gittin* 68a);[7] but in the apocryphal and pseudepigraphical literature other demonic figures are at the head of the demonic world. For example, Beliar (Belial) holds this position in Jubilees (1:20, 15:33) and the Testaments of the Twelve Patriarchs (2:1[n. a], 4:7[n. c]),[8] and allusions to him occur in the apocryphal literature and the Dead Sea Scrolls. Considerable research has been done on this demonic figure.[9]

The prince of the demons in the writings of the Second Temple period is Mastema, a name that means "animosity"; but it occurs only in the Book of Jubilees (10:1–14[esp. 8], 11:11–13, 17:15–18:13, 48:2,12).[10] Another figure with a limited representation during this period but whose stature would increase exponentially in the rabbinic and mystical literature is Samael. The author of the "Martyrdom and Ascension of Isaiah" referred to him as "Sammael Malkira" (king of evil) (1:8) and mentioned him without this epithet on other occasions (1:11, 2:1, 3:13, 5:15–16, 7:9). Knibb[11] suggested that the names Samael, Beliar, and Satan are interchangeable and all apply to the forces of evil; but in the "Martyrdom and Ascension of Isaiah" Beliar and Samael are struggling with each other and are thus seen to be two distinct forces. Samael is also called "the Prince of the Accusers" (3 Enoch 14:2[n. 14b]) and the "Prince of Rome" (3 Enoch 26:12).

The name Satan, which eventually also took on the meaning of Samael, has retained by and large the nature described in the Hebrew Bible, particularly in Job 1:6–2:10. Satan is the head of the "angels of plague" (1 Enoch 53:3), and "the messengers of Satan, [lead] astray those who dwell upon the earth" (1 Enoch 54:6).

As an evil force, Satan preceded the demonic descendants of the Watchers, and he fell from his position in Heaven because of his temptation of Adam and Eve (Life of Adam and Eve 12–17). Satan is an adversary and challenger of humans, sometimes referred to as "the devil"; he is the head of destroying angels but not of demons, as Asmodeus would be later conceived.[12] An examination of the names of the supreme demonic figure in the Hebrew Bible, the apocryphal literature, and the New Testament has been published.[13]

The literature of the Second Temple period is rife with demonic figures. The Testament of Solomon notes that Solomon "subdued all the spirits of the air" (1:1) and then proceeds to identify some, if not all, of them. This literary corpus also includes an etiological mythology of demons that is relevant to the present tale. The Ethiopic Book of Enoch (1 Enoch) constructs a mythic narrative that contrasts sharply with the biblical narrative on which it is founded. According to the Hebrew Bible, "It was then, and later too, that the Nephilim appeared on earth—when the divine beings cohabited with the daughters of men, who bore them offspring. They were the heroes of old, the men of renown" (Genesis 6:4). But according to 1 Enoch, rather than being heroic, the descendants of the union between divine beings and mortal women were demonic. They were the destructive forces that oppressed humanity; and in response to the outcry of humankind God sent the angel Gabriel to destroy them. As they were lying dead on the earth "Evil spirits [came] out of their bodies (1 Enoch 15:8).

Because they were the direct issue of divine creatures, the "evil spirits" were re-conceptualized during this period as "fallen angels," thus offering a narrative foundation for the dualism of the world of the spirits. However, the available analyses of the names of the heads of the demonic forces and evil spirits in the apocryphal books may not accurately reflect the historical conception of the spirit world because the texts studied were translations.[14] A discussion of Jewish demonology in the context of classical and Christian ideology has been published,[15] and examinations of the figure of Samael (Sammael) in Jewish apocryphal literature, early Gnostic sources, early and late talmudic-midrashic literature, *Heikhalot* and *Merkabah*, and medieval kabbalistic books can be found.[16]

The Talmudic-Midrashic Period

The literature of the talmudic-midrashic period and the subsequent gaonic period witnessed a surge in references to demons. These occur in abundance in the Babylonian Talmud and to a lesser extent in the Jerusalem Talmud. The uneven distribution of references does not necessarily represent the extent of beliefs in demons in these Jewish centers. Rather, the midrashic books, which were edited in the Land of Israel, include a number of references to and narratives about demons. In addition, demons are mentioned in magic books and inscriptions that are designed to combat them, thus extending the literature up to the gaonic period.

It is possible to discern four distinct attitudes toward demons in the literature of the talmudic-midrashic period.

The Canonization of Demons

Although demons did not become an object of religious worship, the knowledge of them and their language were attributed to central figures of the talmudic-midrashic period. Some of these figures are also the subject of stories about interactions with demons. Rabbi Hillel the Elder (late first century B.C.E. to early first century C.E.) and Rabbi Yoḥanan ben Zakkai (first century C.E.), historical cornerstones of Jewish tradition during this time, were supposed to have knowledge of the language of demons: "It was said of Hillel that he had not omitted to study any of the words of the sages, even all languages, even the speech of the mountains, hills and valleys, the speech of trees, and herbs, the speech of wild beasts and cattle, the speech of demons and parables" (BT *Soferim* 16:9); and "[t]hey said of R. Johanan b Zakkai that he did not leave [unstudied] Scripture, Mishna, Gemara, *Halachah, Aggadah*, details of the Torah, details of the Scribes, inferences a minori ad majus, analogies, calendar computations, gamatrias, the speech of the Ministering Angels, the speech of the spirits [original: *shedim*, (demons)]" (BT *Sukkah* 28a). A text from the gaonic period, attributed to Rabbi Akiva, the leading second-century rabbi, includes a series of magical protective antidemonic incantations.[17] Rabbi Shimon bar Yoḥai, an important second-century rabbi, saved the Jewish community of Rome, according to one story, with the help of a demon (BT *Meʿilah* 17b; see also notes to tale IFA 16395 [vol. 1, no. 35]). These and other traditions propelled the idea of discourse with demons from the margins into the foundational core of rabbinical Jewish society.

Demonic Names

During this period the use of earlier terms for demons greatly increased, and some new terms were also introduced. The biblical word *shed* (pl. *shedim*) became commonplace in the Talmud and Midrash. In contrast the use of the term *seʿir* (satyr), more common in the Hebrew Bible, decreased in use and was unfamiliar to speakers of the talmudic era. In fact, explanatory interpretations were necessary to gloss the term for the contemporary audience: "these satyrs are naught but demons, as is borne out by the text which says, *They* sacrificed *unto demons, no gods* (Deuteronomy 32:17), these demons being naught but satyrs, as it says, And the satyrs shall dance there (Isaiah 13:21)" (MR *Leviticus* 22:8). Similarly, the Rabbis felt the need to gloss the biblical words *reshef* and *qetev*:

"And *reshef* refers only to demons" (BT *Berakhot* 5a) and "*qetev* is a demon" (MR *Numbers* 12:3).

Furthermore, older terms that had somewhat ambiguous meanings were more concretely associated with demons, as for example *mal'akhei habalah* (angels of destruction) and *ruah ra'ah* (evil spirit) (1 Samuel 16:14). A new term for demons that is absent from the literature of the previous periods is *mazik* (pl. *mazikkim*), meaning harmful one and referring to the demonic function in relation to human beings. The term is found only once in the Mishnah (*Avot* 5:6) but occurs many times in talmudic-midrashic books.

Hierarchy in the Demonic World

As discussed earlier, the apocryphal literature indicates the concept of a social, even military, organization in the demonic world. In the talmudic-midrashic period, there was an adjustment and consolidation of the hierarchy of evil spirits. Asmodeus became "the king of demons" (BT *Pesahim* 110a; *Gittin* 68a–68b), and he retained that position in later popular medieval tradition.[18] At the same time, however, an earlier tradition equated, or associated, Sammael with Satan and with the Angel of Death and considered him the commanding demon (Enoch 14:2, 26:12; in a later midrash see MR *Deuteronomy* 11:10). Although both Asmodeus and Sammael were thought of as the head of the demonic world, they were considered to be distinct figures with mutually exclusive domains in which they affected the lives of human beings. In subsequent periods, Sammael retained his position primarily within the mystical literature, whereas Asmodeus did so within popular narratives.

Worldview of the Demonic World

The multiple references to demons in the talmudic-midrashic literature articulate a clear conception of the demonic world involving two fundamental views. Both assume the invisibility of demons, considering them to exist in a virtual reality that is rarely seen or heard by mortals and yet affects people in every way. The two models differ in the position of demons in relation to humans.

According to the first idea, demons are lurking everywhere, unseen, and they surround an individual. "If the eye had the power to see them, no creature could endure the demons. Abaye says: They are more numerous than we are and they surround us like the ridge around a field. R. Huna says: Every one among us has a thousand on his left hand and ten thousand on his right hand" (BT *Berakhot* 6a). This is, among other things, a proposition about the relationship between appearance and reality, which casts doubt about the perception of the world through human sensibility.

According to the second conception, demons are inherently liminal spirits. They were created in the twilight on the eve of the Sabbath, in the zone between profane and holy time (*Avot* 5:6), and continue to exist in liminal locations such as in ruins (BT *Berakhot* 3a); in the inaccessible areas of buildings (BT *Hulin*

105a); and in inland water holes, wells, and ponds (MR *Leviticus* 24:3; *Tanhuma, Kedoshim* 9; BT *Pesaḥim* 112a). In some of the tales given in these talmudic sources, as in the story from MR *Leviticus* cited earlier, the demons are conceived as the "owners" of the water source. Discussions of the demonic possession of nature have been published.[19] According to this model, demons are more likely to attack people at night and particularly during in-between times, such as the separation between holy and profane times.

Modern ethnographic studies in Jewish communities cast light on the demonological beliefs of Jewish societies in antiquity. Although there are differences between the modern and the ancient periods, observations made today provide insights into the dynamics of demons in more ancient cultures and societies.[20] Furthermore, the antidemonic magic formulas and incantations found on special bowls and amulets and in prayers offer a rich source for understanding the demonic beliefs of the talmudic-midrashic period.[21]

The Middle Ages

The two main sources for Jewish demonology in the Middle Ages are the writings of a sect of Jewish pietists in the Rhine Valley in the twelfth and thirteenth centuries, whose main book, *Sefer Hasidim,* is attributed to Rabbi Judah he-Hasid (c. 1150–1217), and those of the Jewish mystics in southern France and of Spain, which were consolidated in the Zohar, the main part of which was written between 1270 and 1300 by Moshe ben Shem Tov de Leon (d. 1305). (Note, however, that this view of the composition of the Zohar has been challenged.[22])

Although only a century apart, their demonologies differ radically. While the Jewish pietists in Germany incorporated into their belief systems the spirits and ghosts that populated the medieval German world, the French and Spanish Jewish mystics built on the demonology that was available in Jewish sources from the apocryphal books to the oral tradition. The figures of Sammael, Lilith, and Naama are prominent in kabbalistic writings. Studies of the demonology of the German pietists[23] and of the Kabbalah[24] are available. The concern with demons generated a preoccupation with magical protective means, a concern that was not limited to oral culture in Jewish societies but that also became apparent in the writings of rabbinical Judaism.[25] A study that traces Lilith from early records of the Sumerian epic through the Hebrew Bible and subsequent documents is available.[26]

The Modern Period

Starting in the seventeenth century, popular narratives about demons become available. Among them there are tales about marriages between she-demons and human beings.[27] Popular demonology came into its fuller articulation in Hasidic narratives. The demonic terminology in Hasidic tradition draws on traditional Jewish notions and adds some of its own names. Demons are called *leizim* (mockers), *hizoniyim* (outsiders), and *kelippoth* (shells).[28]

The current story belongs to the Hasidic tradition. The appearance of the demons as two gentile peasants represents a reversal of demonizing the "other" in European societies. From medieval times to the present, Jews have been considered as a demonic other, an attitude that has been at the roots of anti-Semitism.[29] The present tale illustrates that the same fear of the other operates in Jewish society and is the basis of viewing the gentile as a demon.

Timing of Demonic Activity

The appearance of the demons on the very night of the Passover ritualistic meal, the seder, is consistent with the inherent nature of demons and ritual. The Hebrew Bible prescribes the Passover night as a *leil shimmurim* (night of vigil), considering it a ritual in which the believers imitate the divine in their actions: "That was for the Lord a night of vigil to bring them out of the land of Egypt; that same night is the Lord's, one of vigil for all the children of Israel throughout the ages" (Exodus 12:42). However, in their interpretation of the phrase *leil shimmurim* the Rabbis insightfully exposed the nature of the ritual as a liminal state as well as the dangers it brings to the worshipers: "Said R. Nahman: Scripture saith, *[It is] a night of guarding [unto the Lord]:* [i.e.,] it is a night that is guarded for all time from harmful spirits" (BT *Pesaḥim* 109b). Therefore, by neglecting to recite the full *keri'at Shema* (the reading of the *Shema*), the son in the story was vulnerable to demonic powers. Studies of the concept of liminality in ritual are available.[30]

Demonic Activity Associated with Fingernails

The present tale has a straightforward pedagogical function: instructing and warning people to maintain proper hygiene. It does so by employing symbols and beliefs that occur within Jewish tradition and by employing fundamental principles of Jewish demonology. As early as the talmudic period, the sages were aware of and commented about the demonic power of disposed body parts, fingernails among them. In the Babylonian Talmud there is a cautionary statement, attributed to Rabbi Shimon bar Yoḥai, who listed "removing one's nails and throwing them away in a public thoroughfare" as one of five things that "[cause the man] who does them to forfeit his life and his blood is upon his own head." Such an act, later rabbis contended, demonstrates a total lack of care for others: "[this is dangerous] because a pregnant woman passing over them would miscarry." Therefore, "[t]hree things have been said about the disposal of nails: He who burns them is a pious man; he who buries them is a righteous man, and he who throws them away is a wicked man" (BT *Niddah* 17a).

R. Thompson[31] considered these instructions in terms of Jewish magic; however, their prescribed behavior does not involve magic but the fear of and the basic belief about the origin of demons. According to Jewish tradition, demons grow out of human waste that is not properly disposed. There are two well-known myths about the origin of demons: They emerge from the bodies of the giants, the descendants of the divine giants and the mortal women (1 Enoch 15:8) mentioned earlier, and the story of Lilith, who seduces men and has them waste their semen from which demons rise. This latter myth has general applications and is not restricted to the Lilith narrative. "Rabbi Jeremiah b. Eleazar further stated: In all those years during which Adam was under the ban, he begot ghosts and male demons and female demons. That statement was made in reference to the semen which he emitted accidentally" (BT *Eruvin* 18b).

The association between demons and fingernails is likely represented in the puzzling ancient custom of looking at the fingernails in the light of the *Havdalah* service that separates the holy Sabbath from the profane weekdays. This custom and the rabbinical commentary about it have been thoroughly explored. Finesinger[32] associated this practice with magical divination, whereas D. Noy[33] considered it a form of ritualistic blessing; but both, particularly Noy, recognized the association between demons and fingernails that this ritual, at least partially, reflects.

Apparently, the association between fingernails and divination was a more general notion. Dan[34] discussed the descriptions of this divination ritual from several sources. Important to the present narrative is the association between demons and divination that recurs in all these and other sources. Studies of demons in general folklore have been published.[35]

Exorcism

The combat with demons is a theme that is well rooted in Jewish tradition. A number of narratives pit rabbis against either demons or sorcerers.[36] In most cases, exorcism in these tales involves either combating demons or releasing an individual from the possession of an evil spirit or the spirit of a departed person.[37]

However, in the present tale, the act of exorcism differs because it involves the restoration of an individual to his human form. The rabbi performs a magical ritual not to chase away a demon or release a person from his possession but rather to restore the son to his human existence. In this particular case, exorcism results in undoing the act of demonic transformation, and it bears structural and thematic similarities to tales of contest in magic (for example, see tale IFA 863 [vol. 1, no. 16]) or of countering witchcraft. Indeed, the earliest occurrence of this motif in Jewish traditional literature is the story of Rabbi Aaron of Baghdad that appeared in the medieval family's rhymed chronicle, *Megillat Aḥimaaz* (1054).[38] In the story, a witch turns a young man into a donkey. Rabbi Aaron restored the man to human form and returned him to his father.

Folklore Motifs

- D42.2 "Spirit takes shape of man."
- D133.1 "Transformation: man to cow."
- D333 "Transformation: bovine animal to a person."

- D771 "Disenchantment by use of magic object."
- D1713 "Magic power of hermit (saint, yogi)."
- D2176 "Exorcising by magic."
- D2176.3 "Evil spirit exorcised."
- cf. D2176.3.2 "Evil spirit exorcised by religious ceremony."
- F400 "Spirits and demons (general)."
- F402 "Evil spirits."
- F402.1.4 "Demons assume human forms in order to deceive."
- F470 "Night-spirits."
- G302 "Demons."
- P233 "Father and son."
- *P252.2.1 "Four sisters."
- P411 "Peasant."
- *P426.4 "Rabbi."
- R11.2.2 "Abduction by demon."
- V50 "Prayer."
- *V56 "Kaddish: mourners prayer said after the death of a close relative."
- V71 "Sabbath."
- V75.1 "Passover."
- *V75.1.1 "Seder, the Passover Eve ceremonial dinner."
- *V131.3 "Phylacteries (tefillin)."
- *V131.4 "Prayer shawl (tallit)."
- V229.5 "Saint banishes demons."
- *V295 "Elijah the Prophet."
- Z71.1 "Formulaic number: three."
- Z71.2 "Formulaic number: four."

Notes

1. See Hillers, "Demons, Demonology"; Y. Kaufmann, *The Religion of Israel,* 63–67; Kuemmerlin-McLean, "Demons"; and Langton, *Essentials of Demonology,* 35–59.

2. Op. cit., 10.

3. Op. cit.

4. P. Alexander, "The Demonology of the Dead Sea Scrolls"; Reimer, "Rescuing the Fallen Angels"; Fröhlich, "Demons, Scribes, and Exorcists in Qumran"; Nitzan, "Hymns from Qumran"; Nitzan, *Qumran Prayer and Religious Poetry,* 227–272; Baumgarten, "The Qumran Songs against Demons"; Ta-Shema, "Notes to 'Hymns from Qumran'"; and Stuckenbruck, "The 'Angels' and 'Giants' of Genesis 6:1–4 in Second and Third Century BCE Jewish Interpretation."

5. P. Alexander, op. cit., 333.

6. Ibid.

7. Bin Gorion, *Mimekor Yisrael,* 49–51 no. 28, 74–77 no. 40, 373–384 no. 200 (1990 ed.).

8. Charlesworth, *The Old Testament Pseudepigrapha,* 2:932 (index).

9. See Langton, op. cit., 125–128; Osten-Sacken, *Gott und Belial;* Scholem, "Bilar

(Bilad, bilid, BEIAR) the King of the Demons"; and Steudel, "God and Belial." For interpretations of the use of biblical use of this name, see Emerton, "Sheol and the Sons of Belial"; Rosenberg, "The Concept of Biblical 'Belial'"; and D. Thomas, *"Beliya 'al* in the Old Testament."

10. See Langton, op. cit., 124–125.

11. Knibb, "Martyrdom and Ascension of Isaiah," 2:151.

12. Charlesworth, op. cit., 2:992 (index).

13. Fontinoy, *"Les nomes du diable et leur etymologie."*

14. Bamberger, *Fallen Angels;* Gammie, "The Angelology and Demonology in the Septuagint of the Book of Job"; Langton, op. cit., 61–144; D. Russell, *The Method and Message of Jewish Apocalyptic,* 235–262.

15. Flint, "The Demonisation of Magic and Sorcery in Late Antiquity," 277–348, esp. 292–296; and Lange et al., *Die Dämonen/Demons.*

16. J. Dan, "Samael and the Problem of Jewish Gnosticism"; and J. Dan, "The Desert in Jewish Mysticism."

17. Scholem, *"Havdala De-Rabbi 'Aqiva."*

18. Bin Gorion, op. cit.

19. Hultkrantz, *The Supernatural Owners of Nature;* for a similar conception in the Near East, see Canaan, "Haunted Springs and Water Demons in Palestine."

20. Bilu, "Demonic Explanations of Disease among Moroccan Jews in Israel"; Bilu, "The Moroccan Demon in Israel"; Becker, *Wunder und Wundertäter im frührabbinischen Judentum,* 141–183; Ginzberg, *The Legends of the Jews,* 7:111–112 (index); Lange et al., op. cit.; Starck and Billerbeck, *"Kommentar zum neuen Testament aus Talmud und Midrasch";* Teugels, "The Creation of the Human in Rabbinic Interpretation," 113–116; Trachtenberg, *Jewish Magic and Superstition,* 25–68; Urbach, *The Sages,* 72–134; and Yassif, *The Hebrew Folktale,* 144–166.

21. Harari, "Early Jewish Magic," 151–155.

22. Liebes, *Studies in the Zohar,* 85–138.

23. J. Dan, "Demonological Stories in the Writings of R. Yehudah Hehasid."

24. J. Dan, "Samael, Lilith, and the Concept of Evil in Early Kabbalah"; Lachower and Tishby, *The Wisdom of the Zohar,* 2:529–546; Scholem, *Origins of the Kabbalah,* 293–298; and Trachtenberg, op. cit.

25. Bar-Levav, "Magic in Jewish Ethical Literature."

26. Patai, *The Hebrew Goddess,* 221–254.

27. T. Alexander, "Theme and Genre"; Goodblatt, "Women, Demons and the Rabbi's Son;" and Zfatman, *The Marriage of a Mortal Man and a She-Demon.*

28. Nigal, *The Hasidic Tale;* and Nigal, *Magic, Mysticism, and Hasidism,* 67–178.

29. Trachtenberg, *The Devil and the Jews;* Wistrich, *Demonizing the Other;* and, in particular, Cala, *The Image of the Jew in Polish Folk Culture,* 112–151.

30. Gennep, *The Rites of Passage;* Turner, "Betwixt and Between"; and Douglas, *Purity and Danger,* 147–148.

31. *Semitic Magic,* 147–148.

32. "The Custom of Looking at the Fingernails at the Outgoing of the Sabbath."

33. *"Histaklut ba-Zipornayim bi-Sh'at ha-Havdalah"* (Observation of fingernails during the *Havdalah*).

34. "The Prince of Thumb and Cup."

35. Daxelmüller, *"Dämonologie";* and Röhrich, *"Dämon."*

36. Harari, op. cit.; and Yassif, op. cit.

37. Goldish, *Spirit Possession in Judaism,* 445–448; Bar-Ilan, "Exorcism by Rabbis"; and Klutz, "The Grammar of Exorcism in the Ancient Mediterranean World."

38. Klar, *Megillat Ahimaaz,* 13. For studies of this historical literary source, see Yassif, "Folktales in 'Megillat Ahimaaz'"; and Yassif, "Analysis of the Narrative Art of 'Megillat Ahimaaz.'"

6

The Treasure

TOLD BY DVORA FUS

*O*n a side street in a small town there lived a mother with three daughters. People called the girls "the orphans" because their father had died when they were all still very young. The mother had sweated to bring them up. She mended and sewed for the householders; the girls, when they got older, helped her. But as luck would have it, their mother died suddenly, leaving behind three grown-up young ladies. The daughters cried a lot but to no avail. They had no idea how they would manage for themselves. Also, it was nearly time for them to be married, and they had no dowries. They started working the way their mother had and lived on that. No one took any interest in them, but God would not abandon them.

One day, an old man was going around begging. He did not skip their house. Instead of a handout, they gave him a meal to eat. Before he went away, he wished that they might soon have good fortune.

In the middle of the night, when they were all sleeping soundly, the girls suddenly heard someone screaming in a queer voice: "Help us!" The girls and woke up in a fright. But when they were awake, the voice fell silent. Each of them told the same story. Terrified, they went back to bed. When they had fallen asleep, they were again roused by the same voice. This time they could not get back to sleep. The voice kept calling for three nights, until the girls responded and asked who was crying. The voice answered that one of them must come out and go to it. Terrified, they did not reply. They barely made it to daylight.

They decided they should go to the rabbi and do whatever he said. When they came to him, the *rebbe* was surprised to see the girls and asked them to recount what had happened. After the girls told the whole story, he understood that the voice was from Heaven. Without delay, he sent them off with his *shammes* to the big city to see the *rebbe*. When they arrived there, the rabbi knew everything.

"You don't have to be frightened, children," he told them. "Your late mother has prayed for you. When you get home, you must cast lots. Whichever one of you the lot falls on, she should go outside."

48

When they were already on their way back home, it dawned on them that the rabbi's voice resembled that of the old Jew they had fed when he came begging.

Relieved by the rabbi's advice, they reached home in a lighthearted mood. The time came, but no voice was heard. They had almost forgotten about it, when suddenly they were awakened by the voice and had no choice but to cast lots. The lot fell on the youngest. With trembling steps, she moved toward the voice, which drew her to their outbuilding. Suddenly, she froze in fear. It seemed to her that her mother was leading her. She stood still. She saw a large bed with a man lying on it, and the voice came from him. She wanted to take him by the arm and help. But the arm broke off when she touched it, leaving a piece in her hand.

When day came, she saw she was holding an ingot of gold, which dazzled her eyes. The sisters stood behind the door of the house, waiting impatiently. When their sister came in, they saw the gold ingot. Then they realized that they had been sent a treasure. They became rich, married, and lived happily ever after.

COMMENTARY FOR TALE 6 (IFA 8256)

Dvora Fus learned this story at her parental home in Lithuania and wrote it down in Yiddish from memory in November 1968.

Cultural, Historical, and Literary Background

The narrator of this tale combines the literary and rhetorical features of legends with those of folktales, thus creating a story that thematically and structurally resonates with Jewish listeners and draws on Jewish cultural symbols, beliefs, and narrative expectations. Consequently, the story is an example of Jewish fictive and magical folktales. Narrators of legends seek to convince their listeners of the reality of the account and so use the names of historical figures, referential dates, and geographical locations to add to the illusion of veracity. In contrast, narrators of folktales wish their listeners to suspend reality and thus place their characters in situations that transcend time, place, and person. The phrase "once upon a time" and its various cognates is a common opening formula for such tales in Europe; the actions take place in an unknown or magical territory, and the characters, with very few exceptions, remain nameless.

In the present story, the narrator employs the poetic principles of the folktale, yet she places them in the familiar environment of a "*shtetl*," using the Yiddish diminutive; the figures—a widow and three orphan girls—remain nameless, yet they are stock characters in Jewish society and in Jewish tales. The "donors" who help the girls in their plight are a mysterious visitor and the soul of their dead mother; the mother, like ancestors in other stories, assumes a mediating position between her daughters and God in Heaven. The rabbi serves as the interpreter, which is the same role he has in the community.

There is an extensive literature concerning different genres in oral tales.[1] This story involves four elements found in many folktales:

- The magical transformation from poverty to riches through the mediation of a mysterious supernatural figure, here implicitly understood to be Elijah the Prophet.[2]
- The commendable act of hospitality.
- A helpful revenant who represents a deceased family member, here the girls' mother.
- A treasure of supernatural gold.

Similarities to Other IFA Tales

Other tales in the IFA with similar elements are the following:

- IFA 708 (in this vol., no. 1): *The Three-Day Fair in Balta* (Lithuania); a helpful revenant.
- IFA 2420 (vol. 1, no. 20): *Three Hairs from Elihah's Beard* (Eretz Yisra'el, Sephardic); Elijah the Prophet.

- IFA 2830 (vol. 1, no. 18): *Ḥakham Eliyahu Is Born through the Special Virtues of the Cave of the Prophet Elijah* (Eretz Yisra'el, Sephardic); Elijah the Prophet.
- IFA 4426 (vol. 3, no. 65): *He Who Finds a Wife Has Found Happiness* (Morocco);[3] hospitality.
- IFA 4815 (in this vol., no. 56): *The Jewish Innkeeper* (Romania); hospitality.
- IFA 6098 (in this vol., no. 50): *The Three Young Men* (Poland); hospitality.
- IFA 7000 (vol. 1, no. 17): *On Passover* (Greece);[4] Elijah the Prophet.
- IFA 9182 (vol. 1, no. 55): *The Miser Mohel and the Demon* (Eretz Yisra'el, Sephardic);[5] supernatural gold.
- IFA 10087 (vol. 1, no. 56): *The Miraculous Circumcision* (Eretz Yisra'el, Sephardic);[6] Elijah the Prophet; supernatural gold.
- IFA 16408: *The Tenth of the* Minyan (Eretz Yisra'el, Sephardic);[7] Elijah the Prophet.

Folktale Types

- cf. 8256 (Christiansen) "Calling the Dairymaid."
- cf. 1645A* "Priest Points Out Treasure."

Folklore Motifs

- D1252.3 "Magic gold."
- *E323.8 "Dead mother prays for her children."
- E402 "Mysterious ghostlike noises heard."
- cf. *F1068.2.3 "Two individuals have the same dream."
- cf. J1853.1.1 "Money from the broken statute."
- K1817.1 "Disguise as beggar."
- cf. L111.4.2 "Orphan heroine."
- N538 "Treasure pointed out by supernatural creature (fairy, etc.)."
- N543 "Certain person to find treasure."
- N825.2 "Old man helper."
- P160 "Beggars."
- P232 "Mother and daughter."
- P252.2 "Three sisters."
- P320 "Hospitality."
- *P426.4 "Rabbi."
- Q45 "Hospitality rewarded."
- Q111 "Riches as reward."
- T52.4 "Dowry given at marriage of daughter."
- *T52.4.2 "Bride, or bride's family, does not have dowry money."
- T100 "Marriage."
- W12 "Hospitality as a virtue."
- Z71.1 "Formulaic Number: three."

Notes

1. Bascom, "The Forms of Folklore"; Bausinger, *Formen der "Volkspoesie,"* 154–198; Belmont, *Poétique du conte;* Ben-Amos, *Folklore Genres;* Dégh, *Legend and Belief;* Jason, *Ethnopoetry,* 34–41; Jolles, *Einfache Formen,* 23–61, 218–246; S. Jones, *The Fairy Tale;* Lüthi, *Volksmärchen und Volkssage;* Lüthi, *So leben sie noch heute;* Lüthi, *Once Upon a Time;* Lüthi, *The European Folktale;* Lüthi, *The Fairytale as Art Form and Portrait of Man;* Propp, *Morphology of the Folktale*; S. Thompson, *The Folktale,* 7–10; and Zipes, *Why Fairy Tales Stick.*

2. Although Bottigheimer, in *Fairy Godfather,* considered Giovanfrancesco Straparola (c.1480–c.1557) to be the literary innovator of this narrative pattern in Europe, it has been known on the European continent since at least the second or third centuries, as attested by the story of Aspasia, daughter of Hermonitus, in Claudius Aelianus's *Varia Historia* ; see Johnson, *An English Translation of Claudius Aelianus's* Varia Historia, 162–166. See also the notes to tale IFA 6445 (vol. 3, no. 45).

3. Also published in Na'anah, *Ozar ha-Ma'asiyyot* (A treasury of tales), 2:321–323.

4. Published in E. Marcus, *Min ha-Mabua,* 29–31 no. 5. Another translation is in Schram, *Tales of Elijah the Prophet,* 115–117 no. 17.

5. Published in D. Noy, *A Tale for Each Month 1971,* 42–43 no. 7.

6. Published in Attias, *The Golden Feather,* 146–148 no. 17.

7. Also published in Angel-Malachi, *Vidas en Jerusalem,* 81–83.

7

The Bottle of Oil from the Holy Land

TOLD BY ESTHER WEINSTEIN TO YEHUDIT GUT-BURG

A certain widow journeyed to visit the Rebbe* of Stratyn to ask for assistance and advice. When she arrived, she broke into tears and recounted her story. "My husband was ill for a long time. I sold everything we had in the shop and the house, everything of value, trying to save his life. But nothing helped. He passed away and left me with seven orphans—four sons and three daughters. Now I have nothing to put in their mouths, and they are liable, Heaven forbid, to die of starvation. Rebbe, please advise me. How can I support us honorably and raise the orphans? For we have a merciful and compassionate God in Heaven, may He have mercy also on me and on my orphans." The woman broke down in tears and could not continue.

The *rebbe* stood up. It was clear that the story had touched his heart. "What do you have left in the shop?" he asked.

"Only a bottle of olive oil that I must keep at any cost, because I received it as a gift from the Holy Land."

"Go home in peace, my daughter," the *rebbe* said, "and set aside many containers. Pour the oil from that bottle and fill up all of the containers. Then you can sell the oil. In this way you can support yourself honorably. But remember! You must not tell anybody about this, not even your children. And you must lock the door while doing it."

The widow followed the *rebbe*'s advice and everything happened just as he said. The oil from the Holy Land made it possible for her to support herself honorably.

Eternally grateful, the widow came to the *rebbe* with a large donation—to express her gratitude for his advice and blessing. But the *rebbe* refused to accept anything from the widow and sent her back home.

---

*A Hasidic rabbi.

COMMENTARY FOR TALE 7 (IFA 4024)

Recorded by Yehudit Gut-Burg from her mother, Esther Weinstein, who heard the story from her own father, Rabbi Ḥayyim Salz of Safad (1876–1936), who lived on the bottom floor of a building that housed the synagogue of the Stratyn Hasidim.[1]

Cultural, Historical, and Literary Background

Rabbi Judah Zevi Hirsch Brandwein of Stretyn (d. 1854) was a founder of a Hasidic dynasty in eastern Galicia. A disciple of Rabbi Uri ben Phinehas Strelisk (Ha-Saraf) (1757–1826), he was a *shohet* (one who slaughters animals according to the kosher laws), and he inherited his teacher's leadership post after the latter's death. Although the transference of leadership after him was marred by family quarrels, a Hasidic dynasty was, nevertheless, formed.[2] Some of his teachings have been published and discussed.[3] A number of Rabbi Judah Zevi's followers lived in Safed, and their synagogue was in the same building as the narrator's childhood home.

The present tale draws on stories from the biblical period and is a version of a biblical legend of the prophet Elisha and the widow (2 Kings 4:1–7). Acts of the early prophets Elijah and Elisha served as narrative models for tales in praise of the Hasidic *tzadikim*. Another common theme of these tales involves the resuscitation of a child, patterned after 1 Kings 17:17–24 and 2 Kings 4:8–37.[4] The miracle of the oil is the basic theme of the Hanukkah story, as told in BT *Shabbat* 21b, although this miracle is absent from 1 Maccabees 4:36–61 and 2 Maccabees 10.[5]

The present tale also draws on local traditions of the magical provision of food. A talmudic-midrashic story about Rabbi Simeon bar Yoḥai, the second-century *tanna* to whom the writing of the Zohar is traditionally attributed, is an example. The rabbi and his son hid themselves from the Romans by living in a cave and eating the fruits of a miraculous carob tree (BT *Shabbat* 33b); in Safed this is considered a local legend. The story of Joseph, the righteous miller of Peki'in, who received magical stones that provided him with flour as a reward for completing a minyan is another local legend.[6] The tale is narrated by an Arab woman to a group of Jews who passed her on their return from visiting the cave of Rabbi Simeon bar Yoḥai.

Folklore Motifs

- C300 "Looking tabu."
- C423.1 "Tabu: disclosing source of magic power."
- D1030.1 "Food supplied by magic."
- D1171.8 "Magic bottle."
- D1242.4 "Magic oil."

- D1472 "Food and drink from magic object."
- D1482 "Magic object produces oil."
- D1652.1 "Inexhaustible food."
- D1652.1.0.1 "Miraculously increasing of small quantity of victuals or drinks to feed a great number of people."
- D1652.5 "Inexhaustible vessel."
- D1713 "Magic power of hermit (saint, yogi)."
- D2105 "Provisions magically furnished."

——————— **Notes** ———————

1. First published in Weinstein, *Grandma Esther Relates . . .*, 46–47 no. 8.

2. See Piekarz, *Ideological Trends of Hasidim in Poland*, 193–195.

3. Brandwein, *Degel Maḥaneh Yehudah* (The banner of Judah's camp); I. Berger, *Eser Tsaḥtsaḥot* (Ten illuminations); Raphael, *Sefer ha-Hasidut* (The book of Hasidism), 351–355; M. Buber, *Tales of Hasidim: Later Masters*, 150–152; and Newman, *The Hasidic Anthology*, 571 ("Stretiner, Judah Zevi").

4. See, for example, Ben-Amos and Mintz, *In Praise of the Ba'al Shem Tov*, 129–131 no. 105.

5. Goldstein, *I Maccabees*, 272–288; and Lurie, *Meggillath Ta'anith*, 170–180 [Hebrew].

6. Haddad, *Peki'in*, 33–34; Reicher, *Sha'arei Yerushalyim* (The gates of Jerusalem), 52a; and Ben-Yeḥezki'el, *Sefer ha-Ma'asiyyot* (A book of folktales), 5:367–371.

Hasidic Tales

8

Rebbe Shmelke's Matzos

TOLD BY Y. TAMARI

*E*very year, when the month of Nisan arrived, the tzadik Rebbe Moshe Leib of Sasov would take up his walking stick and wallet and set out for Nikolsburg, so he could celebrate Passover with his own master, Rebbe Shmelke. Rebbe Moshe Lieb would fill a bag with wheat that he had harvested and threshed with his own hands and stored all winter in his attic, far from moisture and anything else that might cause it to become *hametz*.* This was very important because this wheat was going to be ground into flour that could be used to bake the special seder-night *matzot shemurot* (made from wheat watched over from the moment of harvesting) for his master, Rebbe Shmelke.

Rebbe Moshe Leib imagined his master's pleasure when he gave him this precious gift and how, on the eve of Passover, in the afternoon, the *rebbe* and his disciples would don their Sabbath finery and work together to bake the *matzot shemurot* for the seder, reciting the *Hallel* psalms as they worked, in a state of great joy and intense devotion. And then, when night fell and the holiday began, his master would sit down to the seder and read the Haggadah** with fervor and enthusiasm. Afterward Rebbe Shmelke would eat the *matzot shemurot* prepared from the wheat in Rebbe Moshe Leib's bag, which he had guarded like the apple of his eye and would never sell for all the money in the world. Thinking of this, Rebbe Moshe Leib was filled with joy and was scarcely aware of the hardships of the journey.

The tzadik Rebbe Moshe Leib traveled on the road to Nikolsburg, going from city to city and village to village. All day he walked; sometimes he got a ride in a passing wagon. At night he would lodge with a farmer or a Jewish innkeeper. In this way, he had almost reached Nikolsburg. When darkness fell and he was looking for a place to spend the night, he passed a hut and heard children crying inside. He entered and

---

*All food and beverages that are forbidden during Passover.
**The book of liturgy, prayers, songs, and rituals used at the Passover seder.

asked them what was wrong. At first the children were confused and silent. But the tzadik pressed gently, until they told him that their mother had gone off early in the morning to the nearby market and had not yet returned. Since then they had had nothing to eat and were famished—but there was no food in the house, because their mother was a poor widow. Overcome with compassion, the tzadik took his wheat, pounded it in the mortar, cooked porridge for the children, and gave it to them to eat. When he arrived in Nikolsburg, he went to the market and bought regular flour for his master.

On the night of Passover the tzadik Rebbe Shmelke sat down to the seder with his disciples. As always, he conducted the seder with great enthusiasm. Everyone present was elated and their faces shone with joy. Only Rebbe Moshe Leib was not in his usual exalted state, because of his pangs of conscience. He was sure that when he ate the *matzot*, his master would realize what he had done and denounce him as a fraud.[*]

They finished reading the first part of the haggadah, and the assembled company washed their hands. The tzadik Rebbe Shmelke took the *matzot* in his hands; recited the invocation before performing a mitzvah,[**] "In the name of the Unity of the Holy One, Blessed Be He"; and recited the twin blessings, over bread and over the special seder-night precept of eating *matzot*, with intense devotion. Then he broke off a piece of the upper *matzot* and a piece of the middle *matzot*, put them in his mouth, and ate them with great relish. Suddenly he stopped chewing and said, as if to himself, "What a strange flavor this *matzot* has. I have never tasted anything like it." The tzadik Rebbe Moshe Leib sat there as if on burning coals, certain that his master had discerned the truth and knew this was not *matzot shemurot* but regular *matzot* baked from ordinary flour. In another moment, he would reveal his act of deception to everyone.

Rebbe Moshe Leib's face changed color. He felt dizzy and was about to faint. Then his master addressed the entire company, "Listen, my students. Never in my life have I tasted anything like the flavor of this *matzot*, until today. Tell me, my dear student Moshele, where did you get the flour from which we baked these *matzot*? Tell me everything and conceal nothing."

So Rebbe Moshe Leib told his master the whole story. He begged his master to forgive him for what he had done—but he had been filled with

---

[*]See Genesis 27:12.
[**]An act of fulfilling a commandment.

compassion for the poor orphan children and would, of course, perform any penance that might be imposed on him.

"No," replied Rebbe Shmelke, "you have done well, my dear student, and deserve only praise. When I made the blessing on the *matzot* I felt a great 'illumination'; and when I tasted the *matzot*, I enjoyed a sweetness such as I have never known. I knew there was a reason for it!"

COMMENTARY FOR TALE 8 (IFA 237)

Y. Tamari wrote down this story in 1958 as he heard it from his grandfather, an immigrant from Hungary.

Cultural, Historical, and Literary Background

The Rabbis

The present tale involves two Hasidic rabbis, a disciple and a master; and two *mitzvot*, one religious, the other social, the fulfillment of which is mutually exclusive.

Rabbi Moses (Moshe) Leib of Sasov (1745–1807) was born in Brody, and after living for a number of years in Opatov,[1] he settled in Sasov[2] and became one of the early *tzadikim* to whom the town owes its reputation as a center of Hasidism. He was the author of several novellae on talmudic tractates, which were published posthumously.[3] In Hasidic legend and lore, as the present story underscores, he had the reputation of being a person with a great concern for the poor, attending in particular to the plight of orphans and widows.

Rabbi Moses Leib has been the subject of many tales, some of which appear in Hasidic narrative anthologies[4] as well as in modern anthologies.[5] Tales about him can still be found in the Hasidic oral tradition of America.[6] Notable in particular is the tale about whether the rabbi when up to Heaven.[7] An opponent of the Hasidim learned that Rabbi Moses Leib had not shown up for the penitential prayers (*Selichot*) before Yom Kippur and wondered if the rabbi would be able to go to Heaven. One night he followed the rabbi and saw that Rabbi Moses Leib had put on peasant garb, went into the forest to cut firewood, and then delivered the wood to the house of a sickly, recently widowed woman. The opponent of the Hasidim then concluded that because of such an act of kindness the rabbi would go even higher than Heaven. I. Peretz's short story "*Oyb Nisht Nokh Hekher*" (If not higher),[8] which has entered into the canon of Yiddish literature and has often been translated,[9] was based on some version, either printed or oral, of that tale.

For thirteen years, Rabbi Moses Leib was a devoted disciple of Rabbi Samuel Shmelke Horowitz of Nikolsburg (1726–1778), with whom he studied both Torah and Kabbalah, while the later was a rabbi in Rychwal (1754) and Sieniawa (1766).[10] Rabbi Shmelke himself was, together with his brother Phinehas ben Zevi Hirsch Horowitz (1730–1805), a student of the Great Maggid, Rabbi Dov Baer of Mezhirech (d. 1772). Rabbi Shmelke, who served as a rabbi in several towns in Galicia, was appointed as the head of the rabbinical court and later as the rabbi of Nikolsburg in Moravia. His writings, published posthumously, are *Divrei Shemuel* (Samuel's words; 1862) and *Nezir ha-Shem* (God's hermit; 1869). Like his famous disciple, he was a subject of legends that appeared in Hasidic books,[11] some of which were later anthologized.[12]

Similarities to Other IFA Tales

There are six additional tales about Rabbi Moses Leib in the IFA.

- IFA 2123: *Against Haughtiness* (Belarus).
- IFA 2126: *Genesis* (Belarus).
- IFA 4804: *How Did Rabbi Moses of Sasov Release a Tenant from Prison?* (Poland).
- IFA 5096: *Stink Discovers the Rapist* (Poland).
- IFA 8015: *A Story about the Conscripts* (Belarus).
- IFA 13128: *The Rabbi of Sasov* (Ukraine).[13]
- IFA 21719: *A Melody for a Wedding, a Melody for a Funeral* (Romania).

Matzah *Shemurah*

The term *matzah shemurah* sometimes rendered *shemurha matzah* in Jewish-American English), refers to matzah that is baked from wheat that was preserved for that purpose from harvest time and guarded against any possible contact with water, which might start the fermentation process. The term draws on the biblical verse "You shall observe the [Feast of] Unleavened Bread, for on this very day I brought your ranks out of the land of Egypt" (Exodus 12:17). The modern translation adds the words "Feast of"; and although this is an adequate interpretation of the text, it obliterates the scriptural connection for the emergence of the expression *matzah shemurah*—namely the phrase *u-shmartem et ha-matzot*.

The early occurrences of the term are in the Zohar (*Raya mehemna*, Leviticus 96, p. 29b) and in the talmudic commentary of Rabbi Asher ben Jehiel (c. 1250–1327) on the tractate *Pesaḥim* (chapter 10 no. 35). After the expulsion and dispersion of the Spanish Jews from the sixteenth century onward, the term was broadly spread and accepted. Ultra-religious people would guard the wheat and bake it only on the eve of Passover. The eating of *matzah shemurah* is an obvious mark of piety. In the present tale, Rabbi Moses Leib sacrificed it for the sake of social good.

Folklore Motifs

- cf. F183 "Foods in other world."
- F851 "Extraordinary food."
- V75.1 "Passover."
- V85 "Religious pilgrimages."
- V400 "Charity."
- *V412.3 "Replaced devotional bread that was given in charity to the poor has heavenly taste."
- V530 "Pilgrimages."

―――― **Notes** ――――

1. Opatow in Polish; Apta in Yiddish.
2. Sasow in Polish.
3. The first among them was *Likkutei Ramal*.
4. Bodek, *Seder ha-Dorot mi-Talmidei ha-Besht* (Successive generations of the Besht's disciples), 70–77; Eherman, *Sefer Devarim 'Arevim* (A book of pleasant subjects), 1:30a–34b.
5. Lipson, *Di Velt Dertzeilt* (The world tells), 210 nos. 385, 386; Lipson, *Medor Dor* (From days of old), 1:278–279 nos. 765–768; 2:150, 168, 221 nos. 1318, 1407, 1584–1586; and 3:264 nos. 2560, 2561.
6. J. Mintz, *Legends of the Hasidim*, 175–177 nos. T13, T14.
7. Lipson, *Medor Dor* (From days of old), 2:221 no. 1586; and Mintz, op. cit., 176–177 no. T14. The tale first appeared in print in Bodek, *Ma'aseh Tsaddikim* (The acts of the just).
8. *Der Yid* 1 (1900).
9. See, for example, Peretz, *Stories and Pictures*, 13–18; Peretz, *Peretz*, 174–181; Peretz, *Selected Stories*, 38–40; and Wisse, *The I. L. Peretz Reader*, 178–181.
10. For a brief biographical description of Rabbi Moses Leib, see Raphael, *Sasov*, 8-12; reprinted in Raphael, *Al Ḥasidut ve-Ḥasidim* (On Hasidism and Hasidim), 365–368; and Raphael, *Sefer ha-Ḥasidut* (The book of Hasidism), 186–190.
11. For example, Mikhalzohn, *Sefer Shemen ha-Tov* (The book of oil of goodness).
12. See Lipson, *Di Velt Dertzeilt* (The world tells), 68–69, 272–273 nos. 103, 511; Lipson, *Medor Dor* (From days of old), 1:97–98, 130, 181, 216 nos. 250, 340, 455, 575, 2:241 no. 1667; 3:49, 98–99, 152–153, 221, 263 nos. 1890, 2032, 2033, 2196, 2410, 2487, 2557.
13. Published in M. Cohen, *Mi-Pi ha-Am* (From folk tradition), 2:53–55 no. 160.

9

The Unforgotten Melody

HEARD BY ZALMAN BAHARAV FROM
DOV-BERL RABINOVITCH

Reb Ḥayyim, who held the lease on a nobleman's distillery, wanted a scholar for his daughter, Zippora, who had reached marriageable age. What did he do? He turned to Rebbe Eliezer, the head of the yeshivah* in the nearby city, and requested a groom: one of the young men who studied all the time, could learn a page of Gemara with the Tosafot commentary, knew how to sing, and was a God-fearing Hasid.

The *rosh yeshivah* complied with his supporter Reb Ḥayyim's request and picked out a student named Yaacov, who was faithful and studious, upright and melodious, with a sweet voice that captivated every heart. The *rosh yeshivah* gave the young man a letter, recommending him as a worthy son-in-law for the leaseholder and suggesting that the father-in-law support the scholar after the wedding until he became a householder in his own right.

The *yeshivah* student came to the house of his intended father-in-law and within a short time married Zippora, the daughter of Reb Ḥayyim the leaseholder. Reb Ḥayyim gave the couple their own room in his house, and Yaacov was allotted a place in the attic to study Torah. They ate their meals at the table of the well-to-do father-in-law. Within three years two children were born to them.

In this fashion, the young scholar led a comfortable and agreeable life, chanting his Gemara** melodiously and committing his learning to memory. From time to time he would travel to visit the *rebbe*, bringing him melodies he had heard and memorized. The *rebbe* used them chiefly at his public feasts, for the third Sabbath meal, and for bidding farewell to the Sabbath Queen.

Three years passed, and the period of support promised by his father-

---

*Jewish school of higher learning.
**Rabbinic commentaries on the Mishnah in the Talmud; colloquially referring to the Talmud.

in-law came to an end. Dressed in his Sabbath finery, Reb Hayyim went to visit a nobleman. After protracted negotiations, requests, and promises, he received a loan of a hundred rubles.

Zippora sewed the money into her husband's vest pocket. He took his tallit* and tefillin** and some pieces of cheese and a loaf of bread as provisions for his journey. He put everything in a bundle and tied this, along with his shoes, to his staff. And in this fashion he set out.

That evening Yaacov arrived at an inn. What did he see there? A group of Hasidim avidly eating the tail of a salt herring and drinking. They were all gathered around the stove, because the evening was cool, and one of them was singing a *nigun*.§

Ai didee dai diggy diggy dai

The melody resonated in Yaacov's soul, spread through his limbs, and carried him away, until he reached a decision: "I must stay here and learn this important melody. I will sing it at the first opportunity when I go visit our *rebbe*, may he live."

Yaacov went over to the Hasid who was singing. "Please, sir! You have restored my soul with your wonderful melody. I would like to learn it by heart."

"What?" the Jew replied. "Just like this, you would acquire such a valuable Hasidic *nigun* without paying for it? Is the tune public property? I spent a long time gathering up sparks of holiness, polishing and improving various melodies that hover in our world. I have devoted many years to this holy labor. And you want my work and the fruit of my toil for nothing! Give me fifty rubles from your wallet and the *nigun* is yours."

Yaacov pleaded with the composer, but in vain. He resisted stubbornly and would not drop his asking price by so much as a kopeck.§§

Yaacov could not control himself. What did he do? He paid the owner of the melody half of all the money he had and purchased the melody from him. Because he did not want to lose his precious acquisition, which had cost half his wealth, he kept singing the *nigun* to himself as he traveled.

Ai didee dai diggy diggy dai . . .

---

*Prayer shawl.
**Small black leather prayer boxes, wrapped around the head and arm, containing passages from the Torah.
§Melody.
§§Small coin, like a penny.

Three days later, Yaacov came to a second inn. What did he see there? A group of Hasidim and businessmen gathered around the stove, where an old Hasid with a yellow beard sat singing a much sweeter melody than the one Yaacov had bought three days earlier:

Ai ai didee dai dai dai diggy dai . . .

If it were possible—the thought crept into Yaacov's mind—if it were possible to combine these two melodies into one, which would restore the soul and expand the heart, how great would be the enthusiasm at the *rebbe*'s court! Yaacov decided: "I will learn this *nigun,* too, and when I bring the two of them to the *rebbe,* joined into one, the song will spread through the worlds of body and spirit, and its power will penetrate even to the repository of souls beneath the Heavenly throne. What is more precious than 'joyous shouts of deliverance resounding in the tents of the righteous,'[*] than 'the sound of mirth and gladness'?"[**]

Yaacov went up to the bearded Jew. "Please," he asked, "would you be so good as to teach me this wonderful *nigun*?"

The Jew responded, "This melody I am singing cost me much money. I assembled and collected its parts from outstanding tunesmiths and invested much time and energy in joining and refining them. I will not part with my melody unless you give me fifty rubles for it."

Yaacov had no choice. He paid the owner of the second *nigun* the amount he demanded and began to rehearse it.

Ai ai didee dai dai dai diggy dai

Yaacov already knew the two melodies quite well, but all the same he feared that he might forget them. What he did he do? On his way back home, he kept singing to himself the two melodies he had purchased for good money, until they fused into a single melody:

Ai didee dai diggy diggy dai
Ai ai didee dai dai dai diggy dai . . .

Yaacov approached his house and knocked on the door. "Who's that knocking in the middle of the night?" called his wife. Yaacov responded with the first melody.

Ai didee dai diggy diggy dai . . .

---

[*]See Psalm 118:15.
[**]See Jeremiah 7:34, 16:9, 25:10, and 33:11.

Zippora opened the door. When she saw her husband she asked, "Yaacov, my dear, what did you buy?"

Yaacov replied with the second melody.

> *Ai ai didee dai dai dai diggy dai . . .*

Zippora let her husband inside and gave him a bowl of soup and a loaf of bread. In the meantime the young man's father-in-law, Reb Hayyim the leaseholder, entered. "How was your journey?" he asked. "What bargains did you purchase? How did you succeed?"

Yaacov replied with the first *nigun*.

> *Ai didee dai diggy diggy dai . . .*

Reb Hayyim began to revile and curse his son-in-law, but Yaacov replied with the second *nigun*.

> *Ai ai didee dai dai dai diggy dai . . .*

The time came to repay the nobleman's loan. What did Reb Hayyim the leaseholder do? He hauled his son-in-law off to the nobleman, who asked him, in a non-Jewish language full of curses and insults: "Yaacov, you Jew, tell me, what did you buy? What did you do with my hundred rubles?"

In reply, Yaacov sang the first melody to the nobleman.

> *Ai didee dai diggy diggy dai . . .*

To the nobleman's vigorous cursing, Yaacov the Hasid responded with the second melody.

> *Ai ai didee dai dai dai diggy dai . . .*

Enraged, the nobleman ordered that the crazy Yaacov be spread-eagled across the bench—may it not happen to us!—with a brawny Cossack on each side. "Flog him to get those melodies out of his head."

But a Hasid like Yaacov would never forget the wonderful *nigun* he was going to bring to his *rebbe*, not even if they tortured him with knouts and whips. The Cossacks flogged away, but Yaacov the Hasid kept singing the melody, which made him oblivious to his misery and pain.

> *Ai didee dai diggy diggy dai*
> *Ai ai didee dai dai dai diggy dai . . .*

As long as he didn't forget the *nigun*!

COMMENTARY FOR TALE 9 (IFA 5794)

Zalman Baharav heard this story from his father, Dov-Berl Rabinovitch, in the shtetl of Klinkovich in Belarus, and he it down from memory in 1963.[1]

Cultural, Historical, and Literary Background

This is a cante fable that involves songs as commodities; for more about this genre and its subtypes in Jewish tradition, see the notes to tale IFA 6976 (in this vol., no. 62). Lehman published six versions of the present tale,[2] two of which have been translated into English.[3] Several earlier versions of this story end with the rabbi granting his daughter a divorce from such a son-in-law. Popular renditions of Hasidic legends about songs in Hasidic life are available,[4] as are modern tales on the same subject.[5]

Although comic in its narration, the story itself has an ethnographic value in reconstructing Hasidic life and teaching. Music and songs have become an integral part of Hasidic religious worship, yet unlike the hagiographic tales about the *tzadikim*, the Hasidim had no way of committing their music to writing. The learning and the performing of songs in Hasidic celebrations were completely oral. Most rabbis could not read or write music; and even if one of their followers could, the rabbis objected to recording the melodies for two reasons: They thought, first, that the written score could not inherently represent the music totally and, second, that a score would reduce the spirituality of music to a material representation. Therefore, compulsive repetition, here exaggerated to a comic degree, reflects the learning process in an oral culture.

The tale also points out the competitive nature of the introduction of songs into Hasidic life. In addition to composing original melodies, Hasidim would present songs they learned from diverse sources during gatherings at the rabbi's court. The melody that would appeal to the rabbi most would become the "rabbi's *nigun*" (melody). Naturally, the Hasid who had introduced the melody would incur prestige among his fellow worshipers.[6] There is a substantial body of literature concerning Hasidic music.[7]

Folktale Type

- cf. 1685A "The Stupid Son-in-Law."

Folklore Motifs

- *N430 "Man buys melody."
- *N445 "Valuable melody learned."

Notes

1. First published in M. Noy, *East European Jewish Cante Fables*, 18–23 no. 2.

2. "*Folk-Mayselekh un anekdoten mit nigunim*" (Folktales and anecdotes with melodies).

3. Ausubel, *A Treasury of Jewish Folklore,* 349–354; and B. Weinreich, *Yiddish Folktales*, 231–232 no. 94.

4. D. Cohen, *Aggadot Mitnagnot* (Melodic legends); and P. Schram, *Jewish Stories One Generation Tells Another*, 367–392, esp. 369–375 for a version of the present tale from Ruth Rubin.

5. A collection on the same subject with some modern tales, often about Hasidim in America, is Staiman, *Niggun,* esp. 255–264.

6. For a description from memory of singing in the *rebbe's* court in Sadagura (Sadigora in Yiddish; Sadagora in German), see Y. Even, *Fun'm Rebin's Hoyf* (From the rabbi's court), 162–166.

7. Avenary, "The Hasidic Nigun"; Geshuri, *Music and Hassidism in the House of Kuzmir;* Geshuri, *La-Ḥasidim Mizmor* (A hymn of Hasidim), 162–166 (bibliography); Geshuri, "*Le-Torat ha-Nigun ba-Ḥasidut*" (About the Hasidic ideas of music); Haidu and Mazor, "The Musical Tradition of Hasidism," Idelsohn, "*Ha-Neginah ha-Ḥasidit*" (The Hasidic melody); Koskoff, *Music in Lubavitcher Life;* and U. Sharvit, *Chassidic Tunes from Galicia;* C. Vinaver, *Anthology of Hassidic Music.*

10

The Power of a Melody

HEARD BY ZALMAN BAHARAV FROM

DOV-BERL RABINOVITCH

At his receptions to bid farewell to the Sabbath Queen on Saturday night after the Sabbath, Rebbe Shneur Zalman of Lyady, the founder of Ḥabad, would relate Torah novellae and Hasidic insights to the Hasidim who were sitting around the table. Once, while he was speaking, the *rebbe* spied an old Jew who was not one of his close circle of Hasidim. This Jew was sitting at the corner of the table, his brow furrowed, his eyes focused on the *rebbe*. His face revealed the pain of a man who does not understand what he is hearing, despite his great efforts.

After *Havdalah*,* the *rebbe*** called the stranger over to him. "I saw in your face, Reb Jew, that you did not understand what I was saying when bidding farewell to the Sabbath Queen."

The Jew acknowledged as much. "Holy Rebbe," he said, "when I was a small child, my parents sent me to the religious school of the best teacher in town so I could learn Torah. And indeed my soul thirsted for Torah, and I made great progress in my studies. But it was my bad luck that my parents died of an infectious disease and my relatives apprenticed me to a wagon driver. When I married, I followed the same profession. I drove a horse and wagon until I reached old age. Now I have free time, and my children (may they live) support me. So I have joined your community of Hasidim to hear words of Torah from your holy mouth. But what can I do if I cannot fathom their depth? Please guide me, sainted and revered Rebbe, in the ways of your Torah, so that I may understand them.

What did the *rebbe* do? He began singing a *nigun*.§

---

*The ceremony that marks the end of the Sabbath.
**A Hasidic rabbi.
§*Nigun* in Hebrew is melody.

Ai didee dai diggy diggy dai
Ai ai didee dai dai dai diggy dai . . .

The old wagon driver's face lit up when he heard the melody, and he sang it back along with the *rebbe*.

Ai didee dai diggy diggy dai
Ai ai didee dai dai dai diggy dai . . .

And as he sang, the wagon driver found that he understood the secret meaning of Torah that the *rebbe* had spoken.

From that Sabbath on, Rebbe Shneur Zalman of Lyady would introduce his discourse at the farewell feast with that melody, which is still known today as the "*rebbe's nigun.*"

Ai didee dai diggy diggy dai
Ai ai didee dai dai dai diggy dai . . .

Why? So that everyone present could understand the teachings of Hasidism.

COMMENTARY FOR TALE 10 (IFA 5793)

Zalman Baharav heard this story from his father, Dov-Berl Rabinovitch, in the shtetl of Klinkovich in Belarus, and he wrote it down from memory in 1963.

Cultural, Historical, and Literary Background

The narrator-recorder of the tale was not a Hasid. Although he grew up in a traditional home in Belarus, his father was not a follower of any Hasidic rabbi either. He immigrated to Israel as a secular Jew, fired up by Zionistic-socialistic ideals, but he still remembered the regional Hasidic narratives told about Rabbi Shneur Zalman of Lyady. The narrator could relate the story, which circulated in his district in an abbreviated form, but recalled the melody only partially.

Rabbi Shneur Zalman (1745–1813) was born in Liozna, in the Vitebsk district of Belarus. He was a leading Hasidic rabbi in Lithuania, Belarus, and Ukraine and was a disciple of the Great Maggid, Rabbi Dov Baer of Mezhirech (d. 1772). Rabbi Shneur Zalman founded a distinct trend in Hasidism known as Ḥabad, an acronym for "*Ḥokhmah Binah Daʻat*" (wisdom, insight, knowledge). He added the aspect of study to the ecstatic religious practices of Hasidism and formulated the concept of "intermediary" ethical and religious conduct (*beinoni*), a degree of piety that is attainable by everyone and takes into consideration the ethical choices a person makes as he or she is caught in the struggle between positive and negative values. In his systematic thought, Rabbi Shneur Zalman made ethical and spiritual living attainable by all, not just the *tzadikim*, who possess unique spiritual qualities. A bibliography of the rabbi is available.[1]

His fundamental book, *Likkutei ammarim* (Collected sayings), was published first anonymously in Slavuta in 1776. It was later known as the *Tanya,* and went through numerous printings, becoming one of the basic books of Hasidic thought. There are eight manuscripts predating the first printed edition.[2] A substantial body of scholarly and Hasidic literature about Rabbi Schneur Zalman of Lyady and his teachings has been published.[3]

Rabbi Schneur Zalman of Lyady considered music to be a complement for mystical contemplation and regarded the singing of melodies to have a high spiritual value. According to Zalmanoff, "While the Besht made melody come spiritually alive, Rabbi Schneur Zalman came along and made the melody more profound, revealing to all the inner soul of melody."[4] The Hasidim attribute the composition of ten melodies to Rabbi Schneur Zalman, all of which are steeped in mystical symbolism.[5]

The narrator of the present tale remembered only one stanza of the song, and the transcription of M. Noy[6] varies somewhat from the transcription of Zalmanoff.[7] The melody included in this story is known by several titles in Ḥabad circles—for example, the *"Rav's Nigun"* (The rabbi's melody), the *"Alter Rebbe's Nigun"* (The old rabbi's melody), the "Melody of the Four Stanzas," and

10 / The Power of a Melody

the "Melody of the Four Gates." Instrumental and vocal renditions of the song have been produced.[8] The rabbi's *nigun*

> is the fundamental and principal melody of Habad Hasidim. It was composed by the *alter rebe,* author of the *Tanya,* and it connotes some profound meanings. Each of its movements is devoted to a sublime spiritual subject. Habad Hasidim sing or play it with utmost precision and on specific occasions such as the last day of each pilgrimage holidays [Passover, Shavuot, and Sukkot], Purim, 19th of Kislev [anniversary of the release of Rabbi Shneur Zalman from prison], 12th of Tammuz [birthday and anniversary of the release of Rabbi Joseph Isaac Schneersohn from Soviet prison], weddings and the like.[9]

After this explanation, Zalmanoff quoted at length a letter of Rabbi Joseph Isaac Schneersohn (1880–1950) that was published in 1937. The letter contains valuable interpretive commentary:

> The Old Rabbi's melody is devoted to the four worlds, *azilut* [emanation], *beri'ah* [creation], *yezirah* [formation], and *assiyah* [completion]. Each stanza of the song corresponds to a particular world.
>
> Each of the four worlds—*azilut, ber'iah, yezirah,* and *assiyah*—corresponds to one of the four letters of the Tetragrammaton. Each of the four letters of the Name is lit in each of the four spiritual stages, *nefesh* [soul], *ruach* [spirit], *neshamah* [breath], *hayim* [life], which are part of the soul of every Jewish man and woman.
>
> The Old Rabbi's melody corresponds to each of the four worlds, *azilut, ber'iah, yezirah,* and *assiyah,* and we must sing them with great precision because they correspond with each of the letters of the Tetragrammaton, the four worlds, and the four stages of the soul.
>
> The singing of the melody with inner excitement is the proper time for repentance and connection [with God]; the singing of the melody with a sincere purity of the heart, after "clearing the ashes of the alter" [BT *Yoma* 22a] in the *Tikun Hazzot* service,[10] or after a truthful bedtime *ker'iat Shema*[11] and a deep and faithful prayer, could also be a time for making a personal request.
>
> The melody that the Rabbi composed was in the upward scale, ascending in the order of prayers: *barukh she-amar,*[12] *Pesukei de-Zimra,*[13] *Berakhot Ker'iat Shema,*[14] *Keri'at Shema,* and Eighteen Benedictions, to which the four worlds—*azilut, ber'iah, yezirah,* and *assiyah*—correspond in an upward order.
>
> In general, each of the melody's stanzas has a potential for a personal act, either internally or indirectly.
>
> The first stanza involves a shift and deepening [of meaning]. At the beginning of singing, there is a need to make a slight shift, to move from

one's position, in order to get out of the profane surrounding . . . the continuation of the first stanza involves a deepening in thoughts about the needs at home and the meaning of one's existence in the world.

The second stanza belongs to the first in the sense that it is possible to hear some bitterness at the beginning of the stanza, but immediately the stanza continues with hope and upward movements. The bitterness and the hope are consequences of the shift and the deepening of the first stanza.

The third stanza involves spiritual loftiness, although the second stanza still resonates in the third when the sense of bitterness continues to be felt. Nevertheless, the main aspects of the third stanza are the emotions—loftiness of spirit and effusion of soul.

The fourth stanza corresponds to the world *azilut,* which is the highest level in the hierarchy of the four worlds, *assiyah, yezirah, ber'iah,* and *azilut.* . . .

When the rabbi finished talking, he instructed [them] to sing the song slowly and to repeat twice the first three stanzas and three times the fourth stanza. They sang the *nigun* three times, one after the other; and after the third time, they repeated the forth stanza ten times one after the other so that it would be vested in all ten energies of the soul.[15]

The story about the wagon driver and Rabbi Shneur Zalman has been told among the Hasidim. A version recorded during the Jewish Ethnographic Expedition (1911–1914) in Volhynia and Podolia headed by An-ski is available.[16]

Similarities to Other IFA Tales

Another version of this tale appears in the IFA :

- IFA 1199: *The Rabbi's Melody* (Russia).[17]

Folklore Motifs

- L111.4 "Orphan hero."
- *N445 "Valuable melody learned."
- *P416 "Wagon driver."
- *P426.4 "Rabbi."
- V71 "Sabbath."
- *V71.5 "Escorting the Sabbath ritual."

──────── Notes ────────

1. Mondschein, *Torat Ḥabad;* see Schneur Zalman, *Likutei Amarim (Tanya).*

2. Schneur Zalman, *Likkutei Amarim First Versions;* and Loewenthal, "Rabbi Schneur Zalman of Liadi's Kitzur Likkutei Amarim."

3. For selected studies, see Elior, *The Paradoxical Ascent to God*; Etkes, "Rabbi Shneur Zalman of Lyady as a Hasidic Leader"; Elior, "The Rise of Rabbi Schneur Zalman

of Lyady as a Hasidic Leader"; Foxbrunner, *Ḥabad;* Glitsenshtein, *Sefer ha-Toladot: Rabbi Schneur Zalman mi-Lyady* (The biography of Rabbi Schneur Zalman of Lyady); Hallamish, *Path to the Tanya;* Lindeberg, "Rabbi Shneur Zalmans Anthropologi"; Loewenthal, *Communicating the Infinit*; Mindel, *Rabbi Schneur Zalman*; Steinsaltz, *Opening the Tanya;* and M. Teitelbaum, *Der Rabh von Ladi.* For a brief survey of Rabbi Shneur Zalman of Lyady's writings and recent scholarship about his teaching, see Faierstein, "The Literary Legacy of Shneur Zalman of Lyadi." The rabbi was also the subject of a modern play: *"Ha-Rabi mi-Ladi"* (The rabbi of Lyady), by Z. Cohen. The play concludes with the singing of the rabbi's melody.

4. Zalmanoff, *Sefer Hanigunim,* 19.

5. Zalmanoff, op. cit., 43–46 (scores, pp. 1–7).

6. M. Noy, *East European Jewish Cante Fables.*

7. Op. cit., 1.

8. *The Precise Melodies of the Chabad Rebbes*, CD. Information available at *nigun@netvision.net.il.*

9. Zalmanoff, op. cit., 43.

10. "Midnight service," recited in mourning of the destruction of the Temple.

11. "Hear, O Israel! The Lord is our God, the Lord alone" (Deuteronomy 6:4).

12. "Blessed be He who spoke"; the opening formula of *Pesukei de-Zimra.*

13. "Verses of songs"; a collection of hymns from Psalms recited daily at the beginning of the morning service.

14. "The Blessing of *Shema*"; the first tractate of the Mishnah, order of *Zera'im.*

15. Zalmanoff, op. cit., 43–44. For a musical analysis of this melody, see E. Koskoff, *Music in Lubavitcher Life,* 89–92.

16. Rechtman, *Jewish Ethnography and Folklore,* 259–261; another version is in Indritch, *"Nigun Devekut shel ha-Rabi mi-Liadi"* (The Rabbi of Lyady's devotional melody).

17. Published in M. Noy, op. cit., no. 1 n. 38.

11

The Happy Man

Told by Esther Bergner-Kish to Malka Cohen

At the start of World War I, some Galician Hasidim who had been conscripted were traveling to the front. They rode in third class. Even though they were on their way to the front, they sang and had a jolly time, because it was Hanukkah. Everyone who saw them thought they must be people without a care in the world.

A high-ranking officer was traveling in first class. He, too, was en route to the front. He heard the singing and noise that the Hasidim were making and, knowing that they were headed for the front, went to their carriage. "Why are you so merry?" he asked. "Don't you know that you are going to the front to fight?"

The Hasidim told him the following story about the happy man.

Once there was a merchant who traveled with his clerk. They carried a chest full of money to buy merchandise in the city. While they were traveling through a thick forest, the chest disappeared. The clerk was very much distressed by the loss, but the merchant himself only laughed. They stopped for the night at an inn. The clerk, who was too upset to close his eyes, went back to the forest to search for the chest of money. At last he found it, and not a single penny was missing.

The next morning the clerk brought the chest to the merchant, who began to cry. "Shouldn't you be happy, now?!" asked the clerk. "Why are you crying?"

"Finding the chest after it was lost—and with all the money in it, too—that is too much good fortune," he explained. "That's why I am crying."

After that, the merchant's luck did indeed turn, until he was compelled to sell his business. It was his former clerk who purchased it. The merchant left town. The clerk had nothing but good fortune and became very rich.

Years passed.

Once, on a Friday afternoon, the former clerk heard a loud noise.

Peering out the window he saw a group of beggars chatting outside his window, and among them he noticed his former employer. He called his servant. "Go give that beggar, the one I'm pointing at, a gold zloty,* and silver coins to the other beggars."

About two hours later, the clerk again heard noise outside his window. He looked and saw the merchant, his former employer, stripped naked from head to toe, dancing and singing merrily, while the townsfolk—thinking him mad—were afraid to approach him.

The former clerk said to his servant, "Take some clothes, dress this old man, and invite him to dinner."

When the old man entered, the clerk asked him, "Do you recognize me? I was once your clerk, and you can see how rich I have become. But I have no family. I will give you half of my fortune if you'll explain why you laughed, years ago, when the chest full of money disappeared and why you cried bitterly when it turned up and nothing was missing."

"When the chest disappeared," the old man replied, "it was a great disaster. I laughed because I thought no greater disaster could happen to me. When the chest was found, though, and not a single penny was missing, that was such incredible luck that I immediately felt a presentiment that I would go bankrupt—as indeed happened. That's why I left town. Today, when you sent me a gold coin, but only silver pennies to the other beggars, they asked me to share with them equally. I refused and went to the bathhouse to get ready for the Sabbath. While I was there, the beggars stole all of my tattered clothes, along with the gold coin. So I lingered in the bathhouse. The attendant, seeing that the Sabbath was about to begin and I was not leaving, threw me out. There I was in the street, stark naked. At once I knew that nothing worse could happen to me. I was happy, and danced and pranced, as you saw."

"You see," the Hasidim told the officer, "now we should be sitting with our *rebbe*,** lighting the Hanukkah candles, eating potato latkes, playing at *kvitlakh*,§ and so on. Instead we are sitting in a train that is taking us to the front. There could be nothing worse than this—so, as you see, we are happy!

---

*A Polish coin.
**A Hasidic Rabbi.
§A card game.

COMMENTARY FOR TALE 11 (IFA 12214)

Told by Esther Bergner-Kish from Budapest, Hungary, and recorded by Malka Cohen in Tel Aviv in 1978.[1]

Cultural, Historical, and Literary Background

This tale combines a frame story, which is grounded in the history of the Jews of Galicia, and a fable that draws on a basic classical mythic image. See the notes to tale IFA 960 (in this vol., no. 14) for a discussion of the literary principle of the frame and framed story.

As the tale relates, during World War I, the Jews of Galicia were often reluctant conscripts in the Austrian-Hungarian army.[2] Implicit in the fable the Hasidic conscripts tell is the mythic image of the wheel of fortune, which has it roots in the cult and image of the Roman goddess Fortuna and her symbolic wheel.[3] Fortuna's wheel was apparently known to the Rabbis of the Mishnah and the Talmud, because it is implied in the following story about Rabbi Akiva, though he articulated the reversal of fortune in terms of prophecy fulfillment.

> Long ago, as Rabban Gamliel, R. Eleazar b. 'Azariah, R. Joshua and R. Akiba were walking on the road, they heard the noise of the crowds at Rome [on traveling] from Puteoli, a hundred and twenty miles away. They all fell a-weeping, but R. Akiba seemed merry. Said they to him: Wherefore are you merry? Said he to them: Wherefore are you weeping? Said they: These heathens who bow down to images and burn incense to idols live in safety and ease, whereas our Temple, the "Footstool" of our God, is burnt down by fire, and should we then not weep? He replied: Therefore, I am merry. If they that offend him fare thus, how much better shall fare they that do obey him? Once again they were coming up to Jerusalem together, and just as they came to Mount Scopus they saw a fox emerging from the Holy of Holies. They fell a-weeping and R. Akiba seemed merry. Whereupon, said they to him: Wherefore are you merry? Said he: Wherefore are you weeping? Said they to him: A place of which it was once said, *And the common man that draweth nigh shall be put to death* [Numbers 1:51] is now become the haunt of foxes, and should we not weep? Said he to them: Therefore am I merry; for it is written, *And I will take to Me faithful witnesses to record, Uriah the priest and Zechariah the Son of Jeberechiah* [Isaiah 8:2]. Now what connection has this Uriah the priest with Zechariah? Uriah lived during the times of the first Temple, while [the other,] Zechariah, lived [and prophesied] during the second Temple; but Holy Writ linked the [later] prophecy of Zechariah with the [earlier] prophecy of Uriah. In the [earlier] prophecy [in the days] of Uriah it is written, *Therefore shall Zion for your sake be ploughed as a field* etc. [Micah 3:12; Jeremiah 26:18–20]. In Zechariah it is written, *Thus saith the Lord of Hosts, There shall yet old men and old*

women sit in the broad places of Jerusalem [Zechariah 8:4], so long as Uriah's [threatening] prophecy had not had its fulfillment, I had misgivings lest Zechariah's prophecy might not be fulfilled; now that Uriah's prophecy has been [literally] fulfilled, it is quite certain that Zechariah's prophecy is also to find its literal fulfillment. Said they to him: Akiba, you have comforted us! Akiba, you have comforted us (BT *Makkot* 24a–24b).

In the culture of the Yiddish-speaking Jews, the tale articulates an idea that is represented in the proverb *Erger vi shlekht ken nit zayn* (It cannot be worse than woeful).[4] Indirectly, the tale relates to the paradoxical narrative represented in tale type 844 "The Luck-Bringing Shirt," which tells about a search for the shirt of a happy man, but when the man is located, it turns out that he has no shirt. In a brief study, Jakobsdóttir[5] considered the Jewish versions of this tale type as mediating between Eastern and Western renditions.

The name of the game they played, "*kvitlakh*" is the Yiddish word for the notes that Hasidim submit to their *rebbes* requesting cures to their ills, fertility blessings, and advice on family or business matters. The same word is also used to refer to playing cards.[6] Normative rules in Jewish society did not condone card games; however, they were commonly played, as Rivkind has demonstrated.[7]

Similarities to Other IFA Tales

The following tales in the IFA are related to the present story:

- IFA 1039: *Wheel of Fortune* (Yemen).
- IFA 4447: *Why Did the Landlord Laugh and Why Did He Cry?* (Poland).
- IFA 5524: *The Impoverished Rich Man* (Romania).
- IFA 6369: *The Story of the Leading Merchant Rabbi Samuel* (Poland).
- IFA 8110: *Harun al Rashid and Ja'afar al-Barski* (Iraq).
- IFA 8723: *The Life Ups Are Followed by Downs and the Downs by Ups* (Iraq).[8]
- IFA 15734: *Luck on a Seesaw* (Poland).

Folktale Types

- 736*B (IFA) "The Peak of Good Luck, the Bottom of Misfortune."
- 736*B(IFA) (Jason) "The Peak of Good Luck."
- cf. 754 (Jason) "The Happy Friar."
- 2157 (Tubach) "Fortune, Wheel of."

Folklore Motifs

- *N103 "The peak of good luck."
- *N104 "The bottom of misfortune."
- N111.3 "Fortune's wheel."
- *N135.2.2 "Discovery of lost treasure as omen for loss of good luck."

- N203 "Lucky person."
- N211 "Lost object returns to its owner."
- N250 "Persistent bad luck."
- N350 "Accidental loss of property."
- P431 "Merchant"
- P461 "Soldiers."
- *V75.6 "Hanukkah."

--- **Notes** ---

1. First published in Estin, *Contes et fêtes Juives*, 145–148 no. 31.
2. For example, see Schmidl, *Juden in der K. (und) K. Armee 1788–1918*, 82–85, 142–145.
3. Miranda, "Fortuna"; Patch, "The Tradition of the Goddess Fortuna in Roman Literature and the Transitional Period"; and Patch, *The Goddess Fortuna in Mediaeval Literature*, 145–180.
4. I. Bernstein, *Jüdische Sprichwörter und Redensarten*, 282 no. 3854.
5. "The Luck-Bringing Shirt."
6. Stutchkoff, *Thesaurus of the Yiddish Language*, 565 no. 516, col. 2.
7. *The Fight against Gambling among the Jews.*
8. Published in Cheichel, *A Tale for Each Month 1968–1969*, 126–129 no. 20.

12

How Rothschild Became Wealthy

TOLD BY HINDA SHEINFERBER TO HADARAH SELA

A certain Hasid of the Rebbe* of Kozientz** used to go to the *rebbe*'s court for every festival. One day he fell ill and died. He left several children. They were very poor, and the neighbors took pity on them. One of them identified a child with talent, but the neighbor couldn't pay his school fees. This man, taking pity on the child, journeyed to the *rebbe*'s court and told him that so-and-so had passed away and left behind a very talented boy. What could be done so he could continue his studies?

"Bring him here," the *rebbe* said. "Let him live with me."

The neighbor brought the boy to the *rebbe*. The boy was maybe eight or ten. In the interim, before he started studying with the *rebbe*, the *shammes*§ got the boy to help out. One day the *shammes* told the child, "Go make the *rebbe*'s bed."

So he made up the *rebbe*'s bed for the night. The next day, the *rebbe* asked his *shammes*, "Who made my bed last night?"

The *shammes* was very frightened. Who knows how the child had made up the bed? "Don't be frightened," the *rebbe* said. "Just tell me."

"Anshel," he replied.

"From now on, I always want Anshel§§ to make up my bed for the night."

The *rebbe* began to take care of the boy and teach him as if he were his own son. The child grew up with the *rebbe*, making his bed for him and learning many secrets. Because he was very clever, the *rebbe* asked Anshel what he thought about every important matter.

Whenever people visit a *rebbe* and give him a heart-rending note, they also make a contribution. If they give the *rebbe* gold, he puts it aside to use as dowries for poor brides.

---

*A Hasidic Rabbi.
**Yiddish for the Polish town of Kozienice.
§Synagogue caretaker.
§§Yiddish for the name "Amschel."

Once a man came and said that he was going to marry off his daughter but had no money. The *rebbe* went to the place where he hid the money, but it wasn't there. He searched and the money wasn't there. He was very sad and told everyone. He thought that maybe it was Moshe who had taken it, or perhaps Yaacov, or Yitzhak—who knew who it might be? They thought and thought and thought. Finally his associates told him, "It must be Anshel who took it." He had married by that time and was living in a different city. They all agreed that Anshel was so close to the *rebbe* that he must be the one who took it.

This pained the *rebbe* very much, but he had to go see. When the *rebbe* came to Anshel and told him why he had come, he replied, "Yes, Rebbe, I took it. But I don't have it. I spent it. I have a store now. I'll pay it back in installments."

The *rebbe* was very upset. He had made Anshel's wedding. He had had so much joy from him, and he knew everything—and he had taken his money! He was ashamed to go back to his hometown. He was ashamed to go to his own house. But he went home and told the story.

In the meantime, in the same city, there was a restaurant where people ate and drank. Many gentiles came on Sunday, and one of them paid in gold. The owner accepted it. The next week, on Sunday, the same man came with gold coins again. Once this was against the law, just as it's against the law now. Back then it was against the law. The owner told the police. A policeman came in civilian clothes and stood there watching the gentile pay in gold. "Sir, where did you get that?" he asked.

"I found it."

"Where did you find it?"

"In the village," he said, where his family had land. He had plowed before planting and found a bag full of gold coins.

The policeman took it. The *rebbe*'s name was on the bag. So they summoned the *rebbe* to the police and asked him if he was missing something.

"Yes," he said, "I'm missing something."

And before he could ask whether they had found it, they showed him the bag. "Is this yours?"

"Yes," he said, quite astounded, because he thought Anshel had taken it, but they had found it with the gentile.

The *rebbe* went back to Anshel. "Why did you say you had taken it?" he asked.

"Look," Anshel replied. "The *rebbe* knows that it is forbidden to harbor suspicion. If a person misses something, he's not allowed to suspect that maybe it was Yaacov, maybe Moshe, maybe Yitzhak who took it. If I had said I hadn't taken the money, the *rebbe* would have suspected other people. So to keep the *rebbe* from sinning, I took it on myself."

The *rebbe* said to him, "By the merit of your saving me from such transgression, may you be rich for generations, may you know what to do with money, and may you educate your children in the same way."

COMMENTARY FOR TALE 12 (IFA 18601)

Told in Yiddish by Hinda Sheinferber to Hadara Sela in 1992 in Haifa.

Cultural, Historical, and Literary Background

History of the Tale

Other versions of this tale have been published,[1] including a longer version.[2] In the earlier printed versions, the rabbi in whose house the young Mayer Amschel (1743 or 1744–1812) served is Rabbi Zevi Hirsch Ha-Levi Horowitz of Czortkow, the father of Rabbi Samuel Shmelke Horowitz of Nikolsburg (1726–1778) and of Rabbi Pinḥas ben Zevi Hirsch Ha-Levi Horowitz (1730–1805).

The figures in both the earlier versions and the present version are historical characters from the eighteenth century. The earlier versions, which appeared in print at the beginning of the twentieth century, represent nineteenth-century traditions; the present tale was recorded from oral tradition late in the twentieth century. It is difficult to date with any precision the year in which this tale was first told, but it is possible to assume with certainty that the story about Rothschild and his Hasidic mentor could not have been told before the meteoric rise of Mayer Amschel Rothschild as a financial force in Europe by the end of the eighteenth century.

Though its time in oral circulation has been relatively short, this story has been subject to the familiar processes of oral transmission. Information, misinformation, and creative association transform the relations among historical personalities, facts, and partial truths into fictional associations that advocate the principles of ethical behavior.

The replacement of one personality with another is one of the most common narrative transformations that occur in oral transmission. Rothschild began his independent business dealings in Frankfurt am Main. Hence, it is likely that the early tales of his rise to wealth involved Rabbi Pinḥas ben Zevi Hirsch Ha-Levi Horowitz (1730–1805), who was a rabbi in Frankfurt starting in 1772, rather than his father who was a rabbi in Czortkow, or the *rebbe* from Kozienice, as in the present tale. The present tale is about Rabbi Israel ben Shabbetai Hapstein (1733–1814), who was a disciple of Rabbi Samuel Shmelke Horowitz of Nikolsburg.[3]

The reference to Rothschild and the identity of the person who represents him in the tale are also problematic. As N. Ferguson suggested, "For most of the century between 1815 and 1914, [Rothschild's] was easily the biggest bank in the world. Strictly in terms of their combined capital, the Rothschilds were in a league of their own, until, at the earliest, the 1880s."[4] The family name derived from a banner with an insignia of a red shield that apparently hung over the house the family founder owned in the sixteenth century. The family's accumulation of wealth began with the financial dealings of Mayer Amschel, who was sent by his father to study in the yeshivah at Fürth.

Correctly, as the tale accounts, Mayer Amschel lost his parents when he was boy. One died in 1755 and the other in 1756, victims to an epidemic that swept through Germany. But his father, Amschel Moses, was not poor. Rather, upon his death, he left Mayer Amschel a small inheritance. Records indicate that the family had had a residence in Frankfurt since the sixteenth century; it was built by the founder of the family, Isaac son of Elhanan (d. 1585). After the death of his father, Mayer Amschel moved to Hanover, where he began learning the rudiments of business in the firm of Wolf Jacob Oppenheim and where he began dealing with rare coins and medals—a line of business that put him in contact with the social and economic elite. In 1764, Mayer Amschel returned to Frankfurt and began to develop his own business.

The Rothchilds have been the subject of historical studies, literature, and even music. The history of the House of Rothschild has been extensively researched.[5] The family name "Rothschild" was, and to some extent still is, a subject of folklore and literature.[6] For example, Anton Chekhov (1860–1904) wrote the short story "Rothschild's Violin" (1894)[7] in which an impoverished coffin-maker peasant, who plays with a village orchestra, leaves his violin to an equally poor Jewish flutist, ironically nicknamed "Rothschild." Benjamin Fleischmann (d. 1942?) began to rework the tale into an opera, but he died in the defense of Stalingrad (now named Volgograd). His teacher, Dmitri Shostakovich (1906–1975), completed and orchestrated the work at the end of the war; however, the opera was performed for the first time only in 1968.[8] Reflecting Rothschild's image in eastern European Jewish society, Shalom Aleichem (Sholem-Aleykhem or Shalom Rabinovitz, 1859–1916) published a satirical monologue in 1902 titled *"Ven ikh bin Roytshild"* (If I were Rothschild).[9]

Similarities to Other IFA Tales

In nineteenth- and twentieth-century Jewish verbal traditions, it is possible to discern, both in print and in oral circulation, eight types of Rothschild narratives. Some of these thematic clusters are associated with a specific social group, such as the Hasidim, or a specific folk-literary genre.

The Origin of Wealth in the Rothschild Family

The first group of tales deals with the origin of the Rothschild family wealth and can be divided into three subtypes. The first subtype is made up of tales from the Hasidic tradition that appropriate the Rothschilds to Hasidic society.[10] The present tale falls into this category. Other tales in the IFA from this subtype are the following:

- IFA 11723: *The Origin of Rothschild's Wealth* (Ukraine).
- IFA 13140: *From Where Does Rothschild's Wealth Come?* (Lithuania).[11]

In these Hasidic versions Mayer Amshcel takes note of the talmudic proposition "He who entertains a suspicion against innocent men is bodily afflicted" (BT *Shabbat* 97a; *Yoma* 19b) by trying to give the rabbi a ground for his unjustified suspicion.

Another tale in the IFA about physical suffering, even death, as a consequence of unjustified suspicion is tale IFA 5563: *A Person Who Suspects the Innocent* (Belarus).[12]

The second subtype notes that the family's wealth had its basis in a tricky business transaction. Only one version in the IFA is available: tale IFA 435: *The Origin of Rothschild's Wealth* (Romania).

The final subtype notes that the origin of wealth was in the family founder's trustworthiness or generosity, for which he was blessed by a Hasidic *rebbe* or an ancestor of a Hasidic *rebbe*. As it appeared in earlier manuscripts and oral traditions, this version of the tale did not simply appropriate the Rothschild family to Hasidic society but functioned as a claim on their financial and political power, demanding a recompense for the blessing that initiated the accumulation of wealth.

Mikhalzohn appended his book *Ohel Avraham* (Abraham's tent)[13] with a letter that Rabbi Ḥayyim ben Leibush Halberstam of Nowy Soncz[14] (1793–1876) had sent to the Baron James (Jacob) Rothschild (1792–1868), whom the rabbi assumed was in Vienna but who actually lived in Paris. In this letter, the rabbi claimed that when his maternal grandfather, Zevi Hirsch ben Jacob Ashkenazi (1660–1718)—known as Ḥakham Zevi—quarreled with the Jewish community of Amsterdam, he found shelter in the house of Mayer Amschel Rothschild. Grateful for the hospitality, and in another version also for financial support, he blessed his host with continuous prosperity. Now the rabbi demanded that in recompense James Rothschild should intervene with the Austrian king on behalf of a Jew who was involved in litigation. Mikhalzohn confirmed the veracity of the story of this letter as a testimony from oral tradition. Another version of this subtype was published in a book by Zevi Hirsch ben Aryeh Loeb Levin (1721–1800).[15]

In the IFA the following tales are versions of the same theme:

- IFA 635: *The Origin of Rothschild's Wealth* (Eretz Yisra'el, Ashkenazic).
- IFA 2326: *What Is the Basis for Rothschild's Reputation for Reliability?* (Poland).
- IFA 2922: *Elijah the Prophet Blesses the First Rothschild* (Eastern Europe).
- IFA 5161: *The Origin of Rothschild's Wealth* (Eretz Yisra'el, Islamic).

An Encounter between Rothschild and a Poor Man or Woman

The most popular narrative about Rothschild, occurring mostly in jokes, involves an encounter between Rothschild and a poor person.[16] The following tales of this type are in the IFA:

- IFA 633: *Why Did Rothschild Give the Beggar a Lot of Money?* (Eretz Yisra'el, Ashkenazic).

- IFA 634: *Rothschild's Estate* (Eretz Yisra'el, Ashkenazic).
- IFA 2791: *The Girl from Poland and the Generous Baron* (Eretz Yisra'el, Ashkenazic).[17]
- IFA 4460: *Rothschild and the Honored Beggar* (Eastern Europe).
- IFA 4474: *God's Brother-in-Law* (Romania).
- IFA 6157: *Open Your Hand* (Iraq).
- IFA 6657: *Rothschild's Favor* (Poland).
- IFA 9213: *Does Rothschild Inherit a Beggar?* (Poland).
- IFA 9216: *A Counsel from the House of Rothschild* (Poland).[18]
- IFA 10384: *The Poor Man and Rothschild* (Poland).
- IFA 10884: *Rothschild and the Poor Man* (Russian).
- IFA 11715: *A Contract with Rothschild* (Ukraine).
- IFA 11724: *Who Is the Heir?* (Ukraine).[19]
- IFA 12993: *He Could Have Been Wealthier than Rothschild* (Ukraine).[20]
- IFA 13818: *The Heir* (Poland).
- IFA 13827: *The Scratching Ones* (Poland).
- IFA 14278: *Matchmaking with the House of Rothschild* (Poland).
- IFA 14542: *The Coachman and Rothschild* (Poland).
- IFA 21234: *A Recipe for Eternal Life* (Israel, eastern European heritage).

A subtype of this theme involves verbal play during the encounter between Rothschild and a poor man[21] and is popular in the oral tradition. The following versions are found in the IFA:

- IFA 2912: *A Verbal Play in Donation Solicitation* (Eastern Europe).
- IFA 9447: *One Word* (Poland).
- IFA 10961: *Rabbi Mayer Amschel Rothschild and the Gemara* (Poland).
- IFA 13816: *Gemara* (Poland).

Rothschild's Generosity

Other Rothschild stories focus on his generosity. Tales in the IFA that incorporate this theme are the following:

- IFA 2791: *The Girl from Poland and the Generous Baron* (Eretz Yisra'el, Ashkenazic).[22]
- IFA 2922: *Elijah the Prophet Blesses the First Rothschild* (Eastern Europe).
- IFA 5049: *The Pen Is Mightier Than the Sword* (Czechoslovakia).
- IFA 7162: *The Blood Libel in Shiraz* (Iran).
- IFA 9272: *Ḥakham Simeon the Translator and Rothschild* (Bukhara).
- IFA 10813: *Rabbi Mayer Amschel Rothschild the Banker and His Friend the Prince* (Ukraine).
- IFA 13141: *A Letter to God* (Lithuania).[23]
- IFA 15342: *Sarah Bernhardt and Rothschild* (Poland).
- IFA 18162: *Rothschild and the Sick Mother* (Poland).

Rothschild Maintains His Jewishness in Dignity

The next type of tale involving Rothschild focuses on his Jewishness.[24] The following tales in the IFA have this theme:

- IFA 7374: *Rothschild and the King of Italy* (Greece).
- IFA 7375: *The Penalty for Ignorance* (Greece).
- IFA 12942: *Neither a Jew nor a Pig* (Libya).

Rothschild's Frugality

Rothschild's tendency for frugality is another common topic for stories. The tales with this theme in IFA are the following:

- IFA 3510: *Rothschild Selects His Treasurer* (Poland).
- IFA 4828: *The Orphan Rothschild* (Eretz Yisra'el, Ashkenazic).
- IFA 5599: *Rothschild and the Small Coin* (Germany).
- IFA 14681: *Rothschild's Alms* (Ukraine).
- IFA 17758: *The Rothschilds: Grandfather, Father, and Son* (Israel, second generation).

Rothschild's Gaudiness

Rothschild's gaudiness is the subject of two tales in the IFA:

- IFA 418: *Rothschild's Shoes* (Poland).
- IFA 855: *Rothschild's Shoes* (Eretz Yisra'el, Ashkenazic).

Rothschild in the Land of Israel

Another group of stories involves Rothschild's relationship with the Land of Israel.[25] The tales in IFA on this theme are the following:

- IFA 13690: *When the Lord Restores the Fortunes of Zion (Psalm 126:1)* (Eretz Yisra'el, Ashkenazic).
- IFA 13695: *About the Proselytes in the Galilee* (Eretz Yisra'el, Ashkenazic).
- IFA 13737: *Biblical Exegesis in Rosh Pina* (Eretz Yisra'el, Ashkenazic).
- IFA 14332: *Baron Rothschild and the Farmers of Kefar Tavor* (Eretz Yisra'el, Circassian).
- IFA 14742: *The Land Was Our Gift from the Start* (Eretz Yisra'el, Ashkenazic).
- IFA 21568: *Rothschild Street* (Israel, eastern European heritage).

Rothschild's Death Inside a Locked Safe

The story of Rothschild's death occurs primarily in Yiddish folk songs, though some storytellers have reported it in prose.[26] In the IFA, there are two tales about this subject:

- IFA 7331: Rothschild's Death (Poland).
- IFA 16794: Rothschild's Death (Israel, eastern European heritage).

Within the IFA collection there is one tale that relates to none of the common themes:

- IFA 4169: *Mrs. Rothschild Wishes to Age Well* (Hungary).

The Rothschild of Warsaw

The present story appears to appropriate the founder of the central and western European House of Rothschild to Hasidic society. Most likely, however, this is a late narrative development, representing both a loss of collective memory and a character substitution.

During the eighteenth century, while Mayer Amschel built the foundation for the fortune of his descendants in Western Europe, another Jew amassed wealth in Poland. Known as "The Rothschild of Warsaw," Samuel Zbitkower (c. 1730–1801) moved to that city from the village of Zbitkie[27] —hence his name—and during the second half of the eighteenth century became the wealthiest Jewish merchant in Poland. He was a banker, an army purveyor, and an owner of large estates and different industries; he controlled the production of his wares from the raw materials to the final products. As a man of wealth, he also became an influential community leader, and legends about Zbitkower circulated.[28] Unlike the Rothschilds, Zbitkower's descendants did not maintain or expand the family business. His son born to his first wife, Dov Ber Berek (Sonnenberg), continued in his father's footsteps; however, successive generations and his children from his second wife turned in other directions. His grandson was the Polish pianist and composer Michael Bergson (1820–1898) and his great-grandson was the French philosopher Henri Bergson (1859–1941).

It was the Rothschild of Warsaw, not the Rothschild of Frankfurt, that legends associated with the Maggid of Kozienice. Ringelblum[29] reported an oft-quoted story—attributed to the Maggid—that in 1794, during the Kosciuszko Revolt, Zbitkower sat with two barrels in front of him, one full of silver coins and the other of gold coins, and gave the Ukrainians a golden coin for every living Jew and a silver coin for every dead Jew, saving in this way eight hundred people.[30]

In current oral tradition, Samuel Zbitkower is all but forgotten. With the rise of the House of Rothschild, an unspecified Rothschild has become the subject of jokes and legends as well as of tales that connect Mayer Amschel Rothschild to Hasidic society.[31]

Folklore Motifs

- *C416 "Tabu: harboring suspicion."
- H961 "Tasks performed by cleverness."

- J706 "Acquisition of wealth."
- J1113 "Clever boy."
- L111.4 "Orphan hero."
- N440 "Valuable secrets learned."
- N534 "Treasure discovered by accident."
- *N534.7.2 "Man plows his field and discovers treasure."
- N550 "Unearthing hidden treasure."
- P150 "Rich men."
- *P426.4 "Rabbi."
- Q20 "Piety rewarded."
- *Q38.1 "Reward for helping a holy man avoid a sinful act."
- Q111 "Riches as reward."
- T52.4 "Dowry given at marriage of daughter."
- *V28 "False confession: a person confesses to a sin not committed to help a wronged person."

―――――― **Notes** ――――――

1. Mikhalzohn, *Sefer Shemen ha-Tov* (The book of oil of goodness), 51 no. 93.

2. Mikhalzohn, *Sefer Dover Shalom* (The book of the speaker of peace), 66–68 no. 152. The longer version can also be found in Ben-Yeḥezki'el, *Sefer ha-Ma'asiyyot* (A book of folktales), 1:132–140; Zevin, *Sippurei Hasidim* (Hasidic tales), 2:270–273 no. 300; Litvin, *Yudishe neshomes* (Jewish souls), 5: no. 11; C. Bloch, *Das Jüdische Volk in seiner Anekdote*, 102–104; and Newman, *The Hasidic Anthology*, 503–504 no. 191:4.

3. For information about Rabbi Samuel Shmelke Horowitz of Nikolsburg, see the notes to tale IFA 708 (in this vol., no. 1).

4. *The House of Rothschild 1798–1848*, 1:3.

5. For a selection of studies in English, see Corti, *The Rise of the House of Rothschild;* Cowles, *The Rothschilds;* A. Elon, *Founder;* N. Ferguson, op. cit.; Heuberger, *The Rothschilds;* Morton, *The Rothschilds;* Schwartzfuchs, "Rothschild"; and D. Wilson, *Rothschild*.

6. For example, see N. Ferguson, op. cit., 1–31; and Glanz, "The Rothschild Legend in America."

7. Hingley, *The Oxford Chekhov*, 7:91–101; Garnett, *Anton Chekhov*, 245–255.

8. Fleischmann, *Rothschild's Violin* (CD).

9. Reprinted in 1919 in Odessa, *Ven ikh bin Roytshild* and included in his *Ale verk fun Sholem Aleykhem* (Collected works of Sholem Aleykhem), 5:129–133. For an English translation, see Howe and Wisse, *The Best of Sholom Aleichem*, 129–132; for a reading by the Vilna Troupe actor Noah Nachbush (1885–1970), see Nachbush, *Noah Nachbushe's Gems of Yiddish Poetry and Folklore*.

10. See Mikhalzohn, *Sefer Shemen ha-Tov* (The book of oil of goodness); Mikhalzohn, *Sefer Dover Shalom* (The book of the speaker of peace); Ben-Yeḥezki'el, op. cit.; C. Bloch, op. cit.; and Newman, op. cit.

11. Published in M. Cohen, *Mi-Pi ha-Am* (From folk tradition), 3:101–103 no. 306.

12. Published in Baharav, *Mi-Dor le-Dor*, 72–74 no. 23.

12 / How Rothschild Became Wealthy

13. See 54–55 (27b–28a) in the 1967 edition. See also Ben-Yehezki'el, op. cit., 1:141–144.
14. Zanz in Yiddish.
15. *Sefer Tsava Rav* (The book of multitudes), 9a (17); see also Ben-Yehezki'el, op. cit., 1:127–131.
16. Ausubel, *A Treasury of Jewish Folklore*, 394–396; C. Bloch, op. cit., 98–102; Druyanow, *Sefer ha-Bedihah ve-ha-Hidud* (The book of jokes and witticisms), 1:94–95, 101, 115–116 nos. 247, 260, 299, 300; 2:44, 53, 56–57 nos. 462, 483, 484, 494; Landmann, *Der Jüdische Witz,* 276–280; Learsi, *Filled with Laughter,* 214–215; Olsvanger, *Rosinkess mit Mandlen,* 43–45 nos. 76–80; Olsvanger, *Röyte Pomerantsen or How to Laugh in Yiddish,* 49–52 nos. 75–78; Präger and Schmitz, *Jüdische Schwänke,* 103–105; Rawnitzki, *Yidishe Witzn (Jewish Wit),* 2:42–43 no. 458; Richman, *Laughs from Jewish Lore,* 118–120; Richman, *Jewish Wit and Wisdom,* 115–116; and Spalding, *Encyclopedia of Jewish Humor,* 30–31.
17. Published in Weinstein, *Grandma Esther Relates . . . ,* 41–43 no. 5; and Rush, *The Book of Jewish Women's Tales,* 171–172 no. 46.
18. Published in Keren, *Advice from the Rothschilds,* 35–36 no. 8.
19. This tale, IFA 9213, and IFA 13818 are almost exactly the same story.
20. Published in M. Cohen, op. cit., 3:44–45 no. 233.
21. Olsvanger, *Rosinkess mit Mandlen,* 43–44 no. 78; and Richman, *Jewish Wit and Wisdom,* 396.
22. Published in Weinstein, op. cit., 41–43 no. 5; and Rush, op. cit., 171–172 no. 46.
23. Published in M. Cohen, op. cit., 74–75 no. 276.
24. For example, see Druyanow, op. cit., 3:141, 161 nos. 2449, 2513.
25. E. Davidson, *Sehok le-Yisrael* (Laughter of Israel), 11–13, 146 nos. 46–56; and Druyanow, op. cit., 3:186–187 no. 2596.
26. Prilutski, *Yidishe folkslider,* 2:149–151 nos. 183, 184; [Weinreich and Mlotek], "*Lider*" (Songs), 5–6 no. 4 (1954); [Weinreich and Mlotek], "*Lider*" (Songs), 32 (1955); Poliva, "*Hamishah Shirim mi-pi Abba*" (Five songs my late father sang); and M. Noy, "Bibliographical References to the Song of Rothschild's End."
27. The editor was unable to confirm the spelling or existence of this village.
28. Ringelblum, "Samuel Zbitkower"; and M. Landau, "Zbitkower, (Joseph) Samuel."
29. Op. cit., 256 n. 45.
30. See also Sokolow, *Ishim* (Personalities), 102–103.
31. Cf. the tale of the origin of Lord Whittington's wealth; see notes to tale IFA 7763 (vol. 3, no. 49).

13

Why Rebbe Levi Yitzḥak of Berdichev Deviated from His Custom

TOLD BY AZRIEL BEROSHI TO ZALMAN BAHARAV

*T*he Hasidim of Rebbe Levi Yitzḥak of Berdichev asked him: "Master, why don't you perform the mitzvah of true and disinterested benevolence? Why don't you follow deceased Jews to the cemetery?"

Rebbe Levi Yitzḥak answered them: "I don't attend the funerals of rich men, even if they left money for *tzedakah*,* to keep the heirs from getting puffed up and saying, 'The *rebbe* is honoring our father because he was very rich.' Nor do I attend the funerals of poor people, to keep the synagogue wardens and community leaders from being angry with me and saying that I am biased in favor of the poor, who were never able to support their families respectably. And because the Jews of our town are either rich or poor, I am not able to perform this mitzvah."

But when Yosef Halperin, a very rich man who owned a lot of property, died, Rebbe Levi Yitzḥak set aside all his other engagements and studies and, contrary to his custom, attended the funeral. Seeing the astonishment of his disciples, Rebbe Levi Yitzḥak explained, "Reb Yosef Halperin's special merit compels me to deviate from my custom."

To explain himself to his associates, Rebbe Levi Yitzḥak told them three stories about the man's character and habits.

"Once a Jew whose business was selling grain to stores and bakeries lost two hundred rubles that he owed one of the wholesalers. Extremely distraught, he made a public announcement that he had lost his money. When Yosef Halperin, the local magnate, heard about this, he notified the *rebbe* that he had found the money. The merchant was happy that his money had turned up and Reb Yosef gave him two hundred rubles in bank notes.

"A few hours later, when the merchant called on a bakery, he found the money he had lost on top of a bag of flour. He wanted to return the two

---
*Charitable giving.

hundred rubles to Reb Yosef, but the latter refused to accept them. The two asked me to render a verdict on the matter. Reb Yosef Halperin's argument was, 'I renounced any title to the money the moment it left my possession. If the grain dealer doesn't want it, let him distribute it anonymously to needy people.'

"And once there was a teacher, a desperately poor man with a large family. He had taught in the elementary religious school for many years but had never been able to make a decent living in his native town. He decided to try his luck elsewhere.

"When he left home, he told his wife, 'Don't worry, dear wife, you won't want for anything. The magnate Reb Yosef Halperin has promised to give you twenty rubles a month.'

"The woman believed her husband, although in fact the teacher was just trying to placate her and had not spoken to the magnate at all. He had faith that his valiant wife would muddle through somehow.

"The teacher packed up his clothes with his tallit* and tefillin** and some food for the way and headed for a nearby town that was home to several Jewish leaseholders, hoping that there he would be able to accumulate a decent sum to support his family. When several weeks passed and she had not received a single penny from the teacher, his wife went to Reb Yosef Halperin's office. 'You promised my husband you'd give me twenty rubles a month until he completes his term as a teacher in that town,' she told him, 'and I haven't received anything yet.'

"Even though he knew absolutely nothing about the matter, Reb Yosef didn't miss a beat. He gave the woman the first twenty rubles and promised to have his clerk bring her twenty rubles every month. He even confirmed that there was an 'agreement' between himself and the teacher, although he knew very well that the husband had left his wife in the lurch and was taking advantage of him. For the next six months, the magnate adhered faithfully to the 'agreement.'

"When Passover, which marks the end of the school term, approached, the teacher returned home with his wages from his pupils' fathers and presents for his wife and children, who, he was sure, had been living in penury the whole time. To his astonishment, he found that his wife and children were clothed decently, the house was neat and clean, and the table was covered with good food. 'How did you manage to maintain the

---

*Prayer shawl.
**Small black leather prayer boxes, wrapped around the head and arm, containing passages from the Torah.

family so well for the six months I was gone?' he asked his wife. 'I left you without a cent in the house?!'

" 'But you told me that the magnate Reb Yosef Halperin had promised you a monthly stipend of twenty rubles, remember? He paid me every month, just as the two of you agreed.'

"The teacher went to Reb Yosef Halperin to return the one hundred and twenty rubles, but Halperin refused to take a single penny. This time, too, he argued that the money no longer belonged to him, because he had renounced title to it six months earlier.

"When the two came for a hearing before me, Reb Yosef advanced the same argument as before.

"Yet another story about the same Reb Yosef Halperin. A certain cloth merchant, one of the most important householders in the city, lost everything and was declared bankrupt. In his distress, he decided to go to the magnate Reb Yosef Halperin and ask for a loan of several hundred rubles to pay off his creditors. 'Who will guarantee that you will repay the loan when it comes due?' Reb Yosef asked.

"The borrower replied, 'The Holy One, Blessed Be He, will serve as my guarantor. With His help I will return the sum you lend me.'

" 'I accept your guarantor,' replied Reb Yosef. 'I am confident that He will indeed assist you to repay the loan.'

"He took out several hundred-ruble bank notes and gave them to the merchant.

"When the loan came due the merchant had already recouped the amount and even more. He came to the magnate to repay him, offering profuse thanks and blessings. This time, too, the magnate refused to accept anything, asserting as before that he had renounced title to the money and needy people should benefit from it."

When Rebbe Levi Yitzḥak finished telling the three stories about Reb Yosef Halperin, he added, "Don't the deeds of this Jew, who appeared before me in the three cases, merit that I deviate from my self-imposed rule and repay him with true and disinterested benevolence?"

COMMENTARY FOR TALE 13 (IFA 7612)

Told by Azriel Beroshi from Belarus and recorded by Zalman Baharav in Tel Aviv in 1967.[1]

Cultural, Historical, and Literary Background

This story is a nineteenth-century variation on a narrative theme that occurs in the talmudic-midrashic and the medieval traditions, often known, following Rashi, as *Raḥmana de liba baei* (The Merciful wishes the heart, BT *Sanhedrin* 106b). Studies of this theme and comparable versions are given in the notes to tale IFA 10089 (vol. 1, no. 28). In most versions of the tale, the reward for good deeds is an honorable position in paradise—tale type 809*–*A (IFA) "The Companion in Paradise"—whereas in the present tale and its analogues the reward is a respectable funeral—tale type 759*D (IFA) "Three Cases of Generosity." A similar reward is given in the twelfth-century medieval tale *Sefer Sha'ashu'im* (Book of delight) by Joseph ben Meir ibn Zabara (born c. 1140).[2]

Funerals and Social Standing

Both the medieval story and the present tale underscore an aspect of funerals that is not acknowledged by religious normative laws and regulations but that, nevertheless, is very much an integral part of social practice—namely the function of the funeral as a means of social control. There is a direct correspondence between a person's adherence to social values and the respect awarded at his or her funeral. By avoiding attending funerals, Rabbi Levi Yitzḥak of Berdichev sought to avoid any involvement in differential social recognition of any members of his community.

There is a paucity of historical-ethnographic studies of the actual funeral practices of eastern European Jewish societies. However, preliminary explorations and a case study of a single community have been published.[3]

Charity

The relatively recent versions of this tale share the principle of *matan ba-seter* (secret charity), which is the most valuable form of charity in Jewish societies. According to rabbinic tradition such secret charity was not just an ideal value but a practical form of philanthropy during the period of the Second Temple. "There were two chambers in the Temple, one chamber of secret gifts and the other chamber of the vessels. The chamber of secret gifts—sin fearing persons used to put their gifts therein in secret, and the poor who were descended of the virtuous were supported there from in secret" (Mishnah *Shekalim* 5:6; Sifre *Re'eh*, no. 117, p. 176).

Later, and perhaps by the rabbinical period, donation in secret obtained an ideal and metaphoric form of charity. Not only, as Rabbi Assi (late third century to early fourth) said, "Charity is equivalent to all other religious precepts combined" (BT *Bava Batra* 9a) but, as Rabbi Eleazar (second century?) said, "A man who gives charity in secret is greater than Moses our Teacher" (BT *Bava Batra* 9b). Additional references to the value of charity in Jewish society are given in the notes to tales IFA 2604 (vol. 1, no. 30) and IFA 7202 (in this vol., no. 48).

Within the narratives of this cycle, it is possible to distinguish two subtypes; the first concerns acts of charity and the second involves charitable conduct.

Charitable Acts

Tales of the first subtype describe a sequence of charitable acts, which, according to Schwarzbaum,[4] are the following:

1. The assumption of the guilt of theft, the repayment of stolen or lost goods or money, and refusing return of debt or compensation.
2. The assumption of the support of a traveling salesman's wife, and refusing her husband's repayment.
3. Accepting God as surety.

Within this subtype, the tales from Eastern Europe are associated, as the present version is, with Rabbi Levi Yitzhak of Berdichev.

Similarities to Other IFA Tales

The following stories about Rabbi Levi Yitzhak of Berdichev are on deposit in the IFA:

- IFA 681: *Give the Soul of a Poor Man Whatever It Desires* (Iraq).
- IFA 2324: *The Three Rulings of Rabbi Yitzhak of Berdichev* (Ukraine).[5]
- IFA 2619: *A Rich Man Donates in Secret* (Syria).[6]
- IFA 2910: *Rabbi Levi Yitzhak of Berdichev Vindicates a Rich Man* (Galicia, Poland).
- IFA 10002: *Why Did the Rabbi Join the Funeral of Ezekiel the Blacksmith?* (Romania).

Individual Acts of Charity

In Jewish narrative tradition, each of the three episodes within the sequence of charitable acts can also occur independently. For example, the first episode, returning lost property to its owner (Deuteronomy 22:1–3), is the subject of two narratives learned from oral tradition.[7] In the first narrative, the judging rabbi is Rabbi Joseph Saul Nathanson (1810–1875), who was one of the greatest *posekim* (judging rabbis) of his generation.[8] In the other narrative, Rabbi Levi Yitzhak of Berdichev is the judge and Joshua Eliezer is the pious merchant.[9]

The second episode appears independently in a tale about Rabbi Nahaman of Horodenka (d. 1780), who offers weekly support to the wife of an imprisoned merchant.[10]

The third episode is the most popular of the three and has a broad international as well as current Jewish circulation.[11] This type of tale is also seen in talmudic-midrashic and medieval Jewish literature.[12] In modern times, the theme occurs primarily in humorous discourse.[13]

Similarities to Other IFA Tales

There are four versions of this tale on deposit in the IFA:
- IFA 1455: *The Ocean Is a Good Surety* (Yemen).[14]
- IFA 2609: *God Is a Good Surety* (Syria).[15]
- IFA 9766: *The Guarantor Has Already Returned the Money* (Lithuania).[16]
- IFA 10700: *God as Surety* (Morocco).

Charitable Conduct

The second basic version of this tale involves not a cycle of charitable acts but a character who displays continuous charitable conduct. Often this character supports the poor people in the town by using one or more merchants as a front. A number of these tales have been published.[17] Kleinman[18] noted that he found an example of this story in the *pinkas* (community record) of the Cracow community. In that version, copied from an unspecified manuscript, the rich miser secretly finances the apparent generosity of a butcher, which in Hebrew is *KaZaV*. Kleinman interpreted the noun to be an acronym of *"kiyem zeddakah ba-seter"* (his charity was in secret). Most of the texts in Ben-Yehezki'el are from other books; this is one of the few that is from oral tradition.[19]

Similarities to Other IFA Tales

The following tales in the IFA feature an individual who displays continuous charitable conduct:

- IFA 271: *The Rich Miser and the Shoemaker* (Russia).[20]
- IFA 4945: *The Rich Miser* (Eretz Yisra'el, Ashkenazic).[21]

The Rabbi

Rabbi Levi Yitzhak of Berdichev (1740–1809) was a famous Hasidic rabbi from the town of Berdichev, in the Volhynia district of Ukraine. There are few references to Jews in Berdichev from around the beginning of the seventeenth century; but by 1721 there was clearly a Jewish community in the area. By 1765 there were 1,220 Jews in the town, making up almost 80 percent of the total population. At the end of the eighteenth century and the beginning of the nineteenth, the town became an important center of Volhynian Hasidism.[22]

Rabbi Levi Yitzhak was the most prominent Hasidic rabbi in this town, and the growth of the Jewish community there is a likely consequence of his reputation and influence. His sermons appeared in the book *Kedushat Levi* (Levi's holiness).[23] His literary and traditional image is that of a "defender of his people," an advocate who pleaded before God the religious and ethical values inherent in even the poorest and most ignorant Jews.[24]

An Hasidic biography and exposition of Rabbi Levi Yitzḥak's teaching is available,[25] as are narratives taken from oral traditions and Hasidic literature.[26] The rabbi also figured in literary, dramatic, and poetic works.[27] The African American singer Paul Robeson (1898–1976) included in his repertoire a melody to the prayer of Rabbi Levi Yitzḥak appealing to God on behalf of his people.[28]

Similarities to Other IFA Tales

Some of the tales listed above involve Rabbi Levi Yitzḥak of Berdichev. The following IFA tales are also about the rabbi; many of these are available in Hasidic chapbooks and have been anthologized.

- IFA 389: *The Slave Buyers in Court* (Galicia, Poland).[29]
- IFA 552: *Either in Jerusalem or in Berdichev* (Russia).
- IFA 1643: *Ivan Will Blow the Shofar* (Poland).
- IFA 2109: *Rabbi Yitzḥak Refuses to Recite Lamentations* (Poland).
- IFA 2455: *A Burial for a Dog* (Eretz Yisra'el, Ashkenazic).
- IFA 2705: *Rabbi Levi Yitzḥak of Berdichev Curses a Person Who Did Not Follow His Command* (Galicia, Poland).
- IFA 3097: *Rabbi Isaac Yitzḥak of Berdichev Celebrates Passover Night* (Romania).
- IFA 3204: *The Humility of Rabbi Levi Yitzḥak of Berdichev* (Galicia, Poland).
- IFA 3550: *Rabbi Levi Yitzḥak of Berdichev* (Poland).
- IFA 3591: *Two Kopeks* (Eretz Yisra'el, Ashkenazic).
- IFA 4937: *The Death of Rabbi Levi Yitzḥak of Berdichev* (Eretz Yisra'el, Ashkenazic).
- IFA 4941: *The Death of Rabbi Levi Yitzḥak of Berdichev* (Eretz Yisra'el, Ashkenazic).
- IFA 6678: *Rabbi Levi Yitzḥak of Berdichev Explains the Burglar's Intention* (Galicia, Poland).
- IFA 9629: *Rabbi Levi Yitzḥakof Berdichev and the Honest Jew* (Galicia, Poland).
- IFA 9630: *Rabbi Levi Yitzḥakof Berdichev and the Coachman* (Galicia, Poland).
- IFA 9796: *Indeed, He Saw Elijah the Prophet* (Ukraine).[30]
- IFA 9805: *Rabbi Levi Yitzḥak and the Polish Land Lord* (Romania).[31]
- IFA 10383: *Rabbi Levi Yitzḥak and the Rude Innkeeper* (Ukraine).
- IFA 10656: *Matchmaking* (Poland).
- IFA 11034: *How Great Is the Faith in God among Jews!* (Eretz Yisra'el, Ashkenazic).
- IFA 12297: *Jews in Exile* (Belarus).[32]

- IFA 13026: *Aaron's Greatness because He Never Changed His Ways* (Poland).[33]
- IFA 13066: *Looking for the Drunks* (Ukraine).[34]
- IFA 13083: *He Will Reach a Higher Rung* (Lithuania)[35]
- IFA 13103: *Next to Elijah the Prophet* (Poland).[36]
- IFA 13139: *Rabbi Levi Yitzhak of Berdichev Was Right* (Lithuania).[37]
- IFA 14833: *Rabbi Levi Yitzhak of Berdichev Admonishes God* (Poland).
- IFA 15379: *Rabbi Levi Yitzhak of Berdichev and the Shoemaker* (Poland).
- IFA 18164: *Two Friends* (Poland).
- IFA 20707: *Don't Judge Your Fellow Until You Reach His Place* (Romania).

Folktale Types

- 759*D (IFA) "Three Cases of Generosity."
- cf. 809*–*A(IFA) (Jason) "The Companion in Paradise."
- 849* "The Cross as Security."
- 940* "The Forgiven Debt."
- 940* (Jason) "The Forgiven Debt."
- 2318 (Tubach) "God as Security."
- cf. 3469 (Tubach) "Nicholas, St. as Security."

Folklore Motifs

- *J21.53 "Judge not thy fellow until thou art come to his place [Avoth 2:4(5)]."
- *J1559.2.1 "God as surety."
- N131.5 "Luck changing after change of place."
- P150 "Rich men."
- *P165 "Poor men."
- * P423 "Teacher."
- *P426.4 "Rabbi."
- P431 "Merchant."
- cf. P510 "Law courts."
- Q42 "Generosity rewarded."
- Q68.2 "Honesty rewarded."
- cf. *V28 "False confession: a person confesses to a sin not committed to help a wronged person."
- V60 "Funeral rites."
- V75.1 "Passover."
- V400 "Charity."
- V410 "Charity rewarded."
- *V417 "Secret charity is superior to public donation."
- W11 "Generosity."
- Z71.1 "Formulistic number: three."

Notes

1. First published in Cheichel, *A Tale for Each Month 1967*, 57–60 no. 3; reprinted in Baharav, *Mi-Dor le-Dor,* 193–195 no. 71; and Schram, *Stories within Stories*, 318–322 no. 48.

2. I. Davidson, *Sepher Shaashuim*, 59–63; J. Dishon, *The Book of Delight*, 108–114, 238–239; and Hadas, *The Book of Delight*, 29, 95–98

3. Michalowska, "Charity and the Charity Society"; S. Goldberg, *Crossing the Jabbok;* N. Rubin, *The End of Life.*

4. *Studies in Jewish and World Folklore,* 98–99.

5. Published in N. Gross, *Maaselech un Mesholim,* 19–24. Copious comparative notes can be found in Schwarzbaum, op. cit (in this version, the dead man, Joshua Eliezer, was known in the Berdichev community for his generosity); and Zevin, *Sippurei Ḥasidim* (Hasidic tales), 1:53–55 no. 46.

6. Published in Na'anah, *Ozar ha-Ma'asiyyot* (A treasury of tales), 2:64–67.

7. They have been anthologized in Ben-Yeḥezki'el, *Sefer ha-Ma'asiyyot* (A book of folktales), 3:198–204, 4:195–202.

8. For more about him, see Wygodzki, "Nathanson, Joseph Saul."

9. Kitov, *Ḥassidim ve-Anshei Ma'aseh* (Men of spirit, men of merit), 1: 129–131; another version in which the merchant is anonymous but the rabbi is Rabbi Levi Yitzḥak is in Zevin, op. cit., 1:488–491 no. 504.

10. See Schwarzbaum, op. cit.; and Lipson, *Medor Dor* (From days of old), 2:256–257 no. 1706.

11. Schwarzbaum, op. cit.; Tubach, *Index Exemplorum.*

12. For example, see Rashi's interpretation on BT *Nedarim* 50a; and M. Gaster, *The Exempla of the Rabbis,* 96, 128, 222 no. 183.

13. C. Bloch, *Das Jüdische Volk in seiner Anekdote,* 279–280; and C. Bloch, *Ostjudischer Humor,* 175.

14. Published in D. Noy, *Jefet Schwili Erzählt,* 163–164 no. 66.

15. Published in Na'anah, 1:37–40.

16. Published in M. Cohen, *Mi-Pi ha-Am,* 1:43 no. 12; and see Schwarzbaum, op. cit., 182–184.

17. Daniyel, *Emunat ha-Teḥiyah* (The belief in resurrection), 14a no. 24; and Eherman *Sefer pe'er ve-kavod* (The book of glory and honor), 47b–48a.

18. *Sefer Zikaron la-Rishonim* (A memorial book for the early [*zaddikim*]), 37 (19a).

19. Op. cit., 5:315–320, 440.

20. Published in D. Noy, *Folktales of Israel,* 11–12 no. 5.

21. Published in Weinstein, *Grandma Esther Relates . . . ,* 55–57 no. 13.

22. See Yaari, "Berdichev."

23. A modern edition is available as *Sefer Kedushat Levi ha-Shalem.*

24. See Luckens, "The Life of Levi Yizhaq of Berdichev"; Dresner, *Levi Yitzhak of Berdichev;* and Rubinstein, "Levi Isaac ben Meir of Berdichev."

25. Guttman, *Biographie des Gs. Berühmten Heiliger Grosrabiner Lewi Itzchac Oberrabiner zu Berditschew (Russland).*

26. M. Buber, *Tales of Hasidim: Early Masters,* 203–234; Lipson, op. cit., 1:2, 97, 181–182, 209–210; 216, 242, 273 nos. 2, 249, 456, 457, 551–553, 578, 579, 662, 750; 2:20, 27, 46, 103–104, 149–150, 172, 218–219, 241 nos. 885, 886, 907, 977, 978, 1157,

1158, 1309, 1310, 1312, 1418, 1572, 1668; 3:3–4, 13, 120, 123, 134–137, 139–144, 155–157, 161–162, 164–166, 173–174, 177–178, 262, 288 nos. 1746, 1774, 2096, 2103, 2144, 2145, 2150, 2158, 2161, 2162, 2165–2169, 2203–2205, 2216–2218, 2229, 2230, 2252, 2253, 2264, 2551, 2663; and Newman, *The Hasidic Anthology,* 563–564 (index).

27. For a play, see Z. Cahn, "*Ha-Rabi me-Berdichev*" (The rabbi from Berdichev).
28. Composed by L. Engel (1910–1982) and recorded on January 27, 1942; available on Robeson, *Songs of Free Men* (CD).
29. Published in E. Marcus, *Jewish Festivities,* 17–18 no. 1.
30. Published in M. Cohen, op cit., 1:29–30 no. 1; and Estin, *Contes et fêtes Juives,* 230–232 no. 56.
31. Published in M. Cohen, op. cit., 1:50–52 no. 17.
32. Published in M. Cohen, op. cit., 2:29 no. 127.
33. Published in M. Cohen, op. cit., 2:43 no. 148.
34. Published in M. Cohen, op. cit., 2:80 no. 189.
35. Published in M. Cohen, op. cit., 3:64 no. 264.
36. Published in M. Cohen, op. cit., 2:89–90 no. 203.
37. Published in M. Cohen, op. cit., 3:18–19 no. 210.

14

The Blessing of Elijah the Prophet on Yom Kippur

TOLD BY DVORA FUS

*I*t was right before the Shavuot* festival. Many of the Hasidim were making preparations to travel to the *rebbe*'s** court and spend the Holiday of the Giving of the Torah with him. Two Hasidim, who had once been very rich but had lost their wealth, remembered their bygone days of affluence when they used to travel to the *rebbe* by carriage, bearing many gifts, their trunks full of delicacies. Now, however, they made their way to the *rebbe* on foot, empty handed.

The two were so engrossed in their conversation and thoughts that at first they did not notice that night had fallen. When they did, they found themselves near an inn at a crossroads. Seeing a light shining in the window, the two decided to enter and rest for a while.

The old innkeeper greeted the two cordially, gave them a good meal, and found them a place to sleep. When he heard that the guests were on their way to the *rebbe* and would arrive on Shavuot eve, he took a bottle of wine from the cupboard and asked them to give it to him. The two Hasidim were glad to accept this commission. How wonderful it would be not to come to the *rebbe* with nothing to offer him!

The next day the Hasidim resumed their journey and reached the *rebbe*'s court by late afternoon. Wherever you looked, the place was jammed with Hasidim eager to see the *rebbe*. The tzadik§ sat in his study, sunk in his thoughts, while his *shammes*§§ stood outside the door and collected the Hasidim's petitions. When it was the two travelers' turn, they gave him their requests, along with the bottle of wine.

---
*The holiday celebrating Moses' receiving the Ten Commandments at Mount Sinai.
**A Hasidic rabbi.
§Rabbi.
§§Synagogue caregiver.

14 / The Blessing of Elijah

After the evening service, hundreds of Hasidim crowded around the *rebbe*'s table for the holiday meal. The table was covered with entrees and side dishes of every sort and many bottles of wine. But wonder of wonders! The *rebbe* drank only from the small flask that our two Hasidim had brought. What is more, after every sip he whispered, "The taste of Paradise! The taste of Paradise!" This went on at every meal for the entire holiday.

The two Hasidim were astonished. Why had the simple innkeeper's wine merited such distinction and praise from the *rebbe*? But they did not dare ask for an explanation, of course.

When Shavuot was over, the two Hasidim received the *rebbe*'s blessing and set off for home. They decided that they would stop off at the same inn and purchase several bottles of wine from the innkeeper.

When they reached the inn, they asked the host for several bottles of the wine he had sent to the *rebbe*. Of course, they would pay the full price. But here they were disappointed. He had had only one bottle of that wine, he said, and proceeded to tell them the following story.

"When I was a young man, many years ago, I worked as a *shoḥet*[*] and *mohel*.[**] Once, on Yom Kippur eve, I was busy from early morning slaughtering chickens for the *kapparos*[§] ritual; there was a long line of people waiting, with hens or roosters in their hands. Along came a village Jew in his cart, pleading, with tears in his eyes, that I come circumcise his son. I knew that his village was far away. But was it possible to leave a Jewish infant uncircumcised? Without giving the matter much thought, I left everything in the hands of the other *shoḥet* in town and set out.

"When I reached the village, the only Jew there was the mother of the newborn. At such a time, the eve of the holy day, who would make the effort to go to such an isolated place? Everyone leaves and goes to the nearby shtetl, to attend services in the synagogue. The problem was that no one was left to serve as *sandak*[§§] and hold the baby during the circumcision. Time was passing, and I still had to get home for the prefast meal.

"Suddenly, an old man appeared at the door and agreed to serve as the *sandak*. When the ceremony was over, the old man disappeared. I was astonished by this. None of the other villagers knew who the old man was

---

[*]One who slaughters animals according to the laws of kashrut.
[**]Circumciser.
[§]An old-fashioned ritual of swinging a chicken over one's head to symbolically transfer one's sins to the bird.
[§§]The person given the honor of assisting the *mohel*.

or had seen him before. I gave instructions to the mother and father and quickly left the place, because I wanted to get back home in time.

"When I got home, whom should I meet at the door of my house but that very same man who had been the *sandak*. I invited him at once to share our meal, but he declined. He took a small flask of wine from his pocket and gave it to me with a blessing: "This is a reward for the great mitzvah you performed today, preferring a kindness to a village Jew over the money you would have earned for slaughtering chickens. May you merit to drink the wine in this bottle on many happy occasions until you marry off your youngest grandson."

"His blessing was fulfilled to the letter. Decades have passed since then, and at every joyous celebration—the weddings of my sons and daughters, and after that of my grandsons and granddaughters—I drank the sweet wine from that small bottle. It was always full and never ran dry. . . .

"On the evening when you came to my inn we had just celebrated the wedding feast for my youngest grandson. When you told me where you were going I saw it as a sign from Heaven that I should send the last of the bottle to the *rebbe*."

The two Hasidim looked at each other and understood everything. The wine was the wine of Elijah the Prophet, so it was no wonder that for the *rebbe* it had the flavor of Paradise.

COMMENTARY FOR TALE 14 (IFA 960)

Recorded from memory by Dvora Fus as heard in the shtetl of Lewdow from her mother.[1]

Cultural, Historical, and Literary Background

The Structure of the Tale

The tale consists of two stories—the pilgrimage to the Hasidic rabbi's court and the innkeeper's tale—one embedded in the other. This is a recurrent, though not necessarily frequent, form of storytelling in many societies as well as in Jewish traditions; for examples, see tales IFA 2623 (vol. 1, no. 25), IFA 7755 (in this vol., no. 44), and IFA 10611 (vol. 3, no. 54).

For analytical purposes, it is convenient to distinguish between framed and embedded stories, both of which, when they occur in literary works, recapitulate oral storytelling. These are not mutually exclusive categories because embedded stories can and do occur within framed narratives. The embedding of a story within a story is found in oral and written sources; however, the framing of tales—when a series of tales follow each other within an imagined storytelling situation—is a literary form or an editorial strategy that provides for the inclusion of a variety of tales within a unifying framework. The frame is often structured so that the characters find themselves in a situation that is conducive for storytelling.

Among the better known frame narratives are books of the *kathá* literature of classical Sanskrit, whose style is relatively simple and direct and is geared to a popular audience. Well-known examples are the anonymous Sanskrit *Panchatantra* (100 B.C.E. to 500 C.E.),[2] *The Book of Sinbad* (c. fifth century B.C.E.; extant version in Syriac, tenth century C.E.),[3] *The Life of Secundus* (second century C.E.),[4] Ksemendra's *Vetalapancavimsati* (eleventh century),[5] the *Shuka Saptati* (The seventy tales of the parrot) (late twelfth century),[6] *The Thousand and One Nights* or *The Arabian Nights' Entertainment* (fourteenth century),[7] Petrus Alfonsi's *Disciplina Clericalis* (twelfth century),[8] Boccaccio's *Decameron* (1349–1353), Chaucer's *Canterbury Tales* (1387–1400),[9] Giovanni Francesco Straparòla's *Le Piacevoli Notti* (The nights of Straparola) (1550–1553),[10] and Giambattista Basile's *Lo cunto de li cunti* or *Il Pentamerone* (1634).[11]

Many studies on the use of framing in literature have been conducted.[12] Studies and collections of embedded tales are also available.[13]

The Hasidic Court System

In the present tale, the social life in the Hasidic court serves as the framing context for the story. At one time, the Hasidic court system served as the main social, religious, and political structure of Hasidic life. Likely built on earlier precedents, it emerged into full force in Hasidic life with the transformation of the role of the tzadik from a wondering *ba'al shem* (an itinerant preacher) to a settled community leader in the late eighteenth century.[14] For the next century, and, in fact, well into the 1900s, the Hasidic rabbi's court[15] served as a central gathering site for community life. Accounts of the social activities within the court appear in memoirs and literary writings and are similar to the scenes the narrator of the present tale describes. One of the earliest descriptions is found in the autobiography of Solomon Maimon (1754–1800), an enlightened Jew who, in his youth, was attracted to the Hasidic way of life.[16] Fictional, anecdotal, and historical accounts of Hasidic court life, some focusing on specific dynasties or rabbis, have also been published.[17]

Because the tzadik played such a central role in Hasidic social life and thought, this figure became the focus of extensive scholarship, although most of it focused on the ideology and theology of leadership, rather than the historical ethnographic and anthropological aspects. Important information, scholarly debates, and insights are found in the writings of Hasidic authors and the scholars who study them and their societies. Several essays can be recommended as a starting point for the analysis of the Hasidic court as a site of cult and pilgrimage, especially those by D. Assaf.[18] Studies concerned with the historical development of the Hasidic court in the eighteenth and nineteenth centuries are also available.[19]

Most immigrant groups dissolve their social structure in their new land; but the Hasidim have preserved many aspects of their social structure, especially maintaining in their American communities the centrality of the rabbi (*rebbe*) and his court in both religious and social life.[20]

The Innkeeper's Story

The innkeeper's story is presented as a personal narrative, but the plot follows the pattern of tales about liminal child delivery, or, in Jewish folklore, the rite of circumcision. Typically, the urgent request for help is made at a liminal time, often at midnight or, as in this tale, on the eve of Yom Kippur. Next, the mortal helper is taken or directed to an isolated locale. In most of these stories, the human then offers help to a being that is "between and betwixt"—that is, between the mortal and the supernatural worlds, such as an infant born out of the union of a human and a demon. In the present story, this dimension is absent; however, the man who helps at the circumcision and who brings the reward is interpreted as being Elijah the Prophet—a liminal figure who exists in and between the two worlds and, in the narrative, in and between the two stories.

These stories generally end with a reward of food or drink. There is usually some kind of instructions for, or restrictions on, ingesting this reward. For example, the hero may be forbidden to ingest it in the liminal locale, lest he or she stay there forever; in the present tale, the innkeeper is told to drink the wine on happy occasions and that the wine will not last forever. In some stories food scraps, such as onion peels, turn into gold when the hero returns to the human world. For more

14 / The Blessing of Elijah

on this type of story, see the notes to tales IFA 9182 (vol. 1, no. 55) and IFA 10087 (vol. 1, no. 56).

For more on stories involving Elijah the Prophet, see the notes to tales IFA 2420 (vol. 1, no. 20), IFA 2830 (vol. 1, no. 18), IFA 7000 (vol. 1, no. 17), and IFA 16408 (vol. 1, no. 1).

Folklore Motifs

- cf. A154 "Drink of the gods."
- D1040 "Magic drink."
- D1046 "Magic wine."
- D1171.8 "Magic bottle."
- D1472.1.17 "Magic bottle supplies drink."
- D1652.2 "Inexhaustible drink."
- D1652.5 "Inexhaustible vessel."
- *P426.4 "Rabbi."
- *P449 "Innkeeper."
- *V54.1.1 "Elijah serves as a *sandak*."
- *V75.2 "Day of Atonement."
- cf. *V76 "Pentecost."
- V82 "Circumcision."
- V85 "Religious pilgrimages."
- *V295 "Elijah the Prophet."
- *V536 "Pilgrimage to a holy man."

Notes

1. First published in *Omer* (Sept. 30, 1960).
2. Edgerton, *The Panchatantra Reconstructed;* Hertel, *The Panchatantra: A Collection of Ancient Hindu Tales;* Hertel, *The Panchatantra—Text of Purnabhadra;* Sternbach, *The Kavya-Portions in the Katha-Literature,* 25–62; and W. Brown, "The Panchatantra in Modern Indian Folklore."
3. Clouston, *The Book of Sindibad;* M. Epstein, *Tales of Sendebar;* Niedzielski et al., *Studies on the Seven Sages of Rome;* Perry, "The Origin of the Book of Sindibad"; Runte et al., *The Seven Sages of Rome and the Book of Sindibad;* Steinmaetz, *Exemple und Auslegung;* and Upadhyaya, "Indic Background of *The Book of Sindibad.*"
4. Perry, *Secundus, the Silent Philosopher.*
5. Riccardi, *A Nepali Version of the Vetâlapañcavimsati.*
6. Individual tales from this series date from much earlier periods; the work was translated into Persian in the fourteenth century by Ziya'u'd-din Nakhshabi's as *Tuti-name, the Tales of a Parrot.* See Haksar, *Shuka Saptati;* and Simar, *Tales of Parrot by Ziya' U'D-Din Nakhshabi.*
7. A reference to this tale collection by name occurs in the ninth century; see Dodge, *The Fihrist of al-Nadim,* 713. The currently available translated and reproduced manuscript is from the fourteenth century; see Haddawy, *The Arabian Nights;* and Haddawy, *The Arabian Nights II.*

8. Hermes, *The 'Disciplina Clericalis' of Petrus Alfonsi.*

9. Chaucer has been the subject of voluminous scholarship. Among the recent works most relevant for the present discussion is Gittes, *Framing the* Canterbury Tales.

10. For a translation, see Waters, *The Nights of Straparola.*

11. See Basile, *The Pentamerone of Giambattista Basil.*

12. For example, see Belcher, "Framed Tales in the Oral Tradition"; Gittes, "*The Canterbury Tales* and the Arabic Frame Tradition"; Gittes, *Framing the* Canterbury Tales; Haring, "Framing in Oral Narrative"; Hinckley, "The Framing-Tale"; Irwin, "What's in a Frame?"; and Nelles, *Frameworks.*

13. For example, see Bal, "Notes on Narrative Embedding"; Berendsen, "Formal Criteria of Narrative Embedding"; Schram, *Stories with Stories;* Wright and Holloway, *Tales within Tales.*

14. J. Weiss, "Beginning of Hasidism."

15. *Hatzer* in Hebrew; *hoyf* in Yiddish.

16. S. Maimon, *The Autobiography of Solomon Maimon*, 166–179; and Hundert, *Essential Papers on Hasidism,* 11–24.

17. See, for example, M. Buber, *For the Sake of Heaven.* Anecdotal descriptions of several courts of rabbis who belonged to the Twersky Hasidic dynasty of Ukraine and the tales told within their quarters are in Twersky, *Be-Ḥatsar ha-Zaddik* (In the tzaddik's court). An account of life in the Hasidic courts of Sadagura (Sadigura in Yiddish) and of Ruzhin is in Even, *Fun'm Rebin's Hoyf* (From the rabbi's court). An early historical description of the Hasidic court in the life of Hasidic society is D. Dubnow, *Toldot ha-Hasidut* (History of Hasidism), 354–361.

18. D. Assaf, "Hebetim Historyim ve-Ḥevratyim"; D. Assaf, " 'Like a Small State within a Large State' "; and Pedaya, "The Development of the Social-Religious-Economic Model in Hasidism."

19. Rapoport-Albert, "Hasidism after 1772"; Etkes, "The Zaddik"; and Piekarz, *The Hasidic Leadership.*

20. J. Mintz, *Legends of the Hasidim,* 48–63, 89–121; and J. Mintz, *Hasidic People,* 3–4, 29–32, 43–59, 112–125, 154–175.

15

Rebbe Pinḥas'l of Korets

TOLD BY ITZḤAK CHEPLIK TO MALKA COHEN

*R*ebbe Pinḥas'l of Korets was a famous *rebbe*,* with a following in many districts of Russia. His house was always full of Jews asking for assistance. The *rebbe* would receive them and listen to their troubles. Rebbe Pinḥas'l was used to hearing the woes of the common folk. He gave help and encouragement to the masses and did whatever he could for them. He was so busy, both day and night, that he had no time left to attend to his own needs. More than once he had to stop in the middle of the *Amidah,* although in general it is forbidden to interrupt this prayer. This happened mainly when a sick person came, and he had to interrupt his devotions to save a Jewish soul.

One fine day, after many years, Rebbe Pinḥas'l decided that he would no longer receive visitors. After all, according to the sages, "A Jew who stops studying Torah even for one day is sinning before the Lord." He instructed his servants that no one should be allowed to enter his court.

Jews came and Jews went. Soon the rumor spread that the court of Rebbe Pinḥas'l was closed to all. Jews stopped coming to the town of Korets. This pushed the locals, whose living depended on serving the *rebbe*'s visitors, to the verge of bankruptcy. Naturally they were unhappy with him. Things reached the point that some of the residents wondered if perhaps they should set up a new *rebbe*. But how could one do such a thing to Reb** Pinḥas'l?

Time flew, until the High Holy Days, Rosh Hashanah and Yom Kippur, arrived. The *rebbe* came to the synagogue. As was his custom, in this season too he invited guests to dine at his table. But none of the townspeople wanted to join him for the feast. On Yom Kippur, the *rebbe* sensed that his prayer was incomplete and was not being accepted. This made his heart very heavy. The custom was that after the fast many of the leading Jews of the town would come break their fast with him and help him drive the first

---
*A Hasidic rabbi.
**Rabbi or Mr.

nail into his sukkah.* But no one came this evening. Nor did anyone come the next day to help him build his sukkah.

At first the *rebbe* thought he would call a non-Jew to help him build the sukkah, but at once he changed his mind, because this would make the sukkah invalid. With great pains and much effort the *rebbe* built his sukkah all by himself. On the first night of the Sukkot festival, he went to the synagogue and again invited guests. Can any Jew sit alone in his sukkah without guests? But no one accepted his invitation. The *rebbe* was quite disheartened when he came home from the synagogue. Except for his family, he was all alone in his sukkah. In accordance with the custom of all Israel, the *rebbe* poured himself a goblet of wine, looked at the entrance to the sukkah, and waited for the Patriarch Abraham, the first of the seven *ushpizin*—the holiday guests—to arrive. (The *ushpizin* visit Jews' sukkot on each day of Sukkot. On the first day, the visitor is the Patriarch Abraham; on the second day, Isaac; on the third, Jacob; on the fourth, our teacher Moses; on the fifth, the high priest Aaron; on the sixth, it is the righteous Joseph; and on the seventh, King Solomon.)

In the past, the *rebbe* had always felt the presence of the *ushpizin* and seen them in his sukkah; but this time, he saw nothing and felt nothing. He began to tremble. Then he started praying for mercy, but his prayer was not accepted in Heaven. On the second night of the holiday, when he returned from the synagogue to his sukkah, he again made *Kiddush*** over the wine. Then he waited, hoping to see the *ushpiz* for the second day of Sukkot, the Patriarch Isaac. Once again, he saw no one. Again he prayed and wept bitterly, but in vain. On the third night of the holiday, he again returned to his sukkah with no guests. He filled his goblet with wine to make *Havdalah*§ and recited the blessing over it. This time he began to weep and cry: "Our father Jacob! How have I sinned and what is my transgression? Why do you not visit me?"

All of a sudden the *rebbe* sensed that someone had entered his sukkah. He heard a voice calling, "I am your father Jacob—but my name is also Israel. Where are my sons? Why are none of the people of Israel with you, so that I may sit among them?"

---

*The temporary hut of branches and leaves made for the holiday of Sukkot.
**The blessing over the wine.
§The ceremony that marks the end of the Sabbath. See the commentary for tale IFA 5361 (in this vol., no. 17).

15 / *Rebbe Pinḥas'l of Korets* 111

A sukkah.

Then the *rebbe* understood that he had sinned by isolating himself and not giving audience to the Jews who came to pour out their hearts to him, recount their woes, and receive his blessing, along with words of consolation and encouragement.

After the Sukkot festival the *rebbe* again opened his court to all and received Jews as in the past.

Commentary for Tale 15 (IFA 9797)

Told by Itzhak Cheplik from Russia to Malka Cohen in 1973 in Tel Aviv.[1]

Cultural, Historical, and Literary Background
The Rabbi

Rabbi Pinhas'l ben Abraham Abba Shapiro of Korets (Korzec) (1726–1791) was one of the early Lithuanian followers of the Besht. He was born in Shklov, Belarus, and later moved to Korets, Volhynia (then in Poland; currently in Ukraine). He entered into disputes with the followers of Rabbi Dov Baer, the Maggid of Mezhirech (1704–1772), and left town around 1770, first to Ostrog and later to Shepetovka, Ukraine. During his time, and in large measure due to his presence there, the town enjoyed economic growth. According to legends, Rabbi Pinhas'l was one of the early Hasidic leaders who had direct contact with the Besht.[2] He followed the teachings of Jacob Joseph of Polonnoye (d. 1782) and studied Jewish mysticism. Abraham Joshua Heschel examined his teachings and his relations with other Hasidic leaders.[3]

Heschel, however, did not refer to any conflict Rabbi Pinhas'l may have had with his community, which could have served as a historical basis for the current narrative, which first appeared in print in 1930.[4] The story describes in literary rather than historical terms the effect of the Hasidic court on the community. As a destination of pilgrims who sought cures, learning, or inspiration, the court ensured the economic well-being of the town and was, at the same time, an institution with its own economic dynamics.[5]

The *Ushpizin*

The belief in the *ushpizin*, the seven biblical figures who invisibly enter the sukkah, is at the center of the tale. Although the Aramaic term "*ushpizin*" occurs in the Tosefta (*Ma'aser Sheni* 1:13) in the phrase "*ba'alei ushpizin*" (hotel owners), it was first used in the Zohar (late thirteenth century) to refer to the mysterious guests who attend the holiday celebration in the sukkah. It is similar in its connotation to the Latin word "*hospes*," which means "foreign guests, visitors, or strangers," though its reference in Jewish tradition is very specific.[6]

The *ushpizin* theme is a variation on motif V235 "Mortal visited by angel," which occurs in Judeo-Christian traditions; however, within the Jewish tradition, it is analogous to the belief in the revelation of Elijah as a pietistic-mystical vision that individuals can merit.[7] The appearance of the *ushpizin* is time and place specific, directly related to the Festival of the Sukkot and to the sukkah itself (similar to Elijah's appearance at the seder on the first night of Passover), but Elijah's revelation is unpredictable, though desired and expected.

The virtues by which an individual merits the presence of the biblical figures, in this tale as well as in the first documented reference to this idea and custom, is ethical rather than pietistic, involving the charitable act of feeding the poor. As mentioned, this custom was already practiced by the time the Zohar was written; but though the Zohar might have been instrumental in its diffusion in Jewish communities and its incorporation into the canonic prayers, as Hallamish suggested,[8] the idea of helping the poor was established earlier.

Maimonides (1135–1204) had already proposed that hosting poor people and treating them well during a holiday—any holiday not just Sukkot—is spiritually essential for its proper celebration. In the following, he was describing either an established custom or ideal behavior: "When one eats and drinks he must feed the stranger, the orphan, and the widow, together with the rest of the destitute poor. But whoever locks the gates of his yard and eats and drinks with his children and his wife and does not feed the poor and the embittered people, his celebration is not a celebration of mitzvah but of his belly" (*Mishneh Torah, Hilkhot Yom Tov* 6:18).

In the Zohar, this ideal ethical conduct obtains mystical dimensions:

> Observe that when a man sits in this abode of the shadow of faith, the *Shekinah* spreads her Wings over him from above and Abraham and five other righteous ones make their abode with him. R. Abba said: "Abraham and five righteous ones and David with them. Hence it is written, 'In booths ye shall dwell seven days', as much as to say, 'Ye seven days shall dwell in booths', and a man should rejoice each day of the festival with these guests who abide with him." R. Abba further pointed out that first it says "*ye* shall dwell" and then "*they* shall dwell." The first refers to the guests, and therefore Rab Hamnuna the Elder, when he entered the booth, used to stand at the door inside and say, "Let us invite the guests and prepare the table," and he used to stand up and greet them, saying, "In booths ye shall dwell, O seven days. Sit, most exalted guests, sit: sit guests of faith, sit." He would then raise his hands in joy and say, "Happy is our portion, happy is the portion of Israel, as it is written, " 'For the portion of the Lord is his people,' " and then he took his seat. The second "dwell" refers to human beings; for he who has a portion in the holy land and people sits in the shadow of faith to receive the guests so as to rejoice in this world and the next. He must also gladden the poor, because the portion of those guests whom he invites must go to the poor (*Emor* [Leviticus], 103b–104a, 5:135–136).[9]

Initially, the Zohar identified only Abraham the Patriarch and King David as *ushpizin*. The others are simply "five righteous ones." Later, the text refers to Isaac and Jacob as well. Rabbi Meir ben Judah Loeb ha-Kohen (d. 1662), who was the last editor of the Lurianic writings and whose own works were widely spread in Poland and Germany, identified the seven *ushpizin* in his book *Or Zaddikim* (Righteous ones' light) as Abraham, Isaac, Jacob, Moses, Aaron, Joseph, and David.[10] The men he names as *ushpizin* and the order in which he lists them likely reflect the tradition that emanated from the teaching of Rabbi Isaac ben Solomon Luria (Ha-Ari) (c. 1534–1572).

The idea of the *ushpizin* and the custom of greeting them at the sukkah entrance are found in the influential book *Shenei Luḥot ha-berit*[11] by Rabbi Isaiah ben Abraham Ha-Levi Horowitz (1565?–1630). This custom and a welcoming prayer were incorporated into the Sephardic and Hasidic prayer books. Currently, the custom is ubiquitous in all Jewish communities. The *ushpizin* are welcomed, one each day, in the following order: Abraham, Isaac, Jacob (the three Patriarchs), Joseph, Moses, and Aaron (who led the Israelites out of Egypt), and King David (who founded the Israelite royal dynasty and whose descendant will be the Messiah).

The narrator of the present tale placed Joseph after Moses and Aaron, according to the Lurianic tradition. Substituting King David with King Solomon synthesizes two available traditions. A brief discussion of the available permutations of the list and order of the *ushpizin* has been published.[12]

When determining the *ushpizin,* the kabbalists drew on two lists of righteous people available in the talmudic-midrashic literature. The Babylonian Talmud cites a traditional interpretation of Micah 5:4:

> And that shall afford safety.
> Should Assyria invade our land
> And tread upon our fortresses,
> We will set up over it seven shepherds,
> Eight princes of men.

The seven shepherds are "David in the middle, Adam, Seth, and Methuselah on his right, and Abraham, Jacob, and Moses on his left" (BT *Sukkah* 52b). The names of the seven shepherds and the seven *ushpizin* only partially overlap. The first three among the shepherds, who represent the ancestors of humanity, are replaced by three who are associated with the national dawn of the Israelites and the Jews.

According to another tradition, God favors the seventh in cosmological as well as human lists:

> All sevenths are favorites in the world. The seventh is a favorite above, for there are *shamayim, sheme hashamayim, rakia', shehakim, zebul, ma'on,* and *'araboth* [these were regarded as the names of the seven different heavens which were thought to exist in the universe] and of the last-named it is written, *Extol Him that rideth upon the 'araboth, whose name is the Lord* [Psalm 68:5]. On the earth too the seventh is a favorite. For it is called: *erez, adamah, karka', ge, ziyyah, neshiyyah,* and *tebel* [the seven names indicate different aspects of the world], and of the last-named it is written, *He will judge the rebel with righteousness, and the peoples in his faithfulness* [Psalm 94:13]. The seventh is a favorite among the genera-

tions. Thus: Adam, Seth, Enosh, Kenan, Mahalalel, Jare, Enoch, and of Him it is written, *And Enoch walked with God* [Genesis 5:22]. Among the Patriarchs the seventh was the favorite. Thus: Abraham, Isaac and Jacob, Levi, Kohath, Amram, and Moses, of whom it is written, *And Moses went up unto God* [Exodus 19:3]. And among the children the seventh was the favorite, as it says, David the seventh [1 Chronicles 2:15]. And the among the kings the seventh was favorite. Thus: Saul, Ishbosheth, David, Solomon, Rehoboam, Abijah, Asa, and of the last-named it is written, *And Asa cried unto the Lord* [2 Chronicles 14:10]. Among the years the seventh is the favorite, as it says, *The seventh year thou shalt let it rest and lie fallow* [Exodus 23:11]. Among the septennates the seventh is a favorite, as it says, *And ye shall hallow the fiftieth year* [Leviticus 25:10]. The seventh is the favorite among the days, as it says, *And God blessed the seventh day* [Genesis 2:3]. Among the months, too, the seventh is the favorite, as it says, *In the seventh month, in the first day of the month* ([Leviticus 23:24;] MR *Leviticus* 29:11; *Pêsikta dê-Rab Kahâna* 23:10, pp. 359–360 Mandelbaum's edition 2:343–344).[13]

Discussions of the *ushpizin* and of the Sukkot festival are available.[14]

Folklore Motifs

- *C51.1.16 "Tabu: stopping a prayer before its completion."
- *P426.4 "Rabbi."
- Q1 "Hospitality rewarded—opposite punished."
- Q292 "Inhospitality punished."
- V50 "Prayer."
- *V75.2 "Day of Atonement."
- *V75.4 "Rosh Hashanah (New Year)."
- V97 "Studying of Torah as religious service."
- V226 "Saints as hermits."
- V227 "Saints have divine visitors."
- *V235.4 "Mortal visited by patriarchs."
- *V235.5 "Mortal visited by the 'Seven Visitors' (*ushpizin*)."
- W12 "Hospitality as a virtue."
- W158 "Inhospitality."
- Z71.5 "Formulistic number: seven."

——— **Notes** ———

1. Published in M. Cohen, *Mi-Pi ha-Am* (From folk tradition), 1:31–33 no. 2.
2. Ben-Amos and Mintz, *In Praise of the Ba'al Shem Tov*, 131, 146–149 nos. 124, 131.
3. See the following works by Heschel: "Rabbi Pinhas of Korzec"; "*Reb Pinkhes Koritser*"; "*Le-toldot R. Pinhas mi-Korits*" (Toward a biography of Rabbi Pinhas of

Korets); and "*R. Pinḥas mi-Korits ve-ha-Maggid mi-Mezeritch*" (Rab Pinḥas of Korets and the Maggid of Mezeritch).

4. H. Kahana, *Even Shtiyah* (A foundation stone), 109 no. 8. It was also printed in M. Buber, *Tales of Hasidim: Early Masters*, 120–121; and Zevin, *Sippurei Hasidim* (Hasidic tales), 2:112–113 no. 124.

5. For a study of some of these economic functions, see D. Assaf, "'Money for Household Expenses.'"

6. For use of the term and concept in classical Latin poetry, see Gibson, "Aeneas as *Hospes* in Vergil, *Aeneid* 1 and 4."

7. See also the notes to tales IFA 960 (in this vol., no. 14), IFA 2329 (vol. 4, no. 26), IFA 2420 (vol. 1, no. 20), IFA 2830 (vol. 1, no. 18), IFA 3955 (in this vol., no. 63), IFA 6619 (vol. 4, no. 17). Cf., in particular, the traditional texts and their analysis in Scott, "The Expectation of Elija."

8. *Kabbalah*, 323.

9. See also Lachower and Tishby, *The Wisdom of the Zohar*, 3:1305–1308 (3:104a).

10. See 43a no. 38 (2).

11. See 2:75b.

12. See Sperber, *Minhagei Yisrael* (Jewish customs), 3:214–215 n. 202.

13. Bracketed material appeared as footnotes in the original. See also L. Ginzberg, *The Legends of the Jews*, 3:226, 6:81 n. 430.

14. For the *ushpizin*, see Z. Goren, "On *Ushpizin*"; Lewinski, *Sefer ha-Mo'adim* (The festivals book), 4:152–165; and H. Schwartz, *Tree of Souls*, 209–210, 299. For studies about the history of the Sukkot festival, see J. Rubenstein, *The History of Sukkot in the Second Temple and Rabbinic Periods;* and Ulfgard, *The Story of Sukkot*.

16

The Karliner Rebbe's Prescription

TOLD BY YA'AKOV RABINOVITZ
TO YOḤANAN BEN-ZAKKAI

As a shepherd tends his flock, so did the "Babe of Stolin" care for his flock and see to all their bodily and spiritual needs. Nevertheless, he also conducted conversations on secular matters: with one person he would discuss philosophy and ethics; for another he would write down a "prescription"—a charm for physical health.

A Hasid who felt unwell would come to the *rebbe*,* describe his ailments, and ask for a remedy. The *rebbe* would ask questions and make inquiries, arrive at a diagnosis, and write out a tried and true prescription for perfect health.

Once, during the intermediate days of Passover, a brawny Jew came to the *rebbe* with a request: "Rebbe, I am a carter, a man of the whip and harness. I travel the roads and work day and night. In summer I'm consumed by the heat, and in winter I'm seared by the cold. But my strength is failing—may it not happen to you—and I get dizzy when I'm on the road. Would the *rebbe* be so kind and merciful as to write me a prescription to ease my ailments?"

The *rebbe* tore a piece of paper from his notebook, wrote down some words in Polish, and gave it to the Hasid. "Here is your prescription," he told him, "a proven charm against headache. Now go in peace, and with God's help you will be well."

The Jew took a respectful leave of the *rebbe* and went his way.

Summer passed, autumn arrived, and during one of the Ten Days of Penitence the same Jew came to the *rebbe* again. His face made it plain that he was in great pain. The *rebbe* recognized him. "What's the problem, whip master?" he asked. "Why do you look so downcast?"

"Rebbe, the headaches have come back. Please, have mercy on me and write me a note, and my pains will be relieved again."

---
*A Hasidic rabbi.

"But I wrote you a proven remedy. If it has run out, go to the apothecary and ask him to refill the prescription I wrote you during the intermediate days of Passover."

"May the *rebbe* live, could you possibly imagine that I took the *rebbe*'s handwritten note and gave it to some nameless apothecary? Heaven forbid, Rebbe! Heaven forbid that I should do something like that!"

"I am astonished at you. You didn't give the note to the apothecary? What did you do with my prescription?"

"Rebbe, may you live long, what do you mean what did I do with it? I unraveled the seam of my leather cap, stuffed the note deep inside the lining, and wore the cap on my head. I felt better as soon as I put it on. For half a year I was free of pain."

"And where is the hat now?"

"May the *rebbe* live, one cloudy day last month a storm came up, with a driving rain that soaked me. It tore my clothes and blew my hat away. And, woe is me, it carried off the note, written in the *rebbe*'s own hand. Now once again my head is dizzy when I'm on the road. Would the *rebbe* please be merciful and write out the charm again, to bring me relief as before?"

COMMENTARY FOR TALE 16 (IFA 7912)

Ya'akov Rabinowitz told this story to Yoḥanan Ben-Zakkai in 1967 in Tel Aviv.[1]

Cultural, Historical, and Literary Background

The Karlin Hasidic Dynasty

The Hasidic rabbi in this story is Ha-Yenuka of Stolin (the Babe of Stolin), as Rabbi Israel Perlov (1869–1921) was known. He was a scion of the Karlin Hasidic dynasty. His father, Rabbi Asher the Second (1827–1873), died after serving as the head of his Hasidic community for only one year, when Israel was four years old. The Karlin Hasidim kept their loyalty to the rabbinic dynasty and proclaimed the four-year-old child as their rabbi, sustaining satire and ridicule from the Jewish community. As a mature community leader, Rabbi Israel made a name for himself as being intellectual and compassionate, just and tolerant, and steeped in tradition yet open to new ideas. He spoke Russian and German and was able to fend for his community against the local authorities.[2]

The founder of the Karlin Hasidic dynasty was Rabbi Aaron the Great (1736–1772), who was a disciple and follower of the Great Maggid, Rabbi Dov Baer Mezherich (1704–1772). Rabbi Aaron founded a Hasidic congregation in Karlin on the outskirts of Pinsk, Belarus, and from there traveled and preached the teachings of his master, spreading the Hasidic movement in Lithuania and Belarus. His successors were Rabbi Shelomo of Karlin (d. 1792); his brother, Rabbi Asher of Karlin (1760–1827), who moved to Stolin; Rabbi Aaron the Second (1802–1872); Rabbi Asher the Second; and Ha-Yenuka of Stolin, the rabbi in the present story.[3]

The communication between the Hasidic rabbi and his followers was done through the exchange of written notes. When visiting the rabbi, a Hasid would submit a note (*a kevitel*) and a payment (*pidyon*) for the rabbi's magical cure, therapy, or blessing. The note would have two parts: the first was a declaration of exclusive loyalty that the Hasid declared to the rabbi; the second spelled out the individual's wishes, which often revolved around issues of health, business, marriage, or children. The Hasid submitted the *kevitel* and the *pidyon* in the presence of the *gabbai* (synagogue officer) but otherwise in total privacy. In response, the rabbi would bless his follower orally and might give the Hasid a note, written by a scribe, that would include a blessing and a therapeutic magical formula.[4]

Misuse of a Prescription

Tales in which the patient believes the prescription for medicine is actually the medicine itself or in which he or she misuses it in some way are widely known. Ranke,[5] however, considered this tale type to be of nineteenth-century vintage.

In *The Types of International Folktales*, Uther[6] distinguished four subtypes of this theme:

- A patient eats one of the (uncooked) leeches the doctor prescribed to him and asks his wife to roast the others.
- The patient takes the physician's written prescription with water and gets well.
- A woman follows the instructions on the medicine "to shake before use" by shaking her husband instead of the medicine.
- A farmer brings the door on which the physician wrote the prescription, because of the lack of paper, to the pharmacist.

Although the present tale bears thematic similarity to this tale type, it involves a unique variation that represents the personality of Rabbi Israel Perlov, Ha-Yenuka of Stolin. As a twentieth-century Hasidic rabbi, he was aware of science, medicine, and the modern world. In Hasidic tradition, he is remembered as "completely different from his father. He even dressed differently. He went like a businessman. He wore a kaftan but did not dress in resplendent fashion as Rebbes did."[7] Among the other legends about him, there are at least two more that involve prescriptions that the rabbi gave to generals in the Russian army.[8] Thus, as a modern rabbi, he gave his follower a medical prescription, but the Hasid considered it a traditional amulet. For more on amulets in Jewish societies, see the notes to tales IFA 4425 (vol. 1, no. 41), IFA 6306 (in this vol., no. 23), IFA 8792 (in this vol., no. 5), and IFA 9158 (vol. 1, no. 12).

Similarities to Other IFA Tales
- IFA 4059: *Only the Similarity* (Iraq).[9]
- IFA 4793: *The Doctor and the Peasant* (Eretz Yisra'el, Sephardic).

Folktale Types
- 1349N* "Leeches Prescribed by Doctor Eaten by Patient."
- 1349N* "The Mistaken Prescription" (new ed.).
- 1349N* (Jason) "Leeches Prescribed by Doctor Eaten by Patient" ["Prescription Treated as Charm"].

Folklore Motifs
- *D1273.7 "Magic script."
- D1502.1.1 "Charm for headache."
- J2469.2 "Taking the prescription."
- *P416 "Wagon driver."
- *P426.4 "Rabbi."
- V75.1 "Passover."

Notes
1. First published in Cheichel, *A Tale for Each Month 1967*, 60–62 no. 4.

2. Ben-Ezra, *Ha-"Yenuka" me-Stolin* (The babe of Stolin); and Rabinowitsch, *Lithuanian Hasidism,* 100–106.

3. Rabinowitsch, op. cit. In the United States, the Karlin Hasidim are known as the Stolin community; see J. Mintz, *Hasidic People,* 112–120.

4. See D. Assaf, *The Regal Way,* 315–321; J. Mintz, *Legends of the Hasidim,* 107–108; and Pedaya, "The Development of the Social-Religious-Economic Model in Hasidism."

5. *"Blutegelkur."*

6. At 2:150–151.

7. J. Mintz, *Legends of the Hasidim,* 292 no. H69.

8. J. Mintz, *Legends of the Hasidim,* 292–298 nos. H76, H77.

9. Published in D. Noy, *Jewish-Iraqi Folktales,* 91–92 no. 42.

17

The Merit of the Third Sabbath Meal

TOLD BY MALKAH LEVI TO YA'AKOV AVITSUK

*O*nce there was a merchant who was very meticulous about observing the precepts. Of all of them, however, he was most meticulous about *shalosh se'udot*—the third Sabbath meal—and the *melavah malkah** ceremony when the Sabbath was over. He always endeavored to have the *melavah malkah* table set attractively, with plenty of food and drink for guests who came home from the synagogue with him. He never went any place on Saturday night until he had enjoyed a proper *melavah malkah*. He always made sure to purchase fine spices and candles for *Havdalah*.

Once, when he came home from the synagogue after the Sabbath, his wife began to set the table for the *Havdalah* and then for the *melavah malkah*. His children were already waiting around the table. As he approached it, however, he heard someone knocking at the door. One of the children went and opened the door. Two well-dressed men entered, said good evening, and announced that they wanted to speak with the master of the house. "Wait a while, please," he told them. "First I must eat *melavah malkah,* and then I will talk with you."

They replied that they were merchants from a certain city and in a great hurry.

The householder set the *Havdalah* cup down and went over to talk to them. They urged him to accompany them to a nearby city, where a train full of merchandise had just arrived, and he stood to make a great profit from the shipment.

Again he asked them to wait until he had finished the meal. But they demurred and finally persuaded him to leave with them without delay. While he was changing out of his Sabbath clothes and dressing for the trip, his wife took the wine and hallah, fish and meat, and other dishes and put it all in a basket so her husband would have food for the journey. The merchants said he would come back home the next afternoon.

---

*"Escorting the Queen." The final Sabbath meal.

The man's servant hitched the horses to his carriage and got everything ready for the trip. The merchants said there was no need for the servant to come along, because they had come in their own carriage and the man would be returning during daylight the next day.

The merchant took leave of his wife and children, kissed the mezuzah, and started on his way. He climbed into his coach. The horses knew the way and set out, their master urging them on with whistles and singing *melavah malkah* hymns.

The merchants sat in the second carriage and traveled ahead, leaving him to follow them. After they left town, they took a side road and then turned onto a forest path. Suddenly, their carriage pulled up short and the two merchants jumped down. With drawn pistols they came up to the Jewish merchant. "You're trapped," they told him. "Give us your money, or we'll kill you here!"

The poor merchant was terrified. He wanted to run away and jerked on the reins. The horses began to gallop, but the men shot and killed one horse and the second stopped. The merchant jumped from his carriage and tried to flee; but they grabbed him, tied his hands, and took all his money. Then they dragged him into the forest, where there was an abandoned house. They threw him inside and tossed the basket with food after him. "Eat it before your guest does," they said. Then they opened the door and a huge bear entered.

The merchant was frightened out of his wits and fainted dead away. When he came to his senses everything was dark, except for the stars shining though the tall window. Gradually he remembered what had happened to him. "It's all because I didn't eat *melavah malkah* the way I usually do," he thought. "God has punished me."

He began to weep and suddenly felt hungry. He reached out his arms to the side and found his basket, only to again be overcome by terror and nearly faint when he heard the bear growling next to him. So he sat quite still and tried not to move a muscle. Eventually, though, his hunger got the better of his fear, and he again groped for the basket and pulled out the bottle of wine. With tears in his eyes he began to recite the *Havdalah* in a stifled voice: "Behold, God is my salvation; I will trust, and will not be afraid."* While he chanted the rest of the introductory verses, followed by the blessings of the wine and spices and candles, he could hear the bear growling. Shivering with fear, he almost spilled the wine as he sipped it.

---

*Compare Isaiah 12:2.

He could sense the bear coming closer. "Into Your hand I entrust my spirit,"* he said and prepared to die, sensing that the bear was right beside him. After long moments of panic, he realized that the bear had stopped coming closer. Once again he reached out to the basket; he took out the hallah, made the blessing over bread, and threw the bear a large piece. The bear snatched up the piece of hallah and gobbled it down. Next the man took out the fish, took a small bite, and threw the rest to the bear, which grabbed it and ate it quickly. "If I give him all the food," the merchant thought, "he'll leave me alone." And that's what he did. He tasted only a morsel of each item and put the rest aside. Sure enough, the bear ate everything and did not harm him.

All of this took several hours, during which the stars kept moving in the sky. When the merchant saw through the window that it was almost daylight he thought about escaping. He crawled around looking for the door, which proved to be unlocked. The thieves had trusted in their bear.

The merchant left the house and heard the bear following him. He was startled—but after he had recited the deathbed confession he no longer cared about anything. In the meantime, it was full daylight, and the merchant looked for his horse and carriage, with the bear still following him.

He found the live horse, with the dead one next to it. He undid the reins and left the dead horse there. Then he led the other horse hitched to the carriage back to the path. He climbed into the carriage to return to town. He looked behind: There was the bear running after him. Just before he reached town the bear jumped up on the carriage. The merchant was sure that his end had come.

Then he heard the bear moaning and groaning in pain. Reining in the horse he listened closely to the bear's whimpers. Suddenly he heard the bear talking in a human voice, speaking Yiddish: "I am a Jewish soul," he told him. "I died many years ago but came back to this world to fulfill one precept that I had not fulfilled, that of *melavah malkah*. Now that I have done so, even in the body of a bear, I can return to my resting place on high. Please, I beg you, give me a Jewish burial." With that the bear grew silent, fell on its face, and died there in the carriage.

The merchant returned to his town at a walking pace. After telling his wife what had happened, he went to the burial society and made sure that the bear was buried in a location appropriate to such a soul.

After this incident he became even more meticulous about observing the precept of *melavah malkah*.

---

* See Psalm 31:6.

Commentary for Tale 17 (IFA 5361)

Recorded by Yaakov Avitsuk as he heard it from his sister, Malkah Levi, in 1962 in Moshav Arugot, on the southern coastal plain of Israel. Levi heard the story from their father, David Itskovitz.[1]

Cultural, Historical, and Literary Background
End of Sabbath Rituals

The narrator of the present tale notes the merchant's strict observance of three rituals that must be performed at the conclusion of the Sabbath: *shalosh se'udot* (*shalosh se'udos* in Yiddish, the third meal), *Havdalah* (distinction), and *melaveh malkah* (escorting the Sabbath Queen, or the final meal). Evidence for the practice of each of these rituals can be traced to the talmudic-midrashic period. Traditional sources from that time document and explicate the significance of each ritual separately, as have medieval and modern authorities.

Shalosh Se'udot (The Third Meal)

In the late antiquities, Jews in Palestine likely ate two meals a day, whereas the ruling Romans ate four—breakfast (*ientaculum*), lunch (*prandium*), an afternoon snack (*merenda*), and dinner (*cena*).[2] In light of this information, it is possible only to speculate on the value and meaning of the debate between the sages and Rabbi Ḥidka, a *tanna* of the second century, as it is reported in the Babylonian Talmud:

> Our Rabbis taught: How many meals must one eat on the Sabbath? Three. Rabbi Ḥidka said: Four. Rabbi Johanan observed. Both expound the same verse: *And Moses said, Eat that to-day; for to-day is a Sabbath unto the Lord: To-day ye shall not find it in the field* [Exodus 20:25]. R. Ḥidka holds: These three "to-days" are [reckoned] apart from the evening; whereas the Rabbis hold, they include [that of] the evening (BT *Shabbat* 117b–118a).

Both sides resort to the authority of the biblical text, but the opinion of the Rabbis prevailed. Other authorities asserted their rulings in different forms.

> R. Simeon b. Pazzi said in the name of R. Joshua b. Levi in Bar Kappara's name: He who observes [the practice of] three meals on the Sabbath is saved from three evils: the travails of the Messiah, the retribution of Gehinnom, and the wars of Gog and Magog (BT *Shabbat* 118a).

Later, Rabbi Jose reiterated: "May my portion be of those who eat three meals on the Sabbath" (BT *Shabbat* 118b).

While the talmudic discussion revolves around authority for one form of celebrating the Sabbath or another, and the means of doing so, could it be that the debate between the sages and Rabbi Hidka had some more profound ramifications? Although the sages insisted on maintaining traditional peasantry customs, Rabbi Hidka wished to follow the Roman model of having three meals during the day and a festive dinner at night, thus honoring the Sabbath by imitating the ruling foreign elite. The sages, who rejected his inference from the text, advocated a conservative attitude toward the Sabbath celebration—keeping it within the means of peasant society and following more traditional customs—by counting the Sabbath eve dinner as an additional festive meal of the holy day. Rabbi Hiidka, however, excluded the Sabbath eve meal from the count and proposed celebrating the Sabbath with four meals on the Sabbath day itself. Any way they counted, eating a third meal during the Sabbath was considered a special merit.

To follow the prescription of eating three meals on the Sabbath day—excluding the Sabbath eve dinner—it became customary in the Middle Ages in Spain and Italy (and likely in other countries) to divide breakfast into two meals. The later meal, eaten after the afternoon prayer (*Minhah*), was then considered the third meal.[3]

The third Sabbath meal acquired a mystical significance in the Kabbalah.

> Rabbi Judah said: One should take delight in this day and eat three meals of the Sabbath, in order to bring satisfaction and delight to the world on this day. Rabbi Abba said: ... Whoever subtracts a single meal damages the world above, and great will be his punishment. Therefore, everyone should prepare a table three times from the inception of the Sabbath; the table should not be left empty. Then blessing will rest upon him during the remaining days of the week. It is through this that faith appears in the world above and upon this it depends.
>
> Rabbi Simeon said: If a man completes these three meals on the Sabbath, a voice issues forth and makes a proclamation about him, saying "You shall take delight in the Lord"—this is one meal, that represents *Atika Kadisha*, the most holy of the holy ones; "and I will make you ride upon the high places of the earth"—this is the second meal that represents the field of sacred apples; "and I will feed you with the heritage of Jacob your father" (Isaiah 58:14)—this is the perfection that is completed in *Ze'ir Anpin*. One should perfect each meal in relation to these, and take delight in the meals and rejoice in each one of them, because this is the perfect faith.[4]

Contemporary scholars in Spain and in Germany also emphasized the significance of the third Sabbath meal, either attributing to it a mystical significance or simply documenting it as a prevailing custom. Thus Rabbi Bahye ben Asher ben Hlava (thirteenth century) from Spain drew a correspondence between the three Sabbath meals and the three *sefirot* that make up the central core of the sefirotic tree: Sabbath eve dinner corresponds to *malkhut* (kingdom), breakfast to *tiferet* (glory), and the third meal to *keter* (crown).[5] The third meal on the Sabbath had become an established custom by then, as can be inferred from the response literature.[6]

In the sixteenth century, Safed mystics continued and elaborated this tradition.[7] Their influence on Jewish communities in countries of Islam on the one hand and on the Hasidic movement on the other hand practically secured the practice of *shalosh se'udot* as part of the Sabbath customs. In Hasidic society, the third Sabbath meal around the Hasidic rabbi's table became a religious as well as a social institution. Early Hasidic narratives refer to the third meal as an established time for storytelling and singing.[8] Studies of *shalosh se'udot* are available.[9]

Havdalah (Distinction)

Like the third meal, the *Havdalah* is a ritual prayer of great antiquity. The Mishnah (*Hullin* 1:7) and the Tosefta (*Berakhot* 33b) both refer to the practice of the *Havdalah* as a prayer for distinguishing between the Sabbath and the weekdays.[10] In the Babylonian Talmud (*Berakhot* 33b), Rabbi Shaman ben Abba, an *amora* of the third and the fourth centuries C.E., attributed the institution of the *Havdalah* into the Saturday night evening prayer to the men of the Great Assembly, which might have been historical and, if so, existed at the time of or after the period of Ezra (fifth or fourth centuries B.C.E.). In the talmudic-midrashic period, the sages attributed to these men the canonization of several biblical books (BT *Bava Batra* 15a); the institution of key prayers, including the *Havdalah* (BT *Berakhot* 33a); and the categorization of oral tradition into midrash, *halakhah*, and *aggadah* (JT *Shekalim* 5:1, 48c).[11]

Rabbi Shaman ben Abba and Rabbi Ḥiyya ben Abba, both *amoraim* at the beginning of the fourth century, cast the history of the liturgical position of the *Havdalah* in economic terms, the latter quoting his teacher, Rabbi Joḥanan, the leading *amora* of the third century:

> The Men of the Great Synagogue instituted for Israel blessings and prayers, sanctifications and *Havdalahs*. At first they inserted the *Havdalah* in the *Tefillah*. When they [Israel] became richer, they instituted that it should be said over the cup [of wine]. When they became poor again, they inserted it in the *Tefillah*; and they said that one who says *Havdalah* in the *Tefillah* must [also] say it over the cup [of wine] (BT *Berakhot* 33a).

The historical veracity of this historical interpretation of the *Havdalah* not withstanding, various sages, quoting their respective teachers, offer testimonies, observations, and opinions that indicate that initially the recitation of the *Havdalah* was inserted into the evening prayer of the Eighteen Benedictions on Saturday night (BT *Berakhot* 29a, 33a, 33b). In the second century, the *Havdalah* was known and practiced as a distinct ritual but was still subject to variation (*Berakhot* 8:5).

The House of Shammai said the blessing over the lights, over the food (grace), and over the spices and then said the *Havdalah*. The House of Hillel, however, said the blessings in a different order: lights, spices, and food (grace) and the *Havdalah* (BT *Berakhot* 52b).

The actual text of the *Havdalah* prayer was not consistent. Rabbi Eleazar, an *amora* of the late third century, said in the name of Rabbi Oshaia, a leading rabbi of the previous generation: "He who would recite but few [distinctions] must recite not less than three; while he who would add, must not add beyond seven" (BT *Pesaḥim* 103b). The three basic distinctions are formulated paradigmatically in the prayer, contrasting the holy and the non-holy, the light and the darkness, and Israel and the nations. The seven distinctions add these four distinctions: between "the seventh day and the six working days, between unclean and clean, between sea and dry land, between the upper waters and the nether waters, between Priests, Levites and Israelites" (BT *Pesaḥim* 104a; cf. JT *Berakhot* 5:2). Studies of the *Havdalah* are available.[12]

Melavah Malkah (Escorting the Sabbath Queen, the Fourth Meal)

Unlike the first two rituals, the *melavah malkah* meal is not obligatory; and its performance, though meritorious, is only optional. In the talmudic-midrashic literature, there are only casual suggestions to eat a meal at the conclusion of the Sabbath. Rabbi Ḥanina, an *amora* of the early third century, recommended that every man should set his table at the conclusion of the Sabbath, even if he needs to eat no more than an olive (BT *Shabbat* 119b). Medieval interpreters and kabbalists refer to this meal as the fourth meal of the Sabbath recommended by Rabbi Ḥidka, or as the banquet of King David, who having been told by God that he would die on the Sabbath, marked the completion of each Sabbath with a festive celebration (BT *Shabbat* 30a).

The term *"melavah malkah"* (escorting the Sabbath Queen) occurs in Hebrew from the Middle Ages onward, designating the dinner and singing associated with the festive occasion. Among the kabbalists and the Hasidim, this meal acquired mystical and spiritual value, prolonging the Sabbath spirit.[13]

The Spices of the *Havdalah*

The use of spices, particularly *hadas* (myrtle), in the *Havdalah* stands out as a unique practice in these three canonic rituals for ending the Sabbath. While sanctification of wine and grace over food are acts that occur repeatedly in Jewish religious and festive celebrations, the use of spices occurs only in the *Havdalah*. In the Mishnah there is a reference to the use of the *mugmar* at the conclusion of a dinner (*Berakhot* 6:6); this term can be understood as "burning spices," from its use in the Tosefta (*Shabbat* 1:23).[14] In the mishnaic description of the *Havdalah* ritual, the term *"besamim"* (plural) means "fragrances or spices," suggesting a different use and a significance that is specific to the *Havdalah*.

In most communities, myrtle leaves are used for the spice. Myrtle was a sacred plant in Roman life, having symbolic significance in religion, politics, romance, and culinary practices. Today it has completely disappeared as a spice used in Roman and Italian life.[15] Its use in Jewish religious ceremonies is a reflection of the Roman influence on Jewish culture during the talmudic-midrashic period. Yet the particular use of myrtle in the *Havdalah* ceremony has remained somewhat enigmatic. The Hebrew term for the plant, *hadas,* has a cognate in several Semitic languages.[16] The rabbinic explanation for its use is grounded in the religious conception of the Sabbath, suggesting that the fragrance compensates individuals for the departure of the additional soul with which people are endowed during the Sabbath (BT *Bezah* 16a; *Ta'anit* 27b).

The present story and its analogous narrative tale IFA 8792 (in this vol., no. 5, and discussed below) expose another possible aspect of the use of spices in the *Havdalah* ritual. The significance of the spices becomes apparent when each of the three rituals for concluding the Sabbath is viewed not individually but sequentially, as stages in a single continuous rite. From such a perspective, each corresponds to a stage in a transitional ritual as conceived in the model Arnold Van Gennep proposed in his *The Rites of Passage* and on which Victor Turner elaborated in *The Ritual Process*[17] and *From Ritual to Theatre*.

Although the three rituals are part of a weekly passage rather than a life passage, the conclusion of the Sabbath follows the stages and principles of reintegration into the daily profane social world after a period of seclusion in the temporal domain of the holy. Accordingly, the *shalosh se'dot* is a ritual of departure from the Sabbath, the *Havdalah* is the ritual of transition between the holy and the profane, and the *melavah malkah* represents the incorporation of life back into the workweek.

The ritual of transition exposes people to a high level of danger, usually from supernatural forces, and the fragrance of the burned spices offers the needed protection. It chases away the demonic forces to which humans are most vulnerable.[18] The twilight hour—the period of transition between light and darkness during which, according to the Mishnah (*Avot* 5:6), the demons were created—had other hazards as well. In the world of medieval Jewry in France and Germany, it was believed that this was the time in which the dead returned to Hell after their Sabbath respite; and they drank water to cool themselves from the fires of their fate. Thus it was not advisable for humans to drink water at that time.[19]

The use of spices and fragrance in the *Havdalah* ritual is ancient. References to special containers—first of glass, then special metal boxes—are available from the twelfth century.[20]

For discussions of the idea of the redemptive reincarnation of the soul, see the notes to tales IFA 2634 (vol. 1, no. 22) and IFA 2644 (vol. 1, no. 23).

Similarities to Other IFA Tales

The present tale can be compared to tale IFA 8792 (in this vol., no. 5). One shared theme of the stories involves the acts of evil agents: The characters in tale IFA

8792 are demons; but in the present narrative, they are robbers. In both cases, the evil agents punish an individual for not observing a ritual that serves, among other purposes, as protection against harmful forces. In the present tale, the causal relation between the violation of the ritual and the punishment is made explicit.

Another common element to the tales is the transformation of man to animal. In tale IFA 9797 (in this vol., no. 15), the motif is D133.1 "Transformation: man to cow"; the transformation is punishment for not following the ritual of cutting one's nails. In the present story, the principal character's punishment is violent robbery, and the theme of human transformation is the punishment of a secondary character: the bear who proclaims to be the reincarnation of a human soul (motif E612.8 "Reincarnation as bear").

Another version of the present tale in the IFA is the following:
- IFA 4000: *Melavah Malkah* (Romania).

Folktale Types

- 760* "The Condemned Soul."
- 839*C (IFA) "Miraculous Rescue of Person."

Folklore Motifs

- B211.2.3 "Speaking bear."
- B435.4 "Helpful bear."
- D313.3 "Transformation: bear to person [reversed]."
- *E606.3 "Reincarnation for restoration of soul (*tikkun*)."
- E612.8 "Reincarnation as bear."
- E731.8 "Soul in form of bear."
- K1817.4 "Disguise as merchant."
- P431 "Merchant."
- P475 "Robber."
- V71 "Sabbath."
- *V71.5 "Escorting the Sabbath ritual."
- *V131.5 "Mezuzah."

--- **Notes** ---

1. First published in Na'anah, *Ozar ha-Ma'asiyyot* (A treasury of tales), 2:455–457; and later in Avitsuk, *The Fate of a Child*, 26–27 no. 15.

2. Bouquet, *Everyday Life in New Testament Times*, 70–76; Faas, *Around the Roman Table*, 38–101; and Safrai et al., *The Jewish People in the First Century*, 2:801.

3. Gartner, "The Third Sabbath Meal."

4. Lachower and Tishby, *The Wisdom of the Zohar*, 3:1287–1288. See also Hecker, *Mystical Bodies, Mystical Meals*, 116–141, 164–165.

5. Gartner, op. cit., 19 n. 95.

6. For example, see the response of Rabbi Meir ben Baruch of Rothenburg (1215–1293), quoted in H. Pollak, *Jewish Folkways in Germanic Lands (1648–1806)*, 60.

7. Gartner, op. cit., 20–23.

8. Ben-Amos and Mintz, *In Praise of the Ba'al Shem Tov*, 351 (Third Meal); J. Mintz, *Legends of the Hasidim*, 95–99; and J. Weiss, *Studies in East European Jewish Mysticism and Hasidism*, 31–35.

9. Gartner, op. cit.; Sperber, *Minhagei Yisrael* (Jewish customs), 1:82–87; and Ta-Shema, "Miriam's Well."

10. Lieberman's edition and Zuckermandel's edition, respectively.

11. For more on the men of the Great Assembly, see Finkelstein, *The Pharisees*, 2:578–580; Finkelstein, *Ha-Perushim ve-Anshe Keneset Ha-Gedolah* (The Pharisees and the men of the Great Synagogue); Krauss, "The Great Synod"; and Mantel, "The Nature of the Great Synagogue."

12. Anonymous, "*Havdalah*"; Elbogen, "*Eingang und Ausgang des Sabbats nach talmudischen Quellen*"; Elbogen, *Jewish Liturgy*, 92–94; Fleischer, "*Havdalah-Shiv'atot* According to Palestinian Ritual"; E. Goldschmidt, "*Kiddush ve-Havdalah*"; Lauterbach, "The Origin and Development of Two Sabbath Ceremonies"; Ta-Shema, "Havdalah"; Wieder, "The Old Palestinian Ritual"; Yehuda, "The Ritual and the Concept *Havdalah*"; and Zulay, "*Le-ḥeker ha-Sidur ve-ha-Minhagim*" (Toward the study of the prayer book and customs).

13. B. Landau, "*Melavveh Malkah*" (Escorting the Sabbath Queen).

14. Zuckermandel's edition.

15. Faas, op. cit., 159–160.

16. Testen, "Semitic Terms for 'Myrtle.' "

17. At 94–130.

18. Lauterbach, op. cit.

19. See Ta-Shema, "Miriam's Well"; Ta-Shema, "Havdalah"; and Zlotnik, "*Me-aggadot ha-Shabat u-Minhageah*" (Sabbath legends and customs).

20. Benjamin, *Towers of Spice*, 9; Doleželová, "Spice Boxes from the Collections of the State Jewish Museum"; and Narkiss, "The Origin of the Spice Box Known as the 'Hadass.' "

18

The Apostate Who Made the Tenth for a Minyan

TOLD BY ESTHER WEINSTEIN TO YEHUDIT GUT-BURG

One evening the *rebbe*[*] told his *shammes*,[**] "Hitch up the horses to the wagon and we'll start out." Where? The next day was Erev Yom Kippur.[§] No one knew and no one asked.

The *shammes* hitched up the horses and told the *rebbe* that everything was ready for the journey. The *shammes* loaded the wagon with the *rebbe*'s Yom Kippur *maḥzor*,[§§] his tallit,[***] and provisions for the journey. The *rebbe* climbed into the wagon, followed by the *shammes*, who served as his driver. The horses set off at a fast pace. All night, they traveled this way.

Toward morning, they reached an isolated village where only a few Jewish families lived. The village Jews, who had never seen the holy *rebbe*, did not recognize him and had no idea who the newcomers were. Nevertheless, they were delighted by the arrival of two more Jews whom they could include in a minyan for Yom Kippur and greeted them cordially.

During the morning, the *rebbe* rested from the long drive. As evening approached, he put on his holiday finery, which was as white as snow, and went to the synagogue, accompanied by his *shammes*. All the villagers arrived for the *Kol Nidrei*[§§§] service—but they were one short for a minyan. What could they do? "Do any other Jews live around here?" the *rebbe* asked. "None," was the reply.

"There is one apostate," remembered one of the worshipers, "but he

---

[*]A Hasidic rabbi.
[**]Synagogue caretaker.
[§]Yom Kippur eve.
[§§]A special prayer book used for Rosh Hashanah, Yom Kippur and other holidays.
[***]Prayer shawl.
[§§§]Opening prayer of Yom Kippur eve worship service.

hates Jews. Anyway, who will go call him? His yard is full of dogs and no one dares enter."

"I'll go," said the *rebbe*.

They all cried out in warning, "Don't go! You are putting yourself in mortal peril!" But the *rebbe* did not listen. He took up his walking stick and set out.

When he reached the apostate's house, the dogs jumped on him and threatened to tear him in pieces. But he raised his stick, and the dogs fell silent and did not dare touch him. The apostate came out and saw a Jew in his yard. "You filthy Jew, get out of here!" he shouted. "Who needs you?"

The *rebbe* replied quietly, "We are short one Jew for a minyan for *Kol Nidrei*. I came to ask you to come complete the minyan. Don't forget—tomorrow is Yom Kippur, the day of judgement, the Sabbath of Sabbaths for the Jewish people. You must come with me!"

"Certainly not! Now get out of here before I break all your bones!" yelled the apostate, who proceeded to curse the Jews heartily. The *rebbe* paid no attention. "You will come with me to complete the minyan," he said, quietly but forcefully. "Do you hear me?"

The *rebbe* began walking back toward the synagogue, with the apostate following him.

The apostate did not go back home after Kol Nidre. Instead, he spent the night in the synagogue, together with the *rebbe* and his *shammes*. All night, the three prayed with great intensity and enthusiasm, and so too all the next day. When Yom Kippur was over, after the *Ne'ilah* service, the *rebbe* ordered his *shammes* to hitch up the wagon. This time, however, it had three passengers—the *rebbe*, the *shammes,* and the apostate.

Toward morning, they reached the *rebbe*'s house. The apostate repented and became a loyal Hasid. For the rest of his life, he performed the precepts faithfully and took care of the poor.

COMMENTARY FOR TALE 18 (IFA 4936)

Recorded by Yehudit Gut-Burg from her mother, Esther Weinstein, who heard the story from her father, Rabbi Ḥayyim Saltz.[1]

Cultural, Historical, and Literary Background

Recurrent motifs in Jewish tradition have unusual representations in this story. Commonly, supernatural figures like Elijah the Prophet, or, in Hebron, Abraham the Patriarch, mysteriously appear to play the role of the tenth person who completes a public prayer quorum; for example, in tales IFA 16408 (vol. 1, no. 1) and IFA 10604 (vol. 3, no. 1). In Hasidic tales, the narrators shift the emphasis from the figure who completes the minyan to the spiritual power of the rabbi who is able to fill the quorum by finding or convincing an unexpected individual to join the group, thereby extolling the rabbi's influence. In one such story the Besht uses a paralyzed individual to complete the minyan.[2] In the present tale, the rabbi reaches out to a sinner, the opposite of a holy man, seeking him out to complete the *minyan* and by so doing drawing him out of the depths of his sinful life as an apostate.

Voluntary conversion to Christianity was part of the social-religious reality in eighteenth- and nineteenth-century Jewish society and encompassed both genders. Anecdotal biographies of Jewish apostates are available,[3] as are general studies of this phenomena;[4] Stanislawski[5] stated that "in the nineteenth century more Jews converted to Christianity in the Russian Empire that anywhere else in Europe." He distinguished five types of voluntary Jewish apostates: those who wanted professional and educational advancement, those who desired economic success, criminals, believers, and the poor and destitute. Jewish society despised the apostates and sought to bring them back into the fold. A study of Jewish apostasy in Germany has been published.[6]

The attitude toward apostates, as represented in Jewish narrative traditions, is uncompromising: They are either a welcomed repentant or a condemned and despised outcast. The most well-known late medieval tale about an abducted and baptized Jewish child who achieved greatness yet returned to his roots is *The Story of Pope Elhanan,* which was widely circulated and studied.[7] Another tradition, particularly Hasidic, considers the achieving apostate as an offspring of incestuous relations.[8] A survey of nineteenth-century Hasidic tales about apostates is available.[9]

Similarities to Other IFA Tales

Most of the tales about apostates in the IFA represent the negative attitude that prevailed in Jewish societies toward such individuals. The many apostate tales in the archives can be grouped into several categories as noted below. The following tales can be thought of as tale type *1768 (IFA) "Jokes about Apostates." Note that several of these are actually different versions of the same joke.

- IFA 10558: *Miracles and Wonders* (Poland).
- IFA 12154: *Feeling Like a Christian* (Poland).
- IFA 13086: *The New Christian* (Lithuania).[10]
- IFA 13731: *The Power of Habit* (Morocco).
- IFA 14337: *Bon Appetite, Apostate* (Poland).
- IFA 14429: *The Apostate and the Christian Old Maid* (Eretz Yisra'el, Ashkenazic).
- IFA 15338: *The Apostates* (Poland).
- IFA 15440: *The Apostate Who Converted in Order to Qualify for a Medical License* (Romania).
- IFA 15553: *Better to Be a Professor in St. Petersburg Than a Melamed in a Shtetl* (Lithuania).
- IFA 15630: *Moshe Converted First* (Poland).[11]
- IFA 15956: *The Three Apostates* (Poland).
- IFA 15988: *The Professor Apostate* (Poland).
- IFA 16052: *A Taunt and a Retort* (Poland).
- IFA 17124: *Will a Jew Change His Skin?* (Iraq).
- IFA 19955: *I Don't Know* (Poland).
- IFA 20204: *The Meat That Transformed to Fish* (Greece).[12]
- IFA 20241: *The Chicken That Changed into Fish* (Eretz Yisra'el, Sephardic).
- IFA 21073: *Hold the Stick in Both Ends* (Eretz Yisra'el, Circassian).

As the oral versions in the IFA indicate, despite the central function of Christianity in these anecdotes, similar tales have been told in Islamic countries and among non-Jewish ethnic groups in Israel.[13] A humorous rendition of the idea that any apostate was in fact not a Jew to begin with has been published.[14] A Yiddish proverb asserts this belief: "*A Yid shmadt zikh nit, a klorer vert nit meshuge*" (A Jew does not convert [to Christianity], and a sane person does not become crazy).[15]

The following tales in the IFA relate the idea that the apostate is a son of a Christian who raped a Jewish woman:

- IFA 12159: *The Apostate Son Is an Offspring of a Christian* (Poland).
- IFA 12468: *The King's Jewish Counselor* (Morocco).

In some tales, the Jew converts to Christianity because of a romantic encounter.

- IFA 10829: *The Jew Who Converted to Christianity for the Sake of a Beautiful Woman* (Ukraine).
- IFA 14213: *The Apostate Who Returned to Judaism* (Morocco).
- IFA 15064: *Thanks to the Sabbath Candles* (Belarus).

In another group of tales, the apostate is helpful:

18 / The Apostate

- IFA 13780: *The Jewish Spark* (Poland).
- IFA 14446: *The Chain of Crosses* (Eretz Yisra'el, Ashkenazic).
- IFA 16475: *An Apostate Appeals to Rabbi Meir Baal ha-Nes* (Iraqi Kurdistan).
- IFA 18805: *Why Did the Rabbi Convert to Islam?* (Iran).

In some tales, the apostate is repentant. A historical study relating to repentant apostates is available.[16]

- IFA 200: *The Apostate and the Tailor* (Yemen).
- IFA 1168: *An Apostate Informs about the Jews and Then Cancels His Own Testimony* (Yemen).
- IFA 10831: *The Merit of the Coachman* (Russia).
- IFA 10845: *The Fate of the Apostate Who Revealed Secrets to the Christians* (Ukraine).
- IFA 14213: *The Apostate Who Returned to Judaism* (Morocco).

Another theme is the punishment of the hostile apostate.

- IFA 246: *The Apostate from Me'a She'arim* (Eretz Yisra'el, Ashkenazic).
- IFA 1640: *Lo Yanum . . .* (Eastern Europe).
- IFA 3795: *Tears and Laughter* (Morocco).[17]
- IFA 4573: *The Apostate and the Swine* (Eretz Yisra'el, Ashkenazic).
- IFA 4639: *Hakham Yosef* (Iran).
- IFA 4935: *The Nullified Decree* (Eretz Yisra'el, Ashkenazic).[18]
- IFA 10705: *The King and the Torah Scrolls* (Morocco).
- IFA 10834: *A Blood Libel in Jerusalem* (Eretz Yisra'el, Ashkenazic).
- IFA 12472: *The Wicked Apostate Vizier and the Rabbi* (Morocco).
- IFA 20239: *Purim of Saragossa* (Eretz Yisra'el, Sephardic).[19]

The following tale is about a half-hearted apostate:

- IFA 13017: *The Apostate* (Romania).[20]

One tale is about a pragmatic apostate:

- IFA 13349: The Apostate (Iraqi Kurdistan).

For an even more dramatic confrontation between a rabbi and a convert who became a bishop, see tale IFA 2623 (vol. 1, no. 25). Note that among Yiddish-speaking Jews, the present tale is unique, although there are many different tales about apostates.

Folklore Motifs

- *V54 "Public prayer requires a quorum of ten (*minyan*)."
- *V54.3 "Apostate completes a minyan for the Yom Kippur service."
- V331 "Conversion to Christianity."

- V336 "Conversion to Judaism."
- *V336.1 "Jewish apostate returns to Judaism."

――――― **Notes** ―――――

1. First published in Weinstein, *Grandma Esther Relates* . . . , 51–53 no. 11.
2. See, for example, Ben-Amos and Mintz, *In Praise of the Ba'al Shem Tov,* 213–215 no. 212; and Rubinstein, *In Praise of the Ba'al Shem Tov,* 270–272 no. 176.
3. Ginsburg, *Meshumadim in tsarishn Rusland* (Apostates in tsarist Russia); and Tsitron, *Meshumadim* (Apostates).
4. Agursky, "Conversions of Jews to Christianity in Russia"; and Stanislawski, "Jewish Apostasy in Russia."
5. Op. cit., 190.
6. C. Cohen, "The Road to Conversion."
7. Bin Gorion, *Mimekor Yisrael,* 238–242 no. 129 (1990 ed.); D. Lerner, "The Enduring Legend of the Jewish Pope"; and Lipsker, "The Unreflecting Mirror."
8. Elstein, "The Gregorius Legend."
9. Nigal, *The Hasidic Tale,* 225–238. See also Ashni, *Be-Simta'ot Tzfat* (In the alleys of Safed), 119–121, which is a comparable tale told by a family member of the narrator of the present tale. An historical case of a Hasid who converted to Christianity is discussed in D. Assaf, "Convert or Saint?"; see also FailedMessiah.com (www.failedmessiah.type-pad.com/failed_messiahcom/).
10. Published in M. Cohen, *Mi-Pi ha-Am* (From folk tradition), 3:62 no. 261.
11. Published in Murik, *Yiddishe Hochme* (Yiddish wisdom), 83.
12. Published in Koen-Sarano, *Kuentos del folklor de la famiya Djudeo-Espanyola,* 266.
13. For Arabic versions, see Schmidt and Kahle, *Volkserzählungen aus Palästina;* and Barash, *Arabic Folk Tales,* 82.
14. Izbits, *Der lustiger hoyz-fraynd* (The delightful family friend), 60 no. 209.
15. See Einhorn, *Mishlei-'Am be-Yidish* (Yiddish folk proverbs), 66 no. 278; C. Bloch, *Das jüdische Volk in seiner Anekdote,* 230; Druyanow, *Sefer ha-Bediḥah ve-ha-Ḥidud* (The book of jokes and witticisms), 2:171 no. 1430; Rawnitzki, *Yidishe Witzn* (Jewish Wit), 1:36 no. 67; and Schwarzbaum, *Studies in Jewish and World Folklore,* 341.
16. Fram, "Perception and Reception of Repentant Apostates in Medieval Ashkenaz and Premodern Poland."
17. Published in D. Noy, *Jewish Folktales from Morocco,* 118–119 no. 64.
18. Published in Weinstein, op. cit., 49–51 no. 10.
19. Published in Koen-Sarano, *Konsejas i Konsejikas del mundo djudeo-espanyol,* 266–269, (*Purim sheni*); see also Schwarzbaum, op. cit., 341–342, and tale IFA 15346 (vol. 1, no. 4).
20. Published in M. Cohen, op. cit., 2:61 no. 168.

Holocaust Tales

19

The Fireflies on Rosh Hashanah Night in Lodz Ghetto

TOLD BY ḤAYYIM DOV ARMON (KASTENBAUM)

During the Holocaust, the Nazis would not allow the Jews in the Lodz Ghetto to light candles. First of all, to make the Jews miserable, and, second, out of fear of aerial bombardment.

In a narrow room in the Lodz Ghetto, several dozen men gathered for services on the first night of Rosh Hashanah 5704 (September 1943). Every heart was crying out: May the old year and its curses be ended, and may a new year and its blessing begin. But the Gestapo and the *Judenrat* (the Jewish "self-governing" council in the ghetto) had issued a harsh decree: Not even the smallest candle could be lit. So the Jews who were shut up tightly in the dark and bitter ghetto had to pray in the dark on that first night of the New Year. But as soon as the *ḥazzan*[*] began the traditional melody of the invocation at the start of *Ma'ariv*—"Blessed be the Blessed Name"—tens of thousands of fireflies flew in through the open windows and illuminated Reb[**] Melekh Roitbart's narrow rooms on Dworska Street. At first, the worshipers did not understand what was going on. Soon, however, they realized that they were witnessing a miracle: The fireflies were emissaries of the Holy One, Blessed Be He, come to light up the holy festival. Of course, the Jewish police and the Gestapo perceived at once that the Jews had evidently violated the order and lit candles before praying. A whole company of SS men, accompanied by Jewish police, arrived, shouting at the top of their voices. "Jews, put out the light, or we'll shoot!"

And then came the second miracle: The fireflies landed on the uniforms of the SS men, their vehicles, and their vicious faces.

Only then did the SS men understand that something extraordinary was taking place here. How could there be such a large swarm of fireflies

---
[*]Cantor.
[**]Rabbi or Mr.

at this time of year? wondered Friedrich Schulze, the head of the SS detachment. He swore that this must be the start of the bitter end. Suddenly the God of the Jews, Who had been making Himself as if blind and deaf, was working wonders and miracles for His chosen people. Schulze gave the order to withdraw and allowed the Jews to complete the service.

Rabbi Mordechai, one of the survivors of the Lodz community, reported that the miracle of the fireflies on the first night of Rosh Hashanah brought light to the hearts of the few who had been spared from the murderous *Aktionen*.* He also said that in his opinion they were not fireflies at all. There was an old carter named Reb Yoel who lived in the Lodz Ghetto; everyone was certain that he was a *lamed-vav tzadikim,* one of the thirty-six hidden righteous men by whose merit the world exists, because he had survived all the dangers and *Aktionen*. He trudged from house to house, helping, rescuing, encouraging, comforting, and instilling hope. He was the source of the great light that eyes of flesh and blood perceived as a swarm of fireflies.

May it be God's will that the light of the hidden righteous man Reb Yoel shine for us as well. May we merit a year of light and joy, of radiance and never-ending happiness for our people in the State of Israel and wherever Jews may be.

---

*Nazi roundups of Jews to be deported.

Commentary for Tale 19 (IFA 2361)

Recorded by Ḥayyim Dov Armon (Kastenbaum) from memory.

Cultural, Historical, and Literary Background

The narrator, an observant Jew, apparently heard the story from a survivor of the Lodz Ghetto and was not recalling a personal experience that he had cast in legendary terms. For example, the dating of the event in the tale is problematic. The narrator wrote down this story from memory and conflated the Jewish and Gregorian calendars; in fact, there is a gap of three to four months between them. The Jewish year of 5704 began on September 30, 1943. By September 18, 1944, when Rosh Hashanah was again celebrated, the Nazis had completed the liquidation of the Lodz Ghetto.

Dobroszycki[1] collected and published the bulletins for the ghetto, and the last one is dated July 30, 1944. Dobroszycki added the following note:

> *The Daily Chronicle Bulletin* for Sunday, July 30, 1944, which is given in its entirety here, is the last *Chronicle* entry to have been preserved and was almost likely, in fact, the final entry. On the next day, Monday, it was already known that the fate of the Lodz ghetto had been sealed. The final *Daily Chronicle Bulletin*, that of July 30, 1944, listed 68,561 inhabitants in the ghetto of Lodz. They were deported to Auschwitz-Birkenau, with the exception of about 700 people[2] whom the Gettoverwaltung selected to clean the ghetto after the deportation and some 200 who successfully avoided the deportation action by hiding, as well as about 500 men and women[3] sent to Sachsenhausen-Oranienburg and Ravensbrück. The Jewish community of Lodz was brought to an end.

Unless the original narrator of the story was among the cleaning crews who stayed behind, the historical basis of the legend is minimal. Yet, the practice of holding services in private homes and small shuls was common. According to a formal registration, there were about 130 *minyanim* holding services in private homes. The three major synagogues in Lodz—the Old Town Synagogue, the Temple, and the Vilker shul, on Wolborska, Kosciuszko, and Zachadenie Streets, respectively—were burned, the first two in 1939, and the third in 1940.[4]

During September 1943, a relative calm prevailed in the ghetto. The Germans apparently did not forbid the making and selling of candles, and several thousand families used to light candles on Sabbath eve and major holidays. The following item from the October 11, 1943, edition of the *Daily Chronicle Bulletin* is particularly poignant:

> The eve of Yom Kippur, 1943, was a Friday, that is, a Sabbath eve. Young boys stood in the doorways, at the gates, and in the courtyard entrances, hawking *"Lekht! Lekht!"* [Yiddish for "candles"]. These are short, thin,

homemade tallow candles, which are used for the Sabbath. This time they served a double function: to usher in both the Sabbath and Yom Kippur. They were lit at twilight, their modest glow lighting rooms, the tender little stalks visible behind thin curtains.[5]

Additional studies and documents of the Lodz Ghetto are available.[6] The Jewish council, or the *Judenrat,* mentioned in the tale, was headed in Lodz by Chaim Mordecai Rumkowski (1877–1944). This council had a decisive role in ghetto life. A general study of the *Judenrat* has been conducted.[7]

The individuals mentioned in this tale can be only partially verified. A person by the name of Rotbard Majlech is listed as a carpenter living on Lotnicza Street; a German by the name of Friedrich Schultz does not appear to be associated with the ghetto.[8]

Legendary narratives about miracles during the Holocaust have been published.[9] The narrator of the present tale draws on the universal idea of light versus dark as the symbol of the fight between good and evil. This is a prevailing thought in Jewish culture and is manifest particularly in the Hanukkah festival. For information about the tradition of the thirty-six hidden righteous men, see the notes to tale IFA 10085 (vol. 1, no. 48).[10]

Folklore Motifs

- F574 "Luminous person."
- F900 "Extraordinary occurrences."
- F969.3 "Marvelous light."
- *V229.15.1 "Thirty-six incognito saints preserve the integrity of the world."

―――― **Notes** ――――

1. *The Chronicle of the Lodz Ghetto 1941–1944,* 535. First published in D. Noy, "Ba'alei Nissim be-Sippureinu ha-Amamiim" (Miracle workers in our folktales), 84–85.

2. In the Hebrew edition it is 870.

3. In the Hebrew edition it is 700.

4. Adelson, and Lapides, *Lodz Ghetto,* 69–71. Trunk lists other synagogues in which Jews prayed (*Ghetto Lodz,* 402–412).

5. Dobroszycki, op. cit., 395.

6. Adelson, *The Diary of Dawid Sierakowiak;* Unger, *The Last Ghetto;* Unger, "The Internal Life in the Lodz Ghetto 1940–1944"; Unger, "Religion and Religious Institutions in the Lodz Ghetto."

7. Trunk, *Judenrat.*

8. I thank Michal Unger for this information.

9. For example, see Eliach, *Hasidic Tales of the Holocaust;* and J. Mintz, *Legends of the Hasidim,* 356–380.

10. I would like to thank Michal Unger for her help in preparing the notes for this tale.

20

The Miracle of the White Doves

Told by Itzḥak-Isidore Feierstein
to Abraham Keren

*N*othing moved in the streets of Mielnice. The only sound in the town was the howling of the dogs, as if they wanted to signal the impending catastrophe.

The inhabitants of Mielnice knew that that night, November 9, 1941, Hitler's Germany was getting ready to celebrate its great holiday, the holiday of its victory.

The townspeople had heard alarming reports that something would happen. Doors and gates were slammed shut. Darkness ruled every house, like a living grave.

Suddenly, the deadly quiet was shattered by a gunshot, issuing from near the barracks. Every heart froze in panic. Soon they heard the noise of doors being forced open, followed by the piercing cries of women and children. They were all driven to the square in front of the *beit midrash.**

A Jew with a pot on his head pulled down over his eyes like the brim of his hat, so he would not be able to see, was accompanied by the wild laughter of Germans.

A crowd of Jewish children had been forcibly assembled outside the *beit midrash*. Girls had been forced to dance naked on the tables. All was a hell of rapes, until the Heavens and *beit midrash* walls echoed with the screams. The locked *beit midrash* was pried open and all the holy books were tossed onto a heap by the window. A Torah scroll was dragged out of the Holy Ark and the holy parchment was spread on the street.

The assassins ordered the Jews to kneel and await their fate.

The "show" began with the Germans in their muddy boots strutting back and forth on the parchment and calling out, "Where is the Jews' God?" They accompanied their shouts with howls of laughter.

Then the Germans led out the Jew with the pot on his head and, accompanied by shrieks of amusement from the Germans and Ukrainians,

---
*Religious school.

led him over to the Torah parchment.

They also took two Jews and ordered them to say, within five minutes, whether there is a God. They stood the two next to the wall and told them that all the Jews would be shot if they answered incorrectly.

A shot rang out. A bullet had pierced the skull of the unfortunate Jew in the pot. He collapsed, his blood soaking the Torah scroll.

The murderers sang the Horst Wessel song with wild abandon. "Where is the Jews' God?" they called out in triumph.

Next they hurled a gasoline-soaked rag through the window of the *beit midrash* onto the pile of books. Heavy black smoke poured from the windows. The fumes choked everyone; even the laughing Germans coughed hard.

Then a miracle happened! The books and the *beit midrash* failed to catch fire and were not burned! Suddenly the *beit midrash* was surrounded by a flock of white doves, hovering in the air and beating their wings. The sight and noise stunned the onlookers into silence.

The Germans' frenzy that the *beit midrash* was not burning was accompanied by the noise of the fluttering white doves and the reek of the smoke. Bewildered, the local people panicked and began running away. Still kneeling, the Jews called out: "Angels! Angels!"

In the commotion, the Germans lost their confidence and courage.

"Yes, there is a God, a jealous and vengeful God," one of the Jews replied.

One of the Germans, pale, had to admit that, "Yes, the answer is correct." He slapped the Jew in the face and said, "The Jews wanted a war and they got a war."

The white doves kept flying noisily around the *beit midrash*, as if they wanted to protect the Jews and shield the holy place.

The commander of the murderers ordered the detail to march away and sent the Jews back to their homes. Quiet returned to the town.

After the war, the five Torah scrolls that had not been burned, half-covered with soot, were taken from Mielnice to Bytom (in Silesia). But the miracle of the white doves was not repeated for the 1,470 Jews, who were later transported from the ghetto to Belzec.

COMMENTARY FOR TALE 20 (IFA 11165)

Told in Yiddish by Itzhak-Isidore Feierstein to Abraham Keren in 1977.

Cultural, Historical, and Literary Background
The Town of Mielnice

Mielnice is a small town in Ukraine, on the bank of the Dniester River in the province of Tarnopol (Ternopol). Jews settled there in 1767, when Mielnice changed its status from a village to a township, with a weekly market day and an annual fair. During the nineteenth century, the general and Jewish population increased substantially and then decreased because of migration to urban centers and overseas. At the beginning of the 1930s, the Jews made up about 42 percent of the town's population of approximately 4,000 people. In 1935 a large fire broke out in Mielnice, and it is quite possible that its recollection resonates in the present tale.

At the break of World War II, the Red Army entered the town, and the Soviets confiscated Jewish businesses, closed Jewish community institutions, and arrested several Jewish leaders. When the Russian army retreated after the beginning of "Operation Barbarosa" on June 22, 1941, local nationalist Ukrainians attacked and killed many Jews. The Hungarian troops that entered the town on July 7, 1941, put an end to the riots against the Jews; but after two weeks of relative calm, they forced the Jews to provide their men with food and labor. The condition of the Jewish population in Mielnice worsened considerably when the Germans took control of the town in August 1941.[1]

German History

The narrator dates the beginning of the events that unfold in this tale to November 9, 1941. In modern German history, November 9 has become a memorable date, on which several critical events occurred: the start of the German revolution in Berlin that ended the German Empire and was the first phase in the formation of the German Republic (1918),[2] Hitler's Munich Beer Hall Putsch (1923),[3] Crystal Night (1938),[4] and the beginning of the fall of the Berlin Wall (1989).[5] The second and third of these events are directly relevant to the present story, and the first is important in so far that it was the origin of the cycle of political upheavals that culminated in World War II.

Each year that he was in power, "Hitler returned to Munich to lead the raucous co-conspirators who had been with him on November 8 and 9, 1923, in a reenactment, there to honor the dead rebels who had been interred in a nearby temple of honor."[6] The reenactment in 1939 nearly ended in Hitler's assassination,[7] and his escape could have been another cause of ominous celebration.

Whatever the basis, at that time there was no shortage of excuses for the Germans to engage in celebrations and reasons for the Jews to fear them.

However, according to the documents summarized in *Pinkas Hakehillot* the murderous attack on Jewish homes occurred in December 1941, though the arrest and shipment of young men to work camps had begun the month before. The last action of deportation to extermination camps took place in Mielnice in September 25–26, 1942.[9] Before their deportation, the Jews hid a few Torah scrolls under the floor of the great synagogue, and other scrolls were taken to the neighboring town of Borszczow.[10]

The Horst Wessel Song

The narrator of the present story mentioned that the Germans sung the "Horst Wessel song." This song—originally titled "*Die Fahne hoch*" (The flag high), from its opening phrase—became the second part of the national anthem during the Third Reich. It was composed by the storm trooper Horst Wessel, probably in March 1929 and was first published on September 23, 1929, as "*Der Unbekannte SA-Mann.*"

Horst Wessel was born on October 9, 1907, in Bielefeld and joined the Bismarckjugend in 1922 and the Nationalsozailistische Deutsche Arbeiterpartei (NSDAP) on December 7, 1926. He was a very popular and successful leader in this organization. In the course of his recruitment rounds in bars and cafes, he met an eighteen-year-old prostitute, Erna Jänicke, with whom he developed a close friendship; by October 1929 the two were sharing an apartment. On January 14, 1930, a communist, who was also quite likely a pimp, shot him in this apartment, and Wessel died on February 23, 1930. Because of his high profile in the Berlin SA (*Sturmabteilung*), Goebbels made efforts to elevate Wessel to the status of a martyr and his song to be the second part of the national anthem.

Die Fahne hoch!

I

Die Fahne hoch! Die Reihen fest geschlossen!	The flag high, the ranks tightly closed.
SA marschiert mit mustig-festem Schritt Kameraden, die Rotfront und Reaktion erschossen Marschieren im Geist in unseren Reihen mit.	SA marches pluckily at a firm pace. Comrades, shot dead by Red Front and Reaction March in spirit with us in our ranks.

II

Die Strasse frei den braunen Bataillonen	The street clear for the brown Battalions,
Die Strasse frei dem Sturmabteilungsmann! Es schaun	The street clear for the SA man. Already millions are looking to the

aufs Hakenkreuz voll Hoffnung Schon Millionen	swastika full of hope,
Der Tag für Freiheit und für Brot bricht an!	The day of freedom and bread is dawning.

III

Zum letzten Mal wird nun Appell geblasen!	For the last time the roll-call is sounded,
Zum kampfe stehen wir alle schon bereit!	We are all ready for the fight.
Bald dlattern Hitlerfahnen über Barrikaden	Soon Hitler flags will fly over Barricades;
Die Kneechtschaft dauert nur noch kurze Zeit!	The servitude has only a short time to last.

IV

Die Fahne hoch! Die Reihen fest geschlossen!	The flag high, the ranks tightly closed.
SA marschiert mit mustig-festem Schritt	SA marches pluckily at a firm pace.
Kameraden, die Rotfront und Reaktion erschossen	Comrades, shot dead by Red Front and Reaction
Marschieren im Geist in unseren mit.	March in spirit with us in our *Reihen* ranks.[11]

A detailed biography of Wessel, a study of his song and its variations, and a bibliography of its publication and studies are available.[12]

The White Doves

The miracle of the white doves, the central episode in the present story, draws on Christian rather than Jewish symbolism. In Jewish tradition, the significance of the dove builds on its biblical actions and metaphors. Its role in the Flood myth made the dove a symbol of reconciliation and the receding of God's wrath (Genesis 8:8–12). Ritualistically, doves or pigeons were accepted as an atonement sacrifice (Leviticus 5:7,11, 12:8, 14:22, 15:14,29; Numbers 6:10). Poetically, the dove has been a metaphor for innocence (Songs of Songs 2:14, 5:2, 6:9) and a simile for eyes (Songs of Songs 1:15, 4:1, 5:12). In the talmudic-midrashic period, the dove was a symbol for the Jewish community (BT *Berakhot* 53b; *Shabbat* 130a; *Gittin* 45a; MR *Song of Songs* 1:63).[13]

In Christianity, on the other hand, the dove has emerged as a central symbol in religious art and belief, representing the Holy Spirit itself in its divine protective capacity. The Holy Spirit was seen descending at the baptism of Jesus "in a bodily shape like a dove upon him, and a voice came from heaven, which said, Thou art my beloved Son" (Luke 3:22).[14] A pre-war tale about the fire-fighting doves is available.[15]

The Fate of the Torah Scroll and the People of Mielnice

The narrator concluded the story by mentioning the fate of the Torah scrolls and the Jews of Mielnice. According to the story, the scrolls were taken to Silesia in western Poland rather than to the nearby town of Borszczow, as other accounts suggest. According to the present tale, 1,470 of the Jews of Mielnice were taken to the extermination camp of Belzec. Other sources set the number of deported Jews at 1,200, 1,400, and 2,000.[16]

The construction of the extermination camp of Belzec, a small town in the southeast of the Lublin district, began on November 1, 1941. By March 1942, it was ready to absorb its first transport and to kill Jews in gas chambers. During the nine months of its operation (March to December 1942), 600,000 Jews were killed there. "From January to July 1943 the center was liquidated and evidence of the crime was destroyed; all the corpses were taken from the mass graves and burned, the buildings were removed and the grounds were planted."[17]

Kurt Gerstein (1905–1945), who joined the Nazi party to witness and report about the extermination of the mentally ill, the Jews, and other nationalities, tried to send reports to the Allies about the extermination camp in Belzec.[18] Unfortunately, no one believed him.

Folktale Type

- *730B (IFA) "Jewish Community Miraculously Saved from Mob's Attack."

Folklore Motifs

- A165.2.2 "Birds as messengers of gods."
- B450 "Helpful birds."
- B457.1 "Helpful dove."
- D1812.5.1.12.1 "Howling of dog as bad omen."
- D1841.3.3 "Sacred book or manuscript does not burn in fire."
- F883.1 "Extraordinary book."
- F883.1.4 "Books unscathed by water and fire."
- F900 "Extraordinary occurrences."
- F964 "Extraordinary behavior of fire."
- cf F979.5.1 "Unconsumed burning bush."
- cf. F989.14 "Birds hover over battlefield."
- F989.16 "Extraordinary swarms of birds."
- R122 "Miraculous rescue."
- R168 "Angels as rescuers."
- S110 "Murders."

- T471 "Rape."
- V112.3 "Synagogue."
- *V112.3.1 "Miracles at synagogue."
- *V151.2 "Sacred writings: the Torah."
- *V151.2.1 "Desecration of the Torah."
- V230 "Angel."
- V231.1 "Angel in bird shape."
- cf. V232.1 "Angel as helper in battle."
- V340 "Miracles manifested to non-believers."
- V350 "Conflicts between religions."
- Z142."Symbolic color: white."

――――― **Notes** ―――――

1. *Pinkas Hakehillot,* 320–322.

2. E. Bernstein, *Die deutsche Revolution von 1918/1919;* and H. Friedlander, *The German Revolution of 1918.*

3. Dorenberg, *Munich 1923;* H. Gordon, *Hitler and the Beer Hall Putsch;* and Hanser, *Putsch!*

4. Thalmann and Feinermann, *Crystal Night;* and J. Mendelsohn, *The Holocaust.*

5. See H.-J. Koch, *Der 9. November in der deutschen Geschichte 1918–1923–1938–1989.*

6. Dorenberg, op. cit., 339.

7. Duffy and Ricci, *Target Hitler,* 25–34.

8. At 321.

9. *Pinkas Hakehilot,* 322; and Arad, *Belzec, Sobibor, Treblinka,* 384.

10. *Pinkas Hakehilot.*

11. Broderick, "*Das Horst-Wessel-Lied.*"

12. Broderick, op. cit.; and K. Mann, "Die Mythen der Unterwelt."

13. See also Ginzberg, *The Legends of the Jews,* 4:108; 6:268 n. 110.

14. Sühling, *Die Taube als Religiöses Symbol im Christlichen Altertum.*

15. Cahan, *Jewish Folklore,* 149 no. 25; English translation in B. S. Weinreich, *Yiddish Folktales,* 346 no. 163.

16. *Pinkas Hakehillot,* 322; and Arad, op. cit., 384.

17. Reder, *Belzec,* 81; Arad, op. cit., 23–29; and Arad, " '*Mivtsa Reinhard*' " (Operation Reinhard).

18. Friedländer, *Kurt Gerstein,* 87–121; Schäfer, *Kurt Gerstein—Zeuge des Holocaust;* and Hey et al., *Kurt Gerstein (1905–1945).*

Historical Tales

21

The Exodus on Purim in the Town of Yampol

Told by Mrs. Hayyim Leizer Bezditnichke to
Shalva Polshtinski

In our town, like all towns, there is a street where the gentiles live. We used to call it "dog street," but "wolf street" would have been more appropriate because they were such murderers that the wicked Haman was a poodle by comparison.... And just to provoke us, it seemed, their church was smack in the center of town, so every Sunday, whether you liked it or not, you couldn't help bumping into drunken, bloody, murderous assassins, and it was no treat having to be afraid of them. You know, of course, that when you chop wood, the chips fly; when they used to beat their heads against the wall, chips flew into Jewish windows—and not everyone has shutters. You don't have to ask how terrified we were. And who do you think was responsible? Their scoundrel of a priest (may his name be blotted out!), who had such an end—it should only have happened to his late ancestors.

Every Purim the priest used to rage as only a gentile could. He had taken Haman's grievance as his own, because Haman had been killed on account of Mordechai. He could not forgive this. There always seem to be Hamans assailing the world, and the Haman who came to our town was bad enough to be a punishment for every Jew in the whole world. That Esau raged, especially at Purim, and he decided that was the time to take revenge against the Jews. He stirred up all the gentiles, even though they used to look forward to Purim, when the Jews would treat them to hamantashen* and other pastries. The priest persuaded them that the hamantashen were poisoned. The Jews wanted to poison all the gentiles. You would never believe that such a pogrom could take place today.

In our town, there were all sorts of Jews, respectable people—the rich,

---

*A triangular pastry filled with poppy seeds that is eaten during Purim.

21 / The Exodus on Purim

of course. There were *rebbes** and ritual slaughterers, humble people, artisans, and even—this should stay between us—thieves. But a Jewish thief is better than their priest. Confidentially, they say that their grandfathers, may they rest in peace—let me put it delicately—that a strange horse happened to get lost in their direction. . . . It's all a lie. In short, there was a fine young man in their family—if you didn't know him you would have taken him for a squire: tall, healthy, two highly polished boots, just like all the gentiles. The gentiles were a particular pain for him. His name was Isaac Ḥalomish, after his grandfather. But I can't tell you what Halomish means (spare us the evil eye). It's a Latin word. Still, whoever crowned him with the name knew what he was doing.

Isaac had a Jewish head but (spare us the evil eye) gentile strength. So the priest fell into the hands of Isaac Ḥalomish, whom he took for a non-Jew. He didn't pray, he dressed like a nobleman—but what a Jewish heart he had! Always ready for one Jew to overwhelm a hundred priests. He had a strong desire to give our priest a sound thrashing, so he devised a plot against him. What could he do, so no bird would know anything about it?

He thought about it, dressed up like a gentile, and took some cheap brandy around to the priest. They drank together and the priest took him for a rich villager. The Jew promised the priest a hefty payback, and he *certainly* didn't deceive him. When they were in the woods, Ḥalomish tossed the priest out of the sleigh. Then he poured a glass of brandy on him, pummeled him like a juicy apple, set a bottle of spirits near him, and left him lying there like a pig.

At daybreak, two gentiles were on their way to the city to sell eggs. When they saw the creature, they crossed themselves until they noticed the brandy. Then they forgot about everything and got good and drunk, the way they do. They gave each other such hearty slaps that they broke the eggs. Embraced by troubles, they started singing. And then a shepherd came across this holy trinity, all of them dead drunk.

The authorities arrived and arrested them. We all relished the effort it cost the priest to wipe away the stain. Things became very quiet, because the cleric could not get rid of the disgrace and fear.

The scoundrel understood that Isaac Ḥalomish blessing on his deeds—had played a part in the affair. Soon he would see him in the other world. The way he slaughtered gentiles, he was just like Samson. The scoundrel kept his eye on him. In fact, the priest was doomed—he might

---

*Rabbis.

as well have been six feet under already. He would have such an end as should only have happened to his late ancestors. But he had not lost his hope that one Purim he would have his revenge on the Jews, and he waited impatiently for it to happen.

When there are pogroms against the Jews, there is no mercy in the verdict. One town after another was destroyed, and Heaven and earth cried out.

There had not been such a cold spell as long as Yampol had existed. Our river never freezes over; but that winter, it was like an iron floor. Were it not for Reb* Sanderl the water carrier, the common folk would have had nothing to drink. But he, Sanderl the water carrier, risked his life, chopping wood and carrying water for the common folk without taking a penny for his efforts. He was indeed a righteous man. As we shall see, it was by his merit that many towns were saved from the pogromists.

During one of the most terrible frosts, there was no living soul to be seen outside in the street, except for Sanderl with his water barrel. A gentile came by with a pail. "*Zhidek!*" he said. "Sell me a bucket of water, because my children are begging for something to drink."

"I don't sell water," replied Sanderl.

As the gentile turned to trudge home, Sanderl filled his bucket with water. "Where do you get your water?" the gentile asked him, shivering.

"It isn't my water," Sanderl answered. "The owner of the water and of everything else is in Heaven. You must pay Him for it."

Some time later, when people heard that the mobs were approaching our town, the priest was very merry. From minute to minute, the Jews turned blacker with fear. Isaac Halomish assembled the young people to fight against the pogromists and promised he would kill the priest with his own hands.

One night, Sanderl had a dream. His grandfather came, gave him a kiss for his good heart (he had given water even to gentiles), and told him: "Today you will have a severe fright, but only a fright. The priest will summon you. You must all go, except for the little children and the frail women. Leave them at home. When the priest says something, all the Jews should cry out, *Shema Yisra'el*."**

Before dawn, Sanderl went to the *rebbe* and told him about his dream.

They both shed hot tears. "Reb Sanderl," the *rebbe* told him, "we will be saved by your merit. Tell me, what should we do?"

---

*Rabbi or Mr.
**Literally, "Hear, O, Israel," the first words of the *Shema*, the most sacred Jewish prayer.

21 / *The Exodus on Purim*

Reb Sanderl asked the *rebbe* to decree a one-day fast, so that his grandfather's dream would come true. In the meantime, the gentile Ivan ran in, threw himself on his knees, and said that the priest had called all the peasants together and told them to get ready with axes, shovels, clubs, stones, all the malice in their hearts. The mob would arrive on Purim itself. They were all to stand on the river. The priest and the Jews would be standing next to the river. "But the priest will deceive you. He'll promise to help you. But you must not trust him, because he has shown us the ax he has prepared for Isaac. He'll kill him personally. He told us that if any of you hides, even one Jew, he'll cut off his limbs, one every day. Now, sir *rebbe*, how can I help you?"

The gentile did not want to leave, but the *rebbe* asked him to spread the news. The gentile did whatever he could to help the Jews.

When the day came, all the Jews assembled. The *rebbe* told them the whole story and proclaimed a fast for the day. Isaac Ḥalomish, who had never fasted in his life, was the first to speak up. "Rebbe, whatever you decree, I will do." And so it was.

As soon as the fast was over, the priest showed up and made a speech about how he was the Jews' best friend and hoped he would be able to save them from the gang that was already standing on the river. "And we, along with you Jews, must take all our children with costly gifts, and I hope that you will be saved."

The Jews thanked him and wished that he might himself experience what he wanted to see happen to the Jews. They did as had been instructed in Sanderl's dream: The women and children stayed home. A brilliant sun glistened on the ice. Standing on the river, the murderers were getting drunk and making merry. When they noticed the Jews they went simply berserk with joy. The priest stood in front of the Jews, took off his hat, bowed, and shouted: "Kill the *zhids*."* The Jews, for their part, cried out, "*Shema Yisra'el*."

Suddenly, there was a burst of lightning, followed by thunder. It splintered the frozen river, with all the murderers standing on it, into tiny fragments. Soon they were all buried under the ice as if they had never been there.

Isaac Ḥalomish gave the priest a fine how-do-you-do on his head, leaving him frozen on the spot like a statue. To this day no one knows what

---

*An English transcription of the Polish *"żyd"* (Jew); the translator used the English plural, *"zhids."* In Polish, the plural form in this sentence would have been *"żydow."* Although many Jews think this is a derogatory term, it in fact is not.

happened to him. In any case, no one could drag him away. He cast a pall of dread on all the remaining murderers, who scattered to all the winds and warned their children and their children's children to beware of that river, where Moses watched over his Jews. As a result, all the nearby towns were saved from the gangs and the local gentiles were terrified of the Jews.

Even when Hitler came, the gentiles told him that Moses was in the river and would send the plagues of Egypt against anyone who harmed or even touched the Jews. *Nu,* that's what they say—should we say otherwise? A miracle like that, which we saw with our eyes, isn't it like the exodus from Egypt and the splitting of the Red Sea?

This story was told by Mrs. Ḥayyim Leizer Bezdinichke, who swore by her one and only son, the apple of her eye, who was also born by a miracle, thanks to Marika the witch—about whom she told separately.

21 / The Exodus on Purim

COMMENTARY FOR TALE 21 (IFA 3892)

Told in Yiddish by the wife of Ḥayyim Leizer Bezdinichke from Berdichev, Ukraine, during an air raid on Odessa during World War II. Shalva Polshtinski, who heard the story at that time, wrote it down from memory in 1962 in Tel Aviv.

Cultural, Historical, and Literary Background

Ms. Polshtinski wrote this tale down from memory. She first heard it while sitting in an air-raid shelter in Odessa during World War II. At that time, people told stories to calm themselves down. The present tale conveyed a message of encouragement and hope about the miraculous rescue of a Jewish community, raising the spirits of the group. Because she wrote down the story about twenty years after hearing it, the recorder could not faithfully represent the oral narrative style. Nevertheless, she attempted to approximate the "narratives of spontaneous conversational storytelling" and hence created a relatively "natural" discourse.[1] To achieve this effect, Ms. Polshtinski sprinkled the tale with proverbs and proverbial phrases such as "When you chop wood, the chips fly (*as men hakt holz fallen schpener*)[2] and "A Jewish thief is better than their priest" (*a yiddisher ganef iz besser vi zeier galekh*), which structurally follows the pattern of Yiddish proverbs.[3] She also alluded to a biblical verse—"For a bird of the air may carry the utterance" (Ecclesiastes 10:20)—and included invocations against the evil eye, which are distinctive of Yiddish oral discourse, particularly of women's speech. For studies of the concept of the evil eye, see the commentary to tale IFA 10085 (vol. 1, no. 48).

The narrator told the story as if it were a historical account of events in her own shtetl, referring to the specific personalities but omitting any particular dates. There are several small towns in Ukraine named Yampol (or Yampil). She specifically mentioned Yampol in the Vinnitsa district, near the border of Moldovia, about 180 miles southwest of Kiev. Her reference point was the train station at Zhmerynka, which was the largest railway junction in the region, approximately 55 miles north of Yampol. Jewish settlement in this town probably began in the late seventeenth century, likely after the pogroms of 1648–1649, during the Cossack rebellion against the Polish rulers headed by Bogdan Khmelnytsky[4] (1595–1657). Several bloody conflicts between the Jews and the Ukrainians likely happened, but their documentation is sparse. In recent history, the Jews of Yampol were the target of attacks on November 6, 1917, and December 19, 1919, during the waves of pogroms that swept through Ukraine during and after World War I and the Bolshevik revolution.[5] Twenty years later, these events became part of the town's collective memory and might have been at the historical core of the story.

Available studies do not mention the acts of a townsman named Isaac Ḥalamish (Ḥalomish in Yiddish) as either a trigger for or a leader of Jewish self-defense. The name is Hebrew for "flint." Although neither the narrator nor the recorder recognized the term, in modern Hebrew the word has become a symbol of strength, resonating its biblical use (Deuteronomy 8:15, 32:13; Isaiah 50:7; Job 28:9).

The tale's narrator or recorder synthesized the modern movement of self-defense with traditional notions of divine protective intervention. The trend toward Jewish self-defense first became apparent in Ukraine during the 1903–1906 riots.[6] Memoirs, studies, and documents concerning the Ukrainian pogroms of 1919–1920 are available.[7]

Divine Protection

The traditional aspects of divine protective intervention are manifest in this story in two forms: (1) through repeated allusions to biblical models of community or national rescue and (2) by representation of postbiblical examples of the rescue of a Jewish community.

The repeated allusion to the story of the Book of Esther and its two antagonists—the royal minister Haman and the Jewish Mordecai—is an example of modeling current reality in terms of archetypical biblical narratives (form 1). This narrative allusion draws not only on the biblical account itself but also on everyday Yiddish speech patterns. The idiom "*a goy, a Haman*" ([every] gentile [is] a Haman) was commonly heard in Yiddish-speaking *shtetls*.[8]

Furthermore, the very climatic scene of divine retribution is the inversion of the story told in Exodus 14: In the Bible, the Israelites went through the sea as if it were land; in the present tale, the gangs attacking the Jewish community initially moved on the ice as if it were land, but then, as punishment for their acts and as magical protection of the Jewish community, they fell through the breaking ice. Their sinking recalls another biblical divine retribution of an oppositional group within the Israelite community: the story of Korah and his followers (Numbers 16).

Postbiblical and oral narratives about divine protection of a Jewish community (form 2) are designated as tale type *730B (IFA) "Jewish Community Miraculously Saved from Mob's Attack." Analyses of this and related tale types have been conducted.[9] Within this general classification, it is possible to distinguish two patterns: (1) the direct destruction of the enemy through divine intervention and (2) the indirect defeat through magic.

Pattern 1 has its antecedent in the biblical account of the wars against the Southern Kingdom. When King Sennacherib of Assyria besieged Jerusalem "an angel of the Lord went out and struck down one hundred and eighty-five thousand in the Assyrian camp, and the following morning they were all dead corpses" (2 Kings 19:35).[10] The talmudic-midrashic narratives of communal and national history are steeped in tragedy, which legendary narratives could not redeem. Hence, although miracles abound in the literature of this period, none involves a miraculous community rescue.

After a long period in which such tales were absent, Jews began to retell stories about the rescue of communities from the sixteenth century onward. Examples of tales and studies about "second Purims" are given in the notes to tale IFA 15348 (vol. 1, no. 5).[11]

Pattern 2 involves some sort of magic or miracle. For example, the enemy may perceive a protective wall of fire surrounding a community or a holy man may have immunity against bullets. The enemy flees upon seeing such magical sights (compare motifs D1840 "Magic invulnerability," D1840.1 "Magic invulnerability of saints," and V228 "Immunities of saints [holy men]").

Similarities to Other IFA Tales

Related tales in the IFA are the following:

- IFA 2213: *Mori David Ḥautar Protects the Jewish Quarter* (Yemen); pattern 2.
- IFA 3699: *The Miracle of the Rabbi Simeon Bar Yoḥai's Menorah* (Jerba); pattern 2.[12]
- IFA 3794: *Danger during the Prayer of Eighteen Benedictions* (Ukraine); pattern 2.
- IFA 3837: *The Hateful King and Elijah the Prophet* (Bulgaria); pattern 2.
- IFA 5052: *Elijah the Prophet Protects the Jews* (Poland); patterns 1 and 2.
- IFA 5724: *The Verses of Psalms Are Protection from Gun and Cannon Shots* (Morocco); pattern 2.[13]
- IFA 7460: *The Bow of Rabbi Mordecai ben Attar* (Morocco); pattern 2.
- IFA 7990: *Simeon Berakhah's Lion Roar* (Libya); pattern 2.
- IFA 8101: *Ezra the Scribe's Bloody Sword Protects the Jews* (Iraqi Kurdistan); pattern 2.
- IFA 9152: *Rabbi Meir Ba'al ha-Nes' Tomb Protects the Jew of Tiberia* (Eretz Yisra'el, Sephardic); pattern 2.
- IFA 9155: *How Were the Jews of Tiberia Saved?* (Eretz Yisra'el, Ashkenazic); pattern 2.
- IFA 9414: *A Fire Wall Saved the Jews on Passover Night* (Yemen); pattern 2.
- IFA 9844: *They Wished to Destroy the Jews but Ended up Destroying Their Own Ovens* (Yemen); pattern 2.
- IFA 10882: *The Yemenite Diaspora* (Yemen); pattern 2.
- IFA 10905: *Abu Ibrahim's Tomb* (Druze); pattern 2.
- IFA 13633: *Rabbi Aharon the High Priest Protects the Jews* (Morocco); pattern 2.[14]
- IFA 13918 (vol. 5, no. 61): *The Thwarting of the Riots on the Eve of Shavuot* (Iraqi Kurdistan); pattern 2.
- IFA 13921: *The Rescue of the Erbil Jews during the Rashid Ali Riots* (Iraqi Kurdistan); pattern 2.
- IFA 13928: *The Rescue from a Pogrom* (Iraqi Kurdistan); pattern 2.

Folktale Type

- *730B (IFA) "Jewish Community Miraculously Saved from Mob's Attack."

Folklore Motifs

- D1810.8.2 "Information received through dream."
- D2071 "Evil eye."
- F610 "Remarkably strong man."
- *F900.1.4 "Miracles during Purim."
- F932 "Extraordinary occurrences connected with rivers."
- G200 "Witch."
- K1816.9 "Disguise as peasant."
- *K1817.6 "A Jew disguises as a gentile."
- *P125 "Priest is left in the cold in revenge for his mistreatment of Jews."
- P412 "Shepherd."
- *P417 "Water-carrier."
- P426.1 "Parson (priest)."
- *P426.4 "Rabbi."
- P440 "Artisans."
- *P476 "Thief."
- P623 "Fasting (as means of distrait)."
- P715.1 "Jews."
- *P715.2 "A hater of Jews."
- *V75.5 "Purim."
- V365 "Jewish traditions concerning non-Jews."

——————— Notes ———————

1. For further analysis of this concept, see Fludernik, *Towards a "Natural" Narratology*.
2. This phrase is in I. Bernstein, *Jüdische Sprichwörter und Redensarten*, 73 no. 1075.
3. B. Weinreich, "Toward a Structural Analysis of Yiddish Proverbs."
4. Also spelled Chmielnicki or Khmelnitski.
5. Tcherikower, *The Pogroms in the Ukraine in 1919;* and Tcherikover, *Yehudim be'Itot Mahapekhah* (Jews in periods of revolution), 421–557.
6. Dinur, *Sefer Toldot ha-Haganah* (The history of defense forces), 1:154–175; J. Goren, *Testimonies of Victims*, 36–44; Halpern, *Sefer ha-Gevurah* (The book of heroism), esp. 2:47–108; Klier and Lambroza, *Pogroms,* 392 (index); Lambroza, "Jewish Self-Defense during the Russian Pogroms of 1903–1906"; Shazar, "Defenders of the City"; and Smoliar, " 'In Every Generation.' "
7. Carou and Slutsky, "Bloody Jubilee."
8. Cahan, *Der Yid* (The Jew), 25 no. 176.
9. E. Marcus, "The Confrontation between Jews and Non-Jews"; and D. Noy, "*Bein Yisrael le-'Amim be-Aggadot-Am Shel Yehudei Teiman*" (Conflicts between the Jews and other peoples in the legends of the Yemenite Jews).

10. For a controversial interpretation of this event, see Velikovsky, *Worlds in Collision*, 230–243.

11. See also Yassif, *The Hebrew Folktale*, 304–305.

12. Published in Baharav, *Sixty Folktales*, 102–103 no. 18; E. Marcus, *Jewish Festivities*, 122 no. 71; and Rush and Marcus, *Seventy and One Tales for the Jewish Year*, 226–228 no. 56.

13. Published in Baharav, *Mi-Dor le-Dor,* 95–96 no. 33.

14. Published in Lassri, *Bimḥitsat Ḥakhamim ve-Rabanim* (In the company of rabbis), 110–112.

22

What Really Caused World War I

TOLD BY ELIMELEKH FAYGENBOYM TO YIFRAḤ ḤAVIV

*T*he Holy One, Blessed Be He, is sitting in Heaven, surrounded by the heavenly host, discussing the affairs of the world.

The accusing angel appears and delivers an indictment: "The world is not good. Sinners, transgressors, as usual."

Counters the defender: "That's not true. That's not how it is. That's not how it is."

Their debate heats up.

One jumps up to oppose the accusing angel. "Have you been there?" he calls.

"No."

"Have you seen it with your own eyes?"

"No."

"If so, go down and see it with your own eyes."

"All right," says the accusing angel.

He puts on a *bekeshe* and a *kapote*[*] (which is how people dress in Galicia) and goes down to Berdichev, a famous Jewish town. It's winter, rain and wind and cold and darkness, very early in the morning.

The accusing angel turns round and round, looking for shelter. Then he sees, far away, a light twinkling. He goes there and opens the door, and sees Jews sitting and learning: one is studying *halakhah*,[**] another is reciting Psalms. It will soon be morning light, and one Jew goes up to the lectern to lead the morning service.

The accusing angel tells himself, "In matters between man and God, everything is in order. Those who wear a *tallit*[§] and have beards pray and observe the commandments. But what about relations among human beings?"

He went out and observed, during the course of the day, that those

---

[*]Both words refer to a long coat; a *bekeshe* is lined with fur.
[**]Jewish law.
[§]Prayer shawl.

same Jews who observed the ritual precepts were lying, cheating, stealing, committing fraud in their business, and committing every sin.

He went back to Heaven and said: "In matters between man and God all is in order, but among human beings, especially in business, they are incorrigible sinners."

"Do you know what?" they told him. "Those aren't the only Jews. There are also Jews in Germany. Go there."

"Where?" he asked.

"To Frankfurt, a famous Jewish city."

He went down there early in the morning and started looking for a shul—but he couldn't find one. He kept asking until he finally found someone who could answer him: "You're looking for a synagogue?"

"Yes."

"Come and I'll show you where it is."

He showed him a synagogue with a sign posted outside in German: "Prayers on the Sabbath, closed during the week."

The accusing angel decided to see how these Jews behaved in relations among human beings. What were the Jews engaged in? Commerce. He looked and saw that their word was their bond. They treated others fairly. There was no cheating and no lying in their business dealings.

He went back to Heaven and submitted his report: "In matters between man and God they are sinners! But in relations among human beings they are absolutely in order."

What does the Holy One, Blessed Be He, do?

"We have to mix the two groups together."

"How?"

"We make a war. The Jews of Galicia and Poland will go to Germany and the Jews of Germany will go to Galicia and Poland, and they will learn from one another."

World War I broke out. They met each other—and just the opposite happened: The Jews of Galicia and Poland stopped praying, and their relations with God went sour; while the Jews of Germany began to lie and cheat in their business dealings and became corrupt in relations among human beings.

COMMENTARY FOR TALE 22 (IFA 14026)

Told by Elimelekh Faygenboym from Kuznica, Poland (today Belarus) to Yifraḥ Ḥaviv in 1982 in Bet Keshet.

Cultural, Historical, and Literary Background

This tale is a humorous account of the cause of a historical event. It draws on the traditional image of God as a judge and on a two-centuries-old conflict between eastern and western European Jews, particularly those from Poland and Germany. Each group had a negative image of the other.

The causes of World War I lie in a complex system of alliances, diplomatic pacts, and economic and political tensions, which dominated European politics at the end of the nineteenth century and the beginning of the twentieth. The conflict had nothing to do with the position of Jews in Europe. Unlike World War II, Jews were neither an excuse for nor a target of the hostilities among European states, and Jews fought in the armies of both warring sides. Studies on the causes of World War I are available.[1]

In the present tale, however, the narrator conceives the origin of the war in terms of Jewish theology. World War I was part of the divine design, at the center of which is Jewish social-religious interests and well-being.

The image of God as a supreme and omnipotent judge has its roots in the Hebrew Bible. The verse "for He is a God who judges" (Psalm 50:6) succinctly conveys a dominant idea in Israelite and late Jewish religion and theology. The notion of a supreme judge permeates Jewish written and oral traditions and popular belief.[2] The narrator's image of God sitting on a throne in Heaven and sending emissaries to earth to check on human behavior follows the opening narrative scene in the Book of Job (1:6–12).

The conflict between eastern European Jews (the *Ostjuden*) and central European Jews has deep historical and cultural roots, yet it became most poignant in the nineteenth and the twentieth centuries. The origins of the Jewish population in Poland are the subject of legends.[3] There are some references from the eighth and ninth centuries to Jews in the area, and clearer documentary evidence of Jewish settlement in the region exists from the end of the eleventh century to the beginning of the twelfth. Jews migrated to Eastern Europe from multiple directions and over several historical periods. Jews came to Poland from Western and Central Europe and from eastern countries such as Russia, Ukraine, and probably even the Balkan Peninsula.[4]

In Germany, on the other hand, Jewish communities are known to have existed since the fourth century.[5] They were subject to medieval demographic fluctuations, pogroms, and economic pressures and at other times enjoyed protection. During the sixteenth century, Sephardic Jews immigrated to Germany after their expulsion from Spain; and after the 1648–1649 pogrom in Ukraine headed by Bogdan Khmelnytsky[6] (1595–1657) westward migration increased the presence of Polish Jews in Germany.[7] For more on the Ukrainian pogrom, see the notes to tale IFA 8915 (in this vol., no. 29). The processes of emancipation, enlightenment, and assimilation that Jews in Germany experienced contributed to their enculturation into the country's way of life and created a cultural rift between eastern and western European Jews. Discussions of these trends in European Jewry,[8] studies of countertrends,[9] analyses of Jewish enlightenment,[10] and examinations of Jewish assimilation into European society are available.[11]

The cultural schism between Polish and German Jewish societies perpetuated their mutual negative perceptions into the twentieth century and up to the Holocaust.[12] As the present tale notes, World War I indeed brought together eastern and western European Jews in unexpected ways. "Germany's occupation of Poland in 1915 provided a radically new context for an old problem. Instead of the ghetto coming to Germany, Germany came to the ghetto. Prussian soldiers, impoverished inhabitants of countless shtetls, and middle-class German Jews were flung together—an unprecedented situation."[13]

Folklore Motifs

- A101 "Supreme god."
- A187.1 "God as judge of men."
- A661 "Heaven."
- P421 "Judge."
- V230 "Angel."
- V235 "Mortal visited by angel."

――――― Notes ―――――

1. Albertini, *The Origins of the War of 1914*; Copland, *The Origins of Major War*, 56–117; Fay, *The Origins of the World War*; Hamilton and Herwig, *The Origins of World War I*; and Joll, *The Origins of the First World War.*

2. Nielsen, *YAHWEH as Prosecutor and Judge.* For related studies, see Adamiak, *Justice and History in the Old Testament;* Malchow, *Social Justice in the Hebrew Bible*; Reventlow and Hoffman, *Justice and Righteousness*; and Weinfeld, *Social Justice in Ancient Israel and the Ancient Near East.*

3. Bar-Itzhak, *Jewish Poland*; and Weinryb, "The Beginnings of East-European Jewry."

4. Balaban, "*Korot ha-Yehudim bi-Yemei ha-Beinaim*" (The history of the Jews in the Middle Ages); Balaban, *A History of the Jews in Cracow and Kazimierz,* 1:11–19; Halpern, "The Jews in Eastern Europe"; Gieysztor, "The Beginnings of Jewish Settlement in the Polish Land"; D. Kahana, *Perakim be-Toldot ha-Yehudim be-Polin* (Chapters in the history of the Jews of Poland), 13–64; Mahler, *History of Jews in Poland*, 9–29; and Wyrozumski, "Jews in Medieval Poland." See also the introduction to this volume.

5. Balaban, *A History of the Jews in Cracow and Kazimierz,* 11.

6. Also spelled Chmielnicki or Khmelnitski.

7. Shulvass, *From East to West.*

8. Elon, *The Pity of It All,* 259–295; J. Katz, *Emancipation and Assimilation.*

9. M. Brenner, *The Renaissance of Jewish Culture in Weimar Germany*; Volkov, *Jüdisches Leben und Antisemitismus*, 111–180; and Volkov, "The Dynamics of Dissimilation."

10. Feiner, *The Jewish Enlightenment.*

11. Frankel and Zipperstein, *Assimilation and Community*; Mosse, "Jewish Emancipation"; Schoeps, *Deutsch-Jüdische Symbiose Oder die Mißglückte Emanzipation*; Sorkin, "The Genesis of the Ideology of Emancipation"; Sorkin, *The Transformation of German Jewry 1780–1840*; and Sorkin, "Emancipation and Assimilation."

12. Adler-Rudel, *Ostjuden in Deutschland*; Aschheim, *Brothers and Strangers*; Aschheim, "Eastern Jews, German Jews and Germany's Ostpolitik in the First World War"; Löw et al., *Deutsche—Juden—Polen*; Sorkin, "The Rediscovery of the Eastern Jews"; Y. Weiss, *Deutsche und Polnische Juden vor dem Holocaust*; Y. Weiss, *Citizenship and Ethnicity;* Y. Weiss, "Polish and German Jews between Hitler's Rise to Power and the Outbreak of the Second World War"; Y. Weiss, "The 'Emigration Effort' or 'Repatriation' "; Werthheimer, *Unwelcome Strangers;* and Frankel, "Symposium: *Ostjuden* in Central and Western Europe."

13. Aschheim, *Brothers and Strangers*, 139.

Tales between Jews and Non-Jews

23

The Shofar of the Messiah

Told by Pinḥas Gutterman

*I*n our town there was a Jewish physician whose grandfather had been Zalman the blacksmith. The physician had long since forgotten that he was the grandson of the Jewish blacksmith and the son of Lipke, the Jewish mill owner.

The old men in town told how the physician's father had become wealthy thanks to the grandfather. The grandfather, Zalman the blacksmith, was very poor. But by virtue of the blessing he received from the holy Ba'al Shem (of blessed memory), the physician's grandfather, Zalman the blacksmith, discovered a treasure—a large ingot of pure gold hidden in a heap of rusty old iron.

The physician's father was very rich. The physician was rich because he inherited silver and gold from his grandfather and father, who, thanks to their faith in the God of Israel, had received the blessing of the holy Ba'al Shem and become rich from this treasure they had found in their smithy, among the rusty old iron.

This physician, the son of Lipke the miller, did not acknowledge that he was a Jew. He was ashamed of his family, of his father and his grandfather. This physician believed in nothing, not even the religion of Israel. He changed his name to a gentile name, a non-Jewish one. The language spoken in his home was that of the gentiles. The festivals celebrated in his home were not the Sabbath and the holidays of his people, the Jews. Instead, he began to celebrate his own holidays—though not, Heaven forbid, the Christian holidays.

The children of the physician, the son of Lipke the miller, were taught the language of the gentiles. They received their education and culture from non-Jewish teachers who taught them their language and lore.

These unfortunate children did not know that they were of Jewish stock. They knew that they were the children of the rich physician, who had received his inheritance and wealth from his father and grandfather.

Once, when the children were already grown, something extraordinary

23 / *The Shofar of the Messiah*

happened. In late summer, as evening approached, a large rock fell through the physician's window, shattering the panes into tiny fragments.

When the physician heard the sound of the breaking glass he went outside to see what had happened. He saw that the pane had been shattered by a large rock that someone had hurled through the window.

Furious that someone had dared to throw a rock at his house, he went back inside to where it lay on the floor. He saw that it was wrapped in white paper. When he picked up the rock the paper came off and he saw that it was a note, written in the gentile language: "Filthy Jew, get out of here and go to Palestine. Clear out of our sacred land, you accursed physician, you and all your sons of bitches!"

The physician gripped the sheet. He was ashamed to tell anyone about it and afraid that someone might see this message. With the note in his hand he went home and told no one in his family about it.[*]

Evening came. The physician paced through his house, full of anger and fury, and thought about this despicable act. He walked back and forth in his room until he was worn out. Then he sat down in his chair, bitter and humiliated, and fell asleep.

As he slept, the physician suddenly heard the sound of a shofar.[**] The sound of a shofar roused him from his sleep. He opened his eyes and stared in every direction, trying to figure out which side of his house the sound was coming from. When he listened closely he realized that it was coming from the cellar.

When the physician heard the unwavering sound of the shofar coming from the cellar, he got up and made his way to the cellar door. When he reached the stairwell he could hear the shofar more clearly and more strongly. He lit the candle he held in his hand and went down the stairs to the cellar.

Standing in the cellar was a plain wooden cabinet that had belonged to his father, who had inherited it from his grandfather. When the physician got rid of everything that had belonged to his father, even the pictures of his mother and father, he had tossed them into the damp and dark cellar.

---

[*]Either the narrator forgot that the physician who went *outside* has already returned home and found the note on the floor or the broken window was not in the residential part of the house but in his clinic. And he went out from the clinic to the home.

[**]Ram's horn, traditionally blown for celebration and communication, most notably on the High Holy Days—Rosh Hashanah and Yom Kippur.

He had also discarded this cabinet, which contained a few items that had belonged to his father and his grandfather.

The dazed physician went over to the old cabinet and opened it. Suddenly the shofar was silent. By the light of the candle in his hand he found the shofar, on which the following words were carved: "The shofar of the Messiah."

That night, the physician found out, was *Kol Nidrei.**

At once he began the *Kol Nidrei* prayer. In a tearful voice he begged forgiveness and absolution for the enormous transgression that was his entire life.

---

*Yom Kippur eve. The evening service is commonly referred to by the prayer Kol Nidrei, which starts the service

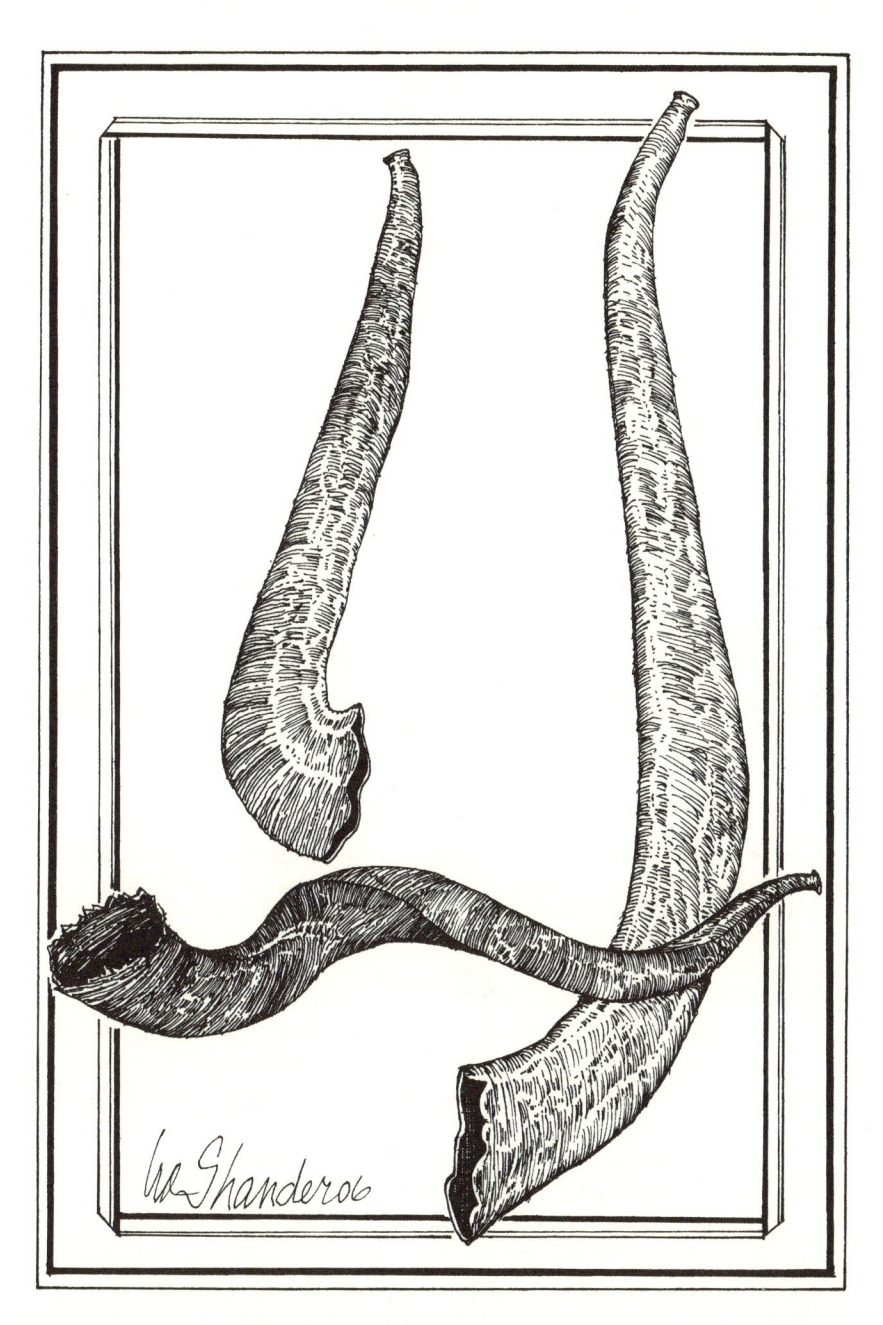

Shofarot—rams' horns.

Commentary for Tale 23 (IFA 6306)

Written down from memory by Pinḥas Gutterman, who heard this story from his grandfather, who told it every year on Yom Kippur eve.

Cultural, Historical, and Literary Background

The narrator reported that this tale was performed annually at his parental home on the eve of Yom Kippur. For him, its telling was part of a family ritual, although none of its characters was a family member and the story does not preserve any memory of his own family history. Rather, the rationale for narrating the tale at this particular time is the *Kol Nidrei* prayer that precedes, or opens, the service on Yom Kippur eve and with which the tale ends.

The performance of the tale occurred in a private family space, but thematically the story presents information about general Jewish history and sociology, religious institutions and beliefs, and national aspirations.

The Transformation of Eastern European Jewish Society

In the introduction to the tale, which sets the genealogy of the principle figure, the story presents the economic, social, and religious modernization of eastern European Jewry as it transformed from a village craft economy, through rural businesses, to the economy of learned professions. The subsequent tale is a religious-social criticism of those who made the full transition to modernity while abandoning their commitment to Jewish culture and religion. Its conclusion is a call for cultural and religious recovery and reawakening. Studies about the economic and professional transformation of eastern European Jewry are available.[1]

Jewish Professions

The tale mentions three specific professions for the successive generations: blacksmith, miller, and physician. Information about and descriptions of Jewish craftsmen in Eastern Europe must be inferred from nineteenth- and twentieth-century literary sources and community memoirs. Historical documentation of their life, organization, and economic condition is scant and scattered, as noted by the few historians who address this topic.[2]

Economically, millers were a notch above craftsmen in the hierarchy of eastern European Jewish society. They leased their mills from the feudal magnets, who owned the land as well as the villages and towns on it. The craftsmen kept as profit any amount that was above the annual rent they paid to their landlords. General studies of these economic relations, not necessarily pertaining to millers specifically, have been published[3] as have examinations and reflections of these relations in Jewish literature.[4]

The interest in medicine in Jewish culture is evident in Jewish literature from ancient to modern times, embracing both folk and learned healing.[5] Although traditional Jewish society highly valued medical knowledge, the acquisition of this knowledge at a university often meant a departure from traditional ways of life, as described in this story. Such a process was common in the nineteenth century and added to the antagonism between traditional and medical healers, between rebbes and modern doctors. By the nature of their education, modern Jewish physicians joined the ranks of the Jewish Enlightenment (Haskalah); and even when they did not abandon their religion completely, such professionals severed their ties with traditional life.[6] Nevins[7] cited the case of Rabbi Israel ben Ze'ev Wolf Lipkin (Salanter) (1810–1883), the leader of the Musar movement who mourned his son when he went to Berlin to study medicine (for more, see the notes to tale IFA 21021 [in this vol., no. 66]). Comparative notes and statistics regarding the position of the Jewish physicians in Russian medical institutions are available.[8]

The Ba'al Shem

The story does not specify the identity of the Ba'al Shem, but within Hasidic society the epithet implies a reference to the Ba'al Shem Tov, the founder of the Hasidic movement. Legends and studies about him are readily available.[9]

The earliest known reference to *ba'al shem* as a socially recognized category of miracle workers occurs in the eleventh century in a question that the Kairouan community of Tunisia, addressed to Rabbi Hai ben Sherira Gaon (939–1038).[10] He dismissed such people and their claims for working miracles as "idle talk," even if the men were righteous people. In his time, the use of divine names for magical purposes was known in Jewish societies; however, in texts dated to the late antiquities the term *ba'al shem* is missing, either because of the absence of self-reference or because the term was not yet coined. Examples of magical texts exist[11] as do studies of names in Jewish magic.[12] A list and interpretation of magical names has been published.[13]

In the sources listed in the endnotes, there are elaborations about the use of names in magic, but the specific term *ba'al shem* is not mentioned. However, the term was apparently in use. It occurred in texts that emanated from Jewish communities in North Africa in the eleventh century, mentioned above, and in the Spanish-Jewish community in the twelfth and thirteen centuries. Like Rabbi Hai Gaon, these poets and mystics considered the *ba'alei shem* to be spiritually inferior. For example, the poet Judah Halevi (before 1075–1141) noted: "[Another group that erred were] those who used name incantations [in their belief that power to perform miracles was from the right incantation]. When they heard about a prophet who had uttered certain words and then a miracle occurred to him, they thought that his words alone were the reason for the miracle." In the original Judeo-Arabic, the term is *"azhab al shemot"* which translates into Hebrew as *ba'alei ha-shemot*.[14]

Similarly, in his evaluation of the Kabbalah as superior to philosophy, Rabbi Abraham ben Samuel Abulafia (1240–c. 1292) condemned the *ba'alei shemot* as people who use names without really comprehending their significance. He wrote: "Then [after learning and being able to appreciate the Kabbalah] I understood the great error that a few people, who call themselves in certain countries by a name that is well known in its kabbalistic ways, BA'ALEI SHEMOT, whom I am reluctant to malign. Their mistake is thinking that they can perform wonders with the power of names and invocations, uttering them in their mouth without any knowledge and understanding of their meanings."[15]

It is significant that, as much as we can ascertain, the term *ba'al shem* is absent from *Sefer Hasidim*,[16] in which the subjects of magic and protection against demonic forces frequently occur. The book emerged among a pietistic group in the Rhine Valley headed by Rabbi Judah ben Samuel he-Ḥasid (1150–1217), during a time when the term was in use among the Jews in Spain. Rabbi Eleazar ben Judah of Worms (c. 1165–c. 1230), who was a student of Rabbi Judah he-Ḥasid, wrote a book about the magical use of holy names, *Sefer ha-Shem*, which is still in manuscript;[17] but the term does not occur in his writings either. On the other hand, Rabbi Abraham ben Azriel (thirteenth century), a student of Rabbi Eleazar who used Jewish-Spanish books and manuscripts extensively, mentioned the term *ba'alei ha-shem* in his chrestomathy *Arugat ha-bosem* (Spice garden) (1234) in reference to two Italian poets: Shephatiah ben Amittai (d. 886) and his son, Amittain ben Shephatiah (late ninth century).[18]

The early use of the term did not apparently take root in the central and eastern European Jewish communities of the time. The term began to appear there only in the sixteenth century, after the expulsion of the Jews from Spain in 1492, and is found in popular, rather than mystical and philosophical, writings as an epithet for individual personalities. In these historical, literary, and geographical transitions, the term *ba'al shem* lost its negative connotation and took on a positive, or at least neutral, value and was used to describe a familiar role in Jewish societies.

Moreover, writers also began to use the term *ba'al shem* to refer to historical individuals, applying sixteenth-century terminology to thirteenth-century people. Thus, for example, the term was applied to Judah he-Ḥasid in a sixteenth-century story.[19] The same tale appeared in the Yiddish *Ma'aseh Book* of 1602, but without the term *ba'al shem*.

However, in the Yiddish collection of wonder stories written in the mid-seventeenth century by Yiftah Joseph Juspa Halevy of Worms (1604–1678),[20] the term *ba'alei shemot* was used in positive terms to refer to Rabbi Gedaliah, who led the miracle makers in a magical war of self-defense during the 1615 expulsion of the Jews from Worms. One tale described Rabbi Eleazar ben Judah of Worms using the magical power of names to save himself from a fiery execution, but the story does not use the term *ba'al shem*.[21]

By the sixteenth century, the *ba'alei shem* had become a familiar character in European Jewish communities. However, until the eighteenth century, information about the extent of their social and religious impact is scarce. Some of these men were wandering healers, others were also known as established rabbis in their communities. The earliest personality about whom there is some historical and legendary information is Rabbi Elijah ben Rabbi Judah Aaron of Helm (or Chelm) (b. 1550). Descriptions of pre-Hasidic *ba'alei shem* can be found in the literature.[22]

Legends grew about the *ba'alei shem*. One such tale about a fictional *ba'al shem*, Rabbi Adam of Bingen, was published in a seventeenth-century chapbook in Amsterdam; it was later incorporated in *In Praise of the Ba'al Shem Tov*.[23] In the eighteenth century, most of the *ba'alei shem* traveled through various eastern European Jewish towns; however, unique among them was Ḥayyim Samuel Jacob Falk (d. 1782), known also as Doctor Falk, the Ba'al Shem of London. He was born in Poland to a family of Sephardic origin and traveled to and settled in London.[24]

Anti-Semitism

The incident related in the present tale illustrates dramatically the theory that anti-Semitism maintained and reinforced Jewish national identity. Many studies about anti-Semitism have been conducted.[25]

The description of the anti-Semitic attack in this story is generic rather than historically specific; however, the mention of Palestine suggests events that occurred in the modern era, after the inception of the Zionistic immigration to the Land of Israel and before the Holocaust. Studies about late nineteenth- and early twentieth-century pogroms in Eastern Europe are available.[26] Kann[27] specifically examined the relationship between assimilation and anti-Semitism, albeit not in Eastern Europe.

Messianic Expectations

The dream and subsequent events in the present story suggest linguistic associations that connote messianic expectations. The verb *gnz* (to store away, to hide) functions as an associative link for relating objects and figures that traditional literature considers hidden. The personal, paternally inherited wooden cabinet (*aron*) resonates the Temple Ark (*aron ha-kodesh*), about the fate of which there were two traditions in the Babylonian Talmud. Rabbi Simon Bar-Yoḥai (second century) noted that "the Ark went into exile in Babylonia," whereas Rabbi Judah ben Il'ai, or ben-Lakish (both second century) suggested that "the Ark was hidden [buried; *nignaz*] in its own place" (BT *Yoma* 53b). According to a *tannaitic* tradition, "the bottle containing the Manna, and that containing the [anointment oil], the staff of Aaron with its almonds and blossoms, and the chest which the Philistines had sent as a gift to the God of Israel" (BT *Yoma* 52b) were all stored in the Ark. The shofar was not in the Ark. In another tradition, however, there is a clear association between the Ark and the Messiah: "Every place where the Messiah is, the ark is, and every place where the Messiah is not, the ark is not"

(JT *Ta'anit* 2:1). The verb *nignaz* (stored away) occurs in reference to both the Messiah and the Holy Ark (Midrash *Lamentations Zuta* 1:1; BT *Yoma* 53b). The present tale also includes the notion of the exile and messianic expectations.

The verb *gnz* is associated with the Messiah in traditional legends. The idea that the Messiah, called Menaḥem ben Amiel, is stored away occurs first in the Book of Zerubbabel, likely written in 629 C.E.; but in this text, the verb *zpn'* a synonym of *gnz,* conveys the same idea. In the tenth-century Midrash *Lamentations Zuta,* the term *gnz* occurs in this context. In earlier versions of the tales about the birth and disappearance of the Messiah the verb *gnz* is absent (JT *Berakhot* 2:4; *Lamentations Rabbah* 1).[28]

In the story, the shofar stands in synecdochical relation to the Messiah himself and is hidden until the coming of the Messiah. The notion that the sound of the shofar will proclaim the appearance of the Messiah draws on the biblical verse "And in that day, a great ram's horn shall be sounded" (Isaiah 27:13). But because this is a Yom Kippur narrative, the shofar in the tale resonates with the biblical proclamation of the jubilee year: "Then you shall sound the horn loud; in the seventh month, on the tenth day of the month—the Day of Atonement—you shall have the horn sounded throughout your land and you shall hallow the fiftieth year. You shall proclaim release throughout the land for all its inhabitants" (Leviticus 25:9–10). In an earlier tradition, articulated in a responsa by Rabbi Hai ben Sherira Gaon (939–1038), Zerubbabel will blow the shofar, announcing the coming of the Messiah.[29] Elijah assumes this role in a Jewish Persian apocalyptic book *Ma'aseh Daniel*[30] (tenth century) and in the later traditions, concurring with the prophecy of Malachi 3:23–24. See also the notes to tale IFA 4813 (in this vol., no. 24).

According to available sources, four locations have been suggested as the place where the eschatological Messiah is awaiting the moment of his appearance in the world. Talmudic legend places him at the gates of Rome, sitting among the wretched of the earth (BT *Sanhedrin* 98a); medieval narratives find him in the fifth chamber of paradise[31] or in prison.[32] According to mystical literature, he is in the Palace of Radiance and in the "bird's nest."[33] Additional sources for the Messiah and messianic movements are cited in the notes to tale IFA 14460 (in this vol., no. 41).

Kol Nidrei

Textually, the *Kol Nidrei*—the most ominous and awe-striking recitation in the Jewish synagogue services—is not a prayer. Its words neither appeal to God nor appease the Divine; none of God's names or epithets appears in the Aramaic version. The contrast between its seemingly legalistic wording and its emotional impact has puzzled its interpreters, who refer to it as an enigma, a paradox, or a riddle.[34]

There have been several attempts to solve the *Kol Nidrei* riddle. J. Bloch[35] proposed that the recitation emerged among crypto-Jews out of their ambivalence, resulting from forced conversion to Christianity and loyalty to their Jewish faith. He considered seventh-century Spain as the provenance for the recitation of the *Kol Nidrei,* when the Visigoths pressured the Jews to become Christians. To stay alive they did convert; but to redeem themselves for the world to come, they annulled their oath of conversion.

Krauss,[36] followed by J. Mann[37] and Baron,[38] considered the nullification of vows on Yom Kippur eve in the context of the controversy with the emerging fundamentalist sect of the Karaites. Reik[39] suggested a psychoanalytical explanation, drawing on the conflicts among the id, ego, and superego in which the collective reading is a confession of covert wishes to break the covenant with God; in other words, he considered Jews as having a subconscious wish to break the covenant with God, and this wish (of which Jews are ashamed) manifests itself in the prayer. Deshen[40] explained the *Kol Nidrei* enigma in terms of its context in ritual performance, considering it a transitional recitation through which the worshipers pass from the mundane to the holy, shedding their obligations in the profane world before entering the state of intense religiosity of Yom Kippur. Merḥaviah, opposed this notion in his essay " '*Kol Nidrei*.' " The *Kol Nidrei* has been the subject of extensive scholarship.[41]

The apparent duplicity that the nullification of vows involved gave rise to a whole corpus of medieval and postmedieval rationale for this unique ritual, rooted in the religious practices of the sixth and seventh centuries and the linguistic representations of those vows. Although the Hebrew Bible recognizes vows (*nedarim*) of different kinds,[42] and the Mishnah and Jerusalem and Babylonian Talmuds, respectively, devote whole tractates to both Yom Kippur worship and the use and laws of vows, the recitation the *Kol Nidrei* is not mentioned in either tractate. The absence of the reading from early services of the Day of Atonement was noted by Stökl.[43] Furthermore, the absolution of vows and oaths requires the authority of a sage or a committee of three knowledgeable laymen (*beit din*) (Mishnah *Neg'im* 2:5; *Nedarim* 2:5; BT *Shevu'ot* 28a; *Bekhorot* 36b–37b; *Gittin* 35b); vows cannot be invalidated through a communal ritual.[44]

The earliest documentation of the *Kol Nidrei* recitation is the ninth-century Hebrew text *Seder Rav Amram,* the earliest prayer book, which Rabbi Amram Gaon, Amram ben Sheshna (d. 875), prepared in response to the request of Rabbi Isaac ben Simeon of Spain.[45] The next known version is in Aramaic, found in a citation in a thirteenth-century source, *Shibbolei ha-Lekket,* by the Italian legal scholar Zedekiah ben Abraham, who attributed the text to Rabbi Hai Gaon. This rabbi is either Rabbi Hai ben Sherira (939–1038), Gaon of Pumbedita, or Rabbi Hai bar Nachshon, Gaon of Sura (in the years 871–879).[46] This Aramaic version was a primary influence on the classical *Kol Nidrei* text in Ashkenazic prayer books.[47] *Maḥzor Vitry,* composed by Simḥah ben Samuel of Vitry, France, in the eleventh century, includes the instruction that the recitation be repeated three times, first in a whisper, next slightly louder, and finally in a clear and loud voice (section 351). By the thirteenth century, the *Kol Nidrei* recitation was universally known and practiced in Jewish communities in Europe, including Spain and Italy, and in the Near East.[48]

However, before its admittance into the Yom Kippur service, the *Kol Nidrei* had to overcome rabbinical objections, such as the dismissal of its validity and significance. Even Rabbi Amram Gaon, who included it in his *seder,* invalidated the *Kol Nidrei*, pointing out that "the holy academy has informed that this custom is complete nonsense and is prohibited."[49] Apparently, as Goldschmidt pointed out, "this ritual originated in a popular custom and the leading rabbinical authorities objected to it."[50]

The canonization of the *Kol Nidrei* appears to be a classical example of a popular folk custom that forced itself into the culture of the upper social and rabbinical echelons and the synagogue canon. The historical reconstruction of this process, necessarily tentative, may suggest a convergence, and perhaps confusion, of the traditions of two distinct Jewish communities—one in ancient Palestine and the other in Babylonia—that drew on two strands of cultural beliefs: law and magic.

Discoveries of texts and material objects in the nineteenth and twentieth centuries cast new light on the history of the *Kol Nidrei*. First are halakhic fragments discovered in the Cairo Geniza known as *Sefer ha-Ma'asim li-Bhnei Erez Israel* (A book of ruling precedents for the people in Palestine). These fragments have become the subject of intensive research.[51] Among these post-talmudic textual fragments are a few that comment either positively or negatively on the legal-religious status of the nullification of past or future vows and the ritualistic observance of this act on the eve of Rosh Hashanah rather than Yom Kippur. The text of one fragment[52] prohibits the performance of the ritual on Sabbath eve but allows it at the end of the Sabbath, taking the very performance of the ritual as a given.[53]

In Babylonia a different attitude prevailed. While the Babylonian Talmud resonates a similar custom, stating that "he who desires that none of his vows made during the year shall be valid, let him stand at the beginning of the year and declare, 'Every vow which I may make in the future shall be null' [his vows are then invalid]" (BT *Nedarim* 23b). But after the editing of the Babylonian Talmud, in the eighth century, Rabbi Yehudai ben Naḥman, who was the Gaon of Sura in 757–761, explicitly objected to the principle of the nullification of vows, but did not refer to the *Kol Nidrei* reading by name.[54] By the ninth century, the recitation had acquired a title (its opening phrase) by which it was known, although it was not necessarily tolerated by the authorities. Rabbi Natronai bar Hillai, Gaon of Sura in 853–858, mentioned the recitation by name and as a known custom that was performed in the services of either Rosh Hashanah or Yom Kippur; however, he denied its practice in either "the two academies or anywhere else."[55] Rav Amram himself, as noted earlier, dismissed the recitation of the *Kol Nidrei*.

A controversial case notwithstanding,[56] it appears that by the ninth century the rabbinical opposition to the *Kol Nidrei* was wavering. While Rabbi Paltoi of

Pumbedita (842–857) noted it as an established custom,[57] Rabbi Saadia (ben Joseph), Gaon of Sura (882–942), excluded the text from his prayer book but permitted its use for the annulment of erroneous vows.[58] By the end of the tenth century and the early part of the eleventh, Rabbi Hai ben Sherira (939–1038), who dominated the Pumbedita academy, apparently gave his stamp of approval to the *Kol Nidrei*, though, as mentioned above, his attitude is known only from a thirteenth-century book.

The last forceful objections to the *Kol Nidrei* came from the French Tosafist Rabbenu (Jacob ben Meir) Tam (1100–1171), who argued that the recitation did not meet halachic standards; therefore, he made a significant change in its text, annulling future rather than past vows. Later, Rabbi Levi ben Gershom (1288–1344) denied the reading any legal validity.[59]

Contemporaneously with the halachic deliberations, the term *neder* (vow) and the nullification of vows occurred in a different context, in which the term and the practice had completely different meanings and cultural values—namely, that of magical incantations and formulas. These magical texts were discovered in archaeological excavations in 1888 and 1889 at Nippur in Babylonia, in what is assumed to have been a Jewish settlement. Studies and texts of the magical bowls are available,[60] as are studies of Aramaic magic formulas and bowls from Palestine.[61] Benovitz[62] dismissed the notion that *Kol Nidrei* draws on the meaning of the term *neder* in incantation formulas, but he did not offer a clear reason for his opposition to this idea.

The incantations on these bowls and amulets contain the terms that constitute the opening formula of the *Kol Nidrei,* either as nouns or verbs: *ndr, hrm asr, shv'a, qdsh,* and *qym.* However, within a magical context, these are verbal acts uttered or performed by the speakers or magical specialists and directed at other people. Therefore, an individual would need protection against such negative incantations and, in a moment of grace, could mutually nullify any such incantation that he or she had uttered in the past.

The texts of these bowls expose the magical negative meanings of the words. For example:

- "[Appointed is this bowl for the sealing and guarding] of the house, dwelling and body of Ḥuna son of Kupitay, that there should go out from him the tormentors, evil dreams, [curses,] vows, spells, [magic practices, devils,] demons, liliths, encroachments, and terrors" (ll. 1–2).
- ". . . and there shall go out from him the tormentors, evil dreams, curses, vows, spells, magic practices, devils, demons, liliths, encroachments and terrors" (l. 11).
- "May there lie in the dust the injuries of vows of every place."[63]
- " . . . devils, afflictions, satans, bans, tormentors, spirits of barrenness, spirits of abortion, sorcerers, vows, curses, magic rites, idols, wicked pebble spirits, errant spirits, shadow spirits, liliths, educators[?] and all evil doers of harm."

- "... from evil liliths, both male and female from all evil sorceries and evil magic acts, from curses and vows and accidents."
- "... ban and annul all mysteries of sorcerers and kinds of sorceries, falsities, knots, blows, spells, vows, necklace charms, accidents, curses, all satans, evil spirits, malicious spirits, all magical acts and all destroyers."
- "... spells and all vows and necklace charms and evil accidents and all blast demons and evil destroyers and all mighty satans and every thing."
- "Bound, seized, attached, pressed down, thrashed, exorcised are all the male idols and the female goddesses. Ladders[?] and vows and curses and afflictions and . . . charms and evil spirits and impious charms and all exorcisms and all curses, exorcism, binding vow, calamity, curse, affliction that is[?] in the world, [magical] words, invocation."
- "In the name of . . . who exist with strife[?]. Bound are the vows, curses, calamities from the same Sergius son of Barandukh."
- "... in appearances and from the spirit of uncleanness[?] and from demon and the vow and the devil and the shadow-spirit[s] and from . . . evil occurrence."
- "... dews, evil spirit, vow with witchcraft, and all other spirits and all other harmful [spirits] that the God of Israel created in the world."[64]
- "Upset, upset is the earth. Upset is the earth, R Q Y' WS. Upset are all the vows."
- "By 'HY'! The words of the vow that they have vowed and performed against 'Abn son of 'Awirti and against Mehisay daughter of . . ."
- "And again blinded are all the idols, male and female, and sorceries and vows and curses and the evil spirit. [They are] bound and tied and sealed. Their mouth[s] are shut and their eyes are blinded and their ears are deafened so that they cannot hear [anything] against 'Amtur daughter of Silta and against her seed and against her house and her property."
- "... and lilies and from the hand of all idols and strokes and from the curses and invocation and vow and spell and from the evil envious eye and from everything bad."[65]

The Hebrew and Aramaic texts of the *Kol Nidrei* recitation have a fair degree of ambiguity in the phrase *al nafshatana* (on our soul). The common interpretation renders the phrase "[all the vows . . .] that we took." However, in light of the incantation texts, it is possible to understand the phrase in the following sense: "that we brought upon our soul." Furthermore, performed within a communal setting, the ritual has an added dimension of mutuality. On the one hand, it nullifies all the negative thoughts and verbal acts that were uttered against an individual, thereby making void all those that were directed against him or her. On the other hand, in the second part of the recitation, the speakers nullify all thoughts and speeches that they uttered publicly or privately against others. This is thus a moment of cleansing for self-protection and for forgiveness toward others.

The rabbinic authorities in the gaonic and medieval periods, as well as in subsequent generations, and most of the scholars who addressed the case of the *Kol Nidrei* considered the recitation within the framework of Jewish law. Although *hatrat nedarim* (the nullification of vows) is a halachic principle,[66] religious law is not the appropriate framework for the interpretation of the reading. This incongruity generated an attitude that considered the reading as paradoxical or enigmatic.[67] The very antagonism of the rabbinical authorities to the *Kol Nidrei* may have been generated by their objection to admit into a religious service, which is governed by religious rules, a ritual that is magical in nature. Thus if the *Kol Nidrei* recitation is viewed as a magical ritual, as Gershon,[68] suggested, then the *Kol Nidrei* could not be considered a legal formula and the meaning of the term *neder* could not be interpreted in terms of its biblical and talmudic uses but rather in light of its magical use in the Land of Israel and Babylonia.

In the magical literature, the term *neder* occurs as a synonym of the other terms in the *Kol Nidrei* as negative wishes, restrictions, and curses directed at other people. Consequently, evoking the principle of communal mutuality, the recitation of the *Kol Nidrei* implies a public denunciation of all the negative thoughts people harbored against each other, thereby cleansing themselves from the negative attitudes directed back at them. Such an interpretation transforms the readers from people who are going back on their word to anxious individuals who would like to rid themselves of any secret negativity. The worshipers are both subjects and objects, denouncing the negative feelings they harbored against their fellow members of the community and expecting them to do the same. The *Kol Nidrei* is a verbal magical ritual of communal protective purification, preparing each and every member of the community for life in the following year. Therefore it is solemn; therefore it is awesome: Life is at the balance.

The *Kol Nidrei* melody is particularly evocative, recalled emotionally by Jews who left traditional life behind them.[69] Scores of the reading as sung in Yemenite, Persian, Sephardic, and Moroccan communities, as well as several other renditions, have been published.[70]

Jewish and non-Jewish composers have rendered the *Kol Nidrei* as instrumental and choral works. For example, Max Bruch (1838–1920) learned the melody from the Jewish members of the choir Sternschen Gesangverein, which he conducted. Bruch wrote his Opus 47 *Kol Nidrei* in 1888. Arnold Schoenbergn (1874–1951) completed his Opus 39 *Kol Nidre: For Rabbi-Narrator, Mixed Chorus, and Orchestra* in 1938; and Mario Castelnuovo-Tedesco (1895–1968) wrote his *Kol Nidre* for cantor, chorus, and organ in 1944.

Folklore Motifs

- *A582 "Messiah: cultural hero (divinity) who is expected to come."
- N135.2.1 "Discovery of treasure brings luck."
- *N511.1.14 "Treasure buried in scrap iron."

- N530 "Discovery of treasure."
- N534 "Treasure discovered by accident."
- *N538.3 "Discovery of treasure as a result of a holy man's blessing."
- P150 "Rich men."
- *P165 "Poor men."
- P424 "Physician."
- P443 "Miller."
- P447 "Smith."
- P715.1 "Jews."
- *P715.2 "Hatred of Jews."
- *P715.3 "Jews in denial of their own culture."
- Q111 "Riches as reward."
- V50 "Prayer."
- *V75.2 "Day of Atonement."
- *V119 "*Shofar* (a ram's horn trumpet)."

――――― Notes ―――――

1. Kahan, *Essays in Jewish Social and Economic History*; and Baron et al., *Economic History of the Jews*.

2. Halpern, *East European Jewry,* 163–194; and Kremer, "Jewish Artisans in Poland in the XVI–XVII Centuries."

3. Ben-Sasson, "Statutes for the Enforcement of the Observance of the Sabbath in Poland"; Cygielman, "Leasing and Contracting Interests (Public Incomes) of Polish Jewry and the Founding of '*Va'ad Arba Aratzot*' "; Ettinger, "Jewish Participation in the Colonization of the Ukraine"; J. Goldberg, *The Jewish Society in the Polish Commonwealth*, 159–170; Rosman, *The Lord's Jews*; Rosman, "The Relationship between the Jewish Lessee (*Arendarz*) and the Polish Nobleman"; and Shmeruk, "The Hasidic Movement and the 'Arendars.' "

4. Bartal, "The Porets and the Arendar."

5. See, for example, Kottek, *Medicine and Hygiene in the Works of Flavius Josephus*; Kottek et al., *From Athens to Jerusalem;* Freudenthal and Kottek, *Mélanges d'histoire de la médecine hébraïque;* J. Preuss, *Biblical and Talmudic Medicine;* and Zimmels, *Magicians, Theologians, and Doctors*. For works that relate to modern times, see N. Berger, *Jews and Medicine;* Friedenwald, *The Jews and Medicine, Essays*; Friedenwald, *Jewish Luminaries in Medical History;* Heynick, *Jews and Medicine;* and Nevins, *The Jewish Doctor.*

6. Mahler, *Hasidism and the Jewish Enlightenment*, 35; Nathans, *Beyond the Pale*, 60, 220, 264–265; Raisin, *The Haskalah Movement in Russia*, 241; and Zalkin, *A New Dawn.*

7. Op. cit.,75.

8. Frieden, *Russian Physicians in an Era of Reform and Revolution,* 130, 252, 332–334.

9. Ben-Amos and Mintz, *In Praise of the Ba'al Shem Tov;* I. Etkes, *Ba'al Hashem;* I. Etkes, "The Role of Magic and *Ba'alei-Shem* in Ashkenazi Society in the Late Seventeenth and Early Eighteenth Centuries"; I. Etkes, "Magic and Magicians in the Haskalah Literature"; A. Kahana, *Rabbi Israel Ba'al Shem Tov (Besht);* Rosman, *Founder*

of Hasidism; Scholem, "Baʻal Shem"; and Scholem, *"Demuto ha-Historit Shel R. Yisrael Baʻal Shem Tov"* (The historical image of Israel Baʻal Shem Tov).

10. B. Lewin, *Otsar ha-Ge'onim* (The gaonic treasure), 4:16; and Trachtenberg, *Jewish Magic and Superstition,* 88.

11. Harari, *Ḥarva de Moses* (The sword of Moses); Margalioth, *Sepher Ha-Razim;* M. Morgan, *"Sepher ha-Razim"*; Naveh and Shaked, *Amulets and Magic Bowls*; and Naveh and Shaked, *Magic Spells and Formulae.*

12. Idel, *Kabbalah,* 96–128, 416 (index); Rohrbacher-Sticker, "From Sense to Nonsense"; Sperber, *Magic and Folklore in Rabbinic Literature,* 80–91; Trachtenberg, op. cit., 78–103; and Urbach, *The Sages,* 124–134.

13. Schrire, *Hebrew Magical Amulets,* 91–135.

14. See Halevi, *The Kuzari,* 3:53, 182; Halevi, *Kitab al-radd wa-ʻl-dalil fi ʻl-din al-dhalil (al-kitab al khazari),* 3:53, 134; and Even-Shmuel, *The Kosari of R. Yehuda Halevi* 3:53, 138.

15. A. Gross, *Gan Naʻul ve-ha-Igeret Sheva Netivot ha-Torah* (The locked garden and the seven Torah paths), 128.

16. Wistinetzki, *Das Buch der Frommen.*

17. J. Dan, *The Esoteric Theology of Ashkenazi Hasidism,* 62–63, 74–76.

18. Urbach, *Sefer Arugat Habosem,* 2:181.

19. Brüll, *"Beiträge zur jüdischen Sagen,"* 32–33 no. 22.

20. Eidelberg, *R. Juspa, Shammash of Warmaisa (Worms),* 72 no. 9.

21. Eidelberg, op. cit., 67–70 no. 7.

22. Eisenstein, *Ozar Yisrael,* 3:137–146; E. Etkes, *Baʻal Hashem,* 15–53; Günzig, *Die "Wundermänner" im jüdischen Volke;* A. Kahana, op. cit., 59–67; Nigal, *Magic, Mysticism, and Hasidism,* 1–32; Oron, *Samuel Falk,* 20–27; and Rosman, *Founder of Hasidism,* 17–26.

23. Elbaum, "The Baʻal Shem Tov and the Son of R. Adam"; Shmeruk, "Tales about R' Adam Baʻal Shem in the Versions of *Shibkhei Ha'Besht"*; and Ben-Amos and Mintz, op. cit., 13–18 nos. 5–7.

24. H. Adler, "The Baʻal Shem of London"; and Oron, op. cit.

25. For example, see S. Cohen, *Antisemitism;* Singerman, *Antisemitic Propaganda;* and Strauss, *A Bibliography on Antisemitism.*

26. Klier and Lambroza, *Pogroms;* R. Weinberg, "Anti-Jewish Violence and Revolution in the Late Imperial Russia."

27. "Assimilation and Antisemitism in the German French Orbit."

28. Jellinek, *Bet ha-Midrasch,* 2:54–57; Even-Shmuel, *Midrashei Ge'ulah* (Midrashim of deliverance), 288–303; and Hasan-Rokem, *Web of Life,* 146–160.

29. Even-Shmuel, *Midrashei Ge'ulah,* 138; B. Lewin, op. cit., 6:70–76, esp. 74.

30. Even-Shmuel, *Midrashei Ge'ulah,* 225.

31. Even-Shmuel, *Midrashei Ge'ulah,* 292–294; Higger, *Halakhot ve-Aggadot* (Laws and legends), 141–150, esp. 147 (extensive bibliography); and Jellinek, *Bet ha-Midrasch,* 2:23–39, 48–51.

32. Higger, op. cit., 123.

33. Even-Shmuel, *Midrashei Ge'ulah,* 294; and Jellinek, op. cit., 3:131–140.

34. See, for example, Deshen, "The Kol Nidre Enigma"; Kieval, "The Curious Case of Kol Nidre"; and Reik, *Ritual,* 167–219, esp. 169.

35. *Kol Nidre und seine Enstehungsgeschichte.*

36. "*Das Problem Kol Nidrei.*"
37. *Texts and Studies in Jewish History and Literature,* 2:52–53 nn. 99–100.
38. *A Social and Religious History of the Jews,* 5:248–249.
39. Op. cit., 167–219. See further comments in Abraham, "The Day of Atonement."
40. Op. cit.
41. Tabory, *Jewish Prayer and the Yearly Cycles,* 235–236 nos. 120–148; Benovitz, *Kol Nidre;* and Gershon, *Kol Nidrei.*
42. Gershon, op. cit., 3–10.
43. *The Impact of Yom Kippur on Early Christianity.*
44. Gershon, op. cit., 19–26.
45. D. Goldschmidt, *Seder Rav Amram Gaon,* 162–163.
46. Gershon, op. cit., 31.
47. Ibid., 29–39.
48. Note that "[w]estern Sephardim recite only the gaonic text referring to vows of the past year, while oriental Sephardim and Yemenites add Rabenu Tam's version"; see Kieval, "Kol Nidrei."
49. D. Goldschmidt, op. cit., 163.
50. *Maḥzor le-Yamim Noraim* (A prayer book for the Days of Awe), 2:26.
51. For bibliographical information and for a description of the current state of research, see Herr, "Matters of Palestinian Halakha during the Six and Seventh Centuries C. E.," esp. nn. 1–6.
52. Published in Margalioth, *Halakhot Erez-Israel min ha-Geniza* (Land of Israel halakhot from the Geniza); and M. Rabinowitz, "*Sepher Ha-Ma'asim Livnei Erez-Yisra'el,*" ll. 10–13.
53. See also Herr, op. cit., 70–76; and Gershon, op. cit., 11–26.
54. B. Lewin, op. cit., 11:19–24 (*Nedarim* nos. 56–66); Abramson, "*Pesakim Kedumim*" (Early rulings); and Abramson, "*Al Birkat Hatarat Nedarim ve-Shevu'ot,*" (About the blessing of nullification of vows and oaths).
55. B. Lewin, op. cit., 11:20–3 nos. 56–65.
56. Gershon, op. cit., 71 n. 11.
57. B. Lewin, op. cit., 11:23 no. 64.
58. Ibid., 11:22 no. 62.
59. Touati, "*Le problème du Kol Nidrey et le responsum inédit de Gersonide* (*Lévi ben Gershom)*"; Gershon, op. cit., 67–91; and Wieder, " 'Kol Nidre.' "
60. Montgomery, *Aramaic Incantation Texts from Nippur.* Selected texts are in Neusner, *A History of the Jews in Babylonia,* 5:217–243, and their analysis is in Levine, "The Language of the Magical Bowls"; C. Gordon, "An Aramaic Incantation"; and C. Gordon, "Aramaic Incantation Bowls."
61. Naveh and Shaked, *Amulets and Magic Bowls;* and Naveh and Shaked, *Magic Spells and Formulae.*
62. Op. cit., 170.
63. Naveh and Shaked, *Amulets and Magic Bowls,* 125 (bowl 1, ll. 1–2, l. 11), 147 (bowl 3, l. 2).
64. Naveh and Shaked, *Magic Spells and Formulae,* 115 (bowl 15, ll. 5–6), 125 (bowl 19, ll. 4, 6–7, 10), 132 (bowl 23, ll. 1–4, 7), 137 (bowl 25, ll. 3, 6).
65. C. Gordon, "Aramaic Incantation Bowls," 117 (text 1, l. 1), 121 (text 4, l. 1).

Gordon noted that "[t]his charm (Iraq Museum no. 9732) is designed to thwart vows (= curses) made against the clients" (124–125 [text 7, l. 9]).

66. Anonymous, "*Hatarat Nedarim*" (Release from vows), *Talmudic Encyclopedia* 11:333–392.

67. Deshen, op. cit.; Kieval, op. cit.; Reik, op. cit.

68. Op. cit., 51–61; and Herr, op. cit., 64–76 nn. 22, 24, 29, 30.

69. Reik, op. cit., 167–173.

70. Gershon, op. cit., 149–157; and Idelsohn, "The Kol Nidre Tune."

24

The Redemption of Captives

TOLD BY RAPHAEL HERBEST TO MOSHÈ RIVLIN

*I*n the great synagogue of Vilna, one Rosh Hashanah many years ago, when the *rebbe* of the synagogue, the righteous Rebbe Joshua (of blessed memory), got up to blow the shofar[*]—precisely at that moment Satan entered, and the *rebbe* could not get a sound out of the shofar, no matter how hard he tried. This astonished everyone, because the righteous Rebbe Joshua had been blowing the shofar for more than fifty years and never before had he been unable to get a sound out of it. What was going on here, the people wondered. What was the reason? There had to be something here. It could not be a matter of chance. An hour passed and then two, but he was still unable to blow the shofar. Other people tried, but none of them could produce a sound either.

When the righteous Rebbe Joshua saw what was happening, he begged the congregation's indulgence. He said he hoped that he would be able to blow the shofar soon, but asked to go off by himself so that he could try to find out why none of them could get a note out of it. The congregation agreed to his request, because of their reverence for the righteous man.

The righteous Rebbe Joshua went home quickly, because he knew the congregation was waiting for him, to pray alone for the short period he had asked them to wait for him. When he arrived in front of his house he saw Monish, the poor Jewish cobbler, the simplest Jew in all of Vilna, an unlettered ignoramus who was never friendly to anyone, with a crying young girl in his arms. He was comforting her and offering her sweets. When the righteous Rebbe Joshua saw this he remembered that he had encountered the same scene on his way to the synagogue that morning, but then it had not occurred to him to ask Monish the cobbler what was going on. Now he wondered whether this was why he could not blow the shofar.

So the righteous Rebbe Joshua went over to Monish the cobbler. "What's the matter?" he asked him. "Why is the girl crying?"

---

[*]Ram's horn, traditionally blown for celebration and communication, most notably on the High Holy Days—Rosh Hashanah and Yom Kippur.

24 / *The Redemption of Captives* 187

The great synagogue of Vilna.

Monish the cobbler answered him, "As I was getting ready to go to the synagogue this morning I saw some people with a little girl. What was interesting was that the people seemed to be gentiles but evidently the girl was Jewish. I wondered what could be going on here. I went up to the people and asked them. They answered that they had passed through some remote town, some poverty-stricken village where there was only one very poor Jewish family. The husband had died and left his widow with one orphan girl and they had nothing to eat. When they were about to depart (the people were merchants), the mother asked them if they would like to buy the girl. The people (the merchants) bought the girl and thought they would take her to a convent so she could grow up among the gentiles and be a nun."

"When I saw and heard this," Monish told the righteous Rebbe Joshua, "I asked the merchants for the girl, but at first they absolutely refused to let me have her. I told them I'd give them whatever they asked. But even so I was barely able to get the girl from them—I had to pay them all the money I had in the house. There's nothing left, not even for a loaf of bread for tomorrow. I also had to give them all my clothes and was left almost naked. My wife, too, helped and gave everything she had, so we could save a Jewish soul from forced apostasy."

When the righteous Rebbe Joshua heard the story he exclaimed, "Blessed is the Lord every day!"* He asked Monish the cobbler to accompany him to the synagogue where the congregation was waiting because without him it would be impossible to blow the shofar. As for the girl, the righteous Rebbe Joshua took her to his house.

When the righteous Rebbe Joshua and Monish the cobbler entered the synagogue together, everyone was dumbfounded. But the righteous Rebbe Joshua told the congregation that now it would be possible to blow the shofar. Indeed, the shofar resounded as it should, like every year. Afterward, he seated Monish next to him.

The girl grew up in the house of the righteous Rebbe Joshua. She married one of his sons and all of her descendants were righteous and upright men.

---

*Popular understanding of Psalm 68:20.

COMMENTARY FOR TALE 24 (IFA 4813)

Narrated by Raphael Herbest from Moshav Kefar Shammai, who learned the story from his father, Zevi Herbest, a native of Czechoslovakia. Recorded by Moshè Rivlin in Kefar Shamai (Moshav) in 1962, when Raphael served as a paratrooper in the Israel Defense Forces.

Cultural, Historical, and Literary Background

The narrator of this tale is from Czechoslovakia, and hence he told the story not as a local legend but as an enchanted narrative about a Jewish community in a faraway place.

Vilna and Rabbi Joshua

The Jewish community in Vilna, the history of which goes back to the second half of the fifteenth century, became one of the major cultural and religious centers of eastern European Jewry. Dubbed by Napoleon (1769–1821) the "Jerusalem of Lithuania," an epithet the Jewish community readily adopted, it became known as "Yerushalayim d'Lita" primarily because of its strength as a cultural and learning center. Basic histories of the Jewish community in Vilna are available.[1]

The great synagogue of Vilna, damaged during World War II and razed to the ground in 1955–1957 in the course of a Soviet reconstruction project for Vilnius, was a unique architectural monument of early seventeenth-century Lithuania. The Jewish community in Vilna built its first synagogue, a wooden structure, in 1573, which was destroyed during a pogrom in 1592. The building was quickly reconstructed but was destroyed again in 1606. The Jewish ghetto was established in 1633 as a way of strengthening the community, and then the Jews were allowed to build a new stone synagogue within its boundaries. The construction of the synagogue had to follow the guidelines that applied to all other synagogues in the country: Their height could not exceed that of surrounding houses, and it could not have the pattern of either a church or a monastery. To comply, the builders set its foundation two meters (about six feet) into the ground.

The rules for construction applied to all synagogues, and the great synagogue of Vilna was the largest. The men's hall measured twenty-five by twenty-two meters, and its height was more than twelve meters. It was surrounded by a women's gallery on the northeast and northwest sides and a vestibule on the southwest side. Although its exterior was simple, its interior was rich and opulent. In the middle of the spacious men's hall, there were four Tuscan columns in a square with a *bimah*. The synagogue had been ransacked, rebuilt, and refurbished during the seventeeth century; in the middle of the next century, it suffered fire and war damage. Yet, each time, it was rebuilt and redecorated, retaining and increasing its famed grandeur. More detailed accounts of its history have been published.[2]

The editor could not establish the historical identity of Rabbi Joshua the righteous in Vilna.

The Shofar

The shofar that is used in the synagogue in the penitential prayers before Rosh Hashanah, during the Rosh Hashanah services, and at the end of Yom Kippur is one of the oldest musical instruments still in use in religious services.[3] Instructions for and descriptions of its use, in ritual and in war, are available in the Bible (Leviticus 25:9; Joshua 6:20) and in numerous passages in the talmudic-midrashic literature.[4]

Any male member of the congregation can blow the shofar. In Hasidic literature, the blowing of the shofar and the anxieties associated with it have become significant narrative themes. Failure to produce sound from the shofar is perceived in mystical and moral terms with ensuing narrative explanations. Some of these stories have anecdotal qualities, whereas others clearly project messianic, cosmic, and moral messages, as the present tale does. Messianic explanations confound the ritual use of the shofar and its use in the utopian condition, heralding the coming of the Messiah. Although an individual shofar blower has the capability to announce the immediate arrival of the Messiah, his generation is not yet ready for this event. See also the notes to tale IFA 6306 (in this vol., no. 23).

The cosmic explanation for the failure to sound the shofar involves a struggle between good and evil, in which Satan prevents the sound of the shofar from reaching the throne of God. Within the moral reasons for failing to sound the shofar, it is possible to distinguish three narrative situations: (1) In the community there is a person who is more troubled than the blower and hence his trumpeting would be more sincere; (2) the shofar blower committed a sin and needs to atone for it before he can succeed in his task; and (3) in the community there is a person who is more virtuous than the blower, of which the present tale is a variation.

Similarities to Other IFA Tales

There are only a few tales on this theme in the IFA, and not all of them are from the Hasidic tradition.

- IFA 1643: *Let Ivan Blow the Shofar* (Poland).[5]
- IFA 5554: *A Tale for Rosh Hashanah* (Irani Kurdistan).
- IFA 6243: *Rabbi Nahum the Coachman from Baghdad* (Eretz Yisra'el, Ashkenazic).[6]

Folklore Motifs

- cf. F321.0.1 "Child sold to fairies."
- cf. G303.9.9.20 "Satan entangles ram horns on altar."
- *N842.2 "Shoemaker as helper."
- P453 "Shoemaker."

24 / The Redemption of Captives   191

- *R131.21 "Shoemaker rescues abandoned or sold child."
- *R132 "Jew rescues a Jewish child from Christians."
- S221 "Child sold (promised) for money."
- cf. S321 "Destitute parents abandon children."
- V50 "Prayer."
- V112.3 "Synagogues."
- *V119 "Shofar (a ram's horn trumpet)."
- *V119.1 "Shofar is blown in the synagogue on the High Holy Days."
- *V119.2 "Satan blocks the shofar's sound."
- cf. *V119.3 "Shofar's sound is blocked: a more meritorious person deserves the honor of blowing it."

Notes

1. I. Cohen, *Vilna*; I. Klausner, *The Jewish Community of Vilno in the Days of the "Gaon"*; I. Klausner, "Vilna"; I. Klausner, *Vilna, "Jerusalem of Lithuania"*; Jeshurin, *Wilno;* Minczeles, *Vilna, Wilno, Vilnius;* and L. Ran, *Jerusalem of Lithuania.*

2. Janekeviciene, *Vilniaus Didzioji Sinagoga;* Krinsky, *Synagoguges of Europe,* 223–225; and Wischnitzer, *The Architecture of the European Synagogue,* 119–120.

3. Adler, *The Shofar;* Finesinger, "The Shofar"; and Reik, *Ritual,* 221–361.

4. M. Gross, *Otzar ha-Aggadah* (The treasure of the Aggadah), 3:1233–1235.

5. Published in Raphael, *Sefer ha-Ḥasidut* (The book of Hasidism), 170; and Lipson, *Medor Dor* (From days of old), 3:2166. This anecdote is told about Rabbi Levi Isaac of Berdichev (1740–1809).

6. Published in E. Marcus, *Jewish Festivities,* 21–22 no. 6.

25

The Long "Ḥad Gadya"

TOLD BY ROSA LIBERMAN TO MOSHE BURT

*I*n the town of Bendzin in Poland there lived many Jews—upright and pious Jews. The city used to belong to Russia, in the time of the czars.

The Polish nationalists wanted to use every means and all their energies to restore Polish freedom, establish a Polish state, and get rid of the Russians. The czar did everything to frustrate this dream.

The Russian people, too, began to rise up against the czar. They too wanted to overthrow the czar and set up a regime of the workers. One of the best-known revolts took place in 1905.

In Bendzin, there were many Jews who belonged to that Polish radical organization. They did their work quietly, in absolute secrecy, because a single wrong move could lead to the death penalty or banishment to Siberia. The group included people who risked their lives for the liberation of Poland, like Pilsudski and his devoted followers. The Jews among them hoped that things would be better for the Jews after the overthrow of the czar.

In Bendzin, there lived a Jew with a beard, David Fischmann. (His family name was somewhat different, but it's better this way, because his family is still alive and lives in Israel.) This David worked with the Polish nationalists and distributed posters calling for the liberation of Poland from the Russians. No one in his house knew anything about it, and if anyone had learned of it they would have been terrified, because czarist agents were everywhere. Then, too, he was a Jew and the father of three children!

Until one day David was arrested. They found illegal posters and pamphlets in his possession—no more and no less. He was sent to the Sherotsk prison.

A year and a half passed and David was still being held, without trial. His wife didn't know what to do. Finally, she gathered up her courage, took her three children, and traveled to Warsaw to see the governor. For a week she wandered the streets of the city until she managed to reach him. The conversation between them went like this:

The governor:	What do you want of me?
The woman:	I am asking for your assistance, my lord.
The governor:	How can I help you? For I am only a man, flesh and blood, like every human being.
The woman:	But you have the power to release my husband.

The governor had reviewed the papers before she came. He said: "Your husband is a major criminal; he raised his hand against our czar."

The woman:	That is true, my lord. I know that he is guilty. But what are the three children guilty of? I am asking for these children to have a father. Release my husband, so that he can work and support his children. If not, we will all die of hunger.
The governor:	Your husband should have thought of that before. I did not imprison him. Now go back home and I will see what can be done with him.
The woman:	My husband is a pious Jew, no revolutionary; it may be that he himself did not know what he was doing.

It was just before Passover. The governor issued an order to release David on furlough until after Passover. His wife prepared a proper seder, for David was a guest in his house, after a year and a half.

Now David had a Christian friend—Tomek, they called him—who was an even more fanatical adherent of the Polish national movement. The czar's secret police learned about him and hunted for him all over Russia; they knew that Tomek was a dangerous propagandist.

Now on this Passover eve, as David's family was getting ready for the seder, Tomek entered their house. He didn't know where to go. He was hungry and tired out from hiding.

The melody of "Had Gadya" was filling the place when suddenly the family turned as pale as death: Someone was knocking at the door. From the sound, it was obvious that it was the police.

David had a paper, covered with official stamps, to the effect that he could stay at home throughout the eight days of the festival. After that he was to return on his own to the Sherotsk prison. But as for Tomek, the gentile—what could be done with him?

David had an idea. He got out his Yom Kippur *kittel** and had Tomek put it on. But this took some time, because the *kittel* was not where it was supposed to be. In the meantime, David's wife went out to the door. There stood soldiers, Cossacks and Circassians. She asked them to wait, because it was forbidden to interrupt "Ḥad Gadya" in the middle. . . . In the next room, they were all singing the many verses of "Ḥad Gadya," "Ḥad Gadya," in a loud voice, while turning Tomek into a person who could not be recognized as a Christian.

The soldiers began shouting. They had to check whether David was at home; they had to come in and see him with their own eyes. But inside they kept dragging out "Ḥad Gadya."

"*Chto eto u vas takoi bolshoi* 'Ḥad Gadya'?"** demanded the soldiers.

When Tomek the gentile was properly arrayed, they stopped singing *Ḥad Gadya* and went on to *Ehad Mi Yode'a*—"Who Knows One?" Then David's wife led the soldiers into the room where they were conducting the seder.

David showed them his papers and everything seemed to be all right. But one soldier kept staring at Tomek, who was swaying back and forth all the time, like a pious Jew, in a white *kittel,* with a hat on his blond head.

"*Kakoi eto nabozhny yevrei, vez borodi?*"§ he asked loudly.

David rescued the situation: "My brother has just recovered from typhus; his beard fell out completely."

In the meantime, the members of the family had poured out brimming glasses of brandy for the uninvited guests. They ate the Passover *knaidlach*§§ and left the place wobbling on their legs.

The long "Ḥad Gadya" had saved the two comrades.

---

*Long white gown worn on special occasions.
**Russian for "Why is your *Ḥad Gadya* so long?"
§Russian for "What kind of pious Jew is this, without a beard?"
§§Matzah ball or dumpling.

A kittel.

COMMENTARY FOR TALE 25 (IFA 7211)

Told in Yiddish by Rosa Liberman from Bendzin, Poland, to Moshe Burt in 1966 in Haifa.

Cultural, Historical, and Literary Background
Poland's Nationalistic Insurrection

The present story is ground in a historical event—the Polish nationalistic insurrection against czarist Russia in 1904–1907, in which Jews participated.[1] Triggered by the recruitment drives of the Russian army to mobilize units for the Russo-Japanese war, the Polish Socialist Party (PPS) organized antiwar demonstrations. On November 12, 1904, the Warsaw police arrested twenty Jews who met to prepare this protest.[2] Bendzin, the locale of the present story, was the county seat of the urbanized and industrialized Dabrowa Basin. During this period, it experienced demonstrations and strikes in which Jews participated, and some Jews were likely arrested together with other national revolutionaries.[3] While the historical accuracy of this particular incident is not verifiable, the available knowledge of the general atmosphere in the country at that time supports the likelihood of such an occurrence.

Among the Polish political leaders, Józef Pilsudski (1867–1935) is mentioned in the story. As a devoted Polish nationalist, he was a fighter in the Polish socialist underground and a military commander who amassed political and military power in interwar Poland, becoming a virtual dictator (1926–1935). In the years after World War I (1918–1922), he reached the peak of his career when he served both as head of state of the Polish Republic and commander-in-chief of its army. As a central figure in Polish nationalistic movement and later political life, Pilsudski drew a large amount of criticism; consequently, there is a large amount of scholarship about his career.[4]

The Songs

To increase the drama of the police search for Polish nationalists, the story draws on two songs that are sung at the end of the seder: "Eḥad Mi Yode'a" (Who knows one?), tale type 2010 Ehod Mi Yode'a (One; who knows?)," and "Ḥad Gadya" (One kid), a variant of tale type 2030 "The Old Woman and Her Pig." Both are formulaic songs that can be expanded with improvisation. The choice of using the latter song to delay the police adds a humorous twist to the tale because in Yiddish slang "Ḥad Gadya" is a code reference to prison.[5]

The scholarship, and likely the history, of these two songs in Jewish tradition are intertwined. The songs' creators are unknown, but they were first printed in the Prague Haggadah (1590). Of the two, "Ḥad Gadya" is found there only in Yiddish. However, Yaari[6] noted that, contrary to all other accounts, the texts of the two songs are in Hebrew and Yiddish.

The songs' origins have been questions that have baffled scholars and generated rigorous literary and historical analysis.[7] Both "Ḥad Gadya" and "Eḥad Mi Yode'a" have parallels in the oral traditions of other nations; they are classified as "cumulative tales." General studies and surveys of this form are available.[8] Perkal[9] distinguished three structural subforms in the cumulative tales: the accumulative tale, the chain tale, and the "clock" tale; "Ḥad Gadya" is, according to her classification, a chain tale.

Fuchs[10] and Gefen[11] wittily observe, that non-Jewish scholars are looking to establish the Jewish origins of these songs, whereas Jewish scholars seek their origins in the folklore of other nations. Their insight is amusing but not entirely accurate. For example, Yoffie[12] concluded that "[t]he Hebrew chant printed in the Passover haggadah [is] the first song to set the pattern for a number-song which has spread over two continents and been transmitted through many languages and among many nations."

These questions are difficult to settle, in spite of, or perhaps because of, the large amount of comparative scholarship that accumulated in the nineteenth and twentieth centuries. Among the Jewish scholars, Zunz[13] was the first to point out the possible influence a German folk song had on "Ḥad Gadya." Gefen[14] demonstrated, however, that the German version to which Zunz referred as evidence was published in the *Wunderhorn* (edited by Arnim Brentano), included Hebrew words such as *shochet* and *malach hammoves*, and was itself a translation of the "Ḥad Gadya" of the Haggadah.

"Ḥad Gadya" is a poem that can also be considered a sorite, a genre that Fischel[15] defined as "a set of statements which proceed, step by step, through the force of logic or reliance upon a succession of indisputable facts, to a climatic conclusion, each statement picking up the last key word (or key phrase) of the preceding one." According to him, the form gained popularity in the Greco-Roman discourses between 50 B.C.E. and 200 C.E. and correspondingly influenced tannaitic and rabbinical discourse. Fischel regarded Ḥad Gadya as a late example of the catastrophic sorite,"[16] a form that has antecedents in tannaitic literature. For example:

R. Judah—also used to say: Ten strong things have been created in the world.
The rock is hard, but the iron cleaves it.
The iron is hard, but the fire softens it.
The fire is hard, but the water quenches it.
The water is strong, but the clouds bear it.
The clouds are strong, but the wind scatters them.
The wind is strong, but the body bears it.
The body is strong, but fright crushes it.
Fright is strong, but wine banishes it.
Wine is strong, but sleeps works it off.
Death is stronger than all, and charity saves from death (BT *Bava Batra* 10a).

The above sorite is quoted in the name of Rabbi Judah bar Ilai (mid-second century C.E.). In a late Palestinian midrash, Rabbi Judah's sorite acquires four more objects and a misogynistic message (cf. also tale IFA 16395 [vol. 1, no. 35]):

> R. Judah said: There are fourteen things which are stronger one than the other, and each one is dominated by the next.
> The ocean-deep is strong, but the earth dominates it because the deep is subservient to it.
> The earth is strong, but the mountains are stronger and dominate it.
> The mountain is strong, but the iron dominates it and breaks it.
> Iron is strong, but fire makes it melt away.
> Fire is strong, but water dominates it and extinguishes it.
> Water is strong, but the clouds carry it.
> The clouds are strong, but wind disperses them.
> The wind is strong, but wall dominates and withstand it.
> A wall is strong, but a man dominates and demolishes it.
> Man is strong, but trouble creeps over [and weakens] him.
> Trouble is strong, but wine dominates it and causes it to be forgotten.
> Wine is strong, but sleep overcomes its effects.
> Sleep is strong, but illness dominates it and prevents it.
> Illness is strong, but the Angel of Death dominates it and takes life away.
> Stronger [i.e., worse] than them all, however, is a bad woman (*Ecclesiastes Rabbah* 7:26).

Such sequences, listing different objects, can take a variety of literary forms, as the following tale types demonstrate:

- 2031 "Stronger and Strongest": The frost-bitten foot—"Mouse perforates wall, wall resists wind, wind dissolves cloud, cloud covers sun, sun thaws frost, frost breaks foot."
- 2031A "The Esdras Chain": Stronger and strongest—"wine, king, woman, truth." In Jewish tradition, a version of this story became the foundation narrative for the return of the Babylonian exile under the leadership of Zerubbabel (1 Esdras 3:1–4:63).[17]
- 2031B "Abraham Learns to Worship God" and 2031B* "The Most Powerful Idol" have religious implications.
- 2031C "The Man Seeks the Greatest Being as a Husband for His Daughter" and 2031A* "Wall in Construction Collapses" are secular parodies on romance. Tale type 2031C occurs in the medieval fable book *Mishlei Shu'alim* of Rabbi Berechiah ha-Nakdan (twelfth to thirteenth centuries). Copious comparative annotations are available.[18]

More recently discovered manuscripts and reexamined texts by rabbinical authorities point to script and oral transmission of "Ḥad Gadya" that predate the song's first publication in the Prague Haggadah. Shmeruk[19] discovered a haggdah manuscript that dated back to the fifteenth century that includes a bilingual (Yiddish and Aramaic) rendition of "Ḥad Gadya." He proposed the priority of the Yiddish text.

Later, reevaluating an oral testimony from 1791, Fuchs[20] proposed, by making reasonable but unconfirmed assumptions, that "Ḥad Gadya" was sung in the seder ceremony by the fourteenth century. This proposal dates the incorporation of the song into the haggadah two hundred years earlier than the Prague Haggadah. The text in question is the Passover haggadah edited by Yedidya Ti'ah Vail.[21] Vail[22] noted that on a manuscript from 1406, found in a beit midrash (house of study) in Worms, there is a reference to the incorporation of the "Ḥad Gadya" song in the seder. This testimony was well known[23] but was not considered reliable. Fuchs proposed that there is a reasonable likelihood that the house of study in Worms was burned in 1349 and rebuilt in 1353–1355; hence the song was sung in the first half of the fourteenth century. Furthermore, reiterating a conclusion that Paris[24] made, Fuchs[25] suggested that "Ḥad Gadya" originated in Provence and from there spread to Worms and then to other European Jewish communities, including those in the Iberian peninsula.

The occurrence of the song in oral tradition might yield unexpected support to Fuchs's hypothesis about the literary history of "Ḥad Gadya." As mentioned, the song does not appear in the *haggadot* of the Italian and Sephardic Jewish communities or in those of Islamic countries until the nineteenth century. However, the song was well known in Sephardic and Italian communities in its traditional form as well as in its variants. Jochnowitz[26] studied the song in Judeo-Italian and Shuadit, or Judeo-Provençal, and noted that the "Jews in southern France who followed the Provençal rite (i.e. who were neither Sephardim nor Ashkenazim but whose ancestors had always lived in the area) sang the traditional "Ḥad Gadya" in Shuadit." It is hence quite possible that "Ḥad Gadya" reached Italian Jewry not from the Ashkenazic tradition, as it is generally assumed, but rather from the Sephardic community—even before the expulsion of the Jews from Spain in 1492. So far, however, this is conjectural history. The more common assumption is that "the 'Khad [Ḥad] Gadya' reached Italian Jews from Ashkenazic sources in Eastern Europe and then—following the usual dispersal lines—moved north to southern France (Provence), and east to the Ottoman Empire and across the Mediterranean to North Africa."[27]

Either migration route is possible. However, the abundance of variations on the literary form in Italian and Sephardic communities suggests the song's occurrence in oral tradition over a long period, the specific text of which was dependent on, but also independent of, the traditional text of the haggadah.[28] Furthermore, in his research, Schwadron[29] found that the western Sephardim exclude this song from their Passover tradition but that the eastern Sephardim—from Italy to Greece and Turkey—know many versions of "Ḥad Gadya" and sing it during the seder and at other times, considering the song to be "rooted originally in their great grandparental familial sources in Spain and Portugal. [Although t]he latter remains questionably assumptive and unconfirmed."

The problem of the origin of "Ḥad Gadya" still awaits conclusive evidence. The search for the song's history is further complicated by the antiquity of the sorite form, its occurrence in many cultures and languages, and the stabilization of the text that Jews provided by incorporating it into the haggadah. Further discussions and surveys addressing this problem have been published.[30] A comprehensive study of the song and its interpretations in the eighteenth and nineteenth centuries has been conducted.[31] Rabach[32] reported a version that is linguistically relevant to the present story.

Folklore Motifs

- K1800 "Deception by disguise."
- P10 "Kings."
- P711 "Patriotism."
- P715.1 "Jews."
- V75.1 "Passover."
- *V75.1.1 "Seder, the Passover eve ceremonial dinner."

――――― Notes ―――――

1. Blobaum, *Rewolucia*.
2. Ibid., 41.
3. Ibid., 79, 84.
4. A selection in English: Dziewanowski, *Joseph Pilsudski*; Jedrzejewicz, *Pilsudski*; Pilsudski, *The Memories of a Polish Revolutionary and Soldier*; and J. Rothschild, *Pilsudski's Coup d'Etat*.
5. Stutchkoff, *Thesaurus of the Yiddish Language*, 479 no. 470.
6. *Passover Haggadah*, 3–4 no. 24. See also Yudlov, *The Haggadah Thesaurus*, 5 no. 32.
7. For a bibliography, see Tabory, *Jewish Prayer and the Yearly Cycle,* 198–199 nos. 33.636–33.665.
8. Clouston, *Popular Tales and Fictions,* 1:289–313; Haavio, *Kettenmärchen-Studien I;* Haavio, *Kettenmärchen-Studien II;* Taylor, "A Classification of Formula Tales"; S. Thompson, *The Folktale*, 229–234; and Wienker-Piepho, "*Kettenmärchen.*"
9. "The Dual Nature of Cumulative Tales."
10. "*Le-Toldot ha-Shirim 'Eḥad Mi Yode'a ve-Ḥad Gadya*" (The history of '*Eḥad Mi Yode'a* and *Ḥad Gadya*).
11. *Transformation of Motifs in Folklore and Literature,* 209.
12. "Songs of the 'Twelve Numbers' and the Hebrew Chant of '*Echod Mi Yodea*,' " 411.
13. *Die gottesdienstlichen Vorträge der Juden*, 300.
14. Op. cit., 204–206. See L. A. Arnim, von, and C. Brentano. *Des Knaben Wunderhorn*; and W. Pape, *Arnim und die Berliner Romantik.*
15. "The Uses of the Sories (Climax, Gradatio) in the Tannaitic Period," 119.

16. Op. cit., 129–132, esp. 130.
17. Bin Gorion, *Mimekor Yisrael*, 81–85 no. 43 (1990 ed.).
18. Schwarzbaum, *The Mishle Shu'alim (Fox Fables)*, 167–178 no. 28; cf. 290–295 no. 53.
19. "The Earliest Aramaic and Yiddish Version of the 'Song of the Kid' (*khad Gadye*)"; and Shmeruk, *Yiddish Literature*, 57–59.
20. Op. cit.
21. *Haggadha shel Pesaḥ* (Passover Haggadah).
22. Op. cit., 47a, 151a.
23. Fuchs, op. cit., 201 n. 6.
24. "*Le 'Chanson du Chevreau.'*"
25. Op. cit., 221.
26. "Had Gadya in Judeo-Italian and Shuadit (Judeo-Provencal)," 241.
27. Schwadron, "'*Khad Gadya,*'" 258.
28. Armistead, "A Judeo-Spanish Cumulative Song and Its Greek Counterpart"; Armistead, *The Spanish Tradition in Louisiana I*, 104, 107; Armistead and Silverman, "A Neglected Source of the Prolog to *La Celestina*"; Pedrosa, "*Pluriliüngismo y paneuropeismo en la canción tradicional de el buen Viejo*"; and Schwadron, op. cit.
29. "Un Cavritico"; and his *Chad Gadya [One Kid]* [sound recording].
30. E. Goldschmidt, *The Passover Haggadah,* 97–98; Kasher, *Hagadah Shelemah,* 190–192; G. Kohut, "*Le Had Gadya et les chansons similaires*"; and G. Kohut, "Had Gadya."
31. Zibrt, *Ohlas obradnich pisni velikonocnich.*
32. "*Had Gadya* in Polish."

26

The Two Friends

Told by Abraham Keren

*I*t happened many years ago, in a town in Galicia. Avrum was a boy from a Jewish family, who lived next door to a Polish family with a son named Wlodek. The two boys were good friends. They played together and got into mischief and indulged in all sorts of pranks suggested by their imaginations.

When the boys grew up, their paths diverged and they went their separate ways. Avrum and Wlodek were both very bright and gifted children. Wlodek studied in the local school. When he finished, his parents sent him to the big city, where he continued his studies and became a priest. Over the years, he rose in the church hierarchy.

Avrum, by contrast, studied in the Jewish religious school. Later, his parents sent him to the yeshivah* to study Torah. After that, he married and had sons and daughters. He never could make a living, though; and he and his family lived in abject poverty, with scant bread and scarce water. Years passed, and Reb** Avrum's family grew larger. But the poverty of his house increased in proportion.

One forenoon Reb Avrum finished his prayers and left the school with his tallit§ and tefillin§§ bag under his arm. He trudged slowly through the street, sunk in gloomy thoughts: Where would his help come from? Where would he find bread for his children? Suddenly, he felt a tap on his shoulder and heard a familiar voice: "Avrumek! How are you?"

Reb Avrum turned toward the speaker—a smiling man in clerical grab. "Don't you recognize me?" the priest asked. "I'm Wlodek." Despite the differences that separated them, Avrum was glad to see his childhood friend and invited him home. The priest accepted the invitation and promised to come that evening for supper.

---

*Jewish school of higher learning.
**Rabbi or Mr.
§Prayer shawl.
§§Small black leather prayers boxes, wrapped around the head and arm, containing passages from the Torah.

26 / The Two Friends

Reb Avrum went home and told his wife about his meeting with the priest, his childhood friend, and that he had invited him home for dinner. His wife listened carefully before replying. "It's fine that you invited him, but we have to entertain and honor him appropriately—and with what? The only thing in this house is poverty."

What could be done? His wife ran to and fro among the neighbors and did what she could. Before the guest arrived the table was set with fine dishes and a royal repast.

When the priest arrived, they greeted him cordially. He surveyed the house and saw that there was poverty in every corner, but nevertheless the table was tastefully set and covered with fine food. He ate and drank and even agreed to sleep there. In the morning, he went away.

After the priest had gone, Avrum's wife went to straighten up the house and make the beds. When she lifted the pillow on the priest's bed, what did she see? A crucifix! It was solid gold, encrusted with precious jewels. And there on the crucifix was the image of the crucified one, with two large diamonds for his eyes! The woman was in a panic and didn't know what to do. Should she run after the priest to return what he had lost? Where should she look for him? Should she touch the crucifix? That was certainly forbidden! It's idolatry and has no place in a proper Jewish house. What should she do? She stood there in perplexity until she decided. She ran to the school and called her husband to come home. When Reb Avrum saw the crucifix, he pondered the matter. Finally he decided: We will set the crucifix aside and wait. The priest will certainly come back for what he lost.

Days passed, and then months. A year went by and still the priest did not return. "It's from Heaven," Reb Avrum told himself then. "I'll sell part of the crucifix to support us and the children."

He did just that. First he removed one eye from the crucifix and sold the diamond. Then he took out the other eye and sold it. When the money was gone he began cutting up the crucifix, piece by piece. Little by little he was able to sweep the poverty out of his house. The house changed beyond recognition and the family began to live comfortably.

Eventually, the priest reappeared in their house. He looked around and saw that the poverty had disappeared and there was no memory of their former indigence. Instead, there was comfort and wealth. The priest turned to Reb Avrum with a victorious and self-confident look. "Avrumek, as my eyes see, your situation is much better now. Tell me, whose God did this for you? Who brought you all of this wealth? Was it not thanks to the crucified one and the cross that all of this came to you?"

"You are mistaken, my friend," replied Reb Avrum. "That's not how it is. My God saw my poverty and he helped me. As for what I received from your god—did he give it to me of his own free will? In order to get anything from him I had to wrench out his eyes, first one and then the other, and finally cut him up limb by limb."

COMMENTARY FOR TALE 26 (IFA 3222)

Written down from memory by Abraham Keren, as heard from his mother, Faya Keren, from the shtetl Bircza, which was located on the road connecting the towns of Sanok and Przemysl.[1]

Cultural, Historical, and Literary Background

In the present version of this story, the two childhood friends belonged to different faiths. In other versions, the friends were both Jewish but one later converted to Christianity;[2] a cycle of such anecdotes about Jews who converted to Christianity is available.[3] Tubach[4] reported a similar story told from a medieval Christian perspective about a Jew who damaged a crucifix.

Not only the crucifix but also other clerical paraphernalia were imagined by Jews to conceal treasures. One example is the story *The Treasure in the Stuff*.[5] Schwarzbaum[6] traced this anecdote to Aesop's fable *How Hermes Bestowed a Treasure*[7] and suggested that it is the earliest known fable in which a treasure is found in a broken idol. The conflict between religions that characterizes the Jewish versions of the tale is absent in the classical version.

Similarities to Other IFA Tales

There are two other versions of this tale type in the IFA:

- IFA 592: *How did Jesus Help a Jew?* (Romania).
- IFA 7490: *The Jew Who Was a Priest as a Way to Making a Living* (Poland).

Folktale Type

- 1565*B (IFA) "Poor Jew Steals from the Statue of the Virgin Mary."

Folklore Motifs

- cf. E544.1.1 "Ghost leaves behind a crucifix."
- *N747 "Accidental meeting of childhood friends."
- P310 "Friendship."
- *P313.2 "Separate paths of childhood friends: one rich, the other poor."
- P426.1 "Parson (priest)."
- cf. Q222.2 "Punishment for heaping indignities upon crucifix."
- cf. V350 "Conflicts between religions."
- X410 "Jokes on parsons."
- *Z71.0.3 "Formulistic number: two."

Notes

1. First published in Keren, *Advice from the Rothschilds*, 30–33 no. 2.
2. N. Gross, *Maaselech un Mesholim*, 131–132; and E. Teitelbaum, *An Anthology of Jewish Humor and Maxims*, 247–249.

3. Druyanow, *Sefer ha-Bediḥah ve-ha-Ḥidud* (The book of jokes and witticisms), 2:395–396 no. 2029, 2:154–177 nos. 1385–1449.

4. *Index Exemplorum*, 110 no. 1373 (crucifix, bleeding, and Jew).

5. Cahan, *Yidishe folksmasiyyot* (Yiddish folktales), 125–127 no. 24 [1931 ed.] and 155–157 no. 35 [1940 ed.].

6. *Studies in Jewish and World Folklore*, 152–153 no. 133

7. Perry, *Aesopica*, 432 no. 295; Perry, *Babrius and Phaedrus*, 154–157 no. 119; and Weinert, *Die Typen der griechisch-römischen Fabel*, 137–138.

27

The Gentile Beggar's Secret

TOLD BY ESTHER WEINSTEIN
TO YEHUDIT GUT-BURG

A poor Jew with many children came to see the *rebbe*. The Jew was a tailor by profession—he patched up the garments of poor Jews and gentiles—and his name was Ḥayyim Yankel. His circumstances could hardly have been worse, yet they got more serious from day to day. So it was no wonder that the Jew complained to the *rebbe* about his bitter lot.

The *rebbe* pressed the tailor's hand. "The old beggar Ivan is ill," he said, "and will die soon. They will sell his clothes for almost nothing. You must go buy them. Rip his clothes apart, and with God's help you'll be rich. But don't tell anyone what I have said."

The tailor Ḥayyim Yankel swore to keep the secret. "But Rebbe," he added, "I don't even have money to buy the clothes." The *rebbe* put his hand in his pocket, took out a few coins, and gave them to the tailor. "Use this money to buy the clothes. But don't wash them and don't shake them. To be doubly safe I'll send my *shammes** to help you."

The *rebbe* blessed the tailor, and he set off, accompanied by the *rebbe*'s *shammes*.

The two set out. They traveled all night by train, reaching the tailor's town at daybreak. What should they hear, but that the poor gentile, Ivan the beggar, had died, and there was no money for a coffin. Ḥayyim Yankel and the *shammes* went to the deceased's hovel, where they found an old man who was watching the corpse and sighing that there was no money to pay for the funeral.

"How much do you need?" Ḥayyim Yankel asked the old man.

"Fifty gulden."

"What will you give me for that sum?"

"There is nothing except for these rags," said the watcher, pointing to the tattered clothes in the bare room.

---
*Synagogue caretaker.

Hayyim Yankel paid over the sum requested, took the bundle of worn-out clothing, and went home with the *shammes*.

Late that night, after midnight, the two ripped the clothes apart. Sewn into them they found many bank notes, along with a brief note and an amulet. According to the note, its owner was a Jew who had been kidnapped by Gypsies when he was a child and had grown up with them. When he was eleven, his grandfather came to him in a dream. "You are a Jew," he told him. "Run away from this place to the Jews. Tell them that you are a Jew and have to put on tefillin* in two more years. After that go off someplace where they don't know you, put on gentile clothes, and wear them for the rest of your life."

While Hayyim Yankel and the *shammes* were reading this document, the *rebbe* showed up. The three set out for the Christian cemetery, removed Ivan's body from its coffin, and took the corpse to the Jewish cemetery. Of course they left the coffin in the Christian cemetery. They erected a stone over the new grave in the Jewish cemetery, with Ivan's Jewish name, as written in the note.

The next day, they distributed the bank notes to poor people, orphans, and widows.

A number of years later, some Jews, the brothers of the kidnapped Jew, happened to visit the Jewish cemetery. On the gravestone they saw the name of their brother who had been kidnapped by Gypsies when he was a child. They were very glad that he had at least had a Jewish burial and told the *rebbe* so.

The *rebbe* sighed. "I brought your brother to a Jewish grave with my own hands," he said. "I learned about him from an old peasant, who told me that he was a Jew but no one knew, because outwardly Ivan behaved like a gentile in every respect. Once he had a wife and two daughters, but he died alone, in a tiny bare room, because his wife left him and took their daughters with her. He was poor and needy all his life and suffered greatly. May his memory be blessed, for he was a righteous man, one of the thirty-six righteous men by whose merit the world exists. He spent his money to help the poor, while he himself went hungry. All his days he was a penitent, since, having spent his childhood among the gentiles, he did not know he was a Jew and committed many transgressions."

The *rebbe* related all this to the man's family. "He performed many good deeds for the poor," he added. "Needy Jews used to say about him,

---

*Small black leather prayer boxes, wrapped around the head and arm, containing passages from the Torah.

'This gentile is a good gentile, but such good deeds prolong the exile. It is because of those like him that the Messiah cannot come.' When he heard this, the beggar would smile inwardly, enjoying the fact that no one knew he was a Jew. When he died, we searched his garments and found his true name written on a scrap of paper sewn into the lining of his coat."

The brothers wept, distressed that they had not known anything about their brother while he was alive. "It would have been better had he died in childhood," they said, "and not lived as a gentile all his life."

"No," the *rebbe* said. "His soul went straight to Paradise, for the man was righteous and penitent. Be proud of him and rejoice in his lot."

COMMENTARY FOR TALE 27 (IFA 4541)

Recorded by Yehudit Gut-Burg from her mother, Esther Weinstein, who heard the story from her father-in-law, Moshe Weinstein, who heard the story told by Hasidim in the court of the rabbi in Dandowka.[1]

Cultural, Historical, and Literary Background

Two major conflicting themes of the Hasidic narrative tradition converge in this tale: secret righteousness and conversion to Christianity.

Secret Righteousness

The theme of unpublicized righteous conduct has its roots in biblical and talmudic-midrashic traditions, discussed in the notes to tales IFA 10085 (vol. 1, no. 48) and IFA 10089 (vol. 1, no. 28). Although this idea continued in medieval narratives, in Hasidic thought and literature it acquired new religious and social meanings and became a cornerstone of Hasidic theology.[2] The hero of the present tale lived a concealed identity and with hidden piety not as a prelude to public recognition of his righteousness but as a lifelong secret as a consequence of childhood abduction. The story tells us that the beggar was one of the thirty-six righteous people.

Kidnapping and Conversion to Christianity

The present tale brings up a curious confluence of traditions about the "other"— alien peoples within European societies—among whom the Jews and the Gypsies were the most prominent. European traditions held that such ethnic groups harmed children: The Jews kidnapped them and slaughtered them for ritualistic purposes, a phenomenon known as "blood libel"; the Gypsies abducted children. The history and study of blood libel are discussed in the notes to tales IFA 10086 (vol. 1, no. 36), IFA 10611 (vol. 3, no. 54), IFA 15347 (vol. 1, no. 15), and IFA 16405 (vol. 1, no. 14). In the present tale, apparently one alien society (the Jews) has adopted the beliefs about another alien society (the Gypsies) held by the mainstream population (Christian Europeans).

The tales about the abduction of Jewish children in nineteenth-century Europe were also rooted in historical fact, involving not the Gypsies but rather the Jews themselves. For a period of twenty-nine years (1827–1856), Jews in the service of the community leadership (*kahal*) kidnapped Jewish children for service in the Russian Army. Under an 1827 act of legislation by Czar Nicholas I, Jewish communities had to fulfill an annual conscription quota of young Jewish males for military service. The leaders of each community were responsible for filling the quota, but they delegated the actual draft to Jewish kidnappers (*khappers*), who preyed primarily on the children of poor families. The *khappers* abducted young children, known as "cantonists," who were then raised in

27 / The Gentile Beggar's Secret 211

non-Jewish households before they began their twenty-five-year service at the age of eighteen.

Converting the Jews to Christianity was a hidden agenda of this legislation, and many boys were pressured to convert. While some maintained their Jewish religion, others succumbed. Their lives in the army and after their discharge became a subject of folk songs, folktales, literary writings, and memoirs.[3] An example of such a song follows:

Thrären giessen sich in die Gassen,	Tears flow in the streets,
In kindersche Blut ken men sich waschen.	We can wash in children's blood.
Gewald, wos is dos far a klog—	Help! What a disaster—
Zi denn wt kein mol mit weren Tog?	Will the day ever rise?
Kleine Eifelech raisst men fun Cheider,	Young chicks are torn away from school,
Men thut sei on jwonische Kleider.	They dress them up in "Greek" uniforms.
Unsere Parneissim, unsere Rabonim	Our leaders, our *rebbes*,
Helfen noch opzugeben sei far Jwonim.	Only help to give them up to the "Greeks."
Bai Suche Bakower sainen do sieben Bonim, Zushe.	Zashe Bakover has seven sons.
Is vun sei nit einer in Jwonim;	None of them is in a "Greek" [uniform];
Nor Leie-die-Almone's einzige Kind	Only the single son of Leah the widow
Is a Kapore far koholsche Sind.	Is an atonement for the community.
Es is a Mizwe opzugeben Prostakes,—	"It is right to sacrifice the simple folk," [Say the rich people]
Schuster, Schnaider sainen doch Laidakes;	"The shoemakers, the tailors—they are only bums;
Krätzige Chaiziqlech vun a Mischpoche a Sheiner	[But] leper animals of a fine Family,
Tor bai uns nitawekgeihn nit einer.	We must not give up, even one."[4]

A more literary translation of this song is available.[5] Discussions of the cantonists have been published.[6] The gentile beggar in the present tale fits with the image of a discharged cantonist, who lived somewhere between the societies of Jews and Christians.

Similarities to Other IFA Tales

In the IFA there are only a few tales about such abducted children:

- IFA 9806: *The Jewish Priest* (Romania).[7]
- IFA 18140 (in this vol., no. 28): *The Boy Who Was Kidnapped and Brought to Russia* (Poland).

Folklore Motifs

- A1674 "Tribal characteristics—stealing."
- cf. A1674.1 "Why it is not a sin for a Gypsy to steal."
- E755.1 "Souls in Heaven."
- cf. J2093 "Valuables given away or sold for trifle."
- K1817.1 "Disguise as beggar."
- *K1827.4 "A Jew disguises as a gentile."
- N524.1 "Money is found in the dead beggar's coat."
- P160 "Beggars."
- *P165 "Poor men."
- P251 "Brothers."
- *P426.4 "Rabbi."
- P441 "Tailor."
- Q172 "Reward: admission to Heaven."
- R10.3 "Children abducted."
- R10.3.1 "Children abducted by Gypsies."
- U60 "Wealth and poverty."
- U110 "Appearances deceive."
- V60 "Funeral rites."
- *V229.15.1 "Thirty-six incognito saints preserve the integrity of the world."
- V400 "Charity."
- V410 "Charity rewarded."

Notes

1. First published in D. Noy, *A Tale for Each Month 1962*, 31–33 no. 4. Reprinted in Weinstein, *Grandma Esther Relates . . .* , 33–36 no. 2.

2. Nigal, *The Hasidic Tale*, 252–263. For anthologized narratives that draw on the Hasidic tradition, see Ben-Yeḥezki'el, *Sefer ha-Ma'asiyyot* (A book of folktales), 2:7–82.

3. Levitats, *The Jewish Community in Russia, 1772–1844*, 57–68, esp. n. 46; Litvak, "The Literary Response to Conscription"; and Ginzburg and Marek, *Yiddish Folksongs in Russia*, 42–52 nos. 43–50 (songs about the cantonists).

4. Ginzburg and Marek, op. cit., 51–52 no. 50.

5. Levitats, op. cit., 65. Another version of this song is in A. Lewin, *Kantonistn* (Conscripts), 228.

6. Baron, *The Russian Jew Under Tsars and Soviets*, 35–38; Ginsburg [Ginzburg],

"*Yidishe Kantonisten*" (Jewish conscripts); Greenberg, *The Struggle for Emancipation,* 48–52; Keep, *Soldier of the Tsar,* 330–331; A. Lewin, op. cit.; A. Ofek, "Cantonists"; Stanislawski, *Tsar Nicholas I and the Jews,* 13–34; and Slutsky, "Cantonists."

7. Published in M. Cohen, *Mi-Pi ha-Am* (From folk tradition), 1:79–80 no. 36.

28

The Boy Who Was Kidnapped and Brought to Russia

TOLD BY HINDA SHEINFERBER TO HADARAH SELA

*O*nce some kidnappers came and snatched an only child. He was already past thirteen. He left the synagogue with his tefillin.* But they grabbed him, gagged him so that he wouldn't scream, put him in a wagon, and carried him off to distant Russia.

They gave the boy to a childless family, who took care of him. He cried a lot because he missed his parents and wanted to go home. He wouldn't eat their food because it wasn't Jewish food. He didn't want to eat. He became thin and sickly. He ate only bread and water. The man loved the boy very much. He called in a physician, who told him, "If you want him to be your son, do what he wants. Buy him new dishes, a plate and a pot and a spoon and a fork, and let him prepare his own food, so he'll start eating."

The boy said that if he watched them milk the cow he'd drink the milk. So they began to cook potatoes with milk. And he could eat butter, too, because when they make butter, it doesn't absorb anything from the goy.** So he was already eating butter and potatoes and drinking milk straight from the cow. He began to be in a better mood and started studying. The man brought him a teacher to teach him Russian because the boy knew only Yiddish.

He grew up. In Russia they went to the army for twenty-five years. He was seventeen or eighteen when they took him for a soldier. But what could he do with his tefillin? He found a metal box and put them inside, dug a hole, and marked the place. He buried his tefillin there and went off to the army.

He grew old—well, not really old, but he had a long beard, and his

---
*Small black leather prayer boxes, wrapped around the head and arm, containing passages from the Torah.
**A non-Jew, often meant disparagingly.

28 / The Boy Who Was Kidnapped

army uniform was too big and so were the boots, so he looked old. The night before he was mustered out of the army he went to the gentile's house and dug up the tefillin and ran away from there. He wanted to find his parents, he wanted to be among Jews—he had never forgotten this all his life.

He traveled from town to town. The dust and filth and mud got on his boots and his clothes, of course. He slept in the woods as he traveled from town to town, but he did not find his parents.

Once he came to a certain town. It was cold and snowing and he was hungry. He saw a light and went and knocked on the door. There was an old couple inside. They were always afraid at night. Who could be knocking? Maybe it was thieves! But he kept knocking. They said to themselves, "When Jews want to do a mitzvah,* 'He commanded us to live'—a person is meant to live. So even if it's a thief or murderer—we'll open the door for him anyway."

They opened the door and saw a gentile. The man and woman whispered to each other: "Should we let him in? Should we leave him outside?" So again they said—"He commanded us to live. We have to save him."

They let him in, made him tea, gave him food, and showed him to a small room with a bed (their own). He closed the door and slept. The old folks did not sleep all night. They were terrified that he would kill them in the middle of the night. But he was quiet.

In the morning he didn't open the door. They put their ears to the door and heard nothing. The woman opened it quietly and looked in. She saw that he was standing like a statue—she couldn't see his face, but he was standing erect and motionless. She called her husband to come and see. Without speaking he gestured to her to come in. She went in a few steps and stopped. Then she took a few more steps, until she was almost next to the table where he was standing. When she saw the tefillin bag there, she almost fainted.

What was this? She held her head at an angle, squinted, and cried out, "It's embroidered with Hebrew letters." No longer able to control herself, she moved even closer and made out her son's name on the tefillin bag. She looked at his face and saw him standing there in his tefillin, standing erect and motionless because he was reciting the *Amidah* prayer. She fainted. He revived her—he had found his parents.

---

*Good deed (literally, "commandment").

COMMENTARY FOR TALE 28 (IFA 18140)

Told by Hinda Sheinferber to Hadarah Sela in 1991 in Haifa, Israel.

Cultural, Historical, and Literary Background

Historical Perspective

This tale serves as a counternarrative to a traditional tale type and implicitly contrasts Jewish with non-Jewish parental behavior. In fact, the only other version of this tale type on record in the IFA is emphatically about a non-Jewish family—IFA 2346 *A Hostile Goy Kills His Son Unknowingly* (Poland)—and adheres to the more widely known narrative pattern in which the parents kill their guest, vying for his money, only to discover later that he was their long-lost son. The contrast between Jews and non-Jews is sharp and detailed: The Jewish parents are compassionate and loving, whereas the non-Jewish parents are greedy killers. In both versions of this tale, it is the mother who first spots the son's bag. In the present version, it is a tefillin bag (prayer boxes bag); but in the other versions, it is a bag of money. In European tales, the mother is also the driving force behind the assassination plot, although the father is often the actual murderer; in the current version, she is the one who recognizes and welcomes her son.

The tale that the present story counters has a unique history, which has been explored in detail;[1] a poetic-semiotic analysis of the tale, which includes seven more versions, is also available.[2] The story first appeared in print in 1618, just before, or at the start of, the Thirty Years' War. It was published in a popular anonymous pamphlet in English as *News from Perin in Cornwall of A most Bloody and un-exampled Murther very lately committed by a Father on his owne Sonne (who was lately returned from the Indyes) at the Instigation of a merciless Stepmother.*[3] Lillo[4] drew on this version of the story when he reprinted the tale in the eighteenth century. The story was also reprinted in the following century[5] and later summarized.[6] In the second version, published by Sir William Sanderson[7] (1586?–1676), a Jewish merchant buys some booty from the pirate-son, who returns to his non-Jewish parents.

A month after the British pamphlet was printed, a French brochure, *L'histoire admirable et prodigieuse de Nîmes,*[8] appeared in Paris. In this version of the tale, similar, though not identical, events took place in Nîmes.[9] On June 18, 1621, another small French pamphlet appeared, *Diversitez historiques ou Nouvelles Relations de quelques histories de ce temps,* which included a fifth variation of the tale written by Jean Baudoin (1590–1650); this tale is related to the present theme.[10]

The year 1618 seems crucial, either for historic, symbolic, or literary reasons, for the narration of this story. The first English and French versions appeared in print during that year, and later versions of the story date the tragic events to the same time period. The story *Polish Soldier of Pultusk,* another variation, was told to Antoine de Balinghem (1571–1631) and written down on May 14, 1618; it was published in 1621 and later printed in Latin by Georgius Stengelius (d. 1651), a German Jesuit.[11] In 1634, Johann Ludwig Gottfried published his *Historiche Chronica,* in which he tells a similar story, also dated to 1618, about the "soldier of Leipzig." Gottfried's tale was reproduced several times.[12]

In early versions of the tale, the son goes to sea, becoming a pirate and traveling to the West Indies or to India. In American versions, he is an outlaw, and in the European balladic tradition he is a legitimate soldier. These early oral variations have no narrative connection to a particular war or any other military experience; however, as noted above, the first published versions of the tale coincided with the start of the Thirty Years' War. Such later versions were current in landlocked central and eastern European countries and thus associated the son's absence with military service. In the present version, the events unfold against the historical background of the Jewish conscription law and its implementation in czarist Russia from 1827 to 1856. For more information about this law, see the notes to tale IFA 4541 (in this vol., no. 27). In light of the Russian experience, the opening episodes of the present tale are rooted in historic fact.

During the eighteenth and early nineteenth centuries, writers recognized the dramatic intensity of the tale and cast it into theatrical plays. In 1736, both George Lillo (1693–1739) in England and Piotr Kwiatkowski (1664–1747) in Poland published dramatizations.[13] Later, the Italian writer Vincenzo Rota (1703–1785) retold this tale as a short story,[14] and in 1809, the German writer Friedrich Ludwig Zacharias Werner (1768–1823) published his play *Der vierundzwanzigste Februar* (The twenty-fourth of February).

Besides the printed versions of the tale, the story circulated orally in prose and balladic forms in Western, Central, and Eastern Europe as well as in America. These stories and songs were recorded during the nineteenth and twentieth centuries. In Germany in 1804, a local journal included a ballad that associated the story's events with a particular building called "Jerusalem";[15] other German balladic variations followed.[16]

From the late nineteenth century and into the twentieth, incidents of filicide were reported in newspapers, circulated in oral tradition, and became a literary theme for authors and poets. In that respect, stories and ballads about these murders can be considered among the prominent "newspaper legends" (*Zeitungssage*), a term L. Schmidt[17] used to describe a ballad about murdering parents; it was likely coined by Görner.[18] Kosko[19] surveyed media and traditional accounts about such incidents in China, Germany, the Netherlands, Norway, Czechoslovakia, Poland, Hungary, the Baltic countries, the Balkans, France, Italy, England, the United States, Canada, Portugal, and Brazil.

The tale continued to circulate in English oral tradition as well as in print; the influences of the seventeenth-century chapbook version are evident in both media.[20] The tale reached the United States via several routes. Stories based on the English balladic tradition told about one of two figures: "Young Edmond" or

"Billy Potts."[21] Other oral versions reached the United States via Polish immigrants, who drew on the well-known tradition that the present version counters.[22]

A third route is from Robert Penn Warren's[23] story told in "Ballad of Billie Potts." In the preface to the poem, Warren wrote: "When I was a child I heard this story from an old lady who was a relative of mine. The scene, according to her version, was in the section of western Kentucky known as 'Between the Rivers,' the region between the Cumberland and the Tennessee. Years later, I came across another version in a book on the history of the outlaws of the Cave Inn Rock, or the Cave-In-Rock."[24] Studies relating the literary ballad to folklore traditions are available.[25]

The story was also a subject of drama.[26] In 1942, Albert Camus referred to such an incident as it was reported in a Czech newspaper and had his character Meursault read it in his prison cell.[27] Comparative studies of these plays have been conducted.[28]

Jewish Themes

The strict dietary laws that the kidnapped boy follows have their roots in the Hebrew Bible (Exodus 23:19; Leviticus 3:17, 7:23–27, 11:13–23, 17:10–14; Deuteronomy 14:4–21) and have been further developed and articulated in the talmudic-midrashic and medieval Jewish literature.[29] A modern anthropological explanation of these laws has been proposed.[30]

Toward the conclusion of the story, the returning son prays the *Amidah* (Standing prayer); it is popularly known among Ashkenazic Jews as the *Shemoneh Esrei* (Eighteen [benedictions]). As its name indicates and as described in the tale, the worshiper stands up and faces Jerusalem while praying. It is a silent prayer that must not be interrupted for whatever reason. It is recited individually at each of the three daily services. In the tale, the returning son is praying at the morning service (*Shaḥarit*). Discussions of the history, variations, and development of the *Amidah* have been published.[31]

Folktale Types

- 939A "Killing the Returned Soldier."
- 939A (Krzyzanowski) "*Niespodzianka*" (The surprise).

Folklore Motifs

- C220 "Tabu: eating certain things."
- cf. C221.1.1.5 "Tabu: eating pork."
- *H96.1 "Identification by tefillin."
- cf. J21.2 "Do not act when angry."[32]
- J1115.2 "Clever physician."
- cf. M444 "Curse of childlessness."

- cf. N321 "Son returning home after long absence unwittingly killed by parents."
- P210 "Husband and wife."
- P231 "Mother and son."
- P233 "Father and son."
- P424 "Physician."
- R10.3 "Children abducted."
- T670 "Adoption of children."
- V50 "Prayer."
- *V131.3 "Phylacteries (tefillin)."

Notes

1. Kosko, *Le fils assassiné (AT 939 A)*.
2. Fabre and Lacroix, *"Sur la production du recit populaire."*
3. Originally printed in 1618 by "E. A. to be sold at Christ-Church gate." The pamphlet is in the Bodleian Library in Oxford, UK.
4. *The London Merchant or the History of George Barnwell and Fatal Curiosity*, 221–238. See also Kosko, op. cit., 40–52, 55.
5. Hunt, *Popular Romances of the West of England*, 442–444.
6. Briggs, *A Dictionary of British Folk-Tales*, B:2:304–305.
7. *A Compleat History of the Lives and Reigns of Mary Queen of Scotland, and of Her Son and Successor, James the Sixth, King of Scotland*, 463–465; republished anonymously, but likely edited by Thomas Frankland (1633–1690), in *The Annals of King James and King Charles the First*, 33.
8. Printed in 1618 and now in the Bibliothèque Nationale (Paris).
9. Kosko, op. cit., 62–64.
10. Ibid., 65–79.
11. Ibid., 79–90.
12. Ibid., 90–103.
13. Lillo, op. cit.; Kosko, op. cit., 266–281.
14. Kosko, op. cit., 112–123; and Dunlop, *History of Prose Fiction*, 2:231–232.
15. Kosko, *"L'auberge de Jérusalem à Dantzig"*; and Kosko, *Le fils assassiné*, 128–144.
16. Meier et al., *Deutsche Volkslieder: Balladen*, 4:260–298 no. 85 (*Die Mordeltern*); for a bibliographical note, see 4:298 n. 2. See also Röhrich and Brednich, *Deutsche Volkslieder: Texte und Melodien*, 1:255–259 no. 44; Cheesman, "The Return of the Transformed Son"; and Cheesman, *The Shocking Ballad Picture Show*, 85–118, 119–160.
17. "Zu der Ballade 'die Mordeletern.'"
18. "Ulrich von Lichtenstein in Zerbst." See also Petzoldt, *"Mord-Herbergen"*; and Shojaei Kawan, "Contemporary Legend Research in German-Speaking Countries."
19. *Le fils assassiné*, 124–239.
20. See Hunt, op. cit.; Briggs, op. cit., B:1:516–517; and Briggs and Tongue, *Folktales of England*, 64–66 no. 26.
21. Randolph, *Ozark Folksongs*, 2:59–64 no. 140; Randolph, "Bedtime Stories from Missouri"; Randolph, *Who Blowed Up the Church House*, 23–24; and Rothert, *The

Outlaws of Cave-in-Rock, 294–298, 301.

22. Dorson, "Polish Wonder Tales of Joe Woods."

23. *Selected Poems:1923–1943,* 3–17.

24. See Rothert, op. cit.

25. Bisanz, "Robert Penn Warren"; Clark, "A Meditation on Folk-History"; and Sarnowski, "Things Exist in You without Your Knowing It."

26. Rostworowski, *"Niespodzianka"* (Surprise), written in 1929; and Camus, *Le Malentendu.*

27. Camus, *L'Étranger,* 113–114.

28. Brednich, *"Mordeltern"*; Frauenrath, *Le fils assassiné;* Krejci, "*Putování sujetu o 'synu, zavrazdeném rudici'* "; Virtanen, "Camus' *Le Malentendu*"; Kosko, "A propos du malentendu"; Kosko, *Le fils assassiné,* 266–329; and Prince, "Meursault and Narrrative."

29. Anonymous, *The Book of Kashrut;* Dresner, *The Jewish Dietary Laws;* and Rabinowicz, "Dietary Laws."

30. Douglas, *Purity and Danger.*

31. Fleischer, "The *Shemone Esre*"; J. Heinemann, "Amidah"; Elbogen, *Jewish Liturgy,* 24–54; Finkelstein, "The Development of the Amidah"; and Kohler, "The Origin and Composition of the Eighteen Benedictions."

32. See the notes to tale IFA 3576 (vol. 1, no. 38).

29

The Jew Who Returned to His People

Told by Efraim Orenstein to Mariana Juster

*O*nce there was a Jew who lived in a small house on the banks of the Dniester River, on the Russian side, near the border between Russia and Romania. He lived there contentedly with his family, after having served twenty years in the czar's army. All his neighbors were gentiles, but they got along well, even though the Jew lived in constant fear of them. But the Jew was king in his own house, which was like a small kingdom where he, his wife, and two children lived in the spirit of the Jewish faith and tradition. Every Sabbath was blessed with bright candlelight, prayer, and a rich and festive meal. The holidays he celebrated with other Jews in a nearby town, where all respected and admired him.

But one day the serenity of the small house evaporated. Some Jew-hating Cossacks surrounded the Jew's house and looked for excuses to quarrel with him. All of his attempts to appease them were fruitless, and they beat him severely until he died. They threatened his wife that they would abduct her son if she told the authorities what they had done.

Thus began a difficult and bitter life for the widow and orphans. They found themselves among enemies, with nowhere to turn for help in their distress. The widow was especially troubled by thoughts of how she could save her son from the wicked anti-Semites. Her sleepless nights were haunted by the vision of how they would take her son for the army and remove him from his family and Jewish faith. Then, during her terrified nights, she had an idea of how she could save her son: run away! Run away to some far-off place, outside Russian territory. It would have to be done soon, because with every day the danger lurked nearer.

One day, the widow took her two children—her five-year-old son and three-year-old daughter—and went to the river. She hid them in the bushes while she looked for a narrow and accessible spot where she could swim across to the Romanian side of the river. When she was certain that no one could see her, she took the boy and swam across with him. Then she told the child to wait quietly until she returned with his sister. But when she went back to get her daughter, the Cossacks seized her.

The only thing that carried across to the Romanian side were the echoes of distant cries of pain. The boy waited for an hour, for two hours; but when darkness fell and his mother still had not returned he began to cry and call for her. All was in vain—his mother did not return. The frightened child called for help. Because no one came, he began walking toward the lights that blinked here and there on the horizon. The boy reached a Romanian village where he found shelter. The farmers did their best to help the foundling, but he really belonged to no one. Because no one knew his name they called him "Pripshila," meaning "an abandoned child."

Pripshila soon learned that he had to work if he wanted to get his daily portion of *mamaliga*,* small as it was. He took care of the geese, cleaned the cowsheds, and did whatever else needed doing. Nevertheless he was often hungry and cold.

The years passed, and the boy almost forgot who he was and where he had come from. When he was almost thirteen he worked as a shepherd and roamed with the sheep far into the hills of Moldavia. One day, while he was watching the sheep, he saw that his favorite lamb had disappeared. He searched and searched for it, but did not find it until the afternoon. Somehow it had gone astray.

The next day, the shepherd was astonished to see that his favorite lamb had disappeared again. He searched all day and found it only in the evening.

On the third day, he kept his favorite lamb close to him, but in the blink of an eye it again vanished. He searched and searched, but there was no sign of it. He climbed hills and went down into valleys. He searched in wooded areas. But the lamb—it was as if the earth had swallowed it up. The more he searched, the farther he got from his flock. The stars came out and the shepherd was still looking for the lamb. He panicked, because he realized that he didn't know the way back. Suddenly, in the darkness, he saw a white spot that looked like the lamb but was somehow different from it. The spot approached, and then receded like a shadow, with the boy running after it. The "lamb" flew like a ghost, with the shepherd in pursuit.

At midnight, when the exhausted shepherd collapsed to the ground, he suddenly heard someone calling him, as if from the direction of the white spot: "Ḥayyim!"

---

*Cornmeal mush.

It was a voice from a distant world—but nevertheless familiar, melodious, and seductive—"Ḥayyim! Ḥayyim!" It was the same voice that had accompanied his childhood. The shepherd got up and resumed his pursuit of the white spot, but it fled more quickly. All the while the voice kept calling, "Ḥayyim, come! Ḥayyim, come!"

Ḥayyim climbed up hills and went down into valleys, until the spot merged with the half-light of morning. The hills and meadows vanished, replaced by a town that materialized before the eyes of the tired and confused shepherd boy. He entered the first house, from which wailing voices could be heard; it was the sound of the morning prayers that this child from the banks of the Dniester had heard long ago, every morning, from his father.

Curious Jews surrounded the gentile boy who had burst into their synagogue. They peppered him with questions. Ḥayyim remembered the sad story of how he had crossed the Dniester. One of the Jews told him about a mother who had been seized by the Cossacks and tortured to reveal where her son was. She had not told them, of course. The boy remembered his mother's cries, "Ḥayyim! Ḥayyim!" Now the meaning of the mysterious events of the past night was clear to him.

Ḥayyim was adopted by a Jewish family, celebrated his bar mitzvah, and remained in the town. When he grew up, he married and had a family, of which he was very proud. Some of his grandchildren and great-grandchildren still live there, in that distant town, while others moved to Israel.

COMMENTARY FOR TALE 29 (IFA 8915)

Recorded by Mariana Juster from her father, Efraim Orenstein, in 1970 in Holon.[1]

Cultural, Historical, and Literary Background

Historical Perspective

The narrator of this tale grew up in a small town in Moldavia, Romania, the region to which the boy in the story fled. Although no other analogues to this tale are available in the IFA or, to the best of my knowledge, in any local tale collections, the story projects the impression of being a regional Jewish narrative, mixing historical fact with fiction.

The references to the father's military service and to the Cossacks' attack on Jewish homes and villages are grounded in fact. The narrator is mistaken, however, in the number of years Jewish soldiers served in the imperial army of the czar: Until 1874, the service in the Russian Army was twenty-five years. However, after the Milyutin Reform, service was reduced to fifteen years, with variable adjustments for education.[2] It is quite likely that the father was among the Jewish boys who were conscripts to military service in the czar's army during the rule of Nicholai I (see the notes to tale IFA 4541 in this vol., no. 27]).

The Cossacks were neither a tribe nor an ethnic group; they did have a culture but not a language of their own. They were frontier fighters and border guards whose historical origins are sufficiently mysterious that any theory about them often projects an ideological position as much as facts. Their vocabulary included Turkic and Tatar terms—such as *"ataman"* (hetman; chief) and *"esaul"* (lieutenant)—suggesting that the Cossacks were derived from or at least had contact with these groups. Romantics viewed them as Christian knights of the border and servants to the czar; the Russian revolutionaries emphasized their egalitarian tradition. They have been considered precursors of Ukrainian nationalism, and Soviet historians attributed their origins to peasant revolts.[3] Common to all of the origin theories is the historical observation that the Russian Cossacks first appeared in the middle of the fifteenth century, two hundred years after the fall of Kiev to the Tatars. "The circumstance of their appearance is shrouded in mist, surrounded by complexity, but the Cossacks were evidently sons of mother Russia, sired as it were, by the Tatars of the steppes."[4]

Quite likely they were renegade Tatars, "free-warriors" of non-Tataric origin, who hired themselves as defenders of the Muscovites, the Lithuanians, and the Poles, who were under seasonal devastating attacks of the swift Tatars. By the sixteenth century, the original Cossacks were outnumbered by the Slavs who joined them, and at the close of the century, the Muscovites imposed stricter rules on their peasants, many of whom, in revolt, responded to the call of the wild and joined the Cossacks. A number of historical and cultural studies are available.[5]

The Cossacks' attitude toward the Jews evolved into open and violent hostility. Initially, on the steppes "Jews were pioneers and first settlers, just as the Cossacks were: they sometimes joined Cossack detachments and generally cooperated with the Cossacks in defending their settlements against Tatar raids."[6] But the tension that simmered and occasionally erupted between the Jews and the Cossacks in the sixteenth century acquired momentum at the beginning of the seventeenth century, when the alliance between the Cossacks and the Orthodox hierarchy intensified. One of the first such attacks occurred in 1621,[7] and they culminated during the Cossack rebellion against the Polish rulers (1648–1649), which was headed by Bogdan Khmelnytsky[8] (1595–1657). During those years, the Cossacks destroyed Jewish villages and decimated the Jewish population in the region. Much has been written about these pogroms. The Jewish historical testimony from that period is by Nathan Nata Hannover,[9] and major Jewish histories describe these events.[10]

Khmelnytsky is considered a national Ukrainian hero even today; hence Ukrainian historians offer a different interpretation of his activities and occasionally challenge the accuracy of the descriptions in Jewish sources. Modern studies and interpretations of the Cossack rebellion and its effects on the Jewish community have been conducted.[11] From the seventeenth century to the modern era, Jews in Ukraine were subject to anti-Semitism and periodic pogroms. A number of publications treat this subject.[12]

Fictional Elements

The fictional themes in the present tale involve the rearing of a Jewish child by a non-Jewish family and the discovery of a Jewish community by seeking a lost sheep.

The first theme—a Jewish child being reared in a non-Jewish home—hovers between fiction and reality, representing a situation that likely did occur, though not commonly, in a heterogeneous population of Jews and non-Jews. However, as a result of the conscription process during the cantonist period, this was more widespread. For more on the conscription laws, see the notes to tale IFA 4541 (in this vol., no. 27). Stories about these incidents often follow the patterns established in Jewish medieval and Hasidic narrative traditions (see the notes to tale IFA 2644 [vol. 1, no. 23]). In the present tale, the Jewish child enjoys the hospitality of his non-Jewish family; but unlike in the model pattern, he returns to a Jewish community before achieving any distinguished status in non-Jewish society.

The second fictional element combines themes known in both Jewish and Romanian folklore. In the present version, the journey of the boy, who follows a domesticated animal, is somewhat truncated, ending in a Jewish community in Moldavia. In other oral tales, an animal—usually a goat—takes a youth through secret passages all the way to the Land of Israel. The idea of caves and underground passages leading to the Holy Land is found in early Hasidic tradition.[13]

A local legend in Sczbrzeszyn tells about a pious Jew who tested whether or not a cave led to the Holy Land by first sending a goat through it. After three days, the goat had not returned, so the man followed it into the cave and was never seen again.[14] S. Y. Agnon (1888–1970) rendered a literary version of the tale, titling it *Pi ha-Me'arah o Ma'asseh ha-'Ez* (The cave opening or the fable of a goat).[15] The tale involves a youth who follows a goat to the Holy Land. He sends a message back home, tucked in the goat's ear, which is discovered only after the animal is slaughtered. The tale has appeared in English translation[16] and has often been reprinted.[17] Agnon sometimes relied on the Yiddish and Hebrew chapbook tradition; but this story seems to be known only in oral tradition. Literary and semiotic analyses of this story have been published.[18]

Similarities to Other IFA Tales

There are six versions of this tale in the IFA:

- IFA 310: *How the Goat Led the Way to the Ten Tribes* (Poland).[19]
- IFA 532: *The Two She-Goats from Shebreshin* (Poland).[20]
- IFA 4119: *The Goat on the Way to Jerusalem* (Poland).
- IFA 4943: *The Mysterious Cow* (Eretz Yisra'el, Ashkenazic).[21]
- IFA 5842: *A Story with a Goat* (Yemen).[22]
- IFA 12003: *The Cow That Knew the Way to Jerusalem* (Morocco).

In the other tales in the IFA, a goat or a cow leads the youth to the Land of Israel. The use of a sheep in the present version is not accidental. Moldavia, where the events in the tale occurred and the birthplace of the narrator, is a sheep-herding country. One of the most popular ballads in Romania, "Miorita," is about a helpful sheep and her shepherd. The story told in the ballad differs from the present tale, yet suggests the central place of sheep in Moldavian culture.[23] An English translation of "Miorita" has been published,[24] as has a comprehensive study of the ballad.[25]

Folktale Types

- 178*C (IFA) "The Slaughtered She-goat."
- 839*C (IFA) "Miraculous Rescue of a Person."

Folklore Motifs

- B184.6 "Magic sheep."
- B412 "Helpful sheep."
- D1162 "Magic light."
- cf. E323.2 "Dead mother returns to aid persecuted children."
- E402.1.1 "Vocal sounds of ghost of human being."
- cf. E421.3 "Luminous ghosts."
- E545 "The dead speak."

- F401.2 "Luminous spirits."
- F585 "Phantoms."
- F966 "Voices from Heaven (or from the air)."
- F969.3 "Marvelous light."
- L111.1 "Exile returns and succeeds."
- L111.2 "Foundling hero."
- L111.3 "Widow's son as hero."
- L111.4 "Orphan hero."
- *N768.1 "Abandoned children accidentally discovered by good people."
- N774.2 "Adventures from seeking (lost) domestic beast (bull) [sheep]."
- *N793 "Adventure from pursuing moving light at night."
- N854 "Peasant as helper."
- N854.1 "Peasant as foster father."
- P200 "The family."
- P210 "Husband and wife."
- P230 "Parents and children."
- P231 "Mother and son."
- P411 "Peasant."
- P412 "Shepherd."
- *P412.4 "Geese herder."
- P461 "Soldiers."
- P715.1 "Jews."
- R131.6 "Peasant rescues abandoned child."
- R153.4 "Mother rescues son."
- S110 "Murders."
- *S351.2.2 "Abandoned child reared by peasants."
- V71 "Sabbath."
- Z71.9 "Formulistic number: thirteen."

Notes

1. First published in D. Noy, *A Tale for Each Month 1970*, 77–80 no. 10 (with extensive note by O. Meir, 112–114).

2. Keep, *Soldiers of the Tsar*, 375–378; and Lincoln, "Nikolai Alekseevich Milyutin and Problems of State Reform in Nicholaevan Russia."

3. Longworth, *The Cossacks,* 7.

4. Ibid., 12.

5. Longworth, op. cit.; Seaton, *The Horsemen of the Steppes;* and O'Rourke, *Warriors and Peasants.* For the Ukrainian national perspective, see Hrushevsky, *History of Ukraine-Rus'*, vols. 7–8.

6. Plokhy, *The Cossacks and Religion in Early Modern Ukraine*, 193–194. See also Ettinger, "The Legal and Social Status of the Jews of Ukraine"; and Weinryb, *The Jews of Poland*, 185–205.

7. Plokhy, op. cit., 194.

8. Also spelled Chmielnicki or Khmelnitski.

9. *Abyss of Despair (Yeven Matzulah)*.

10. For example, see the bibliography in Ettinger, "Chmielnicki (Khmelnitski), Bogdan (1595–1657)."

11. L. Gordon, *Cossack Rebellions,* 53–57; Nadav, "The Jewish Community of Nemyriv in 1648"; Plokhy, op. cit., 190–206; Raba, *Between Remembrance and Denial*; Sysyn, "The Khmelnytsky Uprising and Ukrainian Nation-Building"; and Weinryb, "The Hebrew Chronicles on Bohdan Khmel'nyts'ki and the Cossack-Polish War."

12. Potichnyj and Aster, *Ukrainian-Jewish Relations in Historical Perspectives;* Tcherikover, *Antisemitism un pogromen in Ukraine, 1917–1918* (Anti-Semitism and pogroms in the Ukraine, 1917–1918); and Tcherikower, *The Pogroms in the Ukraine in 1919.*

13. Ben-Amos and Mintz, *In Praise of the Ba'al Shem Tov,* 23–24 no. 11.

14. Cahan, *Jewish Folklore,* 147 no. 20.

15. *Polin,* 35–37; see also Agnon, *Kol sippurav shel Shmuel Yosef Agnon* (Agnon's collected tales), 373–375.

16. Agnon, *Twenty-One Stories,* 26–29.

17. Arnon, *Bibliography of Samuel Josef Agnon and His Work,* 87–88.

18. Aphek and Tobin, "The Realization of Messianism as a Semiotic System in a Literary Text"; and Elstein, *Structures of Recurrence in Literature,* 118–130.

19. Published in Harel-Hoshen and Avner, *Beyond the Sambatyon,* 28 (Hebrew), 69 (English).

20. D. Noy, *The Diaspora and the Land of Israel,* 13–17 no. 3; D. Noy, *Folktales of Israel,* 4–7 no. 2; and Jason, *Märchen aus Israel,* 131–134 no. 40.

21. Published in Weinstein, *Grandma Esther Relates . . . ,* 53–55 no. 12.

22. Published in Seri, *The Holy Amulet,* 44–47 no. 11.

23. Amzulescu, *Balade populare romînesti,* 2:463–486 nos. 146 (196)–152 (196).

24. Buhociu, *The Pastoral Paradise,* 3–5 (titled *Mioritza: The Canticle of the Sheep, the Enchanted Ewe*)

25. Fochi, *Miorita.*

30

The Boots Made from a Torah Scroll

TOLD BY DVORA FUS

There was a peasant family living in a village. They had three sons and one daughter. Like all the peasants in the village, they cultivated their fields. When a pogrom broke out in the neighboring town and everybody went off to plunder the Jews' property and bodies, the peasant took his three sons along. When he came back home and started to go over his loot, among the items he found a new Torah scroll. He was perfectly aware that this was the Jews' most sacred object. Holding it in his arms, he called over his sons and daughter and told them that he thought he would make boots out of the new parchment. The sons, ruffians just like their father, voiced no objections. But when the daughter heard his plan, she sobbed and begged her father to return it, because one must not make anything out of such holy objects. But they all laughed at her.

When things had quieted down a little in the town, the *rebbe* there noticed at once that the Torah scroll, which he had been supposed to bring to the synagogue, was missing. He didn't mourn about anything else that had been lost, but he could not stop thinking about the Torah scroll. He fasted and cried and mourned the holy object. When he went to sleep, his heart burdened with his heavy grief, he dreamed that he heard a voice telling him, "Go to the village and take a minyan* of Jews with you. Perhaps you will be able to retrieve the Torah scroll." When he woke up he remembered everything perfectly, even the name of the village and the peasant. At once he assembled a minyan of Jews and set out for the village.

He inquired after the peasant. When they were standing face to face, the *rebbe* asked him to give back the sacred object. But the peasant also laughed at the *rebbe* and told him straight out that the best thing would be to make boots out of it. When the *rebbe* realized that all was lost with the peasant, he pronounced a curse on him—that none of his descendants would live long. Then the *rebbe* went back home. He soon fell ill and died of sorrow.

---

*Quorum of ten Jewish men, which constitutes a prayer group.

After the peasant cut up the Torah scroll for boots, his daughter gathered the scraps that were left and put them in a small bag. She hid the bag where her father would not find it, because she was very afraid.

Years passed. None of the family lived long. As soon as anyone put on the boots, his feet became paralyzed. Only the daughter was left. No one in the village would marry her because they were infected with dread of the curse. Old, sick, and alone, she decided to take the little bag with the scraps of the Torah scroll to the *rebbe* and ask him to convert her, so that she would be a Jew and atone for her family's sins.

By now she was rich. Wearing her peasant clothes, she came to the town and asked where the *rebbe* lived. When she came to his house, they told her that the old *rebbe* was long since dead and the current *rebbe* was in the synagogue. She did not hesitate but went straight off to the shul.* When she entered, she threw herself down next to the Holy Ark and burst into tears. The *rebbe* didn't know what was going on. He went over and saw a peasant woman lying there and crying. He and the *shammes* picked her up and asked what had brought her there. Crying, she told them the whole story of the sin and the curse on the family and that, being left alone, she wanted to convert.

The *rebbe* explained that he was not allowed to do that. Then from inside her dress she took out the small bag with the scraps of the Torah scroll. The *rebbe* did not let her go back to the village. She lived in a small room next to the synagogue. She began studying the laws and she was converted. She sold her possessions and donated everything to the synagogue. The little bag with the scraps of the Torah scroll was buried in the cemetery. And when the convert died, at an old age, they laid her to rest not far from the tiny grave of the Torah scroll. On the tombstone they inscribed these words: "Here lies a holy convert who merited to be the last survivor of a peasant family. She was a righteous woman who rescued scraps of the parchment of a holy Torah scroll."

---

*Yiddish for "synagogue."

A Torah scroll.

COMMENTARY FOR TALE 30 (IFA 8257)

Written down from memory in Yiddish by Dvora Fus in November 1968 in Moshav Aseret.

Cultural, Historical, and Literary Background

In the present tale, the narrator sheds some of the traditional version's distinctive legendary features and casts the story into a folktale form. Consequently, the tale represents the state of generic transformation: the shift from a narrative in which the storyteller claims historical veracity to a narrative that takes place in an unidentifiable locale and time. For a discussion of such generic distinctions in folktales, see the notes to tale IFA 8256 (in this vol., no. 6); a discussion of generic shifts in Jewish folklore in antiquities has been published.[1]

Although eastern European Jewish populations experienced plenty of pogroms (see the notes to tales IFA 6306 [in this vol., no. 23] and IFA 8915 [in this vol., no. 29]), the present tale does not ground the events to any specific pogrom, nor does it identify the location and the time it happened. Rather, the narrator sets the scene in a generic village and selects as her primary characters the members of a formulaic "peasant family," consisting of a father and his three sons and one daughter. This patterned set of characters approximates the dramatic personae found in Slavic folktales.[2]

The heroine's indignation at her father's and brothers' cruel and sacrilegious behavior and her consequent conversion to Judaism follows a long line of literary, mythical, and historical proselytes who accepted on themselves the Jewish faith, sometimes at great personal sacrifice or danger—even death. Studies about proselytism and conversion to Judaism are available.[3]

The term *ger,* which in later periods referred to a proselyte, did not carry its specific religious connotation in the Hebrew Bible. Rather, it had a broader semantic range. The verb *gur* meant looking for temporary residence in search of sustenance (Genesis 12:10; Ruth 1:1; 2 Kings 8:1; Jeremiah 42:17) or shelter (Judges 17:8). The noun *ger* referred primarily to either non-Israelites who joined the Israelites in their wanderings from Egypt to the Land of Canaan (Exodus 12:48) or to remnants of the tribes that lived in the land before the arrival of the Israelites (1 Chronicles 22:2; 2 Chronicles 2:16, 30:25). As a minority alien population, the Israelites had a status in the Land of Israel that resembled the social position of *gerim* (plural), which they had in Egypt (Exodus 22:20, 23:9; Leviticus 19:34; Deuteronomy 10:19).

The reference to a unique category of a resident alien (*ger ve-toshav*) occurs several times in the Bible (Genesis 23:4; Leviticus 25:6,23; Psalm 39:13); in the mishnaic period, the term takes on a distinct meaning. Biblical law and the Prophets insist on just, compassionate, and nondiscriminatory treatment of such aliens (Exodus 23:9,12; Deuteronomy 24:14, 27:19; Jeremiah 7:6; Zechariah

7:10, Psalm 94:6), even including them in festivities (Deuteronomy 16:11,14). However, the Lawgiver recognized the aliens' distinct, and more permissible, dietary laws (Deuteronomy 14:21).

In the postbiblical *halakhah,* the term"*ger* and the Aramaic term *giora* (fem. *gioret*) refer specifically to a person who desires to join the Jewish community and accept Judaism as his or her religion. In their retelling of the biblical narrative and in discussing historical or current cases in their own society, the Rabbis recognized four kinds of proselytes:

- Righteous proselyte (*ger zedek*), who desires to convert to Judaism because of a change of faith.
- False proselyte (*ger sheker*), who claims religious conversion for material gain.
- Resident proselyte (*ger toshav*), who resides in the Jewish community yet does not have to follow all its religious rules (the halakhic meaning of this biblical term).
- "Lion proselyte," a Samaritan who converted to Judaism after being attacked by the lions (2 Kings 17:25).[4]

The heroine of the present story certainly qualifies as a righteous proselyte.

Within Jewish tradition and history, there are numerous cases of and narratives about converts to Judaism. In her personality and actions, the heroine of the present tale embodies three features that recur in traditional conversion stories: women proselytes are wealthy, enemies of the Jews become proselytes, and proselytes are engaged directly with the Torah.

Women Proselytes Are Wealthy

In traditional narratives about conversion, a recurring character is the wealthy female proselyte. The most famous female proselyte is Queen Helena (first century B.C.E.), the sister and wife of King Monobaz I, who ruled Adiabene, a vassal kingdom within the Parthian Empire. Josephus recorded her conversion to Judaism and her assistance to the people of Jerusalem during the famine of 45 B.C.E. (*Jewish Antiquities* 20, 2,1–5). Her conversion and generosity resonates in the tannaitic tradition.[5] Although she died in Adiabene, her remains were interred in Jerusalem in a mausoleum she built for that purpose; it is known today as The Tombs of the Kings (Josephus, *Jewish Antiquities*, 20:4,3).

Josephus also related the story of Fluvia, a wealthy Roman woman who converted to Judaism (*Jewish Antiquities* 18:3,5). She fell victim to four Jewish swindlers who embezzled the donation she sent with them to the Temple in Jerusalem.

Another example of a wealthy female proselyte is Valeria, whose slave performed ablutions to convert to Judaism before her; thus the sages concluded that they gain their freedom. (BT *Yevamot* 46a).

Enemies of the Jews Become Proselytes

Stories of enemies of the Jews, or their descendants or other relatives, becoming proselytes were common. According to a talmudic tradition, Nebuzaradan, the commander of the Babylonian army who burned the Temple, the king's palace, and all the houses of Jerusalem and who took the remnants of the Jerusalemites into exile (2 Kings 25:8–11), became a righteous proselyte (BT *Gittin* 57b; *Sanhedrin* 96b). The Rabbis further noted that "descendants of Haman learnt the Torah in Benai Berak; "descendants of Sisera taught children in Jerusalem; descendants of Sannacherib gave public expositions of the Torah. Who were these? Shemaya and Abtalion" (BT *Gittin* 57b; *Sanhedrin* 96b), who were in the chain of transmission of the Torah, were the teachers of Hillel and Shammai (Mishnah *Avot* 1:10–11). Rabbi Meir, a second-century C.E. *tanna* and a distinguished disciple of Rabbi Akiva, is said to have been a descendant of the Roman emperor Nero (BT *Gittin* 56a). A late tradition suggests that Rabbi Akiva himself was a son of a proselyte.[6]

One of the most famous proselytes who, according to tradition, was the descendant of an oppressor of the Jewish people was Onkelos, who translated the Pentateuch to Aramaic and who was said to be the nephew of Titus (40–81), the Vespian commander who destroyed Jerusalem in 70 C.E. Equally well known, Aquila, who translated the Pentateuch into Greek, was the nephew of the Roman emperor Hadrian (76–138), who suppressed the Jewish revolt in 132–135 C.E. Discussions of these two figures, whom current scholarship considers to be the same person, are available.[7]

Proselytes Are Engaged Directly with the Torah

Another common traditional theme about Jewish proselytes is that they later become engaged directly with the Torah—by teaching, translating, or simply saving it physically. Among the figures mentioned early, Shemaya, Abtalion, Rabbi Akiva, Rabbi Meir, and Onkelos/Aquila all fit this description.

One of the most celebrated proselytes in Lithuania was Count Valentin Potocki (d. 1749), who studied Torah and became a martyr because of his refusal to return to Christianity. He has become the subject of legends, fiction, and history.[8]

Folktale Types

- 771 (IFA) "Desecration (Sacrilege) Punished."
- 960*C (IFA) "Crime Punished."
- 960*E (IFA) "The Convert."

Folklore Motifs

- D1792 "Magic results from curse."

- D1814.2 "Advice from dream."
- D2072 "Magic paralysis."
- D2601.2.4 "Death by cursing."
- M410 "Pronouncement of curses."
- *M411.24 "Curse by a rabbi."
- P150 "Rich men."
- *P233.12 "Like father like son(s)."
- P251.6.1 "Three brothers."
- P253.0.3 "One sister and three (four) brothers."
- P411 "Peasant."
- *P426.4 "Rabbi."
- P623 "Fasting (as means of distrait)."
- Q551.7 "Magic paralysis as punishment."
- Q556 "Curse as punishment."
- cf. *V54 "Public prayer requires a quorum of ten (minyan)."
- *V151.2 "Sacred writings: the Torah."
- *V151.2.1 "Desecration of the Torah."
- V315 "Belief in the Atonement."
- V336 "Conversion to Judaism."
- Z71.1 "Formulistic number: three."

Notes

1. Ben-Amos, "Historical Poetics and Generic Shift."

2. I. Dan, "The Innocent Persecuted Heroine"; Jason, "Precursors of Propp"; Maranda, *Soviet Structural Folkloristics*; Nikiforov, "Towards a Morphological Study of the Folktale"; and Propp, *Morphology of the Folktale*.

3. Bamberger, *Proselytism in the Talmudic Period*; Ben-Zeev, *Conversion to Judaism*; Braude, *Jewish Proselyting in the First Five Centuries of the Common Era*; S. J. Cohen, "The Rabbinic Conversion Ceremony"; Eichhhorn, *Conversion to Judaism*; M. Finkelstein, *Proselytism;* Goodman, "Proselytising in Rabbinic Judaism"; Homolka et al., *Not by Birth Alone*; and Jacob and Zemer, *Conversion to Judaism in Jewish Law*.

4. See also Urbach, *The Sages*, 541–554.

5. Schiffman, "The Conversion of the Royal House of Adiabene."

6. Bamberger, op. cit., 238; and Safrai, *Akiva ben Yosef*, 12.

7. Silverstone, *Aquila and Onkelos;* and L. Rabinowitz, "Onkelos and Aquila." For further information about Onkelos/Aquila, see Bin Gorion, *Mimekor Yisrael,* 150–151 no. 76 (1990 ed.).

8. Karpinowitz, *The Story of the Vilnian Righteous Proselyte Count Valentine Potocki*; and Prouser, *Noble Soul.*

31

The Gentile Who Wanted to Screw the Jew

Told by Hinda Sheinferber to Hadarah Sela

*E*very village has a tavern run by a Jew. All over Poland there are villages with a tavern run by a Jew. The tavern serves food and drink.

Once a gentile came and asked the Jew to let him have a glass of arrack* on credit. He was going to sell his cow in town and would come back with the money and pay for the drink.

"You're going to sell the cow?" asked the tavern keeper. "I'll buy it." So he bought it and paid for it.

The next day, the gentile went to the priest and told him that his cow had been stolen. It was missing. The whole village went looking for it and found the cow with the Jew. There was a big commotion because the Jew had stolen this gentile's cow. They arrested him and held a big trial.

If there's a trial you have to hire a lawyer. There was a really big lawyer who defended only royalty and important people. He never came for an ordinary trial. But if there was some kind of blood libel against a Jew, then he would appear without a fee.

They brought this lawyer, but he couldn't save the man. The man was found guilty, and the sentence was that he would be sent to prison in Russia for many years.

"His wife will have to move to the city," the lawyer told the judges. "If he is sent to prison in Russia, she won't be able to keep the tavern, and she'll have to move to the city. Can everyone here please give something and help her out?"

Everyone took out a bank note and handed it to the lawyer. When the lawyer reached the man who said his cow had been stolen, the man took out a banknote. The lawyer had been looking at every banknote to make

---

*Brandy of the Near East; term used in Israel by people from countries of Islam. It is of interest that the narrator, who is from Poland, used the term *arrack* rather than one of the Yiddish words for brandy, such as *konyak* or *"vishniak"* (cherry brandy).

sure it was not counterfeit. But he looked really closely at the banknote from the man with the cow.

"Look," he told the judges, "I think this banknote is counterfeit."

The judges, too, began to examine it, one after another. "You can't tell. You can't be sure without testing it." But it didn't look right to them somehow.

"Where did you get this money?" the judges asked the gentile.

"It's true that the man paid me for the cow," he answered. He thought that if he said that the Jew had given him counterfeit money, he would be punished even more severely.

But the lawyer was very clever. The money was not counterfeit; and the judges, too, had already realized that. So the gentile was punished.

COMMENTARY FOR TALE 31 (IFA 18136)

Told by Hinda Sheinferber from Mogielnica, Poland, to Hadarah Sela in 1991 in Haifa.

Cultural, Historical, and Literary Background

The court is a social institution in which and about which stories are told. The tales told in the courts are supposed to tell the truth, but tales told about the courts unfold the twists of truth. There is a substantial amount of scholarship discussing the narrative qualities of testimonies and counter-testimonies.[1]

King Solomon's Judgment

The fundamental court case narrative in Judeo-Christian tradition is the biblical story of King Solomon (1 Kings 3:4–28), which is tale type 926 "Judgment of Solomon." In this tale, two prostitutes each gave birth to a son, but one boy dies. The women come before King Solomon asking him to decide to whom the surviving infant belongs. In his wisdom, Solomon issues a sentence to cut the baby in half and divide him between the two of them. One mother accepts the sentence, but the other protests; Solomon decides that the true mother is the one who protests and wishes the baby to live. Biblical scholars consider the text to be orally derived.[2] Rhetorically, it indeed unfolds in dialogue, an earmark of the oral tradition; however, to the best of our knowledge, literary archaeology has not yet discovered any text that would precede or be contemporaneous with the biblical version.

Although the "dream request" story—in which Solomon asks God to grant him "an understanding mind to judge Your people, to distinguish between good and bad" (1 Kings 3:9)—that precedes Solomon's judgment in the biblical tale has parallels in Egyptian royal accession narratives,[3] the story of the actual judgment is the only example of this tale type from the ancient Near East. Comparative research points to parallel versions in early literary sources from India and China as well as in the oral traditions of these countries, which were recorded in the nineteenth and twentieth centuries.[4] Versions of this tale also occur in Greek and Roman sources of late antiquity.[5]

Later sources in the Jewish tradition consider the two women in the biblical story not as mortal beings but as demonic spirits, creating a confluence of the images of King Solomon as a wise man and as a magus.[6] The biblical version of the judgment of Solomon story is also the earliest "court ruse" tale within Jewish traditional literature, in which a judge or a lawyer causes the litigants or witnesses to trip over their own words. Studies of the biblical story are available.[7]

The child Daniel exposes the falsity of the accusing elders in the story of Susanna, which appears in the Greek translations of the Bible—the Septuagint, which dates to 250 B.C.E., and the Theodotion, which is likely from the middle of the second century C.E.—in the Additions to the Book of Daniel (13:1–64).[8] The tale concerns the beautiful and chase wife of Joakim, who was accosted by two aging judges, insisting that she have sex with them or they would accuse her of adultery with a young lover. She dismissed them; but in the trial that followed, she was found guilty and sentenced to death. The boy Daniel challenged the verdict and exposed the falsity of the elders' testimony. Following the law, the elders were stoned to death instead of Susanna. This story has been canonized by the church but remained outside the Jewish biblical canon. Nevertheless, it recurred in Jewish and Samaritan traditions. Bibliographical discussions of this tale have been published.[9]

The Charity Ruse

The "charity ruse" that characterizes the present story occurs in the oral traditions of Jewish communities in Europe, the Near East, and North Africa, as the other versions of the story in the IFA indicate. Within the previously published versions, it is possible to distinguish two groups of tales. The first group involves, as the present story does, a Jewish and a non-Jewish litigant.[10] In the second group, the two litigants are Jewish: one a wealthy wine merchant and the other a poorer man who hid his saved money in a wine barrel. The merchant steals the money and blames his non-Jewish servants or wagon drivers for the theft. The judging rabbi declares the wine nonkosher for drinking by Jews; and to avert the sentence, the merchant confesses.[11]

So far the editor has not been able to identify any written or printed Jewish source that could have been a contributing factor to the diffusion of the clever ruse tale. Thus he is inclined to attribute the spread of the tale to oral transmission, either among Jewish communities alone or with the assistance of similar versions that are current in the oral traditions of non-Jewish peoples.

Similarities to Other IFA Tales

Other tales in the IFA that involve clever judgments are the following:

- IFA 1757: *How Did the Judge Discover the Embezzler?* (Iraq).
- IFA 2275: *How Did Heinrich Ettinger Become a Famous Lawyer in Poland?* (Poland).
- IFA 4788: *The Judge's Wisdom* (Ertez Yisra'el, Sephardic).[12]
- IFA 7790: *He Who Steals from a Gentile Is Not Dismissed* (Romania).
- IFA 7865: *The Counterfeited Bill* (Morocco).[13]
- IFA 8420: *Truth Comes to Light* (Iraq).
- IFA 9124: *The Story of the Jewish Sage and the Arab Judge* (Iraqi Kurdistan).
- IFA 12827: *The Judge's Wisdom* (Iraq).
- IFA 12274: *The Jew Who Paid the Arab for His Cow* (Iraq).
- IFA 13993: *The Wisdom of the Jewish Policeman* (Tangier, Morocco).

Folktale Types

- cf. 926C "Cases Solved in a Manner Worthy of Solomon."[14]
- cf. 926C–*A (Haboucha) "The Lost Purse."
- 926*E–D (IFA) "The Counterfeited Money."
- 926* E–D (Jason) "The Counterfeited Money."
- 926*E–E (Haboucha) "The Thief's Gesture."

Folklore Motifs

- J1140 "Cleverness in detection of truth."
- J1141 "Confession obtained by a ruse."
- K2100 "False accusation."
- P411 "Peasant."
- P421 "Judge."
- P422 "Lawyer."
- P426.1 "Parson (priest)."
- *P449 "Innkeeper."

───────── **Notes** ─────────

1. Amsterdam and Bruner, *Minding the Law*, 110–193; Brooks and Gewirtz, eds,. *Law's Stories;* Bruner, *Making Stories*, 37–62; Posner, *Law and Literature*, 114–174; Scheppele, "Legal Storytelling"; and West, *Narrative, Authority, and Law*.

2. Cogan, *1 Kings*, 196; and Porten, "The Structure and Theme of the Solomon Narrative," 99.

3. Fensham, "Legal Aspects of the Dream of Solomon"; Herrmann, "*Die Königsnovelle in Ägypten und Israel*"; Kenik, *Design for Kingship*, 27–56; and Zalevsky, "The Revelation of God to Solomon in Gibeon."

4. T. Gaster, *Myth, Legend, and Custom in the Old Testament*, 491–494, 551 no. 150; and Goebel, *Jüdische Motive im märchenhaften Erzählungsgut*, 21–34.

5. Hansen, *Ariadne's Thread*, 227–232.

6. Ginzberg, *The Legends of the Jews*, 4:130–131, 6:284 n. 26; and Torijano, *Solomon the Esoteric King*.

7. Beuken, "No Wise King without a Wise Woman"; Deurloo, "The King's Wisdom in Judgment"; Dubarle, "*Le jugement de Salomon*"; Fontaine, "The Bearing of Wisdom on the Shape of II Sam. 11–12 and I Kings 3"; and Lasine, "The Riddle of Solomon's Judgment and the Riddle of Human Nature in the Hebrew Bible."

8. C. Moore, *Daniel, Esther and Jeremiah the Additions*, 77–116.

9. Bin Gorion, *Mimekor Yisrael*, 79–81 no. 42 (1990 ed.); and Wills, *The Jewish Novel in the Ancient World*, 40–67.

10. N. Gross, *Maaselech un Mesholim*, 389–390; Schwarzbaum, *Studies in Jewish and World Folklore*, 339–340; Sadan, *Ka'arat Egozim o Elef Bediḥah u-Bhdiḥah* (A bowl of nuts or a thousand and one jokes), 347 no. 633; Richman, *Laughs from Jewish Lore*, 229–232; Wanwild, *Ba ync Jid'n* (Among us Jews), 63–64 no. 38; and E. Teitelbaum, *An Anthology of Jewish Humor and Maxims*, 23–25. See also Lipson, *Medor Dor* (From days of old), 1:154–156, no. 389, in which the two litigants are Jewish, and it is the rabbi who

uses the charity ruse. The clever rabbi who detects the truth has been thought to be the Lithuanian Elijah Ḥayyim Meisel (1873–1912), appointed as rabbi of Lodz, Poland.

11. Ben-Yeḥezki'el, *Sefer ha-Ma'asiyyot* (A book of folktales), 3:171–178, 430–431; E. Davidson, *Sehok Pynu (Our Mouth's Laughter)*, 1:178 no. 651 (anthologized from Hasidic books published in L'vov [1877] and Warsaw [1880]; the clever judgment is attributed to Rabbi Moses Zvi of Savran [d. 1838]); and Ḥayyim, *Nifla'im Ma'assekhah* (Wonderful are your acts), 111–112 no. 73.

12. Published in Na'anah, *Ozar ha-Ma'asiyyot* (A treasury of tales), 2:476–477.

13. Published in Rabbi, *Avoteinu Sipru* (Our fathers told), 2:272–273 no. 185.

14. An extensive expansion can be found in the new edition, 560–562.

Moral Tales

32

The Old Couple and Their Children

Told by Naftali Bornstein to Pinḥas Gutterman

When he reached old age, Barukh the carpenter divided his substantial property among his children. He allotted some of the buildings and some of the money to each son and daughter. He divided it all fairly, lest there be—Heaven forbid!—less for one and more for another. After he registered his property in the name of his children, who were all married and had their own children, he told them: "Now my heart is quiet, because when I die you will not have any trouble or aggravation with my property. You are my children and after my death you might come to quarrel because of my property and deprive me of rest in my grave. This way my soul will have its repose in the world to come."

You should not think that Barukh the carpenter had transferred all of his property to his children and left over nothing for himself. No, Barukh the carpenter kept something for himself, too. He reserved for himself a portion equal to what he gave each child, so that he and his wife could manage as long as they lived. He left himself the small house where he lived, which was also where he had his carpenter's shop. He told his children, with a quiet heart, "I have kept for myself a share of my property equal to what I have given each of you."

After that, Barukh the carpenter was at peace with his property, knowing that his children would not quarrel after his death. He kept working in his trade, carpentry. Despite his years he was a healthy man—Barukh the carpenter had never been sick in his life—so he kept working and made a good living to support himself and his wife.

Each morning, he got up early and went to the synagogue for the first morning minyan.[*] As soon as the service was over he returned from the synagogue, carrying his tallit[**] and tefillin.[§] When he got home, he put his

---
[*]Quorum of ten Jewish men, which constitutes a prayer group.
[**]Prayer shawl.
[§]Small black leather prayer boxes, wrapped around the head and arm, containing passages from the Torah.

tallit and tefillin away in their place and began working. This is what he had done all his life since the age of twelve, when he started working in the carpenter's shop. And then, all of a sudden, Barukh the carpenter took ill and lay in bed night and day.

As old age approached, Barukh the carpenter came down with a bad case of the grippe. His children brought a first-rate physician to examine their father. He wrote him a prescription and Barukh recovered and got out of bed. He got out of bed after his illness—but he could no longer work. The children brought their father all sorts of good things. Barukh continued to live with his old wife until she died, suddenly, of a chronic illness. Barukh the carpenter was left by himself after his wife's death, all alone in his house. His children asked their father to come to their homes, to live with them, to eat and sleep there.

Having no real choice, Barukh the carpenter, left all alone, went to live with his firstborn son and eat at his table. Barukh the carpenter cried bitter tears when he left his dear house, where he had lived all his life with his wife and his children in harmony and joy. In this house, he had raised his sons and daughters and married them off and celebrated the festivals and joyous occasions with his family, all of them together. But now he had to leave his dear house and had no choice but to go live with his son.

With a great ache and bitter tears Barukh the carpenter left his house, taking his tallit and tefillin with him, and went to live with his oldest son. When he arrived there, his son's family greeted him warmly. His son's wife was very glad to see her father-in-law. She took him in willingly and cooked for him and saw that he had everything he needed. Everything was fine—except that everything the old man took into his hand would fall and break. That is, whenever the old man picked up a cup or plate his hands shook and the cup or plate fell out of his hand and shattered.

His eldest son came up with the idea of making him a wooden plate and a wooden cup. After he made these wooden dishes he brought them home. Pleased with himself, he told his wife, "Now I'm sure that the old man won't break these dishes."

The old man was wretched as he ate his first meal with these simple and crude wooden dishes. In the middle of the meal the old man left the table and went to his room. He fell on his bed, crying bitterly. "What a sorry state I have come to," he told himself. "I would rather die than live with such shame and humiliation."

Barukh the carpenter's son came home from his carpentry—he too followed his father's old trade—for lunch. "How is the old man?" he asked his wife. "Did he enjoy eating from the wooden dishes?"

"Yes," said his wife. "He ate just now and didn't break anything."

Berl, the carpenter's eldest son, finished eating his meal and went back to his carpenter's shop to resume work. Suddenly, he saw his oldest son and the other children making wooden plates and cups. "What are you doing, children?" he asked them in astonishment.

"We're making a wooden plate and cup," the children answered their father, "so that when you, too, are old, or you're sick and your hands shake with palsy, you too will have wooden dishes to eat from!"

COMMENTARY FOR TALE 32 (IFA 3364)

Told by Naftali Bornstein of Poland to Pinḥas Gutterman in October 1961 in Tel Aviv.

Cultural, Historical, and Literary Background

In their folktale classification system, Aarne and Thompson[1] proposed that tale types 980A "The Half-Carpet" and 980B "Wooden Drinking Cup for Old Man" were two distinct, albeit related, types. Surely each form of "grandfather abuse" has its narrative-logical consequences, but it is also possible to consider them as interchangeable offenses. In the new edition, Uther[2] groups subtypes A–C into one tale type: 980 "The Ungrateful Son (Previously Ungrateful Son Reproved by Naive Actions of Own Son)." In the present story, the narrator says that the old man was a carpenter, assigning him a profession that would correspond to the wooden utensils the son had prepared for him. The moral of the story corresponds to the fifth commandment: "Honor your father and your mother, that you may long endure on the land that the Lord your God is assigning to you" (Exodus 20:12; cf. Deuteronomy 5:16), which has several narrative representations in the talmudic-midrashic literature.[3]

Had the story been known in Jewish societies in the late antiquities and Middle Ages, it could have been, quite likely, included in any of the editions of *Midrash of the Ten Commandments;* however, to the best of the editor's knowledge, it does not occur in any of them. The text of this tale type in M. Gaster's *The Exempla of the Rabbis*,[4] appears in the section "K: Diverse Sources,"[4] but Gaster does not offer any information about the provenance of the stories. Later, Ausubel copied Gaster's text into his own anthology.[6] Quite likely, the tale had been known in Jewish oral traditions, yet it appears in print only as of the nineteenth and early twentieth centuries.[7]

The earliest documentation of this tale in Europe is in the fable and exemplum traditions of the thirteenth century. A version of the tale in fable collections is available;[8] stories in the sermon and exempla literature have also been published.[9] Later in the fifteenth and sixteenth centuries the tale appeared in jokes and anecdotes books.[10] And in the seventeenth century it was even rendered into a German ballad.[11]

The Brothers Grimm drew their version of this tale from a literary source.[12] A collection of fifteen versions of the story from the Middle Ages to the nineteenth century in French, German, and Latin has been published.[13]

Similarities to Other IFA Tales

The IFA includes sixteen additional versions of this tale.

- IFA 1713: *A Youth Teaches His Parents to Honor His Grandfather* (Turkey); tale type = 980A.

- IFA 2161: *A Youth Teaches His Parents to Honor His Grandfather* (Hungary); tale type = 980A.
- IFA 3257: *The Story of the Expelled Grandfather* (Egypt); tale type = 980A.[14]
- IFA 3969: *Honor Thy Father* (Iraq); tale type = 980A.
- IFA 3969: *Honor Due to the Father* (Iraq); tale type = 980A.[15]
- IFA 6037: *Respect for Father* (Morocco); tale type = 980A.
- IFA 6171: *As You Do So Will Be Done to You* (Libya); tale type = 980B.
- IFA 6743: *Respect for Father* (Eretz Yisra'el, Sephardic); tale type = 980A.
- IFA 7014: *The Grandson Who Took Half a Blanket from His Grandfather* (Romania); tale type = 980A.
- IFA 7095: *A Wooden Spoon* (Spanish Morocco); tale type = 980B.[16]
- IFA 7368: *Honor Thy Father and Your Children Will Honor You* (Afghanistan); tale type = 980A.
- IFA 7432: *Grandfather's Spoon* (Romania); tale type = 980B.
- IFA 7668: *Honor Your Father* (Afghanistan); tale type = 980A.[17]
- IFA 7833: *Respecting Father (Half a Coat)* (Afghanistan); tale type = 980A.
- IFA 8189: *Respecting Father* (Poland); tale type = 980B.[18]
- IFA 9133: *A Spoon for a Wooden Plate* (Belarus); tale type = 980B.

Folktale Types

- 980 "The Ungrateful Son (Previously Ungrateful Son Reproved by Naive Actions of Own Son" (new ed.).
- 980 (El-Shamy) "The Ungrateful Son."
- 980A "The Half-Carpet."
- 980A (El-Shamy) "The Half-Carpet."
- 980A (Haboucha) "The Half-Carpet."
- 980A (Jason) "The Half-Carpet."
- 980B "Wooden Drinking Cup for Old Man"
- 980B (El-Shamy) "Wooden Drinking Cup for Old Man."
- 980B (Jason) "Wooden Drinking Cup for Old Man."
- 2001 (Tubach) "Father in Stable."

Folklore Motifs

- J121 "Ungrateful son reproved by naive action of his own son."
- J121.1 "Ungrateful son reproved by naive action of his own son."
- P210 "Husband and wife."
- P233 "Father and son."
- P236 "Undutiful children."
- P291 "Grandfather."
- *P299 "Grandson."

- P424 "Physician."
- P456 "Carpenter."
- Q588 "Ungrateful son punished by having a son equally ungrateful."
- S21 "Cruel son."
- cf. S140.1 "Abandonment of aged."
- W154 "Ingratitude."

Notes

1. *The Types of the Folktale,* 344–345.
2. *The Types of International Folktales,* 610–611.
3. Bin Gorion, *Mimekor Yisrael,* 176–177 nos. 92–93 (1990 ed.).
4. At 171 no. 437 (tale type 980A).
5. At 162–183.
6. *A Treasury of Jewish Folklore,* 383.
7. Hayyim, *Nifla'im Ma'assekhah* (Wonderful are your acts), 43–44 no. 37 (tale type 980A); Uziel, *"Ha-Folklor Shel ha-Yehudim ha-Sefardim"* (The folklore of the Sephardic Jews), 333 (tale type 980A); N. Gross, *Maaselech un Mesholim,* 272–273 (tale type 980A or 980B); and Nahmad, *A Portion in Paradise and Other Jewish Folktales,* 123 (tale type 980A). See further, Schwarzbaum, *Studies in Jewish and World Folklore,* 254–255, 477.
8. J. Jacobs, *The Fables of Odo of Cheriton,* 153 no. 109; Hervieux, *Les Fabulistes Latines,* 4:245 no. 73b; Perry, *Aesopica,* 642 no. 624; and Perry, *Babrius and Phaedrus,* 549–550 no. 624.
9. T. Crane, *The Exempla or Illustrative Stories from the Sermons Vulgares,* 121, 260 no. 228 (extensive references to medieval sources).
10. See, for example, Pauli, *Schimpf und Ernst.,* 1:257–258, 2:359–360 no. 436.
11. Rölleke, *"Die Volksballade von der Wiedervergeltung"*; Rölleke, *"Das Exempel vom undankbaren Sohn"*; and Delpech, *"L'elimination des veillards."*
12. Grimm and Grimm, *The Complete Fairy Tales,* 288–289 no. 78 (The Old Man and His Grandson); Bolte and Polivka, *Anmerkungen zu den Kinder- u. Hausmärchen,* 2:135–140 no. 78; Uther, *Grimms Kinder- und Hausmärchen,* 4:149–150; and Rölleke, *"Das Exempel vom undankbaren Sohn."*
13. Röhrich, *Erzählungen der späten Mittelalters,* 1:92–112, 262–267.
14. Published in Rush, *The Book of Jewish Women's Tales,* 131–134 no. 32.
15. Published in E. Marcus, *Min ha-Mabua,* 120–121 no. 28.
16. Published in Haviv, *Never Despair,* 37–38, 61–62 no. 6.
17. Published in Yehoshua, *The Father's Will,* 66–67 no. 13.
18. Published in Gutter, *Honor Your Mother,* 24 no. 10.

33

With the Rebbe's Power

TOLD BY TONY SALOMON-MA'ARAVI

*I*n our town, the Hasidim used to beam with joy whenever anyone returned from a long journey and brought back with him some miracle worked by the *rebbe's** power.

One day the worshipers in the tailors' synagogue found out that a young man from Dorohoi had been suggested as a match for Reb** Henokh Stoller's daughter, Idislen. Because Reb Henokh had relatives and lots of acquaintances in that town, he went to Dorohoi to learn something about the proposed match.

Of course, he set out on a lucky day—a Tuesday. And because he left us on a Tuesday, he would arrive on Thursday, so that on Friday, when people come to the synagogue early to pray, he would be sure to learn something.

And that's just how it was. His relatives and acquaintances received him warmly. They all gave him helpful information and advised him that on the Sabbath he should pray at the *rebbe*'s *kloyz*.§ They would send the synagogue wardens a note asking that he be admitted to the *rebbe* right after *Havdalah*.§§ He should tell the great rabbi about the match that had been proposed for his young daughter.

When Reb Henokh came to the *kloyz,* the wardens greeted him: "Where are you from? What request do you want to make of our great tzadik?"*** Smiling, the chief warden told him, "Our *rebbe*, may he have a long life, is truly an emissary of God. Listen what a miraculous event occurred because of him:

"Here in the town we had a Jew, a tailor, a truly pious man. But he had three grown daughters and, what is more, was as poor as the night. And

---

*A Hasidic rabbi.
**Rabbi or Mr.
§Hasidic house of prayer.
§§Ceremony that marks the end of the Sabbath.
***Great scholar or holy person.

truth is truth, the poor tailor never complained to God. Heaven forbid! He was always content, steadfast in his faith, and an optimist. But after his daughters started turning thirty he never left the *rebbe* alone and kept asking him for a great blessing. Because only with a blessing would his daughters find a match.

"Three days before Rosh Hashanah the tailor came to the rabbi and told him, amid great sobs: 'Rabbi, our great tzadik, the year is almost over. A new year is coming and my daughters are all still without a head covering.' He burst into tears like a little boy.

"Our *rebbe* pondered for a while. Then, as if waking from a deep sleep, he told the poor tailor, 'Look, my brother, here are a hundred lei.* Tomorrow morning go pray with the first minyan.** Afterward go straight down the street and buy whatever you are offered. Then God will help you.'

"The tailor did as the *rebbe* said. The next morning, right after the first minyan, he went out with the hundred lei in his hand and started looking for something to buy.

"He passed a rich man who was standing by the door to his shop. When the latter noticed the poor tailor, he asked him, almost jeering, 'Nu, little tailor, what are you looking for so early in the street? Have you already finished all your work? Here it is almost Rosh Hashanah, and you're going for a stroll.'

"Like an idler, the tailor answered him. 'Oh, I want to buy something for a hundred lei.'

" 'So you have a hundred lei? Nu, what can you find to buy in town so early? You know what? I'll sell you my share in the world to come.'

"The tailor, feeling very blue, remembered that the *rebbe* had advised him to buy whatever he was offered. He gave the rich man the hundred lei and started for home.

"The city started bustling. Business was brisk, like any holiday eve. The rich man told everyone he met about his good fortune in meeting the little tailor.

"People started making fun of him.

"What can I tell you, my dear friend," the first synagogue warden continued. "An important man, when people in town laugh at him—he doesn't like it at all. He ran to the poor tailor and asked him to take back the

---

*A relatively small sum.
**Quorum of ten Jewish men, which constitutes a prayer group.

hundred lei and return his share in the world to come. When the tailor refused to hear of the idea, the rich man said he was prepared to give him, instead of a hundred lei, two hundred, three hundred, four hundred. . . . Rosh Hashanah was coming and he mustn't play such tricks.

"Meanwhile the town was all agog. People were talking, people were excited, people were laughing, and the sharp wits advised the tailor to tell the foolish rich man: 'Absolutely not! A deal is a deal.'

"And there, as people say, Rosh Hashanah eve was knocking at the door and the town was seething like a boiling kettle.

"Other quick thinkers advised the rich man to run to the *rebbe* and ask him, the holy *rebbe*, to issue a ruling. Because soon it would be the holy day and he would be left for an entire year without a share in the world to come.

"The *rebbe* suggested that they select three pious men to render a verdict.

"The whole town came to hear how the affair would end.

"The three pious Jews ruled that if the rich man wanted to get back the world to come he had sold, he must make weddings for the tailor's three daughters. Having no choice, the rich man agreed.

"Matchmakers looked for and found grooms. At the betrothal ceremony, the tailor announced that he was returning the rich man's share in the world to come.

"From that time on, the rich man was a very different person and stopped making fun of poor people. The *rebbe* blessed him with health and a secure livelihood, because he had made weddings for three old maids.

"Nu, Reb Henokh, what do you say about our *rebbe*?

"Now, dear Jew, you may go in to the *rebbe*. May our eternal God help your daughter be successful in her match."

Reb Henokh Stoller had great pride and satisfaction from his son-in-law and never forgot the Dorohoi *rebbe*'s blessing.

COMMENTARY FOR TALE 33 (IFA 19892)

Written down from memory by Tony Salomon-Ma'aravi from Romania in 1994.

Cultural, Historical, and Literary Background

This tale is an example of a story embedded within another story. A discussion of the literary principles of embedded and frame narratives is provided in the commentary to tale IFA 960 (this vol., no. 14). The present story illustrates, among other issues, the use and function of storytelling within the court of a Hasidic rabbi and among the Hasidim. For more on storytelling in Hasidic societies, see the commentaries to tales IFA 960, IFA 2623 (vol. 1, no. 25), IFA 7755 (this vol., no. 44), and IFA 10611 (vol. 3, no. 54).

Within the frame and the embedded narratives, there are references to traditional practices and beliefs that have been an integral part of Jewish society on different levels: the significance of an auspicious day, the concern for a daughter's dowry, and the idea of having an individual share in the world to come (*helek ba-'olam ha-ba*).

The Significance of an Auspicious Day

Tuesday has acquired its "good omen value" from a scriptural reference. The Bible describes God's creation of the world, concluding each day's work with the formula "God saw that . . . was good" (Genesis 1:4,10,12,18,21,25). On Tuesday, this formula is repeated twice, vesting the day with a double amount of God's good will. Therefore, in some Jewish societies, the day has become the preferred day of the week for performing wedding ceremonies, for starting new ventures, and, as the present tale illustrates, setting off on a journey.

Concern for a Daughter's Dowry

In the poverty-stricken Jewish society of Eastern Europe, the need for a dowry to marry off a daughter was a major family concern. Three daughters meant triple trouble, as is succinctly expressed in the Yiddish saying, *"Drei techter is nisht kein gelechter"* ([Having] three daughters is not a joke). *Hakhnasat Kallah*, a fictive narrative epic by Agnon, presents this concern vividly and profoundly.[1]

A Share in the World to Come

The idea that the righteous have personal shares and personal positions in the world to come occurs also in the talmudic-midrashic literature. Rabbi Ḥanina ben Dosa miraculously received part of his share in the world to come, a golden leg of his heavenly table, while still on earth. Because he did not wish to forfeit it, the golden table leg was restored in Heaven for him (BT *Berakhot* 17b; *Ta'anit* 24b–25a; *Yoma* 53b). The story became popular with medieval narrators and editors of anthologies.[2]

Similarities to Other IFA Tales

In the IFA the following tales have a similar theme.

- IFA 5415: *Joseph the Righteous Innkeeper* (Romania).
- IFA 11439: *Selling a Share of the World to Come* (Poland).
- IFA 11447: *The Rich Man Who Sold His Faith* (Afghanistan).

Folktale Type

- *776 (IFA) "Divine Reward."

Folklore Motifs

- *A694.2 "Jewish paradise."
- *A694.3 "Selling one's share in paradise."
- J21 "Counsels proved wise by experience."
- *J21.26.1 "Buy the first thing you are offered."
- N127.1 "Tuesday as auspicious day."
- P150 "Rich men."
- *P165 "Poor men."
- P234 "Father and daughter."
- P252.2 "Three sisters."
- *P426.4 "Rabbi."
- P441 "Tailor."
- *T52.4.2 "Bride, or bride's family does not have dowry money."
- T53 "Matchmakers."
- T61.4 "Betrothal ceremony."
- T100 "Marriage."
- T135 "Wedding ceremony."
- V71 "Sabbath."
- V112.3. "Synagogues."

──────── **Notes** ────────

1. Holtz, *Mar'ot u-Mekorot* (References and sources). See also commentary for tale IFA 708 (in this vol. no. 1).
2. Bin Gorion, *Mimekor Yisrael*, 136–137 no. 66 (1990 ed.).

34

Gossip Is Worse Than Profaning the Sabbath

TOLD BY SERL ROCHFELD-HAIMOVITS
TO HER HUSBAND ZVI MOSHE HAIMOVITS

*O*nce there were two women, a mother and daughter. They were both widows and desperately poor and lived in a ramshackle hovel at the edge of town, near the forest. They eked out their living by weaving *tallitot*.* To earn their meager crusts, they had to work sixteen hours a day, day in and day out.

The local rabbi, who was very fond of his Sabbath nap, used to walk as far as the nearby forest. One Sabbath afternoon, as he passed the hovel in which the two widows lived, he noticed that it shone with an intense and supernatural light. This, thought the rabbi, must be a place of Torah, where some hidden righteous man or *lamed-vovnik*** lives. The rabbi detoured toward the hut and was about to enter and discuss Torah with its resident. But he was astounded to see through the open window two Jewish women working at their looms. "What is going on here?" cried the rabbi. "Isn't today the Sabbath?"

Ashamed and remorseful, the two looked at the rabbi and did not know what to answer him. When the rabbi noted their confusion, he lowered his voice and asked why they were working on the Sabbath. The mother and daughter replied that it was because they worked sixteen hours a day and never went out, even to visit the neighbor across the way. "Rabbi," said the mother, "even working this hard we scarcely have anything to eat."

"You can see with your own eyes that all your exhausting labor does not bring you wealth."

"You have spoken truly, Rabbi," they replied. "But this keeps us from gossiping."

---

*Prayer shawls.
**One of the thirty-six hidden righteous men. For a discussion of their position in Jewish thought and folklore, see the notes to tale IFA 10085 (vol. 1, no. 48).

"It is possible to go visit the neighbor without gossiping," the rabbi said.

"All right, Rabbi," they said. "We'll try to do that."

The rabbi went on his way but decided that the next week he would go and see whether they were keeping their promise to him. When the rabbi came to the hovel of the two widows' the next Sabbath, he observed that they were not working, but—their hut was no longer shining with a light like that of the Divine Presence.

34 / *Gossip Is Worse* ❧ **257** ❧

Tallitot—prayer shawls.

COMMENTARY FOR TALE 34 (IFA 5609)

Told by Serl Rochfeld-Haimovits to her husband, Zvi Moshe Haimovits, in 1962 in Ein Iron.

Cultural, Historical, and Literary Background

This tale modifies traditional themes and motifs that occur in talmudic-midrashic and medieval folk narratives to articulate Hasidic theology and ideology. The basic narrative antagonistic tension in the story is between the two widows and the admonishing rabbi. In their reply to him, the two poor women weigh the values of two biblical commandments against each other: resting on the Sabbath day and avoiding slander.

Obeying the Commandments

The observation of the sanctity of the Sabbath is a principal Jewish religious duty. The obligation to refrain from any work on the Sabbath is the substance of the fourth commandment: "Remember the sabbath day and keep it holy. Six days you shall labor and do all your work, but the seventh day is a sabbath of the Lord your God: you shall not do any work—you, your son or daughter, your male or female slave, or your cattle, or the stranger who is within your settlements. For in six days the Lord made heaven and earth and sea and all that is in them, and He rested on the seventh day; therefore the Lord blessed the sabbath and hallowed it" (Exodus 20:8–11). The Pentateuch specifies only four kinds of work from which the Israelites were required to abstain on the Sabbath: plowing and harvesting (Exodus 34:21), fire making (Exodus 35:3), and wood gathering (Numbers 15:32–36).

Later, Jeremiah (17:21–22,27) added the prohibition to carry loads on the Sabbath day. Nehemiah (13:15–18) was outraged when he witnessed work—running winepresses, loading goods onto asses, and trading in the markets—on the Sabbath. The Book of Jubilees (2:17–33, 50:6–11; mid-second century B.C.E.) enumerates other forbidden activities on the Sabbath: cooking, drawing and carrying water, sexual intercourse, and market trading.

By the end of the second century C.E. the Mishnah enumerated thirty-nine principal categories of labor (*avot malkhah*) that Jews should not perform on the Sabbath, weaving being one of them (Mishnah *Shabbat* 7:2).

The Hebrew Bible also contains some admonitions against gossip, slander, and calumny. These statements do not occur in texts that are as prominent as the Ten Commandments, yet their language is equally strict:

- "You must not carry false rumors" (Exodus 23:1).
- "Do not go about talebearer among your countrymen" (Leviticus 19:16; alternative translation).
- Jeremiah condemned those who "are going about with slanders" (6:28, old

JPS translation) and "bend their tongues like bows" (9:2). He warned that "every neighbour goeth about with slander" (9:3; old JPS translation).
- Ezekiel declared that "[i]n thee have been talebearers to shed blood" (Ezekiel 22:9; old JPS translation).
- The Book of Psalms (50:20) reads: "You are busy maligning your brother, defaming the son of your mother," and the Book of Proverbs (11:13, 20:19; 1917 JPS translation) condemns "He who goeth about as a talebearer."

The rabbis in the postbiblical period did not waver from their condemnation of slander (*lashon ha-ra*) as a primary evil, considering it a social, not a religious, transgression.[1] Furthermore, in the Yom Kippur prayer, slander (*lashon ha-ra*), idle gossip (*siah siftoteinu*), and tale-bearing (*rekhilut*) are among the sins for which Jews ask forgiveness. Analyses of gossip and rumor are available.[2]

In terms of strict Orthodox Judaism, it appears that the two widows violated a fundamental Jewish religious prohibition; but from the perspective of Hasidic theology, they worshiped God with equal devotion as the most pious Jews would and even surpassed them. According to the teachings of the Great Maggid, Rabbi Dov Baer of Mezherich (1704–1772), and particularly his disciple Rabbi Nahum of Chernobyl (1730–1798), the way to attain religious spiritual devotion is not only through prayer, ecstatic singing, dancing, and storytelling but also through corporeality (*gashmiyut*) by eating, drinking, having intercourse, performing daily activities, and engaging in craft.[3]

Radiant Light

Through their weaving, the two widows were in fact worshiping God and attained a high state of holiness, manifested by the light that shone over them. The idea that light emanates from a human body or in the air surrounding it after contact with divinity is mentioned in the biblical verse that describes Moses after his descent from Mount Sinai:

> So Moses came down from Mount Sinai. And as Moses came down from the mountain bearing the two tablets of the Pact, Moses was not aware that the skin of his face was radiant, since he had spoken with Him. Aaron and all the Israelites saw that the skin of Moses' face was radiant; and they shrank from coming near him. But Moses called to them, and Aaron and all the chieftains in the assembly returned to him and Moses spoke to them. Afterward all the Israelites came near, and he instructed them concerning all that the Lord had imparted to him on Mount Sinai. And when Moses had finished speaking with them, he put a veil over his face.
>
> Whenever Moses went in before the Lord to speak with Him, he would leave the veil off until he came out; and when he came out and told the Israelites what he had been commanded, the Israelites would see how radiant the skin of Moses' face was (Exodus 34:29–35).

In postbiblical literature, Moses is associated with light from birth (BT *Megillah* 14a).

Postbiblical rabbinical Judaism transformed the relationship between light and holy people. The sages conceived of the light not as emanating from holy people but as hovering above them as a sign from on high, indicating their attainment of a high degree of piety. In traditional texts, a group of interchangeable terms on the one hand and a single term on the other hand signify this light. The terms are "light," "radiance," "fire," "candle," and "halo," which describe, in most cases, the holiness of a person who overcame sexual desire.[4] Art and archaeology demonstrate that the halo, as a symbol of holiness and supernatural qualities, occurred in European and Near Eastern paganism and continued in Christianity; but it did not have significance in Jewish visual art, though there are verbal allusions that associate light with holiness in different representations, and the halo could be one of them.[5]

The single term is *shekhinah*, which refers to a specific aspect of holiness that light signifies. Such a light, known as the *ziv ha-Shekhinah* (the light of the *Shekhinah*) ends the present story. The *Shekhinah* itself is a concept of many meanings. Linguistically, the word is a noun constructed out of the root *sh-kh-n* (to dwell, to reside); and the text of the Hebrew Bible employs it numerous times to indicate the presence of the Divine among the people of Israel, as in the verse "And let them make Me a sanctuary that I may dwell among them" (Exodus 25:8). The temporary sanctuary in the desert was called in Hebrew "*mishkan*," a noun that is constructed from the same root. Consequently, the term *Shekhinah*, which developed in the postbiblical period, referred to the numinous immanence of God in the world, which was shapeless, formless, and nonsensual yet spiritual and holy. Light was an acceptable visual sign for the presence of the *Shekhinah*. In addition, the rabbis and mystics conceived of the *Shekhinah* as the feminine principle of God; however, they did not fully accept that theory. An overview of the concept of the *Shekhinah* is available.[6] Examinations of the idea in rabbinical Judaism[7] and in Jewish mysticism[8] have been published, as has a discussion of the association of the *Shekhinah* with other feminine configurations of divinity.[9]

In a second form, the light emanates from the person's body rather than hovering above as a divine sign of his or her holiness, and it occurs in the Hasidic tradition about the Ba'al Shem Tov. The story of his revelation involves light radiating from him or engulfing him while he is praying,[10] and later light engulfs him when he is engaged in a profound devotional mystical prayer.[11] This theme also occurs in early Christian traditions;[12] studies of light in Judaism and Christianity have been conducted.[13] Judaism shares with other religions the attribution of holiness to light and fire; a comparative study of the symbolic value of light in religion has published.[14]

The elevation of the two widows who profaned the Sabbath with their work to a high degree of piety, signified by the light of the *Shekhinah* hovering over, parallels the theme known in Jewish narratives as "God requires the heart," or

Raḥmana liba baei (the Merciful desires the heart), which is discussed in the commentaries to tales IFA 10089 (vol. 1, no. 28) and IFA 10085 (vol. 1, no. 48).

One of the patterns of this narrative cycle involves a rabbinical rational interruption of naive worship, as in the present tale. In tale IFA 10089, the rabbi is punished for his action; but in the present case, there is a loss of the primary innocence of belief, and the sign of holiness is removed from the widows. The story is steeped with Jewish traditional values and their formulation in Hasidic thought and belief, yet the dichotomy between holiness and gossip has parallels in Christian legends. While the observance of the Sabbath and tale-bearing have, respectively, positive and negative values, in Jewish tradition they are not conceived as binary opposition to each other. Such a view, however, has parallels in Christian and Greek legends.[15]

The Rabbi's Nap

In the original Hebrew, the narrator refers to the rabbi's motivation for taking his after-meal walk by the forest as his wish to take an afternoon nap, because "*shenah be-shabat—ta'anug*" (a nap on the Sabbath is a delight). This is a widespread proverb, which transforms the Hebrew letters of the word for the Sabbath into an acronym of this phrase. Creating acronyms is the thirty-first interpretive mode outlined in the eighth-century summary of thirty-two forms of biblical exegesis.[16]

Similarities to Other IFA Tales

Other comparable tales in the IFA are the following:

- IFA 5211: *Better to Work on the Sabbath* (Romania).
- IFA 5596: *The Besht Instructs a Maiden How to Observe the Sabbath* (Ukraine).

Folktale Types

- 796* (old ed. only) "Angels on the Widow's Roof."
- 796* (Andreev) "Angely na krishe vdovy" (Angel on the Widow's Roof).
- 796* (Jason) "Angels on the Widow's Roof."
- 796* (Krzyzanowski).

Folklore Motifs

- C58 "Tabu: profaning sacred day."
- C631 "Tabu: breaking the Sabbath."
- F969.3 "Marvelous light."
- *P165.1 "Poor women."
- P232 "Mother and daughter."
- *P426.4 "Rabbi."

- P445 "Weaver."
- cf. Q223.6 "Failure to observe holiness of Sabbath punished."
- Q393.2 "Gossiping punished."
- V71 "Sabbath."
- *V222.1.5 "Supernatural light rests above a righteous person."
- *V229.15.1 "Thirty-six incognito saints preserve the integrity of the world."

––––––––– **Notes** –––––––––

1. M. Gross, *Otzar ha-Aggadah* (The treasure of the Aggadah), 2:613–616.
2. R. Abrahams, "A Performance-Centered Approach to Gossip"; G. Fine et al., *Rumor Mills*; and Stewart and Strathern, *Witchcraft, Sorcery, Rumor, and Gossip*, 1–58, 194–203.
3. D. Assaf, *The Regal Way*, 218–225; Elior, "Between 'Divestment of Corporeality' and 'Love of Corporeality' "; Schatz-Uffenheimer, *Quietistic Elements*, 14–18, 54–58; Schatz-Uffenheimer, *Maggid Devarav Le-Ya'akov;* Green, *Menahem Nahum of Chernobyl;* and Piekarz, *The Beginning of Hasidism,* index (*gashmiyut*).
4. Lipsker " 'Light Is Sown for the Righteous.' "
5. Collinet-Guérin, *Histoire du nimbe.*
6. Horwitz and Dan, "Shekhinah."
7. Abelson, *The Immanence of God in Rabbinical Literature*; A. Goldberg, *Untersuchungen über die Vorstellung von der Schekhinah;* and Urbach, *The Sages*, 37–65.
8. Scholem, "*Shekhinah.*"
9. Patai, *The Hebrew Goddess*, 96–111.
10. Ben-Amos and Mintz, *In Praise of the Ba'al Shem,* 27–28 no. 14.
11. Ibid., 28–31 no. 15, 45–46 no. 31, 78–80 no. 60, 136–137 no. 114, 242–245 no. 237.
12. Budge, *The Book of Paradise,* 1:798 no. 611, 2:950 no. 440.
13. Bultmann, *"Zur Geschichte der Lichtsymbolik in Altertum"*; Davy et al., *La Thème de la lumière*; and Aalen, *Die begriffe 'Licht' und 'Finsternis.'*
14. Eliade, *The Two and the One*, 19–77.
15. Klaar, *Christo und das verschenkte Brot*, 194–195.
16. Enelow, *The Mishnah of Rabbi Eliezer.*

35

The Tailor Who Was Content with His Lot

TOLD BY DVORA FUS

*I*n a village there lived a poor couple. They had never had children, but this did not keep them from leading a contented life. His trade was tailoring, which he practiced for the gentiles of the village. At home they had plenty of good things. When they had a guest for the Sabbath, he never went away hungry, while they learned all the news about events in the big city from the wayfarer.

There was also a poor woman from the next town who used to come begging door to door. The housewife would feed her well and give her more to take back home. This went on for years.

Then the tailor's wife died suddenly, and he was left alone. He took his loss very hard and began looking for a match. He was considering the neighbor woman, until he had a dream in which a heavenly voice told him: "You must not look for a match. You must marry the woman who comes every week asking for alms." He woke up from his sleep in a fright. But when the voice called three times, saying, "If you don't marry the woman, you will die," he began to change his mind. Still, how could he marry a woman who went begging door to door, and he a respectable householder? What would people say? On the other hand, would it be better to die?

When the woman came around, as usual, he didn't give her a handout right away. He asked her to sit down, and started up a conversation with her: "Perhaps you should marry me? Then you wouldn't have to beg. You'd be a housewife."

The woman thought he was making fun of her. "Go on! Can't you find a better match?" But when she saw that he was serious, she told him: "If you want to marry me, you must go begging with me for a year. You are obviously a clever man. Life is full of talk. You will always be calling me 'the tramp,' and I won't stand for that. If we're going to be happy together, you have to agree to come begging with me. We'll go far away so no one will know about it. In a year, we'll get married and come back to town. You can resume working as a tailor, and we'll live happily."

They made their preparations to go away. They didn't need to take anything with them, because what do you need when you go begging from door to door? They set out on the long and tiresome yearlong trek. They never spent a day and night in the same place.

Finally, she relented and told him they could get married and go back home now, in time for the holidays. "What's the rush?" he asked. "The High Holy Days are coming and people are generous with their handouts. We don't have time for that now!"

COMMENTARY FOR TALE 35 (IFA 8255)

Written down from memory in Yiddish by Dvora Fus, in 1967, as she recalled it told in her father's house.

Cultural, Historical, and Literary Background

In this tale, irony provides an intersection between moral tales and humor. The moral tale, or exemplum, is one of the principle forms of Jewish traditional narratives.[1] Such tales present, in narrative terms, normative ethical values. The actions of the protagonists become religious and moral models for behavior, embodying articles of faith that inherently cannot become objects of ridicule or of humor. But in this tale, the tailor's last statement introduces an ironic inversion, transforming merit into profit, thereby casting humor upon morality.

Attitudes toward the Poor

The principal action of the story involves beggary. Mendicancy has existed in Israelite and Jewish societies from biblical to modern times. However, culturally, throughout history and tradition, the normative regulations and the canonic sources present the poor from the perspective of the affluent classes and the authoritative social and religious institutions. These groups have an ambivalent attitude toward beggars. For the relatively rich, beggars are the object of both compassion and repulsion. They are considered a social blight, yet deserving charity, and their support has become one of the fundamental Jewish values. Tales in which motifs V400 "Charity" and V410 "Charity rewarded" occur touch on this theme; see also the commentaries to tales IFA 2604 (vol. 1, no. 30), IFA 7202 (this vol., no. 48), and IFA 7612 (this vol., no. 13). Furthermore, compassion toward the poor is instrumental because it might save the living from the tortures of hell in the afterlife. The biblical phrase "*tsdaka tatsil mi-mavet*" (righteousness saves from death) (Proverbs 10:2, 11:4) has been adopted in Jewish funerary customs to mean "charity saves from death," and it has served as a means of solicitation for the poor during funerals.[2]

The Bible does not include specific descriptions of beggary and mendicancy, but it refers to these acts when instructing us to treat the poor charitably. For example, farmers are told "not [to] reap all the way to the edges of your field, or gather the gleanings of your harvest. You shall not pick your vineyard bare, or gather the fallen fruit from your vineyard; you shall leave them for the poor and the stranger" (Leviticus 19:9–10; also Leviticus 23:22), and Ruth (2:5–19) is allowed and encouraged to gather the gleanings in Boaz's field. The Book of Deuteronomy (14:28–29, 15:7–11, 24:19–21, 26:12–13) in particular insists on the of offering assistance to the needy poor.

In the postbiblical period, the mishnaic tractate *Pe'ah* articulated in detail the amount of food that the farmers ought to donate to the poor, with specific instructions concerning the amount to be given to a poor man. The occurrence of such detailed instructions in the oral Torah implies the prevalence of mendicancy at that period.[3]

In the medieval period, beggary and mendicancy continued to be an integral part of Jewish community life, as evidence by the development of social organizations and customs to handle these problems.[4] During the sixteenth century, many European countries restricted begging to the local poor or declared it illegal all together.[5] Some Jewish communities tried to follow suit, but to no avail.[6] Beggary, vagrancy, and mendicancy continued to increase in Europe up to and during the Industrial Revolution,[7] and similar trends followed in the Jewish communities.[8]

Literary References

In nineteenth-century eastern European communities, beggary and mendicancy became so prevalent that they acquired presence in literature. In Hasidic literature, for example, Rabbi Naḥman of Bratslav (1772–1811) employed the poor symbolically and allegorically in the tale *The Seven Beggars*.[9] This complex and enigmatic tale involves the abdication of the throne by a king in favor of his seemingly incompetent son, the abandonment of a young couple in the forest, and the couple's encounter with a series of deformed or disabled beggars, each of whom has his own story to tell. Interpretations of this tale are available.[10]

Fiction writers have included beggars for symbolic-satirical purposes and for a dramatic presentation of the clashing of classes in Jewish society. In 1869, Mendele Mokher Seforim[11] published *Fishke der Krumer* (Fishke the Lame) in Yiddish; it was published in Hebrew in 1907 as *Sefer ha-Kabzanim* (The beggars' book). Mendele used satire to describe the complex world of the beggars, as if from their own perspective. Moreover, like in the present tale, Fishke the Lame is lured into the world of beggary by a woman, in his case, his blind wife. An English translation of the novel is available.[12]

Early in the twentieth century, An-Sky incorporated beggars into his folk-mystical drama *The Dybbuk*.[13] The characters were depicted as hovering around the edges of Jewish community life.

In contrast to the normative and literary perspectives, the current tale presents beggary from the point of view of the poor, without criticism or ridicule. The humor that the tailor's comment generates is ironic, and if any satiric criticism is involved, it is directed toward the tailor rather than the beggar woman. Irony is popularly considered typical of Jewish humor.[14] But, in fact, irony is an ancient mode of discourse that is still current in many societies. Although it is possible to discern irony in the Bible—as is amply demonstrated by Good[15]—its use in speech and in the description of social situations is neither exclusively nor typically Jewish.

The term "irony" itself is derived from the Greek "*eironeia*," and occurs in oral and in written traditions throughout many cultures. Examinations of the concept in classical literature and philosophy[16] and in modern societies have been published.[17] Other sources include studies of the concept and the term in context[18] and discussions of irony in philosophical discourse.[19] In literary criticism, irony is a central analytical term that has been a subject of both theoretical and general research.[20]

A complex and layered idea, irony fundamentally involves, as succinctly summarized by Knox,[21] "a conflict of two meanings which has a dramatic structure peculiar to itself: initially, one meaning, the *appearance*, presents itself as the obvious truth, but when the context of this meaning unfolds, in depth or in time, it surprisingly discloses a conflicting meaning, the *reality*." Several permutations and refinements of these basic relationships are possible. In the present tale, the irony has a generic dimension, creating a shift from an exemplum to a joke, which is rare in the Jewish narrative tradition.

Similarities to Other IFA Tales

Other comparable tales in the IFA are the following:

- IFA 1555: *Begging Is the Best Occupation* (Yemen).
- IFA 3387: *The Rich Man's Only Son* (Iraq).[22]
- IFA 8579: *The Way to Live in Peace* (Iraq).
- IFA 9330: *The Prince and the Poor Man's Daughter* (Syria).[23]

Folktale Types

- *857 (IFA) "Wooer Wins Girl by Performing Tasks."
- *857(IFA) (Jason) "Wooer Wins Girl by Performing Tasks."
- *857(IFA) (Jason) "Realistic Suitor's Tasks."
- *857A (Jason) "Beggar-Suitor."

Folklore Motifs

- D1810.8.3 "Warning in dreams."
- D1814.2 "Advice from dream."
- J414 "Marriage with equal or with unequal."
- P160 "Beggars."
- *P165.1 "Poor women."
- P210 "Husband and wife."
- P441 "Tailor."
- T100 "Marriage."
- T121 "Unequal marriage."
- Z71.1 "Formulistic number: three."

Notes

1. Yassif, *The Hebrew Folktale,* 120–132, 283–297.
2. See I. Marcus, *The Jewish Life Cycle,* 211: illustration of the funeral of Malka Asch, mother of the author Sholem Asch.
3. Urbach, "Political and Social Tendencies in Talmudic Concepts of Charity."
4. B. Abrahams, *Jewish Life in the Middle Ages,* 331–347.
5. Geremek, *Poverty,* 123.
6. Baron, *The Jewish Community,* 2:321–322.
7. Geremek, op. cit., 122–124, 146–147, 163–167; and Rheinheimer, *Arme, Bettler und Vavanten.*
8. Baron, op. cit., 2:319–333; and Friedberg, "Begging and Beggars."
9. Band, *Naḥman of Bratslav,* 251–282, 321–324.
10. J. Dan, *The Hasidic Story,* 144–171; and J. Dan, "Rabbi Naḥman's Third Beggar."
11. Or Mendele Moykher Sforim in Yiddish, the pen name of Shalom Yaakov Abramowitsch (1836–1917).
12. Zuckerman et al., *The Three Great Classic Writers of Modern Yiddish Literature,* 169–312.
13. See 20–29.
14. A. Berger, *The Genius of the Jewish Joke,* 66–67; Bermant, *What Is the Joke?,* 6–7; and Eilbrit, *What Is a Jewish Joke?,* 71.
15. *Irony in the Old Testament.*
16. Thomson, *Irony.*
17. Fernandez and Huber, *Irony in Action.*
18. Knox, *The Word Irony and Its Context;* and Barbe, *Irony in Context.*
19. Colebrook, *Irony in the Work of Philosophy.* Prominent among the philosophical studies of irony is Kierkegaard, *The Concept of Irony;* for analyses of his work, see Perkins, *International Kierkegaard Commentary;* and Schleifer and Markley, *Kierkegaard and Literature.*
20. Abrams, *A Glossary of Literary Terms,* 80–84; Booth, *A Rhetoric of Irony;* Colebrook, *Irony;* Dane, *The Critical Mythology of Irony;* Handwerk, *Irony and Ethics in Narrative;* Schoentjes, *Poétique de l'irone;* Holland, *Divine Irony;* Knox, "Irony"; Muecke, *Irony and the Ironic;* and Muecke, *The Compass of Irony.*
21. "Irony," 626.
22. Published in D. Noy, *Jewish-Iraqi Folktales,* 122–123 no. 59.
23. Published in Cheichel, *A Tale for Each Month: 1972,* 45–46 no. 6.

36

A Poor Man's Wisdom Is Scorned

TOLD BY YEHUDAH HERMANN TO YIFRAḤ ḤAVIV

*I*n the Middle Ages there lived a great poet, Abraham ibn Ezra, who was dreadfully poor. He had absolutely nothing except for his staff and his bag, with which he wandered from place to place. All his life, Ibn Ezra was troubled by the verse "A poor man's wisdom is scorned."* "Why is the wisdom of the poor man scorned?" he kept asking himself. "Why did King Solomon write that?" He never could find an answer to his question until the following incident occurred.

Once, during his wandering from city to city, through mountains and wastelands, he met a man who, like him, was traveling with a bag. But with one difference—this fellow had two purses tied together, one on his back and another on his chest.

Ibn Ezra fell into step with him. As they walked, he asked the man, "Who are you?"

"I am a very rich man," he replied, "from very far away. I sold all my property and everything I owned and used the money to buy precious stones. I am carrying these gems in the bag on my back. The other one, on my chest, is full of rocks, of the same weight as the gems."

"Why?" asked Ibn Ezra.

"So that the weight will be equally divided and the gems on my back will not weigh me down."

Ibn Ezra said to him, "Wouldn't it be better to divide the gems into two equal parts? Half in front of you and the other on your back? The weight would still be balanced but your burden would be lighter."

"You're right!" replied the rich man. "Why didn't I think of that? But tell me, are you poor or rich?"

"The poorest of the poor! No one is poorer than I!" Ibn Ezra answered.

"I have learned from my ancestors," the rich man said, "never to heed the advice of a poor man!"

Ibn Ezra was astonished by this answer, but said nothing. The two kept

---

*Ecclesiastes 9:16.

walking until they reached a port city. They went down to the shore and found a ship. Both decided to sail in it to a foreign country. The rich man paid for his passage, while Ibn Ezra, who was dreadfully poor, hired himself out as an oarsman.

The ship raised anchor and set sail. A few days later a storm swept the sea. What did the passengers and sailors do? Each man prayed to his god. But their prayers were not accepted. Quite the opposite! The sea grew stormier and stormier!

"We have to jettison half of the cargo," the captain notified the passengers. "Everyone throw half of what he has overboard."

The rich man came to the captain and showed him his two packages. "The two are of equal weight, aren't they?"

The captain weighed them in his hand. "Yes, you're right. Throw one into the water."

The rich man gave him the bag full of plain rocks. The captain tossed it into the water, leaving the rich man with all his gemstones.

"Had I listened to the advice of that beggar," proclaimed the rich man, "I would have lost half of my wealth now!"

Ibn Ezra heard this and sighed. "Now I understand the verse 'A poor man's wisdom is scorned.'"

COMMENTARY FOR TALE 36 (IFA 13498)

Told by Yehudah Hermann to Yifrah Haviv in 1981 in Kibbuz Bet Keshet.[1]

Cultural, Historical, and Literary Background

The biblical proverb "A poor man's wisdom is scorned" (Ecclesiastes 9:16) frames this tale, occurring in its opening and in its closing. The biblical verse is extracted from the fable of the besieged city that the poor man's wisdom could have saved had the people listened to him (Ecclesiastes 9:14–16). Rabbi Abraham ibn Ezra (1089 or 1092–1165 or 1176) employed this biblical verse in one of his poems.[2] The present tale justifies the rejection of the poor man's advice, rationalizing a negative ethical attitude toward the poor. This attitude contrasts with biblical and talmudic-midrashic law and ethos, which advocates compassion and justice toward the poor; however, it may represent a new elite and urban viewpoint, current in wisdom literature, toward the poorer economic classes.[3] For a discussion of the rhetorical strategy of proverb usage in narrative text, see the commentary to tale IFA 6814 (this vol., no. 55).[4]

Ibn Ezra, one of the leading Hebrew poets in medieval Jewish Spain, was a grammarian, a philosopher, a scientist, and an interpreter of the Bible (biographical sketches of the poet have been published).[5] In his poetry, Ibn Ezra presented himself as a very poor and luckless person—an image that probably had some basis in reality—and folk tradition contributed to this portrayal in legends. The poet has been the subject of a number of works, including an analysis of his contribution to science,[6] a critical edition of his poetry,[7] and general evaluations and appreciation of his works.[8] For further discussion and scholarship about him and his works, see the commentary to tale IFA 12727 (vol. 1, no. 60).

In general, the principal theme in the tales about Ibn Ezra is his deceptive appearance: His poverty masks his superior wisdom and intelligence (compare motifs J260 "Choice between worth and appearance"; K1816.0.4 "Scholar disguised as a rustic along road answers questions of school inspector in Greek, Latin, and Hebrew"; and K1817.1 "Disguise as beggar"). However, in the present tale, he himself puts to test his own intelligence and finds it wanting. The narrative involves an inversion of the failed-trickster narrative pattern. The apparent irrational decision to increase the weight of the burden, rather than dividing it into two equal parts, proves correct, making this tale unique among the internationally known versions of this tale type.

The basic situation in this tale appears to be modeled after the story in the Book of Jonah. However, in the Ibn Ezra narrative cycle, there is another tale in which the poet faces a similar dilemma while sailing on a ship in a stormy sea. In the second tale, however, Ibn Ezra's cleverness serves him well. The ship's captain decided to throw into the deep half of the thirty passengers onboard, who happened to be made up of two equal groups: rascals and Jewish students. Ibn Ezra made use of his mathematical knowledge to save the Jewish students; he arranged all the passengers in a line and suggested that the captain throw off every ninth person. The poet managed to arrange all the passengers in such a way that he saved the students (4 students, 5 rascals, 2 students, 1 rascal, 3 students, 1 rascal, 1 student, 2 rascals, 2 students, 3 rascals, 1 student, 2 rascals, 2 students, 1 rascal).[9]

Folktale Types

- 1242A "Carrying Part of the Load."
- 1242A "Relief for the Donkey" (new ed.).
- 1242B "Balancing the Mealsack."
- 1242B (El-Shamy) "Balancing the Mealsack [with a Rock]."

Folklore Motifs

- *J20 "Counsels proved wrong by experience."
- *J21.37.1 "Do not take a poor man's advice."
- J191.1 "Solomon as wise man."
- J1230 "Clever dividing."
- P150 "Rich men."
- *P165 "Poor men."
- P427.7 "Poet."

——————— **Notes** ———————

1. First published in Haviv, *Taba'at ha-Kesem be-Golani* (The magic ring in Golani), 41–42 no. 6.
2. Is. Levin, *Abraham ibn Ezra: His Life and His Poetry*, 206.
3. Pleins, "Poverty in the Social World of the Wise"; and Pleins, "Poor, Poverty."
4. See also Savran, *Telling and Retelling*.
5. Is. Levin, op. cit., 9–46; Weinberger, *Twilight of a Golden Age*, 1–11.
6. S. Sela, *Abraham ibn Ezra and the Rise of Medieval Hebrew Science*.
7. Is. Levin, *The Religious Poems of Abraham ibn Ezra*; I. Levin, *Abraham ibn Ezra: Reader*; and J. Schirmann, *Ha-Shirah ha-'Ivrit bi-Sefarad uvi-Provans* (Hebrew poetry in Spain and in Provence), 1:569–623.
8. Esteban, *Abraham ibn Ezra y su tiempo/Abraham ibn Ezra and His Age*; and Tomson, *Abraham ibn Ezra savant universel*.
9. Ben-Menachem, *Avraham even-Ezra* (Abraham ibn-Ezra), 17–20.

37

A Change of Place Is a Change of Luck (?)

Told by Mordechai Hillel Kroshnitz to Ayelet Oettinger

Once there was a Jew who never succeeded at anything. Whatever he did, it was always—as they say in Yiddish, *mit der puter a rop*—with the buttered side down (that's what happens when you drop your bread and butter on the ground). In short, bad luck. Whatever business he tried his hand at, he failed. Plain bad luck.

This Jew decided that he would run away from his bad luck. How? Simple. This was the time when everybody was immigrating to America. He would go too, even though he had no relatives there, no friends.

Somehow he reached America by boat. He debarked, left the port—and suddenly this fellow comes up and greets him:

"Hello there! Welcome to America." And he hugged him.

The man looked at him. "Who are you? I don't know you."

"What? You don't recognize me? But I've been your companion for your whole life!"

"But who are you?"

"I'm your bad luck. What did you think? That you could run away from me? I've come to meet you here in America, so we can always be together."

COMMENTARY FOR TALE 37 (IFA 14260)

Told by Mordechai Hillel Kroshnitz to his granddaughter Ayelet Oettinger in 1983 in Kiryat Ḥayyim.

Cultural, Historical, and Literary Background

Luck, Place, and Time

The idea expressed in the proverb "A change of place is a change of luck" (BT *Rosh Ha-Shanah* 16b; JT *Shabbat* 6:9) contrasts with the idea of astrological predetermination and represents a conception of destiny that empowers individuals to change their fate and fortune. Simultaneously with the belief in a single God Almighty who controls and guides world affairs and individual lives, which is conceived as *hashgaḥah elyonah* (providence), past and present Jewish societies also believe in astral magic. These beliefs were not confined to a single sect, class, or rank in Jewish societies but cut across them, occurring in popular wisdom as well as in philosophical speculations and mystical meditations. Although the idea of divine providence is fundamental to Judaism and is discussed in many studies of Jewish thought, it can be contrasted with astrology, as articulated in the writings of Shem-Tov ibn Falaquera (c. 1225–1295).[1]

As in astrological systems, the belief in astral magic implies temporal predetermination of destiny. According to divine providence, the moment of birth has a decisive role in shaping the personality of and course of the individual's life, as a result of the effect that stars and constellations have on Earth at that point in time. The sages articulated two basic opinions regarding the influence of birth time on human life. Rabbi Joshua ben Levi (third-century *amora*) was reported to propose predication of a person's future and temperament on the day of the week he or she was born, based on the story of Creation as told in Genesis 1. For him, there was a correspondence between an individual and the objects God created on the day of the week on which he or she was born. Thus each individual was a microcosm of the universe. In contrast, his peer Rabbi Ḥanina argued in favor of astral magic and noted the influence the planets had on human life (see BT *Shabbat* 156a). Discussions and studies of astral magic in Jewish tradition and thought are available.[2]

Unlike the correspondence between destiny and time, the relation between space and destiny has not been the subject of much philosophical discussion, nor has it been the focus of systems of folk thought. The proverb that motivates the action of the Jew in this story also inspires the main character in tale IFA 2603 (vol. 3, no. 11); however, in the latter tale, prosperity is the consequence of the change of place. In the present tale, the proverb is implicit; the narrator describes the Jew as one for whom everything falls with "the buttered side down," which is a common Yiddish proverb.[3]

The relative paucity of discussions by the sages and medieval rabbis of the

37 / A Change of Place

correspondence between geographic location and luck may be the result of both semantics and beliefs. Astral magic, destiny, and fortune (in terms of fate as well as of riches) are all included in the meanings of the Hebrew word for "luck" (*mazel*). This lexeme connotes the constellations, the signs of the Zodiac, and a fortunate turn in life. The word *mazel* thus represents a deeply rooted belief that Jews share with other peoples. The idea of "A change of place is a change of luck" cannot be expressed in Hebrew by only a single word. The present tale conveys the idea that it is useless to attempt to shift one's luck from astral magic to geographic location.

The Personification of Luck

Within Jewish and international folk narrative traditions, it is possible to distinguish three plot clusters involving the relationships between a locale, a person, and luck.

- The treasure hunt in a far distance place. This story line involves tale types 745A "The Predestined Treasure," 1645 "The Treasure at Home," and 745*B (IFA) "The Predestined Treasure." For a discussion of these tale types, see the commentary to tale IFA 2603.
- The discarded treasure. The tale types associated with this plot cluster are 842 "The Man Who Kicked aside Riches" and 947A "Bad Luck Cannot Be Arrested." For a discussion of this tale cycle, see the commentary to tale IFA 12727 (vol. 1, no. 60).
- Bad luck personified refuses to desert its victim. In these tales, the bad luck has demonic qualities and possesses its victim as a demon inhabits or attacks a person. For a discussion of Jewish demonology, see the commentaries to tales IFA 779 (this vol., no. 4) and IFA 8792 (this vol., no. 5).

The humorous quality of the present tale mitigates the harsh relationships between human and supernatural beings that typically dominate demonic tales.

The earliest record of a story about personified bad luck is available from the end of the seventeenth century in the tales of Rabbi Juspa of Worms, who served as a *shammash*.[4] The Yiddish proverb *"Das Schlimm-Massel geht mit"* (The bad luck comes along) epitomizes Rabbi Juspa's tale.[5] Both an English summary[6] and a literary versified rendition[7] of the tale have been published. In Rabbi Juspa's version, the personified bad luck jumps on the Jew's wagon as he is about to leave town, traveling with him instead of meeting him in his new place. A similar rendition occurs in a twentieth-century recording of tales.[8] Schwarzbaum[9] compiled an extensive bibliography on the representation of bad luck and destiny in Jewish folklore.

The tale types 947A* "Bad Luck Refuses to Desert a Man" and 735A "Bad Luck Imprisoned" appear to be in contrast with each other; but in some Jewish tales they are actually complementary, as when the hero tricks and imprisons the bad luck that refuses to leave. For an example, see the tale *The Rich and the Poor Brothers: Second Tale.*[10] Additional comparative notes[11] and a general discussion of the tale types about luck are available.[12]

Similarities to Other IFA Tales

Other versions in the IFA are the following:

- IFA 1293: *Lentil Is the Poor Man's Luck* (Yemen).[13]
- IFA 6547: *There Is No Escape from Bad Luck* (Belarus).
- IFA 7188: *The Poverty in the Attic* (Poland).[14]
- IFA 7659: *The Shlemiehl* (Poland).
- IFA 8751: *Poverty Grows* (Romania).[15]

Folktale Types

- cf. 735A "Bad Luck Imprisoned."
- 947A "Bad Luck Cannot Be Arrested."
- 947A (El-Shamy) "Bad Luck Cannot Be Arrested."
- 947A (Jason) "Bad Luck Cannot Be Arrested."
- 947A* (old ed. only) "Bad Luck Refuses to Desert a Man".
- 947A* (El-Shamy) "Bad Luck Refuses to Desert a Man."
- 947A* (Jason) "Bad Luck Refuses to Desert a Man."

Folklore Motifs

- N112 "Bad luck personified."
- cf. N131.5 "Luck changing after change of place."
- N250 "Persistent bad luck."
- *N250.5 "Bad luck welcomes man in his new place."

─────── **Notes** ───────

1. See Freudenthal, "Providence, Astrology, and Celestial Influences on the Sublunar World."

2. Fishof, *Written in the Stars*; Ness, *Written in the Stars* (esp. "Astrology in Synagogue Art," 1–38; "Jewish Astrology," 137–174); D. Schwartz, *Studies on Astral Magic in Medieval Jewish Thought*; S. Sela, *Astrology and Biblical Exegesis in Abraham Ibn Ezra's Thought;* and Stuckrad, *Frömmigkeit und Wissenschaft.*

3. I. Bernstein, *Jüdische Sprichwörter und Redensarten*, 41 no. 10.

4. Eidelberg, *R. Juspa, Shammash of Warmaisa (Worms)*, 84 no. 20.

5. Tendlau, *Sprichwörter und Redensarten*, 392–393 no. 1060.

6. Waxman, *A History of Jewish Literature,* 2:655–656; and Zinberg, *A History of Jewish Literature*, 7:200–201.

7. Tendlau, *Das der Sagen und Legenden*, 257–260 no. 53.

8. N. Gross, *Maaselech un Mesholim*, 281.

9. *Studies in Jewish and World Folklore*, 259–278.

10. Published in J. Cahan, *Jewish Folklore*, 111–112 no. 5; an English translation can be found in B. Weinreich, *Yiddish Folktales,* 26–27 no. 14.

11. Schwarzbaum, op. cit., 266.

12. Blum, "*Glück und Unglück.*"

13. Published in D. Noy, *Jefet Schwili Erzählt*, 249 no. 105.

14. Published in Pipe, *Twelve Folktales from Sanok*, 22 no. 4.

15. Published in Cheichel, *A Tale for Each Month 1968–1969,* 135–136 no. 22.

38

God Will Help

Told by Hinda Sheinferber to Hadarah Sela

*T*his is a story for which a person has to believe that things will work out. To think only this.

Once there was an inn. The innkeeper leased it from the governor of the town. But he didn't have the rent money. Whenever the governor came to demand the rent, the innkeeper would say, "God will help me." It was always, "God will help me."

The *poritz** was getting angrier. Several months had passed already. The man kept saying, "You will see that God will help me."

The *poritz* had already stopped going every day. Passover drew near, and the *poritz* said that he wanted to see how the man would celebrate Passover when he had so little and kept saying that God would help him. He wanted to see how.

In the meantime, the *poritz* had sold a broad tract of land, a large forest, and had been paid in silver and gold. If you want to know whether coins are counterfeit you put them in your mouth. Now this *poritz*, the governor, had a clerk. It was the clerk who had to test the money. He sat in a special room. There was a parrot in the room. The parrot watched every time he tested the money. After the clerk left the room, the parrot flew down. It thought that when the man put the money in his mouth he swallowed it. The bird swallowed so many coins that its stomach swelled up, and it fell down dead.

The *poritz* saw this as a way to be nasty to the innkeeper. He would throw him the dead parrot. At the very least, the innkeeper would be frightened. The next day, he threw it through the window. The bird's belly split open, and all the money spilled out.

So the man was able to celebrate Passover like a king, with wine and lots of good food. That night, the *poritz* went to see the innkeeper's Passover. There was bright light, and the table was set as for a royal feast.

---

*Polish landlord.

One truly must believe in God, he thought. No doubt someone had helped. But he wanted to know what, where from.

The next day, the governor went to see the innkeeper. "Why didn't you pay your debt if you had so much money?"

"I haven't had time yet," the man replied. "On the eve of the holiday, I still didn't have any money. When I got up the day before Passover, I found a dead parrot, with a pile of money next to it."

"Now I will start believing that God really does help," the governor told him.

The man was able to pay the rent and live comfortably.

COMMENTARY FOR TALE 38 (IFA 18130)

Told by Hinda Sheinferber from Poland to Hadara Sela in 1991 in Haifa.

Cultural, Historical, and Literary Background

The narrator frames the present story with a statement of its message of trust in God and His just reward to His faithful. In a narrative mode, the tale articulates in concrete terms the eleventh of the thirteen principles of Judaism as formulated by Maimonides (1135–1204) in his commentary on the Mishnah *Sanhedrin* 10. According to this article of faith, "God rewards those who fulfill the commandments of the Torah and punishes those who transgress them."[1]

The implicit acceptance of temporary suffering also underscores the fundamental acceptance of the ways of God to His believers, regardless of its unexplainable hardship. This is one aspect of theodicy, a term formulated by Gottfried Wilhelm Leibniz (1646–1716) to articulate the concept of vindication of divine justice in face of adversity. Analyses of the theodicy in Jewish folk traditions and in Judaism in general are available,[2] as is a discussion of theodicy in the biblical world.[3] A survey of recent scholarship about the issue has been published.[4]

The present tale features two of the most familiar roles in Jewish society of Eastern Europe: the innkeeper and the landlord (for more on innkeepers, see the commentary to tale IFA 4815 [this vol., no. 56]). The test case for having complete faith in God is the perennial anxiety in Jewish life of having sufficient provisions for the celebration of the Passover seder (for a discussion of this concern, see the commentary to tale IFA 7000 [vol. 1, no. 17]). As other versions of this tale in the IFA demonstrate, the exemplum was well known in Jewish communities from Afghanistan to Poland and Russia. In most of them, exotic animals or birds bring the treasure. The disposal of a gold-filled animal carcass in the yard of a Jewish home serves as an inversion of anti-Semitic blood libel accusations, which involved the disposal of a dead Christian in Jewish quarters (blood libel in history is discussed in the commentary to tale IFA 15347 [vol. 1, no. 15]).

Similarities to Other IFA Tales

Other versions of this tale can be found in the IFA:

- IFA 450: *Having Faith in God's Help* (Afghanistan).
- IFA 988: *Happy Is He Who Believes in God* (Iraq).
- IFA 2245: *The Great Miracle* (Russia).
- IFA 2316: *A Magic Help for Passover* (Tunisia).
- IFA 2790: *A Treasure in the Monkey* (Eretz Yisra'el, Ashkenazic).
- IFA 5212: *Golden Coins in the Monkey's Belly* (Romania).
- IFA 5317: *The Rabbi, the Landlord, and the Monkey* (country of Islam in Eretz Yisra'el).
- IFA 5932: *The Poor and the Rich Families* (Iraqi Kurdistan).

- IFA 7260: *The Poor Jew and the Rich Gentile* (Morocco).[5]
- IFA 7273: *The Story of the Poor Jew* (Egypt).
- IFA 8150: *The Monkey* (Tangier, Morocco).
- IFA 10324: *The Monkey and the Golden Coins* (Republic of Georgia).
- IFA 11251: *The Jew and the Christian and His Dog* (Morocco).
- IFA 11463: *Everything Is up to God* (Iraqi Kurdistan).
- IFA 11847: *The Merit of Studying the Torah* (country of Islam in Eretz Yisra'el).[6]
- IFA 13481: *I Have Never Seen a Righteous Man Abandoned* (Iraq).
- IFA 14854: *The Gold in the Dead Mouse* (Eretz Yisra'el, Karaite).

Folktale Type

- 841*B (IFA) "Treasure in a Dead Monkey."

Folklore Motifs

- *B339.2 "Death of a pet animal (bird) from eating gold coins and precious stones."
- *N529.3 "Treasure found in a carcass of an animal (bird)."
- N530 "Discovery of treasure."
- *P449 "Innkeeper."
- Q22 "Reward for faith."
- V75.1 "Passover."
- *V75.1.1 "Seder, the Passover eve ceremonial dinner."

Notes
---

1. See L. Jacobs, *Principles of the Jewish Faith,* 350–367; and Altmann, "Articles of Faith."

2. D. Noy, "The Hidden Zaddik in Theodicy Legends"; Schwarzbaum, "Jewish and Moslem Versions of Some Theodicy Legends"; and Sherwin, "Theodicy."

3. Laato and de Moor, *Theodicy in the World of the Bible.*

4. Whitney, *Theodicy.*

5. Published in Avitsuk, *The Fate of a Child,* 11–12 no. 5.

6. Published in Rabbi, *Avoteinu Sipru* (Our fathers told), 3:46–47 no. 20.

39

The Poisoned Cake

Told by Dvora Fus

The nobleman's castle was in a village near the shtetl. His widow lived there with her only son. The steward and his assistants handled all her business affairs; her son was at school in a distant city. He never came home except during the summer vacation, when his sole pleasure was to go hunting in the nearby forests.

The son was the noblewomen's only comfort, and she expected that he would bring her great honor and satisfaction. On his account, she was extremely devout, to the point of fanaticism. Every Sunday, she went to church and distributed very large sums in alms. She never turned away a beggar and was accordingly much beloved in the village.

Among those to whom she gave alms was a certain Jewish woman, who came to the noblewoman once a week and received what she needed for an entire week. But this Jewish woman never thanked the noblewoman. Instead, she repeated the same Yiddish phrase: "Everything you're doing—you're doing it for yourself and not for me." (In other words, the reward of a good deed is a good deed,* and the true reward is tendered in Heaven.)

The noblewoman did not understand what the Jewess was saying, of course, and kept giving her what she needed every week. Many years passed this way. Throughout this time, the son came home each year for his holiday, and he grew into a handsome young man. He continued to go hunting every summer when he was home. The Jewish woman continued to receive her weekly stipend from the noblewoman.

The noblewoman was curious to know what the Jewess was saying. When she finally found out, she was furious. She decided to pay back this ungrateful Jewish woman, who had never once said thank you to her benefactor. The next time the Jewish woman came she would give her a poisoned cake.

---

*Mishnah *Avot* 4:2.

So she baked a delicious-looking white cake laced with a deadly poison. When the Jewish woman came, as she did every week, she was given this cake as well. And she said, as always, "Everything you are doing—you are doing for yourself and not for me," and went her way.

As she was walking back home from the village, passing through the forest, she suddenly spied a man lying unconscious on the ground. Although she did not know who it was, she began to take care of him at once. When he recovered consciousness he told her, "I am the noblewoman's son. I was hunting in the forest, but I lost my way; and I'm very hungry because I haven't had anything to eat in hours. That's why I fainted." Without a moment's hesitation, the woman took out the mouthwatering cake and gave it to the young man, to satisfy his hunger, and continued on her way. The young man ate the poisoned cake and died.

When they brought the corpse to her castle, his mother finally understood the Jewess's words: She had poisoned the cake for her only son and for no one else.

COMMENTARY FOR TALE 39 (IFA 551)

Written down from memory in 1958 by Dvora Fus.

Cultural, Historical, and Literary Background

In 1946, S. Thompson[1] stated that tales similar to the present one were apparently confined to Estonia. But in subsequent years, new versions from different countries became available.[2] The proposition "He who does good to another does good to himself"—or in German, "*Was man auch tut, tut man sich selbst*"—with some variations, plays a crucial role in these tales.[3] The same adage occurs in the original Yiddish text of the present story as well: *Was du tust, tustu dokh zikh ober nit mir* (Whatever you do, you do it for yourself and not for me). However, when such a traditional saying appears in a folktale, its meaning may become somewhat ambiguous, taking on different nuances and significance as the story develops.

Tales about a person who bites his or her own poisonous bait occur in medieval midrashic anthologies from Yemen and from Europe. It is said that Rebecca's father, Bethuel, offered a poisoned dish to Eliezer, Abraham's servant and messenger, but ended up eating the dish himself (*Yalkut Shimoni* 1:109).[4] These versions of the tale, however, do not include the proverbial-prophetic proposition that the beggar in the present story pronounces.

The first time the poor woman utters her statement she simply questions the altruism of the donor, implying that charity itself has its own reward. In saying so, the beggar woman alludes to a broad range of biblical and postbiblical verses and statements that touch on a similar idea. Thus, for example, the biblical verses "One is repaid in kind for one's deed" (Proverbs 12:14) and "righteousness saves from death" (Proverbs 10:2, 11:4) suggest direct reward for good deeds. In the postbiblical oral tradition, the idea becomes even more explicit, for example: "By that same measure by which a man metes out [to others], they mete out to him" (Mishnah *Sotah* 1:7) and "all the labour [performance of good deeds] you do is done for your own benefit" (MR *Leviticus* 34:15).

Despite the implied cynicism in such statements, casting doubt on the whole-heartedness of charity, the proposition is essentially an expression of gratitude through blessing. However, within the context of interethnic and intercultural contact of the present tale's narrative situation, the donor interprets the blessing as ingratitude and is intent on avenging her perceived insult. After the poisoning attempt and the self-infliction of retribution, the adage becomes a statement of revenge that draws its meaning from a different set of propositions, also given in the Bible. For example, "If anyone maims his fellow, as he has done so shall it be done to him" (Leviticus 24:19); "Woe to the wicked man, for he shall fare ill; As his hands have dealt, so shall it be done to him" (Isaiah 3:11); "As you did, so shall it be done to you" (Obadiah 1:15); "A kindly man benefits himself; A cruel man makes trouble for himself" (Proverbs 11:17); and "He who digs a pit will fall in it" (Proverbs 26:27). This tale demonstrates the semantic indeterminacy of proverbs. Theoretical and analytical explorations of this aspect of speaking in proverbs have been published.[5]

The tale also appears in the Hasidic tradition; for example, it is in the appendix that Rabbi Jacob Joseph of Polonnoye,[6] a disciple of the Besht, titled "Words That I Heard from My Teacher." He attributed the story directly to the founder of Hasidism. Later the tale entered, with variations, the literary Hasidic tradition.[7] Texts from non-Hasidic circles are also known.[8] Additional studies of this tale are available.[9]

Similarities to Other IFA Tales

Other versions of this tale occur in the IFA:

- IFA 1222 (vol. 3, no. 37): *A Measure for Measure* (Egypt).
- IFA 1913: *The Poisoned Cake* (Lithuania).[10]
- IFA 2002: *The Poisoned Cake* (Republic of Georgia).
- IFA 2486: *The Poisoned Bread* (Romania).
- IFA 2849: *A Man's Actions Affect Him Alone* (Poland).
- IFA 3562: *A Man's Actions Affect Him Alone* (Poland).
- IFA 3921: *The Shining Egg* (Iraq).
- IFA 5004: *Don't Do Unto Others What Is Not Good for You* (Sierra Leone).
- IFA 5527: *High Price* (Libya).[11]
- IFA 5791: *A Man's Actions Affect Him Alone* (Germany).
- IFA 6015: *The Poisoned Cake* (Turkey).[12]
- IFA 6605: *The Man Who Hurt Himself* (Iraqi Kurdistan).
- IFA 8358: *Whatever You Do—You Do It to Yourself* (country of Islam in Eretz Yisra'el).
- IFA 8793: *The Lesson of the Lady* (Poland).
- IFA 9170: T*he Story of a Righteous Jewess and Arab Emir* (Iraq).
- IFA 11402: *The Story of the Widow* (Iran).
- IFA 11725: *The Story of the Hallah* (Ukraine).
- IFA 12605: *Everybody Gets the Reward He Deserves* (Bulgaria).[13]
- IFA 12896: *The King and the Pauper* (Bukhara).
- IFA 14811: *The Poisoned Cake* (Yemen).

Folktale Types

- 837 "How the Wicked Lord Was Punished."
- 837 "The Beggar's Bread" (new ed.).
- 837 (El-Shamy) "How the Wicked Lord Was Punished [Poisoner's Son Unwittingly Poisoned]."
- 837 (Haboucha) "How the Wicked Lord Was Punished."
- 837 (Jason) "How the Wicked Lord Was Punished."
- 837 (Krzyzanowski) "*Kara za Otrucie*" (Punishment with Poison).

Folklore Motifs

- H580 "Enigmatic statements."
- H592 "Enigmatic statement made clear by experience."
- K1600 "Deceiver falls into own trap."
- N300 "Unlucky accidents."
- N320 "Person unwittingly killed."
- N330 "Accidental killing or death."
- N332 "Accidental poisoning."
- cf. N332.1 "Man accidentally fed bread which his father has poisoned."
- N825.3.1 "Help from old beggar woman."
- N826 "Help from beggar."
- P60 "Noble (gentle) ladies."
- *P150.1 "Rich women."
- P160 "Beggars."
- *P165.1 "Poor women."
- P231 "Mother and son."
- Q211.8 "Punishment for desire to murder."
- Q261.1 "Intended treachery punished."
- Q402 "Punishment of children for parents' offense."
- Q411 "Death as punishment."
- Q411.3 "Death of father (son, etc.) as punishment."
- S111 "Murder by poisoning."
- cf. S111.1 "Murder with poisoned bread."
- W10 "Kindness."
- Z64 "Proverbs."

――――― **Notes** ―――――

1. *The Folktale*, 132.

2. See the tale types listed for this tale (below) and Ranke, "*Brot des Bettlers*."

3. For example, Davidson and Phelps, "Folktales from New Goa, India," 36–37 no. 13; and Hertel, *Indische Märchen*, 183–184 no. 54.

4. See also Theodor and Albeck, *Bereschit Rabba*, 651 (notes); Margulies, *Midrash Haggadol on the Pentateuch: Genesis*, 1:403, 2:403; S. Buber, ed. *Lekach-Tob (Pesikta Sutarta)*, 1:56a; S. Buber, *Agadischer Commentar*, 59 no. 53; and Ginzberg, *The Legends of the Jews*, 1:295, 5:261–262.

5. Krikmann, "On the Denotative Indefiniteness of Proverbs"; Kirkmann, "Some Additional Aspects of Semantic Indefiniteness of Proverbs"; and Kirkmann, "The Great Chain Metaphor."

6. *Sefer Toldot Yaakov Yosef*, 416.

7. Anonymous, *Sefer Ge'ulat Yisrael* (The book of the redemption of Israel), 35a–35b (last tale); Klainman, *Zikaron la-Rishonim* (Commemoration for the early [righteous people]), 34a; Newman, *The Hasidic Anthology*, 424 no. 5; and Ben-Yeḥezki'el, *Sefer ha-Ma'asiyyot* (A book of folktales), 6:435–436, 450–451.

8. N. Gross, *Maaselech un Mesholim*, 362–363; Larrea Palacin, *Cuentos populares de los Judios del Norte de Marrueccos*, 72–73 no. 18; and B. Weinreich, *Yiddish Folktales*, 189 no. 64.

9. Schwarzbaum, *Studies in Jewish and World Folklore*, 332–333 no. 425.

10. Published in D. Noy, *Folktales of Israel*, 40–41 no. 17.

11. Published in D. Noy, *Jewish Folktales from Libya*, 140–141, 204 no. 62.

12. Published in Stahl, *Stories of Faith and Morals*, 36–37, 119–121 no. 10.

13. Published in Alexander and Noy, *The Treasure of Our Fathers*, 125, 261–262 no. 27.

40

There Is No Truth in the World

TOLD BY WOLF SOSENSKI TO DINAH BEHAR

A man was traveling a long way. It was a very warm day, and he grew tired. He came to a pile of rocks and sat down to rest. Suddenly, he heard a voice from underneath the stones: "Help me get out of here! The rocks are crushing me."

The man's heart was filled with mercy. He stood up and lifted a stone. A snake emerged and slithered away. The man thought no more about it and continued his journey. A short time later, when he lay down to rest, he felt something on his neck. He looked down and saw the snake wrapped around it. "What do you want?" he asked.

"I want to strangle you," replied the snake.

"I saved you—and you want to repay me evil for good?"

"There is no truth in the world," replied the snake.

"It is forbidden to sit in judgment alone," said the man. "Come, let us travel together and find someone to judge between us. If he says you should strangle me, you may do so; otherwise, you'll let me go." The two traveled together until they met a horse, standing there browsing on the grass. The man went up to the horse, told him the story, and asked, "Please, judge between us."

"Strangle him!" said the horse to the snake. "There is no truth among human beings! When I was a colt, they took care of me and children played with me; but when I grew up, they made me work and I brought profit to my master. But now, when I can plow no more, they don't feed me and I have to chew bitter grass."

"Perhaps you have a bad master," said the man. "But there are also good men in the world who don't behave like that. Come, let us continue our journey. Perhaps we will find another animal that has a different opinion of human beings." The three—the man, the snake, and the horse—continued on their way. They met a large dog that was digging with its paws, searching for food. The three went up to him and the man told him what had happened. The dog's answer was the same as the horse's. Turning to the snake, he said, "Strangle him! When I was a puppy, they took care of me and loved me. When I grew up, they put a chain on me and I guarded the sheep and barked when anything approached. But now, when I am old and can no longer bark and run, they have thrown me out. This is why I have to look in the fields for dead rats to eat. Is there any truth, justice, or righteousness in the world? Strangle the man!"

"Perhaps the dog had the same master as the horse," objected the man, "and he didn't treat them fairly. Come, let us go to the forest and look for animals that have never served human beings. Perhaps their verdict will be different."

The snake rejected the proposal. "Don't be too hasty to kill me," interjected the man. "You can always do so later."

They went on and met a fox. The man with the snake wrapped around his neck said to him, "Two judges have already rendered a verdict between me and the snake, and now I want you too to judge."

"How can I judge when I didn't see how it happened?" replied the fox. "Let us go back to where it happened, and after I see how it happened I will issue my verdict."

So they all went back. When they came to the place, the fox told the man, "Pick up the stone and show me how it happened." Then he told the snake, "I want you to go back to the place where you were lying, so I can see exactly what the situation was."

The snake did as the fox instructed. "Leave him there under the stone!" the fox told the man. The man did as the fox suggested and the snake was left to suffocate under the stone.

The man went happily on his way, with the fox accompanying him. As they walked along together, on the way the fox said, "I saved your life. You should pay me for saving you."

"How can I pay you?" asked the man.

"I don't need much," the fox replied. "One chicken a day is enough for me." The man agreed. "Gladly," he said. "A tiny payment like this will not bear heavily on me."

The fox went back to the forest and the man kept on until he arrived back home. He recounted his adventure to his wife and sons. They were all happy. "Yes," the woman said, "I have sixty chickens. We can satisfy the fox every day."

That night they heard the fox yapping in the yard. "Do you hear?" she asked her husband. "The fox is demanding the chickens we promised him."

They sent one of the children to tie up a chicken and bring it to the fox. They did this every day, until finally the woman said to her husband, "We had sixty chickens, but now the fox has eaten all of them. We only have one left. What can we do? Take the ax and kill the fox! Then we'll have a fine pelt we can sell, and we'll also save the last hen."

That night the man hid in the henhouse. When the fox came as usual to get his chicken, the man brought the ax down on its head and killed it.

From this we see that there is indeed no truth in the world.

COMMENTARY FOR TALE 40 (IFA 8004)

Recorded by Dinah Behar from Wolf Sosenski in 1968 in Jerusalem.[1]

Principal Tale Types

The separation of tale types 155 "The Ungrateful Serpent Returned to Captivity" and 331 "The Spirit in the Bottle" into two different categories ("Animal Tales" and "Ordinary Folk Tales," respectively) obscures the affinity between them. Both involve a creature rescued from captivity—a variety of animals in the first case and a supernatural figure in the second. The narrative conclusions of these types of tales are inversions of each other. In tale type 155, the rescued animal threatens its rescuer (who eventually punishes it); in tale type 331, the supernatural being rewards its rescuer.

According to S. Thompson,[2] both tale types have literary origins; and in both cases, the oral versions of the tales owe their worldwide circulation to their literary preservation. Tale type 155 is "definitely [a] literary fable," and tale type 331 "has been frequently told in every century since the Middle Ages.... Oral versions are only occasionally encountered and these are likely to be closely related to some literary retelling."[3] This may be a valid observation for non-Jewish oral traditions; however, in Jewish societies these tales are told orally, as the twenty-six versions in the IFA evidence (see below).

Moreover, in Jewish folk literary tradition, there is a clear thematic and historic distinction between the literary and the oral versions. For example, the written texts found in the medieval *Mishlei Shlomoh ha-Melekh* (Parables of King Solomon)[4] belong to the narrative cycles of Solomon either as a "wise king" or as a "wise prince." The oral tales, however, resonate with variations that are available in the traditions of many nations, and King Solomon figures only in one oral version: IFA 9871 *King Solomon's Judgment between Man and Snake*, from Yemen. In most of the other versions, an animal, often the fox, serves as the just judge.

Contrary to the impression that the recurrence of the tale in nineteenth- and twentieth-century anthologies creates, the literary rendition of this tale is not "extremely popular" in Jewish tradition.[5] Its popularity is limited to the editors of those anthologies, who copied the texts from each other and assumed—perhaps correctly—a similar attitude among their readers. Consequently, in the modern period, the literary tale is available in only two basic versions, which scholars and writers reproduce again and again (see below).

In their commentary on the European versions of the tale, Bolte, Liungman, and Delarue and Tenèze each proposed a secondary typology for tale type 155 "The Ungrateful Serpent Returned to Captivity." Bolte[6] and Delarue and Tenèze[7] considered the final act to be the tale's distinctive feature, whereas Liungman[8] proposed the alleged antiquity and the animal character to be the basis of differentiation.

Narrative Models

On the basis of the approaches taken by Bolte, Liungman, and Delarue and Tenèze, it is possible to distinguish three narrative models.

I. Snake and man[9]
   A. The frozen snake kills its rescuer
   B1. The rescuer and the snake bring their case before one judge
   B2. The rescuer and the snake bring their case before several judges
   C. The rescued man is ungrateful and kills or harms the judge who granted him a reprieve
II. The animal tale[10]
   A. A tale about a crocodile and a fox[11]
   B. A tale about a lion or a tiger and a jackal
   C. A tale about a snake with any of the following acting as judge: Western traditions—horse, ox, dog, or fox; Eastern traditions—tree or buffalo
   D. A tale about a frozen snake, which follows either IIA or IIC
III. Man and animals (not necessarily a snake)[12]
   A. The man is too trusting and is tricked
   B. The animal is ungrateful and is tricked
   C. The judge or arbitrator is too trusting and is tricked

Subtypes in Jewish Tradition

In the Jewish literary tradition, we find two subtypes of these tales, which differ in the number of arbitrators between the rescuer and the snake. In the first subtype, the rescuer and the snake bring their case before one judge; in the second, the rescuer and the snake bring their case before several judges. Versions of the first subtype include several motifs that are found in tale type 285D "Serpent (Bird) Refuses Reconciliation," such as motifs B103.0.4 "Gold-producing snake," B103.0.4.1 "Grateful snake gives gold piece daily," B491.1 "Helpful serpent," B765.6.1 "Snake drinks milk," and F480.2 "Serpent as house-spirit." These motifs appear in medieval tales rendered in both Latin and vernacular languages, indicating literary contact between the European and the Jewish fable traditions (see below).

The folk-literary versions of the first subtype in Hebrew and Yiddish sources are available from the beginning of the fifteenth century. Examples of tale type 155 that involve King (Prince) Solomon are the following:

- *Judgment before King Solomon;* captive = snake, rescuer = man, judge = King Solomon.[13]

- *The Old Man and the Snake and the Judgment of Solomon;* captive = snake, rescuer = an old man, false judges = an ox, an ass, King David, judge = young prince Solomon.[14]
- *The Man, the Snake, and Solomon's Judgment;* captive = snake, rescuer = man, judge = King Solomon.[15]

In contrast to the written versions, the oral narratives that are available in the IFA follow the patterns seen in the folk narratives originally told in European and Asian languages. There are at least three preliminary studies of the comparative history of tale type 155.[16]

In his analysis, McKenzie[17] suggested that "even if at the beginning[,] the story was told with one judge . . . , nevertheless at a very early period it assumed the form with three judges." These variations, which are also found in Jewish oral tradition (see narrative model IB above), thus suggest that the tale type be further subdivided into two groups, based on the number of judges that appear in the story.

Considering the publication history of this tale type and its representation in the IFA, the following tale types could be classified as variations, or subtypes, of tale type 155:

- Tale type 285D "Serpent (Bird) Refuses Reconciliation."
- Tale type 331 "The Spirit in the Bottle."

The occurrence of any of these subtypes in the literary history of this narrative cycle does not, of course, represent the tale's oral circulation. Quite likely, several variations were available as oral narratives in Asian and European cultures before they were documented in the literature. Yet, the following discussion of the elements and variations of this tale offers a preliminary idea of the history of this narrative cycle and suggests the possible interactions that took place between Jewish and non-Jewish folktale traditions.

The Frozen Snake Kills Its Rescuer

In the earliest documented form in this thematic cluster, the snake kills its rescuer. The story line occurs within the ancient Aesopic tradition and was rendered in Greek by Babrius (early first century C.E.) and in Latin by Phaedrus (late first century B.C.E. to early first century C.E.).[18] These fables conclude with the moral "I suffer what I deserve for showing pity to the wicked."

Although absent from the fifth-century collection of fables of Avianus,[19] the tale was included in medieval literary anthologies. For example, it appeared in the collection of Odo of Cheriton (c. 1185–c. 1247);[20] studies about this fabulist have been conducted.[21] In 1483, this version was published in Caxton's translation and edition of Aesop's fables.[22] Note also that the tale was illustrated in an eleventh-century fresco in the refectory of the monastery of Fleury at St. Bénoir-sur-Loire, not far from Orléans, France.[23]

The Rescuer and the Snake Bring Their Case before One Judge

The twelfth-century *Disciplina Clericalis* of Petrus Alfonsi (Rabbi Moshe ha-Sefardi) included the first documented European variation of the tale in which there is a single judge.[24] The thirteenth-century *Gesta Romanorum*[25] is the first documented non-Jewish European version that includes a human—a philosopher who judges between the two litigants. In 1488, this subform appeared in the first printed Spanish edition of *Esopete ystoriado*,[26] published in Toulouse by Johann (John) Parix and Stephan (Estevan) Clebat.

The Rescuer and the Snake Bring Their Case before Several Judges

An early literary rendition of the tale in which there are several judges can be found in a fifteenth-century Persian epic, *Anvár-i Suhailí*,[27] likely transmitting a fable that was known earlier in India. This version also appeared in the 1481 Caxton edition of *Reynard the Fox*.[28] The *Anvár-i Suhailí* contains many tales that derive from the *Panchatantra* and the *Hitopadesha*.

McKenzie[29] proposed that a selection of tales from *Anvár-i Suhailí* that appeared in France as *Livre des lumières* (1644) inspired Jean de la Fontaine (1621–1695) to write his fable *L'Homme et la Couleuvre* (The man and the garter snake), making the story famous in seventeenth-century literary Europe.[30] This of course, might be a possibility. However, a version of this tale in which there were several judges was known in Europe as early as the fifteenth century, when it was included in a manuscript in Florence; this source serves McKenzie as the starting point for his comparative analysis. That tale was also added to the sixteenth-century Codex Gudianus and the seventeenth-century Codex Harleianus 3521, manuscripts that also included the fables of Odo of Chriton.[31] If the manuscript tradition indicates a general knowledge of the story, then the emerging print versions reflect the increased popularity and diffusion of the story.

The European Beast Epic

The version of the tale that includes several judges also appeared in Caxton's edition of a popular medieval beast epic.[32] Relevant to Jewish folklore and to the medieval tradition of the tale is the reference to the ideal wise man as being "salamon, Auycene or aristotiles."[33] This is a tradition that resonated in Ms. 261 De Rossi in Parma, in the *Gesta Romanorum*[34] version of the tale, and later in the Yiddish *Ma'asseh Book*.[35] A comparative analysis of the oral versions of this tale form is available.[36]

The fox functioned as an animal trickster in European beast epics by the eighth century; for example, see the poem "Aegrum Fama Fuit."[37] In the eleventh century, the fox was a figure in the *Ecbasis* story proper, in which he skinned the wolf to cure the lion (tale type 50 "The Sick Lion").[38] In *Ecbasis*, this fable serves as an etiological tale, explaining the animosity between the wolf and the fox. However, no subform of tale type 155 was yet a part of an epic, nor was it incorporated into the beast epic *Ysengrimus*[39] (1148–1149), which unfolded the antagonism between the wolf and the fox. When the story of Reynard the Fox became available in vernacular languages in the twelfth century, the present tale—or fragments of it—began to appear in a cluster of literary works. The early Reynard the Fox story used as its initial scene the fable of the sick lion or tale type 50 "The Sick Lion."

The composition of *Roman de Renart* apparently began around 1170 and continued until around 1250; it eventually consisted of twenty-six separate fragments ("branches") that included some forty tales. The German beast epic *Reinhart Fuchs* was written around 1180; and in the thirteenth century, the story was rendered in Middle Dutch in two versions: *Reinaert I* (before 1274) and *Reinaert II* (late fourteenth century).[40] A prose retelling of *Reinaert II* appeared in print in 1479 at Gouda, which served as the source for the 1481 Caxton edition; the latter version included three judges. There is an extensive scholarly and popular literature about the *Roman de Renart* (see below); however, relevant to this particular tale is Branch X—written after 1180 and hence not included in *Reinhart Fuchs*—in which the third episode of tale type 154 "Bear-Food" appears, corresponding to the concluding segment of the current tale.[41] A woodcut illustration of the parable of the farmer who freed a trapped serpent (tale type 155 "The Ungrateful Serpent Returned to Captivity") can be found in Caxton's edition.[42]

In India, the tale continued to be current in oral tradition;[43] however, available indexes do not indicate which subtypes of the tale were more prevalent.

The Rescued Man Is Ungrateful and Kills or Harms the Judge Who Granted Him a Reprieve

According to McKenzie,[44] the tale form that includes the ungrateful rescued man who harms the judge, which the present tale illustrates, is exclusively European. The Italian manuscript text that was the starting point of his study contained the chicken episode, as did German texts of the fifteenth and sixteenth centuries.[45]

Tale type 285D "Serpent (Bird) Refuses Reconciliation"

Tale type 285D first occurred in the medieval Aesopic tradition.[46] Perry[47] pointed out that the texts of this tale type are also found in Codex Wissemburgensis, ascribed to Romulus (tenth century) and Codex Ademari (eleventh century).[48] In the twelfth century, Marie de France included a similar tale in her collection: fable 72, *De homine et serpente* (The man and the snake).[49] The medieval Hebrew fabulist Rabbi Berechiah ha-Nakdan, likely of the thirteenth century, included a story of this tale type in his book *Mishlei Shu'alim (Fox Fables)*.[50] Note that in the fourteenth-century manuscript tradition, the snake forgives the man.[51] This tale type is current in the Greek oral tradition.[52] Compare this tale type with tale IFA 1709 (vol. 1, no. 37).

Tale Type 331 "The Spirit in the Bottle"

The earliest documented evidence of tale type 331 occurs in the first to third centuries C.E. in *The Testament of Solomon*, relating the magical prowess of King

Solomon.[53] Although the image of King Solomon as a powerful magician occurs in later talmudic-midrashic literature, this particular tale type is absent from these sources.[54] Tale type 331 does appear in The Arabian Nights cycle as *The Story of the Fisherman and the Jinni*.[55] Gerhardt[56] pointed out that the association between tale types 331 and 155 is directly evident in the narrative text of the Arabian Nights. The Brothers Grimm[57] recorded the tale from an unidentified tailor in Bäkendorf. Further comparative notes and discussion are available.[58]

Similarities to Other IFA Tales

Other oral versions in the IFA are listed below.

- IFA 107: *A Fox Tricks the Demon Asmodeus* (Yemen); tale type = 155/331; captive = the demon Asmodeus; rescuer = poor man; false judge(s) = seven human judges; judge = demonic fox; reward = marriage to princess; punishment = impoverishment (for not keeping promise to judge).[59]
- IFA 185: *An Ungrateful Man* (Tunisia); tale type = 155; captive = snake; rescuer = man; false judge(s) = horse; judge = porcupine; punishment = ungrateful man kills porcupine.
- IFA 1117: *The Ungrateful Woodcutter* (Iraq); tale type = 154III; captive = snake; rescuer = woodcutter; false judge(s) = ass; judge = fox; punishment = ungrateful woodcutter turns dogs against fox.[60]
- IFA 1184: *Muhammad and the Snake* (Afghanistan); tale type = 155; captive = snake; rescuer = Muhammad (there is no trial; the snake bites Muhammad, who sucks the poison and spits it out; an olive tree grows where the spittle lands).
- IFA 3690: *The Snake and Its Rescuers* (Egypt); tale type = 155; captive = snake; rescuer = woodcutter and his children; false judge(s) = ass, ostrich; judge = fox; punishment = return to captivity.
- IFA 4509: *The Ungrateful Lion* (Iraq); tale type = 75, 150, 155; captive = lion; rescuer = hare; judge = fox; punishment = ungrateful lion burned to death.[61]
- IFA 5319: *The Litigation between a Snake and a Man* (Iraq); tale type = 155, 161; captive = snake; rescuer = man; false judge(s) = cow, tree; judge = fox; punishment = ungrateful man tells hunter of fox's hiding place.[62]
- IFA 5560: *Speaking Animals* (Zimbabwe); tale type = 155; captive = wolf; rescuer = duiker; false judge(s) = giraffe, antelope; judge = hare; punishment = wolf returned to captivity and dies.
- IFA 5744: *The Ungrateful Man and Lion and the Porcupine* (Morocco); tale type = 155; captive = lion; rescuer = man; false judge(s) = horse, dog; judge = porcupine; punishment = ungrateful man bitten by snake.
- IFA 6207: *The Litigation of the Prey and Domesticated Animals* (Libya); tale type = 155; captive = tiger; rescuer = fox; false judge(s) = bull, hen; judge = horse; punishment = tiger returned to trap.[63]
- IFA 6259: *Ungrateful* (Romania); tale type = 155; captive = snake; rescuer

40 / *There Is No Truth in the World* ⋙ **297** ⋘

- IFA 6282: *The Palace of Tears* (Morocco); tale type = 331, 303; captive = demon; rescuer = poor fisherman (there is no trial; a magic fish helps discover the queen's witchcraft and unfaithfulness).
- IFA 6620: *Why Is It impossible to Give Up Smoking?* (Afghanistan); tale type = 155; captive = snake; rescuer = Muhammad (there is no trial; the snake bites Muhammad, who sucks the poison and spits it out; a tobacco plant grows where the spittle lands).
- IFA 7530: *King Solomon, the Demon, and the Fisherman* (Bukhara); tale type = 331; captive = demon; rescuer = fisherman; judge = fisherman's son acts as counselor; punishment = returned to captivity.[64]
- IFA 9869: *The Hungry Lion and the Fox's Sentence* (Yemen); tale type = 155; captive = lion; rescuer = man; judge = fox; punishment = returned to captivity.[65]
- IFA 9871: *Solomon, the Young Prince, Judges between an Old Man and a Snake* (Yemen); tale type = 155; captive = snake; rescuer = old man; false judge(s) = ass, ox, King David; judge = young Solomon; punishment = killed.[66]
- IFA 9992: *Ali and the Tiger* (Eretz Yisra'el, Arabic); tale type = 155; captive = tiger; rescuer = Ali; false judge(s) = tamed bear, hen, fruit tree; judge = fox; punishment = returned to captivity.
- IFA 11304: *The Fox as a Judge* (Yemen); tale types = 155, 331; captive = tiger; rescuer = Jew; false judge(s) = female camel, dried up tree; judge = fox; punishment = returned to captivity and crushed.[67]
- IFA 11501: *Man Is Unreliable* (Morocco); tale type = 155; captive = lion; rescuer = farmer; false judge(s) = dog, horse; judge = porcupine; punishment = farmer bitten by snake (for wishing to harm porcupine's children).
- IFA 14803: *The Man, the Snake, the Horse, and the Dog* (Romania); tale type = 155; captive = snake; rescuer = old man; false judge(s) and judge = old horse, old dog; punishment = returned to captivity.[68]
- IFA 14937: *Ungrateful Snake Returns to Captivity* (Iraq); tale type = 155; captive = snake; rescuer = poor man; false judge(s) = lion, wolf; judge = fox; punishment = returned to captivity.
- IFA 14951: *The Cruel Man* (Ethiopia); tale type = 155; captive = snake; rescuer = man; judge = fox; reward = n/a; punishment = ungrateful man turns dog against fox.
- IFA 19348: *The Death Penalty Is Too Light a Sentence for a Man* (Ethiopia); tale type = 155; captive = snake; rescuer = man; judge = fox; punishment = ungrateful man turns dog against fox.
- IFA 19362 (vol. 5, no. 32): *The Man, the Snake, and the Fox* (Ethiopia); tale type = 155; captive = snake; rescuer = man; judge = fox; punishment = ungrateful man turns dog against fox.

Comparison to Other Tales

Wolf Sosenski (1890–1969), the narrator of the present tale, was born Lithuania, joined a cultural-national Belarus student movement, and served in the Russian Army during World War I. A comparison of his version with those told by narrators in Russia, Belarus, and even Ukraine would be valuable. Several sources are available for such an analysis.[69]

The Fox

The fox, or jackal in Asia, which appears as the just judge in several oral versions in the IFA and in the traditions of other peoples, is an Indo-European trickster figure.[70] General studies on the trickster in myth and oral traditions have been conducted.[71]

Testimonies for the trickster's role in literary and oral traditions are available from four geographical regions and historical periods: the ancient Near East, Mediterranean antiquities, medieval Europe, and medieval India. In modern times, the fox still preserves its image as a cunning animal in metaphors and fables, particularly in children's literature. This idea is also found in idiomatic English expressions, such as "to out fox someone," "to be foxy (sly)," "to be as cunning (artful) as a fox," "to be as sharp as a fox," "to be as shrewd as a fox," "to be crazy (stupid) like a fox," "to be as sly as a fox," and "to be as wily as a fox."[72]

Ancient Near East

The earliest testimony to the fox's image occurs in the isolated language of Sumeria, in cuneiform tablets copied around 1700 B.C.E., though known to have earlier origins.[73] Gordon[74] argued that "the fox of the Sumerians seems to have rather little in common with the clever and cunningly sly little fox of the later European folklore; although in quite a number of ways, he is akin to the fox in several of Aesop's fables, including the 'Sour Grapes' fable." Falkowitz[75] pointed out that in the Sumerian fables "[t]he fox appears to have had two different symbolic values. On the one hand, it symbolized slyness, while in the Rhetoric Collections a more consistent image is that of cowardly and braggadocio." The fox appears in this dual image in Sumerian proverbs as well.[76]

The fragmentary nature of the literary evidence is due not only to the incomplete archaeological record but also, as Lambert[77] suggested, to the fact that "the academicians of the Cassite period, who either developed or suppressed genres of literature, had no respect for anything which circulated orally among the common people." A survey of studies of ancient fables from Mesopotamia is available.[78]

Mediterranean Antiquities

Much later, in Greece and Rome, the fable acquired a somewhat greater literary, rhetorical, and intellectual respect, and consequently the records are better preserved. In the Greek and Latin fable traditions, beginning with Aesop, the fox appears in the trickster role in which he is at times the duper, at times the duped. The first known collection of Aesop's fables was made by Demetrius of Phalerum in the fourth century B.C.E.[79] However, the stories were known and transmitted even earlier, with testimonies dating back to the seventh century B.C.E. Evidence of these tales is available in the dramatic, historical, and philosophical writings of classic Greece.[80] Babrius and Phaedrus, respectively, rendered the fables into Greek and Latin metric forms during the first centuries B.C.E. and C.E.

With the influence of Hellenistic culture, language, literature, and folklore on Jewish society of Palestine, beginning late in the fourth century B.C.E. and lasting with variable intensity until the decline of the Roman Empire, the fox became the trickster figure during the talmudic-midrashic period and the namesake of the fable as a genre: *misheli shu'alim* (fox fables). Leading rabbis such as Hillel the Elder (first century), Rabbi Yohanan ben Zakkai (first century), and Rabbi Meir (second century) were famous for their special expertise in fables (Tractate *Sofrim* 17:9; BT *Sukkah* 28a; *Bava Batra* 38b, 134a).

Accounts report that fables were used as political rhetoric as well as for entertainment. For example Rabbi Joshua ben Hananiah (first to second centuries C.E.) told the fable *The Wolf and the Heron*[81] to calm a an angry crowd (MR *Genesis* 64:10), and Rabbi Akiva (second century) told a fable about a fox trying to lure a fish onto dry land to escape from the fishermen (BT *Berakhot* 61b).[82] The popular fable *The Fox with the Swollen Belly* interprets the biblical verse "As he came out of his mother's womb, so must he depart at last, naked as he came" (Ecclesiastes 5:14; MR *Ecclesiastes* 5:14).[83] Batany[84] proposed that Jews in medieval France built on these early traditions when creating the narrative cycle about Reynard the Fox, which emanated from their circles as satiric stories about the contemporary ruling class.

Medieval Europe

Initially, the medieval European manuscript tradition preserved the Aesopic fables in two languages: Greek and Latin. The basic Greek prose fables in the tenth-century collection known as *Augustana* likely date back to a source from the second century.[85] At the beginning of the fifth century, Flavius Avianus translated forty-two tales from Greek to Latin, but the major medieval Latin collection was based on the fables of Phaedrus, which were attributed to Romulus.[86] The Romulus collection was first edited by Heinrich Steinhöwel in 1476–1477 and is still available.[87] In addition, as already mentioned, thirteen-century fabulists, such as Odo of Cheriton and Marie de France, included stories about the fox in their writings. A literary history of the European fable has been published.[88]

Medieval India

In Indian medieval tradition, the fox or the jackal functions both as a narrator of moral tales and fables and as a trickster hero. The best-known pair is Karataka and Damanaka, jackals who are ministers to the lion, the king of the animals, and who are the narrators of instructive fables within the frame story of the *Panchatantra*. These characters became known in Europe as Kalila and Dimna through Pelhavi, Arabic, Hebrew, and Latin translations of the tales. A description and analysis of the Arabic and Persian manuscripts is available.[89] For information about *Panchatantra,* see the commentaries to tales IFA 1709 (vol. 1, no. 37) and IFA 960 (this vol., no. 14); a detailed history of the cycle's translation has been conducted.[90]

The present tale is designated by Bødker[91] as tale type 1150, which refers to a story about a man (or animal) who rescues a tiger (or other animal). Once safe, the tiger breaks its promise and decides to eat the man. Several advisers confirm the tiger's intentions, and the jackal makes the man return the tiger to its former predicament and leave it there to die.

To reiterate, Indian and Greek literature may have influenced the spread of the image of and the narratives about the trickster fox in European traditions, but the literary history of animal tales suggests that oral traditions and folklore also contributed to the diffusion of these tales. As of the eighth century, the fable *The Sick Lion*[92] and tale type 50 "The Sick Lion" had become the subjects of literary narratives—first in short forms and later in long ones, either in the main story or in shorter episodes of longer tales. Eventually the fox became a major hero and the wolf's primary antagonist. As noted above, the earliest literary rendition of such a tale is in the eighth-century poem "Aegrum Fama Fuit";[93] and in the eleventh century the tale became part of *Ecbasis*.[94] By the following century, the fox appeared as a trickster figure in medieval beast epics. Studies of the fox as a trickster figure in the medieval beast epic are available.[95] The medieval texts and illustrations that feature the trickster fox have been the subject of a rich and active scholarship; and the International Reynard Society, founded in 1975, focuses on the study of beast epic, fable, and fabliau.[96] Several publications have collected essays and analytical papers about the character of the fox.[97]

Folktale Types

- 48 (Eberhard and Boratav) *"Die Schlange und der Mann"* (The Snake and the Man).
- 154 "Bear-food."
- 154 "The Fox and His Members" (new ed.).
- 154 (Andreev), *"Muzhik, medvedh i lisa"* (Peasant, Bear, and Fox).
- 154 (Smith) "Bear-Food."
- 155 "The Ungrateful Serpent Returned to Captivity."
- 155 (Andreev) *"Staraya khleb-sol zabyvaetsya"* (Old [Custom] of Bread Salt Is Being Forgotten).
- 155 (Haboucha) "The Ungrateful Serpent Returned to Captivity."
- 155 (Jason) "The Ungrateful Serpent Returned to Captivity."

- 155 (Kerbelytė) "*Už Gera Piktu Užmokama*" (Return Evil for Good).
- 155 (Krzyzanowski), "*Waż, cztowick I Lis*" (Snake, Man, and Fox).
- 155 (Marzolph) "*Die Undankbare Schlange*" (The ungrateful snake).
- ET293 (Weinert) "*Der Bauer von der Undankbaren Schlange*" (The Farmer of the Ungrateful Snake).
- 331 "The Spirit in the Bottle."
- 331 (Andreev) "*Dukh v butylke*" (The Spirit in the Bottle).
- 331 (Jason) "The Spirit in the Bottle."
- 331 (Kerbelyte) "*Dvasia Butelyje*" (The Bottle's Spirit).
- 331 (Krzyzanowski) "*Duch w Butelce*" (Spirit in the Bottle).
- 4256 (Tubach) "Serpent, frozen."

Folklore Motifs

- B274 "Animal as judge."
- B279 "Covenant with animals."
- B336 "Helpful animal killed (threatened) by ungrateful hero."
- J1172.3 "Ungrateful animal returned to captivity."
- K231.1 "Refusal to perform part in mutual agreement."
- cf. K235.1 "Fox is promised chickens: is driven off by dogs."
- K713.1 "Deception into allowing oneself to be tied."
- M205 "Breaking of bargains or promises."
- Q281 "Ingratitude punished."
- W154 "Ingratitude."
- W154.2.1 "Rescued animal threatens rescuer."
- W154.2.2 "Man ungrateful for rescue by animal."

––––––––– **Notes** –––––––––

1. First published in Cheichel, *A Tale for Each Month 1968–1969*, 60–63 no. 2. Reprinted, with an extensive analysis, in D. Noy. *The Jewish Animal Tale of Oral Tradition*, 65–67, 170–176 no. 25. Another English translation is in Schram, *Stories within Stories*, 175–178 no. 27.
2. *The Folktale.*
3. Ibid., 47, 226.
4. Yassif, "Parables of Solomon."
5. Schwarzbaum, "International Folklore Motifs in Petrus Alfonsi's '*Disciplina Clericalis*,' " 21:297 (rpt. 269); and Schwarzbaum, *The Mishle Shu'alim (Fox Fables)*, 132.
6. See Pauli, *Schimpf und Ernst*, 2:420–421 no. 745.
7. *Le conte populaire français.*
8. *Die Schwedischen Volksmärchen.*
9. Pauli, op. cit., 2:420–421 no. 745 (includes important bibliographical information).
10. Liungman, op. cit., 23–25 (tale type 155 "*Undankbares Tier Wieder Eingefangen*"); for a review of the original Swedish edition, see Taylor, "Review of Varifrån Kommer Våra Sagor."

11. Note that this subtype of Liungman's is, in fact, another tale altogether, tale type 91 "Monkey (Cat) Who Left His Heart at Home"; in the *Panchatantra* version, it is a tale of ingratitude but otherwise does not belong to this narrative cluster. See Edgerton, *The Panchatantra Reconstructed,* 1:371–385, 2:393–397.

12. These tales are of type 155. Delarue and Tenèze, op. cit., 3:424–425.

13. Available in Ms. 261 De Rossi in Parma, printed in S. Buber, *Midrasch Tanḥuma,* 79a. Also published in Bin Gorion, *Mimekor Yisrael,* 36–37 no. 23 (1990 ed.); M. Gaster, *The Exempla of the Rabbis,* 175–176 no. 441a; Ginzberg, *The Legends of the Jews,* 4:134–135, 6:286 n. 31; and Grünbaum, *Neue Beiträge zur semitischen Sagenkunde,* 236–237.

14. Published in M. Gaster, *Ma'aseh Book,* 1:276–280 no. 144; Maitlis, *The Book of Stories,* 100–103 no. 31; M. Gaster, *The Exempla of the Rabbis,* 176 no. 441b; Tendlau, *Fellmeiers Abende,* 77–81; Pappenheim, *Allerlei Geschichten Maasse-Buch,* 147–149 no. 149; and B. Kuttner, *Jüdische Sagen und Legenden,* 17–19 no. 47.

15. Published in N. Gross, *Maaselech un Mesholim,* 53–54 (submitted by a newspaper reader); and Schwarzbaum, *Studies in Jewish and World Folklore,* 113–114, 463.

16. Krohn, *Mann und Fuchs,* 40–60; McKenzie, "An Italian Fable"; and Draak, "Is Ondank 'S Werelds Loon?" Although not addressing this particular tale type, two further studies are relevant to the tale type's place in oral traditions: Uther, *"Fuchs"*; and Tomkowiak *"Fuchs und Glieder."*

17. Op. cit., 523.

18. Perry, *Babrius and Phaedrus,* 187 no. 143, 332, 333 no. 20; and Perry, *Aesopica,* 390 no. 176.

19. Slavitt, *The Fables of Avianus.*

20. J. Jacobs, *The Fables of Odo of Cheriton,* 136–137 no. 88.

21. Friend, "Master Odo of Cheriton"; Perry, *Aesopica,* 639 no. 617; and Perry, *Babrius and Phaedrus,* 546 no. 617.

22. Lenaghan, *Caxton's Aesop,* 1:80 no. 10.

23. A. Goldschmidt, *An Early Manuscript of the Aesop Fables of Avianus and Related Manuscripts,* 46.

24. Hermes, *The "Disciplina Clericalis" of Petrus Alfonsi,* 116, 183 no. 5; and Schwarzbaum, "International Folklore Motifs in Petrus Alfonsi's '*Disciplina Clericalis.*'

25. Swan and Hooper, *Gesta Romanorum,* 336–337 no. 174.

26. Burrus and Goldberg, *Esopete ystoriado,* 86–87 no. 3 (*Las fabulas extravagantes*).

27. Eastwick, *The Anvár-i Suhailí,* 264–268.

28. *The History of Renard the Fox,* 70–74 no. 30.

29. Op. cit., 499.

30. Spector, *The Complete Fables of Jean de la Fontaine,* 10:502–509 no. 1.

31. Perry, *Aesopica,* 653–655 no. 640; and Perry, *Babrius and Phaedrus,* lxx–lxxi, 558–560 no. 640.

32. Caxton, op. cit., 70–74 no. 30.

33. Ibid., 73 l. 27.

34. Op. cit.

35. M. Gaster, *Ma'aseh Book,* 1:276–280 no. 144; J. Maitlis, op. cit., 100–103 no. 31; and M. Gaster, *The Exempla of the Rabbis,* 176 no. 441b.

36. Krohn, op. cit.

37. Zeydel, *Ecbasis cuiusdam captivi per tropologiam. Escape of a Certain Captive Told in a Figurative Manner*, 97–101.
38. Ibid., 45–87 ll. 392–1097.
39. Mann, *Ysengrimus*.
40. Hellinga, *Van den vos Reynaerde*.
41. Roques, *Le Roman de Renart*, 7–59 ll. 9253–11472.
42. Varty, *Reynard, Renart, Reinaert and Other Foxes in Medieval England*, 236; Varty, "The Earliest Illustrated English Editions of 'Reynard the Fox,' " 179 no. 35, 384; and R. Vedder, *"Die Illustrationen in den frühen Drucken des Reynke de Vos,"* 430 no. 117.
43. Thompson and Roberts, *Types of Indic Oral Tales*, 32; and Jason, *Types of Indic Oral Tales: Supplement*, 23–24.
44. Op. cit., 508–522.
45. Alberus, *Die Fabeln*, 213–219, 371–374 no. 48; Pauli, op. cit., 2:420–421 no. 745; and Gerber, "Great Russian Animal Tales," 26 no. 28.
46. Perry, *Babrius and Phaedrus*, 529–531 nos. 573, 573a; and Perry, *Aesopica*, 614–616 nos. 573, 573a.
47. *Babrius and Phaedrus*, 529.
48. Hervieux, *Les Fabulistes Latines*, 2:155 no. 65, 2:163 no. 12, 2:208 no. 11, 2:254 no. 25, 2:430–431 no. 29, 465–466 no. 29, 2:487 no. 10.
49. Martin, *The Fables of Marie de France*, 187–191.
50. Schwarzbaum, *The Mishle Shu'alim (Fox Fables)*, 123–137 no. 22, 517 n. 15, 547 n. 5.
51. McKenzie and Oldfather, *Ysopet-Avionnet*, 326–327 no. 30.
52. Megas, "Some Oral Greek Parallels to Aesop's Fables."
53. Duling, "The Testament of Solomon," 22:9–15, 1:984.
54. Ginzberg, op. cit., 4:153, 6:292–293 n. 56.
55. Burton, *The Book of the Thousand Nights and Night*, 1:38–45; for comparative notes, see Chauvin, *Bibliographie des ouvrages Arabes*, 6:25 n. 195; and Marzolph and van Leeuwen, *The Arabian Nights Encyclopedia*, 1:183–184.
56. *The Art of Story-Telling*, 390–391 n. 2.
57. Grimm and Grimm, *The Complete Fairy Tales*, 362–367 no. 99.
58. Bolte and Polivka, *Anmerkungen zu den Kinder- u. Hausemärchen*, 2:414–422 no. 99; Scherf, *Das Märchenlexikon*, 1:407–409; Uther, *Grimms Kinder- und Hausmärchen*, 4:188–192; Horálek, *"Geist im Glas"*; and Horálek, *"Zur slavischen Überlieferung des Märchentyps* AaTh 331."
59. Published in D. Noy, *Jefet Schwili Erzählt*, 28–29 no. 6, 86–87 no. 27; and D. Noy, *The Jewish Animal Tale of Oral Tradition*, 55–58 no. 21.
60. Published in D. Noy, *Jewish-Iraqi Folktales*, 110–112 no. 52; and D. Noy, *The Jewish Animal Tale of Oral Tradition*, 62–64 no. 24.
61. D. Noy, *The Jewish Animal Tale of Oral Tradition*, 47–49 no. 16.
62. Published in E. Marcus, *Min ha-Mabua*, 125–126 no. 32; and D. Noy, *The Jewish Animal Tale of Oral Tradition*, 71–72 no. 27.
63. D. Noy, *The Jewish Animal Tale of Oral Tradition*, 68–71 no. 26; and D. Noy, *Jewish Folktales from Libya*, 124–126 no. 53.
64. D. Noy, *A Tale for Each Month 1966*, 65–67 no. 11.
65. Caspi, *Mi-Zkenim Etbonan*, 130–132.

66. Caspi, op. cit., 132–133.
67. Gamlieli, *The Chambers of Yemen*, 79–80.
68. Avitsuk, *The Fate of a Child*, 16–17 no. 8.
69. Kabashnikau, *Kazki pra zhyviol i charadzeinyia kazki* (Fairy tales about animals, and magic fairy tales), 168–169 no. 72; and Berezovs'kyi, *Kazki pro tvarin* (Fairy tales about animals), 256–263 nos. 221–225. I would like to thank Anna Kryvenko and Dr. Olesja Britsyna for these references. See also Kasprzyk, "*L'homme et l'animal*"; and Afanas'ev, *Russian Fairy Tales*, 288–289. J. V. Haney, *Russian Animal Tales*, 128–129.
70. Batany, *Scène et coulisses du "Roman de Renart,"* 30–37.
71. Hyde, *Trickster Makes This World;* Pelton, *The Trickster in West Africa;* and Radin, *The Trickster.*
72. See, e.g., B. J. Whiting, *Modern Proverbs and Proverbial Sayings*, 241.
73. E. Gordon, "Animals as Represented in the Sumerian Proverbs and Fables," esp. 234–236; Kramer, *History Begins at Sumer,* 124–131; and Lambert, *Babylonian Wisdom Literature*, 186–212 (plates 49, 52–54).
74. Op. cit., 236.
75. "The Sumerian Rhetoric Collections," 98.
76. Alster, *Proverbs of Ancient Sumer,* 56–60, 169–172 (esp. 60 no. 2.70, which employs the epithet "the cunning fox); and Perry, *Babrius and Phaedrus*, xxvii–xxxiv.
77. Op. cit., 150.
78. See Falkowitz, "Discrimination and Condensation of Sacred Categories."
79. Perry, "Demetrius of Phalerum and the Aesopic Fables."
80. Perry, *Babrius and Phaedrus,* xii–xiii; Holzberg, *Die antike Fabel;* and Nøjgaard, *La fable antique.*
81. Perry, *Aesopica,* 382 no. 156; and Perry, *Babrius and Phaedrus,* 114–115, 200–201 nos. 8, 94.
82. Perry, *Aesopica,* 415, 419 nos. 241, 252; and Perry, *Babrius and Phaedrus,* 470, 472.
83. Perry, *Aesopica,* 331 no. 24; Perry, *Babrius and Phaedrus,* 107 no. 86; and Schwarzbaum, "Aesopic Fables in Talmudic Midrashic Folk-Literature."
84. Batany, op. cit., 73–107.
85. Perry, *Babrius and Phaedrus,* xvi–xix; Burrus and Goldberg, op. cit., x–xii; and Zafiropoulos, *Ethics in Aesop's Fables.*
86. Perry, *Babrius and Phaedrus,* lxxiii–cii; Burrus and Goldberg, op. cit.
87. Hervieux, op. cit., 2:193–762.
88. Blackham, *The Fable as Literature;* Grubmüller, *Meister Esopus;* and Lewis, *The English Fable.*
89. O'Kane, *Early Persian Painting.*
90. North, *The Moral Philosophy of Doni*, 14–27.
91. *Indian Animal Tales,* 112–113. See also Gupta, "Indian Parallels of the Fox Story."
92. Perry, *Aesopica*, 421 no. 258; and Perry, *Babrius and Phaedrus*, 473–474 no. 258.
93. Zeydel, op. cit., 97–101.
94. Ibid., 45–87 ll. 392–1097.
95. Carnes, *Fable Scholarship;* Varty, *The* Roman de Renart; Best, *Reynard the Fox;* and Flinn, *Le Roman de Renart.*
96. The society's Web site is www.hull.ac.uk/Hull/FR_Web/fox.html, and its journal is *Reinardus: Yearbook of the International Reynard Society.*

97. Levi and Wackers, *The Fox and Other Animals;* Goossens and Sodmann, *Reynaert, Reynard, Reynke*; Goossens and Sodmann, *Third International Beast Epic, Fable and Fabliau Colloquium;* Rombauts and Welkenhuysen, *Aspects of the Medieval Animal Epic;* Varty, "The Death and Resurrection of Reynard in Medieval Literature and Art"; Varty, *Reynard the Fox: A Study of the Fox in Medieval English Art*; Varty, *Reynard the Fox. Social Engagement and Cultural Metamorphoses;* Vardy, "Back to the Beginning of the *Romans de Renart*"; Lodge and Varty, *The Earliest Branches of the* Roman de Renart*;* Simpson, *Animal Body, Literary Corpus;* Varty, "Animal Fable and Fabulous Animal"; and Yamamoto, *The Boundaries of the Human in Medieval English Literature*, 56–74.

41

Everyone Prefers His Own Bundle of Troubles

TOLD BY BEZALEL WEXLER TO ABRAHAM KEREN

The rumor flew through the town: The Messiah was on his way. Soon he would reach their town. The rabbi gathered his flock in the synagogue and told them about the wonderful and exciting event that was about to happen. "My brothers in Israel," he announced, "the end of the exile has arrived, the end and termination of all our troubles has come. Our righteous Messiah is on his way!

"So we can get rid of our troubles, everyone go home and tie them all up in a bundle and put them in a corner of the synagogue. After that, we'll recite psalms and sing the songs of King David. When the Messiah nears our town, we'll all go out to greet him—young and old, men and women and children. Now go home and pack all your troubles in a bundle. When the Messiah comes, we'll leave all our pains behind, here in the Diaspora, and ascend to Zion in joy."

The townspeople scattered to their homes and did as the rabbi had instructed. They all brought their bundles to the synagogue, recited psalms, and waited for the Messiah to arrive.

A day passed, two days passed—and still the footsteps of the Messiah were not heard. The rabbi dispatched messengers to see if he was approaching the town, but they did not find his traces.

After a prolonged wait, the rabbi again gathered his flock in the synagogue. In a voice full of disappointment, choking on tears, he announced: "My fellow congregants, Heaven has postponed the redemption. Satan the accusing angel has once again proved stronger. You must all go back home. Everyone take his bundle of troubles and wait for the end of the exile, for the full redemption."

A great commotion broke out in the synagogue. They all fell on the pile of bundles of troubles, pushing and shouting. "Where is my bundle?

Where is my bundle?" They would not relax until every person had found his own bundle. None of them wanted to exchange his bundle for someone else's. Everyone preferred his own troubles to the next man's.

COMMENTARY FOR TALE 41 (IFA 14460)

Recorded by Abraham Keren from Dr. Bezalel Wexler in 1982 in Haifa.

Cultural, Historical, and Literary Background

The narrator of this tale integrates two distinct themes that have an independent occurrence in Jewish tradition: the anticipation of the Messiah and the attachment people develop to their own personal troubles.

The Messiah

In Judaism, the expectation of the coming of the Messiah has been a fundamental tenant of faith that is inherently connected with the uncertainty principle: Neither the time of his arrival nor his identity is known. The coupling of faith and uncertainty, though an essential feature of religion, has generated in this case false messianic claims that historically created havoc in Jewish societies and in daily life. Furthermore, the convergence of high hopes and uncertainty fostered an attitude of irony and skepticism toward any messianic claims that Jews expressed in narratives, proverbs, and humorous tales such as the present story. A study of individuals who claimed messianic attributes has been conducted.[1]

Jewish history and the position of Jews among the nations have been fertile ground for messianic expectations and movements. Even the national foundation myth, the exodus from Egypt (Exodus 13–15:21), unfolds a story of collective salvation and the transition from slavery to freedom, which are redemptive acts similar to those attributed to the Messiah. However, as a myth of the past, neither the exodus nor Moses, the biblical national leader, has been conceived in messianic terms.

Within Jewish history, as told in the Hebrew Bible, there was only a brief period of national political independence during the rule of King David (ca. 1010–970 B.C.E.) and of King Solomon (970/60–930/20 B.C.E.). The disintegration of the kingdom of David began shortly after Solomon's death, with its division into the Northern and Southern Kingdoms, and their final collapse in 722 and 586 B.C.E., respectively. Already during this biblical period of decline, prophets and poets expressed messianic hopes for utopian restoration of national prominence (for example, Isaiah 2:2–4, 11:1–12, 42:1–4; Micah 4:1–4; Jeremiah 23:5–8, 33:14–16; Zechariah 9:9–10). Later, the deeper the nation sunk into a depressed state, the higher were the messianic hopes, often cast in apocalyptic and eschatological literature and visions. Messianic hopes and visions appeared even in the Dead Sea Scrolls.[2] The apocryphal book Psalms of Solomon (17:21–44), likely written in the first century C.E., after the destruction of Jerusalem in 70 C.E., contains an articulated vision of a messianic figure.

During the talmudic-midrashic period, the Messiah was conceived not only in national but also in universal terms as the figure who will bring the resurrection of the dead. The Messiah, described in terms of his actions rather than by name, became prominent in the central Jewish prayer, the *Amidah,* which was likely formulated during that period. He is specifically mentioned in the prayer's fifteenth blessing: "Speedily cause the offspring of David, Thy servant, to flourish, and lift up his glory by Thy divine help because we wait for Thy salvation all the day. Blessed art Thou, O Lord, who causest the strength of salvation to flourish." The formulation and composition of the *Amidah,* known also as the Eighteen Benedictions, has been the subject of research, and the fifteenth benediction, has been particularly explored.[3]

The reference to the Messiah as the "offspring of David" alludes to Jeremiah's (23:5) prophecy: "See, a time is coming—declares the Lord—when I will raise up a true branch of David's line." (See also Jeremiah 33:15.) In the Middle Ages, Maimonides formulated the thirteen principles of faith in Judaism. The twelfth principle was the belief in the coming of the Messiah.

There is a voluminous scholarship on the figure of the Messiah and on messianic movements in Jewish societies. The first episode in the present tale is a mock narrative of false messianic claims. Anthologies of literary and religious texts about the Messiah are available.[4] Studies of messianic ideas and figures in the Hebrew Bible[5] and in the apocryphal literature and the Mishnah have been published.[6] Analyses of messianic ideas and redemption in the talmudic-midrashic period[7] and in Jewish mysticism have been conducted.[8] Jewish messianic movements have also been examined.[9]

The inherent failure of the Messiah to come, a failure and a constant disappointment that is an integral part of the very idea of utopian redemption, results in the irony that is expressed in proverbs and tales such as the present story.[10]

Similarities to Other IFA Tales

The tales on deposit in the IFA are often similarly ironic, telling about situations of expectation, failure, and frustration:

- IFA 5828: *Then [He] Awoke: It Was a Dream (Genesis 41:7)* (Eretz Yisra'el, country of Islam).
- IFA 7574: *Messiah* (Poland).
- IFA 9627: *A Torn Kapota—An Omen for Redemption* (Galicia, Poland).
- IFA 9989: *This Is for the Better as Well* (Iran).
- IFA 10028: *King Solomon and His Wife Naʻamah [the Birth of the Messiah]* (Morocco).
- IFA 11124 (vol. 4, no. 20): *The Wonderful Acts of the Besht* (Afghanistan).
- IFA 12503: *A Debate about the Coming of the Messiah and the Wonderful Caves* (Iraqi Kurdistan).
- IFA 12795: *The Messiah Will Come* (Iran).
- IFA 12986: *The Grandfather Listened* (Ukraine).[11]

- IFA 14028: *The Difference between a Polish Jew and a Lithuanian Jew* (Poland).
- IFA 14030: *A Difficult but Stable Occupation* (Poland).
- IFA 14090: *A Request for a Slight Delay in the Messiah's Arrival* (Poland).
- IFA 14098: *The Rabbi's Counsel* (Romania).
- IFA 14120: *The Stable Occupation on the Tower of Ḥelem* (Poland).
- IFA 14233: *The Ḥelem Mountain and the Messiah* (Poland).
- IFA 14418: *Yosele de la Reina* (Eretz Yisra'el, Ashkenazic).
- IFA 14451: *As We Were Saved from Haman, so We Will Be Saved from the Messiah* (Belarus).[12]
- IFA 15166: *On the Look Out for the Messiah* (Poland).
- IFA 15182: *We'll Go to Our Ancestral Land Not with an Empty Stomach* (Poland).
- IFA 15392: *When Will the Messiah Come?* (Eretz Yisra'el, Ashkenazic).
- IFA 15693: *The Man Who Never Took an Oath* (Morocco).
- IFA 16076: *Why Does the Messiah Procrastinate?* (Poland).[13]
- IFA 16159: *The Ari Invites His Disciples to Leap from Safed to Jerusalem* (Eretz Yisra'el, Sephardic).
- IFA 17798: *When Will the Messiah Come?* (Russia).
- IFA 18371: *The Messiah's Footsteps* (Israel, second-generation Ashkenazic).
- IFA 18467: *God and the Messiah* (Israel, second-generation Ashkenazic).
- IFA 18738: *The Messiah Is Coming! What Shall We Do?* (Israel, second-generation Ashkenazic).
- IFA 18743: *The Messiah Is Waiting for You* (Israel, second-generation Ashkenazic).
- IFA 18744: *A Position with Tenure* (Israel, second-generation Ashkenazic).
- IFA 19185: *He Cannot Merit to Live in the Era of the Messiah* (Israel, second-generation Ashkenazic).

Personal Troubles

The notion that each person has his or her own share of troubles in life has received proverbial representation, as for example in the German proverb from at least the seventeenth century: *"Jeder hat sein Päckchen zu tragen"* (Each has his own bundle to carry);[14] and in the twentieth century in Yiddish: *"Yeder [id] hot zikh zayn pekl"*; (Each [Jew] has his own bundle).[15] Furthermore, people's preference for their own problems is implicit in the proverb "A man prefers a *kab*[16] of his own to nine of his neighbour's" (BT *Bava Metzia* 38a).

The central element in the present tale, however, is the idea that if people are given the chance to change their lot, they'll select their own bundle of troubles rather than that of someone else. Similar fables are available from the fifth century B.C.E. Despite the meager literary documentation of such tales, it is possible to distinguish three metaphoric descriptions among them.

Troubles in Market

In one form of this tale, the troubles are described in terms of the market. This form is, as far as we could determine, the oldest, dating back to the fifth century B.C.E. Herodotus had already insightfully expressed the idea that, given a choice, people would prefer their own personal sufferings to those of others. In his *History* he wrote: "But this I know full well, if all men should carry their own private troubles to market for barter with their neighbours, not one but when he had looked into the troubles of other men would be right glad to carry home again what he had brought."[17] Similar formulations likely occurred between Herodotus's time and the twentieth century, but we were unable to find documented cases. A text that closely follows Herodotus's metaphor was collected by Stutchkoff.[18]

Airing One's Troubles in Public

The second form, making one's troubles public knowledge, occurs in several proverbs. The core idea is found in the nineteenth-century corpus of Yiddish proverbs cited as *"As men sol aufhengen auf der wand ale peklech (oder: ümgliken), wolt sich itlicher gechapt zü seinem"* (If all the bundles [of troubles or misfortunes] are hanging out in the wind, each person will stick to his own).[19] This form was recorded in New York in English: "If all the troubles were hung on bushes, we would take our own and run."[20]

The Philosopher on the Rooftop

In the final form, a philosopher takes his complaining friend to the rooftop, urging him to select a trouble that would suit him better from those he sees in other people's houses. In Jewish writings, Glückel [Glikl] of Hameln (1646–1724) rendered this form of the fable in her memoirs.[21] The complainer in this tale chooses to keep his own troubles. Turniansky[22] identified two other similar sixteenth-century Yiddish texts but could not confirm that their direct source was Glückel. Turniansky proposed that the fable occurred primarily in oral circulation.

In a variation on this form, God plays the same role the philosopher. A modern version of this variation from Israel was told by a native of Belarus.[23]

There are no other tales in the IFA that relate the idea of preferring one's own troubles to those of others.

Folklore Motifs

- *A183.2 "Messiah invoked."
- *A582 "Messiah: cultural hero (divinity) who is expected to come."
- cf. C428 "Tabu: revealing time of Messiah's advent."
- C897.3 "Calculating time of Messiah's advent."
- *J328 "People prefer their own respective troubles than those of others."
- M363.2 "Prophecy: coming of Messiah."

- *P426.4 "Rabbi."
- V50 "Prayer."

---------- Notes ----------

1. Lenowitz, *The Jewish Messiahs*.
2. Schiffman, *Reclaiming the Dead Sea Scrolls*, 317–366; and Talmon, "Waiting for the Messiah."
3. See L. Finkelstein, "The Development of the Amidah"; Kohler, "The Origin and Composition of the Eighteen Benedictions"; Liber, "Structure and History of the *Tefilah*"; Liebreich, "The Intermediate Benedictions of the *Amidah*"; and Mirsky, "The Origin of the 'Eighteen Benedictions' of the Daily Prayer."
4. Even-Shemuel, *Midrashi Ge'ulah* (Midrashim of deliverance); Patai, *The Messiah Texts;* and Ginsberg et al., "Messiah."
5. Groningen, *Messianic Revelation in the Old Testament*; J. Klausner, *The Messianic Idea in Israel*; and Mowinckel, *He That Cometh*.
6. Neusner et al., *Judaisms and Their Messiahs at the Turn of the Christian Era;* and Oegema, *The Anointed and His People*.
7. Agus, *The Binding of Isaac and Messiah;* Landman, *Messianism in the Talmudic Era;* Neusner, *Messiah in Context;* Urbach, *The Sages,* 649–692; and Zobel, *Gottes Gesalbter*. A comprehensive set of studies on the Messiah in these periods is Charlesworth, *The Messiah*.
8. Idel, *Messianic Mystics;* Scholem, *The Messianic Idea in Judaism;* and Liebes, *Studies in Jewish Myth and Jewish Messianism*. The notes and the bibliographies in these works include references to additional valuable works on this subject.
9. Aescoly, *Jewish Messianic Movements;* Ben-Sasson, "Messianic Movements"; and Sharot, *Messianism, Mysticism, and Magic*.
10. Other examples are available: I. Bernstein, *Jüdische Sprichwörter und Redensarten,* 170 nos. 2401–2403; Cahan, *Jewish Folklore,* 140–141 no. 5; and B. Weinreich, *Yiddish Folktales,* 140–141 no. 5.
11. Published in M. Cohen, *Mi-Pi ha-Am* (From folk tradition), 3:41 no. 227.
12. Published in Estin, *Contes et fêtes Juives,* 232–234 no. 57.
13. Published in Murik, *Yiddishe Hochme* (Yiddish wisdom), 127.
14. Wander, *Deutsches Sprichwörter-Lexikon,* 3:1166.
15. Furman, *Idishe shprichwerter un redensartn* (Yiddish proverbs and sayings), 308 no. 1282.
16. A small measure or quantity.
17. Godley, *Herodotus,* 7:152, 463; I would like to thank Stephanie Craven for drawing my attention to this passage.
18. *Thesaurus of the Yiddish Language,* 531 no. 498.
19. In I. Bernstein, op. cit., 203 no. 2831.
20. Mieder et al., *A Dictionary of American Proverbs,* 612 ("Trouble" no. 6).
21. B. Abrahams, *The Life of Glückel of Hameln,* 90; and Turniansky, *Glikl,* 42–45, 306–307.
22. "Literary Sources in the Memoirs of Glikl Hamel," 168.
23. Cited in Ben-Amos, "Meditation on a Russian Proverb in Israel," 13.

42

Reb Zusha the Shoemaker

TOLD BY AZRIEL ZURIEL TO ABRAHAM KEREN

*I*n those days, they didn't make new shoes. Most people mended their old shoes. My grandfather, the late Reb* Berish, told me that for thirty years he had been mending his boots. In Yiddish they called it *untergeboyt*, that is, resoling.

So most of this cobbler's [Reb Zusha's] work was to sew patch on top of patch on top of patch; and from this, of course, he did not make much of a living. The fact is that he had help. His wife baked bread for the wives of the rich men. His two daughters also helped. They were seamstresses. But even with three trades, poverty reigned in every corner.

A. K.: My friend Azriel told me how even such a destitute man could help others.

"Listen, friend Avrum," he said, "Reb Zusha the shoemaker knew who was ill in the city, he knew the old people and the widows—all those who had nothing, who had no way to prepare the Sabbath meals. Reb Zusha took it upon himself to make sure that those unfortunates would not have to celebrate their Sabbath with weekday fare. This was his mission, the holy mission that brought a little bit of light to those unfortunate people and also filled him with the breath of life.

"Every Thursday afternoon, he would put aside his work and begin his sacred labors, going from door to door. The local women knew that Reb Zusha Shuster** was coming, and they had to get something ready. This one offered a hallah, that one had some *cholent*,§ and another a piece of gefilte fish or chicken soup for a sick person. In this way, he ran around on Thursday and Friday until the afternoon.

"But this arrangement came to an end. Reb Zusha had a brother in New York who managed to make some money. He knew how desperately poor his brother Zusha was. The brother sent him a stream of letters, urg-

---
*Rabbi or Mr.
**Shoemaker.
§A slow-cooked stew for the Sabbath among Ashkenazic Jews.

ing him to come alone to America and save a little money, and then he could bring over his wife and two daughters. 'You have a good trade and you'll be able to escape poverty and destitution. I will send you a steamer ticket. Come to America and change your lot for something better.'

"At long last Reb Zusha agreed. I remember—I was a lad when we accompanied Reb Zusha to the train. We were very sad. Especially sad were all of the sick people and old people. In their distress, they were crying, 'Who will take care of us and give us a tiny bit of the joy of the Sabbath?'

"You probably think that Reb Zusha stayed in America and brought over his wife and his daughters. Why not?

"That's what his wife and daughters thought, too. That's what all the Jews in our town expected. But that wasn't what Reb Zusha Shuster thought.

"One fine day, a year or so later, Reb Zusha came back from America, the land where you could sweep up gold in the streets (at least so people thought). When they asked him, 'Why did you come back from America?' his answer was, '*Dort'n hab ikh nisht gehot vos tsu tun.*[*] That is, my poverty, want, having to do without, not making a living—none of that counts. As I see it, I wasn't really doing anything there. Really doing something means helping the needy and the sick.'"

AK: This story left an unforgettable impression on me. May this story be a monument to his memory.

---

[*]I didn't have anything to do there.

Commentary for Tale 42 (IFA 19949)

Recorded by Abraham Keren from Azriel Zuriel of Poland in 1993 in Jerusalem.

Cultural, Historical, and Literary Background

Jewish Values

Told as a personal memory, the narrator recalls Reb Zusha the shoemaker, who in his way of life made an indelible impression on him. His own destitution notwithstanding, Zusha the shoemaker followed two basic values of the Jewish tradition: charity and the observance of the Sabbath. For discussions of the importance of charity in Jewish life, see the notes to the following tales: IFA 2604 (vol. 1, no. 30), IFA 8391 (vol. 1, no. 11), and IFA 10089 (vol. 1, no. 28); the value of festive food for the Sabbath celebration is addressed in the notes to the following tales: IFA 2623 (vol. 1, no. 25), IFA 5361 (this vol., no. 17), IFA 7602 (vol. 1, no. 47), and IFA 16405 (vol. 1, no. 14).

Immigration to the United States

Immigration to the United States was, before the Holocaust, a cause of major upheaval in eastern European Jewish life. Although there is some scattered information about the presence of Polish Jews in North America early in the eighteenth century, the interest in and the image of America as the *goldene medine* (the golden country) grew during the nineteenth century. One example is found in the popularity of the Yiddish book *Zofnath Paaneach* (1817) by H. C. Hurwitz (1749–1822), which was a translation of the book *Die Entdeckung von Amerika* (The discovery of America; 1781) by Joachim Heinrrich Campe (1746–1818).[1] A sociological-historical analysis of the cultural clash immigrants experienced in North America is available.[2] The return to Europe, the core of the present story, is a phenomenon in Jewish society that has been researched only minimally.[3] A comprehensive bibliography of the subject of returning to the homeland has been published, but it concentrates on the second half of the twentieth century and omits studies focusing on earlier times.[4]

Folklore Motifs

- F111.2 "Voyage to Land of Promise."
- F701 "Land of plenty."
- *F701.3 "America, the land of gold."
- cf. F731.1 "Island covered with gold."
- F761.5.1 "City paved with seeds of gold."
- *F761.5.1.1 "America, where the streets are paved with gold."
- cf. F771.1.1.1 "Castles paved with gold and gems."

- *L212.5 "Choice of charitable life over prosperity."
- L217.1 "Former poverty chosen over new riches."
- *N842.2 "Shoemaker as helper."
- *P165 "Poor men."
- *P165.1 "Poor women."
- P453 "Shoemaker."
- U60 "Wealth and poverty."
- V71 "Sabbath."
- V400 "Charity."
- *V439 "The charitable poor."

Notes

1. Weinryb, "East European Immigration to the United States."
2. Handlin, *The Uprooted.*
3. Sarna, "The Myth of No Return."
4. Gaillard, *Migration Return.*

43

"As Face Answers to Face in Water"*

TOLD BY GERSHON WEISSMAN TO LIMOR WEISSMAN

Gershon: *An old lady...*
Moshe (the brother): *Eventually you'll do penance, after you finish with all your injections, all your vitamins...*
Gershon: *Yes, there really are whale pills, made of a special oil. I'm going to buy some.*
Moshe: *Yes, yes, after you finish all your follies, you'll do penance yet.*
Limor: *Father will decide. What's wrong with that?*
Gershon: *There's a story, there's a story they tell about a woman who had never been in a hotel.*

All her life, she had heard a story about hotels, what a lovely and elegant place they are, where you do nothing but rest, just rest and sleep. It was another place she didn't know, because she was a woman who had to work all the time. Then she decided that for a year she would save a shekel every day so she'd have enough money to go to a hotel. She saved a shekel every day, and another shekel, and another shekel. At the end of the year she had 365 shekels.

She packed her suitcase and went to the hotel.

She went up to the clerk at the reception desk. "I've got money and I want to spend a whole night in the hotel," she told him. "And if I don't have enough money, it's all right with me if you put another woman in my room, as long as she's a nice lady."

"All right," the clerk told her and counted the money. It turned out that she had exactly enough for a room in the hotel, a room for one night and for breakfast. She didn't have to share with another woman. So he called the bellboy. He took the old woman and her suitcase.

---

*Proverbs 27:19.

Gershon: *Nu, Sophie (he calls to his wife, who is some distance from him)—there's a moral here for you.*

They take the woman's suitcase to her room and she goes into the room. The bellboy tells her, "This is your room. Have a good time."

She goes into the room, looks around, and takes a deep breath: wall-to-wall carpets, a large bed, lamps. Suddenly, she sees a woman standing opposite her, with an angry look on her face. "Lady, what are you doing here?" the woman asks the other woman. She sees the woman mimicking her.

"Lady," she tells her, "you behave yourself." She sees that the woman mimics her again.

"Lady, why aren't you being nice?" she says. And again the woman mimics her.

The old woman is irritated. She leaves the room and goes down to the reception desk. "You said you would give me a single room," she tells the clerk. "If I don't have enough money for a single room, I wouldn't mind another woman there, but at least she should be a nice woman. I went up to my room and saw a woman who really isn't nice at all. She keeps mimicking everything I do and behaving rudely."

The desk clerk was smart enough to realize that she was seeing herself in the mirror and that this woman had evidently never seen herself in a mirror before. She didn't know that she was looking at herself. So the desk clerk said to her, "When you go back upstairs and see the other woman, try smiling at her, and she'll smile back at you. Treat her nicely, and you'll see that she'll be nice to you in return. And everything will be all right."

"Fine," said the woman. She went back to her room and saw the woman again. She smiled at the woman and the woman smiled back at her. She invited the woman to sit down, and the woman invited her, too. In this way, she spent a very pleasant evening in the hotel.

The next day, when she went downstairs, she told the desk clerk, "Thank you very much, indeed. I had a wonderful and successful evening. It was everything I imagined about a hotel." Now how does this connect—

Moshe (laughing from a distance): *Wow, to buy a shtreimel* and buy*

---

*Black, board-rimmed hat worn on the Sabbath and special occasions by Hasidic and ultra-Orthodox Jewish men.

	a suit and buy a hat. Gershon, I'll buy you the hat. The hat and the shoes are on me.
Gershon:	*It connects to the exoteric and esoteric aspects of the word* maim.*
Transcriber's comment:	He had explained this part before he told the story. Now both of us go over to sit next to Moshe, because Gershon wants to explain what is special about the word maim to him, too, even though Moshe is making fun at his expense.
Gershon:	*And the verse, "as face answers to face in water," which means that others will treat you the same way you treat them. There was a convention of the advertisers' association about how to deal with the ultra-Orthodox sector. In the past, they didn't give that sector the respect it deserves. They made light of them. . . .*
Father:	*Gershon, do you want Turkish coffee?*
Gershon:	*Turkish coffee, instant coffee, and herbal tea. So Rabbi Yehuda Metzger, the rabbi of north Tel Aviv, said, "Treat this group nicely, because it will vote for you with its feet and buy your products." Then some woman journalist came to the podium and gave an example of the Shefa Mehadrin supermarket chain that caters to the ultra-Orthodox sector. It gives the ultra-Orthodox full kashrut** and full service, a spotless store—something you didn't used to see. And even though they claim—which I totally reject—that there are less expensive stores, the public loves Shefa Mehadrin and votes with their feet for Shefa Mehadrin. Because Shefa Mehadrin gives them added value, more than any other store in that sector. In short, if you write the word maim [in Hebrew], the exoteric and the esoteric are the same. If you take the word maim, the exoteric and esoteric readings are identical.§ It's written with two mems*

---

*Water.

*The body of dietary laws specifying what is kosher.

§That is, the word in Hebrew is a palindrome; it is the same when read forward and backward. The word "radar" is an example of a palindrome in English.

	and one yud. Now the letter mem, the exoteric and esoteric readings are identical. And if you take the letter yud, here, too, the exoteric and esoteric readings are identical: the numerical value of the letter yud is ten, and the value of the other two letters in its name—vav, which is six, and dalet, which is four—also comes out to ten. So maim *is one of the few words in Hebrew whose exoteric and esoteric aspects are identical. If you check according to the Baba Baba—*
Limor:	*You mean the Baba Baruch.*
Moshe:	*The Baba Buba.*
Gershon:	*Now this links up with the sentence "As face answers to face in water," because your reflection appears in water. Once upon a time they didn't have mirrors. So what you see reflected there in front of you is you. And that links up with the moral I mentioned before.*

COMMENTARY FOR TALE 43 (IFA 20439)

Told by Gershon Weissman to his sister Limor Weissman during a family gathering in 1996 in Haifa.

Cultural, Historical, and Literary Background

The Family Context

The present story was told around the family dinner table when the narrator wanted to make a point to his sister; the other family members were either talking simultaneously or lending an ear to the exchange between the brother and his sister. An analysis of the use of fables and anecdotes in intimate family conversation is available.[1]

The narrator elaborated his story with a discussion about the tale's practical, ethical, and mystical dimensions. The narrator apparently heard the story from Rabbi Yehudah Metzger, once the rabbi of north Tel Aviv. The rabbi had addressed a marketing conference, admonishing the audience to treat well the religious sector of the buying public. The rabbi stressed the idea that those you treat well will, in turn, treat you well; and he illustrated his message with the story the narrator related to his family.

Interpretation of the Biblical Verse

The mystical-magical dimension of the present tale involves an explanatory interpretation of the biblical verse "As face answers to face in water" (Proverbs 27:19). In Jewish mystical-magical consideration of biblical, or any other text, the letters themselves may acquire an independent meaning and may be considered as individual symbols, not simply as the consonants and vowels that make up the word. This interpretive system, called *gematria,* is based on the assignment of numerical values to each letter. According to this system, the meaning of a word is derived not from the language but from the numerical relationships among the letters. Thus words with letters that have the same numerical value share related significance, even though their dictionary definitions may reveal no affinity. A discussion, including a brief bibliography, of *gematria* in folktales has been published.[2]

In the interpretation of the biblical verse that makes up the title of this tale, the narrator resorts only partially to *gematria,* perceiving a correspondence between the linguistic and the mystical-magical meanings of the word. The key term is *m[a]im;* (water). Just as water reflects one's image, so the letters of the Hebrew word for water reflect each other, consisting of an initial *mem* and a final *mem.* Palindromes are script-based verbal plays. Their incorporation into an oral dialogue reflects a high degree of script-consciousness. Furthermore, the name of the middle letter, *yod,* also consists of three letters, of which the sum of the last two letters (four plus six) is equal to the value of the first letter (ten); therefore, the letters are a numerical reflection of each other as well. Further information about this and related systems of interpretation is available.[3] A discussion of the use of linguistic symbolism in magic in general has been published.[4]

Mirrors and Reflections

The mirror is one of the most ancient household goods, and its earliest forms were found in Egypt, dating back to the First Dynasty (2920–2770 B.C.E.).[5] It has been used in cultures the world over and was known in European societies from the antiquities through the Middle Ages and the Renaissance.[6]

In the fifteenth century, Lorraine and Venice began manufacturing glass mirrors; but throughout the sixteenth century, Venice gained a monopoly over mirror production. In seventeenth-century France, Jean Baptiste Colbert (1619–1683), the controller of finances under Louis XIV, was able to break the Venetian dominance of the mirror industry and began manufacturing mirrors. For these three hundred years, mirrors were a luxury item, limited to the nobility and the very rich. Even during the eighteenth century, when larger mirrors became part of household decor, they were owned almost exclusively by rich countrymen and burghers.[7] Melchior-Bonnet's[8] observations that "[a]t the end of the eighteenth century, mirrors brought an element of a fairy-tale dream to life as they invaded all spaces of social interaction" and that "[i]n rural society people rarely looked at themselves, and the mirror . . . possessed a poor reputation among them"[9] are relevant to the present story.

The present tale is unique among the versions of tale type 1336A "Man Does Not Recognize His Own Reflection in the Water (Mirror)." The most common versions of this tale type, including those in the IFA, are about a couple. In those tales, the husband finds a handheld mirror and sees his father's image in it; cherishing it, he hides it and observes it from time to time in privacy. His wife spies on him; and when she discovers the mirror, she accuses her husband of having an affair with another woman. They take the mirror to a judge, a rabbi in the Jewish versions, who wonders about the commotion because all he sees in the mirror is an old man.

Eastern Versions of the Tale

Melchior-Bonnet[10] cited a Korean version of tale type 1336A, as did B. Schweig.[11] Other Korean versions are available.[12] Grayson[13] commented on the history of the tale, pointing out that

> [t]his tale has a surprisingly long history with roots going back to India. The earliest recording of the tale type in East Asia is in a Buddhist work, the *Tsa P'I-yü Ching* [Korean: *Chap piyu-gyŏng* (The scripture of collected parables)], which is preserved in the Buddhist canonical collection .the Tripitaka Koreanum of the thirteenth century. The *Tsa P'I-yü Ching*

is available in three translations and is a collection of moralistic tales, teachings and rules for life. The earliest datable translation of this collection into Chinese was the work of the Serindian monk Lokaksema some time in the mid-second century. A Korean version of this tale type is found in Hong Manjong's (1643–1725) collection of stories and folktales, the *Myō ngyōp Chihae* [Collected writings of grass and leaves].

This tale is known also in Japan.[14] In China, the tale has been known since the T'ang era (618–906 C.E.).[15]

Western and Mid-Eastern Versions of the Tale

In the West, reports about tale type 1336A are available, particularly from English-speaking countries, such as England, Ireland, and the United States.[16] One America tale is shorter than other versions;[17] and several other variations in English have been published.[18]

Stories about unrecognized reflections are known from earlier periods, told about simpletons, or their sons, who do not recognize their own image in water or in a looking glass. Some of these tales appear in the Arabic humor tradition.[19] The earliest source that Marzolph cited dates back to 1030. Among the texts from subsequent periods is a late thirteenth-century version that appeared in the collection *Laughable Stories* by John Abu'l-Faraji, whose father, Aaron, was a Jewish physician who lived in the ancient city of Melitene (today known as Malatya, Turkey). Because of his descent, the collector of these tales was known as "Bar 'Ebhrâyâ" or "Bar-Hebraeus."[20] The tale later appeared as part of the Djuha narrative cycle[21] (for more on these tales, see "A General Note on the Tales of Djuha" in vol. 1).

In Jewish traditions, the two forms of reflection—in water and in a looking glass—are thematically distinct. As in non-Jewish tales, the tales about a reflection seen in water usually involve a father and a son, whereas the mirror tales concern a husband and a wife. Versions from Yiddish-speaking communities are available;[22] an Iraqi tale that is analogous to, though not identical with, the present tale is also known.[23]

Similarities to Other IFA Tales

There are twelve related tales on deposit in the IFA:

- IFA 783: *The Way You Look at Others, So They Look at You* (Syria); mirror (brother and sister).[24]
- IFA 2006: *What Is a Mirror?* (Poland).
- IFA 2787: *A Stupid Person Who Does Not Know What Is a Mirror* (Galicia, Poland).
- IFA 5014: *The Demise of a Vain Glorious* (Iraq); mirror.
- IFA 7404: *The Mirror* (Ukraine).
- IFA 7849: *The Couple Who Did Not Recognize Themselves in the Mirror* (Afghanistan).

- IFA 7944: *The Mirror Merchant and the Polish Peasant* (Poland).
- IFA 8179: *The Religious Person and the Mirror* (Poland).
- IFA 8455: *The Bedouin and the Diamond* (Iraq); mirror.
- IFA 9715: *Bewitching* (Poland);[25] mirror.
- IFA 15447: *The Mirror* (Eretz Yisra'el, Ashkenazic).
- IFA 18519: *The Triple Mirror* (Israel).

Folktale Types

- 329 (Eberhard and Boratav) *"Der Spiegel"* (The Mirror); cf. 1284 "Person Does Not Know Himself."
- 1336A "Man Does Not Recognize His Own Reflection in the Water (Mirror)."
- 1336A "Not Recognizing Own Reflection" (new ed.).
- 1337 "Peasant Visits the City."
- 1337 "A Farmer Visits the City" (new ed.).

Folktale Motifs

- *F771.1.1.3 "Hotel as a place of extraordinary pleasure."
- J21 "Counsels proved wise by experience."
- *J21.53.1 "Do unto others what you would like to be done to you."
- J1730 "Absurd ignorance."
- J1742 "The countryman in the great world."
- J1791.7 "Man does not recognize his own reflection in the water."
- J2012 "Person does not know himself."
- *P165.1 "Poor women."
- Q41 "Politeness rewarded."
- *Q96 "Reward for having positive attitude."
- *Q101.2 "Mutuality of reward: done to you as you do to others."

Notes

1. Kirshenblatt-Gimblett, "A Parable in Context."
2. Ben-Amos and Noy, *"Die Zeischen als Metasprache in der Jüdischen Folklore."*
3. Gandz, "Hebrew Numerals"; Idel, *Kabbalah*, 97–103; Scholem, "Gematria"; and Trachtenberg, *Jewish Magic and Superstition*, 147–152, 260–264.
4. O'Keefe, *Stolen Lightning*, 39–61.
5. Schweig, "Mirror."
6. B. Goldberg, *The Mirror and Man*, esp. 95–162; and Melchior-Bonnet, *The Mirror*, 9–18.
7. B. Goldberg, op. cit., 163–176; and Melchior-Bonnet, op. cit., 21–98.
8. On p. 86.
9. On p. 92.
10. Op. cit., 4–5.

11. Op. cit., 257.

12. Choi, *A Type Index of Korean Folktales*, 216–217 (tale type 500 "The People Who Saw a Mirror for the First Time"); and Grayson, *Myths and Legends from Korea*, 356–357 no. 158.

13. Op. cit., 357.

14. Seki, *Folktales of Japan*, 188–189 no. 55. See also Ikeda, *A Type and Motif Index of Japanese Folk-Literature*, 236–237 (tale type 1336A "The Mirror . . . *Matsuyama Kagami; Ama Saiban; Kagami Otoko*").

15. Eberhard, *Folktales of China*, 179, 237–238 no. 69. See also Ting, *A Type Index of Chinese Folktales*, 170–171 (tale types 1336A "Man Does Not Recognize His Own Reflection in the Water [Mirror]" and 1336B "The Peasant, His Relatives, and the Mirror").

16. For example, Briggs, *A Dictionary of British Folk-Tales*, A:2:84; and Briggs and Tongue, *Folktales of England*, 134–135 no. 77.

17. Dorson, *Buying the Wind*, 81–82.

18. Baughman, *Type and Motif Index of the Folktales of England and North America*, 315 (motif J1795.2* "Man finds mirror, thinks it is a picture of his grandfather . . .").

19. Marzolph, *Arabia Ridens*, 2:219 no. 982.

20. Budge, *The Laughable Stories*, 148 no. 583.

21. Wesselski, *Der Hodscha Nasreddin*, 1:177, 276–277 no. 311; Decourdemanche, *Sottisier de Nasr-Eddin-Hodja*, 271 no. 275; and Marzolph, *Nasreddin Hodscha*, 137 no. 317.

22. Olsvanger, *Rosinkess mit Mandeln*, 205 no. 310; Olsvanger, *L'Chayim!*, 102–103, 125 (mirror); N. Gross, *Maaselech un Mesholim*, 413–414 (mirror); and Schwarzbaum, *Studies in Jewish and World Folklore*, 351–352, 480 (includes copious annotation).

23. Ḥayyim, *Nifla'im Ma'assekhah* (Wonderful are your acts), 105–107 no. 69.

24. Analogous to the version in Ḥayyim, op. cit.

25. Published in M. Cohen, *Mi-Pi ha-Am* (From folk tradition), 1:66–68 no. 29.

44

Who Has the Right to Benefit from the Ten Commandments?

TOLD BY MOSHÉ KEREN (EINEHORN)
TO ZALMAN BAHARAV

*H*ershele Ostropoler was on intimate terms with the *rebbe*,* who lived peacefully among his Hasidim in a certain town. The Hasidim guarded their *rebbe* and sat at his table at the *melavah malkah* feast, Saturday night after *Havdalah***, feasting on his leftovers. They also doted on the members of his household. The local magnate, who was fabulously rich, frequented the *rebbe*'s house, too. The mistress of the house, meaning the *rebbetzin,* was a handsome and ample and attractive woman. The rich man, a purveyor who supplied provisions to the imperial army and was close to the authorities, had his eye on the lovely *rebbetzin* and could be found near her whenever possible. From time to time, he would bring valuable gifts to the *rebbe* himself and his family.

The intimacy between the *rebbetzin* and the magnate did not sit well with the Hasidim. But they didn't dare call the *rebbe*'s attention to what was going on, because they were afraid of the magnate and because they didn't want to irritate the *rebbe* and spoil his good mood.

Hershele the jester paid no attention to what was happening. He had his own opinion about the "friendship" between the *rebbetzin* and the tall, broad-shouldered magnate, who turned the eyes of the young women and the gentile maids in rich houses. The Hasidim asked Hershele to stand in the breach and warn the magnate to stop fooling around with the woman, because of the commandment "You shall not covet."

Once, before the Shavuot festival, the Hasidim were sitting and talking idly about the approaching holiday, the festival of the Giving of the

---

*A Hasidic rabbi.
**The ceremony that marks the end of the Sabbath. See commentaries to tale IFA 5361 (in this vol., no. 17) and tale IFA 8792 (in this vol., no. 5).

Torah. Hershele and the magnate were among the group. Hershele began telling a story:

"Back then, before the giving of the Torah, when our teacher Moses ascended Mount Sinai to receive the Ten Commandments in the form of the tablets of the law, he invited the souls of the righteous to be there. One Jew who had left Egypt had owned an inn and tavern in the city of Ramses. When they left Egypt, he liquidated his business and came into the wilderness with all of the holy congregation. That day, all those who had left Egypt were gathered around Mount Sinai. But the ex-innkeeper had an idea.

" 'I'll pitch my tent at a crossroads a little way off from the mountain. Every pious person will pass my inn and come in and have a small drink before he says "We will do and obey."* And on his way back after the giving of the Torah, before he submits to the yoke of the commandments, he'll want to drink another small glass of brandy.' And that's what he [the innkeeper] did.

"When the pious people began returning from the mountain, after they had heard the thunder and lightning and had seen the tablets of the law and what was engraved on them, the innkeeper greeted the first man and asked him, 'What did you hear? And what did you receive?'

"The pious man replied, 'I agreed with everything that was proclaimed at Mount Sinai—"I the Lord am your God who brought you out of the land of Egypt, the house of bondage: You shall have no other gods besides Me." I said, "That makes sense; it is impossible to serve other gods. We must be faithful to the one and only God." '

"The innkeeper turned to the second man, who had arrived in the meantime. 'And what did you hear?'

"The pious man said, 'It is written in the Ten Commandments: "You shall not steal." It is a good idea to observe this commandment. Someone who steals from his fellow is taking another person's property for himself. You benefit, but the other man loses, so what the thief does is unjust.'

"The innkeeper turned to the third pious person who was waiting for a drop to drink—he was a rich man with lots of property: 'Tell me, what did you like best of all in the Ten Commandments?'

"The third man said, 'The commandment "You shall not commit adultery"—that one I don't accept at all. All right—don't steal, don't murder, don't covet! Someone who does that is hurting another person. You steal

---

*Exodus 24:7.

from another person, you kill him and his soul, or you covet his wife. When you do that you are detracting from your neighbor's enjoyment. But "You shall not commit adultery"? I loathe that commandment. Here are two persons, a man and a woman who enjoy each other's love. They do what they do not out of compulsion, but out of love. Why shouldn't they do what they think is good?'

"He was still fuming when our teacher Moses himself walked in. 'What's all the commotion about?' he asked.

"They told Moses about the rich man who was not happy with the commandment 'You shall not commit adultery.' Moses invited the rich man into a side room. 'My friend,' he asked, 'why are you so excited? I didn't mean you. This prohibition applies only to poor people, but rich people are allowed to do whatever they want. So relax and pay no attention to it!'"

Commentary for Tale 44 (IFA 7755)

Recorded by Zalman Baharav from Moshé Keren (Einehorn) in 1966 in Tel Aviv.[1]

Cultural, Historical, and Literary Background

The Rabbi

The tale consists of a story within a story; the first is a historical account into which the second, a fable, is embedded. For a discussion of framed and embedded narratives, see the commentary to tale IFA 960 (this vol., no. 14).

The historical episode is a description of a situation in the Hasidic court of Rabbi Barukh ben Yeḥiel of Medzibezh (1757–1810), the grandson of Rabbi Israel Ba'al Shem Tov, the traditional founder of Hasidism, and the brother of Rabbi Moses Ḥayyim Ephraim of Sudylkow (c. 1740–1800?). The narrator does not name the rabbi, but his identity is inferred from the reference to Hershele Ostropoler, who—according to primarily oral sources—was known to have been a jester in his court.

The testimony of the joke cycles[2] places Hershele in the court of Rabbi Barukh, whom he was supposed to cure from attacks of depression. According to Dubnow,[3] Rabbi Barukh was an arrogant, ignorant, and greedy man who pursued the life of luxury and grandeur. Apparently, he did not always tolerate Hershele's humorous remarks, and Hereshele did not always shield the rabbi from criticism or offense. At one time, when the jester's humor evoked the rabbi's ire, he ordered some thugs among his devotees to throw Hershele down a flight of stairs. Hershele did not recover from the injuries sustained in the fall and died after a lengthy illness.[4] Horodezky[5] described Rabbi Barukh in milder terms. A Hasidic biography that does not mention an association between the rabbi and Hershele has been published.[6]

After the death of his first wife, Rabbi Barukh remarried. The present story does not specify which of the two wives caught the attention of the magnate. Similarly vague is the identity of the wealthy merchant. While Hasidism was primarily a popular movement, it resonated with some of the more affluent classes of Jewish society. For a historical discussion of relationships across the lines of the social classes, see the commentary to tale IFA 18601 (this vol., no. 12).[7]

The Jester and the Use of Humor

Hershele Ostropoler was the best known of the eastern European Jewish jesters. His reputation was greater in Ukraine, but his fame extended beyond its boundaries into many Jewish towns and shtetls in the Pale of Settlement, where he became the ultimate legendary comic figure. Oral tales about his pranks and witty retorts delighted Jewish narrators and listeners throughout the nineteenth century. Many of these stories belong to the international repertoire of trickster jokes. Hershele's rivals for comic popularity were the likes of Ephraim Greidiger (also known as Greidinger or Froy'im Greidiger) from Galicia and Motkeh Ḥabad from Vilna, Lithuania. For more on such figures, see the commentaries to tales IFA 2826 (this vol., no. 64), IFA 6976 (this vol., no. 62), and IFA 7127 (this vol., no. 65); studies about jesters in the courts of political leaders are listed in the commentar to tale IFA 12548 (vol. 1, no. 62).

Hershele was a historical person. Quite likely he was born in Balta, Podolia, but derived his name from the shtetl Ostropol, Poland, where he served as a *shohet*, a kosher ritual slaughterer. His jokes reveal him to be a destitute, hungry man with a shrewish wife; they lived in utter poverty and always dressed in rags. But oral historical information contradicts this image. At least two editors[8] who collected the tales about him during the 1920s and 1930s were able to obtain from elders some oral testimonies about Hershele's appearance and conduct. According to them, there is a discrepancy between his comic image and historical fact. Drawing on their childhood memories, these elders reported their grandfathers' accounts. The grandfathers, in turn, directly met or saw Hershele, extending the testimonial span to about 130 years.

C. Bloch[9] described Hershele as a short and slim man with dark eyes, curly dark hair, and small delicate hands. Sherman corroborated this description with an account by an elder Hasid whose grandfather knew Hershele and used to tell stories about him, adding that he was a "dignified Jew and a distinguished Hasid who was appointed as a treasurer at the court of Rabbi Barukh."[10] Sherman further cited Barukh Schwartz of Balta, who corroborated the description by reporting a eyewitness account given by Moshe Shtifman, who said that Hershele paid a visit to his father's house and that he also saw him in the *beit midrash* (house of study), where he was treated with great respect. Still another person told Sherman[11] that he saw Hershele's tombstone next to the grave of Rabbi Barukh and that women used to place their notes of appeal next to his gravestone as well.

In the present tale, Hershele plays the role not only of a court jester but also of a moralist who uses humor and irony to exert social control. Sociological and anthropological studies on the uses of humor for such a purpose have been conducted.[12]

Throughout the nineteenth century, Hershele was a comic hero of Yiddish oral tradition. Toward the end of that century, book peddlers began to sell collections of his jokes, which printers had published as Yiddish chapbooks (*mayseh bikhlakh*), giving rise to his popularity. From this base in the oral tradition, Hershele became a familiar figure in popular literature as well, starting in Lithuania and Warsaw in Yiddish and eventually becoming known from literary works in other languages, such as German, Hebrew, and English.

As far as the editor could establish, the first Hershele *mayseh bikhl* was published in 1884 by Zeltser.[13] N. Epstein listed four nineteenth-century Yiddish booklets, two of which appeared in Warsaw in 1884 and two in Vilna in 1895.[14]

Editors of Yiddish anthologies included tales about Hershele in collections published before World War I.[15] After the war, Hershele continued to be the principal comic figure in the joke lore of eastern European Jews and their descendants, mainly in Israel. More than a hundred tales about him are on deposit in the IFA. In the United States, the oral circulation of tales about him has declined considerably, and Hershele has become a literary comic figure featured mainly in English-language anthologies of Jewish humor, children's books, and some dramatic works.[16]

Kimmel,[17] an author of Jewish children's literature, expanded Hershele's literary function beyond his comic role, turning him into a demon fighter. Hershele is not so portrayed in traditional Yiddish literature. In a follow-up collection of tales, Kimmel[18] presented more traditional anecdotes about this character.

In Europe and Israel, Hershele was the subject of tales from both oral and literary traditions in a variety of languages. From the nineteenth-century oral and chapbook traditions, stories of his wit and pranks not only entered into anthologies of jokes but also became the subjects of poetry, novels, and plays.[19] He also has appeared in Yiddish literary works.[20] It is surprising that there are relatively few analytical comments about Hershele.[21]

In Israel, where stories about him still circulate, Hershele has been the main figure in only a few printed works.[22] Since the 1990s, there has been a literary revival of Hershele's anecdotes in children's literature in Israel as well as in Argentina.[23]

Women in Hasidic Society

The flirtatious relations between the rabbi's wife and the wealthy Hasid draw attention to the position of women in Hasidic society. An early essay on the subject was written by Horodezky;[24] a modern evaluation of this essay, including a more current restatement of this issue, is available.[25] Most studies of women in Hasidism concern their spirituality,[26] but a discussion of sexuality in Hasidism and in the Hasidic courts has been published.[27]

Similarities to Other IFA Tales

Among the one hundred tales about Hershele Ostropoler in the IFA, there are four versions of the present story, none of which is structured as a tale within a tale. Consequently, they lack the ironic twist with which the present version ends.

- IFA 6389: *The Ten Commandments for the Poor and for the Rich* (Morocco).[28]
- IFA 6744: *The King and His Daughter's Suitors* (Morocco).
- IFA 7614: *The Ten Commandments for the Poor and for the Rich* (Belarus).
- IFA 15636: *Pieces and Shards* (Poland).

Folklore Motifs

- A101 "Supreme god."
- C115 "Tabu: adultery."
- C560 "Tabu: things not to be done by certain class."
- C786 "Tabu: stealing."
- *E755.1.5 "Souls of the pious accompany Moses to Mt. Sinai."
- J80 "Wisdom (knowledge) taught by parable."
- J1124 "Clever court jester."
- P150 "Rich men."
- *P426.4 "Rabbi."
- *P449 "Innkeeper."
- T481 "Adultery."
- V71 "Sabbath."
- *V71.4 "Eating the rabbi's leftovers at the third Sabbath meal."
- *V76 "Pentecost."
- Z71.16.2 "Formulistic number: ten."

Notes

1. First published in Estin, *Contes et fêtes Juives*, 266–269.
2. See, e.g., Sherman, *Hershele Ostropoler*, 67–83.
3. *Toldot ha-Ḥasidut* ("History of Hasidism"), 208–213.
4. Gottlober, *Memoirs and Travels*, 164–166.
5. *Ha-Ḥasidut ve-ha-Ḥasidim* ("Hasidism and Hasidim"), 3:12–17.
6. Breitech, *Sefer Tehilot Barukh* (The book of praises for Barukh).
7. See also, Dynner, '*Men of Silk*,' 88–116.
8. C. Bloch, *Hersch Ostropoler;* and Sherman, op. cit.
9. Op. cit., 10.
10. Op. cit., 8.
11. Op. cit., 8–9.
12. Davies, *Jokes and Their Relation to Society;* Douglas, "The Social Control of Cognition"; G. Fine, "Sociological Approaches to the Study of Humor"; Martineau, "A Model for the Social Functions of Humor"; Mulkay, *On Humor,* 73–119, 152–177; Paton et al., *The Social Faces of Humor;* Powell and Paton, *Humor in Society;* and Stephenson, "Conflict and Control Functions of Humor."
13. *Hershele Ostropoler.*
14. "*Bemerkungen zu di vitzen un vitzike mayselach*" (Notes to the jokes and comic tales), 319. See also S[human], *Dos Freylikhe Hershele Ostropoler* (The merry Hershele Ostropoler); Anonymous, *Hershele Ostrapoler* (n.d.); and Anonymous, *Hershele Ostrapoler* (1925).
15. Marinov and Vohliner, *Humor un satire* (Humor and satire), 135–142.
16. E.g., Ausubel, *A Treasury of Jewish Folklore*, 304–319; Howe and Greenberg, "Stories of Hershel Ostropolier", 614–620; Learsi, *Filled with Laughter,* 159–185; Richman, *Laughs from Jewish Lore*, 354; and Richman, *Jewish Wit and Wisdom*, 115–121.
17. *Hershel and the Hanukkah Goblins.*

18. *The Adventures of Hershel of Ostropol.*

19. Works devoted exclusively to Hershele and other jesters: C. Bloch, op. cit.; Holdes, *Bajki i anegdoty Herszla z Ostropola;* Botoschansky, *Herschele Astropolier;* and Shtern, *Hershele Ostropoler un Motke Habad* (Hershele Ostropoler and Motke Habad). Joke collections: Cahan, *Jewish Folklore,* 200–201 nos. 16–18; Landmann, *Jüdische Anekdoten und Sprichwörter,* 38–47; Mark, *Le-Vediḥut ha-Da'at* (For entertainment),140–147, 160, 192 nos. 291–310, 312, 313, 343, 401; Olsvanger, *Rosinkess mit Mandlen,* 15 no. 27, 36–37 no. 63; [Präger and Schmitz], *Jüdische Schwänke,* 252–255; Olsvanger, *Röyte Pomerantsen or How to Laugh in Yiddish,* 40–44 nos. 60, 63, 64; and Präger and Schmitz, *Jüdische Schwänke,* 252–255. Comparative notes are available in the following: Schwarzbaum, *Studies in Jewish and World Folklore,* 538 (index, "Hershele Ostropoler"); and Cahan, *Studies in Yiddish Folklore,* 266–274 (esp. 266–267, 272, 299).

20. Manger, *Lid un Balade,* 200–201; and Trunk, *Der Freilechster id in der velt* (The happiest Jew in the world).

21. See the introductions in C. Bloch, op. cit., and Sherman, op. cit.; see also Sfard, *Studia i szkice* (Studies and notes), 176–179.

22. Sherman, op. cit. (important introduction and bibliography); Herceberg, *Hershele ha-Ostropoli;* Druyanow, *Sefer ha-Bediḥah ve-ha-Ḥidud* (The book of jokes and witticisms), 3:26–33 nos. 2131–2149; and Mark, op. cit.

23. Abbas, *Hershele;* Ofek and Ben-Ner, *Harpatka'otav shel Hershele* (Hershele's adventures); Ofek and Ben-Ner, *Hershele;* and Fingueret and Toker, *Las picardías de Hérshele.*

24. Op. cit., 4:67–71.

25. Rapoport-Albert, "On Women in Hasidism."

26. Loewenthal, "Women and the Dialectic of Spirituality in Hasidism" (n. 1 includes references to further studies on this subject).

27. Biale, *Eros and the Jews,* 121–148.

28. Published in Rabbi, *Avoteinu Sipru* (Our fathers told), 1:212 no. 145.

45

The Neighbor in Paradise

TOLD BY ESTHER WEINSTEIN TO YEHUDIT GUT-BURG

The *rebbe** of Stretyn once asked, "Who will be my neighbor in the world to come?"

A heavenly voice replied, "Eliezer the water carrier will be your neighbor in the world to come. He will sit next to you in Paradise."

The *rebbe* ordered his *shammes*** to hitch up the horses to the wagon. "I'm leaving on a journey at once." The *shammes* and the Hasidim were astounded and perplexed. But one does not ask questions of the *rebbe*, neither where nor why. He knows very well what he is doing, even when his Hasidim do not understand his enigmatic deeds. The *rebbe* put on his coat and warm hat and took his tallit,§ tefillin,§§ and siddur.***

The two flew like eagles, passing through towns and villages, crossing woods and mountains. The *rebbe* spent the whole time singing songs of praise to the Creator of the universe and all creation.

Finally, the *rebbe* took a flask from his pocket, poured out a bit of water, washed his hands, took a piece of cake from his bag, gave a piece to his *shammes,* and told him, "Wash your hands and we'll eat."

The two finished their meal with a cup of tea, said the grace after meals, fed and watered the horses, and continued their journey.

At last they reached their destination. The horses stopped, and the *shammes* got down, followed by the *rebbe*. The two entered a small room, where a woman sat by a table, along with two boys and a girl.

"Welcome to those who arrive," they called to the two visitors, rising to greet them.

---

*A hasidic rabbi.
**Synagogue caretaker.
§Prayer shawl.
§§Small black leather prayer boxes, wrapped around the head and arm, containing passages from the Torah
***Prayer book.

"Welcome to those who are already present," replied the *rebbe*. "Where is the master of the house?"

"He will come soon. He is still working. It is true that the Holy One, Blessed Be He, gives us everything that we need, for he is a merciful and compassionate God Who sustains and supports His people and all the universe. But nevertheless we must do our part to earn our keep."

The *rebbe* sat down and waited for the master of the house. The family, too, sat down.

After a while, the householder entered, washed his hands, recited the benediction, sat down at the table, and began to eat, for he was very hungry. When he finished, he said the grace after meals. Then he turned to his guests: "What brings you to my house? Of course, guests are always welcome; but there are so many rich householders here, as well as the rabbi and the rosh yeshivah,* and I am no more than a poor and insignificant water carrier. So why have you chosen me? Who am I? What is my strength and what are my good deeds?"

The *rebbe* of Stretyn replied, "You, Reb Eliezer, will be my neighbor in the world of truth. So I have come to see you and inquire into the good deeds by which you have merited this."

The water carrier sank in thought and then began to tell his tale:

"Every morning I get up early, say my prayers, and go out to gather wood in order to heat the school. Only after that do I begin my regular work. I take empty buckets and bring water to the houses. I also distribute free firewood to the poor people of the town. One day, when I was walking in the forest, I heard people moaning and crying. I went toward the voices and found a woman with three children—two sons and a daughter—lying on the ground, exhausted. They no longer had the strength to walk. I put the woman on my back and the three small children on my shoulders and brought them here. Ever since they have been living in my house, and I support them, with the help of God, may He be blessed. Here they are, sitting by our table. Those are all my good deeds.

"And now, Rebbe," concluded the water carrier, "bless me, Rebbe, that we may merit complete redemption and the coming of the Messiah, speedily in our days."

The *rebbe* of Stretyn understood that there was good reason why Reb

---

*Jewish school of higher learning.

Eliezer had been chosen to be his neighbor in the world to come. He fully merited that.

The rabbi blessed his future neighbor that he should have a comfortable living, a long life, and a good old age. Then he returned to his wagon, followed by his *shammes*. The horses flew back toward the *rebbe*'s house.

After the *rebbe*'s visit to the water carrier's house, the townsfolk discovered that the simple and self-effacing water carrier who lived among them was a righteous man who supported and honored the woman he had saved from death and was raising her orphans to knowledge of the Torah, observance of the commandments, and performance of good deeds.

COMMENTARY FOR TALE 45 (IFA 5377)

Recorded by Yehudit Gut-Burg from her mother, Esther Weinstein, who learned this story from her father, Rabbi Ḥayyim Salz.[1]

Cultural, Historical, and Literary Background

Rabbi Judah Zevi Hirsch Stratyn (Brandwein) (1780–1844) was the son of Rabbi Samuel Zanvil and the favored disciple of Rabbi Uri (Ha-Saraf) ben Pineḥas of Strelisk (1757–1826). Rabbi Judah was the founder of a Hasidic dynasty in eastern Galicia. This particular story is an example of the modeling process in the Hasidic tradition in which narrators construct episodes from the lives of Hasidic rabbis—sometimes entire biographies—following the patterns of prominent talmudic-midrashic and medieval figures. For studies, narrative parallels, and comparative analyses of the idea of a companion in Paradise, see the commentaries to tales IFA 10089 (vol. 1, no. 28) and IFA 7612 (this vol., no. 13). The water carrier in this story assumes the role played by individuals from other humble, even despised, professions found in earlier versions of this story.

Folktale Types

- 809*–*A (IFA) "The Companion in Paradise."

Folklore Motifs

- A694.2 "Jewish paradise."
- *H1258 "Quest for the identity of neighbor in paradise."
- *P417 "Water carrier."
- *P426.4 "Rabbi."
- Q53 "Reward for rescue."
- Q172.2 "Man admitted to heaven for a single act of charity."
- R130 "Rescue of abandoned or lost persons."
- R131 "Exposed or abandoned child rescued."
- *R131.10.2 "Water carrier rescues abandoned children."
- S301 "Children abandoned (exposed)."
- S431.2 "Wife and children exposed in forest."
- *V131.3 "Phylacteries (tefillin)."
- *V131.4 "Prayer shawl (tallit)."
- *V131.6 "Prayer book (siddur)."
- V400 "Charity."

Note
---

1. First published in Weinstein, *Grandma Esther Relates...*, 57–59 no. 14.

46

A Trial in Heaven

TOLD BY YEHUDAH HERMANN TO
YIFRAḤ ḤAVIV

A certain man died—may it not happen to us—and went up to Heaven.

He came to the guardians of Heaven. There were two angels standing in front of him, the good angel and the bad angel, with a scale in front of them. The bad angel began: "This man must go to Hell."

"Why?"

"Because he is wicked and a miser." And he tossed many sins onto one pan of the scale.

Said the good angel, "I have something that will weigh down my pan." He brought a man, a woman, and six children, and put them on the pan of the scale.

"What's this?" asked the bad angel.

"The good deed performed by this 'wicked man,' as you would have him, that is of equal weight to all the sins that you brought."

"How can that be?"

"Do you see this family? They were on the verge of death. They almost died of hunger. The father came to our deceased man and asked for *tzedakah*.* He gave it to him gladly. They bought food and lived. After that they had luck and became rich and blessed your wicked man all the time."

"All right. If that's how you're going to play, I too have someone." He went and brought a certain man and put him on his pan of the scale. "You see this?" he asked.

"What is it?" asked the good angel.

"You're asking who this is?"

"Yes, who is he, and what does he have to do with wickedness?"

"This man—the wicked man asked him for a loan. He gave it to him; but the wicked man did not repay it, and the lender died on account of him. So what is your good deed worth if this man died because of him?"

---

*Charity.

They began to argue.

One said, "I'm right." The other claimed, "No, I'm right."

What happens in a case like this?

They pass it on to obtain a verdict from "behind the veil"—from the Holy One, Blessed Be He Himself.

"Tell me your arguments," the Holy One, Blessed Be He, told them.

The bad angel presented his case. And after that, the good angel did likewise.

When they were done, the Holy One, Blessed Be He, said to them, "A gift is greater than a loan. Why? Because one extends a gift with one's entire heart and seeks only good for the recipient and his family. But as for a loan—did this dead man want the lender to die? Heaven forbid. He merely delayed paying back the loan, because he was doing good business with it and didn't think about the lender's death. So he is not a murderer.

"Having said this, I rule: Put all the souls on the pans of the scale and see which weighs more."

So the good angel put back the family that had received the donation from the deceased man, and the bad angel put back the loan money and the profits. The good angel's pan weighed more, so the soul of the deceased man was allowed to enter Paradise.

COMMENTARY FOR TALE 46 (IFA 19585)

Told by Yehudah Hermann to Yifraḥ Ḥaviv in 1994 in Kibbutz Bet Keshet.

Cultural, Historical, and Literary Background

In antiquities, in biblical times, in the era of the Second Temple, and in talmudic-midrashic and medieval times, Jewish religion—particularly Jewish mysticism—had a highly developed and articulated angelology. There were numerous named angels with clearly defined tasks who oversaw every aspect of human life and mediated between people and God.[1] The information about angelology in Jewish belief from antiquities up to the Middle Ages is available primarily from literary sources, so it is quite possible that the study of the hierarchical system of angels was always esoteric and limited to sages and mystics. Thus folk societies, whose spiritual life has rarely been directly documented, never gained access to the secrets of the heavenly angels. If this were not the case, and knowledge about heavenly angels were widespread in Jewish societies, then the text of the present story and other evidence from nineteenth- and twentieth-century oral tradition would indicate the decline of the general population's familiarity with such angels.

Functionally, angels continued to serve as the managers of the upper worlds and as mediators between God and people. But information about their specific roles and the particular task of each angel has been lost, as the present tale demonstrates via the dichotomy between a good angel and a bad one. The angels in the present story function as the defender and the accuser of the dead at the gate of Heaven. The tale describes a popular conception of the heavenly court; comparable narratives are available.[2]

Folktale Types

- cf. 1501 (Tubach) "Deeds Weighed (King Coenred's Knight)."
- 4180 (Tubach) "Scale of Judgment."
- cf. 4198 (Tubach) "Scholar Saved by Alms."

Folklore Motifs

- A661.0.1 "Gate of heaven."
- *A661.0.6 "Angel as porter of heaven."
- *A661.0.1.3.1 "Angels measure on a heavenly scale the good and the bad deeds."
- cf. A671 "Hell."
- cf. A671.1 "Doorkeeper of hell."
- A694.2 "Jewish paradise."
- E755 "Destination of the soul."
- E755.1 "Souls in heaven."

- E755.2 "Souls in hell (Hades)."
- F177.1 "Court in other world."
- Q42 "Generosity rewarded."
- *Q42.8.1 "Angel gives a man all his credit for good deeds so that the man may go to Heaven."
- Q172 "Reward: admission to Heaven."
- Q172.2 "Man admitted to Heaven for a single act of charity."
- cf. Q286 "Uncharitableness punished."
- V230 "Angel."

Notes

1. Bamberger et al., "Angels and Angelology"; Margaliot, *Mal'akhei 'Elyon* (Heavenly angels); and, generally, Marshall, *Angels*.

2. Schwarzbaum, *Studies in Jewish and World Folklore*, 158–159.

47

White Flowers, Red Flowers

Told by Hinda Sheinferber to Hadarah Sela

In our town there was a physician who had a son. The son went abroad to study. During the summer, he came home for vacation—two months. There were two young women he was friendly with. They spent the two months together. When he left, the two women went to the train station with him. The boy had two bouquets of flowers, one white and one red. Because he didn't know the language of flower colors, he gave the white flowers to one girl and the red flowers to the other. Then he went away.

Red means love and white means friendship. But he gave the white bouquet to the young woman who loved him and the red bouquet to the one who really wasn't interested in him. The girl who received the white flowers was very upset and very sad. She almost fell ill. Her parents sent her to America, to stay with family there. After several years there, she moved to Eretz Yisra'el.

When the son came home for his next vacation, he found only the young woman he wasn't really interested in. When he learned that the other woman was in America he went there to look for her, but didn't find her.

When she reached Eretz Yisra'el she opened a flower shop, because she had been so badly hurt by flowers. Once a man entered and asked for a bouquet of flowers. "What do you want them for?" she asked.

"It doesn't matter," he replied

"What color?"

"That doesn't matter."

"Yes it does. If you have time I'll tell you a story." So she told him this story—and he was her lost love!

Commentary for Tale 47 (IFA 18156)

Told by Hinda Sheinferber to Hadarah Sela in 1991 in Haifa.

Cultural, Historical, and Literary Background

This tale is grounded in modern Jewish life in Eastern Europe, America, and Israel. In the original Hebrew text, the narrator mentions the shtetl's rabbi, but accords him no narrative function within the story, shifting the focus immediately to a father and his son, who is studying abroad.

The tale itself hinges on a symbolic system that was part of western and central European popular culture and that apparently had diffused into lower- and middle-class Jewish society of Eastern Europe, where it was known during the twentieth century. This is not to say, however, that colors and flowers did not have symbolic value in traditional Jewish cultures.

Biblical poetry suggests the romantic use of flowers. In Song of Songs (6:2) the beloved sings about her lover:

> My beloved has gone down to his garden,
> To the beds of spices,
> To browse in the gardens
> And to pick lilies.

It is implied that he will present the flowers to his beloved. The Hebrew word of the flower in this verse is *shoshan*, which in modern Hebrew means rose; but quite likely in biblical Hebrew this word referred to the white lily (*Lilium candidum*).[1] Thus the modern and the biblical symbolic values of the colors are reversed: In biblical times, white flowers were for lovers, as they still were in some cultures in the nineteenth century, evidenced by the following nursery rhyme:

> Blue is true,
> Yellow's jealous,
> Green's forsaken,
> Red's brazen,
> White is love,
> And black is death![2]

Berlin and Kay[3] studied color terms from a variety of languages. According to them, the distinction, perception, categorization, and naming of colors across a number of cultures indicate that there are eleven basic color terms: white, black, red, green, yellow, blue, brown, purple, pink, orange, and gray. This influential study stimulated further research examining both the physical neurological basis of color distinctions and the linguistic representation and literary use of color terms.[4]

Modern Hebrew has all eleven basic color terms.[5] In biblical Hebrew, only the first eight are in use, and of them only four—black, white, red (with its two hues, *argaman,* purple, and *shani,* crimson) and blue—acquire symbolic meanings in poetry and ritual. However, none of them is associated with flowers. Blue was the dominant color in the Tabernacle (Exodus 26:31–36; Numbers 4:5–12), representing Heaven, the abode of God. The colors of the sunrise and sunset also have representation in the ritualistic context of the Tabernacle. White, black, and red occur occasionally as metaphors in biblical poetry; white represents purity, red represents sin (Isaiah 1:18; Psalm 51:9), and black refers to the color of tanned or dark skin (Song of Songs 1:5–6). In his prophetic visions, Zechariah (6:6) used colors in a unique way: black symbolized the north, and white the west. Furthermore, in this and in an earlier vision (Zechariah 1:8), the prophet described horses, not flowers. A. Brenner[6] analyzed the use of red, white, black, green, and yellow in the Hebrew Bible.

Talmudic-midrashic literature amplified the symbolic meanings of colors. Blue became the national color (MR *Exodus* 49:2), and red and its hues had a broad spectrum of symbolic use, ranging from the sun (MR *Numbers* 12:4) to desire (MR *Numbers* 20:7) and to royalty (MR *Numbers* 12:4). White represented sunlight (MR *Numbers*), holiness, and purity (BT *Yoma* 19a), whereas black, its ultimate opposite, symbolized death (BT *Yoma* 39b). Kabbalistic writings intensified the symbolic use and meanings of colors.[7]

The symbolic value and use of colors in society are culture bound. The book *The Realms of Colour,* edited by Portman and Ritsema, includes essays about color symbolism in several religions, systems of thought, cultures, and sciences. Turner's article, "Color Classification in Ndembu Ritual: A Problem in Primitive Classification," published later, is an important methodological essay in the analysis of color symbolism.[8]

The symbolic values of the colors and flowers in the present story, however, are based not on Jewish but on western European popular culture. These values were outlined in Charlotte de Latour's[9] *Le langage des fleurs* (1819), which became fashionable in France and England. According to B. Seaton,[10] who has extensively studied the tradition of the "language of flowers,"

> There is a great deal of misinterpretation of the nineteenth-century language of flowers in today's cultural history.... [Many people] think that the language of flowers was a socially agreed-upon symbolic language which men and women actually used to communicate with one another concerning matters of love and romance.... [However, studies show otherwise.] Instead of a universal symbolic language, the language of flowers was a vocabulary list, matching flowers with meanings, differing from book to book. Originating among the journalists catering to the genteel reader in Napoleonic France, the language of flowers was almost certainly a creation of writers of popular books. Belonging to the genre of

literary almanacs and their offspring, the gift annuals, language of flower books were intended as suitable gifts, perhaps to entertain the genteel female reader for a few dull afternoons. There is almost no evidence that people actually used these symbolic lists to communicate, even if the parties agreed upon what book to use for their meanings.

Further studies by B. Seaton are available.[11]

Goody[12] attributed the introduction of the language of flowers to England to Lady Mary Worterly Montagu (1689–1762), who reported in her letters from Turkey on the use of objects, including flowers, as a code language between lovers. Goody pointed out that the Orientalist Joseph Hammer-Purgerstall (1774–1856) later modified this perception and suggested that the harem women in Iran used flowers as a system of communication among themselves.

The present tale acquires special significance in consideration of Seaton's well-researched conclusion. It demonstrates the occurrence of two cultural trends: (1) the filtering down of a western European upper-middle-class literary tradition into an eastern European Jewish middle-class oral tradition. and (2) the actual interpretation of flowers as a language conveying either a conventional or an idiosyncratic meaning. As the story unfolds, we learn that the knowledge of and care for the language of flowers differs between the genders. The man was unaware of the symbolism of the flowers he presented to the young women; the women, however, noticed all the possible nuances.

Folklore Motifs

- J1820 "Inappropriate action from misunderstanding."
- P310 "Friendship."
- T10 "Falling in love."
- T24.1 "Love-sickness."
- Z100 "Symbolism."
- Z141 "Symbolic color: red."
- Z141.4 "Red rose as symbol of love."
- Z142 "Symbolic color: white."
- *Z142.3 "White rose as symbol of friendship."

--- **Notes** ---

1. Zohary, *Plants of the Bible*, 176–177.
2. Halliwell-Phillips, *Popular Rhymes and Nursery Tales*, 228.
3. Berlin and Kay, *Basic Color Terms*.
4. E.g., Hays et al., "Color Terms Salience"; Jernudd, "The Concept of Basic Color Terms"; Kay, "Synchronic Variability and Diachronic Change in Basic Color Terms"; Kay and McDaniel, "The Linguistic Significance of the Meanings of Basic Color Terms"; McManus, "Basic Colour Terms in Literature"; Moss, "Basic Colour Terms"; Pawlowski,

"The Quantitative Approach in Cultural Anthropology"; Shields, "Indo-European Basic Colour Terms"; Thorson-Collins, "Color Terms in British Folk Tales and Legends"; Wattenwyl and Zollinger, "Color Terms Salience and Neurophysiology of Color Vision"; and Wyler, "Old English Colour Terms and Berlin and Kay's Theory of Basic Colour Terms."

5. Berlin and Kay, op. cit., 94–95, 120.
6. *Colour Terms in the Old Testament.*
7. Scholem, "Colors and Their Symbolism in Jewish Tradition and Mysticism."
8. Turner, "Color Classification in Ndembu Ritual."
9. Perhaps the pseudonym of Louise Cortambert.
10. *The Language of Flowers,* 1–2.
11. "The Flower Language Books of the Nineteenth Century"; "French Flower Books of the Early Nineteenth Century"; "A Nineteenth-Century Metalanguage"; and "Considering the Lilies."
12. "The Secret Language of Flowers"; and *The Culture of Flowers,* 232–253.

Folktales

48

The King's Three Daughters

TOLD BY SIMA GOLDENBERG TO ZALMAN BAHARAV

A certain king ruled his kingdom with a heavy hand. His subjects suffered under the yoke of the many taxes he levied on them. But the king didn't care, because he wasn't interested in how they made a living. Only a few people—the excise men, tax collectors, and clerks—knew how to get by. The rich lived in palaces; the poor in tents and miserable shacks.

Three daughters were born to the king and queen, but they had no sons who could inherit the throne when the time came. The daughters grew into beautiful and shapely young ladies and were educated as befits the daughters of a royal house. The king and queen were sad because they did not know what would happen to their precious daughters when they received marriage proposals.

One day, the king had an idea. "I want my daughters to find themselves suitable husbands who can rule the kingdom after my death—each according to his ability. One can be the commander of the army, one can hold the reins of the economy, and the best will be king after me when I am old and frail."

The king summoned his three daughters, the oldest, the middle, and the youngest. "My dear daughters, you have grown up and matured," he told them. "The time has come to think about the important matter of what your futures hold in store for you. I have decided to test you. To each of you I will give a precious gem, a pearl worth a fabulous sum. Each of you may do as you wish with the pearl you receive from me. From this I will learn how well you can prepare for what may happen to you soon."

"My lord father," said the oldest daughter, "I will go to the goldsmith and ask him to take the pearl you have given me as a present and set it in a locket attached to a gold chain. I will hang the chain around my neck and keep the pearl safe."

"And I," said the second daughter, "I will command that a high tower be built. At its summit I will place a golden spire, and at the tip of the spire I will mount the lovely pearl, so that it will dispel the darkness of night and its glow will be visible from afar. This will add to the renown of my lord father's capital city."

The third daughter did not know what to do with her gift. She asked her father to give her time to think about how to guard the valuable pearl.

The king did not want to wait for his youngest daughter to decide. He gave the first pearl to his oldest daughter and told her, "Daughter, I will not prevent you from doing as you wish. Go to the goldsmith and have him make an ornate locket where you can place the pearl I have given you and keep it safe."

The king ordered his masons to build a tall tower. The artists inset the pearl that the king had given to his second daughter into a golden rod, and fastened the spire to the roof of the tower. The pearl lit up the dark night for miles around, to the honor and glory of the king's capital city.

The youngest daughter took the pearl that her father gave her but did not tell him what she would do with it. "I'll give my youngest daughter time to think about it," mused the king, "and see what happens."

The king's youngest daughter began roaming through the capital, visiting the distant suburbs and the alleys that were home to the neediest people, the dreadfully poor and the beggars.

One day, she went into a shack. The stifling air in this house of poverty irritated her sensitive nose. The king's daughter sneezed. Then she opened her eyes to see what was happening in the dark room. She saw a young mother lying on her sickbed. Around her swarmed seven young children, with no clothes to cover their bodies and crying for bread to still their hunger. The mother was wrestling with her pains and had no answer for her infants' entreaties for a crust of bread. Soon death would overpower her diseased body, and the children would be left orphans. They, too, were doomed. The young princess took pity on them. Without delay, she went to the market, took the precious pearl from her purse, and exchanged it for a large sum of money. She bought medicine, food, and clothing and began to care for the whole family until she had restored the mother's health and satisfied the needs of her frail and naked children. Nothing was left of all the money she had received for the pearl. The young princess went back to her father's palace with empty hands. The father raged at his spendthrift daughter and banished her from the palace.

The girl wandered through the kingdom looking for shelter. She traveled from city to city and village to village. Her fine clothes wore out, her lovely shoes became full of holes, her manicured hands and feet grew rough from much walking and the manual labor she performed to earn her food.

One day the princess, tired and broken, left with only a single thin shift to clothe her body, sat down to rest in the shade of a huge tree that grew on the side of a hill. She saw a tiny man rolling large stones from the top of the hill down into the valley. Whenever a sufficient number accumulated he would come down and pile them one on top of another to build a fence around a plot of land. Even though her strength was quite exhausted, the princess, observing his backbreaking toil, could not bear the little man's pain.

She went to help him with his excruciating work.

The dwarf was grateful to the girl for her good heart. "Thank you, miss," he told her, "for your good heart and assistance, which is a sign that God has blessed you with a sense of compassion. Because the suffering of human beings moves you, I will give you a precious gift."

He took from his neck a small wooden box, inlaid with gold, and gave it to her.

"This is a magical box," the dwarf told her. "When you feel that your distress is unbearable and would lament your bitter fate, open the box and let a single tear fall inside. The tear will turn into a priceless diamond. Sell it and use the money to support yourself, along with other poverty-stricken people who have nothing."

The young princess took the box from the dwarf and hung it around her neck. She bade him farewell and went on her way. When she passed an orchard she saw the owner abusing his workers, beating them with his riding crop while they dug ditches and sighed.

The young princess was overcome with pity for the suffering laborers and almost choked on her tears. Remembering the small box that hung round her neck, she opened the cover and let a single hot tear fall inside. At once it turned into a sparkling diamond.

The compassionate princess went to the market and sold the diamond for a high price. She distributed most of the money to the workers in the orchard, keeping the rest to buy herself food.

The princess behaved similarly in many cases. Her fame spread throughout her father's kingdom.

One day, the oldest princess, the one who wore the locket with the pearl around her neck, went bathing in the sea. A storm blew up. The heiress took the locket off her neck and grasped it in her hand. Suddenly she was knocked over by a large wave, and the pearl was swept away into the depths of the sea.

A large eagle flying at a great altitude saw a shining orb in the golden steeple on top of the tower. He thought this must be the eye of another eagle, his enemy; he had already pecked out one of its eyes and was eager to peck out its other eye as well. He stuck his beak, which was as hard as iron, into the top of the golden spire and swallowed the pearl that had been the king's gift to his second daughter. She too returned to her father's palace with empty hands. Thus the pearls that had been the king's gift to his two daughters were both lost.

The king of the neighboring kingdom realized that the father of the three princesses had grown old and feeble and had no sons to manage the kingdom the way he had done when he was young and vigorous. This king decided to send his army to invade and conquer it. He declared war and named his own son and heir to command the army.

The first king saw that his country was menaced with invasion and mobilized his subjects to fight the enemy. But the people did not want to fight, because they were all too familiar with the arbitrary cruelty of the king's officials. The young men hid in caves and gullies and did not want to go out and face the enemy.

The young princess, who knew that the people respected her for her good deeds and her charitable work for the wretched and miserable, addressed a proclamation to the nation. Their homeland was in danger, she said, and must be saved from a heartless invader who wanted to enslave its inhabitants. She promised that she would rule with kindness and humanity.

The princess's proclamation resonated in the hearts of the young men. They streamed into the encampments. The knights donned their armor, girded on their weapons, and went out to face the enemy resolutely. No one stayed home.

The invading king and his son saw the neighboring country's troops and battalions standing guard at the border, their morale high, and had second thoughts about assaulting the old king's fortresses and invading his kingdom.

The praises of the merciful princess, so beloved by the people and blessed with peerless beauty and grace, reached the ears of the young prince. Desirous of marrying her, he sent ambassadors to the old king, requesting the hand of his wise youngest daughter. The king agreed and said that it was a good match. The two kings concluded a treaty of peace and friendship, sealed by the marriage of their children.

So the compassionate and gentle princess became the wife of the neighboring king's son. When the time came, they managed jointly the affairs of the two kingdoms, which had merged into one, with humility and compassion.

The other two princesses died old maids.

COMMENTARY FOR TALE 48 (IFA 7202)

Told by Sima Goldenberg from Tulcea, Romania, to Zalman Baharav in 1965, in Ashkelon.

Cultural, Historical, and Literary Background

The present tale consists of several narrative roles, functions, and motifs that are at the core of tale type 923 "Love Like Salt," such as the father, his three daughters, the outcast heroine who outlasts her more privileged sisters and comes to the rescue of her father, and finally the prince and the concluding function of marriage. However, this tale is unique in a crucial point: The plot turns not on a test of love but on a test of competence. The youngest daughter succeeds by performing charity, a central value in Jewish society (*tzedakah*). Analyses of the position of charity in Jewish society and culture have been conducted.[1]

Within European literature, Shakespeare canonized the theme of the royal love test and its tragic consequences in *King Lear* (1605/6–1608). The first time the tale of King Lear, his daughters, and their husbands occurred in written literature was in *Historia Regum Britanniae* (1135–1139) by Geoffrey of Monmouth (d. 1155).[2] Geoffrey claimed he had merely translated into Latin the ancient book *Britannici Sermonis*.[3] Whether such a book ever existed is questionable; Geoffrey likely drew on several sources.[4] Perrett[5] argued that "there is a trace of the Lear-story in Welsh national literature . . . [and] we should not regard the story as drawn from Welsh tradition current in Geoffrey's time."

Motif H592.1 "Love like salt" is absent from both the *Historia* and *King Lear*. In both texts Cordelia, the outcast heroine, responds by stating her love in legal terms: "*Est uspiam, pater mi, filia quae patrem suum plus quam patrem preaesumat diligere?*" (Father mine, is there a daughter anywhere that presumeth to love her father more than a father?).[6] Nearly two hundred manuscripts and numerous translations in Welsh and other languages attest to the popularity of the *Historia Regum Britanniae* in the Middle Ages;[7] yet, in as far as what motivates the favorite daughter's response, there is a clear difference between the written and the oral traditions. In European traditions, motif H592.1 occurs only in the oral narratives. It is absent from the literary renditions of such stories from the fifteenth century, with which Shakespeare was possibly and probably acquainted.[8] Even the fourteenth-century version, which is included in the more popular collection of tales *Gesta Romanorum,* does not include this motif.[9]

In contrast, motif H592.1 "Love like salt" occurs in the oral renditions of this tale, which were recorded mostly in the nineteenth century but likely date to earlier folk traditions. Most notably, the motif is found in the Brothers Grimm's *Kinder-u. Hausemärchen.*[10] The Brothers Grimm did not record this tale directly from an oral version. Including the tale only in the 1843 edition of their anthology, they drew on a text that appeared in a collection by H. Keltke (*Almanach deutscher Volksmärchen*), which contained a High German rendition of a tale originally told in dialect[11] and published in 1833.[12] The responses that appear in these texts are as follows: *"ich hab' den Vater so gern wie's Salz"* (I am fond of father like salt; Keltke) and *"habe ich den Vater so lieb wie Salz"* (I love father like salt; Brothers Grimm).[13]

During the nineteenth century, it became apparent that motif H592.1 is part of tale type 923, as it was told in several European countries.[14] Hartland[15] categorized the narratives based on this theme into five types, of which the "Value of Salt" is the second. Cox considered these tales to be a distinct group—which she titled "Cap o' Rushes"—within the Cinderella narrative corpus.[16] Later this group was identified as tale type 510 "Cinderella and Cap o' Rushes."[17]

The theme also occurs in Indian oral tales.[18] On the basis of sources cited in indexes of these tales, Cosquin[19] suggested an Indian origin of such stories. A psychoanalytical interpretation of such tales is available.[20]

Yiddish versions of this story do not necessarily follow the pattern of the current tale; rather, many are similar to the more common European forms in which the royal father seeks confirmation of his daughters' love.[21] Other such tales combine themes current in several European narrative traditions with values typical of Jewish society.[22]

Similarities to Other IFA Tales

In the IFA there are sixteen versions of tale type 923 "Love Like Salt":

- IFA 346: *Who Is Blessed with the Realm, Riches, and Honor?* (Yemen).[23]
- IFA 2453: *A Daughter Loves Her Father Like the Torah* (Egypt).
- IFA 2567: *A Daughter Loves Her Father Like Excrement* (Eretz Yisra'el, Sephardic).
- IFA 2875 (vol. 3, no. 39): *A Daughter Waits the Gift of God* (Egypt).[24]
- IFA 3084: *Wife Brings Home Luck* (Afghanistan).
- IFA 3274: *God's Gift Is Greater Than Man's Gift* (Tunisia).
- IFA 3477: *The King and His Daughter* (Iraq).
- IFA 4492: *She Loves Him Like Salt* (Iran).[25]
- IFA 5225: *Love Is Like Salt* (Afghanistan).[26]
- IFA 5691: *Love Like Salt* (Poland).[27]
- IFA 5956: *The King and His Three Daughters* (Romania).
- IFA 8002: *Love Is Like Salt* (Belarus).
- IFA 9380: *She Loves Him Like Salt* (Iraq).
- IFA 10291: *Love Is Like Salt* (Eretz Yisra'el, Sephardic).
- IFA 12008: *The Youngest Daughter and Her Love for Her Father* (Iraq).[28]
- IFA 14896: *The Princess Who Loved Her Father Like Salt* (Morocco).

Folktale Types

- 256 (Eberhard and Boratav) *"Der Faule Mehmet"* (The Lazy Mehmet).
- 923 "Love Like Salt."
- 923 (Andreev) "Kak Sol" (Like Salt).

- 923 (Jason) "Love Like Salt."
- 923 (Krzyzanowski) "*Drogi Jak Sól*" (Dear Like Salt).
- 923 (Schullerus) "*Wie das Salz Lieben*" (Loving Like Salt).
- 3006 (Tubach) "Lear and Daughters."

Folklore Motif

- D475.4.5 "Tears become jewels."
- D812.12 "Magic object received from dwarf."
- D817 "Magic object received from a grateful person."
- D1174 "Magic box."
- F451 "Dwarf."
- F451.3.4 "Dwarfs as workmen."
- cf. H592.1 "Love like Salt."
- *H921.2 "Task set by king to daughters to determine heir to kingdom."
- J414 "Marriage with equal or with unequal."
- L50 "Victorious youngest daughter."
- cf. M21 "King Lear judgment."
- P10 "Kings."
- P234 "Father and daughter."
- P252.2 "Three sisters."
- Q40 "Kindness rewarded."
- T100 "Marriage."
- *T104.3 "Foreign prince marries princess instead of waging war."
- V400 "Charity."
- V410 "Charity rewarded."
- Z71.1 "Formulistic number: three."
- Z71.5 "Formulistic number: seven."[29]

--- **Notes** ---

1. See L. Rabinowitz, "*Gemilut Hasadim*"; and Ben-Sasson and Levitats, "Charity."
2. Hammer, *Geoffrey of Monmouth Historia Regum Britanniae*, 46–52 (II.10–15).
3. Hammer, op. cit., 22 (I.1).
4. Perrett, *The Story of King Lear from Geoffrey of Monmouth to Shakespeare*, 1–2.
5. Op. cit., 19.
6. Hammer, op. cit., 47 (II.10.151–152). See S. Evans, *Histories of the Kings of Britain by Geoffrey of Monmouth*, 30; and *King Lear* (I.i.92–93): "I Love your Majesty according to my bond, no more nor less."
7. Griscom, *The Historia Regum Britanni*, 551–580; Hammer, "Some Additional Manuscripts of Geoffrey of Monmouth's *Historia Regum Britanniae*"; and Hammer, "Remarks on the Sources and Textual History of Geoffrey of Monmouth's *Historia Regum Brit Anniae*."
8. Bullough, *Narrative and Dramatic Sources of Shakespeare*, 7:269–420; D.

Hamilton, "Some Romance Sources for *King Lear*"; Perrett, op. cit.; and A. Stewart, "The Tale of King Lear in Scots."

9. Swan and Hooper, *Gesta Romanorum*, xxxix–xl.

10. See Grimm and Grimm, *The Complete Fairy Tales,* 562–570 no. 179 (The Goose Girl at the Spring).

11. Bolte and Polívka, *Anmerkungen zu den Kinder-u. Hausemärchen,* 3:305–308.

12. Schumacher, *D'Ganshiadarin.*

13. Rölleke, *Grimms Märchen und ihre Quellen,* 374–375.

14. Hartland, "The Outcast Child."

15. Op. cit.

16. *Cinderella: Three Hundred and Forty-Five Variants.*

17. I(c), II, III, IV, V, VI. Ibid., 80–86, 137–139, 167–172, 175–176, 196–199, 214, 226–227, 264, 306–307, 317, 335–336, 374–375, 415–416, 423 nos. 208–226, 314, 315, 318.

18. Thompson and Balys, *The Oral Tales of India,* 228 (motif H592.1); and Thompson and Roberts, *Types of Indic Oral Tales,* 115 (tale type 923).

19. "*La theme de 'la princesse qui ame son pere comme du sel'* "; and C. Schmitt, "*Lieb wie das Salz.*"

20. Dundes, " 'To Love My Father All.' "

21. Olsvanger, *Rosinkess mit Mandlen,* 253–254 no. 361; Olsvanger, *L'Chayim!,* 143–144 no. 171; and B. Weinreich, *Yiddish Folktales,* 85–88 no. 32.

22. Cahan, *Yidishe folksmasiyyot* (Yiddish folktales), 56–63 no. 13 (1931 ed.), 91–98 no. 24 (1940 ed.).

23. Published in D. Noy, *Folktales of Israel,* 257–161 no. 57.

24. Published in Rush, *The Book of Jewish Women's Tales,* 207–209 no. 57.

25. Published in Avitsuk, *The Fate of a Child,* 22–23 no. 12.

26. Published in Kort, *Sippurei 'Am mi-Pi Yehudei Afghanistan* (Folktales of the Jews of Afghanistan), 80–84.

27. Published in Rush, op. cit., 201–203 no. 55.

28. Published in Agassi, *Sent with the Wind,* 72–76.

49

A Boy and Girl Who Were Destined for Each Other

TOLD BY HINDA SHEINFERBER TO HADARAH SELA

*O*nce there were two friends. They were very close until they grew up, when each of them married in a different city. But they wrote to each other. Once a week, once every two weeks, once a month. Finally they stopped. Things went well for them. One of the two friends had no children. He went to visit the *rebbe*.* There he met his friend, and they were very happy to see each other, because they were such good friends.

"Why are you here?"

"Why are *you* here?"

They had both come for the same reason. Neither of them had children. So they told each other, "If we have children—one of us a son and the other a daughter—we will make a match between them."

God helped them. A son was born to one, and a daughter to the other. The father of the son was rich, but the father of the daughter was poor. This son, an only child, was pampered by his parents. They sent him to yeshivah.**

At the yeshivah there was a certain woman who sold bagels from a basket to the yeshivah students. She had a daughter. The mother took sick. There was no father, because he had passed away. So the daughter came to sell bagels. One young man saw her and started looking at her, which is not appropriate for a yeshivah student. But he had seen her before. He had seen her once when she was sitting on the second story, knitting, and the skein of yarn fell from her hand. He ran to pick it up—and then he saw her. When he saw her with the bagels and saw that she was very beautiful, very lovely, he fell in love with her.

The mother found out, since he kept walking near their house, but she knew that the young man was rich and would never marry a poor girl. She began to arrange a match for her daughter with an old man, because they

---
*A Hasidic rabbi.
**Jewish school of higher learning.

Yeshiva boys, studying.

were poor. The girl told the young man about the match, in strictest confidence. They began talking. He said he wanted to marry her. "Has the old man come already? Has he bought you a present?"

The girl's grief made her ill. They sent her to a rest home, and he came to visit. Her mother would not let her look at the boy from the yeshivah. But she loved him, and he loved her. Still, she had to marry the old man. The boy traveled home and told his father that there was a girl he wanted to marry.

But the father would not agree: "What, a poor girl? We're rich." He argued and would not give his consent. By no means would he agree.

But when the two friends had agreed on the match, before their children were born, they had shaken hands on it. When you shake hands, it's like an oath in the Bible. The young man got up during the night. He knew that the wedding was going to be the next day. He got up during the night, took some money—just enough—and rushed back to the town where his yeshivah was. The procedure is that first they escort the groom to the *huppah*.* So the rich groom was already standing there and the young man went and stood next to him. When they brought the bride, they had to place her next to the young man. So he was the one who married her.

That night the young man's father dreamt that he was shaking his friend's hand. But there was sadness mixed with the dream on account of his son, who had stolen his money. The next day, he traveled to the town where the yeshivah was. He arrived after the wedding ceremony was over. The next day, they made a great feast, and the father brought the money. "Maybe it really is her," he thought.

In the morning, before the feast, they didn't pray in the yeshivah, but in the bride's home. One of the guests stood like this,** next to the wall, which was covered with wallpaper. He ripped open the wallpaper and uncovered a hole behind it. He put his hand inside and took out a box. When they opened the box, they saw it contained money and a letter.

When the bride's father was still alive, it happened that a rich son from another city went to the army and didn't want his father to know that he had so much money. He asked the father of the bride, that same faithful man, to hide the money for him. If he did not return, the money would be his. If he did return, he would get half. Time passed, and he did not return. So the father of the bride hid it, so no thief would take it. But when the man found it (they say that it was Elijah the Prophet) . . .

---
*Wedding canopy.
**Evidently, the narrator demonstrated the guest's action.

COMMENTARY FOR TALE 49 (IFA 18132)

Told by Hinda Sheinferber from Poland to Hadarah Sela in 1990 in Haifa.

Cultural, Historical, and Literary Background

Marriages are made in Heaven but happen on earth. The Yiddish proverb "*a zivug min ha-shamayyim*" (a match from Heaven)[1]—its humorous extension "*der hatan iz oyf ayn oyg blind, un di kalah iz oyf ayn oyer toyb*" (the bridegroom is with a blind eye, and the bride is with a deaf ear), notwithstanding—and the Yiddish word "*bashert*" (destined [mate]) reiterate an ancient conception of God. The idea that marriages are decreed by God occurs in the story of the mission to Abraham's native land to bring a wife for his son Isaac (Genesis 24:50). In the Book of Tobit (6:18), the angel Raphael reassures Tobias that he will not meet the tragic end of Sarah's seven previous bridegrooms because "she was set apart for him from the beginning."

The notion of divine predestination of marriage occurs several times in the talmudic-midrashic literature. In a debate between a Roman noblewoman and Rabbi Yose ben Ḥalafta (second-century *tanna*), the rabbi argues that God's continuous involvement in running the world's affairs manifests itself in matchmaking (MR *Genesis* 68:4; MR *Leviticus* 8:1; MR *Numbers* 3:6). Or, simply put, "A man's marriage partner is from the Holy One. . . . Sometimes a man goes to his spouse and sometimes it is the reverse" (MR *Genesis* 68:3; see also BT *Mo'ed Katan* 18b; BT *Sotah* 2a). The proverb "marriages are made in Heaven" has been documented in English at least since the sixteenth century.[2]

Yet, human beings are not privileged to the divine plan and have to discover it for themselves. This lack of correspondence between human knowledge and divine arrangement has generated narratives about predestined spouses.

In his study of such tales, A. Taylor[3] distinguished several narrative cycles of tale type 930A "The Predestined Wife": far-eastern (China, Japan), northern (Northern Europe from Finland to Iceland), and the southern (modern Greek, Spanish, Portuguese, English, and Scottish Gaelic). However, these geographical cycles are not necessarily thematically or spatially separate and often fuse into each other, as can be expected in oral traditions. A. Taylor noted subvarieties of this tale type, represented by Armenian, Russian, Finnish, and Arabic tales.

With some variation, the common pattern in these tales involves a wandering mature man of noble birth who finds refuge in a house of a poor family. When a baby girl is born there, he receives a prophecy that she will be his future wife. He tries to kill the baby, but only wounds her. Years later, the man falls in love and marries a beautiful maiden who has a scar that identifies her as the infant he tried to murder. In the IFA, only tale IFA 7964 from Irani Kurdistan fits this pattern.

Brednich[4] researched the theme of the predestined wife in international folk traditions, including an analysis of tale type 931 "Oedipus," within which he formulated three new subtypes: 931* "A The Legend of Judas Iscariot," 931*B "The

Legend of Saint Andreas," and 931*C "The Legend of Patricide." He further studied tale type 933 "Gregory on the Stone," made several distinctions within tale type 934 "The Prince and the Storm," and reexamined tale type 930 "The Prophecy."

In an essay, Shazar[5] delineated four additional Jewish subtypes of the present story: 930*E "Predestined Marriage: Magic Separation," 930*F "The Well and the Weasel as Witnesses," 930*H "An Unsuccessful Human Trial in Match-Making," and 930*J "Taming the Father-in-Law." None of these subtypes is applicable to the present story or to its parallel texts in the IFA, partially because the idea of predestination is implicit rather than explicit in these tales.

Within the IFA, there are two groups of tales that involve explicit marital predestination. In both cases, the narratives involve relations that cross the economic line between poor and rich. In the first case, predestination involves divination; whereas in the second case, there is a prenatal parental pact. For a discussion of the first form, see the commentary to tale IFA 4735 (vol. 1, no. 45). The predestination that dominates the second form is neither astral nor divine but a consequence of an agreement between two humans, as seen in the present tale. Such a pact acquires a supernatural power because it is consummated through a vow, taking on the characteristics of divine predestination. Breaking of the vow—intentionally or unintentionally—has tragic consequences. These tales have five or six narrative episodes.

- Initial childlessness.
- Conditional parental pact.
- Birth of the offspring.
- Separation by class, distance, or death.
- Resolution.
- Happy consequence.

or

- False resolution.
- Tragic consequence.

Narrators who immigrated to Israel from eastern European countries told stories that parallel the present tale. One such tale was recorded in Ukraine by Solomon Zainwil Rappoport[6] (1863–1920), who is better known by his pseudonym An-Sky. He led the Jewish Ethnographic Expedition (1912–1914) into Ukraine under the auspices of Baron Naftali Horace Günzburg. That tale served as a basis for his play *Tsvishn Tsvey Veltn* (Between two worlds), which was produced by the Vilna troupe in 1920 as *Der Dybbuk*.[7] H. N. Bialik translated the play into Hebrew;[8] it is also available in English.[9] A comparative study of the play is available;[10] as is information about An-Sky's ethnographic expedition.[11]

Similarities to Other IFA Tales

Other versions of this story in the IFA are the following:

- IFA 881: *No Escape from Destiny* (Yemen).[12]
- IFA 1767: *The Vow of Two Friends* (Eastern Europe).
- IFA 7012: *The Mountain of the Besht* (Romania).[13]
- IFA 7964: *There Is Escape from Fate* (Irani Kurdistan).[14]
- IFA 9041: *The Promise of the Two Neighbors* (Morocco).
- IFA 9997: *A Match Enforced by Destiny* (Poland).
- IFA 9998: *The Princes and the Pauper's Son* (Poland).
- IFA 13131: *The Handshake* (Romania).[15]
- IFA 13797: *The Bride and the Bridegroom Who Were Destined for Each Other* (Poland).
- IFA 13798: *The Help of Elijah the Prophet* (Poland).

Folktale Types

- 930A "The Predestined Wife."
- 930A (El-Shamy) "The Predestined Wife" (Prince Is to Marry a Poor Girl).
- 930A (Haboucha) "The Predestined Wife."
- 930A (Jason) "The Predestined Wife."
- 930A (Krzyzanowski) "*żona z przeznaczenia*" (The Destined Wife).

Folklore Motifs

- D1810.8.4 "Solution to problem discovered in dream."
- D1925.3 "Barrenness removed by prayer."
- *K1915.4 "Lover tricks an unloved bridegroom out of the marriage ceremony."
- cf. L162 "Lowly heroine marries prince (king)."
- M205 "Breaking of bargains or promises."
- M444 "Curse of childlessness."
- N517.2 "Treasure hidden within wall (under floor) of house."
- N538. "Treasure pointed out by supernatural creature (fairy, etc.)."
- *N747 "Accidental meeting of childhood friends."
- P150 "Rich men."
- *P165.1 "Poor women."
- P232 "Mother and daughter."
- P233 "Father and son."
- P233.2 "Young hero rebuked by his father."
- P310 "Friendship."
- *P313.2 "Separate paths of childhood friends: one rich, the other poor."

- T10 "Falling in love."
- T22 "Predestined lovers."
- T22.1 "Lovers mated before birth."
- T22.2 "Predestined wife."
- T22.3 "Predestined husband."
- T24.1 "Love-sickness."
- T52.4 "Dowry given at marriage of daughter."
- *T52.4.2 "Bride, or bride's family does not have dowry money."
- T61.5.3 "Unborn children promised in marriage to each other."
- T91 "Unequals in love."
- T91.6 "Noble and lowly in love."
- cf. T91.6.2 "King (prince) in love with a lowly girl."
- *T98 "Father opposed to son's marriage."
- T100 "Marriage."
- *V295 "Elijah the Prophet."

Notes

1. I. Bernstein, *Jüdische Sprichwörter und Redensarten*, 98 no. 1451.

2. Mieder et al., *A Dictionary of American Proverbs*, 407 no. 11. For a brief history, see I. Abrahams, *The Book of Delight*, 172–183.

3. "The Predestined Wife."

4. *Volkserzählungen und Volksglaube von den Schicksalsfrauen.*

5. "The Jewish Oicotype of the *Predestined Marriage* Folktale."

6. Yiddish: Shloyme-Zanvl Rappoport.

7. Sandrow, *Vagabond Stars*, 217–221; for the production of the same play two years later in Habima theater see E. Levi, *The Habima—Israel's National Theater*, 32–37.

8. An-Sky, "*Bein Shnei Olamot*" (Between two worlds).

9. An-Sky [An-Sky], *The Dybbuk and Other Writings*; Landis, *The Dybbuk and Other Great Jewish Plays*, 15–68; and Neugroschel, *The Dybbuk and the Yiddish Imagination*, 1–52.

10. Werses, "S. An-Ski's 'Tsvishn Tsvey Veltn.' "

11. Beukers and Waale, *Tracing An-Sky;* An-Ski, *The Enemy at His Pleasure.*

12. Published in D. Noy, *Jefet Schwili Erzählt*, 238–239 no. 98.

13. Published in D. Noy, *A Tale for Each Month 1966*, 56–57 no. 7.

14. Published in Cheichel, *A Tale for Each Month 1967*, 64–66 no. 7.

15. Published in M. Cohen, *Mi-Pi ha-Am* (From folk tradition), 2:57 no. 162.

50

The Three Young Men

TOLD BY NAḤUM PELZ TO
HIS DAUGHTER, ḤANNAH PELZ

Once upon a time, there were three young men, orphans left to their own devices. Wanting to earn an honorable living, they wandered from village to village in search of work, but could not find anything to do.

One day, when they were in the forest, they met an old man. "What are you doing in the forest?" he asked them.

"We have been looking for work for many days, but in vain. We have passed through many villages but have yet to find any employment."

The old man agreed to be like a father to them and support them. The four wandered through the forest until they reached a clean white hut. They stopped and looked at it. The door opened and a beautiful young woman came out to meet them. The eldest son was much taken with her.

So he told the old man and his brothers, "I would be happy to live in this hut. I would build other huts and become rich."

"All right, my son," the old man said. "May it be as you wish."

The old man married the eldest son to the girl from the hut. Before he left him, he said, "Hate falsehood and love truth."

The old man and the two brothers continued through the forest. A few days later they came to the bank of a stream. On the other side was a clean hut, with a flour mill alongside it. While they stood there considering what to do, a lovely young woman came out of the mill with a jar of flour in her hand.

"How happy I would be to live with this woman," the middle son said. "I would build more flour mills and get rich."

"So may it be, my son," replied the old man.

The old man married the middle son to the girl with the jar of flour. When he parted from him he told him, "My son, hate falsehood and love truth."

The old man and the youngest son continued their journey. When they

363

reached the edge of the forest they saw a ramshackle and decrepit hut. The door of the hut opened and a beautiful girl in humble clothes came out.

"I would be happy to live with this girl," said the youngest son, "and share everything with her, both joy and sadness, happiness as well as pain. And whatever we had, we would share with the poor."

"May it be as you wish," responded the old man. "Marry this girl. But always remember: Hate falsehood and love truth."

The old man married the youngest son to the girl and disappeared.

About a year later the old man decided to go back and see how his adopted sons were doing. He passed by the house of the eldest and saw that many new buildings had been constructed near the hut. He understood that the eldest son had become rich.

The old man disguised himself as a beggar. "Honored sir," he entreated, "please give a poor hungry man a loaf of bread."

The son lost his temper and chased the old man away from his house, yelling after him, "Don't dare come back and bother me. I don't have time for idlers like you!"

The old man climbed the nearby hill and looked down at the house. At once all the buildings went up in flames.

The old man went to see how the second son was doing. He noted many flour mills all around, with many servants working in them. The old man went up to the master and asked him for a little flour. The son lost his temper and threw the old man out, shouting after him: "I barely have enough for myself and I have to share with you and all the other paupers who come to me?!"

The old man climbed the nearby hill and looked down at the house and the mills. They all went up in flames at once.

The old man continued toward the youngest son's house. There he saw that the young couple were still living in the same small hut and sharing their bread with the poor. The old man knocked on the door and asked for some bread. The youngest son and his wife invited him in. "Sit down and eat," they told him. "We'll give you some soup, too."

The youngest son's wife ran and brought the old man some clean clothes, because his old ones were torn and filthy. When the old man took off his shirt, the husband and wife saw a great sore on his chest. Taken by surprise, they asked him, "Can we help heal your wound?"

"It is possible," he replied. "Anyone could do it, but no one wants to."

"What remedy is needed?" asked the young man.

"Burn down the house," replied the old man, "and put the ashes on the sore."

The young man was silent, at a loss for words. But his wife told him, "Human life is more precious than a house. We can build another house—but if the old man dies we won't be able to bring him back to life."

The young man agreed with her. They took their son with his cradle and a few other essential possessions out of the hut. Then the young man lit a match and set the house on fire.

The old man saw that the son and his wife had compassionate hearts. He looked at the burning house—and a new house, all clean and white, emerged from the flames.

The young man and his wife, bewildered by the sight, looked for the old man, but he had vanished. Then they understood that the wonderful old man was a messenger of God and thanked God for his kindness.

Commentary for Tale 50 (IFA 6098)

Recorded by Ḥannah Pelz from her father, Naḥum Pelz, from Zakroczym, Poland, in 1963 in Tel Aviv.

Cultural, Historical, and Literary Background

In the various versions of the present story, the narrators advocate a set of priorities of social values, positioning generosity above wealth and even learning. The former is thought to be a fundamental tenet of Judaism as stated in a proposition attributed to Simeon the Just, who said that the three pillars of Judaism are "Torah, divine service and the practice of kindliness [*gemilut hasadim*]" (Mishnah *Avot* 1:2). In this tale, the narrators generally reverse the ancient order, positioning *gemilut hasadim* (acts of lovingkindness) as the primary value of Judaism. Brief surveys of the importance of this tenet in Judaism and Jewish societies are available.[1]

In Jewish tradition, tale types 550A "Only One Brother Grateful" and 750D "Three Brothers Each Granted a Wish by an Angel Visitor" have three basic forms, which are represented in written texts from about the seventeenth to the nineteenth centuries and in oral tradition. Most of the narrators are from Mediterranean countries and from countries of Islam; only a few of them are from inland Europe, particularly from Eastern Europe. The narrator of the present text is from Poland, a country in which the tale is widely known—twenty-five versions are listed in the type index of Polish folktales. Out of the thirty-six versions in the IFA, there is only one other from an eastern European country, Belarus. A Russian version[2] (compare with tale IFA 8021 [this vol., no. 51]) and Greek versions[3] have been published.

Megas[4] noted sixty-seven similar texts in the Folklore Archives of the Academy of Athens. The version in Dawkins[5] concludes with motif S268 "Child sacrificed to provide blood for cure of friend," prompting the suggestion that the theme of child sacrifice spread from India to Europe.[6] This motif does not occur in any of the Jewish versions or in the version from Egypt.[7]

The basic form of the tale involves three men (brothers or friends), each of whom receives a gift from a revered or supernatural character. Elijah the Prophet is usually implicitly, if not explicitly, identified as playing this role. Later, the donor checks on the conduct of the men and withdraws his gift from the two who have not complied with his instruction to perform charity, hospitality, and *gemilut hasadim*.

Three Subforms

There are three subforms of this tale type in Jewish traditions. In the first, the donor acts as a matchmaker, assigning each of the individuals a wife, according to their respective choices. Upon testing, only the most modest young man and his wife are hospitable, even self-sacrificing. The present tale is the only version of this subform in the IFA. The couple sacrifices their own house to cure the donor. This dramatic concluding episode also occurs in the Greek version cited above.

The wife-testing theme, which is included in this subform, has precedents in Jewish and Islamic traditions in the stories about Ishmael's wives and their approval by Abraham the Patriarch. This narrative occurs in the eighth-century midrash *Pirkei de-Rabbi Eliezer*.[8] A study of this tale has been conducted.[9]

In the second subform, the donor gives the three young men magical objects that enable them to achieve their respective goals of wealth, learning, and family. In a few of these versions, the donor matches the young man with a wife directly without magical mediation. The first literary documentation of this subform is in a Persian manuscript that M. Gaster[10] dated from the sixteenth to eighteenth centuries. A truncated Yiddish version exists; Gaster[11] suggested that he may be able to complete the tale with a passage from a manuscript in his possession.

Similarities to Other IFA Tales

Oral versions of the second subform appear in the IFA:

- IFA 167: *The Tale about the Three Brothers Who Are Robbers* (Libya); donor = an old man.[12]
- IFA 1796: *Elijah Bestows Wealth upon His Disciples and Then Tests Them* (Iraq); donor = Elijah the Prophet.
- IFA 2112: *Elijah the Prophet's Gifts* (Tunisia);[13] donor = Elijah the Prophet.
- IFA 2464: *The Wishes of the Three Beggars* (Iraq);[14] donor = Elijah the Prophet.
- IFA 3092: *The Three Gifts* (Yemen); donor = Elijah the Prophet.
- IFA 3578: *The Acts of Elijah the Prophet* (Turkey); donor = Elijah the Prophet.
- IFA 4911: *A Woman of Valor* (Iran); donor = Elijah the Prophet.
- IFA 5097: *A Woman of Valor* (Tunisia); donor = Elijah the Prophet.
- IFA 5605: *The Selfish Men* (Spanish Morocco);[15] donor = Elijah the Prophet.
- IFA 5934: *The Three Sons* (Iraqi Kurdistan); donor = Elijah the Prophet.
- IFA 6086: *The Three Brothers and the Angel* (Iraqi Kurdistan); donor = an angel; third wish = to meet their dead father.
- IFA 6406: *The Three Gifts of Elijah the Prophet* (Egypt); donor = Elijah the Prophet; third gift = candles; outcome = the wealthy person complies with the command for charity.
- IFA 6936: *The Two Brothers* (Morocco); donor = an old man; outcome = the learned man complies.
- IFA 7597: *The Three Gifts of Elijah the Prophet* (Morocco); donor = Elijah the Prophet.

- IFA 8021 (this vol., no. 51): *The Poor Man Who Became Rich* (Belarus); donor = father; gifts = learning, medicine, music (the last one preferable).
- IFA 8439: *The Three Wishes* (Iraq); donor = Elijah the Prophet.
- IFA 8747: *A Woman of Valor* (Morocco); donor = Elijah the Prophet.
- IFA 9188: *Elijah the Prophet Fulfills the Wishes of Three Men* (Morocco); donor = Elijah the Prophet.
- IFA 9886: *He Who Found a Wife, Found Happiness* (Yemen); donor = Elijah the Prophet.
- IFA 11295: *A Girl from a Good Home* (Yemen);[16] donor = Elijah the Prophet.
- IFA 11678: *He Who Found a Wife Found Happiness* (Yemen);[17] donor = Elijah the Prophet.
- IFA 12098: *The Three Friends* (Bukhara); donor = Elijah the Prophet.
- IFA 12333: *The Three Vagabonds* (Yemen); donor = an old man.
- IFA 13041: *The Gifts of Elijah the Prophet* (Iran);[18] donor = Elijah the Prophet.
- IFA 13660: *The Three Men Who Lost Their Luck* (Yemen); donor = Elijah the Prophet.
- IFA 14052: *Elijah the Prophet and the Three Beggars* (Yemen); donor = Elijah the Prophet.

In the third subform, the donor gives three impoverished individuals a magical object that enables them to restore themselves to their previous positions—at least temporarily. The three individuals are a rich and generous man, a scholar who sold his books, and a righteous God-fearing Jew who escapes his cantankerous wife. The donor gives them, respectively, a magic coin, a magic book, and a magic ring. Upon testing them in later visits, only the God-fearing man, whose wife was no longer quarrelsome, meets the required standard of generosity, hospitality, and *gemilut hasadim*. Published versions of this story are available.[19]

Similarities to Other IFA Tales

Oral versions of the third subform in the IFA are the following:

- IFA 6473: *The Tale about Three Men* (Turkey);[20] donor = Elijah the Prophet.
- IFA 13369: *Elijah the Prophet Gives Three Gifts* (Morocco); donor = Elijah the Prophet.
- IFA 14569: *Elijah the Prophet and the Three Jews* (Morocco); donor = Elijah the Prophet.

Exemplary Tales

The narrators of such tales as described here applied the functions, motives, and roles seen in fantastic tales, as defined and articulated by Propp,[21] to ethical didactic purposes. Within the Hasidic world, the best-known storyteller who followed these literary principles was Rabbi Nahman of Bratslav (1772–1810), who infused his stories with allegory and mystical meanings. An edition of his tales[22] and a biography[23] are available. However, the literary tradition of transforming the fantastic into exemplary tales preceded Rabbi Nahman and is not unique to the Hasidic narrative tradition.

Folktale Types

- 110 (Eberhard and Boratav) "*Hizir und die Drei Brüdere*" (Hizir[24] and the Three Brothers).
- 550 (Andreev) "*Ivan-Tsarvich i seryi volk*" (Tsarevich Ivan and the Gray Wolf).
- 550 (Krzyzanowski) "*Ptak Ztotopióry*" (The Golden Bird).
- 550A "Only One Brother Grateful" (old ed. only).
- 550A (El-Shamy) "Only One Brother Grateful."
- 750D "Three Brothers Each Granted a Wish by an Angel Visitor."
- 750D "God (St. Peter) and the Three Brothers" (new ed.).
- 750D (Haboucha) "Three Brothers Each Granted a Wish by an Angel."
- 750D (Jason) "Three Brothers Each Granted a Wish by an Angel."
- 750D (Krzy_anowski) "*Pan Bóg Go_ciem*" (The Lord [Is] a Visitor).
- *841 (Marzolph) "*Das Schicksal Liegt Allein Bei Gott*" (Fate Is with God Alone).

Folktale Motifs

- D1271 "Magic fire."
- D1500.1.2.2 "Magic healing ashes."
- *D2082.3 "Magic glance reduces estate to ashes."
- *D2082.4 "Magic glance reduces flour mill to ashes."
- F541.1.1 "Eyes flash fire."
- H1552 "Tests of generosity."
- H1564 "Test of hospitality."
- J151 "Wisdom from old person."
- cf. J751.1 "Truth the best policy."
- K1816.9.1 "Wise men disguised as peasants."
- K1817.1 "Disguise as beggar."
- N825.2 "Old man helper."
- P320 "Hospitality."
- P336 "Poor person makes great effort to entertain guests."
- Q1.1 "Gods (saints) in disguise reward hospitality and punish inhospitality."
- Q2 "Kind and unkind."
- Q40 "Kindness rewarded."
- Q42 "Generosity rewarded."

- Q45 "Hospitality rewarded."
- Q111.2 "Riches as reward (for hospitality)."
- Q292 "Inhospitality punished."
- Q292.1. "Inhospitality to saint (god) punished."
- W11 "Generosity."
- Z71.1 "Formulaic number: three."

——————— **Notes** ———————

1. L. Rabinowitz, *"Gemilut Hasadim"*; and Ben-Sasson and Levitats, "Charity."
2. Haney, *Russian Wondertales*, 2:296–300 no. 354 (designated as tale type 654 "The Three Brothers").
3. Dawkins, *Modern Greek Folktales*, 415–419 no. 70; and Megas, *Folktales of Greece*, 134–136 no. 42.
4. Op. cit.
5. Op. cit.
6. Winsted, "The Self-Sacrificing Child."
7. Published in El-Shamy, *Folktales of Egypt*, 128–132 no. 21. For other Arab versions, see Basset, *Mille et un contes*, 3:500–501 no. 302.
8. Higger, *"Pirkei de Rabbi Eliezer"*; G. Friedlander, *Pirkê de Rabbi Eliezer* (The chapters of Rabbi Eliezer the Great), 215–219 (chap. 30); and D. Börner-Klein, *Pirke de-Rabbi Elieser*, 341–345 (chap. 30).
9. Schussman, "Abraham's Visits to Ishmael."
10. *The Exempla of the Rabbis*, 17 (44), 131–132, 248 no. 355.
11. *Ma'aseh Book*, 1:313–316 no. 157; anthologized in Bin Gorion, *Mimekor Yisrael*, 3:1225–1226 no. 67 (1976 ed.) and 430–431 no. 221 (1990 ed.).
12. El-Shamy, op. cit.
13. Summarized in Jason, "Elijah in the Israel Folktale Archives"; published in Rush, *The Book of Jewish Women's Tales*, 163–166 no. 42.
14. Published in D. Noy, *Jewish-Iraqi Folktales*, 118–120 no. 57; and Schram, *Tales of Elijah the Prophet*, 37–42 no. 7.
15. Published in Haviv, *Never Despair*, 21–24 no. 1 (extensive note by Cheichel, 51–54).
16. Published in Gamlieli, *The Chambers of Yemen*, 279–281 no. 92.
17. Published in Y. Yarimi, *Me'Aggadot Teiman* (From the legends of Yemen), no. 14, pp. 59–61.
18. Published in M. Cohen, *Mi-Pi ha-Am* (From folk tradition), 3:23–26 no. 214.
19. The first source text is in Anonymous, *Ma'aseh ha-Kedoshim* (The acts of holy men); anthologized in Bin Gorion, op. cit., 3:1226–1232 no. 68 (1976 ed.) and 431–435 no. 222 (1990 ed.). The second is in Anonymous, *Ma'asiyyot me-ha-Gedolim ve-ha-Zaddikim* (Tales about great and righteous men); anthologized in Ben-Yeḥezki'el, *Sefer ha-Ma'asiyyot* (A book of folktales), 1:341–354. The two source books are identical; see Nigal, *The Hasidic Tale*, 40, 48.
20. Published in Na'anah, *Ozar ha-Ma'asiyyot* (A treasury of tales), 3:466–473.
21. *Morphology of the Folktale*.
22. Band, *Naḥman of Bratslav*.

23. Green, *Tormented Master.*

24. A Muslim saint, the most revered figure among the Turks of Turkey, after Muhammad and the caliph Ali; see Walker and Uysal, "An Ancient God in Modern Turkey."

51

The Poor Man Who Became Rich

Told by Wolf Sosenski to Dinah Behar

A man who was working in the field found a treasure. He took it home and became rich. He moved to a different place, purchased a fine large house, and educated and raised his three children. Eventually he sent them to the big city to learn a profession.

The first became a rabbi. The second studied medicine and became a physician. The third studied music and became a great performing artist. They studied for a number of years, until they grew up, married, and built their own homes.

One day, the mother said, "What do we have from our children? We gave them an education and every fine thing, but now we don't see them. Let's go see how they are."

They took some money and went to visit their sons. The first son, who was a rabbi, greeted them warmly and respectfully and brought them to the school, where his disciples sat immersed in their studies and everyone else, too, was engaged in prayer and Torah study. It was as if the whole world were pious and observant.

As for the second, the physician, they came to him and saw how he cared for his patients in the hospital, a place where everyone lay, dressed in white, moaning and suffering. They watched surgical operations and even saw how people die. Their son the physician showed them everything—it seemed as if the whole world were sick. After they saw how they performed surgery, they [the couple] could not stay any longer and went to visit their third son, the musician.

He took them to the theater, which was brightly lit, sat them in the best seats in the house, and asked them to wait until he came to collect them after everyone had left.

Cheerful music resounded through the hall, the atmosphere was happy, and there was dancing and singing on stage. That is how the performance began. Then a man with a patriarchal visage and long white beard came on stage. When the play was over they waited for their son to come collect them.

After the audience had dispersed their son came. "Nu," he asked, "did you like it?"

"Nothing could be finer," they replied.

"And did you see the old man?" asked the son.

"Yes," his parents replied, "we were quite surprised to see an old man like that."

The son laughed. "That was me!"

The parents could not believe it, but the son repeated, "Yes, that was me."

Finally they went back home. "We didn't know what to teach our sons," the woman told her husband. "One is wasting his life in a yeshivah,* and one is wasting his life in a hospital. Only the third has it good today. If we were smart we would have sent all of them to be artists."

---

*Jewish school of higher learning.

COMMENTARY FOR TALE 51 (IFA 8021)

Recorded by Dinah Behar from Wolf Sosenski in 1968 in Jerusalem.

Cultural, Historical, and Literary Background

In "brotherhood tales" (*Brüdermärchen*), numbers count. There is a qualitative, not just a quantitative, difference between tales about two, three, or four brothers or about serial siblings. For example, tales about sibling pairs are tales of conflicting opposites that clash in their sexual, economic, or moral interests (motif P251.5.4 "Two brothers as contrasts"). Tales of three or four brothers are stories of contests that also bring about, in particular narrative circumstances, cooperation and mutual help (motifs P251.6.1 "Three brothers" and P251.6.2 "Four brothers"). In tales that involve a greater number of brothers, the youngest or weakest one faces his older siblings and wins (motifs P251.6.3 to P251.6.7 "Six or seven [up to twelve] brothers," H1242 "Youngest brother alone succeeds on quest," and L10 "Victorious youngest son").

Tales about Two Siblings

The most ancient known tale of two brothers is tale type 318 "The Faithless Wife," in which the conflict is sexual. The earliest available example of this tale is the thirteenth-century B.C.E. Egyptian story "The Two Brothers," about Anubis and Bata. The wife of the elder brother, Anubis, attempts to seduce Bata, the younger brother, who lived with them. When Bata did not succumb to her lure, Anubis's wife turned against him, accusing him of trying to rape her. In his rage, Anubis tried to kill his brother, but a sequence of extraordinary occurrences such as a talking cow (motif B211.1.5 "Speaking cow") and a flight (motif D672 "Obstacle flight") saves the younger man. Anubis discovers the truth and kills his wife; Bata marries his own beautiful wife, whom the king desires and takes away from him. In revenge, Bata transforms himself into a bull (motif D133.2 "Transformation: man to bull"); when the bull is slaughtered, two trees magically grow from two drops of its blood. The king orders that the trees be cut down, and during the process, a chip of wood enters into Bata's wife and impregnates her. A study of the tale's history and geographic distribution,[1] a literary-historical and religious analysis,[2] a comparative survey,[3] and a discussion of its European analogues have been published.[4]

In tale type 303 "The Twins or Blood Brothers," the magical origin of the brothers mitigates against their conflicts and turns sexual rivalry into a chaste and protective relationship.[5] An example from Yiddish folktales is the story *The Orphan Boys*,[6] in which the two brothers are not in opposition; each is granted a magical gift that helps him win a king's daughter (tale types 610 "The Healing Fruit" and 891A "The Princess from the Tower Recovers Her Husband").

Tale type 318 "The Faithless Wife" has a biblical representation in the story of Joseph and Potiphar's wife (Genesis 39), in which the fraternal opposition is transformed into a conflict of class, age, and ethnicity between an older Egyptian master and a younger Hebrew servant. Studies of this tale are available.[7]

Other examples of rivalry between two brothers are the biblical narratives of Cain and Abel (Genesis 4:1–16) and Jacob and Esau (Genesis 27). The talmudic-midrashic literature contains expansions and interpretations of these stories, further illustrating the narrative pattern of pairs of brothers.[8]

The theme of sibling contrasts is rather sparse in medieval Jewish tales; and in modern recordings these stories are concerned with oppositional pairs of rich–poor, wise–fool, and kind–unkind.

Tales of Economic Contrast

Several versions of tales about two brothers follow the plot line of tale type 613 "Two Travelers (Truth and Falsehood)," which was studied by Christiansen.[9] However, in most of the versions that Jews tell or preserve in books, the two main characters are brothers rather than accidental travelers (there is at least one non-Jewish variant that involves brothers). A tale type that focuses on the economic distinction between brothers is 735 "The Rich Man's and the Poor Man's Fortune." Versions of both tale types were and are current in Jewish narrative traditions.[10] There is another version of this tale in the IFA : tale IFA 3598 *Where Is Hell Located?* (Morocco).[11]

Other Contrasts

Other tales of two brothers reveal a contrast in intelligence involving either tale type 480 "The Spinning-Woman by the Spring. The Kind and Unkind Girls" (with male characters)[12] or tale type 1696 "What Should I Have Said (Done)?"[13]

Another common tale of brothers focuses on a contrast in attitude.[14] In a typical tale, the wise brother is heartless, and the foolish brother is kind; each is rewarded according to his attitude.[15] Such stories involve tale type 503 "The Gifts of the Little People."

Tales about Three and Four Siblings

Tales about three and four brothers are absent from the Hebrew Bible and are rare in talmudic-midrashic and medieval narrative traditions. Therefore, the tale about the three brothers who seek King Solomon's wise counsels—tale type 910 "Precepts Bought or Given Prove Correct"—stands out (see also tale IFA 3576 (vol. 1, no. 38).[16]

Segel[17] published a modern folktale involving three or four brothers. Although that tale belongs to tale type 654 "The Three Brothers," it is about *four* brothers, among whom the musician is the preferred sibling. The tall-tale aspect of this tale type (see below) is absent from Segel's version.

In modern collections as well as in the IFA, stories about three and four brothers have two basic themes: inheritance disputes and the acquisition of a profession or skill.

Inheritance Disputes

The theme of inheritance disputes resonates in biblical stories about brothers, and similar stories of different tale types are represented in the talmudic-midrashic and medieval folk literature. For example, a medieval version of tale type 910 "Precepts Bought or Given Prove Correct" was first printed in 1516 in *Meshalim shel Shelomoh* (Parables of King Solomon).[18] For early narratives of tale type 655 "The Wise Brothers," see the commentary to tale IFA 6402 (vol. 1, no. 40). Stories of tale type 920C "Shooting at the Father's Corpse Test of Paternity" occurs as early as the Babylonian Talmud (*Bava Batra* 58a); in Jewish traditions, such tales involve not three or four but up to ten brothers;[19] for another example, see tale IFA 3188 *Dividing the Inheritance* (Iraq).[20]

Acquisition of a Profession or Skill

The present tale's principal theme is the brothers' acquisition of a profession or skill; however the story is unique in modern Jewish folk tradition and in the IFA. Most of the tales on record involve magical or extraordinary skills, rather than the middle-class professions that the brothers acquire in this tale.

Similarities to Other IFA Tales

Listed according to their typological designations, similar tales in the IFA are as follows. Two tales are classed as tale type 653 "The Four Skillful Brothers":[21]

- IFA 2932: *The Four Lazy Sons* (Iraq).
- IFA 3301: *The White King's Son and the Doe* (Tunisia); the story is framed in other tale types.

Nineteen tales are classed as tale type 653A "The Rarest Thing in the World":

- IFA 88: *The She-Demon's Ring* (Yemen);[22] the story is framed within other tale types.
- IFA 464: *Three Brothers* (Poland).
- IFA 932: *Hassan, the Doe, and the Silent Princess* (Eretz Yisra'el, Arabic); the story is framed within other tale types.
- IFA 936: *Who Deserves to Marry the Girl?* (Eretz Yisra'el, Arabic).
- IFA 1310: *The Youth and Three Birds* (Tunisia);[23] the story is framed within other tale types.
- IFA 4494: *The Princess and Her Mistress* (Egypt).[24]
- IFA 5118: *The Binocular, the Plane, and the Magical Cure* (Egypt).[25]
- IFA 6849: *The White King's Seven Sons* (Morocco); a story of seven sons frames a story of tale type 653A with three brothers.
- IFA 7076: *Three Brothers* (Irani Kurdistan).
- IFA 7287: *Who Is the Winner?* (Erez Isra'el, Christian Arab).
- IFA 7608: *Three Friends of the Same Age Save the Princess* (Eretz Yisra'el, Circassia).
- IFA 7631: *Three Brothers* (Irani Kurdistan).

- IFA 7684: *Inducing the Princess to Talk* (Romania).
- IFA 7784: *How Did People Begin to Cultivate Tobacco and Coffee?* (Eretz Yisra'el, Arabic).
- IFA 7900: *The Rich Man's Son Who Wished to Convert to Christianity* (Morocco).
- IFA 7920: *The Book, the Carpet, and Golden Pitcher* (Irani Kurdistan).
- IFA 11549: *The Youngest Brother Induced the Princess to Speak* (Iran).[26]
- IFA 12709: *Who Will Marry the Girl?* (Morocco).
- IFA 13870: *The Sons Who Did Not Obey Their Father* (Morocco).

Tale Type 1525 "The Master Thief"

Related to the acquisition of a profession or skill is tale type 1525 "The Master Thief," which occurs in eastern European Jewish tradition. For example, a story in Lehman[27] follows the pattern of typical tales of two brothers. After a contrast in intelligence, two of the brothers share a single characteristic. A study of such tales in Jewish tradition is available.[28]

Similarities to Other IFA Tales

- IFA 104: *The Master Thief* (Yemen).[29]
- IFA 3627: *The Master Thief* (Iraq).
- IFA 8449: *The Master Thief* (Iraq).

Traditional Basis of the Tale

The present tale, the only version of tale type 654 "The Three Brothers" in the IFA, draws on two traditions. On the one hand, its early representations, as G. Thomas[30] correctly observed, occurred in the European tall-tale tradition, particularly in the stories of Philippe D'Alcripe (Philippe le Picard; sixteenth century). A biographical and bibliographical discussion of D'Alcripe is available.[31] In Italy, a version of this tale type appeared in print in the sixteenth century in the *Piacevoli Notti* (1550–1553),[32] and a story about five brothers whose poor father sent them to learn a trade appeared in *Lo Cunto de li Cunti* (1634–1636), or as it was later known, *Il Pentamerone* (1674).[33] The tale is also known in the later French tradition.[34] The Brothers Grimm[35] recorded it from oral tradition, as told by Ferdinand Siebert. A more general discussion on the theme of brotherhood tales has been published.[36]

On the other hand, the present tale draws on non-European tradition as well. The text lacks the tall-tale aspects that dominate the European representation of tale type 654, and the acquisition of a profession is not competitive among the brothers but rather a demonstration of parental nurturing.

The complex question of the origin and social relevance of this story is an example of a rather common explanatory challenge in folklore, pitting functional theories against comparative theories. Functionally, the choice of professions—physician, rabbi, and musician—may reflect a society in transition, in which medicine and music become realistic career options for Jewish youth along with the more traditional choice of rabbi. During the nineteenth century, the educational opportunities that became open, ever so slowly, to Jews enabled them to acquire professions that were viable in urban society.[37] Indeed, as the story suggests and as historical-sociological studies indicate, medicine and music served as career paths that enabled young Jews to achieve a satisfactory degree of social mobility beyond the tradition boundaries.

A comparative examination, however, reveals that similar career choices existed in Asian traditions. For example, Ting[38] indicated that in the Chinese narrative tradition, the brothers in this tale type learn, accumulatively, eight professions: hunting, beekeeping, barrel making, selling candies, fertilizing farms, weeping, playing music, and becoming a useless pharisee (tale type 654* [Ting] "The Smart Brothers"). One particular tale reflects an even greater similarity. In the opening episode in the story *Three Brothers Learn through Worldly Experiences*,[39] the father sends his three sons to learn professions. They respectively learn to be a coppersmith, a businessman, and a musician. The latter is initially rejected but is later recognized as the most successful of the three.

Folktale Types

- 654 "The Three Brothers."
- 654 "The Three Agile Brothers" (new ed.).
- 654 (Andreev) "Tri iskusnyk bruta" (Three Skillful Brothers).
- cf. 750D "Three Brothers Each Granted a Wish by an Angel Visitor."
- cf. 750D "God (St. Peter) and the Three Brothers" (new ed.).

Folklore Motifs

- B211.1.5 "Speaking cow."
- D133.2 "Transformation: man to bull."
- D672 "Obstacle flight."
- cf. H1210.1 "Quest assigned by father."
- N135.2.1 "Discovery of treasure brings luck."
- N511 "Treasure in ground."
- N530 "Discovery of treasure."
- N534 "Treasure discovered by accident."
- N550 "Unearthing hidden treasure."
- P150 "Rich men."
- *P165 "Poor men."
- P210 "Husband and wife."
- P230 "Parents and children."
- P233 "Father and son."
- P251 "Brothers."
- P251.6.1 "Three brothers."

- P424 "Physician."
- *P426.4 "Rabbi."
- P428 "Musician."

---------- **Notes** ----------

1. Liungman, *Sagan om Bata och Anubis och den Orientalisk-europeiska undersagans ursprung.*
2. Hollis, *The Ancient Egyptian Story "Tale of Two Brothers."*
3. Horálek, "*Brüdermärchen.*"
4. Gehrts, *Das Märchen und das Opfer,* 39–61.
5. Ranke, *Die Zwei Brüder.*
6. B. Weinreich, *Yiddish Folktales,* 93–97 no. 34.
7. Goldman, *The Wiles of Women/The Wiles of Men*; Kugel, *In Potiphar's House*; and Yohannan, *Joseph and Potiphar's Wife in World Literature.*
8. Ginzberg, *The Legends of the Jews,* 1:105–113, 1:311–315, 1:328–340, 1:377–395, 5:132–142, 5:270–274, 5:281–286, 5:303–313.
9. *The Tale of the Two Travellers or the Blinded Man.*
10. Cahan, *Yidishe folksmasiyyot* (Yiddish folktales), 39–41 no. 9 (tale type 735), 143–147 no. 28 (tale type 676 "Open Sesame") (1931 ed.) and 75–77 no. 20, 173–177 no. 39 (1940 ed.). For an English translation of the first of these tales, see B. Weinreich, *Yiddish Folktales,* 10–11 no. 4. See also Cahan, *Jewish Folklore,* 107–113 nos. 4–7 (no. 4 is tale type 735; no. 5 is tale type 735A "Bad Luck Imprisoned"). For a Hebrew translation of nos. 4 and 5, see Zfatman, *Ma'asiyyot kesem* (Magical tales), 223–237 nos. 21–22; for an English translation of no. 5, see B. Weinreich, op. cit., 26–27 no. 14. See also B. Weinreich, op. cit., 98–100 no. 35 (tale types 613 "The Two Travelers [Truth and Falsehood]" and 461 "Three Hairs from the Devil's Beard, III The Questions").
11. Published in D. Noy, *Jewish Folktales from Morocco,* 121–124 no. 66; and D. Noy, *Moroccan Jewish Folktales,* 160–163 no. 66.
12. Cahan, *Yidishe folksmasiyyot* (Yiddish folktales), 60–67 no. 17 (1940 ed.); and B. Weinreich, op. cit., 37–43 no. 17.
13. Cahan, *Yidishe folksmasiyyot* (Yiddish folktales), 12–15 no. 2 (1931 ed.) and 18–21 no. 3 (1940 ed.); and B. Weinreich, op. cit., 57–58 no. 25.
14. Cahan, *Yidishe folksmasiyyot* (Yiddish folktales); and B. Weinreich, op. cit.
15. B. Weinreich, op. cit., 120–122 no. 41.
16. Bin Gorion, *Mimekor Yisrael,* 61–63 no. 35 (1990 ed.).
17. "*Der König und seine vier Söhne.*"
18. Bin Gorion, op. cit.; see also the commentary to tale IFA 3576 (vol. 1, no. 38).
19. Bin Gorion, op. cit., 200 no. 110; and cf. Bin Gorion, op. cit., 35–36 no. 22, 457–459 no. 247.
20. Published in D. Noy, *Jewish-Iraqi Folktales,* 120–122 no. 58.
21. Lehman, "*Ganeivim un gneiva*" (Stealers and stealing), 68–72 no. 4; and Zfatman, op. cit., 275–295 no. 26.
22. Published in D. Noy, *Jefet Schwili Erzählt,* 90–98 no. 29.
23. Published in D. Noy, *Jewish Folktales from Tunisia,* 93–98 no. 27.
24. Published in Avitsuk, *The Tree That Absorbed Tears,* 134–137 no. 34.
25. Published in Haimovits, *Faithful Guardians,* 48–50 no. 6.

26. Published in Shenhar and Bar-Itzhak, *Sippurei 'Am me-Bet-She'an* (Folktales from Bet She'an), 67–80 no. 8.

27. Op. cit., 72–75 no. 5; and B. Weinreich, op. cit., 89–93 no. 33 (also tale type 950 "Rhampsinitus").

28. B. Weinreich, "Four Yiddish Variants of the Master Thief Tale."

29. Published in D. Noy, *Jefet Schwili Erzählt*, 284–291 no. 126.

30. *The Tall Tale and Philippe d'Alcripe*, 83, 169–171 no. 1; and D'Alcripe, *La nouvelle fabrique des excellents traicts de verité*, 13–16 no. 1.

31. Schenda, "*Philippe le Picard und seine Nouvelle Fabrique.*"

32. Waters, *The Nights of Straparola*, 2:71–74 (night 7, tale 5).

33. Basile, *The Pentamerone of Giambattista Basile*, 2:139–143.

34. Delarue and Tenèze, *Le conte populaire français*, 2:554–558 (tale type 653 "*Les quatre frères ingénieux*").

35. Grimm and Grimm, *The Complete Fairy Tales*, 443–444 no. 124; Bolte and Polivka, *Anmerkungen zu den Kinder- u. Hausemärchen* 3:10–12 no. 124; Uther, *Grimms Kinder- und Hausmärchen*, 4:237–238 no. 124; Ranke, "*Brüder*"; and S. Thompson, *The Folktale*, 82.

36. Lüthi, "*Bruder, Brüder*"; and Scherf, *Das Märchenlexikon*, 1:132–138.

37. Nathans, *Beyond the Pale*.

38. *A Type Index of Chinese Folktales*, 115.

39. Stuart and Limusishiden, *China's Monguor Minority*, 104–106.

52

The Stolen Ring

TOLD BY ZINDALE NEUMAN TO MEIR NOY

*O*nce there was a king whose precious signet ring had been stolen. This king had a Jew-hating minister named Dayenu. "Your majesty, the Jews are a stiff-necked people," he told the king. "Their ways are crooked, and they consider every means appropriate to enhance their Passover festival, which is coming soon. Even the poor of Israel must celebrate this festival with great pomp and splendor, so there is no doubt that they stole the ring to sell it."

The king took the wicked minister's words to heart. On seder night, he disguised himself and went to the Jewish quarter, hoping to learn what had happened to his ring.

The king stood outside the window of one of the houses, where the seder was being conducted strictly according to procedure. Inside they were singing a song. The master of ceremonies was asking questions, and all of those seated around the table kept answering, *"Dayenu."*

"What are all these questions?" the king asked himself. "They must be about the thief who stole the ring. And the thief is none other than my minister Dayenu! The Jews are indeed a wise and intelligent people."

The king returned to his palace and sent messengers to search the minister's house. Sure enough, the signet ring was found. The shocked minister admitted that he had thought that he could use the signet ring to launch a rebellion and overthrow the king.

The king had his wicked Jew-hating minister executed. "So may all your enemies perish!"* He gave the Jews many presents, and they had light and gladness** and lived in peace and tranquility. And every year after that, the king's treasury paid out *kimha de-Pis'ha*—money to buy matzah with—to all the poor Jews.

---

*Judges 5:31.
**Esther 8:16.

COMMENTARY FOR TALE 52 (IFA 7812)

Recorded from memory by Meir Noy, who heard the story from his father, Zindale Neuman, in Kolomea, Galicia, Poland.[1]

Cultural, Historical, and Literary Background

The present tale is an example of stories that circulated in the oral narrative traditions of several Jewish ethnic groups without relying, to the best of the editor's knowledge, on any earlier print or manuscript versions. The earliest published rendition appeared relatively late in the anonymous collection of Hasidic tales titled *Sefer Sippurei Kedoshim* (1866).[2] Likely, the book was published in Warsaw; but to outsmart the censor, it bears a Leipzig imprint.

The Song "Dayenu"

At the center of the narrative, is a wordplay in bilingual communities—a pun involving a non-Jewish name and a word that stands out in the Jewish Passover liturgy. In Hebrew, the word *dai* (enough, sufficient) has been in common use from biblical times to the modern period, but the particular declensional form "*dayenu*" (first person plural) is not. The word *dai* appears in biblical Hebrew (Malachi 3:10; Proverbs 25:16), but only the Amoraic literature documents the use of the formation "dayenu" (JT *Berakhot* 9:8; *Ta'anit* 3:9; *Megillah* 1:7; *Sanhedrin* 7:19; BT *Berakhot* 16a; *Yevamot* 63a)—once directly in association with a pilgrimage to Jerusalem (BT *Pesahim* 8b).

In any case, the Passover song in which *dayenu* occurs as a refrain is considered to have been composed in the early rabbinical period, before the destruction of the Temple, or in the pre-Maccabean period. L. Finkelstein[3] narrowed down the date of the song's composition to the period between 198 and 167 B.C.E. E. Goldschmidt,[4] however, did not accept Finkelstein's assumptions and intertextual references, pointing out the rabbinical idioms in the song. He dated the song to the last century of the Temple.

The song is a litany—a liturgical form consisting of call and response. It is sung by a leader, and a congregation responds with a refrain. The form itself is used in Psalm 136, known as "The Great Hallel." "*Dayenu*," named after its refrain, consists of fourteen strophes that reveal highlights in Israelite history, from the exodus from Egypt to the construction of the Temple. The song concludes with a summary passage. "Dayenu" is not mentioned in rabbinical literature, though it is possible that the rabbis referred to the song (see JT *Berakhot* 9:8; *Ta'anit* 3:9; BT *Pesahim* 8b). L. Finkelstein[5] proposed several sources for and references to the song, ranging from Nehemiah 9:10–37 to the tannaitic source *Sifrei Devarim*. However, such segments of highlighted historical events point to a shared past tradition rather than an exact textual relationship.

Early Christian sources from the second century may indicate a knowledge of the "Dayenu" litany. Werner[6] considered the Latin "*Improperia*"—the reproaches of the dying Jesus on the Cross against his people—to be "an old anti-Jewish parody of the "Dayenu" of the Passover Haggadah." He suggested that the source of the *Improperia* is the passa-homily *Peri Pascha* of Melito of Sardes (120–185 C.E.).

Such early dates for "Dayenu" in the Passover haggadah are certainly possible, though there is no internal textual evidence for their validation. The mishnah *Pesaḥim* 10, which describes the tannaitic Passover celebration, does not mention the song. The earliest full text of the song occurs in the first medieval haggadah, which is part of the ninth-century *Seder Rav Amram* prepared by Rabbi Amram Gaon, Amram ben Sheshna (d. 875), in response to the request of Rabbi Isaac ben Simeon of Spain.[7] Rabbi Saadiah Gaon (882–942) included "Dayenu" in his prayer book.[8] In an eighteenth-century interpretation of Maimonides' *Mishneh Torah,* Mas'ud Roke'aḥ[9] noted that he had found out in an ancient manuscript written by Rabbi Abraham (Maimonides' son) that Maimonides had sung the song in its current position in the ceremony. Maimonides' contemporary Rabbi Abraham ben David of Posquieres, known as Rabad (1120?–1198), wrote a responsa concerning the song "Dayenu."[10]

On the basis of the lack of pre-Christian evidence for the song and its relatively late incorporation in the Passover ritual, Yuval[11] suggested that the song be considered as part of the Judeo-Christian dialogue and the Jewish response to the Christian charge of Jewish ingratitude.

Family Customs

The current tale, which builds on the apparent oddity of the word *dayenu,* is known in Ashkenazic and Sephardic communities as well as in Jewish communities in Islamic countries. There are at least two testimonies indicating that the story accompanied the seder celebration within the family, serving as a narrative that supplemented the reading of the haggadah. Gilead[12] recalled the tale as being part of the second seder celebration, and Alexander-Frizer[13] recorded a story that includes a description of the grandmother in Shaul Angel-Malachi's family's telling of the story on the eve of Passover. For other such family customs of storytelling associated with common holidays, see the commentary to tale IFA 6306 (this vol., no. 23).

Discovery of the Crime

Although the present tale and its telling are steeped in Jewish tradition, the narrative principle of discovery of the crime through inadvertent knowledge is part of a theme that has worldwide distribution. Such stories are classed as tale type 1641 "Doctor Know-All." The Brothers Grimm recorded a version from Dorothea Viehmann.[14] S. Thompson[15] pointed out that the tale is known in Asia, Africa, Europe, and the Americas and is recorded in ancient Indian tale collections and European jest books.

A version of the present tale was collected by Halperin[16]—not as a joke about Chelm, the town of fools, but as an exotic narrative about a Jewish community in Bakhehisaray, "the capital of the Tatars" in the Crimea.

Similarities to Other IFA Tales

There are other versions of this tale in the IFA, told by narrators from eleven countries. Most of the stories involve the inadvertent discovery of a lost jewel; two such tales, one IFA 9686 and the other published before the establishment of the IFA in 1953,[17] are concerned with averting a blood libel accusation. For discussion of blood libel tales, see the commentaries to tales IFA 10086 (vol. 1, no. 36), IFA 10611 (vol. 3, no. 1), IFA 15347 (vol. 1, no. 15), and IFA 16405 (vol. 1, no. 14).

- IFA 50: *The Fortune Teller's Luck* (Turkey).[18]
- IFA 255: *The Stolen King's Ring* (Yemen).
- IFA 360: *The Confident Rabbi Nahum (Dayenu)* (Poland).
- IFA 969: *A Jew Finds Forty Thieves and Their Head "Dayenu"* (Iraq).
- IFA 1311: *"Go Forth and Study" on Passover Night* (Tunisia).[19]
- IFA 1573: *Passover Seder and the King's Ring* (Iraq).[20]
- IFA 2003: *The King's Ring and the Minister "Dayenu"* (Republic of Georgia).
- IFA 4415: *The Fortune Teller in the Court of Harun al Rashid* (Iraq).[21]
- IFA 5136 (vol. 4, no. 27): *The Know All Rabbi* (Bukhara).
- IFA 5896: *The Passover Seder Miracle* (Tunisia).
- IFA 6526: *Deliverance Will Come from God* (Morocco).
- IFA 6533: *Shlomo Dahan the Shoemaker and the Arab Thief* (Morocco).
- IFA 6799: *The Hasid Who Found the Stolen King's Treasure* (Morocco).[22]
- IFA 7099: *Dayenu* (Central Europe).
- IFA 7571: *Yehudah the Fortune Teller* (Morocco).
- IFA 8483: *A Jewish Family in Salonika* (Eretz Yisra'el, Sephardic).
- IFA 9112: *Dayenu* (Tangier, Morocco).[23]
- IFA 9177: *The Thief Who Was Captured on Passover Night* (Iraq).
- IFA 9686: *Dayenu* (Iran).
- IFA 11671: *The Lord Will Open for You His Bounteous Store (Deuteronomy 28:12)* (Yemen).[24]
- IFA 12046: *The Minister "Dayenu" Stole a Diamond from the King's Crown* (Ukraine).[25]
- IFA 13058: *A Jew Hater Called "Dayenu"* (Iraq).[26]

Folktale Types

- cf. 311 (Eberhard and Boratav) *"Der Oberastrologe"* (The Serious Astrologer).
- 1641*D (IFA) *"Dayenu."*
- 1641*D (Haboucha) *"Dayenu."*
- 1641*D (Jason) *"Dayenu."*

Folklore Motifs

- K420 "Thief loses his goods or is detected."
- K1812 "King in disguise."
- K1965 "Sham wise man."
- K2127 "False accusation of theft."
- K2248 "Treacherous minister."
- N275 "Criminal confesses because he thinks himself accused."
- N610 "Accidental discovery of crime."
- N611.1 "Criminal accidentally detected: 'that is the first'—sham wise man."
- cf. N688 "What is in the dish: 'poor crab.'"
- P10 "Kings."
- P110 "Royal ministers."
- *P476 "Thief."
- P715.1 "Jews."
- *P715.2 "A hater of Jews."
- Q114 "Gifts as reward."
- Q411 "Death as punishment."
- V75.1 "Passover."
- *V75.1.1 "Seder, the Passover eve ceremonial dinner."

Notes

1. First published in M. Noy, *East European Jewish Cante Fables*, 31–32 no. 6.

2. For a recent edition, see Nigal, *Sefer Sippurei Kedoshim* (A book of saints' tales), 8, 45–47 no. 11. The tale was anthologized from an earlier edition in M. Ben-Yeḥezki'el, *Sefer ha-Ma'asiyyot* (A book of folktales), 2:132–138.

3. "Pre-Maccabean Documents in the Passover Haggadah."

4. *The Passover Haggadah*, 50.

5. Op. cit., 3–5.

6. "Melito of Sardes," esp. 194, 199; Werner, "*Zur Textgeschichte der Improperia*"; Hall, "Melito in the Light of the Passover Haggadah"; and Lieu, *Image and Reality*, 199–240.

7. D. Goldschmidt, *Seder Rav Amram Gaon*, 115.

8. I. Davidson et al., *Siddur R. Saadja Gaon*, 143–144.

9. *Ma'aseh Roke'aḥ*, 252b.

10. Sherwin, "Original Sin."

11. "*Two Nations in Your Womb*," 85–87.

12. "*Dayeynu*" (note).

13. *The Beloved Friend-and-a-Half*, 122–123. For another version of this tale, see Angel-Malachi, *Vidas en Jerusalem*, 97–100.

14. *The Complete Fairy Tales*, 361–362 no. 98. For bibliographical information, see Bolte and Polivka, *Anmerkungen zu den Kinder- u. Hausmärchen*, 2:401–413 no. 98; Uther, *Grimms Kinder- und Hausmärchen*, 4:188 no. 98; Dömötör, "*Doktor Allwissend*"; and Tauscher, *Volksmärchen aus dem Jeyporeland*, 82–84, 181 no. 36.

15. *The Folktale,* 144–145.
16. *Ḥelem ve-ḥakhameha* (Helem and its wise men), 151–157.
17. Gilead, op. cit.
18. Published in T. Alexander and Noy, *The Treasure of Our Fathers*, 181–184 no. 60.
19. Published in D. Noy, *Jewish Folktales from Tunisia,* 98–101 no. 28.
20. Published in Agassi, *Ḥusham mi-Bagdad* (Husham of Baghdad), 67–68.
21. Published in D. Noy, *Jewish-Iraqi Folktales,* 170–173. Note that Harun al Rashid was the caliph of Baghdad from 764? to 809.
22. Published in Estin, *Contes et fêtes Juives,* 205–208 no. 45.
23. Published in Alexander and Noy, op. cit., 91–93 no. 13.
24. Published in Yarimi, *Me'Aggadot Teiman* (From the legends of Yemen), 121–122 no. 38.
25. Published in Warnbud, *Neḥemyah Ba'al Guf* (Nehemyah the Heavy-Set), 127.
26. Published in M. Cohen, *Mi-Pi ha-Am* (From folk tradition), 2:73–74, 127–128 no. 184.

53

The Money Hidden in the Cemetery

TOLD BY ESTHER WEINSTEIN TO YEHUDIT GUT-BURG

A merchant traveled to a large city to buy goods. He arrived there late Friday afternoon, shortly before sunset. He went at once to the bathhouse and put on his Sabbath finery. But what could he do with his money? You're not allowed to keep money in your pocket on the Sabbath. But to whom could he entrust it? He didn't know a soul in town. But how does the saying go? "A learned Jew will always find an idea." The merchant decided to bury his money in the local Christian cemetery. After all, who goes there on the Sabbath?

So the Jew went to the cemetery, dug a small hole near one of the graves, buried his money, and marked the hiding place. In his heart, he was quite confident that no one would steal his money.

Thus he came, all clean and polished, to the house of the *rebbe*,[*] who greeted him cordially. The merchant stayed with the Hasidim until late at night. They didn't go to bed until after midnight.

No sooner had the merchant fallen asleep then he dreamed about his late father: "Why did you put your money next to the grave of a gentile? Go move your money away from there!"

The merchant woke up. It was just a dream. He turned over and fell asleep. Again his father was standing by his bed. "Get up quickly!" he ordered. "Time is short. Go get your money! I command you! Get dressed, go to the cemetery, take out the money, and bring it to the *rebbe*'s house. Your money will be safe there."

The merchant got up and dressed, poured water on his hands, washed his face, said the *Modeh Ani*,[**] opened the door quietly, and started out. The street was quiet and still; everyone was sleeping peacefully.

With rapid steps, he made his way to the cemetery, found the hiding place, dug up his money, put it in his pockets, and turned to go back to his

---

[*] A Hasidic rabbi.
[**] The prayer said by Jews when they first wake up, even before getting out of bed and washing their hands.

lodgings. Just then a gentile appeared. The man looked at the Jew in astonishment. "What are you doing here so early?" he asked. "Isn't today the Sabbath for you Jews?"

"I have to pray very early," replied the Jew, "so I took a shortcut."

The Jew watched what the gentile did. What did he see? The man was digging alongside the grave, precisely where the money had been buried. The gentile dug and dug. It was obvious that he was searching for something. When he didn't find it he became furious and ran after the Jew. "Where does your rabbi live?" he asked. "I want to ask him something."

"Follow me, if you like. I'm going there too."

As they walked together, the gentile asked the Jew, "Does your rabbi know how to interpret dreams?"

"I have no idea. Come ask him, and you'll find out."

The two reached the *rebbe*'s house. "What are you doing here, Ivan?" one of the Jews asked the uninvited guest.

"I want to ask your rabbi something."

"Please come in, then."

Ivan entered, and they offered him a chair. Then the *rebbe* himself came into the room. "What do you want?" he asked the gentile.

"Rabbi," Ivan replied, "I had a dream that my father came to me and said, 'Go to the cemetery first thing in the morning. Next to my grave, where the earth was turned over recently, you'll find a large sum of money. Take it and you'll be very rich. Buy an estate and a house and you'll be a landowner.' My father wouldn't let me sleep all night. He came back in my dreams three times, insisting that I go get the money. Finally I got up early, went to the cemetery, and dug. I searched until I was worn out, but I didn't find anything. So I've come to ask you to interpret my dream. Why didn't I find the money?"

The *rebbe* stood up and answered him. "The money that was buried next to your father's grave didn't belong to you. That's why you didn't find it. One has to work to make money. And because you are an honest man, not a thief, not a murderer, not a highwayman, you didn't find it. You are an honest man, and God will be your help."

Ivan began to believe in the God of Israel and finally became a Jew. The *rebbe* gave him the name Abraham. He studied Torah with the *rebbe*, like a child, until he himself became a scholar. His wife and children, too, followed his lead, and they all lived a happy and contented life.

COMMENTARY FOR TALE 53 (IFA 4032)

Recorded by Yehudit Gut-Burg from her mother, Esther Weinstein, who learned the tale from her father, Rabbi Ḥaim Salz, in 1962 in Safed.[1]

Cultural, Historical, and Literary Background

Travelers, itinerant merchants, pilgrims, and knights in any society would have had difficulty ensuring the safety of large sums of money while they were away from home. Among Jews, this problem was magnified because they were not permitted to carry money on their person on the Sabbath. Commensurate with this real-life issue in antiquities and the Middle Ages were tales in both European and Asian traditions about hiding treasure, deceptive bankers, and recovering money—by luck, alertness, or ruse.

The narratives on this theme revolve around three hiding spots for the money: a cemetery, the home of an entrusted person (rabbi, community leader, or innkeeper), and a honey jar. Corresponding to the hiding places, there are three methods of recovering the treasure: alertness, ruse, and through the courts. In these tales, there is a consistent association between hiding money in a honey jar and recovering it in court; however, the other methods of concealment and return of the money are variable, depending on the number and identity of the characters in the story. Accordingly, on the basis of known tales, it is possible to distinguish four subtypes in the Jewish narrative tradition.

1. The treasure is hidden in the cemetery.
2. The treasure is on deposit with the rabbi, community leader, or innkeeper (tale types 1617 "Unjust Banker Deceived into Delivering Deposits" and 3738 [Tubach] "Philip, King, godfather of").
3. The stolen hidden treasure is recovered by ruse (motifs K1667 "Unjust banker deceived into delivering deposits by making him expect even larger" and K1667.1.1 "Retrieving the buried treasure").
4. The coins are in the jar of honey, oil, or pickles (motifs J1176.3 "Gold pieces in the honey-pot" and J1655.3 "Coins concealed in jar of oil [pickles]").

Treasure in the Cemetery or on Deposit

Tales in which the money is either hidden in a cemetery or given to a trusted person were very popular, and there is ample evidence of their circulation in European and Near Eastern folklore traditions in the Middle Ages. However, as in the case of tale IFA 6402 (vol. 1, no. 40), the earliest known documented version in Jewish tradition is found in the Babylonian Talmud (*Yoma* 83b); another allusion to such a tale is in JT *Berakhot* 2:3.[2] This version involves three travelers who are divided into two groups; each hides and recovers the money following subtypes 1 and 2, respectively:

> Also, R. Meir and R. Judah and R. Jose were on a journey together. (R Meir always paid close attention to people's names, whereas R. Judah and R. Jose paid no such attention to them). Once as they came to a certain place, they looked for a lodging, and as they were given it, they said to him [the innkeeper]: What is your name?—He replied: Kidor. Then he [R. Meir] said: Therefrom it is evident that he is a wicked man, for it is said: *For a generation* [ki-dor] *very forward are they* [Deuteronomy 33:14]. R. Judah and R. Jose entrusted their purses to him [it was on the eve of the Sabbath]; R. Meir did not entrust his purse to him, but went and placed it on the grave of that man's father. Thereupon the man had a vision in his dream [saying]: Go, take the purse lying at the head of this man! In the morning he [the innkeeper] told them [the rabbis] about it, saying: This is what appeared to me in my dream. They replied to him: There is no substance in the dream of the Sabbath night. R. Meir went, waited there all day, and then took the purse with him. In the morning they [the rabbis] said to him: 'Give us our purses.' He said: There never was such a thing! R. Meir then said to them: Why don't you pay attention to people's names? They said: Why have you not told us [before], Sir? He answered: I consider this but a suspicion, I would not consider that a definite presumption! Thereupon they took him [the host] into a shop [and gave him wine to drink]. Then they saw lentils on his moustache. They went to his wife and gave her that as a sign, and thus obtained their purses and took them back. Whereupon he went and killed his wife.

Other versions, or allusions to them, are in the Babylonian Talmud and in the medieval books that drew on the talmudic-midrashic literature. Among them are the ninth-century *Pesikta Rabbati*[3] and a twelfth-century manuscript from Aleppo[4] (both are of subtype 2). An examination of these and other relevant stories is available,[5] as is a discussion of such tales in relation to the "Susanna" story.[6]

In the eleventh century, Rabbi Nissim of Kairouan of Tunisia rendered a similar tale in Arabic (using subtypes 1 and 2).[7] Later, probably around the fourteenth century, the tale was copied by Eleazer ben Asher Ha-Levi into a manuscript known as *Sefer ha-ma'assim*[8] (also subtypes 1 and 2). Yiddish translations with the same subtypes are in the 1602 *Ma'aseh Book*[9] and in an earlier and shorter collection of Yiddish tales;[10] the story is also found in nineteenth- and twentieth-century anthologies.[11]

Another version was told by Enan to Joseph ibn Meir Zabara in the twelfth-century *Sefer Sha'ashu'im* (The book of delights). That tale involves deception and recovery of a necklace through ruse and a court appearance; however, it is a story about a fraudulent business deal rather than an untrustworthy banker.[12] Additional bibliographical discussion is available.[13]

Treasure on Deposit and Recovered by Ruse

Subtypes 2 and 3 (motif K1667 "Unjust banker deceived into delivering deposits by making him expect even larger") were popular in European medieval literature, and such stories generally involve a Muslim pilgrim who briefly stays over in Egypt on his way to Mecca. The earliest tales are from the twelfth-century *Disciplina Clericalis*.[14] In the next century, the Jewish physician Isaac ben Solomon ibn Sahula included it in his book of fables,[15] and an almost identical version can be found in the early-fourteenth-century *Gesta Romanorum*.[16]

Around the same time in Italy, Boccaccio (1313–1375) included a romantic-commercial version of the tale in his *Decameron*[17] (motif K1667). The tale that Franco Sacchetti (1332–1400), a Boccaccio imitator, included in his *Il Trecentonovelle*[18] (written in the 1390s) was based on motif K1667.1.1. In a comparative annotation, Lee[19] focused on this motif, documenting its popularity in medieval European, Asian, and Near Eastern traditions.[20]

This subtype was popular in medieval Jewish tradition as well; for example, a tale with motif K1667.1.1 is found in a printed edition of *Midrash Aseret ha-dibrot* (The midrash of the Ten Commandments).[21] The manuscripts and printed versions of this midrash include different numbers and selections of tales.[22] Already the first printed edition (Verona 1647) includes this tale.[23] In one anthologized version of the story, King Solomon advises a merchant on how to recover his money.[24] This variation has analogues in medieval Near Eastern traditions in *The Tale of the Melancholist and the Sharper*.[25] Clouston[26] recorded a rendition in which the money is discovered when a person digs out tree roots for medical purposes.

In modern Jewish Hasidic tradition, subtype 2 and motif K1667 combine in a narrative of litigation involving the unjust banker, the depositor, and the community rabbi. The rabbi employs a ruse to bring the unjust banker, a prominent community and business leader, into the rabbinical court.[27] In another version, the banker is not unjust but simply dies, and his bereaved widow and children have no knowledge of the deposit.[28] The rabbi solves the problem by inviting the deceased banker to court so that his spirit can reveal that he has left the money tucked in the book he was studying before he died.

Modern parodies of this form that are also anti-rabbinical satire exist. In these stories, the rabbi, or an allegedly unjust banker or friend, mockingly does not side with the victim who lost his money, "just to show him what kind of a rabbi [people] we have in our community."[29]

Similarities to Other IFA Tales

This form of the tale is currently in oral tradition in tales IFA 4334, IFA 9778, IFA 9916, IFA 11663, IFA 12161, IFA 12529, IFA 13772, IFA 13908 (this vol., no. 60), and IFA 13909 (this vol., no. 61). In two tales from Tunisia, the story of an unjust banker became a narrative of ethnic conflict in which the banker is a Christian monk or priest instead of a Muslim.

- IFA 1943: *The Jewish Butcher and the Monk* (Tunisia).
- IFA 2304: *Children Offer a Solution* (Tunisia); tale type = 920*E (IFA) "Children's Judgment."
- IFA 2994: *The Tale about the Jar Case* (Yemen);[30] child judge = Rambam.
- IFA 3427: *Judah Finds the Owner of the Coins* (Afghanistan); tale type = 920*E (IFA) "Children's Judgment."

Other tales involve a ruse in which a third person helps the deceived individual. He pretends that he would like to deposit a very large sum of money with the unreliable banker. The original deceived person appears on the scene while the banker is talking to the pretender; and the banker, wishing to receive the larger amount of money from the third person, agrees to return the deposit to the deceived individual. Once the ruse succeeds, both people leave the banker alone. As noted, such a ruse occurs in medieval literary texts and in some tales in the IFA.

- IFA 1344: *The Deposit with the Hajj* (Yemen).[31]
- IFA 1944: *If a Lame Man Defeated You, Escape to the Red-Headed Who Will Save You* (Tunisia).[32]
- IFA 3068: *The Unjust Pawn Broker* (Egypt).

Treasure in a Container

Jewish narrators associated the tales in which the treasure was hidden in a container with the "wise child" narrative cycles. Initially, these stories were told about the judicial wisdom of King Solomon as a youngster; later such tales featured other figures of local or national fame. The tale first appeared in print in *Meshalim shel Shlomoh ha-Melekh* (Parables of King Solomon), a collection that was published together with *Divrei ha-Yamim shel Moshe Rabbenu* (The chronicle of Moses), M. Gaster summarized the tale in English,[33] and it has been anthologized.[34] Studies of these medieval collections are available.[35] A seventeenth-century Yiddish translation of the tale is in the *Mayseh bukh*.[36]

A century later, a similar narrative about a local hero as the wise child was part of a complex foundation legend of the Jewish community in Prague. The Yiddish story was known as *Ma'aseh Prague*. In this tale, the episode is combined with subtype 2 (tale type 1617). The book, now rare,[37] was published by two women, probably around 1705. A discussion of the tale has been published.[38]

Similar stories, with Solomon or David as the wise child, continued to be printed in Hebrew folk books from a variety of communities. In the seventeenth century, it was included in *Hibbur Ma'asiyot*, and in the nineteenth century, it was anthologized by Ḥuzin.[39] Further bibliographical references can be found.[40]

Motif J1176.3 "Gold pieces in the honey-pot" was known in Europe by the thirteenth century in a text attributed to Etienne de Besancon (d. 1294).[41] The tale is also part of the Arabian Nights tradition; however, it does not occur in early texts. Instead, it is one of the "orphan" stories told to Antoine Galland by the Maronite Hanna and for which no other Arabian source is known.[42]

Similarities to Other IFA Tales

The following versions of this narrative subtype include a variety of characters who act as the judge; in all of them, a trial serves as the narrative resolution.

- IFA 6841: *King Solomon's First Case* (Tunisia).
- IFA 7072: *The Rambam's Wisdom* (Yemen).
- IFA 9138: *Children's Wisdom* (Syria); tale type = 920*E (IFA) "Children's Judgment."
- IFA 11099: *King Solomon and the Coins Trial* (Turkey).
- IFA 12077: *The Pilgrim's Trial* (Yemen); tale type = 920*E (IFA) "Children's Judgment."
- IFA 13685: *The Oil and the Perfume* (Yemen); tale type = 920*E (IFA) "Children's Judgment."

The tales in the following group are very popular among several Jewish ethnic groups and fall into several of the subtypes listed earlier. There are more than twenty versions on deposit in the IFA.

Treasure Hidden in the Cemetery

- IFA 1513: *Never Believe a Gentile* (Morocco).[43]
- IFA 3421: *There Is No Trust in a Gentile* (Iraq).[44]
- IFA 4017: *Don't Trust the Arabs Even Forty Years after Their Death* (Tunisia).
- IFA 4405: *The Corpse in the Grave* (Tunisia).
- IFA 4887: *Three Learned Men: Don't Trust a Gentile for Forty Years* (Turkey).
- IFA 6202: *The Sly Grocer* (Libya);[45] subtypes = 1 and 3.
- IFA 6806: *There Is No Trust in the Gentiles, Even after They Are Dead for Forty Years* (Morocco).
- IFA 7662: *The Clever Beggar Recovers His Stolen Money* (Iraq);[46] subtypes = 1 and 3.
- IFA 7720: *The Clever Washwoman* (Iraqi Kurdistan).[47]
- IFA 8587: *There Is No Confidence in Arabs, Even after Forty Years (Rabbi Abraham ibn Ezra)* (Morocco).
- IFA 9123: *King Solomon's Judgment and the Merchants* (Iraqi Kurdistan).
- IFA 11183: *Only a Wise and Clever Nation* (Syria).[48]
- IFA 11187: *The Wise Washwoman* (Iraqi Kurdistan).[49]
- IFA 11253: *There Should Not Be Any Trust in a Gentile* (Morocco).
- IFA 11500: *There Is No Trust in a Gentile Even after He Has Been Forty Years Dead* (Morocco).
- IFA 11867: *Do Not Trust a Gentile Even If He Is in Grave* (Iraq).
- IFA 11882: *There Is No Trust in a Gentile Even after He Has Been Forty Years Dead* (Eretz Yisra'el, Sephardic).
- IFA 11901: *There Is No Trust in a Gentile Even after He Has Been Forty Years Dead* (Morocco).

- IFA 11963: *There Is No Trust in a Gentile Even after He Has Been Forty Years Dead* (Tunisia).
- IFA 13294: *The Jew and the Treasure* (Iraq).
- IFA 13566: *There Is No Trust in a Gentile Even after He Has Been Forty Years Dead* (Morocco).
- IFA 13882: *Do Not Trust a Gentile* (Morocco).

Treasure on Deposit

The following tales encompass tale types 1617 "Unjust Banker Deceived into Delivering Deposits," 3367 (Tubach) "Money Sack Recovered from Burgher," and 3738 (Tubach) "Philip, King, Godfather of."

- IFA 4334: *The Shepherd and His Flock* (Poland and Hungary).[50]
- IFA 4887: *Three Learned Men: Don't Trust a Gentile for Forty Years* (Turkey); subtypes = 1 and 3 (as in the talmudic version).
- IFA 6217: *The Qadi and the Clever Woman* (Eretz Yisra'el, Ashkenazic).
- IFA 8062: *The Clever Judge* (Iraq).
- IFA 9778: *The Honest Rabbi* (Eretz Yisra'el, Ashkenazic).[51]
- IFA 9916: *The Tenth in a Minyan and the Rabbi* (Canada).[52]
- IFA 11663: *The Rabbi Demonstrates the Character of the Members of His Congregation* (Poland).
- IFA 11884: *Do Not Trust Those Who Are Hyper-Honest* (Iran).
- IFA 12161: *I Just Wanted to Show You Who Is Our Rabbi* (Poland).
- IFA 12529: *The Rabbi* (Greece).
- IFA 12618: *The Man Who Recovered a Jar in Exchange for a Barrel* (Morocco).
- IFA 13681: *The Cheating Sheikh and the Clever Woman* (Yemen).
- IFA 13772: *The Local Rabbi* (Romania).
- IFA 13908 (this vol., no. 60): *What Kind of Congregants I've Got!* (Poland).
- IFA 13909 (this vol., no. 61): *What Kind of Rabbi We've Got in this Town* (Poland).

Folktale Types

- 910*M (IFA) "Do Not Trust a Gentile, Even Forty Years after His Death."
- 910*M (Jason) "Do Not Believe a Gentile, Even Forty Years after His Death."

Folktale Motifs

- D1810.8 "Magic knowledge from dream."
- D1810.8.2 "Information received through dream."
- D1810.8.3 "Warning in dreams."
- D1814.2 "Advice from dream."

- E545 "The dead speak."
- *E545.12.1 "The dead directs man to a hidden treasure."
- F1068 "Realistic dream."
- *F1068.2.3 "Two individuals have the same dream."
- N511 "Treasure in ground."
- N511.1.1 "Treasure buried in graves."
- N531 "Treasure discovered through dream."
- cf. N531.1 "Dream of treasure on the bridge."
- N550 "Unearthing hidden treasure."

Notes

1. First published in Weinstein, *Grandma Esther Relates...*, 47–49 no. 9.
2. See also M. Gaster, *The Exempla of the Rabbis,* 127, 222 no. 181.
3. Braude, *Pesikta Rabbati,* 1:459–460 chap. 22:5; Friedmann, *Pesikta Rabbati,* 111b chap. 22; Ulmer, *A Synoptic Edition of Pesiqta Rabbati,* 1:527–529 chap. 22:7–8; and Shapira, *Midrash Aseret ha-Dibrot (A Midrash on the Ten Commandments),* 84–85.
4. Published by S. Buber as *Midrash Aggadah,* 1:152b; and M. Gaster, op. cit., 83 no. 123, 117 no. 324.
5. Marmorstein, "*Das Motiv vom veruntreuten Depositum in der jüdischen Volkskunde.*"
6. Baumgartner, "*Susanna.*"
7. Hirschberg, *Ḥibbur Yafe me-ha-Yeshuʻah* (An elegant composition concerning relief after adversity), 63–64 no. 23; Brinner, *An Elegant Composition Concerning Relief after Adversity,* 103–104, 108–110 no. 23; Margulies, *Midrash Haggadol on the Pentateuch: Exodus,* 410 (20:7); D. Hoffman, *Midrash ha-gadol zum Buch Exodus,* 221–222; Ibn Sahula, *Meshal ha-kadmoni* (The ancient fable), 222–225; and Ibn Sahula, *Meshal Haqadmoni,* 2:520–533.
8. In the Bodleian Library in Oxford, UK: Oxford 1466, folios 300a–338b. It is summarized in M. Gaster, op. cit., 115, 238 no. 315.
9. M. Gaster, *Maʻaseh Book,* 1:141–143 no. 85.
10. Zfatman, "The Mayse-Bukh."
11. Farḥi, *Oseh Pele* (The miracle worker), 306–308, 311–312; and Bin Gorion, *Mimekor Yisrael,* 2:631–632 no. 95 (1976 ed.).
12. Hadas, *The Book of Delight,* 83–85; I. Davidson, *Sepher Shaashuim,* lxi, 49–50; I. Abrahams, *The Book of Delight and Other Papers,* 41–42; and Dishon, *The Book of Delight,* 94–95 n. 16, 235 n. 41.
13. Schwarzbaum, *Studies in Jewish and World Folklore,* 239–241, 476.
14. Hermes, *The "Disciplina Clericalis" of Petrus Alfonsi,* 128–130 no. 15; Schwarzbaum, "International Folklore Motifs in Petrus Alfonsi's '*Disciplina Clericalis,*'" 31–31; and Schwarzbaum, *Jewish Folklore between East and West,* 286–287 (rich bibliography).
15. *Meshal ha-kadmoni* (The ancient fable), 222–226, and *Meshal Haqadmoni,* 2:521–535 chap. 4:1083–1262.
16. Swan and Hooper, *Gesta Romanorum,* 210–212 no. 118.
17. Day 8, tale 10.

18. On p. 457–463 no. 198.
19. *The Decameron*, 266–270; see also Boccaccio, *Decameron*, 633–647.
20. Marzolph and van Leeuwen, *The Arabian Nights Encyclopedia*, 1:295; Chauvin, *Bibliographie des ouvrages Arabes*, 8:103 no.77; 9:23–25 no. 13.
21. Jellinek, *Bet ha-Midrasch*, 1:87–88 and Shapira, *Midrash Aseret Ha-Dibrot*, 84–85.
22. D. Noy, "General and Jewish Folktale Types in the Decalogue Midrash."
23. D. Noy and Hasan-Rokem, *Midrash Aseret ha-Dibrot* (Midrash of the Ten Commandments), 11.
24. M. Gaster, *Ma'aseh Book*, 2:523–525 no. 215; see also Iraki, *Sefer ha-Ma'asiyyot* (A book of folktales), 22b–23a no. 29, 69a–70a no. 96; Koidonover, *Sefer Kav ha-Yashar* (The book of the straight line), chap. 52; and Ben-Yeḥezki'el, *Sefer ha-Ma'asiyyot* (A book of folktales), 6:72–73.
25. See R. Burton, *Supplemental Nights to the Book of the Thousand Nights and a Night*, 1:264–266 no. 11.
26. *A Group of Eastern Romances and Stories*, 442–446.
27. Sladvonik, *Sefer Ma'aseh Ha-Gedolim He-Ḥadash* (The new gests of the prominent men), 50–51 no. 26; anthologized in Ben-Yeḥezki'el, op. cit., 3:158–163.
28. Ben-Yeḥezki'el, op. cit., 3:399–401.
29. Druyanow, *Sefer ha-bediḥah ve-ha-Ḥidud* (The book of jokes and witticisms), 144–145 no. 368; Olsvanger, *Röyte Pomerantsen or How to Laugh in Yiddish*, 166–167 no. 241; and Landmann, *Der Jüdische Witz*, 101.
30. Published in Jason, *Märchen aus Israel*, 96–98 no. 32.
31. D. Noy, *Jefet Schwili Erzählt*, 306–307 no. 135.
32. D. Noy, *Jewish Folktales from Tunisia*, 163–164 no. 62.
33. *The Exempla of the Rabbis*, 155, 259 no. 403.
34. Jellinek, op. cit., 4:150–151; and Eisenstein, *Ozar Midrashim*, 2:533.
35. Shinan, " 'The Chronicle of Moses' "; and Yassif, "Parables of Solomon."
36. M. Gaster, *Ma'aseh Book*, 2:452–456.
37. The single known copy is in the Bodelian Library, Oxford, UK: Opp. 8°796,7.
38. Zfatman-Biller, "Yiddish Narrative Prose."
39. *Ma'aseh Nissim* (Miracles), 58a–58b no. 37; and Farḥi, op. cit., 1:46–47.
40. Ginzberg, *The Legends of the Jews*, 4:85, 6:250, cf. 6:284–286; Bin Gorion, op. cit., 28–29 no. 17 (1990 ed.); Hendler, "The Jars of Honey"; Seymour, *Tales of King Solomon*, 17; and Ben-Yeḥezki'el, "The Book *And It Came to Pass*," 352.
41. Banks, *An Alphabet of Tales*, 1:182 no. 261.
42. R. Burton, op. cit., 3:405–416 no. 4; Gerhardt, *The Art of Story-Telling*, 13–14, 171; and Chauvin, op. cit., 9:25–26 no. 14.
43. Published in D. Noy, *Moroccan Jewish Folktales*, 48–49 no. 9; and D. Noy, *Jewish Folktales from Morocco*, 40–41 no. 9.
44. Published in D. Noy, *Jewish-Iraqi Folktales*, 62–83 no. 35.
45. Published in D. Noy, *Jewish Folktales from Libya*, 122–124 no. 52; and Baharav, *Mi-Dor le-Dor*, 139–141 no. 51.
46. Published in Haimovits, *Faithful Guardians*, 65–66 no. 12.
47. Published in Rabbi, *Avoteinu Sipru* (Our fathers told), 1:176–177 no. 113.
48. Published in Rabbi, op. cit., 2:213–214 no. 101.

49. Published in Rabbi, op. cit., 2:168–169 no. 84.
50. Published in Bribram, *Jewish Folk-Stories from Hungary,* 29–30 no. 10.
51. Published in M. Cohen, *Mi-Pi ha-Am* (From folk tradition), 1:82–84 no. 40.
52. Published in Shenhar, *A Tale for Each Month: 1973,* 28–30 no. 8.

54

Catch the Thief; or Don't Put Too Much Trust in a Pious Person

TOLD BY SHLOMO ROTSHTEIN TO MORDEKHAI ZEHAVI

*T*his is the story about Groin'm, a woman, and a priest.

Old Groin'm was dying. Full of years and troubles, he called for his son, Ḥayyim Yossel, and in a trembling voice, with not even enough strength to open his mouth, scarcely mumbling, he said, "Ḥayyim'l, my son, I'm dying. I have nothing to leave you except for one thing." He paused to breathe and rest and then continued. "I will give you some advice before I go to the world that is all good. Don't put too much trust in a pious person."

With this, he gave up his pure soul and his head moved no more. Of course, he went straight to Paradise, because he was a righteous man in his generation.[*]

His son, Yossel Ḥayyim, buried him with all the rites. After the thirty days of mourning, he returned to his business.

Yossel was very clever, so he was quite successful in his business. He became a confidant of the wealthy nobleman Kazimierz Wiśniowiecki. Yossel was always willing to flatter the nobleman, so the gentile was fond of him. What counted is that he proceeded from strength to strength[**] and became extremely wealthy.

But in his heart, he wondered about what his father had told him before his death. He couldn't understand what he had meant.

Much water flowed in the river Vistula. The town of Lomza prospered and, as was fitting for a very rich man, a match was arranged for him with a beautiful and pious woman, as was appropriate in those days.

Our Yossel lived in happiness and wealth and loved his wife, for there was none so beautiful and pious as she.

She was so pious that instead of one kerchief on her head she wore two

---
[*]An allusion to Genesis 6:9.
[**]See Psalm 84:8.

of them. And when she was on her way to the synagogue and handsome and elegantly dressed men passed by, she looked only at her feet.

Once Yossel happened to come back from a trip to a nearby town the same day, although he had been supposed to spend the night there. He opened the door quietly, with the diamond he had bought for his wife in his hand. Then he went into the bedroom. What did he see?!

Woe is me! He saw his wife lying in the arms of a strange man.

Then he remembered what his late father had said: "Don't put too much trust in a pious person." The man wept, tore his clothes, and ran away from his house, his mood, black as soot from his disillusionment and heartbreak. Where could he go? "What am I to do?" he wailed bitterly.

He sat on the bench, crying and crying, until he fell into an exhausted sleep.

That night, thieves broke into the governor's apartment and took everything they found, even the diamonds, and left the house empty.

That night, there was a great commotion among the Lomza police. The entire force was called out. How could this happen? A robbery, and in the house of his excellency the governor himself! They raided every place; the whole town was jumping that night. Policemen burst into the park where our friend Yossel was sleeping and snoring. His father appeared in his dream and said, "Nu, now do you remember what I told you—don't put too much trust in a pious person!"

The next moment he was no longer dreaming. The police did not sit idle and decided that he was the thief. They had caught the thief!

They didn't fool around for a minute. They grabbed him, put him in handcuffs, and took him straight to his excellency the governor.

The governor was furious that anyone would dare rob him. He looked at the chained and trembling Jew and gave orders to hang him at once. He would never steal again.

The gallows were soon ready. Instead of a *rebbe** they brought a priest. Yossel looked at him. The priest did not hesitate. In a loud voice he began chanting the Lord's Prayer, [other] prayers, and confession for the repose of the soul of all of those hanged everywhere. The priest knew his job and sang the entire way.

But Yossel knew that he was a great scoundrel, a skirt chaser, and a dealer in stolen property.

---

*A Hasidic rabbi.

The priest was delighted. Soon they would hang another Jew. He was ecstatic.

The priest kept on singing out loud, the Jew following behind in his leg irons, his arms bound, feeling very gloomy.

When they reached the place, they led Yossel to the gallows. The governor and all the townsfolk were there. The soldiers were already beating the drums.

Everything was exactly as it should be. The executioner, with the mask on his face, was ready to put the noose around his neck.

Yossel, who had studied Russian, cried out, "Let me say something." They all looked at his excellency the governor. He hesitated. He wanted to go to sleep, but he ruled that Yossel could speak.

"I am not the thief," he exclaimed. "The priest is the thief!"

Everyone was astonished and a commotion broke out.

But the governor, who was an honest man, said they should go search the priest's house.

They found all the stolen objects in the priest's house. They brought the diamonds and the rest to the governor and hanged the priest.

After they let him go, Yossel went home. On the way, he admitted that his father had been right. One should not put too much trust in a pious person.

COMMENTARY FOR TALE 54 (IFA 14962)

Shlomo Rotshtein heard this story from his grandmother and told it to Mordekhai Zehavi in 1985 in Jerusalem.

Cultural, Historical, and Literary Background

This tale is part of two narrative cycles: counsel narratives and misogynous tales. For an examination and discussion of the counsel narrative cluster, see the commentary to tale IFA 3576 (vol. 1, no. 38). For discussion of misogynous tales in Jewish tradition see the commentary to tale IFA 16395 (vol. 1, no. 35).

Most available versions of the tale are presented as exempla, reaffirming moral values and deriving validity from the moral foundation of the community rather than from history. In contrast, the narrator of the present version localizes the tale, associating it with the town of Lomza in the Bialystok region of Poland. Furthermore, the tale is centered around a historical personality, a locally known nobleman who is likely a descendent of Jeremi Wiśniowiecki (1612–1651), a Polonized Russian prince who was one of the most powerful magnates of Poland-Lithuania in the seventeenth century. Wiśniowiecki owned an enormous estate in Ukraine on the Dnieper River. He defended the Jews living on his estate against the Cossack units under Chmielnicki in 1648–1651 (for more on these attacks, see the commentary to tale IFA 3892 [this vol., no. 21]). Such a deviation from the standard printed versions suggests that the tale had a history in oral tradition that was distinct from its printed transmission.

As discussed in the notes to tale IFA 3576, counsel narratives have been known since the tenth century, and perhaps earlier. However, in Jewish tradition, versions of the present story have been available only since the beginning of the eighteenth century. The story was first published by Koidonover (Kaidenover).[1] The writer presents the narrative as an illustration to the biblical verse "So don't overdo goodness . . . don't overdo wickedness" (Ecclesiastes 7:16–17) and a comment King Jannai (130/120[?]–76 B.C.E.) made to his wife: "Fear not the Pharisees and the non-Pharisees but the hypocrites" (BT *Sotah* 22b). Other editors and scholars included this tale in their books of collected texts with only minor stylistic variations.[2]

Similarities to Other IFA Tales

Other versions of the tale can be found in the IFA:

- IFA 3075: *Son, Listen to Your Father's Counsel* (Iraq).[3]
- IFA 4335: *The Shammash's Wisdom* (Iraq);[4] advice episode is missing.
- IFA 6718: *Whoever Is Careful Not to Step on Small Worms, Does Not Refrain from Stepping on People* (Eretz Yisra'el, Ashkenazic).
- IFA 7104: *Do Not Trust Those Who Are Too Honest* (Iraq).
- IFA 7937: *Do Not Trust the Over Pious* (Iraq).

- IFA 8469: *The Father's Will* (Bukhara); tale type = 910*N (IFA) "Do Not Trust the Over Pious."
- IFA 10242: *The Father's Advice: Beware of the Hypocrites* (Irani Kurdistan).
- IFA 11358: *The Innocent Wife* (Libya).
- IFA 12407: *The Hypocrite* (Bukhara).
- IFA 14113: *Every Exaggeration Is Suspicious* (Poland, Yiddish speaker).

Folktale Types

- 910*N (IFA) "Do Not Trust the Over Pious."
- 910*N (Jason) "Do Not Believe in the Over Pious."
- 910*Q (Haboucha) "Father's Counsel."

Folklore Motifs

- H588 "Enigmatic counsels of a father."
- J21 "Counsels proved wise by experience."
- J21.18 " 'Do not trust the over-holy.'"
- J154 "Wise words of dying father."
- J191 "Wise men."
- K1561 "The husband meets the paramour in the wife's place."
- K2000 "Hypocrites."
- K2051 "Adulteress feigns unusual sensitivity."
- P210 "Husband and wife."
- P233 "Father and son."
- P426.1 "Parson (priest)."
- T481 "Adultery."

──────── **Notes** ────────

1. *Sefer Kav ha-Yashar* (The book of the straight line), 102a & b chap. 53 (in some editions, chap. 52).

2. Cf. Jellinek, *Bet ha-Midrasch*, 6:146–147. Anthologized in Eisenstein, *Ozar Midrashim*, 2:339; Farḥi, *Oseh Pele* (The miracle worker), 4:22–25; Iraki, *Sefer ha-Ma'asiyyot* (A book of folktales), no. 97; Ben-Yeḥezki'el, *Sefer ha-Ma'asiyyot* (A book of folktales), 6:74–77; and Bin Gorion, *Mimekor Yisrael*, 449–450 no. 240 (1990 ed.).

3. Published in D. Noy, *Jewish-Iraqi Folktales*, 66–67 no. 26.

4. Published in Baharav, *Mi-Dor le-Dor*, 69–71 no. 12.

Humorous Tales

55

I Came from Mád and Returned to Mád

Told by Gershon Bribram

*T*here probably wasn't a more common or widespread saying in Hungary than, "I reached the same place as the Jew from Mád."

I heard about the source of this adage from my late grandfather, who was a *shoḥet** in Abauszantó. Here I report exactly what he told me:

The community of Mád was small, but it was well known throughout Hungary. It was in the Tokay district, which is famous for its wines. In that place, there lived a Jew who made his living buying and selling second-hand (*alte zakhen*) goods. He traveled from city to city and village to village, trying his luck and hoping to make enough to live on.

One day, he started for Szantó to try his luck there. To make his load less burdensome, he filled his pipe with tobacco and tried to light it. But it was his bad luck that a strong wind was blowing and he couldn't get the match to light. Refusing to give up, our Jew turned around and faced in the other direction. Standing with his back to the wind he had no trouble lighting his pipe. When he was satisfied with the smoke rising from his pipe he continued his journey.

This was all very well—except that, having forgotten to turn around again, he continued his journey back toward the place he had started from. When he reached his intended destination, you can imagine his astonishment that the place was so similar to Mád. The same houses, the same streets and shops and everything.

Here is the synagogue! This synagogue and that of Mád are as alike as two drops of water. And not only on the outside. Inside, too. There is the same "jesters' pew"** as in Mád—and a synagogue without a jesters' pew is like the Holy Temple without the frankincense (a component of the incense that by itself had a terrible smell).

---

*One who slaughters animals according to the kosher laws.
**In Hebrew: *moshav letzim;* after Psalm 1:1, "Happy is the man who does not sit in the seat of the irreverent."

A Jewish merchant.

In the jesters' pew the poor people were making fun of the rich people and exchanging all the local gossip.

And if he had any slight hope that everything was all right, when he reached his own house, he quickly perceived that the problems were the same as at home. And when he met his own wife, too, he awakened at once to the bitter truth, because she greeted him with the same "refrain" that he could never forget.

And this is the source of the saying, "I reached the same place as the Jew from Mád."

Commentary for Tale 55 (IFA 6814)

Written down from memory by Gershon Bribram from Hungary. He heard the story from his grandfather, Rabbi Israel Jacob Schwarz, who was a cantor and a shoḥet in Abauszantó, Hungary, around the time he celebrated his bar mitzvah.

Cultural, Historical, and Literary Background

The Proverb

The narrator presents this story as an etiological tale, explaining the origin of a proverb. Consequently, the proverb serves as both the opening and the closing formula for the narrative. Subject to theoretical positions and analytical methods, the relations between proverbs and tales have been described in causal, analytical, structural, and rhetorical terms. In the literary Aesopic fables, proverbs occurred as a coda, concisely summing up the moral message of the fable; however, in other narratives traditions, the relationship between the proverb and the tale is more complex. Proverbs may occur in narrative texts in different positions, serving different functions. A study of such relations as they occur in the tales of the IFA has been published.[1] Taylor[2] articulated the basic framework for discussing these relations in general; additional studies[3] and essays[4] on this subject are available.

The proverbial phrase *"Ott vagyunk ahol a mádi zsidó"* (There we are, where the Jew of Mád [is]) is used to mean "we are where we were"—that is, we came back to the same place (in our discussion or actions), we have not made progress. It is, as the narrator attests, a very popular phrase in Hungary that retained its currency in speech throughout the nineteenth and twentieth centuries. Speakers can and do modify the phrase in terms of person and tense, for example:

- *Ott van, ahol a mádi zsidó* (It is there, where the Jew of Mád is).
- *Úgy járt, mint a mádi zsidó* (He ended up like the Jew from Mád).
- *Úgy járunk majd, mint a mádi zsidó* (We will end up like the Jew from Mád).

The first documentation of this saying occurs in 1851 in Erdélyi.[5] It now appears in standard collections of Hungarian proverbs, such as the comprehensive work of Margalits,[6] in which the text is *"Ott leszek, ahol a mádi zsidó"* (I shall be there, where the Jew of Mád is). Gábor[7] recorded a variant relating to another village: *"Ott van, ahol a laki zsidó."*

The Village

Mád is a small village in Zemplén County in the district of Szerencs in northern Hungary. This is the wine-growing area of the Hegyalja, where the world-famous

Tokay is produced. Until World War II, this region had a large Jewish, mainly Hasidic, population that was involved in the wine trade. Few, if any, of these Jews survived the Holocaust.

The Fool

Kovács and Katalin[8] distinguished two subforms of tale type MNK1275/I* "The Reversed Wagon." The first was about the Jew from Mád, which is a variant of the present tale. The other was about the Gypsy Maatee Sarju, who, drunk, drove his horses in the wrong direction, making a roundtrip and getting home a day late only to be spanked by his bossy wife. In both cases, the fools are not Hungarian village people but ethnically the "others" of Hungarian society. A proverbial saying is associated with each of these anecdotes; however, although the one about the Jew is known widely in Hungary, the one about the Gypsy is known only regionally. A study of the image of the Jew in Hungarian proverbs and folklore in general is available,[9] as is a more general discussion.[10]

In eastern European Jewish joke lore, tale type 1275 "The Sledges Turned" is part of the Chelemite narrative cycle.[11] For a bibliographical discussion of Chelm as the "town of fools" in eastern European Jewish tradition, see the commentary to tale IFA 2826 (this vol., no. 64).[12]

Similarities to Other IFA Tales

The other versions of this tale in the IFA are the following:

- IFA 6995: *Shmu'el the Fool from Ḥelem* (Romania).
- IFA 10954: *The Crazy Man's Compass* (Poland).
- IFA 14235: *A Ḥeleite Goes to Warsaw* (Poland).

Folktale Types

- 1275 "The Sledges Turned."
- 1275 "Sledges Turned" (new ed.).
- 1275 (Andreev) "*Poshekhontsy ostavlyayut sani ogloblyami tuda, kuda, edut*" "People from Poshekhon Leave Their Sledges with the Runners Pointed toward Their Destination".
- 1275* (Jason) "Travelers Lose Way and Get Turned Around."
- 1275 (Krzyzanowski) "*Odwrócone wozy*" (The Reversed Wagon).
- MNK1275/I* (Kovács and Katalin) "*A megaforditott kocsi*" (The Reversed Wagon).

Folklore Motifs

- J2333 "The sledges turned in the direction of the journey."
- *P436 "Junk dealer."
- V112.3 "Synagogues."
- Z64 "Proverbs."

---------- **Notes** ----------

1. Hasan-Rokem, *Proverbs in Israeli Folk Narratives*.
2. *The Proverb and an Index to the Proverb*, 27–32.
3. Carnes, *Proverbia in Fabula* (valuable bibliography); Mieder, *Proverbs,* 131–134; Mieder, *Wise Words;* and Norrick, *How Proverbs Mean*.
4. Carnes, "The Fable and the Proverb"; Krżyzanowski, "Sprichtwort und Märchen in der polnischen Volkserzählung," 151–158; Loukatos, "*Le proverbe dans le conte*"; and Permyakov, *From Proverb to Folktale*.
5. *Magyar közmondások könyve* (A book of Hungarian proverbs), 286 no. 5416.
6. *Magyar közmondások és közmondászerû szólások* (Hungarian proverbs and proverb-like sayings), 529 col. 2.
7. *Magyar szólások és közmondások,* 420, 457 no. 1127.
8. *Magyar Népmesekatalógus* (Hungarian folktale catalogue). [Note: according to the University of Pennsylvania library catalog, Katalin was the editor of some these volumes.]
9. Flesch, "*A zsido a Magyar közmondásban*" (The Jew in Hungarian proverbs).
10. Görög-Karady, "Ethnic Stereotypes and Folklore."
11. Ausubel, *A Treasury of Jewish Folklore;* Frid, *Medrcy z Chelma* (The wise men of Chelm), 176–186; Halperin, *Ḥakhmei Ḥelem* (The wise men of Chelm), 30–34; Richman, *Jewish Wit and Wisdom,* 260–262; Rugoff, *A Harvest of World Folk Tales,* 565–569; and Schwarzbaum, *Studies in Jewish and World Folklore,* 189–190, 472–473. For a literary rendition of this anecdote, see Simon, *The Wise Men of Helm and Their Merry Tales,* 89–102.
12. I would like to thank Linda Dègh, Adrienn Mizsei, Gyula Paczolay, Vilmos Voigt, Veronika Karady, and Victor Karady for their invaluable help in the preparation of these notes.

56

The Jewish Innkeeper

TOLD BY YOSEF DAVID TO MOSHÈ RIVLIN

In a large town in Poland there lived a rich landowner who served as mayor. He was a respectable man and was revered by the Jews and the gentiles of the district. He was very fond of hunting and always went hunting once or twice a week. He did it for sport, not to support himself.

Once when he was out hunting, he lost his way. Darkness came, and he had no idea how to get home. He decided to try sleeping in the forest. But that is very difficult at night, when the animals move about more than during the day and you cannot see them. Suddenly, he saw a faint glow in the distance. If there is light there must certainly be people. So he made his way toward the light. When he got there, he found he was in a small and infamous village, the home of thieves and highwaymen and criminals. But the landowner had no alternative to spending the night there. You should know that when he went hunting he dressed differently, so many people did not recognize him as the landowner and mayor.

The landowner knocked on the door of the first house. He told the people there that he had lost his way and asked to spend the night in their house. They would not let him in, even though he was soaked from the heavy rain and shivering in the fierce cold. They shut the door in his face. He tried the neighbors, and the same thing happened, but even worse—they threatened to beat him up. How dare he ask to sleep in their house? The same thing kept happening in one house after another. Meanwhile, the rain was coming down harder. In his misery, he thought that the only thing left to do was to kill himself because they were throwing him out of house after house like a dog, and it was dangerous to go back to town, especially in the driving rain. But he told himself that he would try one more house.

Here, too, his reception was no different from that in all the other houses. Suddenly, he asked whether there was a Jew in the village. They told him that the Jewish innkeeper lived at the edge of the village. He went

A street in a town in Poland.

to the edge of the village and asked whether this was the house of the Jewish innkeeper. Yes, they told him. He asked whether he could spend the night.

But the Jew asked him for one favor. "I'll let you spend the night because I see that you are in a bad way. But Heaven forbid that the people here should find out, because they are wicked people and I could lose my livelihood."

The landowner agreed. He warmed himself and then ate and went to sleep. When the landowner got up in the morning, he thanked the Jewish innkeeper. He gave him his address and asked him to come see him in town as soon as he could. Then the landowner left the house early in the morning so that the villagers would not see that he had spent the night with the Jewish innkeeper.

A few days later, the Jewish innkeeper went to town and inquired for the address. He was quite astonished to learn that the landowner who had slept at his house was the mayor and that not only was he a nobleman and the mayor but also people thought very highly of him throughout Poland. When he arrived at the landowner's house, he was overwhelmed by his great wealth. But the landowner greeted him cordially and asked the Jew what he wanted in recompense for having saved his life. "I'm willing to give you a thousand gulden for the kindness you showed me."

The Jew demurred and did not want to accept the money. "I'll give you two thousand gulden," pressed the landowner. Still the Jew would not agree and refused to accept the money. The landowner raised his offer to ten thousand gulden—an astronomical sum. But once again the Jew declined. "I have enough money of my own," he told the landowner.

Finally, the landowner said, "I'll give you land anywhere you want."

Again the Jew declined, saying he already had enough land.

"So what can I give you?!"

"There is one small thing you can do for me," replied the Jew. "In the village where I live there's another Jew who runs a tavern. If you could get him to move away and leave me alone in the village—that's what I would like you to do."

What happened? The Jew didn't want money or land. All he wanted was to get the other Jew out of the village, because he didn't want another Jew to be making his living there, in such a wicked place.

COMMENTARY FOR TALE 56 (IFA 4815)

Josef David from Romania told this tale to Moshe Rivlin in 1962 in Moshav Kefar Shammai.

Cultural, Historical, and Literary Background

The tale is a satire on social and economic relations among the Jews, employing narrative themes that are current in Jewish and international folktale traditions and that concern social values fundamental to Jewish culture. As in any other society of limited goods and economic resources,[1] in the eastern European shtetl culture, indigence and destitution created competitive relations that often outweighed any other social values, such as solidarity and kindness. Discussions of the shtetl economy[2] and studies of the poverty in central and eastern European Jewish societies[3] have been published.

Within the shtetl society, the innkeeper had a central position as the overseer of a social and economic meeting place[4] and as a mediator between the community and its local, non-Jewish magnate.[5] An examination of the reflection of these relations in Jewish literature is available.[6]

The present story revolves around the cultural value of hospitality and uses two narrative devices: an incognito visitor and wishes and their rewards.

Hospitality

Hospitality is a fundamental value in Jewish culture. It made its first imprint in the Israelite pastoral culture of wanderers as it is represented in the Torah, particularly in the image of the Patriarch Abraham, who is the archetypal host and is described as a person watching out for potential guests whom he could welcome (Genesis 18:1–15). This image was further developed in rabbinical literature.[7]

In settled agricultural and later urban society, hospitality lost some of its essential function, yet narratives about hospitality continue to occur. Within the biblical tradition, the guests are divine, or supernaturally empowered people, and their hosts could be categorized as socially marginal in terms of gender, age, or class. Their wishes, either explicit or implicit, manifest themselves in the reward of offspring. Examples are the story of Abraham; the implicit hospitality in the story of the angel who visited Manoah and his wife, Samson's parents (Judges 13:2–24); the story of the poor woman who offered hospitality to Elijah the Prophet, who revived his hostess's son (1 Kings 17:17–24); and the story of the prophet Elisha, who both prophesied the birth of and later revived the son of the Shunammite (2 Kings 4:8–37). When the hosts are human beings, the consequences of hospitality include marriage (Genesis 24:15–67; Exodus 2:15–21) and thus children. Tales of abuse of hospitality relate the inversion of the conjugal relationship, turning it into sexual abuse (Genesis 19:1–11; Judges 19).[8]

The term for hospitality (*hakhnasat orhim*) became part of the talmudic-midrashic vocabulary. The sages singled out hospitality as the most important social value, expounding on the mishnah "One may clear away even four or five baskets of straw or produce [grain] to make room for guests" (*Shabbat* 18:1).

> R. Johanan said: Hospitality to wayfarers is as "great" as early attendance at the Beth Hamidrash, since he [the *tanna*] states, *to make room for guests or on account of the neglect of the Beth Hamidrash*. R. Dimi of Nehardea said: It is "greater" than early attendance at the Beth Hamidrash, because he states, *to make room for guests*, and then *on account of the neglect of the Beth Hamidrash*. Rab Judah said in Rab's name: Hospitality to wayfarers is greater then welcoming the presence of the Shechinah, for it is written: *And he said, My lord, if now I have found favour in thy sight, pass not away* [Genesis 18:3]. . . .
>
> R. Judah b. Shila said in R. Assi's name in R. Johanan's name: There are six things, the fruit of which man eats in this world, while the principal remains for him for the world to come, viz: Hospitality to wayfarers, visiting the sick, meditations in prayer, early attendance at the Beth Hamidrash, rearing one's sons to the study of the Torah, and judging one's neighbor in the scale of Merit (BT *Shabbat* 127a).

In the available texts of that period the hospitality narratives are not about divine guests, consequently neither are they about wishes for and rewards of children. Rather they are realistic tales, mostly about sages hosting each other. Hospitality becomes its own reward. Such are the tales in MR *Leviticus* (9:3) about the insolent rabbi and his modest guest and the humorous tale in BR *Genesis* (92:6) about trust, or the lack thereof, and hospitality; see also the commentary to tale IFA 4032 (this vol., no. 53).[9] Some of these tales have been anthologized.[10] By the Middle Ages, hospitality narratives about rabbis had turned bawdy and may reflect earlier traditions.[11]

As a cultural value, hospitality—particularly extended to the poor—continued to be an integral part of shtetl culture.[12] An anthology of tales about hospitality has been published;[13] see also tale IFA 9797 (this vol., no. 15).

Incognito Visits

Within the later Jewish tradition, Elijah the Prophet continued to function in his role as a supernatural figure who rewards meritorious people with children or wealth, fulfilling their wishes even though they sometimes stupidly waste their gifts—for example, see tales IFA 960 (this vol., no. 14), IFA 2420 (vol. 1, no. 20) and IFA 2830 (vol. 1, no. 18).[14] Such a divine or supernatural figure appears on Earth in disguise, by definition, as a mortal. But in the narratives of the Middle Ages and later periods, secular rulers begin to appear as disguised or unrecognized guests, who, as in the present story, seek shelter—for example, see tales IFA 10086 (vol. 1, no. 36) and IFA 10611 (vol. 3, no. 54). In the literary medieval epic tradition, knights appear incognito, though in these stories the men are not part of a sequence of assistance, wishes, and rewards.[15]

As a result of this literary-historical development, secular rulers played the roles divine figures held in earlier narratives. In the eastern European Jewish folktale tradition, there are several versions in which non-Jewish rulers, in some cases Napoleon, find shelter in the homes of poor Jews of a variety of professions.[16] Tale IFA 683 *Napoleon's Expensive Coat*[17] tells of a French military coat that has belonged to a Jewish family, now living in Israel, which verifies the story that one of their great-grandfathers gave shelter to Napoleon. Wishes and rewards are not part of the family tradition, though they function in the narratives cited in the endnotes. Historical accounts and a collection of eastern European Jewish tales, jokes, and children's rhymes about Napoleon have been published.[18]

Wishes and Rewards

The innkeeper's wish in the present tale belongs to the cycle of "foolish wishes" made by hosts to a supernaturally empowered or divine figure or to an incognito ruler (see also tale IFA 2420 [vol.1, no. 20]). Within Jewish narrative tradition, it is possible to distinguish four patterns of stupidly absurd wishes: accidental absurd wishes that need to be undone, deliberate absurd wishes that need to be undone, trivial wishes and a cruel curious inquiry, and the trivial competitive wish. The first two forms are discussed in the commentary to tale IFA 2420. Several authors have analyzed the third pattern.[19] The fourth pattern has antecedents in medieval European narratives,[20] and a similar wish concludes a story that involves a Jew and his non-Jewish lord, although not in a hospitality context.[21] Studies of humor in folktales and the use of folktales in humor have been conducted.[22]

Similarities to Other IFA Tales

In the IFA there are sixteen additional versions that follow the third and fourth patterns.

Third Pattern

- IFA 981: *Napoleon and Tailor* (Lithuania).
- IFA 1258: *Kaiser Francis Joseph I and the Jews* (Poland).
- IFA 12768: *Don't Judge Your Fellow Man* (Iran).
- IFA 13033: *The German Kaiser and the Blacksmith Who Saved His Life* (Poland).[23]
- IFA 13502: *How Did the King Feel on the Gallows?* (Poland).
- IFA 14018: *The Jew's Three Wishes* (Poland).

Fourth Pattern

- IFA 78: *Rivalry* (Yemen).[24]
- IFA 1052: *You Shall Not Covet Your Neighbor's House (Exodus 20:14)* (Morocco).
- IFA 1121: *The Graf Pototcki and the Jews* (United States, Ashkenazic).
- IFA 2491: *The Jewish Grocer Who Hid Napoleon* (Eretz Yisra'el, Asian).

- IFA 3709: *Envy* (Romania).
- IFA 4506: *Why Are the Jews Still in Exile?* (Romania).[25]
- IFA 7862: *Francis Joseph I* (Eretz Yisra'el, Ashkenazic).
- IFA 10833: *The King and the Peasant* (Russia).
- IFA 12284: *A Jew Saves the King* (Iran).
- IFA 14291: *Sheik Abas and the Jew Who Saved Him* (Iran).

Folktale Type

- 750*K (IFA) "Granted Any Wish, the Jew Who Saved the King Chooses a Trifle."

Folktale Motifs

- J2076 "Absurdly modest wish."
- cf. K1812.1 "Incognito king helped by humble man."
- P150 "Rich men."
- P320 "Hospitality."
- P414 "Hunter."
- *P449 "Innkeeper."
- *P476 "Thief."
- Q45 "Hospitality rewarded."
- Q111.2 "Riches as reward (for hospitality)" [declined].
- *Q115.4 "Reward: any boon that may be asked—man asks for the removal of a competitor."
- W158 "Inhospitality."

--- **Notes** ---

1. Foster, "Peasant Society and the Image of Limited Good."
2. Kahan, *Essays in Jewish Social and Economic History;* and Baron et al., *Economic History of the Jews.*
3. Jersch-Wenzel et al., *Juden und Armut in Mittle- und Osteuropa.*
4. Shmeruk, "The Hasidic Movement and the 'Arendars.'"
5. Rosman, *The Lord's Jews;* Rosman, "The Relationship between the Jewish Lessee (*Arendarz*) and the Polish Nobleman"; and J. Goldberg, *The Jewish Society in the Polish Commonwealth,* 232–240.
6. Bartal, "The Porets and the Arendar."
7. Ginzberg, *The Legends of the Jews,* 1:240–245, 270–271, 3:479, 5:234, 383; and Bin Gorion, *Mimekor Yisrael,* 4–16 no. 8 (1990 ed.).
8. Anonymous, "Hospitality"; and Koenig, "Hospitality."
9. M. Gaster, *The Exempla of the Rabbis,* 115, 127, 222, 238 nos. 181, 315.
10. Bialik and Ravnitzky, *The Book of Legends,* 679–682 nos. 361–382.
11. Fishman, *Ma'asim al Aseret ha-Dibrot* (Tales about the Ten Commandments), 34–36; Jellinek, *Bet ha-Midrasch,* 1:81–83; Hasan-Rokem, *Midrash Aseret ha-Dibrot* (Midrash of the Ten Commandments), 23–25; A. Shapira, *Midrash Aseret Ha-Dibrot,*

76–79; Abramson, *Nissim,* 491 no. 35 (discussion of the identity of R. Meir, 420); Hirschberg, *Ḥibbur Yafe me-ha-Yeshu'ah* (An elegant composition), 68–70 no. 25; and Brinner, *An Elegant Composition Concerning Relief after Adversity,* 118–120 no. 25.

    12. Zborowski and Herzog, *Life Is with People,* 191–213.

    13. Ben-Yeḥezki'el, *Sefer ha-Ma'asiyyot* (A book of folktales), 1:3–124.

    14. Bin Gorion, op. cit., 427–440 nos. 219–226.

    15. S. Crane, "Knights in Disguise"; Ménard, *Le rire et le sourire,* 333–416, esp. 336–337; and Traxler, "Hide and Get Lost."

    16. Ariel, *Ḥakhamim ve-Tipshim* (Wise men and fools), 57–58; N. Gross, *Maaselech un Mesholim,* 166–167 (the characters are a king and a cobbler); Learsi, *Filled with Laughter,* 66–71 (the characters are Napoleon and a tailor); Learsi, *The Book of Jewish Humor,* 87–91 (the characters are Napoleon and a tailor), Olsvanger, *L'Chayim!,* 24–26 no. 25 (the characters are Napoleon and a tailor); and Ausubel, *A Treasury of Jewish Folklore,* 401–402 (the characters are Napoleon and a tailor).

    17. Published in D. Noy, *The Diaspora and the Land of Israel,* 24–26 no. 7.

    18. Pipe, "Napoleon in Jewish Folklore"; Kobler, *Napoleon and the Jews;* and Schwartzfuchs, *Napoleon, the Jews and the Sanhedrin.*

    19. N. Gross, op. cit.; Learsi, *Filled with Laughter;* Learsi, *The Book of Jewish Humor;* Olsvanger, op. cit.; and Ausubel, op. cit.

    20. Swan and Hooper, *Gesta Romanorum,* 158–159 no. 85.

    21. J. Cahan, *Yidishe folksmasiyyot* 225–227 no. 48 (1940 ed.); and Schwarzbaum, *Studies in Jewish and World Folklore,* 164–166.

    22. Kuhlmann and Röhrich, *Witz, Humor und Komik im Volksmärchen.*

    23. Published in M. Cohen, *Mi-Pi ha-Am* (From folk tradition), 2:69–70 no. 178.

    24. Published in Jason, *Märchen aus Israel,* 75–78 no. 22; D. Noy, *Jefet Schwili Erzählt,* 342–343 no. 169; and Stahl, *Edot Mesaprot* (Tales of ethnic groups), 73–75 no. 38.

    25. Published in Baharav, *Sixty Folktales,* 58–62 no. 2.

57

Little Fish, Big Fish

Told by Aryè Tesler to Gershon Bribram

The head of a certain community was known to be a great miser. All the beggars in the neighborhood told one another about him and publicized the fact far and wide.

Once the head of the community received a great honor: a well-known *rebbe** honored him with a visit. The head of the community had no choice but to invite the honored guest for the midday meal. He took council with his wife, who was even stingier than he was, and the two of them decided that the menu would include fish. In the afternoon they would serve the little fish and keep the big fish for the evening, after the *rebbe* had left, when they could enjoy them.

The *rebbe* peeked into the kitchen, where he saw the dishes cooking on the stove and imagined the fine flavor of the fish. How great was his disappointment when he saw that the platter placed before him contained only small fish. He leaned over and seemed to be carrying on a whispered conversation with them. The astonished couple sat there in tense silence, watching this wonder. A great miracle was taking place in their own house—with their own eyes they could see the *rebbe* conversing with the fish. The story of the miracle in their house would certainly be passed down to future generations.

After a while the head of the community made so bold as to ask the *rebbe*: "Your honor, may you live to be one hundred and twenty, you understand the language of fish and can converse with them?"

"Certainly," sighed the *rebbe*. "Ever since my late brother drowned in the river, I keep asking the fish whether they have seen him."

"And what did the fish reply?"

"They said, 'we weren't born yet when the disaster took place. But there are large fish in the kitchen, and they certainly know the answer.' "

---

*A Hasidic rabbi.

COMMENTARY FOR TALE 57 (IFA 8889)

Recorded by Gershon Bribram as told by Aryè Tesler, in 1970 at Kibbutz Ma'agan.[1]

Cultural, Historical, and Literary Background

This humorous narrative occurs in two main variations: a repartee between a host and his jester guest and a repartee between parents and their clever son.

Repartee between Host and Jester Guest

The documentation of the first form of the tale dates back to classical antiquity. Athenaeus[2] (c. 200 C.E.) reported an anecdote told by the poet Phainias of Eresos (c. 300 B.C.E.), a pupil of Aristotle, about Philoxenus, the poet of Cythera (436–380 B.C.E.), who was a dinner guest of the tyrant Dionysios the Elder (432–367 B.C.E.). Dionysios served Philoxenus a small mullet, while on his own plate was a large one. Philoxenus put his small fish his ear.

> When Dionysios asked him why he did that, Philoxenus answered that he was writing a poem about Galatea and desired to ask the mullet some questions about Nereus [a sea divinity who fathered Galatea] and his daughters. And the creature, on being asked, had answered that she had been caught when too young, and therefore had not joined Nereus's company; but her sister, the one set before Dionysios, was older, and knew accurately all he wished to learn. So Dionysios, with a laugh, sent him the mullet that had been served to him.[3]

In the Middle Ages, the anecdote recurred in Islamic tradition associated with Ash'ab (eighth century), who was likely a historical personality, an entertainer, who later became the central figure in humorous narrative cycles.[4] A version of the present story is included in the tenth-century book of jokes *'Iqd,* by Ibn 'Abddrabbih.[5]

Joke and anecdote collectors have found that the story was current in Europe from the sixteenth to the nineteenth centuries.[6] The tale in the Jewish tradition in Yiddish-speaking communities corresponds to the European variant.[7]

Repartee between Parents and Clever Son

The second form of the tale seems to date from later Middle Eastern humor, often centering around the figure of Djuha.[8] Surveys of this anecdote have been conducted.[9]

Similarities to Other IFA Tales

The following versions are on deposit in the IFA:

- IFA 2427: *A Small Fish Tells a Guest about a Big Fish* (Eretz Yisra'el, Sephardic).
- IFA 4665: *The Conversation with a Fish* (Eretz Yisra'el, Sephardic).
- IFA 4685: *The Emissary from Jerusalem Talks with a Fish* (Eretz Yisra'el, Sephardic).

Talking Fish

In this story, motif B211.5 "Speaking fish" is employed humorously; however, as an idea it is still current in Jewish tradition. On March 15, 2003, a story of a talking fish was published as a front-page news item in the *New York Times*.[10] The article reported about a non-Jewish employee in a fish shop who heard a carp talk. He called the shop owner in alarm, noting that the fish made prophetic pronouncements about the end of the world. "The fish commanded Mr. Rosen [the shop owner] to pray and to study the Torah and identified itself as the soul of a local Hasidic man who died last year, childless. The man often bought carp at the shop for Sabbath meals of poorer village residents." The story, which had its detractors in the community, circulated orally and was the buzz of the town.

Folktale Types

- 401 (Marzolph) "*Der Gierrige*" (The Greedy).
- 1567C "Asking the Large Fish."
- 1567C (El-Shami) "Asking for the Large Fish."
- 1567C (Jason) "Asking the Large Fish."

Folklore Motifs

- B211.5. "Speaking fish."
- J1341.2. "Asking the large fish."

――――― **Notes** ―――――

1. First published in D. Noy, *A Tale for Each Month 1970*, 55–56 no. 4 (extensive notes by Adler et al., 95–98).
2. *The Deipnosophist*, 1.6e–f.
3. Hansen, *Ariadne's Thread*, 38–40.
4. Rosenthal, *Humor in Early Islam*, 17–35.
5. Rosenthal, op. cit., 121 no. 134; I. Yahuda, *Proverbia Arabica*, 1:130–131 no. 547; and Weisweiler, *Von Kalifen Spassmachern und klugen Haremsdamen*, 176–177.
6. Pauli, *Schimpf und Ernst*, 2:7–8, 407–408 no. 700; Millien and Delarue, *Contes du Nivernais et du Morvan*, 215–218; and Ranke, *European Anecdotes and Jests*, 72–73, 157–158 no. 98 (informative note).
7. Bialik, *Ketavim genuzim* (Unpublished texts), 262 no. 2; Druyanow, *Sefer ha-Bediḥah ve-ha-Ḥidud* (The book of jokes and witticisms), 1:303–304 no. 780; Learsi,

Filled with Laughter, 291; Olsvanger, *Rosinkess mit Mandlen,* 28 no. 46; and Rawnitzki, *Yidishe Witzn* (Jewish wit), 1:104 no. 212.

8. Wesselski, *Der Hodscha Nasreddin,* 1:82–83, 247–248 no. 158 (extensive bibliography); Decourdemanche, *Sottisier de Nasr-Eddin-Hodja,* 121–122 no. 72; and Marzolph, *Nasreddin Hodscha,* 112–113 no. 262.

9. Moser-Rath, "Fisch."

10. Kilgannon, "Miracle?"

58

Three Complaints

TOLD BY YITZḤAK BEROSH TO HAIM SCHWARZBAUM

*O*nce a *maggid** came to town and wanted to preach in the synagogue and be paid for his sermon. When the synagogue officer, the *gabbai*, refused to let him speak, he said that he would tell just a quick story:

Once, he said, a poor man, a *mamzer*,** and the *Aleinu* prayer§ lodged complaints against the Master of the Universe.

The poor man claimed that he was relegated to the last seat in the synagogue, right by the door.

The *mamzer* complained, "Where is my guilt? Because my father sinned, I am subject to the verse 'No one misbegotten shall be admitted into the congregation of the Lord'?"§§

Aleinu's grievance: "People sing all the other prayers and treat them with respect. But in *Aleinu* they spit. Why am I of lesser station than all the other prayers?"

The Master of the Universe replied as follows:

"For you, poor man, I have ordained that on Friday night, when people say *bo'i be-shalom*, 'come in peace, Sabbath Queen,' all the worshipers turn and face the door. Then you are in front and have the best place.

"As for you, *Aleinu*," said the Master of the Universe, "when people look into their souls on Rosh Hashanah and Yom Kippur and behave with utmost gravity, they open the Holy Ark and sing, with great devotion, *Aleinu le-Shabe'ah*.***

Finally, the Master of the Universe told the *mamzer:* "And that is why I ordain that every *mamzer* will get to be a *gabbai*!"

---

*An itinerant preacher.
**See the commentary to this tale.
§See the commentary to this tale.
§§Deuteronomy 23:3.
***Here the informant sang "*A-A-lei-nu*" in the special tune for the High Holy Days.

COMMENTARY FOR TALE 58 (IFA 8794)

Told in Yiddish by Yitzḥak Berosh from Warsaw, Poland to Haim Schwarzbaum on July 1, 1969, in Kiron, Israel.

Cultural, Historical, and Literary Background

Jokes and Laughter

This joke is an example of protest humor, a putdown of a central and highly ranked member of the congregation by a marginal figure and a lowly ranked man. Revealing tensions within Jewish society,[1] the narrating *maggid* (itinerant preacher) constructs a reversal of position for the *gabbai* (synagogue officer), hurling him from the center to the periphery of the congregation's social structure. Thereby he achieves what Thomas Hobbes (1588–1679) considered to be the trigger of laughter, "sudden glory," a narrative one-upmanship that allows the lowly narrator to switch positions with the higher person, who becomes the butt of the joke.[2] This tale has appeared in some twentieth-century collections of Jewish humor.[3]

Community Leadership and the Sermon

The hierarchical structure of community leadership consisted of four groups of officers: the *parnassim* (wardens), the *tovim* (notables), *gabbaim* (synagogue officers), and *memunim* (overseers). *The gabbai* was an officer who was in charge of the sacred funds for community charity.[4] Descriptions and analyses of the hierarchical structure of the Jewish community and its leadership are available.[5] For information about the sermon (*derashah*) and preachers (*darshanim*, *maggidim*, and *Ba'al darshan* [Yiddish]), see the commentary to tale IFA 21021 (this vol., no. 66).

The *Mamzer*

The fundamental law of the illegitimate child is stated in Deuteronomy 23:3: "No one misbegotten shall be admitted into the congregation of the Lord; none of his descendants, even in the tenth generation, shall be admitted into the congregation of the Lord." The meaning of the biblical term *mamzer*, translated as "misbegotten," is not clear; and in Jewish law, it evolved to mean the offspring of adultery or incest between Jews. Much discussion of the issues concerning the ambiguity of the term and the evolution of the law has been generated.[6]

Aleinu

"*Aleinu*" (*Alyinu*) is the colloquial reference to the prayer that begins with the phrase "*Aleinu le-Shabbe'ah*" (It is our duty to praise [the Lord of all things]).

Historically, the prayer *Aleinu* first occurred in the *Musaf* (additional) Rosh Hashanah service, and from there it was also taken into the *Musaf* service of Yom Kippur. Only in the Middle Ages did it acquire the function of concluding the morning service (*Shaharit*) and later the afternoon (*Minhah*) and the evening (*Ma'ariv*) prayers.

Quite likely, it is a prayer of great antiquity. A tradition that survived until the thirteenth century attributes the composition of this prayer to Joshua bin Nun.[7] Rosenson[8] pointed out that this legendary attribution is available only from the Middle Ages. Another period in which the prayer may have been composed was suggested by Manasseh Ben-Israel[9] (1604–1657), who dated the *Aleinu* to the era of the "Men of the Great Assembly," during the period of the Second Temple. The absence of hope for the reconstruction of the Temple indicates, among other evidence, the antiquity of the prayer, setting the date of its composition to a period before the Temple's destruction in 70 C.E. Mirsky[10] dated the composition of the prayer to the same period on the basis of its style, which he considered to be transitional between biblical and mishnaic.

The prayer is part of the liturgical verses known as the *Teki'ata de-Vei Rav* (the shofar service of Rav, or the shofar service of *beit midrash*), and its composition has been ascribed to Rav (also known as Abba ben Aivu, Abba Arikha, and Abba the Tall), a Babylonian teacher of the third century (JT *Rosh Ha-Shanah* 1:3; *Avodah Zarah* 1:2).[11] Discussions of the *Aleinu* in the talmudic period[12] and historical documentation of the prayer have been published.[13]

The shift from being an annual prayer to a daily one, which occurred in the fourteenth century, is associated with a mythic narrative about the martyrs of Blois, who in 1171 went to their death chanting *Aleinu*. A version of the prayer written by Jews from northern France who immigrated to England twelve years after the martyrdom in Blois is known.[14] Studies of these events and of Jewish martyrs in the Middle Ages are available.[15]

The prayer was a cause of anti-Jewish sentiments based on information that Jewish apostates provided church authorities. These informers said that the anti-pagan verse in the prayer—"for they prostrated themselves before vanity and emptiness and prayed to a God that saveth not"—was interpreted by Jews to be anti-Christian. In the fourteenth century, the apostate Pesah Peter contended that the word *va-rik* has the same numerical value in *gematria* as "Yeshu" (Jesus in Hebrew), both of which are equal to 316. His accusation and others that followed apparently had roots in Jewish popular traditions. In *Arugat ha-bosem* by Abraham ben Azriel (thirteenth century), there is a mention of a tradition that the complete, slightly modified phrase *la-hevel ve-larik* (vanity and emptiness), which occurs in Isaiah 30:7, equals in *gematria* the numerical value of "Yeshu u-Muahamat," thus expressing both anti-Christian and anti-Islamic attitudes. To add insult to injury, the Hebrew word *rik* has the dual meaning of "emptiness" and "spital," generating the custom related in this tale of spitting at the mention of the word and therefore insulting Christianity with even a greater offense.[16]

Regardless of its role in the present tale as a "complainer" about its low status in the service, the *Aleinu* has an important role in Jewish liturgy, which is represented not only in the frequency of its daily recitation and its position in the Rosh Hashanah and the Yom Kippur services but also in its content, which reaffirms the Kingship and Oneness of God and the distinction of the Jewish people. Many publications focus on the *Aleinu* prayer.[17]

Similarities to Other IFA Tales

One other version of this tale is found in the IFA:

- IFA 4114: *Complaints against God* (Hungary).[18]

Folktale Motifs

- A101 "Supreme god."
- C575 "Tabus of bastards."
- L300 "Triumph of the weak."
- L400 "Pride brought low."
- *P165 "Poor men."
- *P426.5 "Preacher."
- T640 "Illegitimate children."
- V50 "Prayer."
- V71 "Sabbath."
- V112.3 "Synagogues."
- *X501 "Jokes about community leaders."

Notes

1. Ben-Amos, "The 'Myth' of Jewish Humor."
2. For Hobbes's comments on laughter, see Hobbes, *Leviathan,* part I, chap. 6, 43; and Molesworth, *The English Works of Thomas Hobbes*, chap. 6, sect. 13, 45–47 ("Human Nature"). See also Morreall, *The Philosophy of Laughter and Humor*, 19–20.
3. Druyanow, *Sefer ha-Bediḥah ve-ha-Ḥidud* (The book of jokes and witticisms), 1:143–144 no. 367; Miller, *Fun'm Yiddishn Kval,* 242 no. 47; Olsvanger, *Rosinkess mit Mandlen,* 157–158 no. 252; and Rawnitzki, *Yidishe Witzn* (Jewish wit), 1:169–170 no. 345. For additional references to comparable anecdotes, see Schwarzbaum, S*tudies in Jewish and World Folklore,* 367 no. 532.
4. J. Katz, *Tradition and Crisis,* 84.
5. Baron, *The Jewish Community*, vol. 2; and Ben-Sasson, *Hagut ve-Hanhaga* (Thought and leadership), 160–228.
6. D. Katz, "The Mamzer and the Shifcha"; Levitsky, "The Illegitimate Child (Mamzer) in Jewish Law"; Touati, "*Le mamzer, la zona et le statut des enfants issus d'un mariage mixte en droit rabbinique*"; and Passameneck, "Some Medieval Problems in Mamzeruth."
7. Urbach, *Sefer Arugat Habosem,* 470 n. 32.
8. "The *Aleinu* Prayer."

9. *Vindiciæ Judæorum*, 4:2.

10. *HA'PIYUT*, 72–74.

11. D. Goldschmidt, *Mahzor le-Yamim Noraim* (A prayer book for the Days of Awe), 1:28–29.

12. J. Heinemann, *Prayer in the Talmud*, 269–275.

13. Tabory, *Mekorot le-Toldot ha-Tefilah* (Sources for the history of the prayer), 63–68.

14. Hallamish, *"Nusah shel Aleinu Le-Shabe'ah"* (An early version of *Aleinu Le-Shabe'ah*).

15. Blumenkranz, *"Les Juifs à Blois au moyen-âge"*; Chazan, "The Blois Incident of 1171"; Einbinder, "Pucellina of Blois"; Einbinder, "Jewish Women Martyrs"; Habermann, *Gezerot Ashkenaz ve-Zarfat* (German and French decrees), 182–186; Sapir-Abulafia, "Twelfth-Century Christian Expectations of Jewish Conversion"; Spiegel, *"In Monte Dominus Videbitur"*; and Wagenaar-Nolthenius, "*Der Planctus Iudei und der Gesang jüdischer Märtyrer in Blois anno 1171.*"

16. Vidar, *"Be'etyah shel Gimatria Anti-Nozrit ve-Anti-Islamit"* (An anti-Christian and anti-Islamic *Gematria*).

17. Elbogen, *Jewish Liturgy*, 71–72; Freeman, "The Language of Jewish Political Discourse"; Kellner, "Overcoming Chosenness," esp. 149–152; Klein, "Alenu and the Censors"; H. Matt, "Acknowledging the King"; Porten, "The Ideology of Totality-Frontality"; Wachs, "Aleinu"; and Wolfson, "Hai Gaon's Letter and Commentary on 'Aleynu.' "

18. Published in Bribram, *Jewish Folk-Stories from Hungary*, 28–29 no. 9.

59

The Elderly Cantor

TOLD BY MOTEL ADAR

When the Holy One, Blessed Be He, created the world, He assembled all His creatures and assigned them their allotted life span—forty years to each—as well as their tasks on earth. When it was the horse's turn, that animal asked the Holy One, Blessed Be He, "What will my labor be?"

"Human beings will ride on you," replied the Holy One, Blessed Be He.

"If that is what I have been created for," replied the horse, "twenty years are enough."

After the horse came the donkey. He too asked what his task would be. When he heard that he would carry heavy loads on his back he, too, asked to be exempted from twenty years of such toil.

Finally the cantor entered and asked what his mission would be. The Holy One, Blessed Be He, replied, "Yours will be a clean and easy job—singing melodiously."

When the cantor heard this he asked that his years be augmented. What did the Holy One, Blessed Be He, do? He gave him the twenty years returned by the horse and the twenty years returned by the donkey.

And this is why until the age of forty a cantor sings with the voice of a cantor. But when he passes forty he starts neighing like a horse—and eventually he brays like a donkey!

Commentary for Tale 59 (IFA 6655)

Written down from memory in 1965 by Motel Adar, a member of Bet ha-Shittah, originally from Poland.[1]

Cultural, Historical, and Literary Background

In eastern European Jewish societies, the community leaders and religious functionaries, known as *klei kodesh* (instruments of worship), have often been the target of social criticism, satire, and humor.[2] Among these community leaders, the cantors are vulnerable to such attacks because their capacity to fulfill their role declines as they grew older.

As much as this tale appears to specifically target a role in the Jewish community, it has roots in classic fable literature. The Aesopic tradition includes two distinct fables that present two different narrative patterns involving the attribution of animal qualities to human beings through transformation and through reallocation of the life span.

Transformation

According to the transformation fable[3]—which is included in the manuscript known as *Augustana, Recenssion Ia* (probably from the second century C.E.)[4]—at the command of Zeus, Prometheus, who had created too many animals, transformed some of them into human beings. These people, however, retained in their personalities their animal characteristics. In Jewish tradition, this theme pertains mainly to women, in stories of the daughters of Noah, for example (see tale IFA 660 [vol. 1, no. 33]).

Reallocation of the Life Span

In the second Aesop's fable, the horse, the ox, and the dog give man a portion of their respective life allotment in gratitude for his hospitality.[5] Therefore, in his youth, man is haughty in spirit; in his middle years, he works like an ox; and in his old age, he has the life of a dog. This tale has a wide European and Asian distribution. The Brothers Grimm included in their collection a version that was recorded from oral tradition.[6] Comparative information about this tale is available.[7]

The course of transmission of this tale is rather enigmatic. Bolte and Polivka[8] cited, following Köhler,[9] the works of the Spanish Renaissance writer Jayme Juan Falco (1522–1594) as the earliest European documentation of this fable. So far, subsequent scholarship has not uncovered any other medieval renditions of this story. Unless new evidence becomes available, it appears that neither Jewish nor non-Jewish medieval fabulists included this tale in their collections, and the story passed from antiquities to the dawn of the modern period through oral transmission.[10]

In the recorded oral versions from Jewish tradition, fables of reallocation of life years from animals to humans center on the figure of the congregation cantor, as in the present tale.[11]

Human Life Stages

The metaphoric comparison of the stages of human life to animal behavior also occurs in Jewish tradition independently of the theme of the reallocation of the life span. Thus within the talmudic-midrashic and medieval literature, the following comparisons recur with minor variations (see MR *Ecclesiastes* 1:3; Midrash *Tanḥuma, Piqudei* 3; *Yalkut Shimoni, Ecclesiastes* no. 966)[12]:

- In the first year, a child is like a king; in his second year, he is like a pig; in the third, like a kid.
- From five to eighteen, he is like a horse; and from eighteen till forty, like a donkey.
- After forty, he is like a dog; and in his old age, he is like a monkey.

Additional analyses of this tale have been published.[13]

Similarities to Other IFA Tales

Other versions of this tale are found in the IFA:

- IFA 256: *The Span of Man's Life* (Poland);[14] characters = man (not a cantor), donkey, dog, monkey.
- IFA 11508: *The Span of Man's Life* (Iraqi Kurdistan); characters = man, donkey, dog, monkey.
- IFA 14847: *The Span of Man's Life* (Poland); characters = man, *shammes's* wife, *shammes*.

Folktale Types

- 173 "Men and Animals Readjust Span of Life."
- 173 "Human and Animal Life Spans Are Readjusted" (new ed.).
- ET347 (Wienert) "*Pferd, Rind und Hund vom Menschen Beherbergt*" (Horse, Cattle, and Dog Sheltered by Man).
- 828 "Men and Animals Readjust Span of Life."
- 828 (Jason) "Man and Animal Readjust Span of Life."
- 2462 (Krzyzanowski) "*Wiek Ludzki*" (Human Age).

Folklore Motifs

- A1321 "Men and animals readjust span of life."
- cf. B592 "Animals bequeath characteristics to man."

──────── **Notes** ────────

1. First published in English in Rosten, *The Joys of Yiddish*, 81.
2. Ausubel, *A Treasury of Jewish Folklore*, 388–394; Druyanow, *Sefer ha-Bediḥah ve-ha-Ḥidud* (The book of jokes and witticisms), 1:141–224 nos. 361–588; Lipson, *Medor Dor* (From days of old), 1:86–178 nos. 221–448, 2:66–118 nos. 1042–1200, 4:50–74 nos. 2840–2908; Rawnitzki, *Yidishe Witzn* (Jewish wit), 1:125–180 nos. 257–369; Richman, *Jewish Wit and Wisdom*, 96–114, 141–173; and Spalding, *Encyclopedia of Jewish Humor*, 84–100.
3. Perry, *Aesopica*, 415 no. 240; and Perry, *Babrius and Phaedrus*, 469 no. 240.
4. Perry, *Babrius and Phaedrus*, xvi.
5. Perry, *Aesopica*, 362 no. 105; and Perry, *Babrius and Phaedrus*, 92–93, 442 no. 74.
6. Grimm and Grimm, *The Complete Fairy Tales*, 556–557 no. 176.
7. Bolte and Polivka, *Anmerkungen zu den Kinder- u. Hausmärchen*, 3:290–293 no. 176; and Uther, *Grimms Kinder- und Hausmärchen*, 4:325–327.
8. Op. cit.
9. Köhler, "*Zu dem Märchen*."
10. Gutenberg, "Animal Fables as a Historical-Cultural Source"; and Z. Shapiro, "Fables in Jewish Writings."
11. Druyanow, op. cit., 1:200 no. 517 (characters = horse, donkey, cantor); Wanwild, "*Ba ync Jid'n*" (Among us Jews), 107–108 no. 16 (characters = dog, horse, cantor); and Ausubel, op. cit., 391–392 (characters = dog, horse, cantor; likely a translation of Wanwild).
12. E. Davidson, *Sehok Pynu (Our Mouth's Laughter)*, 1:37 no. 153; M. Gaster, *The Chronicles of Jerahmeel*, 21–22 no. 9; Yassif, *The Book of Memory*, 91–92; Jellinek, *Bet ha-Midrasch*, 1:154–155; Eisenstein, *Ozar Midrashim*, 1:243–245; D. Noy, *The Jewish Animal Tale of Oral Tradition*, 90–92 no. 33; D. Noy, *Folktales of Israel*, 62–64 no. 26; andHabermann, *Me-Sippurei ha-Kara'im* (Karaite tales), 108–118. Cf. Schwarzbaum, *Studies in Jewish and World Folklore*, 312–313; see also the commentary to tale IFA 660 (vol. 1, no. 33).
13. Schöne, "*Lebenszeiten des Menschen*"; Schwarzbaum, "The Zoological Tinged Stages of Man's Existence"; Schwarzbaum, "Review of 'Aarne, Anti and Thompson, Stith, *The Types of the Folktale*' "; and Wesselski, "*Das Geschenk der Lebensjahre*."
14. Published in D. Noy, *Folktales of Israel*, 62–64 no. 26; and D. Noy, *The Jewish Animal Tale of Oral Tradition*, 90–92 no. 33.

60

"What Kind of Congregants I've Got!"

TOLD BY SHIMON ḤALAMISH TO NILI ARYEH-SAPIR

A well-to-do merchant who did most of his business on the road and was always traveling once had the bad fortune to be stuck in a town far from his home on a Friday afternoon. Unable to get home, he had to stay there and spend the Sabbath in a foreign place, in some inn.

But what could he do with all the money he was carrying, since it is forbidden to handle money on the Sabbath? He remembered a passage in the Talmud: "If darkness overtakes a man while he is traveling, he must give his purse to a gentile."* Finally he came up with the idea of storing his money in a safe place and went to the house of the local rabbi. The rabbi greeted him cordially. Hearing his request, he agreed to accept the purse, of course. He called over two men who frequented his house. "Look," he told them, "this Jew wishes to deposit his money with me so that he will not, God forbid, come to desecrate the Sabbath." Then he turned to the Jew. "Please, give me your purse, count how much you have in it, and here are your witnesses!"

He opened the drawer in his table and put the purse inside. The Jew went off, wishing him a peaceful Sabbath and promising to return when the Sabbath was over.

When the sanctity of the Sabbath had departed, after *Havdalah*,** the Jew appeared in the rabbi's house and wished him a good week. The rabbi asked whether he wanted to recite *Havdalah*. The Jew said that he had already recited *Havdalah,* but . . .

"What do you want, man?" demanded the rabbi.

The Jew took fright. "Rabbi, before the Sabbath I gave you my purse with my money!"

The rabbi pretended that he did not know what the man was talking about. "Oh, your honor must have had a dream. I will be glad to try to interpret it."

---

*Mishnah *Shabbat* 24:1.
**The ceremony that marks the end of the Sabbath.

The Jew began to plead, "Rabbi, that was all my property!"

The rabbi interrupted him. "Do you have witnesses?" he asked. "Or did anyone see that you left something with me? Tell me! And did you count the money and show them what you were doing?"

"Oy, rabbi," cried the Jew. "You called in two men who were sitting in the next room and counted the money in their presence!"

"All right, let's see," the rabbi replied, and called in the two men. "Come here. Did you see this Jew leave something with me before the Sabbath, a purse or money?"

The two looked in the rabbi's eyes and turned to the Jew. "We saw nothing. You're making it all up." Then the two went back to the other room.

When the Jew heard this, he began to cry hysterically. "How can it be, Rabbi?" he screamed. "You took the purse from me and counted the money and put it into the drawer. Oy, what has happened to me? How will I get home?"

He went to the door to leave the house without wishing the rabbi good-bye. As he reached the door and put his hand on the knob, the rabbi called him suddenly. "Reb Jew, come here." With this, he opened the drawer and gave the man his purse. "Please, count it to make sure it's all there."

The Jew burst out in apology. He asked the rabbi to understand his situation—he had almost given up the ghost in his agony. Why had he done this to him?!

The rabbi smiled. "I wanted you to see what kind of congregants I've got."

COMMENTARY FOR TALE 60 (IFA 13908)

Told by Shimon Ḥalamish of Poland to Nili Aryeh-Sapir in 1982 in Tel Aviv.

Cultural, Historical, and Literary Background

The tale belongs to the narrative cycle about deposits and their recovery; for more information, see the commentary to tale IFA 4032 (this vol., no. 53). The present tale and tale IFA 13909 (this vol., no. 61), told by the same narrator, make a contrasting pair.

Folktale Types

- Cf. 1617 "Unjust Banker Deceived into Delivering Deposits."
- Cf. 1617 (El-Shamy) "Unjust Banker Deceived into Delivering Deposits."
- Cf. 1617 (Jason) "Unjust Banker Deceived into Delivering Deposits."
- Cf. 3367 (Tubach) "Money Sack Recovered from Burgher."
- Cf. 3738 (Tubach) "Philip, King, Godfather of."

Folklore Motifs

- C631 "Tabu: breaking the Sabbath."
- C631.1 "Tabu: journeying on Sabbath."
- *C631.7 "Carrying money on person on Sabbath."
- *K231.16 "Banker refuses to return deposit, claiming it was never made."
- K1667 "Unjust banker deceived into delivering deposits by making him expect even larger" [parody].
- *K2059 "Pretended villainy."
- P431 "Merchant."
- V71 "Sabbath."

61

What Kind of Rabbi We've Got in this Town!

TOLD BY SHIMON ḤALAMISH TO NILI ARYEH-SAPIR

*O*nce there were two friends who were like blood brothers while growing up. They studied together with the same elementary-school teacher and afterward were together in the school with other fine young men, until they got married and their paths diverged: Shlomo married a local girl, while his friend Yitzhak, whom they called "Itzik," married a woman from another town. As a result, they were separated, perhaps forever.

Some fifteen years after they had parted company, Shlomo received an invitation from his friend Itzik, who wrote as follows: Because he was arranging a party to celebrate a happy occasion, and especially so they could get together and remember the past, the youth they had spent together, and all their shared experiences—and, especially, his friend Itzik wrote, because with God's help he was doing very well financially and had even become wealthy, he would pay all of Shlomo's travel expenses and any losses he might incur by being absent from his own business—he would be happy to cover everything. The main thing was that he come and have no worries.

After an exchange of letters, they greeted him and his wife with extraordinary cordiality and they celebrated together. The next day, Shlomo wanted to go home, but Itzik would not hear of it. He asked him to stay for at least another week, claiming that they had not had enough time to talk and be together. Being together was a priceless experience for him. He urged Shlomo to draw up a reckoning and calculate how much he was losing. He would cover it all, and then some, because they had come to visit and given great cheer to him and his family.

Shlomo wanted to go back home because his business needed him, but Itzik urged him to stay a few more days. He repeated that Shlomo need not worry about his business—he would reimburse him because the good Lord had blessed him with wealth and it was worth it to him for them to be together. Nothing bad would happen to him. What was important was that they were together.

After about two weeks, on Saturday night after *Havdalah*,* Shlomo rose and began to take his leave of his friend and his family. Without warning, his good friend Itzik handed him a bill for the days he had spent with him and the nights he had slept in his house and all his other expenses, to the tune of thousands of rubles.

Shlomo was in shock. "Itzik, what's going on?" he cried. "You wrote that you would cover all my expenses. The next day, when I wanted to leave your house you wouldn't let me and promised that you would reimburse me for all the business I lost while I stayed here. I didn't want to stay but you detained me with promises—and now you are not embarrassed to ask me to pay this colossal sum? Shame on you!"

"Let's go to the rabbi and ask him to hear the case," Itzik replied. "I'll do whatever he says."

So they went to the rabbi. After the rabbi listened to their arguments he rendered his verdict: "Reb Itzik is right. You must pay for everything."

When he heard the verdict, Shlomo got up and left the room quickly. He took out his wallet to give Itzik his money and threw the wallet in his face. But Itzik started laughing uproariously.

"What do you think? That I was serious about it all? Heaven forbid that I break my promise. Here is your purse, and also the money I promised you."

"What did you want of me?" retorted Shlomo. "You almost gave me a heart attack."

"I just wanted to show you what kind of rabbi we've got in our town. Please forgive me!"

Itzik gave him the money and took him home for the night. The next day they parted warmly, with many hugs and kisses.

---

*The ceremony that marks the end of the Sabbath.

COMMENTARY FOR TALE 61 (IFA 13909)

Told by Shimon Ḥalamish of Poland to Nili Aryeh-Sapir in 1982 in Tel Aviv.

Cultural, Historical, and Literary Background

Compare the present tale with tales IFA 4032 (this vol., no. 53) and IFA 13908 (this vol., no. 60). Tale IFA 13908 is a version of tale type 1617 "The Unjust Banker," which has been known in Europe since the Middle Ages and has roots in the Near East and North Africa; the present tale, however, is a unique Jewish parody on the classic anecdote.

Folklore Motifs

- *J1705.5 "Foolish rabbi."
- P310 "Friendship."
- P320 "Hospitality."
- P421 "Judge."

62

Half Is Mine and Half Is Yours

TOLD BY ISRAEL FURMAN

First Version

One clear summer day, a Polish Jew came to a town in Germany looking for a way to make some money. He saw that the townsfolk were all *amaratzim*—unlettered ignoramuses when it came to Hebrew and religious matters. What did he do? He pounced on his prey and informed the Jews that the next day was Yom Kippur. The Jews were in a panic—where would they find themselves a cantor?

Hearing this, the Polish Jew immediately offered—for he was a professional cantor—to stay and conduct the services if they paid him a handsome sum.

The local Jews were delighted and agreed to his terms. The next day they celebrated Yom Kippur.

During the services, however, another Polish Jew, a certain Ḥayyim who hailed from the same town as the cantor, happened into the synagogue. What did the cantor do? When he saw Ḥayyim enter, he continued the service without interruption, singing the same melody but changing the Hebrew words:

"Greetings, Reb* Ḥayyim!
I told them today is Yom Kippur.
Half is mine and half is yours:
O Holy One!"

Second Version

A Polish Jew was looking for a way to make a living and began selling candles. One day, he came to a town in Germany and tried to sell giant candles to the local Jews. But who buys such large candles? What did the

---
*Rabbi or Mr.

Jew do? In an astonished voice he told the Jews of the town, "What? Don't you know that tomorrow is Yom Kippur?"

When they heard this, the Jews bought up his entire stock of candles and shared their other concern with him. "What are we to do? Where will we ever find ourselves a cantor?"

The Jew soothed them. "I'll be glad to conduct the service for you, if you pay me well—the amount they offer me in the neighboring town."

The local Jews were delighted and agreed to his terms. The next day they celebrated Yom Kippur.

During the services, however, another Polish Jew, a certain Hayyim who hailed from the same town as the cantor, happened into the synagogue. What did the cantor do? When he saw Hayyim enter, he continued the service without interruption, singing the same melody but changing the Hebrew words:

"Greetings, Reb Hayyim!
I told them today is Yom Kippur.
Half is mine and half is yours:
O Holy One!"

Third Version

Reb Hayyim was a traveling salesman. When he came to a certain city in Germany, he found all the Jewish businesses locked tight.

Astounded, Reb Hayyim asked the Christian shopkeepers, "What does this mean? Why are all the Jewish stores shuttered? What's so special about today?"

"They're all in the synagogue," they told him.

Reb Hayyim went to the synagogue, and what did he see there? The place was filled to overflowing, and a certain merchant, from his own town, was standing at the lectern chanting the Yom Kippur service.

What did the cantor do? When he saw Hayyim enter the synagogue, he continued the service without interruption, singing the same melody but changing the Hebrew words:

"Greetings, Reb Hayyim,
I told them today is Yom Kippur.
Half is mine and half is yours:
O Holy One!"

Without missing a beat, Reb Hayyim joined in the cantor's refrain: "O Holy One!"

Hershele the Cantor *Ḥazzan*

Once, in the middle of the summer, Hershele was hard up—as usual. He had already drawn on every source from which he could dredge up a few pennies. His wife was scolding that she didn't have so much as a nickel to buy bread for the children. As usual in such situations, Hershele left the house and walked around aimlessly until he reached a certain village. There he had a brainstorm. He stepped into the shop of a certain Jew who was busy with his work. "What are you doing?!" he asked. "Here it's Erev Rosh Hashanah,* yet I see that you are working like normal?"

The Jew was taken aback. He had no idea that it was Erev Rosh Hashanah, he said. At once, he put his tools down and went over to a neighbor to tell him that a Jew from the city had just arrived and said that today was Erev Rosh Hashanah. The news spread through the village like wildfire. All the men stopped working and began to get ready for the Day of Judgment. The rub, however, was that they realized they did not have a cantor for Rosh Hashanah. But it was already late and where could they find one now? "Where is that city Jew?" they asked one another. When they found Hershele they made him an offer. "Reb Jew, perhaps you will be our cantor for Rosh Hashanah? We'll pay you well."

At first, Hershele pretended that he was not interested in their offer. Finally he gave in. "What can I do?" he said. "I see that it was ordained in Heaven that I be here precisely on Erev Rosh Hashanah, so I have no right to refuse." He agreed to serve as their cantor for a thousand pounds. That night, when all the villagers entered the synagogue, Hershele led the Rosh Hashanah evening service, and they all enjoyed his singing. The next morning Hershele led the service. In the middle of the service, he noticed that a Jew who was not from the village had entered the synagogue. "I've really gone and done it," he thought. "Now the fraud will come out." But he quickly recovered and, singing in the special holiday melody as if it were part of the liturgy, he hinted to the uninvited guest:

> "A thousand pounds they're paying me.
> Half is yours and half is mine.
> Here today, tomorrow fly!
> O Holy One."

---

*Eve of Rosh Hashanah.

The fellow caught the hint and said nothing. In this way, Hershele made some money and split it with the other Jew. Hershele went home happy, knowing that his wife would be glad to see him now.

COMMENTARY FOR TALE 62 (IFA 6976)

Recorded from memory by Dr. Israel Furman, who heard all four versions in Romania. The second version was told to him by I. Scharf in Bacau, Romania. Dr. Furman wrote down these versions in Yiddish, and Israel Rosenthal translated them into Hebrew.[1]

Cultural, Historical, and Literary Background

The comic imbedding of a secret message within an incantation or a prayer occurs elsewhere in European folklore and literature. The best-known case is the exchange between Mistress Tessa and her lover, Federigo di Nero Pegolotti, who duped the husband, the carpenter Gianni Lotteringhi (or in an alternate version Gianni di Nello) in the first tale of the seventh day of the *Decameron*. Boccaccio's narrator concludes the tale with a confirmation formula: "But a neighbor of mine, a very old lady, tells me that, according to that which she heard when a child, both the one and the other were true,"[2] replicating a conclusion common in oral tales. Comparative notes that examine variations on the theme found in the local folktale tradition of Verona and Vicenza are available.[3] Boccaccio weaves folk songs into his narratives in other tales as well, reflecting usage current in oral tradition.[4]

In Jewish tradition, such a comic imbedding of messages usually occurs in a religious context rather than in a romantic one, although the earliest reported example is in the context of a business transaction. In her memoirs, Glückel of Hameln (1645–1724) recalled that her stepsister overheard two traders who plotted to cheat her father in a business deal and warned him by using a line from the song in the tale.[5] Quite likely, the story was already known orally at that time, and she was able to use common local knowledge to fend off the planned robbery.

Twentieth-Century Collections

The third version of the present tale represents a shift in perspective, but maintain the same narrative sequence. In twentieth-century collections and in oral tales in the IFA, different social tricksters assume the role of the practical joker and different Jewish communities serve as the butt of their humor; the fourth story here, *Hershele the Cantor Ḥazzan,* is an example. Versions of this popular story appear in the following sources:

- Olsvanger:[6] comic hero = Ephraim Greidinger; holiday = Yom Kippur; goods = wax; locale = Chelem.
- Prilutski [Prylucki] and Lehman:[7] comic hero = Hershele Ostropoler; holiday = Yom Kippur; goods = candles; locale = unnamed village.
- Loewe:[8] comic hero = Efraim Greidinger; holiday = Ta'anit (fast of) Esther; goods = receiving hospitality; locale = Chelm.

- Sherman:[9] comic hero = Hershele Ostropoler; holiday = Purim; goods = receiving hospitality; locales = unnamed village, a tax collector's home.
- Druyanow:[10] comic hero = Efraim Greidinger; holiday = Yom Kippur; goods = wax for candles; locale = unnamed town.
- C. Bloch:[11] comic hero = Hershele Ostropoler; holiday = Purim; goods = receiving hospitality; locale = unnamed village.
- Kehimkar:[12] comic hero = Yemenite Jew; holiday = Yom Kippur; goods = charity for himself; locale = Bene-Israel in the Konkan.

Similarities to Other IFA Tales

Other versions in the IFA are the following:

- IFA 1977: *A Beggar Declares a Day to Be Yom Kippur* (Afghanistan); comic hero = beggar; holiday = Yom Kippur; goods = alms; locale = unspecified.
- IFA 4513: *A Dumb Public* (Eretz Yisra'el, Asian); comic hero = emissary from the Land of Israel; holiday = Yom Kippur; goods = collecting donations; locale = unspecified.
- IFA 4595: *The Day of Atonement in the Summer* (Iraq); comic hero = Jew from Baghdad; holiday = Yom Kippur; goods = serving as cantor; locale = Erbil.
- IFA 5366: *A Seder Night with a Villager* (Ukraine); comic hero = Lithuanian Jew; holiday = Passover; goods = prank on individual; local = unnamed village.
- IFA 6658: *Eating Latkes while Kneeling* (Poland); comic heroes = pranksters; holiday = Yom Kipper; goods = prank on old man; locale = unspecified.
- IFA 7245: *Ephraim Greidinger and Hershele Ostropoler on Yom Kippur* (Poland);[13] comic heroes = Ephraim Greidinge and Hershele Ostropoler; holiday = Yom Kippur; goods = serving as cantor; locale = Lesko (Yiddish = Linsk).
- IFA 8583: *Half Is Mine and Half Is Yours* (Irani Kurdistan); comic hero = a Koran reader; holiday = Islamic Day of Mourning; goods = tricking an individual; locale = unspecified village.
- IFA 12863: *A Day of Atonement in the Summer* (Iraq);[14] comic hero = a swindler; holiday = Yom Kippur; goods = serving as cantor; locale = unspecified village.

Local Variations

Although the available recorded versions, both oral and print, center around two of the principle jesters in eastern European tradition, the tale is not exclusive to the Yiddish-speaking communities. More than a third of the tales listed above were told by narrators from communities within Islamic countries.

In most of the tales, the trickster-jester has the upper hand over the community he tricks; however, in two tales (the fourth and sixth listed earlier), an individual host within the community has the upper hand.

Furman, who recalled the present tales, pointed out that in the Jewish underworld argot, the word *kadosh* (holy) is used in the sense of "agreed." Furthermore, Romanian Jews use the phrase "Half is mine and half is yours" when striking an illegitimate deal or offering a bribe.

The Cante Fable

The use of verse to exchange coded messages is one of the methods of integrating prose and song in the cante fable. This narrative form is performed widely in Africa and the Caribbean and to a somewhat lesser extent in Asian, Arabian, medieval European, and more modern European oral traditions. General surveys of this form have been published,[15] and analyses of such tales in African traditions are available.[16]

Olayemi[17] distinguished five song types: introductory songs, narrative songs, magic songs, songs that mark turning points in the tale, and songs of comment.

The classical medieval work that is best known for the interplay of prose and verse is the early-thirteenth-century cante fable *Aucassin et Nicolette,* which was likely written down by a professional minstrel of northeastern France. Several studies have examined this French fable in terms of its versification,[18] parody,[19] and use of the fool.[20] Some authors suggested that the format of interspersing verses in prose narration is influenced by Arabic literature;[21] whereas others pointed out the existence of this form in tenth-century Chinese *pien-wen* (marvelous) tales.[22]

Collections of Yiddish cante fables have been published,[23] as have discussions of Jewish cante fables.[24] Dov and Meir Noy[25] distinguished three types of cante fables in Jewish traditions: etiological narratives that explain the origins of a melody, narratives in which a melody becomes a trade object, and narratives that involve a magical role for a melody.

Similarities to Other IFA Tales

In addition to the fourth version of the present tale, five other cante fables from M. Noy's collection are deposited in the IFA:

- IFA 5793 (this vol., no. 10): *The Power of a Melody* (Belarus).[26]
- IFA 5794 (this vol., no. 9): *The Unforgotten Melody* (Belarus).[27]
- IFA 7300: *The Jew Who Chanted in a Railway-Coach* (Romania).[28]
- IFA 7811: *Moshe Potato* (Galicia, Poland).[29]
- IFA 7812 (this vol., no. 52): *The Stolen Ring* (Poland).[30]

Folktale Types

- 1831*C (IFA) "Ignorance of Holidays."
- 1831*C (IFA) (Jason) "Ignorance of Holidays."

Folktale Motifs

- cf. K1546 "Woman warns lover of husband by parody incantation."
- K1700 "Deception through bluffing."
- *K1961.6 "Sham cantor."
- M200 "Bargain and promises."
- *M241.3 "Dividing the winnings: between the clever person and the visitor who is about to discover his bluff."
- *V75.2 "Day of Atonement."
- cf. X441 "Parson and sexton at mass."

─────── **Notes** ───────

1. First published in D. Noy, *A Tale for Each Month 1965*, 69–71 no. 10.
2. Boccaccio, *Decameron*, 489–493.
3. Lee, *The Decameron*, 185–186; and G. Solinas, "*Da Firenza a Verona e Vicenza sul filo di una novella del 'Decameron.'*"
4. M. Marcus, "Cross-Fertilizations."
5. B. Abrahams, *The Life of Glückel of Hameln*, 19–20; Hamil, *Memoirs and Studies on the Jewish Literature*, 54–56; Kaufmann, *Die Memoiren der Glückel von Hameln*, 34–35; Pappenheim, *Die Memoiren der Glückel von Hameln*, 32–33; Rabinovitch, *Zikhronot Glikl* (Glikl's memoirs), 13; and Turniansky, *Glikl*, 72–75. Note: This incident is omitted in some editions of her memoirs.
6. *Rosinkess mit Mandlen*, 230 no. 347; and Olsvanger, *L'Chayim!*, 128–129 no. 160. In his note (at 159), Olsvanger cites a variant verse that he heard from the author S. J. Agnon. A similar story is also included in Halperin, *Ḥakhmei Ḥelem* (The wise men of Chelm), 93 (without the song).
7. *Studies in Yiddish Philology, Literature and Ethnology*, 3:410 no. 35.
8. *Schelme und Narren mit jüdischen Kappen*, 16–19.
9. *Hershele Ostropoler*, 88–90 no. 84.
10. *Sefer ha-Bediḥah ve-ha-Ḥidud* (The book of jokes and witticisms), 2:82 no. 1213.
11. *Hersch Ostropoler*, 124–127.
12. *The History of the Bene-Israel of India*, 48–49 (written in 1897).
13. Published in Pipe, *Twelve Folktales from Sanok*, 22–23 (extensive bibliographical note, 49–51). In Jewish-Polish folklore Linsk was considered to be a town of fools, like Chelm; see B. Weinreich, *Yiddish Folktales*, 405 n. 3.
14. Published in Agassi, *Ha-Yafah Bat ha-Ruah* (The beautiful daughter of the wind), 38.
15. Baader, "*Cante fable*"; Halpert, "The Cante Fable in Decay"; Lovlace, "Cante Fable"; and Reinhard, "The Literary Background of the Chantefable."
16. Fretz, "Answering in Song"; and Olayemi, "Forms of the Song in Yoruba Folktales."

17. Op. cit.
18, Trotin, "*Vers et prose dans* Aucassin et Nicolette."
19. Spraycar, "Genre and Convention in *Aucassin et Nicolette*" (n. 2 contains bibliographical references).
20. Drogi, *Le Cantique déguisé.*
21. Roques, *Aucassin et Nicolette,* vii–x.
22. Ch'en, "Pien-wen Chantefable and *Aucassin et Nicolette.*"
23. Lehman, "*Folk-mayselekh un anekdoten mit nigunim*" (Folktales and anecdotes with melodies); 410 no. 34 is a version of the present story.
24. D. Noy, "Folktales Including Songs and Melodies."
25. "Introduction."
26. Published in M. Noy, *East European Cante Fables,* 17–18.
27. Published in M. Noy, op. cit., 18–23.
28. Published in M. Noy, op. cit., 24–27.
29. Published in M. Noy, op. cit., 27–31.
30. Published in M. Noy, op. cit., 31–32.

63

A Visit by Elijah the Prophet

TOLD BY SHALOM MOSKOVITZ TO
MENAḤEM BEN-ARYEH

A Jew from the Land of Israel recounted that once, in a village in Europe, on the day before Passover, a Jew came to one of the householders and asked to be put up for the holiday. The family agreed to perform the precept of hospitality and was glad to host him for the seder.

When the householder filled *Kos Eliyahu*—the Cup of Elijah the Prophet—just before they recited "Pour out Your fury on the nations,"[*] the guest fell asleep. Suddenly, the door opened and a tall old man with a long white beard entered, came over to the table, picked up Elijah's Cup, made the blessing over wine, drank, and went out again.

Of course, a fuss broke out at once about how they had had the merit of seeing Elijah the Prophet. The guest, who had fallen asleep before they recited "Pour out Your fury," woke up and asked what the commotion was all about. They told him that they had been granted the privilege of seeing Elijah—that a tall man had entered, drunk from the cup, and left. "Did you ask him for a blessing?" asked the guest. "When you had the merit of seeing Elijah the Prophet it was a propitious time to do so."

"We didn't think of it," they replied, "because we were taken by surprise."

The guest sighed. "What a shame! Had I not fallen asleep I would have known what to ask Elijah. It's too bad that I fell asleep just then." But, he advised them, "Since outside the Land of Israel you have two seders, perhaps Elijah will come again on the night of the second seder. So be alert and pay attention. When Elijah comes again, should you merit that, ask him for some boon."

The whole family waited for the second seder with bated breath. When night came they all sat down together with the guest, who took a place at the corner of the table. They conducted the seder with great joy and waited impatiently for Elijah. When they reached "Pour out Your fury on

---

[*]Psalm 79:6.

the nations" and poured the cup of wine for Elijah, the householder rose with fear and trembling to go open the door in honor of the prophet. To their astonishment Elijah entered again. Again he came, tall and bearded, and, as before, made the blessing over the wine and drained the cup. As he turned to leave, the householder intercepted him and began entreating him, "If we have merited to have Elijah appear to us, we ask Your Honor to give us a blessing."

Elijah consented. Taking a handkerchief from his pocket he said, "Anyone who sniffs this handkerchief is guaranteed long life and everlasting success."

Of course everyone in the house stuck their noses out to smell the handkerchief. No sooner had they inhaled Elijah's pleasant scent than they sank unconscious to the floor. Then the guest rose from the table. He and Elijah gathered up all the valuables in the house, jewels and whatever else there was. They went to the stable, led out the horse, hitched it to the wagon, piled their loot on it, and drove off.

They had not gone far from the village, when the watchmen observed a wagon loaded with goods, traveling after midnight. They recognized that the cart and horse belonged to a certain person from the village, the man who was hosting "Elijah." "Yankel," they called, going up to the wagon, "where are you going at midnight on the holiday? What has happened to you?"

But to their astonishment they saw strangers in the wagon. "Elijah" and his companion began stammering various excuses. The watchmen detained them and took them off to the judge. When their interrogation revealed what had happened, they [the watchmen] arrested them [the strangers]. Then they went to the house of the owner of the wagon, where they found him and his whole family asleep.

When the family woke up, hours later, they told the story about Elijah and how he had them smell his handkerchief and they fell unconscious. "Elijah" was arrested and punished, and the householder got back his stolen goods.

COMMENTARY FOR TALE 63 (IFA 3955)

Told by Shalom Moskovitz of Safed to Menaḥem Ben-Aryeh in 1962 in Safed.

Cultural, Historical, and Literary Background

The present tale, a parody on traditional Elijah tales, combines two of the traditional roles that Elijah the Prophet plays in Jewish tradition: a supernatural visitor at the seder, the Passover eve ritual, and the benevolent donor of folk narratives. For a brief discussion of parody in Jewish literature see the commentary to tale IFA 21021 (this vol., no. 66).

Elijah and the Passover Seder

The association between Elijah the Prophet and the Passover eve ritual is threefold, involving messianic expectations; the ritualistic offering of wine from a designated cup, known as Elijah's Cup (*Koso Shel Eliyahu*); and the ritualistic opening of the door. Currently, all three aspects are interrelated; however, each has its own historical and regional development.

Messianic Expectations

Elijah the Prophet has been associated with messianic expectations since the post-exilic period, approximately 500 B.C.E., as is apparent in the prophecy of Malachi (3:23–24): "Lo, I will send the prophet Elijah to you before the coming of the awesome, fearful day of the Lord. He shall reconcile parents with children and children with their parents, so that, when I come, I do not strike the whole land with utter destruction. Lo, I will send the Prophet Elijah to you before the coming of the awesome, fearful day of the Lord." A summary discussion of the dating and the theological significance of the Book of Malachi in general and this prophecy in particular is available.[1]

Some tannaitic sages, like Rabbi Joshua [ben Ḥananiah] (second century C.E.), give voice to a tradition that the Messiah will come during the Passover celebration (BT *Rosh Ha-Shanah* 11b). Such a tradition represents an analogy between historical or mythical events that share the same calendar time, a principal of analogical thinking that I. Heinemann articulated.[2] Such thinking further draws an analogy between a redemption that is placed in the past, which the Exodus represents, and the apocalyptic redemption that will occur in the future with the coming of the Messiah. Hence, textually, the interpretation of the somewhat vague phrase "*leil shimurim*" (night of vigil; Exodus 12:42) connects the Passover eve ritual with messianic expectations.[3] However, there are no documented indications that Elijah the Prophet was associated with these expectations during the seder until the eleventh century.

Throughout the Passover haggadah there are phrases expressing hope for freedom, but the direct reference to Elijah the Prophet as part of the ceremony occurs after or simultaneously with the recitation of a sequence of biblical verses that call for vengeance on the nations that oppressed the Jews, starting with the phrase "Pour out Your fury" (Psalm 79:6). This sequence does not appear in the text of the Passover haggadah until it was included in *Mahzor Vitry,* thought to be written by Simhah ben Samuel (d. before 1105). In other words, it is absent from the fragmentary texts in the Mishnah *Pesahim* 10; from the haggadah text found in the Cairo Genizah (ninth century);[4] from the siddur *Seder Rav Amram* (ninth century), the earliest prayer book that Rabbi Amram Gaon, Amram ben Sheshna (d. 875), prepared in response to the request of Rabbi Isaac ben Simeon of Barcelona, Spain;[5] and from the siddur (prayer book) of Rabbi Saadiah Gaon (tenth century).[6]

The association of these verses with Elijah the Prophet is not known before the fifteenth century, at which time a link can be found in the illuminated *haggadot*.[7] A readily available example of such an illumination is in "the Washington Haggadah" from north Italy;[8] references to other examples from about the same period are available.[9]

Together with the recitation of these verses, it is customary to pour wine into the cup of Elijha and to open the door for him.

Elijah's Cup

According to mishnaic (*Pesahim* 10:7) and talmudic (BT *Pesahim* 117b) sources, the number of wineglasses that were ritualistically required for the proper performance of the Passover seder was four. However, gaonic responsa suggested the existence of parallel traditions that recommended the drinking of a fifth cup.[10] Later traditions dedicated this fifth, controversial glass to Elijah. Although Wahrmann[11] noted that it was called "Elijah's Cup" (*Kos Shel Eliyahu ha-Navi*) for the first time only in the eighteenth century, the examination of the Washington Haggadah suggests that a wineglass was prepared for Elijah the Prophet much earlier, because the illustration represents a man holding a cup and welcoming the prophet.

Opening the Door for Elijah

The association of the ritualistic door opening with the welcoming of Elijah the Prophet involved attributing a new meaning to an existing custom. It is said about Rabbi Huna (*amora,* third century) that "when he had a meal he would open the door wide and declare. Whosoever is in need let him come and eat" (BT *Ta'anit* 20b). This personal custom does not pertain specifically to the Passover meal. Rabbi Matityahu Gaon (ninth century) referred to such a custom from days long gone.[12] Later, because of security considerations, the celebrants closed their doors; according to Wahrman[13] Jews opened their doors to make sure that no stranger was eavesdropping while they recited the verses of vengeance and only later was such a custom linked to the idea of welcoming Elijha the Prophet. However, as early as the gaonic period, this custom was associated with Elijah as heralding the Messiah.[14]

Relevant to the present tale is a quotation from sixteenth- and seventeenth-century sources[15] describing a customary impersonation of Elijah, in which a visitor would appear at the doorstep in the guise of an old man. If this tradition was well known, then the two scoundrels in the present tale may have roots in this early custom.

The impersonation of Elijah occurred not just on Passover eve. The responsa book of Rabbi Eleazar Moses Horowitz (1817–1890)[16] contains a discussion of a case in which a woman committed adultery with a man who presented himself to her, in the absence of her husband, as Elijah, promising that the Messiah would be born from their union.[17]

Further discussions of these topics[18] and a comprehensive examination of the development of the customs related to Elijah and the seder[19] have been published.

Similarities to Other IFA Tales

Elijah the Prophet is the most popular protagonist in the folktales in the IFA; however, there is only one version of the present folktale on record. For more on Elijah in the IFA, see the commentaries to tales IFA 960 (this vol., no. 14), IFA 2329 (vol. 4, no. 26), IFA 2420 (vol. 1, no. 20), and IFA 6619 (vol. 4, no. 17). An earlier rendition of the present tale has been collected.[20]

Folktale Types

- 46 (Weinreich) "Thief Disguises as Elijah on Passover."

Folklore Motifs

- K310 "Thief in disguise."
- *K311.2 (Weinreich) "Thief disguises as Elijah on Passover eve."
- K331.2 "Owner put to sleep and goods stolen."
- K420 "Thief loses his goods or is detected."
- K1700 "Deception through bluffing."
- K1800 "Deception by disguise."
- K1810.1 "Disguise by putting on clothes (carrying accoutrements) of certain person."
- K1821.8 "Disguise as old man."
- K1827.1 "Disguise as saint."
- *K1827.3 "Disguise as Elijah the Prophet."
- K1930 "Treacherous impostors."
- K1961.1.5 "Sham holy man."
- K2058 "Pretended piety."
- K2058.1 "Apparently pious man (sadhu) a thief."
- *P476 "Thief."

Notes

1. Hill, "Malachi, Book of."
2. *Darekhei Aggadah* (The methods of the Aggadah), 31.
3. Kasher, *Torah Shelemah*, 12:55–58 nos. 210–219.
4. E. Goldschmidt, *The Passover Haggadah,* 73–84.
5. D. Goldschmidt, *Seder Rav Amram Gaon.*
6. I. Davidson et al., *Siddur R. Saadja Gaon,* 130–153.
7. J. Gutmann, "The Messiah at the Seder."
8. *EJ,* 6:651–652 (illustration).
9. J. Gutmann, op. cit., 30–31 n. 3; Metzger, *La Haggada enluminée,* 1:319–327; and Sperber, *Minhagei Yisrael* (Jewish customs), 4:168–184.
10. Kasher, *Hagadah Shelemah,* 161–178
11. *The Holidays and Festivals of the Jewish People,* 160 n. 71.
12. B. Lewin, *Otsar ha-Ge'onim* (The Gaonic treasure), 2:112 no. 303.
13. Op. cit., 149.
14. B. Lewin, op. cit.
15. J. Gutmann, op. cit., 29–30.
16. *Yad El'azar* (El'azar's hand), 60a–61a no. 109.
17. I would like to thank Julie Lieber for this information.
18. D. Noy, "*Eliyahu ha-Navi be-Leil ha-Seder*" (Elijha the Prophet on Passover eve); Fishman, "Seder Customs"; and Goren, "*Shefokh Ḥamatkha*" (Pour out your fury).
19. Avida, *Koso shel Eliyahu ha-Navi* (Elijah's Cup).
20. Lehman, "*Ganeivim un gneiva*" (Stealers and stealing), 75–76 no. 7.

64

The Emissary from the World to Come

TOLD BY ESTHER WEINSTEIN TO YEHUDIT GUT-BURG

*O*nce there was a Jew named Moshke. Desperately poor, he had many children and no way to make a living. One night, sleep deserted him; his wife, too, could not sleep. Winter was approaching, and they had no firewood and no warm clothes, neither for the children nor for themselves. He did not know where his salvation would come from. He thought and thought until at last he fell asleep.

In the morning, he hired a wagon and driver and traveled to the town of Chelm. When he reached its main street he began proclaiming that he had just arrived from the World of Truth, bringing greetings to all the inhabitants of Chelm.

All their relatives (he reported) had asked for winter clothes, because winter was approaching and they had nothing to wear. The townspeople brought him bundles of clothing and parcels of food. There's no firewood either (he hinted). So they also brought him firewood. He piled up the clothes and food and other donations and returned home, where he started unloading the bundles. It was already dark outside but he filled his house with all the gifts—and his family was in heaven.

COMMENTARY FOR TALE 64 (IFA 2826)

Recorded by Yehudit Gut-Burg from her mother, Esther Weinstein, who heard the tale in her childhood from her father, Rabbi Ḥayyim Salz, in the late 1920s in Safed.[1]

Cultural, Historical, and Literary Background

The Town of Fools

Chelm,[2] located about forty miles east of Lublin, was one of the oldest Jewish communities in Poland, possibly dating to the twelfth century. Its position on the trade route between the Black Sea and the Baltic Sea may have contributed to the establishment of the early Jewish community. However, documented archaeological evidence for the existence of a Jewish community in Chelm is available, in the form of dated tombstones, only from the mid-fifteenth century.[3]

Within the eastern European Jewish oral tradition, Chelm was the epitome of a town of fools, similar to Gotham in England, Abdera in Greece, Schildburg in Germany, and Kampen in Holland. The tales of "the wise men of Chelm" represent an inversion of a Jewish community in life, religion, and logic, presenting a model of the ideal "stupid" community. In the nineteenth century, Chelm jokes and anecdotes circulated orally among the Jewish communities of the Pale of Settlements, and the tales' first appearance in print was in a Yiddish booklet titled *Blitzende vitzen oder lakhfilen* (Snappy jokes or filled with laughter) (1867), which included the chapter "*Di khokhmot fun ayner gevissen shtat Kh*" (The wisecracks of a known city, Kh).[4] Since then, the Chelm cycle of witticisms and jokes has appeared in many separate books, for adults as well as for children and adolescents; many such tales were also included in anthologies of humor and folklore.

At the same time, in Israel, Western Europe, and the United States, these tales slowly disappeared from oral tradition. Chelm itself, however, remained the proverbial town of fools to the descendants of eastern European Jews. Now it is a town of fools mostly in literary sources rather than in the oral tradition. Chelm jokes and stories have been published in a variety of works,[5] as have bibliographical discussions and comparative notes for some of these tales.[6]

Somewhat defensive, former residents of Chelm wrote brief essays, comparing the Chelm traditions with those of other towns of fools, wondering, without offering any satisfactory answer, why the Jews of the Pale of Settlement picked on their brethren in Chelm. In general Polish folklore, Chelm is not the town of fools, nor has that image of the Chelm Jewish community entered Polish folk humor.[7] Studies and attempts to explain this attitude about the Chelm community have been published.[8]

The present tale, a variation on tale type 1540 "The Student from Paradise (Paris)," rarely appears in the published Chelm joke cycles, and it is likely that the narrator was familiar with an oral version or modified it herself to adapt it into this body of tales. In eastern European Jewish tradition, this tale is not necessarily part of the Chelm cycle of anecdotes, and other eastern European Jewish versions are available.[9] Weinreich[10] noted that, in the Cahan Archive in YIVO, there is another version of this tale in which the trickster is a demobilized Jewish soldier who returns home after twenty years of service.

The Trickster

The personality that fulfills the trickster role varies, but is frequently Hershele Ostropoler[11] or Froim Greidinger.[12] Tale type 1540 was the subject of a historical-geographic monograph,[13] which noted that the earliest literary documentation of this story is from 1509 and that it was included in other collections of the later sixteenth century. Aarne's study was heavily weighted toward Europe, examining more than 230 European tales but only four Asian versions and one Africa version. Some of the narratives build on the near homophony of the words "paradise" and "Paris," partially explaining the prevalence of such tales in Europe. The Brothers Grimm recorded a version from Dortchen Wild Grimm that was included in the seventh edition of their collection (published in 1857).[14]

Similarities to Other IFA Tales

In the IFA there are nine versions of this tale, recorded from narrators from six countries:

- IFA 116: *The Messenger from Heaven* (Yemen).[15]
- IFA 927: *The Foolish Woman* (Eretz Yisra'el, Arabic); includes tale type 1383*A (IFA) "Foolish Woman Sold New Name by Trickster."
- IFA 1535: *Abu Nawas Takes Revenge from the King* (Yemen).
- IFA 1624: A Folktale (Iran);[16] includes tale types 1384 "The Husband Hunts Three Persons as Stupid as His Wife," 1530 "Holding up the Rock."
- IFA 2430: *An Arab Thinks a Certain Jew Has Returned from Paradise* (Eretz Yisra'el, Sephardic).
- IFA 5060: *A Man Is Looking for a Woman Who Is More Foolish Than His Wife* (Irani Kurdistan); includes tale type 1384 "The Husband Hunts Three Persons as Stupid as His Wife."
- IFA 7332: *Froyim Greidinger and the Misery Husband* (Sanok, Poland).
- IFA 12882: *The Jew Who Tricked an Arab Woman* (Morocco).
- IFA 14959: *The Clever Student* (Ethiopia).

In the IFA there are thirty-one Chelm anecdotes. A number of these were previously recorded and published and have become part of the modern literary tradition about the wise men of Chelm.

- IFA 1494: *How did the Wise Men of Chelm Punish the Rooster?* (Galicia,

64 / *The Emissary*

A storyteller's version of the legendary town of Chelm.

Poland); tale type = 1310 "Drowning the Crayfish as Punishment."
- IFA 3300: *The Broken Eruv Line* (Galicia, Poland).
- IFA 4132: *The Synagogue in Chelm* (Poland); compare tale type 1225 "The Man without a Head in the Bear's Den."
- IFA 6579: *The Construction of a Mikveh in Chelm* (Ukraine).[17]
- IFA 14030: *Poor but Secure Job* (Poland).[18]
- IFA 14114: *Honesty Has a Bad Smell* (Poland); tale type = 1296A "Fools Go to Buy Good Weather."
- IFA 14120: *The City Watch Tower, or a Secure Job* (Poland).[19]
- IFA 14230: *The Foundation Stones of Chelm's Houses* (Poland);[20] tale type = 1243 "The Wood Is Carried Down the Hill."
- IFA 14231: *The Mikveh in Chelm* (Poland).[21]
- IFA 14232: *The Cats in the Fire in Chelm* (Poland);[22] tale type = 1281 "Getting Rid of the Unknown Animal."
- IFA 14233: *The Chelm's Mountain* (Poland),[23] tale type = 1326 "Moving the Church."
- IFA 14234: *The Source of Worries of the Wise Men of Chelm* (Poland).
- IFA 14235: *A Chelmite Goes to Warsaw* (Poland); tale type = 1275 "The Sledges Turned."
- IFA 14236: *The Chelmite and the Down* (Poland); tale type = 1291D "Other Objects Sent to Go by Themselves."
- IFA 14237: *The Chelmites Buy Honesty* (Poland); tale type = 1296A "Fools Go to Buy Good Weather."
- IFA 14238: *The Fire Extinguishing Trumpet* (Poland).
- IFA 14239: *The Stolen Moon of Chelm* (Poland);[24] compare tale type 1335 "Rescuing the Moon."
- IFA 14240: *The Snow in Chelm* (Poland).[25]
- IFA 14241: *The Old Beadle of Chelm* (Poland);[26] compare tale type 1009 "Guarding the Store-Room Door."
- IFA 14516: *A Chelmite Doctor* (Poland); tale type = 1862 "Jokes on Doctors (Physicians)."
- IFA 14517: *The Chelmite at the Doctor's Office* (Poland).
- IFA 15144: *Chelm, What a City* (Poland).
- IFA 15366: *The Excommunication of Chelm's Physician and Pharmacist* (Poland).
- IFA 15441: *The Wise Men of Chelm Move a Mountain* (Romania);[27] tale type = 1326 "Moving the Church."
- IFA 15879: *The Governor's Visit* (Poland).
- IFA 15896: *A Chelmite in Lublin* (Poland).
- IFA 15912: *A Calf's Feet* (Poland).
- IFA 16728: *In Chelm's Poultry Market* (Poland).
- IFA 17609: *The Mountain That Blocks the Sun* (Romania);[28] tale type = 1326 "Moving the Church."

- IFA 21375: *The Moon of Chelm* (Poland);[29] compare tale type 1335 "Rescuing the Moon."
- IFA 21383: *Hershele Ostropoler in Chelm* (Romania).

Folktale Types

- 305 (Wesselski).
- 1540 "The Student from Paradise (Paris)."
- 1540 (Andreev) "*S togo cveta vykhodets*" (A Person from the Other World).
- 1540 (El-Shamy) "The Student from Paradise (Paris)."
- 1540 (Jason) "The Student from Paradise (Paris)."
- 1540 (Krzyzanowski) "*Wystaniec z Raju*" (The Messenger from Paradise).
- 1540 (Marzolph) "*Der Bote aus der Hölle*" (The Messenger from Hell).

Folklore Motifs

- J1700 "Fools."
- J1703 "Town (country) of fools."
- J2326 "The student from paradise."
- K1900 "Impostures."

Notes

1. First published in Weinstein, *Grandma Esther Relates . . .*, 43–44 no. 6.
2. Also spelled Helem and, in Polish, Chelm.
3. Milner, "*Le-Korot ha-Yehudim be-Ḥelem*" (The history of the Jews in Chelm); Freedman, "*Le-Divrei ha-Yamim shel ha-Yehudim be-Ḥelem*" (The history of the Jews in Chelm); and Kalish, "Chelm."
4. Freedman, "*Maʿasiyyot Ḥelem*" (Tales of Chelm), 562.
5. Ausubel, *A Treasury of Jewish Folklore*, 326–342; Bialostotzky, *Jewish Humor and Jewish Jesters*, 95–100, 149–220; Druyanow, *Sefer ha-Bediḥah ve-ha-Ḥidud* (The book of jokes and witticisms), 2:1–36 nos. 1022–1086; Frid, *Medrcy z Chelma* (The wise men of Chelm); Halperin, *Ḥakhmei Ḥelem* (The wise men of Chelm); Halperin, *Ḥelem ve-Ḥkhameha* ("Helem and its wise men"); Landmann, *Der Jüdische Witz*, 243–247; Landmann, *Jüdische Schwänke*, 262–265; Learsi, *Filled with Laughter*, 75–156; Loewe, *Schelme und Narren*, 7–12; Olsvanger, *Rosinkess mit Mandlen*, 231–233 nos. 348, 349; Olsvanger, *L'Chayim!*, 129–131, 135–136 nos. 162, 162, 165; Prilutski, *Zamelbicher far Yidisher folklor*, 2:187–210; Rawnitzki, *Yidishe Witzn* (Jewish wit), 2:100–112 nos. 586–614; Richman, *Jewish Wit and Wisdom*, 9–10; Safrin, *Przy Szabasowych swiecach* (By the light of the Sabbath candles), 119–135; Simon, *The Wise Men of Helm and Their Merry Tales*; Spalding, *Encyclopedia of Jewish Humor*, 111–129; and B. Weinreich, *Yiddish Folktales*, 222–230 nos. 81–93.
6. Schwarzbaum, *Studies in Jewish and World Folklore*, 189–194, 472–473 (see "Helm" in index).
7. Freedman, "*Maʿassyyot Ḥelem*," (Tales of Chelm"); Yenesovitch, "*Sippurei Ḥelem*

ve-ha-Sifrut ha-Yehudit" (Chelm tales and Jewish literature); M. Sela, "*Helem ve-Hakhameha*" (The wise men of Chelm); and Roitman, "*Der tokh fun der khelemer mayseh*" (The essence of the tales of Chelm).

8. A. N. Roth, "*Sanegoria al Hakhmei Helem*" ("A defense for the wiseacres of Chelm); and Veining, "*Dos Poylishe Folkslid 'Wojna zydowska,'* " esp. 461–465.

9. Wanwild, *Ba ync Jid'n* (Among us Jews), 75 no. 6; and B. Weinreich, op. cit., 235–237 no. 97.

10. Op. cit.

11. The trickster-emissary in, for example, Sherman, *Hershele Ostropoler,* 125–127 no. 132.

12. Featured in, for example, Cahan, *Jewish Folklore,* 202–203 no. 21.

13. Aarne, *Der Mann aus dem Paradiese.*

14. Grimm and Grimm, *The Complete Fairy Tales,* 376–380 no. 104; Bolte and Polivka, *Anmerkungen zu den Kinder- u. Hausemärchen,* 2:440–451 no. 104; and Uther, *Grimms Kinder- und Hausmärchen,* 4:199–201 no. 104. See also Chestnutt, "Paradies."

15. Published in D. Noy, *Jefet Schwili Erzähalt,* 297–298 no. 129.

16. Published in Mizrahi, *With Elders Is Wisdom,* 25–27 no. 4.

17. Cf. Druyanow, op. cit., 2:9–10 no. 1034.

65

Froyim Greidinger Revives the Dead

TOLD BY GITSHE AMENT TO SAMUEL ZANVEL PIPE

Froyim Greidinger had an egg that could revive the dead. One day, he told to his wife, "Pretend you're dead."

Then he invited the Jews to pray over her. "My wife has died," he told them, "and I have to bring her back to life."

What he did he do? He took the egg and struck her on the forehead with it—and she came back to life.

He demanded a fantastic sum for the egg. Of course, he received his price.

Once the rabbi's wife took ill and died. They took the egg and tried to bring her back to life, but, of course, it cracked open on her face. Everyone was furious and wanted to kill Froyim. They were going to drown him in the river San. They had already dragged him to its edge when they realized they had forgotten their prayer books. How could they read the confession of the dying with him? What did they do? They nailed him up in a crate and went off to get their prayer books.

Meanwhile, Froyim, shut up inside the crate, kept calling out in Ukrainian: *Ne umyu chitaty, ne umyu pisaty, a khochut mene za krola vybraty.**

A gentile who was passing by heard this. *Ya umyu chitaty, ya umyu pisaty,* he said, *a mene she ne khochut za krola vibraty.***

"You know what?" Froyim Greidinger told the gentile. "Get into the crate, and they'll make you king."

The gentile got into the crate, and the people tossed it into the river and went home. And whom should they see there but Froyim. "What are you doing here?" they demanded.

"It's really marvelous there in the river!" he replied.

What did they do? They all went and threw themselves into the river San.

---

*"I don't know how to read, I don't know to write, and they want to make me king."
**"I know how to read and I know how to write, but they don't want to make me king."

How did that happen? When the first one jumped in and found himself in the deep water, he waved his arms so they would rescue him. The others thought he was calling them to follow him, and they all leaped into the river.

COMMENTARY FOR TALE 65 (IFA 7127)

Recorded by Samuel Zanvel Pipe in 1932 from a fifteen-year-old girl, Gitshe Ament, who heard the story from her mother, a forty-year-old poultry trader.[1]

Cultural, Historical, and Literary Background

Ephraim Greidiger[2]—known as Froy'im Greidiger—was one of the primary practical jokers, or social tricksters, about whom several eastern European Jewish joke cycles have evolved. Initially, each cycle and main character had a limited geographical distribution: Froy'im Greidiger was popular in Galicia, Poland; Hershele Ostropoler in Ukraine (see tale IFA 7755 [this vol., no. 44]); and Motkeh Ḥabad in Vilna, Lithuania. Eventually, the reputations of these figures exceeded their original regions. The personas in the jokes and anecdotes told about them were that of extremely poor tricksters, and much of the humor focuses on their coping with destitution. The stories provide some primary biographical data, although many of such tales have an international distribution and hence belong more to humor than to history. Greidiger is said to have lived in the town of Grodek Jagiellonski, in the Lwow District of Poland, in the mid-nineteenth century; today, this region is part of Ukraine.[3] On the other hand, Druyanow[4] pointed out that some scholars contend that Greidiger is a completely fictional character. A discussion of other Jewish jokers has been published.[5]

Greidiger's popularity in Sanok is evident in Cahan's[6] collection, in which narrators from Sanok told four out of the six anecdotes about the trickster. A comparative annotation of fourteen Greidiger tales is available.[7] Narratives about Greidiger have not been frequently anthologized.[8] Although several chapbooks about Ostropoler have been documented (see the commentary to tale IFA 7755), there is only a single known chapbook of the tales about Greidiger.[9]

Similarities to Other IFA Tales

In the IFA there are only eleven tales about Ephraim Greidiger:

- IFA 7236: *How Did Ephraim Greidiger Trick a Misery Woman?* (Galicia, Poland).[10]
- IFA 7245: *The Day of Atonement in Linsk* (Poland).[11]
- IFA 7332: *Ephraim Greidiger and the Miser* (Sanok, Poland).
- IFA 7333: *A Couple Thinks Ephraim Greidiger Is Elijah the Prophet* (Sanok, Poland).
- IFA 7345: *Ephraim Greidiger Sits on Loaves of Bread* (Sanok, Poland).
- IFA 7401: *Hershele's Underpants* (Russia).[12]
- IFA 9610: *The Lice and the Gold Coin* (Galicia, Poland).
- IFA 9625: *Ephraim Greidiger and the Underwear* (Galicia, Poland).
- IFA 10661: *Ephraim Greidiger, the Plum and the Worm* (Poland).
- IFA 12210: *She Would Not Escape from Your Hands* (Poland).

- IFA 15264: *The Look of Passover* (Poland).
- IFA 16186: *Ephraim Greidiger's Revenge* (Poland).

Other Trickster Characters

With the present story, Ephraim Greidiger joins a long list of tricksters that extends back to *Unibos* (One-Ox), the poor farmer who is the protagonist of a medieval Latin narrative in quatrain verse that likely dates to the tenth century. The tale is available in an eleventh-century manuscript.[13] The Latin original and its German translation[14] and its English translation[15] have been published. The story of *Unibos* is included in two of the milestone collections of European folktales: the Italian *Piacevoli Notti* (1550–1553)[16] and the Brothers Grimm (nineteenth century). The Grimms heard the tale from the Hassenpflug family and from Dorothea Viehmann; the brothers subsequently synthesized these versions into one tale.[17] Hans Christian Andersen[18] (1805–1875) noted that his version of the tale (*Little Claus and Big Claus*) was one of four stories in his collection that he recalled learning in his childhood via the oral tradition; he introduced it as a "real" story. Several comparative studies have been conducted.[19]

In addition to these versions, which were included in prominent collections, S. Thompson[20] noted that the tale "appears in nearly every collection of stories over the whole of Europe and Asia; it is among the most popular stories in Iceland and Ireland, in Finland and in Russia, in India and the Dutch East Indies. It is well known not only on the North African coast but is also found in many parts of central and south Africa," as well as in the Western Hemisphere. Comparative notes on these tales are available,[21] as is an example recorded from the Americas.[22]

The Comic Narrative

The present tale is considered to be a "funny story," or *ridiculum*, a genre that preceded the medieval *fabliaux* and has "close ties with live performance."[23] Essentially, tales of this genre "all depict deception, and usually the deceiver is unmasked at a climatic scene of recognition, yet often the characters' roles are inverted—that is, the deceiver is himself deceived—and hence there is a doubling of lies, of fictions."[24]

Beyer[25] considered the genre *ridicula* within the general German category of *Schwank*, making the distinction between *ridiculum dictum* and *ridiculum factum*—comic speech and comic action (the present tale belongs to the latter subcategory).

On the other hand, Suchomski[26] emphasized the moral rather than the humorous aspect of these tales. Wolterbeek[27] suggested that "Unibos is the earliest version of a folktale that has had worldwide popularity, and later medieval analogues reveal generic distinctions among three types of short comic narrative: *ridiculum, Schwank,* and fabliau." The possible performances and performers of these narratives have been studied.[28] Ziolkowski[29] proposed that, although the vernacular oral version was a popular entertainment, "[i]n Latin verse, [this] story could have been an amusement for highly literate courtiers."

J. Müller[30] conducted a historic-geographic analysis of the tale. In his analysis, which was influenced by his access to German texts (33.1 percent of his sample), Müller examined only European sources, concluding that the tale originated in Indo-European antiquities and spread from Irish Celtic populations to mainland Europe through Flanders and then spread in prongs into the south, west, and north. At the time of the study, he did not have knowledge of the tale from Eastern Europe or from countries of Islam. However, the present text and other versions in the IFA provide evidence that the tale had a wider distribution.

Similarities to Other IFA Tales

Several tales in the IFA are versions of tale type 1535 "The Rich and the Poor Peasant (Unibos);" however, not all of them include "V. Fatal Deception." The following tales include episode V.

- IFA 1288: *How Strange Are the Pathways of Fate* (Libya).
- IFA 1535: *Abu Nuwâs Takes Revenge of the King* (Yemen).
- IFA 1884: *Kachal Sells Excrement* (Afghanistan).
- IFA 5259: *The Resuscitating Cat* (Iraq).
- IFA 5477: *The Two Brothers* (Ukraine).[31]
- IFA 6812: *Two Brothers and Eight Donkeys* (Libya).[32]
- IFA 7594: *The Tricks of Ali Benuet* (Yemen).
- IFA 8725: *He Who Trusts in the Lord Shall Be Surrounded with Favor (Psalm 32:10)* (Iraq).
- IFA 13488: *The Sheik's Clever Tricks* (Iraq).
- IFA 13654: *Abu Al Nuas: The Son Who Hid in His Mother's House* (Yemen).

Folktale Types

- 1297* "Jumping into the River after Their Comrade."
- 1535 "The Rich and the Poor Peasant (Unibos)." (new ed.).
- 1535 (Andreev) *"Dorogaya kozha"* (The Expensive Leather).
- 1535 (El-Shamy) "The Rich and the Poor Peasant (Unibos)."
- 1535 (Jason) "The Rich Man and the Poor Peasant" (episode V is rare in these versions).
- 1535 (Krzyzanowski) *"Sprytny Oszust* (Unibos)" (The Clever Cheat).

Folktale motifs

- J1832 "Jumping into the river after their comrade."
- K113 "Pseudo-magic resuscitating object sold."

- K842 "Dupe persuaded to take prisoner's place in a sack: killed."
- K1860 "Deception by feigned death (sleep)."
- K1865 "Death feigned to establish reputation of false relic."

--- Notes ---

1. First published in Pipe, *Twelve Folktales from Sanok*, 20–21, 44–47, no. 1. Note: This is one of the few tales deposited in the IFA that were not recorded in Israel but in Poland by one of the YIVO *zamlers* (folklore collectors). The present tale's inclusion in the archives and in this volume underscores the continuity in Jewish folklore scholarship and commemorates the scholarly work of a young folklorist and his narrator, who perished in the Holocaust. For local variants of the tales in Pipe's collection, see Bikel, "*Tsvelf folks-mayses fun Sanik*" (Twelve folktales from Sanok).

2. Also spelled Greidinger and, in Yiddish, Greiding.

3. Schwarzbaum, "*Badḥanim ve-Leitzim Mefursamim be-Yisrael*" (Famous Jewish jokers and pranksters), esp. 58–62.

4. *Sefer ha-Bediḥah ve-ha-Ḥidud* (The book of jokes and witticisms), 3:429 n. 1.

5. Lifshitz, "*Badḥonim un leytsim bay Yidn*" (Jesters and jokers among the Jews). Greidiger is not mentioned in this essay.

6. *Jewish Folklore*, 201–204 nos. 19–24.

7. Schwarzbaum, in *Studies in Jewish and World Folklore*, 176–186 nos. 211–224, analyzed the tales that appeared in N. Gross, *Maaselech un Mesholim*.

8. Druyanow, op. cit., 1:306, 316–317, 355, 2:82, 3:290 nos. 787, 815, 927, 1213, 2877; Ausubel, *A Treasury of Jewish Folklore*, 286, 303–304; and Loewe, *Schelme und Narren*, 12–22.

9. Anonymous, *Der berihmter vittsling R. Ephraim Greidiger Z"L* (The famous jokester R. Ephraim Greidiger Z"L).

10. Published in D. Noy, *Sippurim mi-Pi Yehudei Polin* (Tales told by Polish Jews), 49–50 no. 6.

11. Published in Pipe, op. cit., 22–23 no. 5.

12. The same as tale IFA 7236, told about Hershele Ostropoler.

13. Now Ms. 10078-95 9f.38v-42v in the Bibliothèque Royale (Brussels).

14. Langosch, *Waltharius-Ruodlieb Märchenepen*, 251–305, 379–382.

15. Wolterbeek, " 'Unibos' "; and Wolterbeek, *Comic Tales of the Middle Ages*, 150–171 (important discussions, xiii–xvi, 28–35, 124–126).

16. Waters, *The Nights of Straparola*, 1:28–34 night 1, fable 3.

17. Grimm and Grimm, *The Complete Fairy Tales* 247–252 no. 61; Bolte and Polivka, *Anmerkungen zu den Kinder- u. Hausemärchen*, 2:1–18 no. 61; and Uther, *Grimms Kinder- und Hausmärchen*, 2:9–14, 4:124–125 no. 61.

18. *The Complete Fairy Tales and Stories*, 8–19, 1069–1070 no. 2.

19. Honemann, "*Unibos und Amis*"; Wells, "*Die biblischen Wörter im 'Unibos'*"; and Ziolkowski, "A Medieval 'Little Claus and Big Claus.' "

20. *The Folktale*, 165.

21. Liungman, *Die Schwedischen Volksmärchen*, 304–305; and Tauscher, *Volksmärchen aus dem Jeyporeland*, 29–32, 172–173 no. 9.

22. Armistead, *The Spanish Tradition in Louisiana*, 145–147 no. 10.4 (includes a valuable comparative note).

23. Wolterbeek, *Comic Tales of the Middle Ages,* xi.
24. Ibid., 1 (generic analysis, 1–41).
25. *Schwank und Moral,* 73-79; and Beyer, "The Morality of the Amoral."
26 *"Delectaio" und "Utilitas",* 106–110.
27 Wolterbeek, *Comic Tales of the Middle Ages,* 34.
28. Ogilvy, " 'Mimi,' 'Scurrae,' 'Histriones'."
29. Op. cit., 6, 12–13 (quotation from 13). See also Vollmann, "Unibos."
30. *Das Märchen vom Unibos.*
31. Published in Haviv, *Taba'at ha-Kesem be-Golani* (The magic ring in Golani), 43–46 no. 7.
32. Published in D. Noy, *Jewish Folktales from Libya,* 62–66 no. 21.

66

The Death of a Wicked Heretic

TOLD BY ZALMAN BEN-AMOS TO DAN BEN-AMOS

*M*y masters and teachers,

Because I am a *maggid** and go preaching from town to town, I once came to the town of Samakhlalovitch.

Oy, my masters and teachers, I came to the town of Samakhlalovitch. I have to tell you what happened there.

The heretic—may his name and memory be blotted out—had died. He used to eat *treif*** food and desecrate the Sabbath.

And when he died, the family wanted to bury him. Ay, what did they do with him? They buried him in the ground.

Oy, my masters and teachers, in the morning, when the family came to the grave, what did they see? The earth had cast him out.

My masters and teachers, the family didn't know where to put him. They took him, the deceased, the corpse, and tossed him into the river.

The next morning, when they came to the riverbank, what did they see, my masters and teachers? There was the deceased again, lying on the riverbank.

Oy, my masters and teachers, the family didn't know where to put him. They decided, they took him and built a fire, and went and laid him in the fire.

Ay, but he was so wicked, such a sinner, that the fire didn't burn him.

And what, my masters and teachers, is the moral of this? You should be pious, you should not be sinners, you should observe God's Torah.

Oy, my masters and teachers, follow God's way and observe the Torah, so the fire will burn you, the water will swallow you, and the ground will take you.

Speedily in our days, amen.

---

*An itinerant preacher.
**Nonkosher.

COMMENTARY FOR TALE 66 (IFA 21021)

Recorded by Dan Ben-Amos as told by his father, Zalman Ben-Amos (Castrol), during a visit to Philadelphia, Pennsylvania, in the summer of 1968.

Cultural, Historical, and Literary Background

Parodies of Sermons

Parodies of *derashot* (sermons) might have been composed and recited orally by the late antiquities, since the institution of the *derashah* (sermon) in Jewish religious life. However, the Rabbis who edited the literature of that period excluded such works from their exegetical collections. The earliest textual evidence of parody in Jewish literature dates from the twelfth century to the beginning of the thirteenth,[1] but they were not parodies of sermons. Parodies of sermons are available from Christian sources that date to the same period.[2]

Examining medieval sermons, Gilman[3] distinguished between the Latin cathedral and monastic sermons that were preserved through the copying of the works of great preachers and the popular, often vernacular, preaching done in village churches, marketplaces, town squares, and at the sides of dusty roads. The parodies parallel this typology: One group was created by scholastically trained teachers; the other stems from popular tradition. Yet, in Gilman's opinion, the extant texts of both categories are not truly popular creations. "No examples of purely oral tradition have been or could have been preserved, since they were extempore in nature."[4] Their form can interpolated only from preserved literary parodies.

The earliest evidence for parodic sermons is available from 1260, when they were condemned by the council of the Province of Cognac.[5] Within the medieval church, parodies of sermons became part of a ritual and festival when they were performed and developed within the context of the celebration of the *festum innocentium* (feast of the holy innocents). According to Christian tradition, this is celebrated on the twenty-eighth of December in commemoration of the children whom Herod murdered after the apparition of the star to the Wise Men (Matthew 2:16–18). Despite its commemorative nature, during the festival children were permitted to elect a boy-bishop, and the occasion served as the core ritual from which the celebration that was known as the *festum stultorum* (feast of fools) was developed. It was celebrated on or about the feast of circumcision, which took place on the first of January, and it was the feast of fools that included the parodic sermon.[6]

Jewish Parodies

In Jewish society, the festival of Purim served as the occasion for the humorous inversion of religion, ethics, and logic; and many parodies employ the holiday narrative as their basic reference. A bibliographical survey of Jewish parodies in print has been conducted,[7] as has an examination of the genre in general.[8]

The basic reference of the Jewish parodies, of which the present tale is an example, is the institution of the *derashah* in the Jewish religious service in the synagogue. The *derashah*, as performed by *darshanim* (preachers), rabbis, *mokhihim, tzadikim, maggidim,* and *matifim,* has undergone historical, geographical, and social transformations over the long duration of Jewish history, partially represented by preachers' appellations. A selected list of studies on preaching in Jewish religious and social life may be found in the endnotes.[9]

The talmudic-midrashic period was a formative age of the *derashah:* Neither its time in the Sabbath and holiday service nor the role of its speaker was fixed. The literature of the period contains evidence that in the first century the *derashah* was delivered during the Sabbath morning (Luke 4:16–20; BT *Hagigah* 3a); in the second century it was also delivered on Sabbath eve (JT *Sotah* 1:4). Medieval renditions of midrashic sources indicate that sermons took place on the Sabbath during the afternoon prayer (*Yalkut Shimoni, Mishlei* 964). The preachers could have been well-known rabbis (MR *Genesis* 58:3; MR *Song of Songs* 1:64) or itinerate *darshanim*, specializing in either *halakhah* (law) or *aggadah* (legend) (JT *Horayot* 3:7, 48b; MR *Genesis* 12:10, 40[41]; BT *Sotah* 40a).

In the Middle Ages, the preaching situation continued to be governed by custom rather than by law, preserving flexibility and diversity of its position in the service. Sermons were delivered not only on Sabbath and holidays but also on special community occasions and on the celebration of rites of passage.[10]

Sarperstein[11] pointed out that

> [i]t was in the synagogues of the Iberian Peninsula, and later of the Sephardic Diaspora in Italy, Turkey, the Land of Israel, and the Netherlands, where the practice was established that a respected rabbi would deliver a sermon each Sabbath. It was the Sephardim who cultivated the sermon into an art form with a characteristic structure and a set of homiletic and rhetorical conventions. Finally, it was primarily Jews from the Mediterranean basin and not from northern Europe who went to the trouble of writing the texts that enable us to know what they preached.

With the increased Jewish migration to Eastern Europe in the fifteenth and sixteenth centuries and the natural population growth in those regions, traditional ethical preaching evolved as an integral part of religious worship. After the Bogdan Khmelnytsky[12] (1595–1657) pogroms of 1648, the class of itinerant preachers expanded. The emergence of Hasidism in the subsequent century was motivated by this group and then contributed to its further expansion and popularity.[13]

In response to the religious pressure of Hasidism on the one hand and the threat of Haskalah (the Jewish enlightenment) on the other hand, the Musar movement emerged among Lithuanian Jewry, under the leadership of Rabbi Israel ben Ze'ev Wolf Lipkin (Salanter) (1810–1883). The movement, which sought to reemphasize the ethical foundation of Judaism, enlisted not only educators and established rabbis but also itinerant preachers (*maggidim*).[14] Both within and outside of the Musar movement, the *maggidim*—including the popular, itinerant, and well-settled preachers—became an integral part of the social-religious landscape of nineteenth-century Lithuanian Jewry.[15]

Caplan[16] studied immigrant Orthodox Jewish preachers in the United States. He described the rhetorical style, the intonation, and the dramatic performance of the preachers from Lithuania, which the narrator of the present story mockingly imitates.[17]

The *Maggid*

The specific *maggid* whose preaching style is ridiculed in this parody was Rabbi Moshe Yitzḥak ben Noah, known as the Maggid of Kelme (1828–1900).[18] According to Sirkin,[19] in 1859–1860 the rabbi was "a forty year old, short and thin man, with dark complexion, and uncombed dark hair and beard," who wandered and preached around Lithuanian towns. Quite likely, he was born in the town of Kelme, in the district of Kovno. He was a very popular preacher who appealed to pious women in particular. In his sermons, he condemned unethical behavior and specifically criticized the modern conduct of enlightened Jews. Descriptions of Hell featured prominently in his sermons. A disciple of Rabbi Israel Salanter within the Musar movement, he was admired for his tenacity, flamboyant rhetoric, sonorous voice, and uncompromising honesty.[20] A brief mention of his visit to Kamenets and the hospitality accorded to him by one of the community leaders is available.[21] Ten of his sermons have been collected.[22]

The *maggid* was known for his unique style and intonation, which became subjects for imitation and ridicule.[23] Although he was very popular and admired by his followers, the *maskilim* ridiculed him. The present parody appears in a succinct form in a satirical story by Shulman.[24] Quite likely the narrator of the present tale was not aware of the object of his ridicule. However, he grew up in the region in which Rabbi Moshe Yitzḥak ben Noah preached during the late nineteenth century; hence his parody represents a regional oral tradition of the circles of *maskilim* and Zionists. The present tale has been anthologized in books of Jewish wit and humor; and in some of them it has been related directly to the Maggid of Kelme,[25] who was a subject of a cycle of anecdotes.[26] A number of jokes and anecdotes about itinerant preachers and *maggidim* have been published.[27]

Oral Parodies

The performed parody follows similar rhetorical principles that have been observed in medieval parodies: It is in a monologue form, addressing an imaginary audience. The narrator sets the *theme*, which is developed further in the *divisio*. Finally the narrative *dénouement* is an application of the theme, which in this case is a dissolution of logic.[28] Among the published versions, Olsvanger's[29] approximates this structure and the performed style closely. Examples of performed oral parodies of sermons became available for analysis in print only in modern times.[30] Hence the present text is a rare example of an orally recited parody in Jewish folklore.

Formula Tales

The present tale is an example of a "formula tale," a category of tale types (numbers 2009–2340) that employs a narrative device of incremental repetition. This form is more common in balladic poetry than in prose narratives.[31] Note that there is no one tale type number assigned to this style. Poetic examples from a different culture and in song are available.[32]

Similarities to Other IFA Tales

There are two other versions of this parody in the IFA:

- IFA 7745: *The Sinner's Punishment* (Poland).
- IFA 9755: *So Said the Preacher* (Kiev, Ukraine).[33]

Folktale Types

- 1824 "Parody Sermon."
- 1824 (El-Shamy) "Parody Sermon [Fabricated Holy Text]."
- 1824 (Jason) "Parody Sermon."
- 1824 (Krzyzanowski) "*Parodia Kazania*" (Parody Sermon).

Folklore Motifs

- E411.0.6 "Earth rejects buried body."
- *E411.0.6.1 "Water rejects corpse."
- *E411.0.6.2 "Fire does not consume corpse."

---- Notes ----

1. I. Davidson, *Parody in Jewish Literature*, 3–29.
2. Gilman, *The Parodic Sermon in European Perspectives*.
3. Ibid., 11.
4. Ibid.
5. Ibid., 18; and Hoffmann-Krayer, "*Neujahrsfeier im alten Basel und Verwandtes*."

6. Gilman, op. cit., 16–28.

7. Steinschneider, *"Purim und Parodie"*; I. Davidson, op. cit., 209–263 (lists parodies of other liturgical and traditional texts); and Saperstein, *Jewish Preaching 1200–1800,* 91 (n. 4 refers to nineteenth- and twentieth-century literary satires and parodies of famous *maggidim*).

8. Dane, *Parody*; B. Müller, *Parody,* 275–298 (selected bibliography).

9. Ben-Sasson, *Hagut ve-Hanhaga* (Thought and leadership), 34–54; Bettan, *Studies in Jewish Preaching;* Elbaum, *Openness and Insularity,* 242–247; Gliksberg, *Ha-Derashah be-Yisrael* (The sermon in Jewish life); I. Heinemann, *Derashot ba-Tsibur bi-Tekufat ha-Talmud* (Sermon in public in the talmudic period); Saperstein, *Jewish Preaching 1200–1800;* Saperstein, *"Your Voice Like a Ram's Horn";* and Zunz, *Die gottesdienstlichen Vorträge der Juden.*

10. Saperstein, *Jewish Preaching 1200–1800,* 26–44; and Saperstein, *"Your Voice Like a Ram's Horn,"* 149–150.

11. *"Your Voice Like a Ram's Horn,"* 147

12. Also spelled Chmielnicki and Khmelnitski.

13. Piekarz, *The Beginning of Hasidism,* 96–172 (esp. 163–172).

14. Etkes, *Rabbi Israel Salanter;* and D. Katz, *Tenu'at ha-musar* (The Musar movement).

15. Greenbaum, *The Jews of Lithuania,* 110–115; Lewinski, *Encyclopedia of Folklore,* 1:316–317; and Luz, *Parallels Meet,* 149–154.

16. Caplan, *Orthodoxy in the New World.*

17. Ibid., 48–58, 127–131.

18. Other dates: 1829–1880 or 1899.

19. *"Partzufim"* (Portraits).

20. Deinard, *Sichronoth Bat Ami,* 100–105; Etkes, op. cit., 198–204; Gliksberg, op. cit., 453–456; D. Katz, op. cit., 2:395–407; Likhtenshtain, *Pinkas Slonim,* 66–68; and H. Rabinowitz, *Portraits of Jewish Preachers,* 178–181.

21. D. Assaf, *Journey to a Nineteenth-Century Shtetl,* 135.

22 Ben Iloah, *Tokhahat Ḥayyim* (Moralizing for living).

23. Caplan, op. cit., 127 (references to his life and sermons, 178 n. 46).

24. " *'Ikesh u-ptaltol*" (Stubborn and twisted), esp. 284. The story was anthologized in E. Davidson, *Sehok Pynu (Our Mouth's Laughter),* 2:964–965 no. 969.

25. Miller, *Fun'm Yiddishn Kval,* 195 no. 22. For other versions, see Ausubel, *A Treasury of Jewish Folklore,* 382; Druyanow, *Sefer ha-Bediḥah ve-ha-Ḥidud* (The book of jokes and witticisms), 1:184 no. 475; and S. Mendelsohn, *The Merry Heart,* 59.

26. Druyanow, op. cit., 1:187–190 nos. 481, 484, 485; and Lipson, *Medor Dor* (From days of old), 1:18, 73, 163–167, 231 nos. 45, 184, 409–415, 632, 2:42–43, 105–107, 208 nos. 964, 965, 1163–1167, 1538, 3:41, 146, 164, 245–248 nos. 1871, 2179, 2225, 2489–2492.

27. N. Gross, *Maaselech un Mesholim,* 108–118; Richman, *Jewish Wit and Wisdom,* 96–114; Miller, op. cit., 186–196; and Rawnitzki, *Yidishe Witzn* (Jewish wit), 147–160; and Schwarzbaum, *Studies in Jewish and World Folklore,* 147 no. 104.

28. Cf. Gilman, op. cit., 15.

29. *Rosinkess mit Mandlen,* 167–169 no. 263; and *L'Chayim!,* 46–47 no. 51.

30. I. Russell, " 'My Dear, Dear Friends.' "

31. Gerould, *The Ballad of Tradition,* 105–110.

32. Lomax and Lomax, *Negro Folk Songs,* 108–110 ("De Grey Goose"); and R. Abrahams, *A Singer and Her Songs,* 119–129 ("Go Tell Aunt Nancy").

33. Published in M. Cohen, *Mi-Pi ha-Am* (From folk tradition), 1:116 no. 92.

67

Who Had It Better?

TOLD BY ZALMAN BEN-AMOS TO DAN BEN-AMOS

I'm sure you believe that in the other world everything is good for the righteous and bad for the wicked. But let me tell you, you're dead wrong. How do I know? I'll tell you what happened.

One Erev Shabbat,* late Friday afternoon, a righteous man died and went to the other world. When he arrived there in the other world, they all said: "Where will he be sent? To *Gan Eden*,** of course! He was such a righteous and God-fearing man!

But then a fly appeared and said it had something bad to report. What was it?

The fly told its story: "One day, when the rabbi was sitting and learning Torah, I was flying in the room. I felt tired and landed on his forehead. The rabbi gave a slap and killed me. So there is a question about him, and a *beit din*§ must be convened to issue a ruling."

It was Erev Shabbat, and the heavenly tribunal does not sit on the Shabbat. What did the president of the other world court decide? That the righteous man and the fly should be taken and put in a special room together, and, with God's help, a *beit din* would be convened on Sunday and issue a verdict.

One Erev Shabbat a freethinker died and went to the other world. When that sinner arrived there in the other world, they all said: Where will he be sent? Here it is Erev Shabbat, and he is a freethinker, after all. The verdict was to *Gehenna*.§§

Then a fine young *shiksa**** appeared and said she had something good to report. What was it? "When he was a young man, he used to like to ogle the girls bathing naked in the river. He hid among the trees and watched

---
*Yiddish for "Sabbath eve."
**Garden of Eden or Paradise.
§A Jewish court of law.
§§Hell.
***A woman who is not a Jew, usually a derogatory term.

473

them. When I started to go under, he, the sinner, jumped into the water and tried to rescue me." So there was a question about him, and a *beit din* had to be convened to issue a ruling. But now it was Erev Shabbat.

What was decided? That the sinner and the gentile woman should be put together in the same room.

Now ask yourself: Who had the better time? The righteous man with the fly, or the sinner with the *shiksa*?

COMMENTARY FOR TALE 67 (IFA 21022)

Told by Zalman Ben-Amos to his son, Dan Ben-Amos, in June 1968 in Philadelphia.

Cultural, Historical, and Literary Background

This ironic tale inverts the standard ethical principles and social hierarchy of Jewish society by relating to two common themes in Jewish tradition. First, is the principle epitomized in motif Q172.2 "Man admitted to Heaven for a single act of charity" or its opposite—namely that a man could be sent to Hell because of a single transgression or crime. For a discussion of this subject, see the commentaries to tales IFA 5377 (this vol., no. 45), IFA 7612 (this vol., no. 13), and IFA 10089 (vol. 1, no. 28). Although the other tales focus on a general behavior pattern rather than a single event, the present story builds on the talmudic notion that even a single humane act can save a person from the throws of Hell. As "R. Eliezer the son of R. Jose the Galilean said: Even if nine hundred and ninety-nine parts of that angel are in his disfavour and one part is in his favour, he is saved" (BT *Shabbat* 32a). Other tales deal with this issue, albeit not humorously.[1]

The second theme is the use of the gates of Heaven and Hell as a location for a humorous narrative. In Jewish and non-Jewish comedic traditions, there are many tales about political and religious leaders entering or about to enter Heaven or Hell.[2]

Similarities to Other IFA Tales

Similar tales can be found in the IFA, although the following are not humorous.

- IFA 2485: *Moshke the Evil-Doer* (Eretz Yisra'el, Ashkenazic).[3]
- IFA 4941: *Rabbi Levi Isaac of Berdichev before the Heavenly Court* (Eretz Yisra'el, Ashkenazic).[4]
- IFA 4945: *The Rich Miser* (Eretz Yisra'el, Ashkenazic).[5]
- IFA 6002: *In the Heavenly Court* (Hungary).[6]

Folktale Types

- 809* "Rich Man Allowed to Stay in Heaven."
- 809* (El-Shamy) "Rich Man Allowed to Stay in Heaven."
- 809* (Haboucha) "Rich Man Allowed to Stay in Heaven."
- 809* (Jason) "Rich Man Allowed to Stay in Heaven."
- 809** "Old Man Repaid for Good Deeds."
- **809A (Haboucha) "The Two Souls on Judgment Day."

Folklore Motifs

- A661 "Heaven."
- A661.0.1 "Gate of heaven."

- A671 "Hell."
- A671.1 "Doorkeeper of hell."
- E755. "Destination of the soul."
- cf. J2102.3 "Bold man aims at fly: hurts his head."
- Q53 "Reward for rescue."
- Q172.2 "Man admitted to heaven for a single act of charity."
- V71 "Sabbath."
- X370 "Jokes on scholars."

——————— **Notes** ———————

1. M. Gaster, *The Exempla of the Rabbis,* 153 no. 397; and Schwarzbaum, *Studies in Jewish and World Folklore,* 158–160, 470.

2. E.g., Galnoor and Lukes, *No Laughing Matter,* 23, 68–69; and Richman, *Jewish Wit and Wisdom,* 364.

3. Published in Weinstein, *Grandma Esther Relates . . . ,* 38–41 no. 4.

4. Ibid., 37–38 no. 3.

5. Ibid., 55–57 no. 13.

6. Published in Bribram, *Jewish Folk-Stories from Hungary,* 32–33 no. 14.

68

The Shammes Who Became a Millionaire

Told by Bella Ḥaviv to Yifraḥ Ḥaviv

*O*nce a Jew from Poland came to America with his family. He didn't know English and began looking for work. They offered him a job as the *shammes** in a synagogue. To be a *shammes* there you have to be able to read the notes from people who are asking for charity. But the fellow couldn't read or write English. So they told him, "You're fired."

He went out into the world, did what he did and became a millionaire. One day he went to the bank. "Sign here," the clerk told him.

The Jew replied, "That's no great skill! If I knew how to write, I'd still be the *shammes* in the synagogue."

---

*A synagogue caretaker.

Commentary for Tale 68 (IFA 14351)

Recorded by Yifraḥ Ḥaviv in Kibbutz Bet Keshet in 1983 from his mother, Bella Ḥaviv, from Hruszow, Podolia, in Ukraine.

Cultural, Historical, and Literary Background

This anecdote is part of the "American cycle" of eastern European Jewish tales about immigration to and emigration from America (see also tale IFA 19949 [this vol., no. 42]). The tale recurs as an immigration story in the Jewish jokes of the Soviet Union.[1] Similarly, this tale has been a favorite among American collectors of Jewish humor.[2] Moreover, the tale was part of the eastern European humorous tradition pertaining not only to immigration but to any transition, as from rural to urban life.[3]

William Somerset Maugham (1874–1965) used this tale as the basis for his 1929 story "The Man Who Made His Mark" and for his short story "The Verger."[4] The story was also included in the film *Trio* (1951), which adapted three of Maugham's short stories for the screen.[5] The Romanian author Konrad Bercovici (1882–1961) filed a plagiarism suit against Maugham, contending that "The Verger" was based on his own story "It Pays to Be Ignorant." Maugham responded that the tale was "a well-known piece of Jewish folklore" that he heard from his friend Ivor Back, who was a surgeon.[6]

By comparison to the anthologized and the literary versions of the tale, the present rendition appears truncated and literarily underdeveloped. Because the narrator was an accomplished storyteller, as is evident from her other tales in the IFA, narrative incompetence can be ruled out, and other explanations for the present form are necessary. These could be circumstantial, indicating that the narrating and recording situation was inadequate; cultural-social, reflecting the relevance, or rather irrelevance, of the tale to the narrator's social life; or transmittal, representing a decline in the verbal adequacy along the oral transmission sequence. General discussions of these issues in folklore are available.[7]

Similarities to Other IFA Tales

There are four other versions of this tale in the IFA:

- IFA 14355: *How Did an Illiterate Person Become a Millionaire?* (Poland).[8]
- IFA 16660: *The Shammes Who Was Illiterate* (Russia).[9]
- IFA 17210: *The Scrap Iron Millionaire* (Israel).
- IFA 20281: *A Time for Everything* (Eretz Yisra'el, Sephardic).

Folktale Type

- *1799 A (IFA) "A Shammes Becomes a Millionaire."

Folklore Motifs

- N203 "Lucky person."
- N410 "Lucky business venture."
- *N427 "Man cannot hold a lowly job because of illiteracy, pursues his own business and becomes rich."
- V400 "Charity."

――――― **Notes** ―――――

1. Harris and Rabinovich, *The Jokes of Oppression,* 40–41.

2. Ausubel, *A Treasury of Jewish Folklore,* 16–17; Koppman and Koppman, *A Treasury of American Jewish Folklore,* 150–151; F. Mendelsohn, *The Jew Laughs,* 196–197; and Spalding, *Encyclopedia of Jewish Humor,* 430–431.

3. Druyanow, *Sefer ha-Bediḥah ve-ha-Ḥidud* (The book of jokes and witticisms), 1:3 no. 6; and Scheiber, *Essays on Jewish Folklore and Comparative Literature,* 313–314.

4. In *Cosmopolitans,* 221–233; also available in *The Complete Short Stories,* 572–578.

5. The other two stories are "Mr. Know-All" and "Sanatorium."

6. Rogal, *A William Somerset Maugham Encyclopedia,* 295–296; and T. Morgan, *Maugham,* 545.

7. Dégh and Vazsonyi, "Legend and Belief"; Dundes, "The Devolutionary Premise in Folklore Theory"; E. Fine, *The Folklore Text;* Ortutay, "Principles of Oral Transmission in Folk Culture"; and S. Thompson, *The Folktale,* 428–448.

8. Told by the husband of the narrator of the present version.

9. Published in Kabarnit, *Sippurim ve-Zutoth* (Tales and anecdotes), 6–7.

69

I Have No Place to Rest

TOLD BY TONY SOLOMON-MA'ARAVI

The story goes like this: There were two friends, let's call them Moses and Aaron, both of them first-rate scholars, shoemakers by profession, but unsuccessful. Their living, as the saying goes, was in the prayers in the prayer book. The two fellows used to sit and talk: Would they ever manage to get up from the table feeling full?

One fine day, Moses told Aaron that he had decided to go to America and seek his fortune there. He couldn't stand being hungry any more. With tears in their eyes they told each other good-bye and swore they would never forget each other.

So Moses went off to America.

After he was gone, Aaron got married. He lived in respectable poverty with his wife and children and quite forgot that he had ever had a good friend by the name of Moses.

But over there, in golden America, Moses got lucky. After several years, he remembered that he had once had a comrade named Aaron and began to long for him. Moses sent Aaron a ticket and invited him to come visit.

Aaron was so surprised that he fainted away. His wife threw cold water on him. Then she asked him, gently, "What will be, Ar'ele, if you go to America? Did he send you a ship ticket?

"It's all right. Moses has a good head. He'll take care of you there. You'll have what to eat and a place to lay your head. And who knows, maybe when you come back he'll even give you some money."

Aaron took his wife's advice and made the journey. En route he threw up into the black waves even the mother's milk he had once suckled, but finally the voyage was over. His comrade Moses greeted him warmly. He showed him what he had amassed there in golden America. Then he made Aaron a proposal:

"Bring your wife and children over. America is big. America is 'all right.'* You come here a poor man and turn into a respectable person."***

Aaron pondered the matter before replying with a stern no. He was going back. He didn't need America with its luck.

He did just as he said and returned home.

When his wife saw him, she began asking how their Moses was living over there, what things were like there.

Aaron began telling the story to his wife and to the neighbors who had come to greet him.

"God should have mercy on Moses there: Where he eats he doesn't sleep, where he sleeps he doesn't smoke, where he smokes he doesn't work. He simply has no place where he can stop and rest. . . ." And because he could not bear watching Moses suffering so much and being miserable, and since he obviously couldn't help him, he had left him behind in God's care and come home quickly. "In truth, my dear wife, we are really fortunate people. Here, for example, in the very same room we eat, we sleep, we work, you do the laundry and you cook here. Not the way my Moses slaves over there in that dismal America."

And that's how it used to be. . . .

---

*"*Alrayt*" in Yiddish.
***"*Layt*" (respectable person) may have the connotation of "non-Jew."

Commentary for Tale 69 (IFA 18592)

Tony Solomon-Ma'aravi wrote this tale down from memory in Yiddish in 1991 in Petaḥ Tikvah.[1]

Cultural, Historical, and Literary Background

For a discussion of immigration to America and return immigration to Europe, see the commentary to tale IFA 19949 (this vol., no. 42). In both tales, a shoemaker, one of the lowly professions in shtetl society, serves as the returning figure who is unable to adjust, physically or morally, to life in the New World. A characteristic of immigrant humor is the focus on the clash of cultures; most often the newcomer is the target of ethnic jokes, which point out the immigrant's inability to perceive and adjust to a higher standard of living or highlight the differences in style and practice between the new and the old communities. A comparable joke that builds on the separation and combination of residential and business spaces was collected by Dorson.[2]

Folklore Motifs

- F111.2 "Voyage to Land of Promise."
- F701 "Land of plenty."
- *F701.3 "America, the land of gold."
- *P165 "Poor men."
- P310 "Friendship."
- P453 "Shoemaker."
- *P486 "Scholar."
- T100 "Marriage."
- U60 "Wealth and poverty."
- *Z71.0.3 "Formulistic number: two."

--- Notes ---

1. First published in the Yiddish newspaper *Yisrael Shtime* on March 4, 1991.
2. "Jewish-American Dialect Stories on Tape"; and Richman, *Jewish Wit and Wisdom*, 373.

70

Stalin Tests His "Friends"

Told by Mordecai Hillel Kroshnitz
to Ayelet Oettinger

Stalin, when he was alive, wanted to know which nation loved him the most—because there are many nations in Russia. Lots of them. So he summoned people from every nationality and questioned each one.

"Do you love me?" he asked. "Do you know who I am?"

"Yes. You are our leader, the father of all the nations, Stalin."

"Do you love me?"

"Certainly, Father Stalin!"

"Would you give your life for me?"

"Certainly, Father Stalin!"

So he takes the fellow over to the window—it was the fifth floor—and says, "Jump out!"

Everyone looks down and recoils. Nobody wants to jump. Until the Jew came. Stalin asks him all the same questions, and the Jew says, "Yes, Father Stalin. Yes, Father Stalin."

"Are you willing to be killed for me? To give your life for me?"

"Yes, Father Stalin."

He takes him to the window and says, "Jump!"

The Jew hardly stops to think and lifts his leg over the sill, ready to jump!

Stalin grabs hold of him and says, "No, no! I won't let you die. You are wonderful! Now I see that you truly love me. But please explain—what's going on? No one from any of the other nations wanted to jump—why are you the only one?"

He says (with tears), "I'll tell you the truth, Father Stalin. If life is like this, death is better. Death is better."

Commentary for Tale 70 (IFA 14263)

Told to Ayelet Oettinger-Salama by her grandfather Mordechai Hillel Kroshnitz from Poland in 1986 in Kiryat Yam.

Cultural, Historical, and Literary Background

In dictatorial regimes, humor serves as the only political venue for the citizenry; and even then, individuals who practice it openly may pay with their lives. Such was the case in the Germany of the Third Reich[1] and during the Holocaust in other European countries.[2] This was also the case in the Soviet Union during the period of Joseph Stalin (1879–1953) and beyond.[3] Humor, however, functions politically not only in dictatorial regimes but in all other forms of government as well.[4]

The reign of terror during the period that Stalin ruled over Russia was destructive to the lives of many ethnic groups. Several biographies and other works have attempted to assess his life in politics.[5] Studies of the oppressive society his regime created, Stalinism, and the particular humor generated during that time are available.[6]

Within this political environment, the ethnic minorities were of particular concern.[7] Among these ethnic groups, the Jews were a target of special anti-Semitic actions that had their origin in government policies and Stalin's own agenda. Studies of Jewish life in the Soviet Union and Stalin's own attitude toward the Jews have been conducted.[8] The narrator of the present story does not specify the ethnicity of the other three characters, but in its format the tale follows the pattern of ethnic jokes in which the ethnic identity of the figures has cultural and comic significance. Studies of ethnic humor have been published.[9]

Folktale Type

- 1870*A (IFA) "Jokes on Dictators."

Folklore Motifs

- *H1556.0.3 "Test of fidelity (loyalty) of citizen."
- J227 "Death preferred to other evils."
- Q72 "Loyalty rewarded."
- W34 "Loyalty."

——————— **Notes** ———————

1. Hillenbrand, *Underground Humour in Nazi Germany 1933–1945.*

2. It. Levin, *Beyond the Tears;* Lipman, *Laughter in Hell*; and Stokker, *Folklore Fights the Nazis.*

3. Draitser, *Taking Penguins to the Movies;* Harris and Rabinovich, *The Jokes of Oppression;* and Lif, *Forbidden Laughter.*

4. Galnoor and Lukes, *No Laughing Matter;* Mulkay, *On Humor,* 197–212; and Nilsen, *Humor Scholarship,* 53–57.

5. The classic study is Deutscher, *Stalin.* Selected studies that appeared after the fall of the Soviet Union are Medvedev and Medvedev, *The Unknown Stalin*; Radzinsky, *Stalin*; and Rayfield, *Stalin and His Hangmen.* For a relevant bibliography, see Bloomberg and Barrett, *Stalin.*

6. Fitzpatrick, *Everyday Stalinism;* D. Hoffmann, *Stalinism;* Read, *The Stalin Years;* and Sacks and Pankhurst, *Understanding Soviet Society.*

7. Pipes, "Reflections on the Nationality Problems in the Soviet Union"; Rockett, *Ethnic Minorities in the Soviet Union*; Armstrong, "The Ethnic Scene in the Soviet Union"; and Armstrong, "The Soviet Ethnic Scene." For an examination of issues related to ethnicity and nationalism in the post-Soviet era, see Williams and Sfikas, *Ethnicity and Nationalism in Russia.*

8. Lustiger, *Stalin and the Jews;* Pinkus, *The Jews of the Soviet Union;* and Rucker, *Staline, Israël et les Juifs.*

9. Davies, *Ethnic Humor around the World.*

71

Communism and Religion

TOLD BY MORDECAI HILLEL KROSHNITZ
TO AYELET OETTINGER

Stalin wanted to reform religion. What does that mean, "to reform religion"? He wanted the religions to start teaching that Communism had not begun just now, with the Revolution, but that the Bible, too, preaches communism and there has always been Communism.

So he summons the head of the Orthodox Church, which was the most important in Russia. That was their religion. He asks him, he tells the head priest, the patriarch, "You have to reform religion, to teach anyone who studies in the church and comes to you that Communism began long ago and that the Bible preaches Communism."

"I cannot do that," says the patriarch. "Communism is against religion. How can I do such a thing? Distort the Bible?"

He summons the head of the Catholic Church in Russia, and the same refrain is repeated, "I cannot."

He summons the head of the Muslim church (that of Uzbekistan and Kazakhstan and Turkistan), all the Muslims, and he says the same thing. After that he summons the chief rabbi.

There was a chief rabbi in Moscow, for all the Jews. The rabbi says, "Comrade Stalin, we don't have to change anything. We recognize the fact that there was Communism already at the beginning. The Bible tells about it from the first day."

"How can that be?" Stalin asks.

"It is written that Adam and Eve were naked and barefoot and had to make do with one apple, that they shared and went naked and barefoot, and they said they were living in paradise. Nu, that's just the way it is with us here."

Commentary for Tale 71 (IFA 14264)

Told to Ayelet Oettinger by her grandfather Mordecai Hillel Kroshnitz in 1986 in Kiryat Yam.

Cultural, Historical, and Literary Background

In this tale, Stalin's request follows the pattern of the Soviet Union's notorious practice of adjusting history to serve the government's political and ideological purposes. Following the Communist interpretation of Marxist philosophy, the Soviet regime rejected religious worship of any faith and imposed on its citizens an ideology that promoted atheism.[1] Although the present joke underscores the antireligious measures of the Soviet regime, the tale follows the pattern of religious disputation stories in Jewish tradition.

The classic tale involves the ruler of the Khazars, their Khaqan, who converted to Islam in 737 C.E. and then to Judaism three years later. One of the narratives in the Jewish tradition that explains this event involves a religious dispute between representatives of Islam, Christianity, and Judaism, each defending the superiority of his own faith.[2] Other historical cases are known.[3] In the present story, however, the rabbi acts like a figure in modern Jewish ethnic jokes cycles in which he demonstrates his superiority through witty repartee, clever actions, and tricky behavior.[4] References to studies of humor under oppressive regimes are given in the commentary to tale IFA 14263 (this vol., no. 70).

Similarities to Other IFA Tales

Other versions in the IFA are the following:

- IFA 10145: *The Opinion of Soviet Citizen* (Poland).
- IFA 13222: *Who Wrote Yevgeni Oniegin* (Ukraine).
- IFA 14993: *Where Is the Butter? Where Is Ḥayyim?* (Russia).

Folktale Type

- 1870*A (IFA) "Jokes on Dictators."

Folklore Motifs

- A694.2 "Jewish paradise."
- H961 "Tasks performed by cleverness."
- P426.1 "Parson (priest)."
- *P426.4 "Rabbi."

--- Notes ---

1. Bercken, *Ideology and Atheism in the Soviet Union*; Casey, *Religion in Russia*; Hakim, *Islam and Communism*; C. Lane, *Christian Religion in the Soviet Union*; and J. Thrower, *Marxist-Leninist "Scientific Atheism."*

2. Bin Gorion, *Mimekor Yisrael,* 228–231 nos. 122–123 (1990 ed.).

3. Baron, *A Social and Religious History of the Jews* (see index to each vol., "Controversies, socioreligious").

4. Cray, "The Rabbi Trickster"; and L. Mintz, "The Rabbi Versus the Priest." For another version, see Galnoor and Lukes, *No Laughing Matter,* 108.

Abbreviations

AA	American Anthropologist
A&AS	African and Asian Studies
AASOS	The Annual of the American Schools of Oriental Studies
ABD	Anchor Biblical Dictionary
AE	Acta Ethnographica
AfR	Archiv für Religionswissenschaft
AFS	Asian Folklore Studies
AFSBSS	American Folklore Society, Bibliographical and Special Series
AJH	American Jewish History
AJS	American Journal of Sociology
AJSR	AJS Review: The Journal of the Association for Jewish Studies
AL	American Literature
ALing	Anthropological Linguistics
AN	African Notes
APH	Acta Poloniae Historica
ARV	Arv: Scandinavian Yearbook of Folklore
AUR	The Aberdeen University Review
BGDSL	Beiträge zur Geschichte der deutschen Sprache und Literatur
BPIASA	Bulletin of the Polish Institute of Arts and Sciences in America
BYBFS	Bestia: Yearbook of the Beast Fable Society
BT	The Babylonian Talmud
CCM	Cahiers de civilization médiévale
CJ	Conservative Judaism
CJL	The Canadian Journal of Linguistics/La Revue canadienne de linguistique
CJRT	Canadian Journal of Religious Thought
CL	Comparative Literature
CMP	Culture, Medicine and Psychiatry
CQ	The Classical Quarterly
DLMV	Die deutsche Literatur des Middelalters Verfasserlexikon
DSD	Dead Sea Discoveries: A Journal of Current Research on the Scrolls and Related Literature
DV	Das deutsche Volkslied

EBS	Eschel Beer Sheva
EEJA	East European Jewish Affairs
EJ	Encyclopaedia Judaica
EM	Enzyklopädie des Märchens
FFC	Folklore Fellows Communications
FHL	Forum Homosexualitat und Literatur
FJB	Frankfurter judaistische Beiträg
FS	Filologishe shriftn (YIVO)
HTR	Harvard Theological Review
HUCA	Hebrew Union College Annual
HUS	Harvard Ukrainian Studies
IFAPS	Israel Folktale Archives Publication Series
IFR	International Folklore Review
IUFS	Indiana University Folklore Series
JAF	Journal of American Folklore
JAOS	Journal of the American Oriental Society
JBA	Jewish Book Annual
JBQ	Jewish Bible Quarterly
JE	The Jewish Encyclopedia
JFER	Jewish Folklore and Ethnology Review
JFI	Journal of the Folklore Institute
JH	Jewish History
JHCS	Journal of Halacha and Contemporary Society
JHSE	The Jewish Historical Society of England: Transactions
JJGL	Jahrbücher für jüdische Geschichte und Literatur
JJML	Journal of Jewish Music and Liturgy
JJS	Journal of Jewish Studies
JLS	Journal of Literary Semantics
JNES	Journal of Near Eastern Studies
JPOS	Journal of the Palestine Oriental Society
JPS	The Jewish Publication Society
JPSR	Jewish Political Studies Reviews
JQL	Journal of Quantitative Linguistics
JQR	Jewish Quarterly Review
JSHL	Jerusalem Studies in Hebrew Literature
JSJ	Journal for the Study of Judaism
JSJF	Jerusalem Studies in Jewish Folklore
JSJT	Jerusalem Studies in Jewish Thought
JSN	Journal of Soviet Nationalities
JSOT	Journal for the Study of the Old Testament
JSOTSS	Journal for the Study of the Old Testament Supplement Series
JSP	Journal for the Study of the Pseudepigrapha
JSQ	Jewish Studies Quarterly

JSS	*Jewish Social Studies*
JT	*The Talmud of the Land of Israel: A Preliminary Translation and Explanation*
JThS	*The Journal of Theological Studies*
JuB	*Judaica Bohemmiae*
JUS	*Journal of Ukrainian Studies*
JVL	*Jahrbuch für Volksliederforschung*
KR	*The Kentucky Review*
KS	*Kirjath Sepher*
LBIYB	*The Leo Baeck Institute Year Book*
LiS	*Language in Society*
LS	*Language and Speech*
MAQ	*The Morton Arboretum Quarterly*
MGWJ	*Monatsschrift für Geschichte und Wissenschaft des Judentums*
MH	*Mehqere Hag*
MJ	*Modern Judaism*
MLN	*Modern Language Notes*
MLR	*Michigan Law Review*
MP	*Modern Philology*
MR	*Midrash Rabbah*
MT	*Marvels and Tales*
NCFS	*Nineteenth-Century French Studies*
NJ	*Nordisk Judaistik: Scandinavian Jewish Studies*
NMS	*Nottingham Medieval Studies*
NYFQ	*New York Folklore Quarterly*
OGS	*Oxford German Studies*
OT	*Oral Tradition*
P&P	*Past & Present*
PAAJR	*Proceedings of the American Academy for Jewish Research*
PFLS	*Publications of the Folk-Lore Society*
PMLA	*Publications of the Modern Language Association of America*
PR	*The Polish Review*
PTL	*PTL: A Journal for Descriptive Poetics and Theory of Literature*
PZKA	*Philologus: Zeitschrift für das Klassische Altertum*
RAL	*Research in African Literatures*
REJ	*Revue des études juives*
RJV	*Rheinisches Jahrbuch für Volkskunde*
RR	*Romanic Review*
RSPT	*Revue des Sciences Philosophiques et Théologiques*
RTP	*Revue des Traditions Populaires*
SAV	*Schweizerisches Archiv für Volkskunde*
SBL	*Society of Biblical Literature*
SFF	*Studia Fennica Folkloristics* [*SF* as of 1992]

SFQ	*Southern Folklore Quarterly*
SH	*Scripta Hierosolymitana*
SHAHYB	*Sefer Hashanah: The American-Hebrew Year Book*
SJA	*Soviet Jewish Affairs*
S/L	*Ha-Sifrut/Literature*
SP	*Studies in Philology*
TAPA	*Transactions of the American Philological Association*
TE	*Talmudic Encyclopedia*
VS	*Victorian Studies*
VT	*Vetus Testamentum*
WCJS	*World Congress of Jewish Studies*
WF	*Western Folklore*
WZKMU	*Wissenschaftliche Zeitschrift der Karl-Marx-Universität*
YA	*Yeda-'Am*
YAJSS	*Yivo Annual of Jewish Social Sciences*
YB	*Yivo Bletter: Journal of the Yiddish Scientific Institute*
YCS	Yale Classical Studies
YF	*Yidischer Folklor*
YFS	*Yel French Studies*
YIVO	*Yidischer Vissenshaftlecher Institut*
YJS	Yale Judaica Series
YV	*Yad Vashem*
ZÖV	*Zeitschrift für Österreichisch Volkskunde*

Narrators

Adar, Motel. (1912–1964). Born in Rudnik, Poland, a *shtetl* in western Galicia, into a Hasidic family. His father died when he was ten years old, but his mother made every effort that he would continue to receive a traditional religious education. Nevertheless, at a very young age he had to start working in the basket-making industry to help his mother care for the family. As a young adult he joined the He-Halutz-Deror movement, preparing himself to immigrate to the Land of Israel. He was a shepherd in kibbutz Tel Yosef, and later in kibbutz Bet-ha-Shittah. He loved the Hasidic tradition and read Hasidic books, particularly tales, extensively. After his death his family deposited forty-four tales that he had recorded in the IFA.

Altman, Leon. (b. 1906). Born in a village near Bacau, Romania, in the Moldavia region. Further biographical information is unavailable.

Ament, Gitshe. (dates unavailable). Born in Sanok, Poland, she was fifteen years old when she told and sang her stories and songs, most of which she learned from her mother, a poultry trader in the market.

Armon (Kastenbaum), Hayyim Dov. (b. 1899). Born in Dambrowa, Poland, and immigrated to the Land of Israel in 1939. He lived in Tel Aviv, where he worked in the Post-Office Bank. A religiously observant person and an intellectual, he organized the "Maimonides Circle," a home study circle that met weekly for the examination of issues in Jewish philosophy. He edited two books.

Ben-Amos, Zalman [Castrol]. (1898–1983). Born in Minsk, Belarus, and educated there and in the yeshivah of Odessa. During and after World War I, he taught in a rural Jewish school in Lithuania, where he met Rivka Feinzilber, whom he married in 1922. Both were ardent Zionists and immigrated to then-Palestine two years later; after living in Jerusalem for six months, they moved to Tel Aviv, where they remained until 1930, when they moved to Petah-Tikvah, with the hope for a more regular employment. In Jerusalem, Tel Aviv, and Petah-Tikvah, Ben-Amos worked constructing roads and building houses. After moving to Petah-Tikvah, he began working in the quarries of Migdal Zeddek, where he joined the Jewish auxiliary police (*ghafirs*) during the riots of 1936–1939. During World War II, he worked in a factory that served the war effort; and after the war, he became a Solel Boneh laborer. In 1955, he suffered a major head injury when a car hit him from behind; after recovering, he was forced to retire. All of his life, he was active in community life and was a member of numerous committees of the local branch of the Histadrut ha-Kelalit shel ha-Oudim be-Eretz Yisrael (the General Federation of Labor in Israel), yet he never held an appointed office.

Bergner-Kish, Esther. (b. 1909). Born in Budapest, Hungary, and immigrated to the Land of Israel as a teenager in 1926. After her marriage, she was a homemaker. When she became a widow at a young age, she raised her two children alone. To earn a living, she learned secretarial skills, worked as an accountant, and was able to take shorthand dictation in English and in German. After her retirement, she was a volunteer, helping needy people and, in particular, reading to the blind and translating texts from English to Hebrew.

Berosh, Yitzhak. (b. 1901). Born in Warsaw, Poland. Further biographical information is unavailable.

Beroshi, Azriel. (1897–1986). Born in Lyskow, Poland, in the Wolkowysk district (now Belarus). He was one of the first tour guides in Palestine and imparted his love of the countryside, historical sites, and other features of the land to generations of newcomers and native-born Israelis during the Yishuv period and the early days of the State of Israel. He received his primary education in traditional Jewish schools in his hometown but also acquired a broad secular education. He joined the Zionist-socialist movement before the outbreak of World War I but stayed in Lyskow during the German occupation (1915–1917), teaching Jewish schoolchildren. He moved to the Land of Israel in 1920, working first as a pioneer in road building but shortly thereafter joining the educational system as a teacher and principal in the schools of Moshav Balfuriah, Jerusalem, and then Tel Aviv. He taught children, adolescents, and adults. His essays about historical sites in Israel were collected in a small volume, *Ba-Derekh Asher Halakhti* (1968). In 1984 the Tel Aviv City Council bestowed upon him the title of "Tel Aviv Honored Citizen."

Bezditnichke, wife of Ḥayyim Leizer from Berdichev. Biographical information is unavailable.

Bornstein, Naftali. (c. 1880–c. 1960). Born in Poland and immigrated to the Land of Israel in the 1920s during the third Aliya. After the establishment of the State of Israel, he worked in a government office. He learned the tales he told from the Hasidic oral tradition, listening to them in the Hasidic rabbi's court when Hasidim gathered on the Sabbath and during holidays.

Bribram, Gershon. (1885–1983). Born in the small town of Batorkeszi (Batorovekesy) in northwest Hungary. His father was a cantor and a *shoḥet* (ritual animal slaughterer). He had a traditional education in a yeshivah, yet complemented his studies with a general education in a private high school. After completing his studies at the age of twenty-two, he became a *shoḥet* and tutored children privately. He married the daughter of a cantor in 1911 and began to serve as a cantor himself, moving to the town of Hatag (Hatszeg). In 1915, he was recruited to the Austrian army and fought in Italy, where he was seriously wounded.

In 1925, he moved to Arad, Romania. In 1950, he moved to Israel and settled in Kibbutz Ma'agan, where three of his seven children lived. He learned his stories mostly from his parents, who told them in Yiddish. The IFA contains fifty-six tales that he wrote down from memory and fourteen of those tales appeared in Bribram's *Jewish Folk-Stories from Hungary* (1965).

Cheplik, Itzhak. (dates unavailable). Born in Petrikov, Belarus and moved to then-Palestine in 1922. He lived in Tel Aviv. He was a generous and kind man and used to conduct biweekly lessons for Talmud studies in his home.

David, Yosef. Biographical information is unavailable.

Faygenboym, Elimelekh. (b. 1900). Born in Kuznica, Poland, in the Bialystok district. He was the sixth child of Itzhak and Zevia Esther. He and his twin brother studied in a yeshivah until World War I. During the war, he was among the sympathizers of the Germans who entered their town. He and his brother considered the Germans more civilized than the Ukrainians and Poles who attacked the Jews during periodic pogroms. He noticed that the Jewish soldiers in the Austrian army spoke Yiddish and befriended the Polish Jews, whereas the Jews in the German army spoke only German and did not reveal their Jewishness. In 1924, he immigrated to the Land of Israel, living first in Rosh Pinnah, where he was a tobacco farmer. His son, Levi, was born in Safed in 1925. The same year, the family moved to Kiryat Hayyim. Later, Faygenboym moved to Ramat Gan. His life in Israel was entwined with tragedies: His son, Levi, was killed in Bet Keshet's fields on March 16, 1948, during the War of Independence. His grandson Levi (born just after his father's death and named after him), died in 1974, and his other grandson, Amiram (Levi's firstborn), died in 1980.

Feierstein, Itzhak-Isidore. (b. 1903). Born in the village of Lysobyki, Poland, near Tluste in eastern Galicia. He studied in Czernowitz and Vienna and was politically and ideologically involved in the Po'alei Zion party, as a journalist and as a public speaker. During World War II, he was in Mielnica, where he was captured and tortured. After the war he lived in Germany and was involved in the investigation of war crimes and in the welfare of war refugees. He came to Israel in 1971 and settled down in Haifa.

Furman [Fuhrmann], Israel. (1890–1967). Born in Sarata, Romania, in the Bukovina district. After 1920, he lived in Chernovtsy (Czernowitz), Romania. After the war, he worked in Bakoy, Romania, moving to Israel in 1965. From his youth, he was an indefatigable collector of proverbs. His first collection, which he prepared for publication, was lost in the war; but he resumed his project and continued to record Yiddish proverbs. His book *Idishe shprichwerter un redensartn* (1968), which includes 1,778 proverbs with interpretive notes, was published posthumously. A biographical sketch and a selection of his proverbs are in *Yeda-'Am* 10 (1964), 35–41 [Hebrew].

Fus, Dvora. (b. 1913). Born and raised in the *shtetl* of Lewdow near Vilna, Lithuania. During World War I, the members of her family were refugees in

Minsk, Belarus, for three years, after which they returned to their hometown. For seven years before the war (1903–1910), her father lived in America and worked in the sweatshops of New York, trying to support the family he left back in Lithuania. Fus was a member of He-Ḥaluz ha-Za'ir, a Zionist youth movement, and immigrated to the Land of Israel in 1934. She was active in public life, a member of the Yeda-'Am (the Israel Folklore Society), and published poems in Yiddish and a memoir of her life in Lewdow. Seven of the twenty-one tales that she recorded were published in *Seven Bags of Gold* (1969). She learned her tales from her parents, Kalman and Esther Lipkind, both of whom were avid storytellers and known for their hospitality. Fus said that she learned to love folktales at home. "My father was careful to observe the *mitzvah* of being hospitable and my good-natured mother helped him. Our home was open to all, poor and rich alike. On Sabbath evenings and at the close of the Sabbath the house was filled with people who told and listened to stories, and I was among the audience. My mother told me many stories she had heard at her own home as well." In her old age, she lived with her daughter in Moshav Aseret.

Goldenberg, Sima. (b. 1915). Born in Tulcea, Romania, to parents from Romania and Turkey. After twenty-five years of marriage, Goldenberg divorced her husband and raised her only son alone. In Bucharest, she worked as a seamstress, an occupation she continued after she immigrated to Israel and settled in Ashkelon in 1964. Very successful professionally, she later managed a seamstress cooperative. She learned her tales from her customers, to whom she also enjoyed telling stories.

Gutterman, Pinḥas. (1906–1991). Born in Miechow, Poland, in the Kielce district, to a Hasidic family. He remembered his parents as very religious people who worked hard to make ends meet and yet were very generous, extending their hands to widows, orphans, and the sick. On Friday afternoons, they would stop their work and begin their preparations for the Sabbath. In the evening, parents, children, and guests would come home from the synagogue; and after the meal, they would tell Hasidic legends about the Ba'al Shem Tov and other Hasidic rabbis, Maimonides, blood libels, the thirty-six hidden righteous men, Elijah the Prophet, and miracle workers. He started his studies in a *ḥeder* (Hebrew school) at the age of four, and when he was ten years old he entered high school. At the end of World War I, he had to stop his education and work to support his family because his father was sick. In 1919, a year after Poland gained its independence, and then again in 1920 during the Russo-Polish campaign, he witnessed Polish pogroms against the Jews; the experiences left him shocked and confused, shaking his fundamental religious beliefs. He found solace in reading Jewish history and modern Jewish literature. During World War II, he joined the partisans in the Polish forests. After the war, in 1947, he immigrated to the Land of Israel, where he worked as a landscaper. He began writing his memoirs and published his first story in Yiddish in 1950; the next year, he published a collection of his short stories. He lived in Rammat ha-Hayal together with his wife and their only son. Two hundred of his tales are preserved in the IFA.

Halamish, Shimon. (1904–1982). Born in Yanov, Poland, near Lublin. His father died seven days after Halamish was born, and because his mother was busy all day at her store, the boy was reared by his grandparents. He began schooling at a very early age; he excelled and began to study independently, asking older students for help in explaining difficult issues. While studying traditional literature, he began, in secret, to read modern Hebrew and Yiddish writers. At the outbreak of World War I, he and his older brother became agents for the Yiddish newspaper, and thus he became a local expert in politics and current events. Being exposed to modern literature and the newspaper led him to become a secular Zionist; he was active in Zionist circles but, because of restrictions on immigration, was able to settle in then-Palestine only in the 1930s. At that time, unemployment was rampant, so he moved to Tel Aviv, where he began to work as a house painter. He joined the emerging labor movement and volunteered for many roles that later developed into professional administrative positions. In the course of his work, he met Yom-Tov Lewinski, the founder of the Israel Folklore Society, who convinced him to record from memory a version of the text and melodies of the Purim play *The Sale of Joseph* as well as many other stories.

Haviv, Bella. (1909–1986). Born in the *shtetl* of Jerishev, Ukraine, in the Podolsk district. Her father was a *shohet* (ritual animal slaughterer). As a child she experienced both World War I and the Communist revolution, and those events left indelible impressions on her. She lost her father when she was only eleven years old and so began to help her mother maintain their family of six children. Shortly thereafter she decided to immigrate to then-Palestine, following her sister, who went to the Land of Israel illegally. She achieved her goal in 1928 and began to work during the daytime and study in the evenings. She married in 1929 and had two sons and two daughters. The family lived in the village of Givton, near Rehoboth. Her son Yifrah is an avid recorder of folktales, and he wrote down thirty-three tales that Haviv had heard in her childhood in Ukraine from an old woman during the winter nights.

Herbest, Raphael. (b. c. 1940). Born in Czechoslovakia and immigrated to Israel after World War II. He served in the Israel Defense Forces as a paratrooper.

Hermann, Yehudah. (b. 1913). Born in Warsaw. He grew up in a traditional Jewish home and moved to Paris in 1938, where he married Rachel Fuchs a year later. During the war years, they were in Paris and had many close calls eluding the German police. Their three children were born in Paris. In 1955, the family moved to Brazil; but later their children moved to Israel. In 1980, Hermann and his wife moved to Israel and joined their son Daniel in kibbutz Beit-Keshet, of which he was a member. Hermann spoke several languages and was erudite in Jewish traditional literature. As a young man growing up in Warsaw, he heard many Hasidic and general Jewish stories, and during his mature years he enjoyed sharing them.

Keren, Abraham. (b. 1912). Born on July 8 in Bircza, Poland, a town situated in the Carpathian Mountains, on a road that linked the towns of Sanok and Przemysl. During World War I, he and his parents were refugees in Vienna. After the war, they returned to their hometown, where his father was a textile merchant and a community leader and his mother helped in the family business. As a teenager, Keren joined a Zionist organization and continued his studies for a teaching certificate at the Jewish Teachers Seminar in Warsaw. During the Russian occupation (1939–1941), he was a school principal in Bircza, and he spent the later war years in ghettoes and concentration camps. After the war, he was active in education in the camps for displaced persons. He immigrated to Israel after its establishment, where he continued teaching. He was an active collector of folktales, many of which he recorded from his own family.

Keren, Moshé (Einehorn). (b. 1898). Born in Cernovitch, the capital of Bokovina. When he was very young, his family moved to Hungary. He studied in the yeshivah of Syget-Marmucz and served in the Austrian army during World War I. In 1930, he immigrated to the Land of Israel and lived in Haifa. He worked in the Shemen factory while he was active in the Jewish Haganah underground during the period of the British mandate. During World War II, he served with the British forces, and after the establishment of the State of Israel he held different offices in the immigrant town of Hazor.

Kroshnitz, Mordechai Hillel. (1915–1998). Born in Baranowicze, Belarus, formerly Poland, where he received a traditional primary Jewish education and modern schooling in a "Tarbut" high school. He had to leave high school because he organized a student revolt, and he took his matriculation examinations externally. Later, he studied accounting in Warsaw. From a young age he was active in the Zionist-socialist youth movement Frayheyt (freedom). At the age of seventeen he served as the executive secretary of the district council, and at the same time organized the Frayheyt Vilna branch. He joined the Shaḥariya kibuttz in Vilna, where he met Mina-Tamar Faybowitch, whom he married in 1936. At the outbreak of World War II he escaped to Lubcza, Poland (today Belarus), his wife's hometown, and later he escaped, together with his wife and infant daughter, to Samarkand, Uzbekistan. There he joined the Red Army. Later he fought and was wounded in the battle of Leningrad. At the end of World War II he returned to Poland and was sent by the Zionist Party to organize the activities in the Upper Silesia district. He was the manager in a kibbutz that was a gathering point for Jewish survivors in Byten, Poland. He planned to immigrate to Israel and for that purpose he was smuggled to the border with Germany. While there he became one of the leaders of the survivors in Germany, and he was a delegate and lecturer in congresses of the survivors and in the World Jewish Congress in Switzerland (1948). In Germany, he was a founding member of the Association of Jewish Writers and Artists. During the War of Independence he was active in organizing both illegal immigration to Palestine and Gaḥal, the overseas volunteers for the Israel Defense Forces. With his wife and two children, he himself came to Israel in 1949, settling in Kiryat Ḥayyim near Haifa, where he worked as the secretary of the Clerical Workers Union and continued to be a union consultant about Israeli labor laws. Simultaneously with his involvement in public affairs he engaged in literary and journalistic writing. He edited books and newspapers in Yiddish—among them *Bafrayung,* the labor party's journal of the Holocaust survivors in Germany, and the anthology *Haifa,* a yearbook for literature and art. He was a member of the Writers' Association in Israel and the Association of Yiddish Writers. In his literary activities he edited the memorial books for the communities of Krasnobrod, Lubcza, and Delatycze, Poland; he wrote four books in Yiddish: *Doyres*; *Erd*; *Eygns*; *Natur un mentsh*; and he received several literary prizes.

Levi, Malkah. (b. 1927). Born in Vaslui, Moldavia, Romania, to a large family; she had five brothers and four sisters. Her parents were Zionists who encouraged their children to move to then-Palestine, but she could not fulfill this dream before World War II. After the war, she joined the Gordoniah youth movement and worked on a farm, preparing herself for agricultural life in the Land of Israel. Together with her friends, she boarded a ship in a Yugoslavian seaport that was part of an illegal immigration to the Land of Israel. She was arrested with other immigrants and was shipped to a camp in Cyprus. There she met and married Tanḥum Levi. They were among the founders of Moshav Nevatim in the northern Negev; but after abandoning their settlement during the War of Independence they moved to Arugot, where they built their farm and where their three children were born.

Liberman, Rosa. (b. 1900). Born in Bendzin, Poland. She grew up in a traditional Jewish family and attended primary school. At the age of eighteen, she got married and moved with her husband to Berlin, where he had a textile business and she was a midwife. In 1938, she was expelled from Germany to Poland, and she returned to live with her parents. She had two sons and two daughters, but lost her husband, her sons, and her parents during the Holocaust. Together with her younger daughter she was sent to Auschwitz and survived the ordeal until the liberation of the camp in May 1945. At the end of the war, she and her daughter began the long journey to then-Palestine, arriving in Israel in 1948, after spending some time in the camps for illegal immigrants in Cyprus.

Moskovitz, Shalom. (1887–1980). Born in Safed. He grew up in a home steeped in tradition. He worked as a watchmaker, a silversmith, a scribe, and a stone mason. His small workshop was destroyed during the War of Independence, and consequently he decided to make some occupational changes and began producing and selling plywood toys, decorated in Crayon colors; he had once made such toys for his grandchildren. The toys were sold at the Safed

Central Bus Station and caught the eye of the Israeli painter Yossl Bergner (b. 1920), who encouraged Shalom to become an artist. At the age of seventy, he began painting biblical figures and scenes, blending them anachronistically with kabbalistic and Hasidic themes and symbols as well as with contemporary sights. His artwork has been the subject of a book, several exhibitions, several essays, and a brief video recording—for example, Doron and Wiesel's *Images from the Bible* (1980), Rodov's "Origin and Developments in the Work of Shalom Moskovitz from Safed" (1994), and Doron and Eagle's *Shalom of Safed: An Innocent Eye of a Man of Galilee* (video recording; 1988). In 1961, he visited New York for the first exhibition of his works in the Julius Carlebach Galleries. The popular press published several articles about him, including an essay and eight reproductions of his works in *Horzion* 3, no. 6 (1961). He became known as Shalom of Safed, gaining an international reputation as an Israeli naive painter; his paintings and prints are sold in art galleries the world over.

Neuman, Zindale (Zundil, Zygmunt). (1891–1942). Lived in Kolomyja, Poland (today Ukraine). The father of Dov and Meir Noy, he was a very erudite person, with profound knowledge in Jewish tradition. During World War I, he served in the Austro-Hungarian army, as had his father before him. His learning served him and his community well during World War II. While he refused to work for the Judenrat, he agreed to be in charge of the postal services in the ghetto. In this capacity he was able to help the members of the Kolomyja community maintain contact with the outside world and their relatives in then-Palestine. He was able to decipher for the people the code language letter-writers used to avert the German censorship. Thousands of people witnessed how he was shot to death by the Germans when he rushed to save his family.

Orenstein, Efraim. (1908–1968). Born in Frumusica, Romania, a small Jewish town in the Moldavia region. His father was an estate manager of one of Moldavia's rich land owners. He went to high school in Botosani and Iasi; after graduation, he returned to his hometown. Initially, he joined his father's business, but he found himself more interested in music, literature, and art. He obtained a broad knowledge in Yiddish literature and culture and organized a Yiddish library in his town and directed and acted in the local amateur theater. During World War II, he was detained as a political prisoner; when the war ended he moved to Botoshany, where he was in charge of trade and continued his involvement in amateur theater. He immigrated to Israel together with his family in 1962.

Pelz, Naḥum. (b. 1924). Born in Zakroczym, Poland. In 1940, he was taken to the Warsaw ghetto, from which he escaped, although his entire family perished in the Holocaust. Throughout World War II, he hid in different places. After the war, he enlisted in the Polish army and served for three years. In 1946, he married; and in 1957, he immigrated to Israel.

Rabinovitch, Dov-Berl. (dates unavailable). He was the father of the folktale collector Zalman Baharav. According to his son, Rabinovitch was a scion of a rabbinical family who did not follow in his father's footsteps. He lived in the *shtetl* of Klinkovich in Belarus. In his youth, he piloted barges on the river and served in the Russian army. Upon his discharge, he opened a pub and earned his living that way. As a pub owner, he mixed with the local peasants and policemen and thus learned about the impending pogroms in sufficient time to warn the Jewish community. He was a strong man who did not hesitate to fight back and whom local hooligans feared.

Rabinovitz, Ya'akov. (b. 1892). Born in Stolin, Poland (now Belarus) and grew up in a Hasidic family. He moved to Kiev, where he married his wife, Fruma. His son, Barukh, was born in 1922 and grew up to be a talented scientist. During World War II, his son volunteered to serve in the army and was killed in battle in 1943. Shortly thereafter, Rabinovitz's wife died. After the war, he returned to Poland with his second daughter and his son-in-law, and in 1947 they immigrated to the Land of Israel. In Israel, he was involved in maintaining the tradition and community life of the Karlin Hasidim from Stolin.

Reeder, Avigdor. (1895–1977). Born in Szczebrzeszyn, Poland, in the Zamosc district. He studied in a *ḥeder* (Hebrew school) and a yeshivah. He was the fourth of a family of four brothers and eight sisters, all crowded in a small dwelling. When his father died in 1914, he stopped his studies and began to work, traveling to Lublin, where he found a job in a bakery that hardly paid for his basic needs. Thanks to a friend, he moved to a better paying job in another bakery. At that time, he was influenced by the new social and Zionistic ideas that swept through Jewish society in Poland. During World War II, he lost his family—his mother, wife, ten-year-old daughter, and several brothers and sisters and their families. He survived by escaping to Russia; after the war and the establishment of the State of Israel, he immigrated in 1949. In Israel, he lived in Acre and had two daughters. He used to tell stories on the long winter nights and on the Sabbath and holidays.

Reeder, Neḥemiah. (1864–1914). Born in Zamosc, Poland, and lived in Szczebrzeszyn. He studied in the *ḥeder* (Hebrew school) until his bar mitzvah. Shortly thereafter he began to work in manual labor, without learning a profession. He moved to Warsaw and continued his wandering life in the big city until the age of twenty-four. Then he got married and moved back to Szczebrzeszyn, where he had a bakery and was a Hasid. He had twelve children. His grandmother was the wife of the chief rabbi in the Old City of Jerusalem.

Rochfeld-Ḥaimovits, Serl. (b. 1905). Born in Mogielnica, Poland, in the Warsaw district. Her father was a tailor who worked for the Polish nobility in the area. She completed her studies in elementary school and prepared herself for entering high school in Warsaw, but, because of a family tragedy during which six of her siblings died within a short time, she could not leave her parental home. She married Zvi Moshe Ḥaimovits in 1927 and joined her husband in then-Palestine in 1931. Because of severe diabetes, she lost her eyesight; but despite her blindness she continued to be active in family affairs. She loved to tell the stories she had heard from her mother and grandfather, who served as a sailor in the czar's navy for twenty-five years.

Rotshtein, Shlomo. (b. 1914). Born in Lomazy, Poland. In Israel, he lived in Jerusalem and worked in construction. Further biographical information is unavailable.

Salomon-Ma'aravi, Tony. (b. 1912). Born in Bivolari, Romania, in the Moldavia district. She was active in the Zionist movement since childhood, finally arriving in Israel in 1948. She worked as an accountant in Petaḥ Tikvah and also had some literary interests. She authored three books in Yiddish; the first drew on her grandfather's memoirs, the second was an account of Romanian Jewry during World War II, and the third included her own memoirs about her postwar activities and her involvement in illegal immigration to then-Palestine. Her Yiddish short stories appeared in the newspaper *Israel Shtime*.

Salz, Ḥayyim. (1876–1936). Born in Safed, Israel, where he lived all his life. He and his wife, Neḥamah, who was born in Tiberias (Teveryah, Israel), married very young and had four daughters and two sons. In Safed he served as a religious supervisor of animal slaughtering and also tanned cowhides for parchment, processing them for scribes to write Torah scrolls. He was a tolerant, happy, and good-hearted man who loved to study and to tell stories, always finding a ready audience to listen to him. On these, often spontaneous occasions, he would follow his stories with songs, and the listeners would join him. In his community, he was also known as a healer who knew incantations against the evil eye and who used them effectively, protecting those who sought his help.

Scharf, I. (dates unavailable). A silversmith from Chernovtsy (Czernowitz), Romania. Further biographical information is unavailable.

Sheinferber, Hinda. (1904–1996). Born in the *shtetl* of Mogielnica, Poland, near Warsaw. She grew up in a very religious home. In 1926, at the age of twenty-two, she married David Aaron Sheinferber and a week later immigrated to then-Palestine. The young couple lived in Jerusalem, where their two sons were born. Because of economic difficulties, they moved to Haifa, where their daughter was born. Their economic conditions did not improve much, so Sheinferber helped by working in temporary jobs outside the home. She lost a son in the war of 1948; and twenty years later, her husband died after two years of sickness. The death of a grandson in a car accident was an additional tragic blow. Despite these difficulties and tragedies, she was able to maintain a positive attitude and to have an active social life. The religious books and the Yiddish literature that she read constantly were sources of strength and pleasure for her and enriched the repertoire of folktales she had learned from her mother. Most of her tales have didactic purposes, and she felt that through storytelling she was able to state her opinion about current affairs and diverse situations.

Sosenski, Wolf. (1890–1969). Born in Dolhinov, Lithuania, a small *shtetl* in the province of Vilieka in the Vilna district. His father was an expert tailor. Although he began studying in the *ḥeder* (Hebrew school) at an early age, he had to join his father's workshop, learning to be a tailor at the age of nine, after a fire destroyed all of his family's possessions. Nevertheless, he continued to read and became self-taught. At the age of eighteen, he joined a cultural-national Belarus student movement and contributed articles to the movement's journal, working all the while as a tailor. He learned several languages and was known for his pleasant singing voice. He served in the Russian army beginning in 1910, and after participating in several battles in World War I, he was taken as a war prisoner. He married in 1921, and in the interwar years he was active in community affairs and attained a high administrative position in a local bank. During World War II, he was separated from his family, joined the partisans, and later learned about the deaths of his wife and seven children. After that war, he remarried and had one daughter. He continued to work as a tailor until his bad eyesight did not permit him to continue. Encountering further anti-Semitism, he decided to immigrate to Israel in 1966. He left in Belarus a collection of folktales and folk songs that he wrote down from memory, which is now on deposit in the folklore archive of the Belarus Academy in Minsk.

Tamari, Y. (dates unavailable). Came to Israel from Hungary. Other biographical information is unavailable.

Tesler, Aryè. (1879–1957). Born in a *shtetl* in Hungary. His father died when he was just two years old, and his widowed mother raised him and his four siblings. He studied in a *ḥeder* (Hebrew school) and, later, in yeshivahs in Sighet and Bondyhad. He married Rivka Mandel in 1896 and moved to Sighet, where he owned a grocery store. After World War I, he moved from one place to another looking for work. After a forest that he was managing went up in flames, he became a *shoḥet* (ritual animal slaughterer) and a cantor. By that time, he had six sons and three daughters. In 1941, he was deported with all of the Jews who lived in that rural area across the Dniester River, and he became a cantor again. After the war, two of his children immigrated to the Land of Israel, and he and his wife joined them in Kevuzat Yavneh.

Weinstein, Esther. (1906–1966). Born in Safed, on Purim eve, hence her name. Her parents were religiously observant Ashkenazic Jews who had four daughters and two sons. The synagogue of the Stretyner Hasidim (followers of Rabbi Judah Zevi Hirsch Stretyn; d. 1844) was a floor above their home. Weinstein heard many of the tales in her repertoire in that synagogue; among them were stories about Rabbi Ḥayyim Tyrer of Czernowitz (1770–1816), the anniversaries of whose birth and death were observed in that synagogue and were specific occasions for storytelling about him. Uncommon for the period and the community, Weinstein and her sister graduated from a modern religious school, which exposed them to the new Jewish society that had emerged at that time as well as to the geography of the Land of Israel. Like the rest of the Jewish population in Safed, she and her family suffered economically during World War I. At fifteen, she moved to Haifa to live with her sister, where she met her husband, Ḥayyim Weinstein. They lived in Haifa, Safed, Nes Ziona, Kiryat Ḥayyim, and Bat-Shelomo. In Haifa, they lived on the border between the Jewish and the Arab territories, yet her life and the lives of her family were spared during the 1929 and 1936–1939 conflicts because of the good relations she maintained with her Arab neighbors. Eighteen of her tales appeared in her *Grandma Esther Relates*... (1964).

Weissman, Gershon. (b. 1959). Born and educated in Haifa. He was a paratrooper in the Israeli army. After his discharge, he received a B.A. degree in economics and business administration. He married and had two daughters. He loves to recount stories he heard others tell on various occasions.

Wexler, Bezalel. (1908–1987). Born in Vilna, Lithuania. He attended Tarbut High School in his hometown. He continued his studies in the rabbinical college in Wroclaw (German Breslau), in southwest Poland, from which he received his ordination as a rabbi. Later, he studied at the German University in Prague, where he received his doctorate in Oriental studies. He immigrated to the Land of Israel in 1934 and worked as an educator, being a teacher and a school principal in Bat-Yam, Haifa, and Kiryat-Shemonah. He authored several textbooks for teaching the Hebrew language, literature, and Jewish tradition, and he was a prolific translator of German to Hebrew. Among the authors whose works he translated are Heinrich Böll (1917–1985), Max Frisch (1911–1991), Hermann Hesse (1877–1962), Knut Hamsun (1859–1952), and Konrad Lorenz (1903–1989). He was a founding member and a rabbi of the Reform communities in Haifa and Nahariyyah.

Ẓuriel [Zerkandel], Azriel. (1917–1997). Born in Brody, Poland, in the eastern Galicia district. When he was four years old, his family moved to Sanok in central Galicia. His father, Shmuel, was a learned man, and when Ẓuriel had his bar mitzvah, his father taught him the entire Talmud. When he was sixteen, he convinced his mother to let him go to Germany to pursue traditional Jewish and general non-Jewish studies, and he enrolled for that purpose in the rabbinical and teacher's college in Frankfurt am Main. Despite his poor economic conditions, he devoted himself totally to his studies. When Hitler rose to power, he foresaw the consequences and immigrated to then-Palestine on November 27, 1933. In Jerusalem, he began to work in the Post Office, a position he maintained until his retirement. He was a talented storyteller with a phenomenal memory. In particular, he loved to tell stories about common people who had left an indelible impression on him.

Collectors

Aryeh-Sapir, Nili. (dates unavailable). Born and educated in Tel Aviv. She studied Hebrew literature and Jewish philosophy at Tel Aviv University; during her military service, she was an officer teaching in a military boarding school. After her discharge from the military, she continued her studies in the Department of Jewish and Comparative Folklore at the Hebrew University of Jerusalem, specializing in folklore of the Land of Israel. Her doctoral dissertation (completed in 1998) is on stories and ceremonies in Tel Aviv, 1909–1936. She participated in a project preparing a folklore curriculum for teaching folklore in Israeli high schools. Now she teaches at the Department of Jewish and Comparative Folklore at the Hebrew University of Jerusalem and in the Literature Department of Tel Aviv University, specializing in public ceremonies and personal narratives.

Avitsuk, Yaacov. (1924–1993). Born in Vaslui, Romania, in the Moldavia region. He was the sixth child in a family of nine children. His father, an upholsterer, instilled in his children the love for the Land of Israel and the hope to live there. All of his brothers and sisters were members of Zionist organizations and prepared themselves to live in then-Palestine in agricultural settlements, a goal they all fulfilled. Avitsuk grew up in a traditional home, but he did not remember his father as a learned person. He heard stories about his grandfather, who escaped conscription to the Russian army and sought refuge in Romania. His grandfather gained the respect of his non-Jewish neighbors because of his strength and his knowledge of folk medicine—a tradition he passed on to his own son, Avitsuk's father. When Avitsuk was young, his father used to take him to hear wandering Hasidic preachers who visited Vaslui, and from them the boy learned many stories. He also learned many stories from his father, who used to tell them around the family table on Sabbath eve.

Avitsuk remembered that his parents welcomed to their home the city's poor people and travelers, who used to tell stories during their stay. At the end of World War II, he joined a Zionist organization and came to Israel in 1946 onboard an illegal ship. After a short period of confinement in the Atlith Camp, he was released and joined the Haganah underground; after the establishment of the State of Israel he began working as a teacher and as a youth counselor for new immigrants. In 1955, he married his wife, Tamar, and joined Moshav Be'er-Tuviyyah. After participating in the 1956 Sinai Campaign, Avitsuk completed his studies in a teacher's college in Beer-Sheva. He published a book of poems in 1961, began writing short stories about the life of the new immigrants to Israel, and started to record oral tales from his family and from newcomers. He published some of the tales he recorded in *The Tree That Absorbed Tears* (1965) and *The Fate of a Child* (1985).

Baharav, Zalman. (1902–1983). Born in the *shtetl* of Klinkovich, Belarus. Although his father was a descendant of a rabbinical family, he himself was not involved in learning; after his discharge from military service, he owned a tavern. He studied in a reformed *ḥeder* (Hebrew school), where he was exposed to Hebrew literature as well as traditional studies. His mother died when he was thirteen years old, and he began his studies at the yeshivah of Lida in 1915, which were disrupted by the Russian revolution of 1917. In 1922, he joined a he-Ḥalutz group, which engaged in manual labor on the Russian steppe, the Caucasus Mountains, and around the Black Sea. With this group, he immigrated to then-Palestine in 1923 and joined Gedud ha-Avodah. Later, Baharav worked as a shepherd in Tel-Ḥai; in 1926 he moved to Jerusalem, where he worked on an archaeological excavation. Next, he worked in road construction around Jaffa and in the construction of the electric hydraulic station in Naharayyim. In 1929, he joined the moshav (farm cooperative) of Be'er-Tuviyyah. Because of his wife's sickness and then her death at an early age, he could not maintain his own farm and thus worked as a hired laborer in the moshav. After the establishment of the State of Israel, he joined the Shaḥal organization and dedicated himself to the task of the absorption of immigrants, becoming the cultural secretary of the labor council in Ashkelon.

Behar, Dinah. (b. 1929). Born in kibbutz Kiryat Anavim (Israel), where she was educated and lived until 1957, when she moved with her family to Bet Zayit. She worked on the farm for several years and then decided to continue her education at Hebrew University, studying Hebrew language and literature. As a student of Dov Noy, she recorded folktales primarily from Wolf Sosenski .

Ben-Amos, Dan. (b. 1934). Born in Petaḥ Tikvah (now in Israel). He was educated in local schools and, later, at Hebrew University and Indiana University at Bloomington. He is a member of the faculty of the Graduate Group in Folklore and Folklife at the University of Pennsylvania and the editor of this series, *Folktales of the Jews*.

Ben-Aryeh, Menaḥem. (1930–1996). Born in Rosh Pinnah, Israel. A grandson of Rabbi Yehoshua Ben-Aryeh, one of the founders of Rosh Pinanah and the regional village head, representing five Jewish settlements and a dozen Arab villages in the Upper Galilee, Ben-Aryeh was a reporter for the Israeli daily *Ha-Boker* until 1956. He recorded the tales and memoirs of the early farmers in the Upper Galilee who founded such settlements as Metullah, Mishmar ha-Yarden, Mahanayim, Rosh Pinnah, and Yesud ha-Ma'alah; of the founding members of the kibbutzim Kefar Giladi and Ayelet Hashakhar; and of residents of Safed and Tiberias (Teveryah). During this time, he interviewed hundreds of people. Fluent in Arabic, he recorded Arabic proverbs, translated them into Hebrew, and annotated his collection with comparative notes and Hebrew proverbial parallels. He was an avid recorder of folktales, and by 1980 he had deposited 159 tales in the IFA.

Ben-Zakkai, Yoḥanan. (c. 1900–1970). Most of the stories he recorded and submitted to the IFA draw on the tradition of the Karlin Hasidic dynasty of Lithuania. He learned many of them from his father, Rabbi Benjamin Israel Globerman from Poland, who was the assistant of Rabbi Aaron of Karlin II (1826–1872) and the tutor of his grandson, Rabbi Israel Perlov, known as "Ha-Yenuka of Stolin" (the Child of Stolin; 1873–1921). Ben-Zakkai lived in Jerusalem; but after the death of his twenty-year-old daughter in 1948, the family moved to Tel Aviv. He translated Russian tales and fables into Hebrew.

Bribram, Gershon. See "Narrators."

Burt, Moshe. (1916–1998). Born in Warsaw, Poland. His father was a teacher of Russian and a director of amateur Yiddish theatrical productions, first in the city of Gorki, Belarus, and later in Poland. His mother was a seamstress. At the age of thirteen, Burt lost his father and had to start working to help support his family; for eight years, he apprenticed himself to a goldsmith. In 1937, he opened his own workshop, but two years later war broke out. He was the sole survivor of his family, who perished in the Holocaust. At the end of the war, he boarded an illegal ship to come to then-Palestine; but after the ship was caught by the British forces, he was detained in Cyprus, to be released on November 29, 1947, the day the United Nations decided on the establishment of two states, one Jewish, one Arab, in the former Palestine. In Israel, he first joined a kibbutz but a year later joined the police, where he served for twenty-one years. He had a daughter and two sons. He was an aspiring author and published about thirty short stories in the daily *Omer*.

Cohen, Malka. (b. 1908). Born in Be'er-Tuviyyah, Israel. Her father immigrated to the Land of Israel in 1889, coming to the country at the age of thirteen as a stowaway on a Romanian ship. At the age of seventeen, she joined the Labor Brigade; and after her marriage to Raphael Cohen, she settled in Moshav Ein-Vered. Later, they moved to Tel Aviv, where they engaged in the business of agricultural goods. Cohen was an active member of the Yeda-'Am, the Israel Folklore Society, recording tales and memoirs from the elderly and organizing a folklore club in an old-age home. She was also a volunteer, helping the sick and teaching Hebrew to newcomers. Cohen published some of the tales she recorded in *Mi-Pi ha-Am* (1974–1979) and authored six books for adolescents.

Gut-Burg, Yehudit. (b. 1928). Born in Safed. She was a teacher and a member of Kibbutz Gevar-Am in the Upper Galilee, later moving to Kiryat Tiv'on. She recorded more than one hundred tales told by her mother, Esther Weinstein.

Gutterman, Pinḥas. See "Narrators."

Ḥaimovits, Zvi Moshe. (b. 1900). Born in Warsaw a year after his family moved from their *shtetl* of Mogielnica in the Warsaw district. His father studied for the rabbinate but turned to business and leased a large farm that his brother managed. In Warsaw, his father was a trader; but after World War I began, the elder man returned to Mogielnica. In the interwar years, while his father became active in the Jewish religious political parties in Poland, Haimovits joined the Zionist Workers (Po'alei Zion) party. In 1931, he immigrated to then-Palestine and settled in Haifa, where he worked first in a quarry and later became a member of Moshav Ein Iron, to which he moved in 1937. During World War II, he was a watchman for the Jewish Settlement Police coast guard. In 1949, he began working at the Jewish Agency in the Immigration Department; and from 1956 to 1968 he was the director of an old-age home. After 1968, Haimovits returned to Ein Iron and worked on his farm. He had three children and several grandchildren and great-grandchildren.

Haviv, Yifrah. (b. 1930). Born in Tel Aviv, and grew up in Gibbethon near Rehovot. He was educated in the local school system and joined the youth movement Ha-Mahehanot ha-Olim and the underground youth brigade. He stopped his formal studies as the War of Independence started in 1948, and he joined the Palmah. At the end of the war, he returned to his group in kibbutz Hulatah. Since 1950, he has been a member of kibbutz Bet Keshet, where he was an educator and a writer. He began recording folktales after attending a lecture by Dov Noy in 1963; since then, he has recorded more than 620 tales, which are on deposit in the IFA. After his retirement from teaching, he became a librarian in the regional library of the Lower Galilee.

Juster, Mariana. (b. 1932). Born in Frumusica, Romania, a small Jewish town in the Moldavia region. She grew up in a traditional Jewish home and preferred literary and humanistic subjects in school from an early age. At the outbreak of World War II, she was forced to leave her hometown and move to Botosani, the regional capital, where she completed high school. Shortly thereafter she began working as a script writer in the film studios in Bucharest, specializing mainly in documentary films. In 1951, she began her studies at the University of Bucharest, majoring in literature; in that same year she married Solo Juster. During her university studies, she developed an interest in Romanian folklore. Upon graduation, she began working in the Romanian National Film Archive and wrote a few scripts for documentary films on children, youth, and the folk arts. She immigrated to Israel in 1960 and has worked for many years as an operator at the international telephone switchboard.

Keren, Abraham. See "Narrators."

Mark, Nathan. (b. 1897). Born in Galicia, Poland, in a village near Sanok. In his childhood, he received an intensive traditional Jewish education in a *heder* (Hebrew school), and later in a yeshivah. As a teenager, he began to study secular subjects. His studies were interrupted by World War I, during which he served in the army and participated in battles in Italy. He knew four languages: Hebrew,

Yiddish, German, and Romanian. In Romania, he was a teacher of Hebrew and of German in the schools and lectured on literature in teacher's colleges. In 1957, he lost a son, and the next year, he immigrated to Israel, where he was a teacher of various subjects in the humanities.

Noy, Meir. (1922–1998). Born in Kolomyja, Poland. He studied in Lwow, Ukraine; but when the Germans began their military campaign against Russia in July 1941, he returned to the Kolomyja ghetto to be with his parents. After his father was killed, and with the blessing of his mother and grandmother, he escaped to Romania and joined the Russian partisans. At the end of World War II, he was a major in the Red Army, conducting military bands; and later he was appointed a music teacher in the Russian school in Bucharest. At the end of 1947, he escaped from Romania with his fiancée and tried to reach the Land of Israel via illegal immigration. His ship was stopped by the British Navy, and he was incarcerated in the refugee camps in Cyprus, where he met up with his brother, Dov Noy. When the camps closed in 1949 he moved to Israel and joined the Israel Defense Forces, serving with a military entertainment unit. After his discharge, he became a music teacher and established the Jewish Folk Song Archives, which, by the time of his passing, included about 100,000 Hebrew songs and about 50,000 Yiddish ones. This archive is now part of the music department of the Jewish National and University Library.

Oettinger, Ayelet. (b. 1964). Born in Kiryat-Yam, Israel. She has worked as a volunteer in the IFA since the age of fourteen, and she served in the army as a secretary in the Northern Command. She studied Hebrew and English literature at the University of Haifa, where she obtained her M.A. degree, specializing in talmudic and midrashic literature. Later she completed her doctorate degree in the field of Hebrew literature of the Middle Ages (both degrees were granted summa cum laude). From 1987 to 1995, she taught Hebrew literature at the Western Galilee College, and since 1996 she has been a lecturer on the faculty of Hebrew and comparative literature at the University of Haifa. She teaches courses on medieval Hebrew literature and folklore and heads the Hebrew studies program in the pre-academic unit at the University of Haifa. In addition to her academic studies, she writes poetry, paints, and sculpts, and she is the mother of four children.

Pelz, Ḥannah. (b. 1948). Born in Bratslaw, Ukraine, and came to Israel in 1957. She is a resident of Tel Aviv.

Pipe, Samuel Zanvel. (1907–1943). Born in Sanok, Poland. His father was a tailor who taught his daughter and three of his four sons his own trade. In addition, his father instilled in his children his love for traditional Jewish songs, tales, wit, and humor. Beggars and itinerant people who stopped at their house used to tell stories, to which the children listened eagerly. At the age of eighteen, Pipe responded to the challenge of the Yiddisher Visenshaftlikher Institut (YIVO, Institute for Yiddish Research) in Vilna to record and collect all traditional genres of tales in Jewish society, and he became one of the most prolific and broad-ranging collectors. He attended a year-long training seminar at YIVO, and after another year on a fellowship he joined the staff. The folk songs he recorded were published in his *Yiddish Folksongs from Galicia—The Folklorization of David Edelstadt's Song "Der Arbeter" Letters* (1971). The volume includes several essays evaluating his scholarly contributions and further information about him and his family.

Polshtinski, Shalva. (b. 1903). Born in a small town in Russia. She grew up in Odessa, Ukraine. She studied and worked there as a kindergarten teacher until she moved to Tel Aviv in 1960, where she worked as a pedicurist. She recorded from memory the stories she submitted to the IFA, tales she originally heard in shelters in Odessa, when the city was being bombed during World War II. During such times, storytelling was used to calm those who were becoming hysterical from fright.

Rivlin, Moshè. (b. 1924). Born in Jerusalem. He worked as a typesetter in Jerusalem, and in 1958 he moved to Kefar Shammai near Safed to become a farmer. He recorded tales primarily from the residents of his village, most of whom were immigrants from Romania. He is an avid stamp collector and sports fan.

Schwarzbaum, Haim. (1911–1983). Born in Warsaw, Poland, into a Hasidic family. He became one of the most erudite and prolific scholars of Jewish and Islamic folklore. Initially, Schwarzbaum received a traditional Jewish education; but at the age of seventeen, he shifted to a more secular way of life and enrolled at Hebrew Teacher's College in Warsaw, from which he graduated in 1931. He continued his education at the University of Warsaw, studying first Polish and English literature and then Arabic language and literature. When he immigrated to the Land of Israel in 1937, he continued his studies at Hebrew University; he dropped out in 1938 to join the Jewish Settlement Police at the height of the Arab Revolt. During his service, he came in contact with Palestinian Arabs and studied their folklore directly. In 1940, Schwarzbaum began his civil service career, first in the administration of the British government and then as an archivist at the Israel Ministry of Defense, where he worked until his retirement in 1977. Though he never held an academic position, he was a world-renowned folklore scholar. For his publications, see Ganuz's "A Bibliography of Haim Schwarzbaum's Essays and Books in the Realm of Jewish and Arab Folklore," *Yeda-'Am* 22 (1984).

Sela, Hadarah. (b. 1939). Born in Reḥovot, Israel. She studied in the local schools and participated in the activities of the ha-Tenu'ah ha-Me'uhedet youth movement. Her military service was in the Naḥal Division, working in kibbutz Ein-Gev and as a counselor in her youth movement. After her discharge from the army, she studied at Hebrew University and later worked as a high school teacher in and around Haifa. After several years of teaching and raising four children, she enrolled at the University of Haifa, concentrating on Bible studies, literature, and folklore.

Tamari, Y. See "Narrators."

Weissman, Limor. (b. 1971). Born in Haifa to a family of Romanian origin who spoke Romanian and Yiddish. She now lives in Tel Aviv, is enrolled as a doctoral student in the Department of Literature at Tel Aviv University, and works as a freelance copyeditor. She loves to listen to stories, especially personal narratives.

Zehavi, Mordekhai. (dates unavailable). Born in Poland. Further biographical information is unavailable.

Bibliography

Aalen, S. *Die begriffe "Licht" und "Finsternis" im alten Testament, im Spätjudentum und im Rabbinismus*. Vol. 1. Oslo: Dybwad, 1951.

Aarne, A. *Der Mann aus dem Paradiese in der Literatur und im Volksmunde: Eine vergleichende Schwankuntersuchung*. FFC 22. Hamina, Finland: Suomalaisen Thedeakatemian Kustantama, 1922.

———. *Verzeichnis der Märchentypen* (Types of the folktale). FFC 3. Helsinki: Academia Scientianum Fennica, 1910.

———, and S. Thompson. *The Types of the Folktale: A Classification and Bibliography. Antti Aarne's Verzeichnis der Märchentypen*. FFC 184. 2nd rev. ed. Helsinki: Suomalainen Tiedeakatemia, 1961. [Originally published FFC 3.]

Abbas, S., ed. *Hershele: 40 Tales* [Hebrew]. Hod Hasharon, Israel: Agur, 1990.

Abelson, J. *The Immanence of God in Rabbinical Literature*. London: Macmillan, 1912.

Abraham, K. "The Day of Atonement: Some Observations on Reik's Problems of the Psychology of Religion." In *Clinical Papers and Essays on Psycho-Analysis* (2:137–147). Brunner/Mazel Classics in Psychoanalysis 4. Ed. H. C. Abraham. New York: Brunner/Mazel, 1979.

Abrahams, B. Z. *Jewish Life in the Middle Ages*. Rev. ed. London: Edward Goldston, 1932.

———, trans. and ed. *The Life of Glückel of Hameln 1646–1724 Written by Herself*. New York: Yoseloff, 1963.

Abrahams, I. *The Book of Delight and Other Papers*. New York: Jewish Publication Society of America, 1912.

Abrahams, R. D. *African Folktales: Traditional Stories of the Black World*. New York: Pantheon, 1983.

———. "A Performance-Centered Approach to Gossip." *Man* 5 (1970), 290–301.

———. *A Singer and Her Songs: Almeda Riddles Book of Ballads*. Baton Rouge: Louisiana State University Press, 1970.

Abrams, M. H. *A Glossary of Literary Terms*. 3rd ed. New York: Holt, Rinehart & Winston, 1971.

Abramson, S. R. "*Al Birkat Hatarat Nedarim ve-Shevu'ot*" (About the blessing of nullification of vows and oaths). *Sinai* 50 (1962), 185–186.

———. *Nissim: Libelli Quinque* [Hebrew]. Jerusalem: Mekizei Nirdamim, 1965.

———. "*Pesakim Kedumim*" (Early rulings). *Sinai* 49 (1961), 210–218.

Adamiak, R. *Justice and History in the Old Testament: The Evolution of Divine Retribution in the Historiographies of the Wilderness Generation*. Cleveland, OH: Zubal, 1985.

Adelson, A., ed. *The Diary of Dawid Sierakowiak: Five Notes from the Lodz Ghetto*. Trans. K. Turkowski. New York: Oxford University Press, 1996.

———, and R. Lapides. *Lodz Ghetto: Inside a Community under Siege*. New York: Penguin, 1989.
Adler, C. *The Shofar—Its Use and Origin*. Washington, DC: Smithsonian Institution, 1894.
Adler, H. "The Baal Shem of London." *JHSE* 5 (1908), 148–173.
Adler-Rudel, S. *Ostjuden in Deutschland 1880–1940: Zugleich eine Geschichte der Organisationen, die sie betreuten*. Tübingen, Germany: Mohr, 1959.
Aescoly, A. Z. *Jewish Messianic Movements* [Hebrew]. Jerusalem: Bialik Institute, 1987. [Originally published 1956.]
Afanas'ev, A. N. *Russian Fairy Tales*. Trans. N. Guterman. New York: Pantheon, 1945.
Agassi, E. *Ha-Yafah Bat ha-Ruah* (The beautiful daughter of the wind). Tel Aviv: Hadar, 1980.
———. *Husham mi—Bagdad* (Husham of Baghdad). Tel Aviv: Am Oved, 1960.
———. *Sent with the Wind: Jewish Folktales from Iraq* [Hebrew]. Tel Aviv: Am Oved, 1979.
Agnon, S. Y. "*Hakhnasat Kallah.*" *Miklat* 2 (1919), 75–85, 259–276, 401–416. [Published in an extended form in Agnon, *Kol Sippurav shel Shmuel Yosef Agnon* (Agnon's collected tales). Vol. 1–2. Berlin: Shocken, 1931; English translation: Agnon, *Bridal Canopy*. Trans. I. M. Lask. New York: Literary Guild of America, 1937.]
———. *Kol Sippurav shel Shmuel Yosef Agnon: Elu ve-Elu* (Agnon's collected tales: These and those). Tel Aviv: Schocken, 1959.
———. *Polin: Sipure Agadot* (Poland: Legends). Tel Aviv: Hedim, 1925.
———. *Twenty-One Stories*. Ed. N. N. Glatzer. New York: Schocken, 1970.
Agursky, M. "Conversions of Jews to Christianity in Russia." *SJA* 20, nos. 2–3 (1990), 69–84.
Agus, A. *The Binding of Isaac and Messiah: Law, Martydom and Deliverance in Early Rabbinic Religiosity. Hermeneutics, Mysticism and Religion*. Albany: State University of New York Press, 1988.
Albertini, L. *The Origins of the War of 1914*. Trans. I. M. Massey. 3 vols. New York: Oxford University Press, 1952.
Alberus, E. *Die Fabeln: Die erweiterte Ausgabe von 1550 mit Kommentar sowie die Erstfassung von 1534*. Frühe Neuzeit 33. Ed. W. Harms, H. Vögel, and L. Lieb. Tübingen, Germany: Niemeyer, 1997.
Alexander, P. S. "The Demonology of the Dead Sea Scrolls." In *The Dead Sea Scrolls after Fifty Years: A Comprehensive Assessment* (331–353). Ed. P. W. Flint and J. C. Vanderkam. Leiden: Brill, 1999.
———. "Gaster's Exempla of the Rabbis: A Reappraisal." In *Rashi 1040–1990, Hommage á Ephraim E. Urbach* (793–805). Congrès Européen des Études Juives. Ed. G. Sed-Rajna. Paris: Les Éditions du Cerfs, 1993.
Alexander, T. "Theme and Genre: Relationships between Man and She-Demon in Jewish Folklore." *JFER* 14 (1992), 56–61.
———. " 'The Weasel and the Well': Intertextual Relationships between Hebrew Sources and Judeo-Spanish Stories." *JSQ* 5 (1998), 254–276.
———, and D. Noy, eds. *The Treasure of Our Fathers: Judeo-Spanish Tales* [Hebrew]. Jerusalem: Misgav Yerushalayim, 1989.
Alexander-Frizer, T. *The Beloved Friend-and-a-Half: Studies in Sephardic Folk-Literature* [Hebrew]. Jerusalem: Magnes, 1999. [Also published in Beer-Sheva, Israel: Ben-

Gurion University of the Negev Press.]

Almi, I. *1863: Yidishe povstanye-mayselekh* (Jewish tales of Polish insurrection). Warsaw: Goldfarb, 1927.

Alster, B. *Proverbs of Ancient Sumer: The World's Earliest Proverb Collections.* Bethesda, MD: CDL Press, 1997.

Althaus, H. P. *Die Cambridger Löwenfabel von 1382: Untersuchung und Edition eines defektiven Textes.* Berlin: de Gruyter, 1971.

Altmann, A. "Articles of Faith." *EJ* 2:657–660, 1971.

Amsterdam, A. G., and J. Bruner. *Minding the Law.* Cambridge, MA: Harvard University Press, 2000.

Amzulescu, A. I., ed. *Balade populare romînesti.* 3 vols. Bucharest: Editura Pentru Literature, 1964.

Andersen, H. C. *The Complete Fairy Tales and Stories.* Trans. E. C. Haugaard. New York: Anchor, 1974.

Andreev, N. P. *Ukazatel' skazochnykh siuzhetov po sisteme aarne.* Leningrad: Izdanie Gosudarstvennogo Geograficheskogo Obtschestua, 1929. [Reprint ed. Berkeley, CA: Berkeley Slavic Specialists, 1993.]

Angel-Malachi, S. *Vidas en Jerusalem* [Hebrew]. Jerusalem: La Semana, 1987.

Anonymous, ed. *The Book of Kashrut.* N.p., n.d.

Anonymous. *Der berihmter vittsling R. Ephraim Greidiger Z"L zayne khokhmes un glaykhe vortlikh vitsen un anekdoten, zusamengeshtelt fun zayne ktovim* (The famous jokester R. Ephraim Greidiger Z"L, his tricks and equally witty words and anecdotes). Warsaw, 1905.

Anonymous. "*Hatarat Nedarim*" (Release from vows). *TE* 11:333–392, 1965.

Anonymous. "*Havdalah*" [Hebrew]. *TE* 8:67–102, 1957.

Anonymous. *Hershele Ostropoler: Di velt berihmter vittsling beshriben zayne anekdoten, stsenes, und shtukes* (Hershele Ostropoler: All the anecdotes, scenes and pranks of the world famous jokster). Brooklyn: Hebrew Publishing, n.d.

Anonymous. *Hershele Ostropoler: Oder der veltbeuihmter vitsler a naye vitsenbikhel. Ver s'vill gut lakhenun zikh freylekh makhen, zal bald gukh loyfen, dos naye bikhel koyfe, ershter tail* (Hershele Ostropoler: Or a new booklet of the world famous jester, from which you will have a good laugh and will enjoy yourself, that you will run fast to buy this new booklet. First part). Przemyśl, Poland: Freund, 1925.

Anonymous. "Hospitality." *EJ* 8:1030–1033, 1971.

Anonymous. *Meshalim shel Shlomoh ha-Melekh* (Parables of King Solomon). Constantinople, 1516. [Published with Anonymous, *Divrei ha-Yamin shel Moshe Rabbenu* (The chronicle of Moses).]

Anonymous. *Petirat Rabbenu ha-Kadosh mi-Belz* (The death of our holy rabbi from Belz). Lemberg, [Ukraine]: Ehrenpreis, 1894.

Anonymous. *Sefer Adat Zadikkim.* Lemberg, [Ukraine], 1864.

Anonymous. *Sefer Ge'ulat Yisrael* (The book of the redemption of Israel). Warsaw: Knoster, 1907 or 1908.

An-Sky [An-sky, An-Ski], S. "*Bein Shnei Olamot*" (Between two worlds). Trans. H. N. Bialik. *Hatekufah* 1 (1918), 225–296. [Author also known as S. Z. Rappoport.]

———. *The Dybbuk and Other Writings.* Ed. D. G. Roskies. Trans. G. Werman. New York: Schocken, 1992.

———. *The Enemy at His Pleasure: A Journey through the Jewish Pale of Settlement during World War I*. Ed. and Trans. J. Neugroschel. New York: Metropolitan Books/Henry Holt, 2002.

———. *Hurban ha-Yehudim be-Polin, Galitsyah u-Bukovina* (The destruction of the Jews in Poland, Galicia, and Bukovina). Trans. S. L. Tsitron. 4 parts. Berlin: Shtibl, 1929.

———. "On Jewish Folk-Creativity" [Hebrew]. *Chulyot* 5 (1999), 323–362.

———. *Tsvishn Tsvey Veltn (Der Dybbuk)* [Between two worlds (The Dybbuk)]. In *Gezamelte Shriften* (Collected writings) (2:3–109). Vilnius, Lithuania: An-Ski, 1921.

Aphek, E., and Y. Tobin. "The Realization of Messianism as a Semiotic System in a Literary Text." *Semiotica* 59 (1986), 55–67.

Apo, S. "Tale Type." In *Folklore: An Encyclopedia of Beliefs, Customs, Tales, Music and Art* (2:785–787). Ed. T. A. Green. Santa Barbara, CA: ABC-CLIO, 1997.

Arad, Y. *Belzec, Sobibor, Treblinka: The Operation Reinhard Death Camps*. Bloomington: Indiana University Press, 1987.

———. " 'Mivtsa Reinhard': Mahanot ha-hashmadah: Belzec, Sobibor, Treblinka" ("Operation Reinhard": The extermination camps: Belzec, Sobibor, Treblinka). *YV* 16 (1985), 165–192.

Ariel, Z., ed. *Hakhamim ve-Tipshim: Otsar Sippurim Mevadhim, Ma'asiyyot, Guzma'ot, Havalim, Huididim u-Vedihot* (Wise men and fools: A treasury of humorous tales, folktales, tall tales, nonsense, wit and jokes). Tel Aviv: Sreberk, 1950.

Armistead, S. G. "A Judeo-Spanish Cumulative Song and Its Greek Counterpart." *REJ* 137 (1978), 375–381. [Reprinted in Armistead and Silverman, *En torno romancero sefardi* (183–188). Madrid: Seminario Menéndez Pidal, 1982.]

———. *The Spanish Tradition in Louisiana I: Isleno Folkliterature*. Musical transcript by I. I. Kats. Newark, DE: de la Cuesta, 1992.

———, and J. H. Silverman. "A Neglected Source of the Prolog to *La Celestina*." *MLN* 93 (1978), 310–312. [Reprinted in Armistead and Silverman, *En torno romancero sefardi* (76–78). Madrid: Seminario Menéndez Pidal, 1982.]

Armstrong, J. A. "The Ethnic Scene in the Soviet Union: The View of the Dictatorship." *JSN* 1 (1990), 14–65.

———. "The Soviet Ethnic Scene: A Quarter Century Later." *JSN* 1 (1990), 66–75.

Arnim, L. A. von, and C. Brentano. *Des Knaben Wunderhorn: Alte deutsche Lieder. Vollständige Ausgabe nach dem Text der Erstausgabe vone 1806–1808*. Post script by W. A. Koch. Munich: Winkler, 1970. [See also Pape, W.]

Arnon, J. *Bibliography of Samuel Josef Agnon and His Work*. Tel Aviv: Aticot, 1971.

Aschheim, A. S. *Brothers and Strangers: The East European Jew in German and German Jewish Consciousness, 1800–1923*. Madison: University of Wisconsin Press, 1982.

———. "Eastern Jews, German Jews and Germany's Ostpolitik in the First World War." *LBIYB* 28 (1983), 351–365.

Ashliman, D. L. *Folk and Fairy Tales: A Handbook*. Westport, CT: Greenwood Press, 2004.

Ashni, Y. *Be-Simta'ot Tzfat* (In the alleys of Safed). Safed, Israel: Sifriyat Tzfat, 1961.

Assaf, D. *Bratslav: An Annotated Bibliography. Rabbi Nahman of Bratslav, His Life and Teaching, the Literary Legacy of His Disciples, Bratslav Hasidim in Its Context*. Jerusalem: Zalman Shazar Center for Jewish History, 2000.

———. "Convert or Saint? In the Footsteps of Moshe, the Son of Rabbi Shneur Zalman of Lyady" [Hebrew]. *Zion* 65 (2000), 453–515.

———. "*Hebetim Historyim ve-Hevratyim be-Heker haHasidut*" (Social and historical aspects in Hasidic scholarship). In *Zaddik and Devotees: Historical and Sociological Aspects of Hasidism* (9–32). Ed. D. Assaf. Jerusalem: Zalman Shazar Center for Jewish History, 2001.

———, ed. *Journey to a Nineteenth-Century Shtetl: The Memoirs of Yekhezkel Kotik*. The Raphael Patai Series in Jewish Folklore and Anthropology. Detroit: Wayne State University Press, 2002.

———. " 'Like a Small State within a Large State': The Royal Court and Its Residents" [Hebrew]. In *Zaddik and Devotees: Historical and Sociological Aspects of Hasidism* (398–421). Ed. D. Assaf. Jerusalem: Zalman Shazar Center for Jewish History, 2001.

———. " 'Money for Household Expenses': Economic Aspects of the Hasidic Courts." In *Studies in the History of the Jews in Old Poland in Honor of Jacob Goldberg* (14–50). SH 38. Ed. A. Teller. Jerusalem: Magnes Press and the Center for Research and the History and Culture of Polish Jews, 1998.

———. *The Regal Way: The Life and Times of R. Israel of Ruzhin*. Trans. D. Louvish. Stanford, CA: Standford Univeristy Press, 2002.

Assaf, Da. *Sefer ha-Kaddish: Mekoro, Mashma'uto ve-dinav* (The Kaddish book: Its origin, its meaning and laws). Haifa: Makhon le-Heker Kitvei ha-Rambam, 1999.

Assaf, S. "*Le-Korot ha-Rabbanut be-Ashkenaz, Polanya, ve-Lita*" (The history of the rabbinate in Germany, Poland, and Lithuania). *Reshumot* 2 (1927), 259–300.

Athenaeus of Naucratis. *The Deipnosophists*. Loeb Classical Library. Trans. C. B. Gulick. 7 vols. Cambridge, MA: Harvard University Press, 1961–1980.

Attias, M. *The Golden Feather: Twenty Folktales Narrated by Greek Jews* [Hebrew]. IFAPS 35. Ed. D. Noy. Haifa: Ethnological Museum and Folklore Archives, 1976.

Ausubel, N. *A Treasury of Jewish Folklore*. New York: Crown, 1948.

Avenary, H. "The Hasidic Nigun: Ethos and Melos of a Folk Liturgy." In *Encounters of East and West in Music* (158–164). Ed. H. Avenary. Tel Aviv: Department of Musicology, Tel Aviv University, 1979.

Avida [Zlotnik], Y. *Koso shel Eliyahu ha-Navi: Naftule Minhag be-Hitrakmuto* (Elijah's Cup: The twists and turns of a custom formation). Jerusalem: Jewish Agency Publishing House, 1958.

Avitsuk, J. *The Fate of a Child: 28 Folktales by 25 Narrators Collected from the Tribes of Israel* [Hebrew]. Ed. E. Shelly-Neuman. Tel Aviv: Amir, 1985.

———. *The Tree That Absorbed Tears* [Hebrew]. IFAPS 7. Ed. D. Noy. Haifa: Ethnological Museum and Folklore Archives, 1965.

Baader, R. "*Cante fable*." *EM* 2:1167–1168, 1979.

Babbi, A. M., ed. *Paris et Vienne: Romanzo cavalleresco del XV secolo*. Milan: Angelli, 1992.

Baharav, Z. *Mi-Dor le-Dor: One Generation to Another. Seventy-One Folktales Collected in Israel* [Hebrew]. Tel Aviv: Tarbut Vechinuch, 1968.

———. *Sixty Folktales: Collected from Narrators in Ashkelon*. IFAPS 5. Haifa: Ethnological Museum and Folklore Archives, 1964.

Bal, M. "Notes on Narrative Embedding." *Poetics Today* 2, no. 2 (1981), 41–60.

Balaban, M. *A History of the Jews in Cracow and Kazimierz 1304–1868* [Hebrew]. Ed. J. Goldberg. 2 vols. Jerusalem: Magnes Press, 2002. [Originally published as *Dzieje Zydów w Krakowie i na Kazimierzu, 1304–1868.*]

———. "*Korot ha-Yehudim bi-Yemei ha-Beinaim*" (The history of the Jews in the Middle Ages). In *Beit-Yisrael be-Polin* (The Jewish community in Poland) (1:1–16). Ed. I. Halpern. 2 vols. Jerusalem: Youth Department of the Zionist Organization, 1948–1953.

Bamberger, B. J. *Fallen Angels*. Philadelphia: Jewish Publication Society of America, 1952.

———. *Proselytism in the Talmudic Period*. 2nd ed. New York: Ktav, 1968.

———, J. Gutmann, A. Marmorstein, et al. "Angels and Angelology." *EJ* 2:956–977, 1971.

Band, A. J. "Folklore and Literature." In *Studies in Jewish Folklore: Proceedings of a Regional Conference of the Association for Jewish Studies Held at the Spertus College of Judaica, Chicago May 1–3, 1977* (33–44). Ed. D. Noy and F. Talmage. Cambridge, MA: Association for Jewish Studies, 1980.

———, ed. and trans. *Nahman of Bratslav: The Tales*. The Classics of Western Spirituality. New York: Paulist Press, 1978.

———. *Studies in Modern Jewish Literature*. JPS Scholars of Distinction Series. Philadelphia: Jewish Publication Society, 2003.

Banks, M. M., ed. *An Alphabet of Tales. An English 15th-Century Translation of the* Alphabetum Narrationum *of Étienne de Besançon. From Additional MS. 25,719 of the British Museum*. Early English Text Society Series 126–127. London: Paul, Trench, Trüber, 1904–1905.

Barash, A. *Arabic Folk Tales*. Ramat Gan, Israel: Massada Press, 1969.

Barbe, K. *Irony in Context*. Pragmatics and Beyond 34. Amsterdam and Philadelphia: Benjamins, 1995.

Bar-El, E. *Under the Little Green Trees: Yiddish and Hebrew Children's Periodicals in Poland 1918–1939* [Hebrew]. Jerusalem: Dov Sadan Institute and the Zionist Library, 2006.

Bar-Ilan, M. "Exorcism by Rabbis: Talmudic Sages and Magic" [Hebrew]. *Daat* 34 (1995), 17–31.

Baring-Gould, S. "Appendix: Household Tales." In *Notes on the Folk Lore of the Northern Counties of England and the Borders* (299–344). Ed. W. Henderson. London: Longmans, Green, 1866.

Bar-Itzhak [Bar-Yishak], H. "An-ski's Essay on Jewish Ethnopoetics" [Hebrew]. *Chulyot* 5 (1999), 363–368.

———. *Jewish Poland: Legends of Origin: Ethnopoetics and Legendary Chronicles*. Raphael Patai Series in Jewish Folklore and Anthropology. Detroit: Wayne State University Press, 2001.

Bar-Levav, A. "Magic in Jewish Ethical Literature" [Hebrew]. *Tarbiz* 72 (2003), 389–414.

Baron, S. W. *The Jewish Community: Its History and Structure to the American Revolution*. 3 vols. Philadelphia: Jewish Publication Society of America, 1945.

———. *The Russian Jew under Tsars and Soviets*. Russian Civilization Series. New York: Macmillan, 1964.

———. *A Social and Religious History of the Jews*. 2nd rev. ed. 18 vols. Philadelphia: Jewish Publication Society, 1952.

———, A. Kahan, et al. *Economic History of the Jews*. Ed. N. Gross. New York: Schocken, 1975.

Bartal, I. "The Porets and the Arendar: The Depiction of Poles in Jewish Literature." *PR* 32 (1987), 357–369. [Reprinted in I. Bartal and I. Gutman, eds. *The Broken Chain—*

Polish Jewry through the Ages (191–206) (Hebrew). Jerusalem: Zalman Shazar Center for Jewish History, 2001.]
Bascom, W. "African Folktales in America: I. The Talking Skull Refuses to Talk." *RAL* 8 (1977), 266–291.
———. "The Forms of Folklore: Prose Narratives." *JAF* 78 (1965), 3–20.
———. "The Talking Skull Refuses to Talk: More Addenda." *RAL* 9 (1978), 258.
Basile, G. *The Pentamerone of Giambattista Basile*. Ed. N. M. Penzer. Trans. Benedetto Croce. 2 vols. London: John Lane the Bodley Head; New York: Dutton, 1932. [Originally published 1634–1636 and 1644 as *Lo Cunto de li Cunti* and 1674 as *Il Pentameron*.]
———. *Il Pentamerone ossia la fiaba delle fiabe*. Trans. B. Croce. 2 vols. Bari, Italy: Laterza & Figli, 1925. [Originally published 1891.]
Basset, R. *Mille et un contes, récits & legends Arabes*. 3 vols. Paris: Librairie Orientale et Américaine, Maisonneuve Frères, 1924–1926.
Bastomski, S. *Yidishe folkmayses un legends* (Yiddish folktales and legends). Vol. 1: *Legends vegn besht* (Legends about the Besht). Vilnius, Lithuania: New Yiddish Folkschool, 1925.
Batany, J. *Scène et coulisses du "Roman de Renart."* Paris: Sedes, 1989.
Baughman, E. W. *Type and Motif Index of the Folktales of England and North America*. IUSF 20. The Hague: Mouton, 1966.
Bauman, R. "Y. L. Cahan's Instructions on Collecting Folklore." *NYFQ* 18 (1962), 284–289.
Baumgarten, J. M. *Introduction à la littérature Yiddish ancienne*. Paris: Éditions du Cerf, 1993.
———, ed. *Paris un Viene. Verona 1594*. Bologna, Italy: Fonti, 1988. [Facsimile ed.]
———. "The Qumran Songs against Demons" [Hebrew]. *Tarbiz* 55 (1985–1986), 442–445.
Baumgartner, W. "Susanna: Die Geschichte einer Legende." *AfR* 24 (1926), 259–280.
Bausinger, H. *Formen der "Volkspoesie."* Grundlagen der Germanistik 6. Berlin: Schmidt, 1968.
Baviskar, V., and M. Herzog. *The Language and Culture Atlas of Ashkenazic Jewry*. Tübingen, Germany: Niemeyer; New York: YIVO Institute for Jewish Research, 1992.
Becker, M. *Wunder und Wundertäter im frührabbinischen Judentum: Studien zum Phänomen und seiner Überlieferung in Horizont von Magic und Dämonismus*. Wissenschaftliche Untersuchungen zum Neuen Testament 144. 2nd ser. Tübingen, Germany: Siebeck, 2002.
Belcher, S. "Framed Tales in the Oral Tradition: An Exploration." *Fabula* 35 (1994), 1–19.
Belmont, N. *Poétique du conte: Essai sur le conte de tradition orale*. Paris: Gallimard, 1999.
ben-Abraham, J., ed. *Maysey bukh*. Basel: Konrad Waldkirch, 1602. [Reprinted in Zfatman, *Yiddish Narrative Prose* (36–39).]
Ben-Amos, D., ed. *Folklore Genres*. AFSBSS 26. Austin: University of Texas Press, 1976.
———. "Historical Poetics and Generic Shift: *Niphla'ot ve-Nissim*." *Fabula* 35 (1994), 20–49.
———. "Meditation on a Russian Proverb in Israel." *Proverbium* 12 (1995), 13–26.
———. "The 'Myth' of Jewish Humor." *WF* 32 (1973), 112–131.
———, and J. R. Mintz, trans. and eds. *In Praise of the Baal Shem Tov [Shivhei ha-*

Besht]: *The First Collection of Legends about the Founder of Hasidism.* Bloomington: Indiana University Press, 1970.

———, and D. Noy. "*Die Zeischen als Metasprache in der Jüdischen Folklore.*" In *10 + 5 = Gott: Die Macht der Zeichen* (17–34). Ed. D. Tyradellis and M. S. Friedlander. Berlin: Jüdisches Museum Berlin, 2004.

Ben-Ezra, A. *Ha-"Yenuka" me-Stolin* (The babe of Stolin). New York: Author, 1951.

Ben Noah, M. Y. *Tokhahat Hayyim* (Moralizing for living). Vilnius, 1877.

Ben-Israel, M. *Vindiciæ Judæorum, or, A letter in Answer to Certain Questions Propounded by a Noble and Learned Gentleman: Touching the Reproaches Cast on the Nation of the Jevves; Wherein All Objections Are Candidly and Yet Fully Cleared.* London: Printed for W. Bickerton, 1743.

Benjamin, C. *Towers of Spice: The Tower-Shape Tradition in Havdalah Spiceboxes.* Jerusalem: Israel Museum, 1982.

Ben-Menachem, N., ed. *Avraham even-Ezra: Sihot ve-Aggadot* (Abraham ibn-Ezra: Anecdotes and folk legends). Ba-Mishor Series 7. Jerusalem: Mossad Harav Kook, 1943.

Bennett, G. "The Vanishing Hitchhiker at Fifty-Five." *WF* 57 (1998), 1–17.

Benovitz, M. *Kol Nidre: Studies in the Development of Rabbinic Votive Institutions.* Brown Judaic Studies 315. Atlanta: Scholars Press, 1998.

Ben-Sasson, H. H. *Hagut ve-hanhagah: Hashkafotehem h-hevratiyot shel Yehudei Polin be-Shilhei Yemei-ha-Benayim* (Thought and leadership: The social views of the Polish Jews at the late Middle Ages). Jerusalem: Bialik Institute, 1959.

———. "Messianic Movements." *EJ* 11:1417–1427, 1971.

———. "Statutes for the Enforcement of the Observance of the Sabbath in Poland" [Hebrew]. *Zion* 21 (1956), 183–206.

———, and I. Levitats. "Charity." *EJ* 5:338–353, 1971.

Ben-Yehezki'el, M., ed. "The Book *And It Came to Pass*" [Hebrew]. In *Bialik: Critical Essays on His Works* (337–370). Ed. G. Shaked. Jerusalem: Bialik Institute, 1974. [Reprint ed. 1992.]

———. *Sefer ha-Ma'asiyyot* (A book of folktales). 3 vols. Tel Aviv: Dvir, 1925–1929. [Expanded ed. 6 vols. Tel Aviv: Dvir, 1957.]

Ben-Zeev, I. *Conversion to Judaism: Present-Day Problems in the Light of History* [Hebrew]. Jerusalem: World Union for the Propagation of Judaism, 1961.

Bercken, W. van den. *Ideology and Atheism in the Soviet Union.* Religion and Society 28. New York: de Gruyter, 1989.

Berendsen, M. "Formal Criteria of Narrative Embedding." *JLS* 10 (1981), 79–94.

Berezovs'kyi, I. P. *Kazki pro tvarin* (Fairy tales about animals). Kiev: Naukova Dumka, 1979.

Berger, A. A. *The Genius of the Jewish Joke.* Northvale, NJ: Aronson, 1997.

Berger, I. *Eser Tsahtsahbahot* (Ten illuminations). Petrikov, Belarus: Kleiman, 1909.

Berger, N. *Jews and Medicine: Religion, Culture, Science.* Philadelphia: Jewish Publication Society, 1995.

Berlin, B., and P. Kay. *Basic Color Terms: Their Universality and Evolution.* Berkeley: University of California Press, 1969.

Berliner, A. *Selected Writings* [Hebrew]. Jerusalem: Mossad Harav Kook, 1969.

Bermant, C. *What Is the Joke? A Study of Jewish Humour through the Ages.* London: Weidenfeld & Niolson, 1986.

Bernstein, E. *Die deutsche Revolution von 1918/1919: Geschichte der Entstehung und ersten Arbeitsperiode de deutschen Republik.* Bonn: Dietz, 1998.

Bernstein, I. *Jüdische Sprichwörter und Redensarten.* Warsaw: Kauffmann in Frankfurt am Main, 1908.

Best, T. W. *Reynard the Fox.* Twayne's World Authors Series 673. Boston: Twayne, 1983.

Bettan, I. *Studies in Jewish Preaching: Middle Ages.* Cincinnati, OH: Hebrew Union College Press, 1939. [Reprint ed. Lanham, MD: University Press of America, 1987.]

Beuken, W. A. M. "No Wise King without a Wise Woman (1 Kings iii 16–28)." In *New Avenues in the Study of the Old Testament* (1–10). Oudtestamentische Studiën 25. Ed. A. S. Van Der Woude. Leiden: Brill, 1989.

Beukers, M., and R. Waale, eds. *Tracing An-Sky: Jewish Collections from the State Ethnographic Museum in St. Petersburg.* Zwolle, The Netherlands: Waanders Uitgevers, 1992–1994.

Beyer, J. "The Morality of the Amoral." In *The Humor of the Fabliaux: A Collection of Critical Essays* (15–42). Ed. T. Cooke and B. Honeycutt. Columbia: University of Missouri Press, 1974.

———. *Schwank und Moral: Untersuchungen zum altfranzösischen Fabliau und verwandten Formen.* Heidelberg: Winter, 1969.

Biale, D. *Eros and the Jews: From Biblical Israel to Contemporary America.* New York: Basic Books, 1992.

Bialik, H. N. *Ketavim Genuzim* (Unpublished texts). Tel Aviv: Hotsa'at Bet Byalik al-yede Devir, 1970 or 1971.

———, and Y. H. Ravnitzky, eds. *The Book of Legends: Sefer ha-Aggadah. Legends from the Talmud and Midrash.* Trans. W. G. Braude. New York: Schocken, 1992.

Bialostotzky, B. J. *Jewish Humor and Jewish Jesters* [Yiddish]. New York: Cyco, 1963.

Bikel, S. "*Tsvelf folks-mayses fun Sanik*" (Twelve folktales from Sanok). In *Sanok: Sefer Zikaron li-Kehilat Sanok veha-Sevivah* (Sanok: A community memorial book) (515–518). Ed. E. Sharvit. Tel Aviv: Association of Sanok Former Residents in Israel, [1969].

Bilu, Y. "Demonic Explanations of Disease among Moroccan Jews in Israel." *CMP* 3 (1979), 363–380.

———. "The Moroccan Demon in Israel: The Case of 'Evil Spirit Disease.' " *Ethos* 8 (1980), 24–39.

Bin Gorion [Berdyczewski], M. J., ed. *Der Born Judas: Legenden, Märchen und Erzälungen.* Trans. Rahel bin Gorion [Ramberg]. 6 vols. Leipzig, Germany: Insel, 1916–1923. [2nd. ed.: vols. 1–2, 1918; vol. 3, 1919; vol. 4, 1924; 3rd ed.: vols. 1–3, 1924.]

———. *Mimekor Yisrael: Classical Jewish Folktales.* Ed. Emanuel Bin Gorion. Trans. I. M. Lask. 3 vols. Bloomington: Indiana University Press, 1976. [Abridged and annotated ed., prepared by Dan Ben-Amos, 1 vol., Bloomington: Indiana University Press, 1990.]

Biran, R. "*L'affair Berl Verblunsky: Polémique autour du folklore juif entre les deux guerres.*" *CLO* 44 (1998), 59–91.

Birnbaum, P., trans. *Daily Prayer Book: Ha-Siddur ha-Shalem.* New York: Hebrew Publishing, 1949.

Bisanz, A. J. "Robert Penn Warren: The Ballad of Billie Potts." *Fabula* 14 (1973), 71–90.

Blackham, H. J. *The Fable as Literature*. London: Athlone Press, 1985.
Blidstein, G. J. "Kaddish and Other Accidents." *Tradition* 14 (1974), 80–85.
Blobaum, R. E. *Rewolucia: Russian Poland, 1904-1907*. Ithaca, NY: Cornell University Press, 1995.
Bloch, C. *Hersch Ostropoler: Ein jüdischer Till-Eulenspiegel des 18. Jahrhunderts, Seine Geschichten und Streiche*. Berlin: Harz, 1921.

———. *Das Jüdische Volk in seiner Anekdote: Ernstes und Heiteres von Gottsuchern, Gelehrten, Künstlern, Narren, Schelman, Aufschneidern, Schnorrern, Reichen, Frommen, Freidenkern, Täuflingen, Antisemiten*. Berlin: Verlag für Kulturpolitik, 1931.

———. *Ostjudischer Humor*. Berlin: Harz, 1920.
Bloch, J. S. *Kol Nidre und seine Enstehungsgeschichte*. Berlin: Philo, 1922.
Bloomberg, M., and B. B. Barrett. *Stalin: An Annotated Guide to Books in English*. Borgo Reference Guides 1. Ed. M. Burgess and P. D. Seldis. San Bernardino, CA: Borgo Press, 1993.
Blum, E. "Glück und Unglück." *EM* 5:1305–1312, 1987.
Blumenkranz, B. "Les Juifs à Blois au moyen-âge; à propos de la démographie historique des Juifs." In *Études de civilisation médiévale (IXe-XIIe siècles): Mélanges offerts à Edmond-René Labande* (33–38). Poitiers, France: C.E.S.C.M., [1983].
Boccaccio, G. *Decameron: The John Payne Translation*. Ed. C. S. Singleton. Berkeley: University of California Press, 1982.
Bodek, M. M. *Ma'aseh Tsaddikim* (The acts of the just). Lemberg, Poland [now Ukraine], 1864.

———. *Seder ha-Dorot mi-Talmidei ha-Besht* (Successive generations of the Besht's disciples). Lublin, Poland, 1899. [Reprint ed. Jerusalem, 1964 or 1965.]
Bødker, L. *Indian Animal Tales: A Preliminary Survey*. FFC 170. Helsinki: Suomalainen Tiedeakatemia, 1957.
Bolte, J., and G. Polivka, eds. *Anmerkungen zu den Kinder-u. Hausemärchen der Bruder Grimm*. 5 vols. Leipzig, Germany: Dieterich, 1913–1932.
Booth, W. C. *A Rhetoric of Irony*. Chicago: University of Chicago Press, 1974.
Börner-Klein, D., ed. *Pirke de-Rabbi Elieser: Nach der Edition Vendedig 1544 unter Berücksichtigung der Edition Warschau 1852*. Studia Judaica 26. New York: de Gruyter, 2004.
Botoschansky, J. *Herschele Astropolier: Tragicomedia en 4 actos* [Yiddish]. Buenos Aires: Oyfgang, 1927.
Bottigheimer, R. B. *Fairy Godfather: Straparola, Venice and the Fairy Tale Tradition*. Philadelphia: University of Pennsylvania Press, 2002.
Bouquet, A. C. *Everyday Life in New Testament Times*. New York: Scribner's, 1954.
Brandwein, E. *Degel Mahaneh Yehudah* (The banner of Judah's camp), 1912. [Reprint ed. Jerusalem: Ha-Makhon le-Heker ha-Hasidut, 1998.]
Braude, W. G. *Jewish Proselyting in the First Five Centuries of the Common Era: The Age of the Tannaim and Amoraim*. Providence, RI: Brown University, 1940.

———, trans. *Pesikta Rabbati: Discourses for Feasts, Fasts, and Special Sabbaths*. YJS 18. New Haven, CT: Yale University Press, 1968.
Brednich, R. W. "Mordeltern." *EM* 9:876–879, 1999.

———. *Volkserzählungen und Volksglaube von den Schicksalsfrauen*. FFC 193. Helsinki: Suomalainen Tiedeakatemia, 1964.

Breitech, M. A. *Sefer Tehilot Barukh* (The book of praises for Barukh). Brooklyn: Tehilos Baruch, 2002.
Brenner, A. *Colour Terms in the Old Testament*. JSOTSS 21. Sheffield, UK: Department of Biblical Studies, the University of Sheffield, 1982.
Brenner, M. *The Renaissance of Jewish Culture in Weimar Germany*. New Haven, CT: Yale University Press, 1996.
Bribram, G. *Jewish Folk-Stories from Hungary* [Hebrew]. IFAPS 10. Ed. O. Schnitzler. Haifa: Haifa Municipality and Ethnological Museum and Folklore Archives, 1965.
Briggs, K. M. *A Dictionary of British Folk-Tales in the English Language*. 4 vols. 2 parts. London: Routledge & Kegan Paul, 1970.
―――, and R. L. Tongue, eds. *Folktales of England*. Folktales of the World. Chicago: University of Chicago Press, 1965.
Brinner, W. M., trans and ed. *An Elegant Composition Concerning Relief after Adversity*. YJS 20. New Haven, CT: Yale University Press, 1977.
Broderick, G. "*Das Horst-Wessel-Lied*: An Analysis." *IFR* 10 (1995), 100–127.
Bromberg, A. I. *Mi-Gdolei ha-Ḥasidut* (Great Hasidic rabbis). Vol. 18: *Beit Kozhnich* (The house of Kozienice). Jerusalem: Makhon le-Ḥasidut, 1961.
Brooks, P., and P. Gewirtz, eds. *Law's Stories: Narrative and Rhetoric in the Law*. New Haven, CT: Yale University Press, 1996.
Brown, M. K. *The Narratives of Konon*. Beiträge zur Altertumskunde 163. Munich: Saur, 2002.
Brown, W. N. "The Panchatantra in Modern Indian Folklore." *JAOS* 39 (1919), 1–54.
Brüll, N. "*Beiträge zur jüdischen Sagen- und Spruchkunde im Mittelalter*." *JJGL* 9 (1889), 1–45.
Bruner, J. *Making Stories: Law, Literature, Life*. New York: Farrar Straus & Giroux, 2002.
Buber, M. *For the Sake of Heaven*. Trans. L. Lewisohn. New York: Harper & Row, 1953.
―――. *Tales of Hasidim: Early Masters*. Trans. O. Marx. New York: Schocken, 1947.
―――. *Tales of Hasidim: Later Masters*. Trans. O. Marx. New York: Schocken, 1948.
Buber, S., ed. *Agadischer Commentar zum Pentateuch nach einer Handschrift aus Aleppo* [Midrash Aggadah]. Vienna: Fanto, 1894.
―――, ed. *Lekach-Tob (Pesikta Sutarta): Ein agadischer Commentar zum ersten und zweiten Buche Mosis von Rabbi Tobia ben Elieser (Lebte im XI Jahrh)* [Hebrew]. 2 vols. Vilnius, Lithuania: Romm, 1924.
―――. *Midrash Aggadah*. New York: Mada, 1960. [Originally published 1894.]
―――, ed. *Midrasch Tanḥuma: Ein agadischer Commentar zum Pentateuch von Rabbi Tanchuma Ben Rabbi Abba*. 2 vols. Vilnius: Widow & Brothers Romm, 1885. [Reprint eds. 1946, 1964.]
Budge, E. A. W., ed. and trans. *The Book of Paradise, Being the Histories and Sayings of the Monks and the Ascetics of the Egyptian Desert, by Palladius, Hieronymus*. Lady Miux Manuscript 6. London: Drugulin, 1904.
―――, ed. and trans. *The Laughable Stories Collected by Mâr Gregory John Bar-Hebræus Maphrian of the East from A.D. 1264 to 1286*. London: Luzac, 1897. [Reprint ed. New York: AMS, 1976.]
Buhociu, O. *The Pastoral Paradise: Romanian Folklore*. Lakewood, OH: Trandafir, 1966.
Bullough, G., ed. *Narrative and Dramatic Sources of Shakespeare*. 8 vols. New York: Columbia University Press, 1957–1975.
Bultmann, R. "*Zur Geschichte der Lichtsymbolik in Altertum*." *PZKA* 97 (1948), 1–36.

Burrus, V. A., and H. Goldberg, eds. *Esopete ystoriado (Toulouse 1488)*. Madison, WI: Hispanic Seminary of Medieval Studies, 1990.
Burton, R. *Supplement Nights to the Book of the Thousand Nights and a Night*. 6 vols. London: Burton Club, 1886–1888.
Burton, R. F., trans. *The Book of the Thousand Nights and Night*. 10 vols. London: Burton Club, 1885.
Caciola, N. "Wraiths, Revenants and Ritual in Medieval Culture." *P&P* 152 (1996), 3–45.
Cahan [Kahan], J. [Y.] L., ed. *Der Yid: Vegen zikh un vegen andere in zayne shprichtverter un redensarten* (The Jew: About him and about others in proverbs and idioms). New York: YIVO, 1933.
———. "Folksong and Popular Song" [Hebrew]. Trans. G. Hasan-Rokem. *JSJF* 1 (1981), 146–152.
———. *Jewish Folklore* [Yiddish]. Publications of the Yiddish Scientific Institute 9, Philological Series 5. Vilnius, Lithuania: Yiddish Scientific Institute, 1938.
———. *Studies in Yiddish Folklore*. Ed. M. Weinreich. New York: Yiddish Scientific Institute, 1952.
———. *Yidishe folksmasiyyot* (Yiddish folktales). Vol. 1. New York/Vilna: Yidishe Folklor-Bibliyotek, 1931. [Expanded ed. in Cahan, *Gesamlte ktovim* (Collected writings). Vol. 5. Vilna, Lithuania: Yiddish Scientific Institute, 1940.]
———. *Yiddish Folksongs with Their Original Airs, Collected from Oral Tradition* [Yiddish]. 2 vols. New York: International Library, 1912. [Reprint ed. *Yiddish Folksongs with Melodies*. Ed. M. Weinreich. New York: YIVO Institute for Jewish Research, 1957.]
Cahn, Z. "*Ha-Rabi me-Berdichev*" (The rabbi from Berdichev). In *Sheloshah Ketarim: Trilogyah ba-Ḥasidut* (Three crowns: A Hasidic trilogy) (5–195). Ed. Z. Cahn. Tel Aviv: Massada, 1954.
———. "*Ha-Rabi mi-Ladi*" (The rabbi from Lyady). In *Sheloshah Ketarim: Trilogyah ba-Ḥasidut* (Three crowns: A Hasidic trilogy) (197–371). Ed. Z. Cahn. Tel Aviv: Massada, 1954.
Cala, A. *The Image of the Jew in Polish Folk Culture*. Studies of the Center for Research on the History and Culture of Polish Jews. Jerusalem: Magnes Press, 1995.
Caliebe, M. *Dukus Horant: Studien zu zeiner literaruschen Tradition*. Philologische Studien und Quellen 70. Berlin: Schmidt, 1973.
Camus, A. *L'Étranger*. Paris: Gallimard, 1942.
———. *Le Malentendu: Pièce en trios actes; Caligula: pièce en quatre actes*. Paris: Gallimard, 1944.
Canaan, T. "Haunted Springs and Water Demons in Palestine." *JPOS* 1 (1920–1921), 153–170. [Reprinted in *Studies in Palestinian Customs and Folk-Lore 2*. Jerusalem: Palestinian Oriental Society, 1922.]
Caplan, K. *Orthodoxy in the New World: Immigrant Rabbis and Preaching in America (1881–1924)* [Hebrew]. Jerusalem: Zalman Shazar Center for Jewish History, 2002.
Carnes, P. "The Fable and the Proverb: Intertexts and Reception." *Proverbium* 8 (1991), 55–76.
———. *Fable Scholarship: An Annotated Bibliography*. Garland Folklore Bibliographies 8. Garland Reference Library of the Humanities 367. New York: Garland, 1985.
———. *Proverbia in Fabula: Essays on the Relationship of the Fable and the Proverb*. Sprichtwörterforschung 10. Bern: Lang, 1988.

Carou, B., and Y. Slutsky, eds. "Bloody Jubilee." Special issue, *He-Avar* 17 (1970), 3–136.
Casey, R. P. *Religion in Russia*. New York: Harper & Brothers, 1946.
Caspi, M. *Mi-Zkenim Etbonan* (I will observe the elders). Sedeh-Boker, Israel: Midreshet Sedeh Boker, 1968.
Caxton, W. *The History of Renard the Fox*. Early English Text Society 263. Ed. N. F. Blake. London: Oxford University Press, 1970.
Charlesworth, J. H., ed. *The Messiah: Development in Earliest Judaism and Christianity*. The First Princeton Symposium on Judaism and Christian Origins. Minneapolis: Fortress Press, 1992.
———, ed. *The Old Testament Pseudepigrapha*. 2 vols. Garden City, NY: Doubleday, 1983.
Chauvin, V. *Bibliographie des ouvrages Arabes ou relatifs aux Arabes publiès dans l'Europe Chrétienne de 1810 à 1885*. 12 vols. Liege, Belgium: Vallant-Carmanne, 1892–1922.
Chazan, R. "The Blois Incident of 1171: A Study in Jewish Intercommunal Organization." *PAAJR* 36 (1968), 13–31.
Cheesman, T. "The Return of the Transformed Son: A Popular Ballad Complex and Cultural History, Germany 1500–1900." *OGS* 18/19 (1989–1990), 60–91.
———. *The Shocking Ballad Picture Show: German Popular Literature and Cultural History*. Oxford, UK: Berg, 1994.
Cheichel, E., ed. *A Tale for Each Month 1967: Twelve Selected and Annotated IFA Folktales* [Hebrew]. IFAPS 22. Haifa: Ethnological Museum and Folkore Archives, 1968.
———, ed. *A Tale for Each Month 1968–1969: Twenty-Four Selected and Annotated IFA Folktales* [Hebrew]. IFAPS 26. Haifa: Ethnological Museum and Folkore Archives, 1970.
———, ed. *A Tale for Each Month: 1972. Twelve Selected and Annotated IFA Folktales* [Hebrew]. IFAPS 22. Haifa: Ethnological Museum and Folkore Archives, 1973.
Ch'en, L. "Pien-wen Chantefable and *Aucassin et Nicolette*." *CL* 23 (1971), 255–261.
Chestnutt, M. "Parodies." *EM* 10:556–561, 2001.
Choi, I. H. *A Type Index of Korean Folktales*. Seoul: Myong Ji University Publishing, 1979.
Christiansen, R. T. *The Migratory Legend: A Proposed List of Types with a Systematic Catalogue of the Norwegian Variants*. FFC 175. Helsinki: Suomalainen Tiedeakatemia, 1958.
———. *The Tale of the Two Travellers or the Blinded Man: A Comparative Study*. FFC 24. Helsinki: Suomalainen Tiedeakatemia, 1916.
Clark, W. B. "A Meditation on Folk-History: The Dramatic Structure of Robert Penn Warren's 'The Ballad of Billie Potts.'" *AL* 49 (1978), 635–645.
Clouston, W. A. "Appendix: Variants and Analogues." In *Supplemental Nights to the Book of the Thousand Nights and Night* (293–383). Ed. R. F. Burton. London: Burton Club, 1986.
———. *The Book of Sindibad; or, The Story of the King, His Son, the Damsel, and the Seven Vazirs*. London: Author, 1884.
———. *A Group of Eastern Romances and Stories from the Persian, Talmud, and Urdu*. London: Author, 1889. [Reprint eds. Norwood, NJ: Norwood Editions, 1973; Folcroft, PA: Folcroft Library Editions, 1977.]

———. *Popular Tales and Fictions: Their Migrations and Transformations.* 2 vols. Edinburgh and London: Blackwood, 1887.

Cogan, M. *1 Kings.* The Anchor Bible. New York: Doubleday, 2000.

Cohen, C. "The Road to Conversion." *LBIYB* 6 (1961), 259–279.

Cohen, D. *Aggadot Mitnagnot* (Melodic legends). Tel Aviv: Hakibutz Hameuchad, 1955.

Cohen, I. *Vilna.* Philadelphia: Jewish Publication Society of America, 1943. [Reprint ed. 1992.]

Cohen, M. *Mi-Pi ha-Am: Sippurei-Am mi-Pi Edot Israel* (From folk tradition: Folktales of ethnic groups in Israel). 3 vols. Tel Aviv: Alef, 1974–1979.

Cohen, S. J. D. "The Rabbinic Conversion Ceremony." *JJS* 41 (1990), 177–203.

Cohen, S. S. *Antisemitism: An Annotated Bibliography.* The Vidal Sassoon International Center for the Study of Antisemitism. The Hebrew University of Jerusalem. 15 vols. New York: Garland (vols. 1–3); Munich: Saur (vols. 4–15), 1987–2002.

Colebrook, C. *Irony.* The New Critical Idiom. London: Routledge, 2004.

———. *Irony in the Work of Philosophy.* Lincoln: University of Nebraska Press, 2002.

Collinet-Guérin, M. *Histoire du nimbe des origins aux temps modernes.* Paris: Nouvelles Editions Latines, 1961.

Copland, D. C. *The Origins of Major War.* Ithaca, NY: Cornell University Press, 2000.

Corti, E. C. *The Rise of the House of Rothschild.* New York: Cosmopolitan Books, 1928.

Cosquin, E. "La theme de 'la princesse qui ame son pere comme du sel'—'le roi Lear' de Shakespeare." *RTP* 28 (1913), 537–555.

Cowles, V. *The Rothschilds: A Family of Fortune.* New York: Knopf, 1973.

Cox, M. R. *Cinderella: Three Hundred and Forty-Five Variants of Cinderella, Catskin, and Cap o' Rushes, Abstracted and Tabulated, with Discussion of Mediaeval Analogues, and Notes.* PFLS 31. London: Folk-Lore Society, 1892. [Reprint ed. Liechtenstein: Nendeln, 1967.]

Crane, S. "Knights in Disguise: Identity and Incognito in Fourteenth-Century Chivalry." In *The Stranger in Medieval Society* (63–79). Medieval Cultures 12. Ed. F. R. P. Akehurst and S. C. van D'Elden. Minneapolis: University of Minnesota Press, 1997.

Crane, T. F. *The Exempla or Illustrative Stories from the Sermons Vulgares of Jacques de Vitry.* PFLS 26. London: Folk-Lore Society, 1890.

Cray, E. "The Rabbi Trickster." *JAF* 77 (1964), 330–345.

Cygielman, S. A. A. *Jewish Autonomy in Poland and Lithuania until 1648 (5408).* Jerusalem: Author, 1997.

———. *The Jews of Poland and Lithuania until 1648 (5408): Prolegomena and Annotated Sources* [Hebrew]. Jerusalem: Zalman Shazar Center for Jewish History, 1991.

———. "Leasing and Contracting Interests (Public Incomes) of Polish Jewry and the Founding of 'Va'ad Arba Aratzot' " [Hebrew]. *Zion* 47 (1982), 112–144.

D'Alcripe, P. *La nouvelle fabrique des excellents traicts de verité: Livre pour inciter les resveurs tristes et melancholiques à vivre de plaisir.* Ed. F. Joukovsky. Geneva: Librairie Droz, 1983. [Originally published 1574.]

Dan, I. "The Innocent Persecuted Heroine: An Attempt at a Model for the Surface Level of the Narrative Structure of the Female Fairy Tale." In *Patterns in Oral Literature* (13–30). World Anthropology. Ed. H. Jason and D. Segal. The Hague: Mouton, 1977.

Dan, J. "Demonological Stories in the Writings of R. Yehudah Hehasid" [Hebrew]. *Tarbiz* 30 (1961), 273–289. [Reprinted in Dan, *Studies in Ashekanizi-Hasidic Literature* (9–25) (Hebrew). Ramat Gan: Massada, 1975.]

———. "The Desert in Jewish Mysticism; the Kingdom of Samael." *Ariel* 40 (1976), 38–43.

———. *The Esoteric Theology of Ashkenazi Hasidism* [Hebrew]. Jerusalem: Bialik Institute, 1968.

———. *The Hasidic Story—Its History and Development* [Hebrew]. Jerusalem: Keter, 1975.

———. "The Prince of Thumb and Cup." *Tarbiz* 32 (1963), 359–369.

———. "Rabbi Nahman's Third Beggar." In *History and Literature: New Readings of Jewish Texts in Honor of Arnold J. Band* (41–54). Brown Judaic Studies 334. Ed. W. Cutter and D. C. Jacobson. Providence, RI: Brown Judaic Studies, 2002.

———. "Samael and the Problem of Jewish Gnosticism." In *Perspectives on Jewish Thought and Mysticism: Proceedings of the International Conference Held by the Institute of Jewish Studies* (257–276). Ed. A. L. Ivry, E. R. Wolfson, and A. Arkush. Amsterdam, The Netherlands: Harwood Academic, 1998.

———. "Samael, Lilith, and the Concept of Evil in Early Kabbalah." *AJS Reviews* 5 (1980), 17-40. [Reprinted in L. Fine, ed. *Essential Papers on Kabbalah* (154-178). New York: New York University Press, 1995; and J. Dan, *Jewish Mysticism, Vol. III: The Modern Period* (253-282). Northvale, N. J.:] Jerusalem: Jason Aronson, 1999.]

Dane, J. A. *The Critical Mythology of Irony*. Athens: University of Georgia Press, 1991.

———. *Parody: Critical Concepts Versus Literary Practices, Aristophanes to Sterne*. Norman: University of Oklahoma Press, 1988.

Daniyel, M. N. ben. *Emunat ha-Tehiyah: Bo yevo'ar ha-metim, kol minhagehem aḥare tehiyotehem* (The belief in resurrection: Explanation of all the customs concerning the resurrection of the dead). Berdichev, Ukraine: Bi-defus H. Y. Sheftil, 1896.

Danzig, N. "Two Insights from a Ninth-Century Liturgical Handbook: The Origins of Yequm Purqan and Qaddish de-Hadata." In *The Cambridge Genizah Collections: Their Contents and Significance* (74–122). Ed. S. C. and S. Reif. Cambridge, UK: Cambridge University Press, 2002.

Davidson, E., ed. *Sehok le-Yisrael: Yalkut le-Folklor, Havai, Humor u-Vediḥah 'al Medinat Yisrael be-Ḥazon u-v-Metzi'ut le-min Tekufat ha-Meshiḥiyut ve-ad Shnat he-'Asor la-Medinah* (Laughter of Israel: A collection of folklore, folkways, humor and wit about the state of Israel in vision and reality from the messianic era till the first decade of the State of Israel). Ramat-Gan, Israel: Matmonim, 1958.

———. *Sehok Pynu (Our Mouth's Laughter): Anthology of Humour and Satire in Ancient and Modern Hebrew Literature* [Hebrew]. 2nd ed. 2 vols. Hulon, Israel: Biblos, 1972.

Davidson, H. R. E., and W. M. S. Russell, eds. *The Folklore of Ghosts*. Mistletoe Series 15. Cambridge, UK: Published for the Folklore Society by D. S. Brewer, 1981.

Davidson, I. *Parody in Jewish Literature*. Columbia University Oriental Studies 2. New York: Columbia University Press, 1907.

———, ed. and trans. *Sepher Shaashuim: A Book of Mediaeval Lore by Joseph ben Meir ibn Zabara*. Texts and Studies of the Jewish Theological Seminary of America 4. New York: Jewish Theological Seminary of America, 1914.

———, S. Assaf, and B. I. Joel, eds. *R. Saadja Gaon: Kitāb ´gāmi` as-salawāt wat-tasā-bīh* [Hebrew and Arabic]. Jerusalem: Mekitse Nirdamim, 1963.

Davidson, S., and E. Phelps. "Folktales from New Goa, India." *JAF* 50 (1937), 1–51.

Davies, C. *Ethnic Humor around the World: A Comparative Analysis*. Bloomington: Indiana University Press, 1990.

———. *Jokes and Their Relation to Society*. Humor Research 4. Berlin and New York: de Guyter, 1998.
Davy, M. M, et al. *La Thème de la lumière dans le Judaïsme le Christianisme et l'Islam*. Paris: Berg International, 1976.
Dawkins, R. M. *Modern Greek Folktales*. Oxford, UK: Clarendon, 1953.
Daxelmüller, C. "Dämonologie." *EM* 3:237–259, 1979.
Decourdemanche, J. A. *Sottisier de Nasr-Eddin-Hodja: Bouffon de Tamerlan*. Bruxelles: Gay et Doucé, 1878.
Dégh, L. *Legend and Belief: Dialectics of a Folklore Genre*. Bloomington: Indiana University Press, 2001.
———, and A. Vazsonyi. "Legend and Belief." In *Folklore Genres* (93–123). AFSBSS 26. Ed. D. Ben-Amos. Austin: University of Texas Press, 1976.
Deinard, E. *Sichronoth Bat Ami: Memoirs of Jewish Life in Russia* [Hebrew]. St. Louis: Moinseter, 1920.
Delarue, P., and M. L. Tenèze. *Le conte populaire français; Catalogue raisonné des versions de France et das pays de langue française d'outre-mer: Canada, Louisiane, îlots français des États-Unis, Antilles françaises, Haïti, Ile Maurice, La Réunion*. 3 vols. Paris: Maisonneuve & Larose, 1957.
Delpech, F. "L'elimination des veillards: Recherches sur quelques versions Iberiques d'un cycle folklorique tradionnel." In *Litterature orale tradionnelle populaire actes du colloque Paris, 20–22 Novembre 1986* (433–490). Paris: Fondation Calouste Gulbenkian, 1987.
Deshen, S. "The Kol Nidre Enigma: An Anthropological View of the Day of Atonement Liturgy." *Ethnology* 18 (1979), 121–133. [Reprinted in E. Etkes and Y. Salmon, eds., *Studies in the History of Jewish Society in the Middle Ages and in the Modern Period* (136–153) (Hebrew). Jerusalem: Magnes, 1980.]
Deurloo, K. A. "The King's Wisdom in Judgment: Narration as Example (1 Kings iii)." In *New Avenues in the Study of the Old Testament* (11–21). Oudtestamentische Studiën 25. Ed. A. S. Van Der Woude. Leiden: Brill, 1989.
Deutsch, N. "An-Sky and the Ethnography of Jewish Women." In *The Worlds of S. An-Sky: A Russian Jewish Intellectual at the Turn of the Century* (266–280). Ed. G. Safran and S. J. Zipperstein. Stanford, CA: Stanford University Press, 2006.
Deutscher, I. *Stalin: A Political Biography*. 2nd ed. New York: Oxford University Press, 1966.
Dierkens, A., ed. *Apparitions et miracles*. Problèmes d'histoire des religions. Bruxelles: Université libre de Bruxelles, 1991.
Dinur, B., ed. *Sefer Toldot ha-Haganah* (The history of defense forces). 4 vols. Tel Aviv: Am Oved, 1954.
Dishon, J. *The Book of Delight Composed by Joseph Ben Meir Zabara* [Hebrew]. Jerusalem: Rubin Mass, 1985.
Dobroszycki, L., ed. *The Chronicle of the Lodz Ghetto 1941–1944*. New Haven, CT: Yale University Press, 1984.
Dodge, B., ed. and trans. *The Fihrist of al-Nadīm, a Tenth-Century Survey of Muslim Culture*. Records of Civilization, Sources and Studies 83. New York: Columbia University Press, 1970.
Doleželová, J. "Spice Boxes from the Collections of the State Jewish Museum." *JuB* 24 (1988), 42–54.

Domnitch, L. *The Cantonists: The Jewish Children's Army of the Tsar.* Jerusalem: Devora, 2003.

Dömötör, A. *"Doktor Allwissend* (AaTh 1641)." *EM* 3:734–742, 1980.

Dorenberg, J. *Munich 1923: The Story of Hitler's First Grab for Power.* New York: Harper & Row, 1982. [Also published as *The Putsch That Failed: Munich 1923: Hitler's Rehearsal for Power.* London: Weidenfeld & Nicholson, 1982.]

Dorson, R. D. *Buying the Wind: Regional Folklore in America.* Chicago: Chicago University Press, 1964.

———. "Jewish-American Dialect Stories on Tape." In *Studies in Biblical and Jewish Folklore* (109–174). IUFS 13. Memoir Series of the American Folklore Society 51. Ed. R. Patai, F. L. Utley, and D. Noy. Bloomington: Indiana University Press, 1960.

———. "Polish Wonder Tales of Joe Woods." *WF* 8 (1949), 25–52, 131–145.

Douglas, M. *Purity and Danger: An Analysis of Concepts of Pollution and Taboo.* London: Routledge & Kegan Paul, 1966.

———. "The Social Control of Cognition: Some Factors in Jokes Cognition." *Man* 3 (1968), 361–376. [Reprinted in M. Douglas, *Implicit Meanings: Essays in Anthropology* (90–114). London: Routledge & Kegan Paul, 1975.]

Draak, M. "Is Ondank 'S Werelds Loon?" *Neophilologus* 30 (1946), 129–138.

Draitser, E. A. *Taking Penguins to the Movies: Ethnic Humor in Russia.* Humor in Life and Letters Series. Detroit: Wayne State University Press, 1998.

Dresner, S. H. *The Jewish Dietary Laws: Their Meaning for Our Time.* New York: Burning Bush Press, 1966. [Reprint ed. New York: Rabbinical Assembly of America, 1982.]

———. *Levi Yitzhak of Berdichev: Portrait of a Hasidic Master.* New York: Shapolsky, 1986. [Reprint ed. *The World of a Hasidic Master: Levi Yitzhak of Berditchev.* Northvale, NJ: Aronson, 1994.]

Drogi, P. *Le Cantique déguisé: Image et folie dans Aucassin et Nicolette.* Genève: Université de Genève, 1995.

Druyanow, A. A. *Sefer ha-Bediḥah ve-ha-Ḥidud* (The book of jokes and witticisms). 3 vols. Tel Aviv: Dvir, 1935–1938. [Originally published Frankfurt am Main, Germany: Omonuth, 1922.]

Dubarle, A. M. "Le jugement de Salomon: Un Cœur à l'écoute." *RSPT* 63 (1979), 419–427.

Dubnow, S. *Toldot ha-Ḥasidut* (History of Hasidism). Tel Aviv: Hotsa'at Devir, 1960. [Originally published 1930.]

Duffy J. P., and V. L. Ricci. *Target Hitler: The Plots to Kill Adolf Hitler.* Westport, CT: Praeger, 1992.

Duling, D. C. "Testament of Solomon (First to Third Century A.D.)." In *The Old Testament Pseudepigrapha: Apocalyptic Literature and Testaments* (1:977–982). Ed. J. H. Charlesworth. Garden City, NY: Doubleday, 1983.

Dundes, A. "The Devolutionary Premise in Folklore Theory." *JFI* 6 (1969), 5–19.

———. " 'To Love My Father All': A Psychoanalytic Study of the Folktale Source of King Lear." *SFQ* 40 (1976), 353–366. [Reprinted in Dundes, ed. *Cinderella: A Folklore Casebook* (229–244). New York: Garland, 1982.]

———. "The Symbolic Equivalence of Allomotifs in the Rabbit-Herd (AT 570)." *ARV* 36 (1980), 91–98.

Dunlop, J. C. *History of Prose Fiction.* Rev. ed. New York: Franklin, 1970. [Originally published 1896.]

Dynner, G. *Men of Silk: The Hasidic Conquest of Polish Jewry*. Oxford, UK: Oxford University Press, 2006.

Dziewanowski, M. K. *Joseph Pilsudski: A European Federalist, 1918–1922*. Stanford, CA: Hoover Institute Press, 1969.

Eastwick, E. B., trans. *The Anvár-i Suhailí or the Lights of Canopus, Being the Persian Version of the Fables of Pilpay; or the Book "Kalílah and Damnah" Rendered into Persian by Husain Vá'iz U'L-Káshifí*. Hertford, UK: Austin, 1854.

Eberhard, W. *Folktales of China*. Folktales of the World. Chicago: University of Chicago Press, 1965.

———, and P. N. Boratav. *Typen türkischer Volksmärchen*. Wiesbaden, Germany: Steiner, 1953.

Edgerton, F., ed. and trans. *The Panchatantra Reconstructed: An Attempt to Establish the Lost Original Sanskrit Text of the Most Famous of Indian Story-Collections on the Basis of the Principal Extant Versions*. American Oriental Series 2–3. New Haven, CT: American Oriental Society, 1924.

Eherman, D. B. *Sefer Devarim 'Arevim* (A book of pleasant subjects). Perbenik, Republic of Slovakia: Author, 1902 or 1903.

———. *Sefer Pe'er ve-Kavod* (The book of glory and honor). Munkacs [Mukacevo], Ukraine: Maisels and Gartenberg, 1911.

Eichhhorn, D. M., ed. *Conversion to Judaism: A History and Analysis*. New York: Ktav, 1965.

Eidelberg, S. *R. Juspa, Shammash of Warmaisa (Worms): Jewish Life in 17th-Century Worms* [Hebrew]. Jerusalem: Magnes Press, 1991.

Eilbrit, H. *What Is a Jewish Joke? An Excursion into Jewish Humor*. Northvale, NJ: Aronson, 1981.

Einbinder, S. L. "Jewish Women Martyrs: Changing Models of Representation." *Exemplaria* 12 (2000), 105–127.

———. "Pucellina of Blois: Romantic Myths and Narrative Conventions." *JH* 12 (1998), 29–46.

Einhorn, S. *Mishlei-'Am be-Yidish* (Yiddish folk proverbs). Ed. Y. T. Lewinski. Tel Aviv: Devir, 1959.

Eisenstein, J. D., ed. *Ozar Midrashim: Bibliotheca Midraschica* [Hebrew]. 2 vols. New York: Grossman's Hebrew Book Store, 1956. [Originally published 1915.]

———. *Ozar Yisrael: An Encyclopedia of All Matters Concerning Jews and Judaism* [Hebrew]. 10 vols. New York: Eisenstein, 1907–1913.

Elbaum, J. [Y.]. "The Ba'al Shem Tov and the Son of R. Adam—A Study of a Story in Praise of the Ba'al Shem Tov" [Hebrew]. *JSJF* 2 (1982), 66–79.

———. *Openness and Insularity: Late Sixteenth-Century Jewish Literature in Poland and Ashkenaz* [Hebrew]. Jerusalem: Magnes Press, 1990.

Elbogen, I. "Eingang und Ausgang des Sabbats nach talmudischen Quellen." In *Festschrift zu Israel Lewy's siebzigstem Geburtstag* (173–187). Ed. M. Brann and J. Elbogen. Breslau: Marcus, 1911.

———. *Jewish Liturgy: A Comprehensive History*. Trans. R. P. Scheindlin. Philadelphia: Jewish Publication Society, 1993.

Eliach, Y. *Hasidic Tales of the Holocaust*. New York: Oxford University Press, 1982.

Eliade, M. *The Two and the One*. Trans. J. M. Cohen. London: Harvill Press, 1965.

Elior, R. "Between 'Divestment of Corporeality' and 'Love of Corporeality' " [Hebrew].

In *Studies in Jewish Culture in Honour of Chone Shmeruk* (209–242). Ed. I. Bartal, E. Mendelsohn, and C. Turniansky. Jerusalem: Zalman Shazar Center for Jewish History, 1993. [Reprinted in D. Assaf, ed. *Zaddik and Devotees: Historical and Sociological Aspects of Hasidism* (463–495) (Hebrew). Jerusalem: Zalman Shazar Center for Jewish History, 2001.]

———. *The Paradoxical Ascent to God: The Kabbalistic Theosophy of Habad Hasidism.* Trans. J. M. Green. Albany: State University of New York Press, 1993.

Elon, A. *Founder: A Portrait of the First Rothschild and His Time.* New York: Viking, 1996.

———. *The Pity of It All: A History of the Jews in Germany, 1743–1933.* New York: Metropolitan Books, 2002.

El-Shamy, H. M. *Folktales of Egypt.* Folktales of the World. Chicago: University of Chicago Press, 1980.

———. *Types of the Folktales in the Arab World: A Demographically Oriented Tale-Type Index.* Bloomington: Indiana University Press, 2004.

Elstein, Y. "The Gregorius Legend: Its Christian Versions and Its Metamorphosis in the Hasidic Tale." *Fabula* 27 (1986), 195–215.

———. *Structures of Recurrence in Literature* [Hebrew]. Tel Aviv: Alef, 1970.

Emerton, J. A. "Sheol and the Sons of Belial." *VT* 37 (1987), 214–218.

Enelow, H. G., ed. *The Mishnah of Rabbi Eliezer or the Midrash of Thirty-Two Hermeneutical Rules.* New York: Bloch, 1933.

Epstein, L. M. *The Jewish Marriage Contract: A Study in the Status of the Woman in Jewish Law.* New York: Jewish Theological Seminary of America, 1927.

Epstein, M. *Tales of Sendebar: An Edition and Translation of the Hebrew Version of the Seven Sages Based on Unpublished Manuscripts* [Hebrew and English]. Philadelphia: Jewish Publication Society of America, 1967.

Epstein, N. "*Bemerkungen zu di vitzen un vitzike mayselach*" (Notes to the jokes and comic tales) [Yiddish]. In *Jewish Folklore* (319–321). Publications of the Yiddish Scientific Institute 9. Philological Series 5. Ed. J. L. Cahan. Vilnius, Lithuania: Yiddish Scientific Institute, 1938.

Erdélyi, J. *Magyar közmondások könyve* (A book of Hungarian proverbs). Pest, Hungary: Kozma Vazul, 1851.

Erik, M. *Geshichte fun yiddisher literature, fun di eltste zeitn biz der haskoloh-tkufoh* (The history of Yiddish literature from the oldest times until the period of enlightenment). Warsaw: Cultural League, 1928. [Reprint ed. New York, 1979.]

Esteban, F. D. *Abraham ibn Ezra y su tiempo/Abraham ibn Ezra and His Age*: Actas del Simposio Internacional/*Proceedings of the International Symposium, Madrid, Tudela, Toledo. 1–8 febrero 1989.* Madrid: Asociacion Española de Orientalistas, 1990.

Estin, C. *Contes et fêtes Juives.* Paris: Beauchesne, 1987.

Etkes, E. [I]. *Ba'al Hashem: The Besht—Magic, Mysticism, Leadership* [Hebrew]. Jerusalem: Zalman Shazar Center for Jewish History, 2000.

———. "Magic and Magicians in the Haskalah Literature" [Hebrew]. In *Studies in Hasidism* (39–56). Ed. D. Assaf, J. Dan, and I. Etkes. Jerusalem: Institute of Jewish Studies, Hebrew University of Jerusalem, 1999. [Also published in special issue, *JSJT* 15 (1999).]

---. *Rabbi Israel Salanter and the Beginning of the "Musar" Movement* [Hebrew]. Jerusalem: Magnes Press, 1982.

---. "Rabbi Shneur Zalman of Lyady as a Hasidic Leader" [Hebrew]. *Zion* 50 (1985), 321–354.

---. "The Rise of Rabbi Schneur Zalman of Lyady as a Hasidic Leader" [Hebrew]. *Tarbiz* 54 (1985), 429–439.

--- "The Role of Magic and *Ba'alei-Shem* in Ashkenazi Society in the Late Seventeenth and Early Eighteenth Centuries" [Hebrew]. *Zion* 60 (1995), 69–104.

---. "The Zaddik: The Interrelationship between Religious Doctrine and Social Organization." In *Hasidism Reappraised* (159–167). Ed. A. Rapoport-Albert. London: Littman Library of Jewish Civilization. [Originally published in *Zion* 55 (1990), 183–245.]

Ettinger, S. "Chmielnicki (Khmelnitski), Bogdan (1595–1657)." *EJ* 5:480–484, 1971.

---. "Jewish Participation in the Colonization of the Ukraine (1569–1648)" [Hebrew]. *Zion* 21 (1956), 107–142.

---. "The Legal and Social Status of the Jews of Ukraine from the Fifteenth Century to the Cossack Uprising of 1648." *JUS* 17 (1992), 122–130.

Evans, H. *Visions, Apparitions, Alien Visitors*. Wellingborough, UK: Aquarian Press, 1984.

Evans, S., trans. *Histories of the Kings of Britain by Geoffrey of Monmouth*. New York: Dutton, 1912.

Even, Y. *Fun'm Rebin's Hoyf* (From the rabbi's court). New York: Author, 1922.

Even-Shemuel, J. [Y.], trans. *The Kosari of R. Yehuda Halevi*. Tel Aviv: Dvir, 1972.

---, ed. *Midrashi Ge'ulah: Pirke ha-Epokalipsah ha-Yehudit me-Ḥatimat ha-Talmud ha-Bavli ve-'ad Reshit ha-Elef ha-Shishi* (Midrashim of deliverance: Jewish apocalyptic writings from the conclusion of the Babylonian Talmud until the beginning of the sixth millenium). Jerusalem: Bialik Institute/Masadah, 1954.

Faas, P. *Around the Roman Table*. Trans. S. Whiteside. New York: Palgrave, 2003.

Fabre, D., and J. Lacroix. "Sur la production du recit populaire: À propos du Fils Assassiné." In *Approches de nos traditions orales* (91–140). Ed. M. L. Tenèze. Paris: Maisonneuve & Laros, 1970.

Faierstein, M. M. "The Literary Legacy of Shneur Zalman of Lyadi." *JBA* 52 (1994–1995), 148–162.

Falk, F. *Das Schemuelbuch des Mosche Esrim Wearba: Ein biblisches Epos dem 15. Jahrhundert*. Publications of the Bibliotheca Rosenthaliana. 2 vols. Assen: Van Gorcum, 1961.

Falkowitz, R. S. "Discrimination and Condensation of Sacred Categories: The Fable in Early Mesopotamian Literature." In *Entretiens sur l'Antiquité Classique*. Vol. 30: *La Fable* (1–32). Series ed. Francisco R. Adrados. Geneva: Vandoeuvres, 1983.

---. "The Sumerian Rhetoric Collections." Unpublished dissertation. Philadelphia: University of Pennsylvania, 1980.

Farḥi, J. S. 1959. *Oseh Pele* (The miracle worker). 4 parts. Jerusalem: Bakal, 1959. [Originally published Livorno, 1845, 1869, 1870.]

Fay, S. B. *The Origins of the World War*. 2 vols. New York: Macmillan, 1929.

Feiner, S. *The Jewish Enlightenment*. Jewish Culture and Contexts. Trans. C. Naor. Philadelphia: University of Pennsylvania Press, 2002.

Fensham, F. C. "Legal Aspects of the Dream of Solomon." *4th WCJS* 1 (1967), 67–70.
Ferguson, N. *The House of Rothschild 1798–1848*. 2 vols. New York: Viking, 1998.
Fernandez, J. W., and M. T. Huber, eds. *Irony in Action: Anthropology, Practice, and the Moral Imagination*. Chicago: University of Chicago Press, 2001.
Fine, E. C. *The Folklore Text: From Performance to Print*. Bloomington: Indiana University Press, 1984.
Fine, G. A. "Sociological Approaches to the Study of Humor." In *Handbook of Humor Research*. Vol. 1: *Basic Issues* (159–181). Ed. P. E. McGhee and J. H. Goldstein. New York: Springer-Verlag, 1983.
———, et al., eds. *Rumor Mills: The Social Impact of Rumor and Legend*. New Brunswick, NJ: Aldine Transaction, 2005.
Finesinger, S. B."The Custom of Looking at the Fingernails at the Outgoing of the Sabbath." *HUCA* 12–13 (1937–1938), 347–365.
———. "The Shofar." *HUCA* 8–9 (1931–1932), 193–228.
Fingueret, M., and E. Toker. *Las picardías de Hérshele*. Buenos Aires: Ediciones Colihue, 1991.
Finkelstein, L. "The Development of the Amidah." *JQR* 16 (1925), 1–43, 127–169.
———. *Ha-Perushim ve-Anshe Keneset Ha-Gedolah* (The Pharisees and the men of the Great Assembly). Texts and Studies of the Jewish Theological Seminary of America 15. New York: Jewish Theological Seminary of America, 1950.
———. *The Pharisees: The Sociological Background of Their Faith*. The Morris Loeb Series. 2 vols. 3rd ed. Philadelphia: Jewish Publication Society of America, 1966.
———. "Pre-Maccabean Documents in the Passover Haggadah." *HTR* 35 (1942), 291–332; 36 (1943), 1–38.
———, ed. *Sifre on Deuteronomy*. New York: Jewish Theological Seminary of America, 1969, 1993. [Originally published *Siphre ad Deuteronmium. Corpus Tannaiticum. Sectio tertia veterum doctorum ad Pentateuchum interpretationes halachicas continens*. Berlin: Jüdischer Kulturbund in Deutschland, 1939.]
———. "Mi-Torato Shel R. Nehunya ben ha-Kanah" (From the teaching of R. Nehunya ben ha-Kanah). In *Sefer ha-Yovel le-Rabi Hanokh Albek: Mugash 'Al Yede Talmidav Yedidav u-Mokirav li-Melot lo Shiv'im Shanah* (A festschrift for Rabbi Hanohk Albek: Presented by his students, friends, and admirers on his seventieth birthday) (352–377). Jerusalem: Mossad Ha-rav Kook, 1963.
Finkelstein, M. *Proselytism: Halakhah and Practice* [Hebrew]. Ramat-Gan, Israel: Bar-Ilan University Press, 1994.
Finucane, R. C. *Appearances of the Dead: A Cultural History of Ghosts*. London: Junction, 1982.
Fischel, H. A. "The Uses of the Sories (Climax, Gradatio) in the Tannaitic Period." *HUCA* 44 (1973), 119–151.
Fishman, Y. L. *Ma'asim al Aseret ha-Dibrot o Haggadah Shel Shavu'ot* (Tales about the Ten Comandments or aggadah for Shabuoth). Jerusalem: Hotsa'ah me-Yuhedet me-"ha-Tur," 1924.
———. "Seder Customs and the Midrash to the Aggadah." *Sinai* 2 (1939), 329–351.
Fishof, I. *Written in the Stars: Art and Symbolism of the Zodiac*. Jerusalem: Israel Museum, 2001.
Fitzpatrick, S. *Everyday Stalinism: Ordinary Life in Extraordinary Times: Soviet Russia in the 1930s*. New York: Oxford University Press, 1999.

Fleischer, E. "*Havdalah-Shiv'atot* According to Palestinian Ritual" [Hebrew]. *Tarbiz* 36 (1967), 342–365.

―――――. "The *Shemone Esre*—Its Character, Internal Order, Content and Goals" [Hebrew]. *Tarbiz* 62 (1993), 179–223.

Fleischmann, B. *Rothschild's Violin,* compact disc. Completed and orchestrated by D. Shostakovich. Dir. E. Cozarinsky. BMG Music 09026-68434-2.

Flesch, A. "*A zsido a Magyar közmondásban*" (The Jew in Hungarian proverbs). *IMIT Evkönyv* [Yearbook]. Budapest: Franklin, 1908.

Flinn, J. *Le Roman de Renart dans la littèratures Française et dans les littèratures étrangèrs au moyen age.* Paris: Presses Universitaires de France, 1963.

Flint, V. "The Demonisation of Magic and Sorcery in Late Antiquity: Christian Redefinitions of Pagan Religions." In *Witchcraft and Magic in Europe: Ancient Greece and Rome* (277–348). Ed. B. Ankarloo and S. Clark. Philadelphia: University of Pennsylvania Press, 1999.

Fludernik, M. *Towards a "Natural" Narratology.* London and New York: Routledge, 1996.

Fochi, A. *Miorita: Tipologi, circulatie, geneza, texte.* [Bucuresti]: Editura Academiei Republicii Populare Romîne, [1964].

Fontaine, C. "The Bearing of Wisdom on the Shape of II Sam. 11–12 and I Kings 3." *JSOT* 34 (1986), 61–77.

Fontinoy, C. "*Les nomes du diable et leur etymologie.*" In *Orientalia J. Duchesne-Guillemin Emerito Oblata* (157–170). Acta Iranica 23. 2nd ser. Hommages et Opera Minor 9. Leiden: Brill, 1984.

Foster, G. M. "Peasant Society and the Image of Limited Good." *AA* 67 (1965), 293–315.

Foxbrunner, R. A. *Ḥabad: The Hasidism of R. Shneur Zalman of Lyady.* Judaic Studies Series. Tuscaloosa: University of Alabama Press, 1992.

Fram, E. "Perception and Reception of Repentant Apostates in Medieval Ashkenaz and Premodern Poland." *AJSR* 21/22 (1996), 299–339.

Frankel, J., ed. "Symposium: *Ostjuden* in Central and Western Europe." *Studies in Contemporary Jewry* 1 (1984), 3–198.

―――――, and S. J. Zipperstein, eds. *Assimilation and Community: The Jews in Nineteenth-Century Europe.* Cambridge, UK: Cambridge University Press, 1992.

[Frankland, T.] *The Annals of King James and King Charles the First . . . Early English Books, 1641–1700.* London: Braddyll, 1681.

Frauenrath, M. *Le fils assassiné: L'influence d'un sujet donne sur la structure dramatique.* Beihefte zu Poetica 9. Munich: Fink, 1974.

Freedman, P. "*Le-Divrei ha-Yamim shel ha-Yehudim be-Ḥelem: Korotav shel ha-Yishuv ha-Yehudi me Hatḥalato*" (The history of the Jews in Chelem: From the beginning of the Jewish settlement). In *Yizkor Book in Memory of Chelem* (37–56). Ed. S. Kanc and M. Grinberg. N.p.: Irgun Yots'ei Ḥelem be-Yisrael uve-Artson ha-Brit, 1980 or 1981.

―――――. "*Ma'asiyyot Ḥelem*" (Tales of Chelm). In *Yizkor Book in Memory of Chelem* (561–562). Ed. S. Kanc and M. Grinberg. N.p.: Irgun Yots'ei Ḥelem be-Yisrael uve-Artson ha-Brit, 1980 or 1981.

Freeman, G. M. "The Language of Jewish Political Discourse." *JPSR* 1, nos. 1–2 (1989), 63–76.

Fretz, R. I. "Answering in Song: Listener Responses in Yishima Performances." *WF* 54 (1995), 95–112.

Freudenthal, G. "Providence, Astrology, and Celestial Influences on the Sublunar World Is Explored in Shem-Tov ibn Falaquera's *De'ot Ha-Filosofim*." In *The Medieval Hebrew Encyclopedias of Science and Philosophy: Proceedings of the Bar-Ilan University Conference* (335–370). Ed. S. Harvey. Dordrecht: Kluwer Academic, 2000.

———, and S. Kottek, eds. *Mélanges d'histoire de la médecine hébraïque: Études choisies de la Revue d'histoire de la médecine hébraïque (1948–1984)*. Études sur le Judaïsme medieval 24. Leiden: Brill, 2003.

Frid, F. *Medrcy z Chelma* (The wise men of Chelm) [Yiddish]. Warsaw: Idisz Buch, 1966.

Friedberg, M. "Begging and Beggars." *EJ* 4:387–391, 1971.

Frieden, N. M. *Russian Physicians in an Era of Reform and Revolution, 1856–1905*. Princeton, NJ: Princeton University Press, 1981.

Friedenwald, H. *Jewish Luminaries in Medical History: A Catalogue of Works Bearing on the Subject of the Jews and Medicine from the Private Library of Harry Friedenwald*. Baltimore: Johns Hopkins Press, 1946.

———. *The Jews and Medicine, Essays*. 2 vols. Baltimore: Johns Hopkins Press, 1944.

Friedlander, G., trans. *Pirkê de Rabbi Eliezer* (The chapters of Rabbi Eliezer the Great). London: Paul, Trench, Trubner; New York: Bloch, 1916. [Reprint ed. New York: Hermon Press, 1965.]

Friedlander, H. *The German Revolution of 1918*. New York: Garland, 1992.

Friedländer, S. *Kurt Gerstein: The Ambiguity of Good*. Trans. C. Fullman. New York: Knopf, 1969.

Friedman, M. A. *Jewish Marriage in Palestine: A Cairo Geniza Study*. Vol. 1: *The Ketubba Traditions of Eretz Israel*. Vol. 2: *The Ketubba Texts*. Tel Aviv and New York: Tel Aviv University, Chaim Rosenberg School of Jewish Studies, Jewish Theological Seminary of America, 1980–1981.

Friedmann, M. *Pesikta Rabbati, Midrasch für den Fest-Cyclus und die ausgezeichneten Sabbathe*. Jerusalem, 1963. [Originally published 1880.]

———. *Seder Eliahu Rabba and Seder Eliahu Zuta (Tanna d'be Elihau)—Pseudo-Seder Eliahu Zuta*. Jerusalem: Bamberger & Wahrman, 1960. [Originally published *Pseudo-Seder Elihahu Zuta (Derech Ereç und Pirkê R. Eliezer)*. Vienna: Achiasaf, 1904.]

Friend, A. C. "Master Odo of Cheriton." *Speculum* 23 (1948), 641–658.

Frobenius, L., and D. C. Fox. *African Genesis*. New York: Blom, 1937.

Fröhlich, I. "Demons, Scribes, and Exorcists in Qumran." In *Essays in Honour of Alexander Fodor on His Sixtieth Birthday* (73–81). Ed. D. T. Iványi. Budapest: Eötvös Loránd University Chair for Arabic Studies, Csoma de Körös Society Section of Islamic Studies, 2001.

Frumkin, A. L., ed. *Seder Rav Amram ha-Shalem* (The complete prayer book of Rabbi Amram). 2 vols. Jerusalem: Tsukerman, 1912.

Fuchs, M. Z. "*Le-Toldot ha-Shirim 'Eḥad Mi Yode'a ve-Ḥad Gadya be-Yisrael u-ve-Amim*" (The history of "Eḥad Mi Yode'a" and "Ḥad Gadya" in Israel and [other] nations). *Asufot* 2 (1988), 201–226.

Fuks, L. *Das Altjiddische Epos Melokîm-Bûk*. Publications of the Bibliotheca Rosenthalia. 2 vols. Assen: Van Gorcum, 1965.

———. *The Oldest Known Literary Documents of Yiddish Literature (c. 1382)*. 2 vols. Leiden: Brill, 1957.

Furman [Fuhrmann], I. *Idishe shprichwerter un redensartn* (Yiddish proverbs and sayings). Tel Aviv: Hamenora, 1968.
Fus, D. "The Blessing of Elijah the Prophet." *Omer* Yom Kippur Suppl., September 30, 1960.
Gábor, O. N. *Magyar szólások és közmondások.* Budapest: Gondolat, 1966.
Gaillard, A. M. *Migration Return: A Bibliographical Overview.* Occasional Paper 12. New York: Center for Migration Studies, 1994.
Galderisi, C. "*Le 'crâne qui parle': Du motif aux récits, vertu chrétienne et vertu poétique.*" *CCM* 46 (2003), 213–231.
Galiebe, M. *Dukus Horant: Studien zu seiner literarischen Tradition.* Berlin: Schmidt, 1973.
Galnoor, I., and S. Lukes. *No Laughing Matter: A Collection of Political Jokes.* London: Routledge & Kegan Paul, 1985.
Gamlieli, N. B. *The Chambers of Yemen: 131 Jewish-Yemenite Folktales and Legends* [Hebrew]. Tel Aviv: Afikim, 1978.
Gammie, J. G. "The Angelology and Demonology in the Septuagint of the Book of Job." *HUCA* 56 (1985), 1–19.
Gandz, S. "Hebrew Numerals." *PAAJR* 1931–1932, no. 3 (1932), 54–111.
Ganz, P. F., F. Norman, and W. Schwarz, eds. *Dukus Horant.* Tübingen, Germany: Niemeyer, 1964.
———. "Zu dem Cambridger Joseph." *ZdP* 82 (1963), 86–90.
Garnett, C., ed. and trans. *Anton Chekhov: Later Short Stories 1888–1903.* New York: Modern Library, 1999.
Gartner, Y. "The Third Sabbath Meal: Halakhic and Historical Aspects" [Hebrew]. *Sidra* 6 (1990), 5–24.
Gaster, M., trans. and ed. *The Chronicles of Jerahmeel: Or, the Hebrew Bible Historiale: Being a Collection of Apocryphal and Pseudo-Epigraphical Books Dealing with the History of the World from the Creation to the Death of Judas Maccabeus.* Publications [Oriental Translation Fund] 11, new ser. London: Royal Asiatic Society, 1899. [Reprinted. New York: Ktav, 1971.]
———. *The Exempla of the Rabbis.* Leipzig: Asia Publishing, 1924. [Reprint ed. New York: Ktav, 1968.]
———, trans. and ed. *Ma'aseh Book.* 2 vols. Philadelphia: Jewish Publication Society of America, 1934.
Gaster, T. R. *Myth, Legend, and Custom in the Old Testament: A Comparative Study with Chapters from Sir James G. Frazer's* Folklore in the Old Testament. New York: Harper & Row, 1969.
Gefen, M. *Transformation of Motifs in Folklore and Literature* [Hebrew]. Jerusalem: Mass, 1991.
Gehrts, H. *Das Märchen und das Opfer: Untersuchungen zum europäischen Brüdermärchen.* Bonn: Bouvier, 1967.
Geller, E. *Warschauer Jiddisch.* Phonai 46. Tübingen, Germany: Niemeyer, 2001.
Gennep, A. van. *The Rites of Passage.* Trans. M. B. Vizedom and G. L. Caffe. London: Routledge & Kegan Paul, 1960.
Geoffrey of Monmouth. See Griscom, A.
Georges, R. A. "The Universality of the Tale-Type as Concept and Construct." *WF* 42 (1983), 21–28.

Gerber, A. "Great Russian Animal Tales." *PMLA* 4 (1891), 1–101.
Geremek, B. *Poverty: A History*. Oxford, UK: Blackwell, 1994.
Gerhardt, M. I. *The Art of Story-Telling*. Leiden: Brill, 1963.
Gerould, G. H. *The Ballad of Tradition*. Oxford, UK: Oxford University Press, 1932.
Gershon, S. W. *Kol Nidrei: Its Origin, Development, and Significance*. Northvale, NJ: Aronson, 1994.
Geshuri, M. S., ed. *La-Hasidim Mizmor* (A hymn of Hasidim). Jerusalem: Association for Hasidic Music, 1936.

———, ed. *Music and Hasidism in the House of Kuzmir (Kazimierz) and Its Affiliations (Contributions to the History of the Zaddikim-Taub-Dynasty and of the Hasidic Music in Poland)* [Hebrew]. Jerusalem: Association for the Teaching of Hasidism and Its Music, 1952.

———. "*Le-Torat ha-Nigun ba-Hasidut*" (About the Hasidic ideas of music). In *Sefer Ha-Besht: Ma'amarim u-Mehkarim be-Toldot ha-Hasidut u-Mishnata* (The Besht book: Essays and studies about the history and teaching of Hasidism) (70–83). Ed. Y. L. Maimon. Jerusalem: Mossad Harav Kook, 1960.

Gibson, R. K. "Aeneas as *Hospes* in Vergil, *Aeneid* 1 and 4." *CQ* 49 (1999), 184–202.
Gieysztor, A. "The Beginnings of Jewish Settlement in the Polish Land." In *The Jews in Poland* (15–21). Ed. C. Abramsky, M. Jachimczyk, and A. Polonsky. Oxford, UK: Blackwell, 1986.
Gilead [Goldfried], H. "Dayeynu" [Hebrew]. *YA* 1, no. 2 (1953), 64–65.
Gilman, S. L. *The Parodic Sermon in European Perspectives: Aspects of Liturgical Parody from the Middle Ages to the Twentieth Century*. Beiträg zur Literatur des XV bis XVIII Jahrhunderts 6. Weisbaden, Germany: Franz Steiner, 1974.
Ginsberg, H. L., D. Flusser, G. J. Blidstein, J. Dan, and L. Jacobs. "Messiah." *EJ* 11:1407–1417, 1971.
Ginsburg [Ginzburg], S. M. *Meshumadim in tsarishn Rusland* (Apostates in tsarist Russia). New York: CYCO-Bicher Farlag, 1946.

———. "*Yidishe Kantonisten*" (Jewish conscripts). In *Historical Works*. Vol. 3: *Jewish Martyrdom in Tsarist Russia* [Yiddish] (3–135). New York: Ginsburg Testimonial Committee, 1937.

Ginzberg, L. *The Legends of the Jews*. Trans. H. Szold (vols. 1, 2, 4) and P. Rodin (vol. 3). 7 vols. Philadelphia: Jewish Publication Society, 1909–1938.
Ginzburg, S. M., and P. S. Marek. *Yiddish Folksongs in Russia*. Ed. D. Noy. Reprint edition. Ramat-Gan, Israel: Bar-Ilan University Press, 1991. [Originally published: St. Petersburg: Voskhoda, 1901.]
Gittes, K. S. "The *Canterbury Tales* and the Arabic Frame Tradition." *PMLA* 98 (1983), 237–251.

———. *Framing the* Canterbury Tales: *Chaucer and the Medieval Frame Narrative Tradition*. Contributions to the Study of World Literature 41. New York: Greenwood Press, 1991.

Glanz, R. "The Rothschild Legend in America." *JSS* 19 (1957), 3–28.
Glick, S. *A Light unto the Mourner: The Development of Major Customs of Mourning in the Jewish Tradition from after Burial until the End of Shiva*. Efrat, Israel: "Keren Ori," 1991.
Gliksberg, S. Y. *Ha-Derashah be-Yisrael* (The sermon in Jewish life). Tel Aviv: Mossad Ha-rav Kook, n.d. [1940].
Glitsenshtein, A. H. *Sefer ha-Toladot: Rabbi Schneur Zalman mi-Lyady* (The biography of

Rabbi Schneur Zalman of Lyady). Brooklyn: Otzar Ha-Hasidim, 1976. [Includes bibliography of author's books.]

Godley, A. D., trans. *Herosotus*. 4 vols. Loeb Classical Library. Cambridge, MA: Harvard University Press, 1943.

Goebel, F. M. "*Jüdische Motive im märchenhaften Erzählungsgut: Studien zur vergleichenden Motiv-Geschichte.*" Unpublished dissertation. Gleiwitz, Germany [now Poland]: University of Greifswald, 1932.

Goldberg, A. M. *Untersuchungen über die Vorstellung von der Schekhinahin der frühen rabbinishen Literatur: Talmud und Midrasch*. Studia Judaica: Forschungen zur Wissenschaft des Judentums 5. Berlin: de Gruyter, 1969.

Goldberg, B. *The Mirror and Man*. Charlottesville: University Press of Virginia, 1985.

Goldberg, C. "The Forgotten Bride (AaTh 313C)." *Fabula* 33 (1992), 39–54.

Goldberg, J. *The Jewish Society in the Polish Commonwealth* [Hebrew]. Jerusalem: Zalman Shazar Center for Jewish History, 1999.

Goldberg, S. A. *Crossing the Jabbok: Illness and Death in Ashkenazi Judaism in Sixteenth- through Nineteenth-Century Prague*. Trans. C. Cosman. Berkeley: University of California Press, 1996.

Goldfaden, A. *Isegeklibene Shriften* (Collected writings). Buenos Aires: Ateno Literario en el IWO, 1972.

Goldin, J. "Toward a Profile of the Tanna, Aqiba ben Joseph." *JAOS* 96 (1976), 38–56.

Goldish, M., ed. *Spirit Possession in Judaism: Cases and Contexts from the Middle Ages to the Present*. Raphael Patai Series in Jewish Folklore and Anthropology. Detroit: Wayne State University Press, 2003.

Goldman, S. *The Wiles of Women/The Wiles of Men: Joseph and Potiphar's Wife in Ancient Near Eastern, Jewish and Islamic Folklore*. Albany: State University of New York Press, 1995.

Goldschmidt, A. *An Early Manuscript of the Aesop Fables of Avianus and Related Manuscripts*. Studies in Manuscript Illumination 1. Princeton, NJ: Princeton University Press, 1947.

Goldschmidt, D., ed. *Maḥzor le-Yamim Noraim le-fi Minhagei Benei Ashkenaz le-khol Anfeihem* (A prayer book for the Days of Awe according to the customs of all the Ashkenazic branches). 2 vols. Jerusalem: Koren, 1970.

———, ed. *Seder Rav Amram Gaon*. Jerusalem: Mossad Harav Kook, 1971.

Goldschmidt, E. D., ed. "*Kiddush ve-Havdalah*" [Hebrew]. *Mahanayyim* 85–86 (1964), 48–53.

———. *The Passover Haggadah: Its Sources and History* [Hebrew]. Jerusalem: Bialik Institute, 1960.

Goldstein, J. A. *I Maccabees*. The Anchor Bible (vol. 41). Garden City, NY: Doubleday, 1976.

Good, E. M. *Irony in the Old Testament*. Philadelphia: Westminster Press, 1965.

Goodblatt, C. "Women, Demons and the Rabbi's Son: Narratology and 'A Story from Worms.'" *Exemplaria* 12 (2000), 231–253.

Goodman. M. "Proselytising in Rabbinic Judaism." *JJS* 40 (1989), 175–185.

Goody, J. *The Culture of Flowers*. Cambridge, UK: Cambridge University Press, 1993.

———. "The Secret Language of Flowers." *YFS* 3 (1990), 133–152.

———, and S. J. Tambiah. *Bridewealth and Dowry*. Cambridge Papers in Social Anthropology 7. Cambridge, UK: Cambridge University Press, 1973.

Goossens, J., and T. Sodmann, eds. *Reynaert, Reynard, Reynke: Studien zu einem mitte-*

lalterlichen Tierepos. Niederdeutsche Studien 27. Cologne and Vienna: Böhlau, 1980.

———, eds. *Third International Beast Epic, Fable and Fabliau Colloquium, Münster, 1979: Proceedings.* Niederdeutsche Studien 30. Cologne: Böhlau, 1981.

Gordon, C. H. "An Aramaic Incantation." *AASOS* 14 (1934), 141–143.

———. "Aramaic Incantation Bowls." *Orientalia* 10, n.s. (1941), 116–141, 272–284.

Gordon, E. "Animals as Represented in the Sumerian Proverbs and Fables: A Preliminary Study." In *Drevniémini Mir: Festschrift V. V. Struve* (226–248). Ed. N. V. Pigulevskaëïa et al. Moscow: Akademi Nauk, SSSR, Institute [for the study of] the Peoples of Asia, 1962.

Gordon, H. J., Jr. *Hitler and the Beer Hall Putsch.* Princeton, NJ: Princeton University Press, 1972.

Gordon, L. *Cossack Rebellions: Social Turmoil in the Sixteenth-Century Ukraine.* Albany: State University of New York Press, 1983.

Goren, J. *Testimonies of Victims of the 1903 Kishinev Pogrom as Written Down by Ch. N. Bialik and Others* [Hebrew]. Tel Aviv: Hakibbbutz Hameuchad & Yad Tabenkin, 1991.

Goren, Z. "On *Ushpizin*" [Hebrew]. *MH* 10 (1998), 76–90.

———. "*Shefokh Ḥamatkha ve-Kos Eliyahu ha-Navi be-Haggadot lo- Ortodoksiyyot*" (Pour out your fury and Elijah's cup in non-orthodox Haggadah books). *MH* 6 (1995), 94–105.

Görner, O. "*Ulrich von Lichtenstein in Zerbst: Ein methodologischer Versuch.*" *MBVMittledeutsche Blätter für Volkskunde* 5 (1930), 33–48.

Görög-Karady, V. "Ethnic Stereotypes and Folklore: The Jew in Hungarian Oral Literature." *SFF* 1 (1991), 114–126.

Gottesman, I. N. *Defining the Yiddish Nation: The Jewish Folklorists of Poland.* Raphael Patai Series in Jewish Folklore and Anthropology. Detroit: Wayne State University Press, 2003.

Gottlober, A. B. *Abraham Baer Gottlober Memoirs and Travels* [Hebrew]. Ed. R. Goldberg. Jerusalem: Bialik Institute, 1976.

Grayson, J. H. *Myths and Legends from Korea: An Annotated Compendium of Ancient and Modern Materials.* Richmond, Surrey, UK: Curzon, 2001.

Green, A., trans. and ed. *Menahem Nahum of Chernobyl: Upright Practices, the Light of the Eyes.* Classics of Western Spirituality. New York: Paulist Press, 1982.

———. *Tormented Master: A Life of Rabbi Nahman of Bratslav.* Judaic Studies Series 9. Tuscaloosa: University of Alabama Press, 1979.

Greenbaum, M. *The Jews of Lithuania: A History of a Remarkable Community: 1316–1945.* Jeruslaem: Gefen, 1995.

Greenberg, L. *The Jews in Russia.* Vol 1: *The Struggle for Emancipation.* Yale Historical Publications 45. New Haven, CT: Yale University Press, 1944.

———. *The Jews in Russia.* Vol. 2: *The Struggle for Emancipation, 1881–1917.* Yale Historical Publications 54. New Haven, CT: Yale University Press, 1951.

Greenwald, J. *Kol Bo al Avelut* (A compendium on mourning customs and laws). New York: Feldheim, 1973.

Gries, Z. *The Book in Early Hasidism: Genres, Authors, Scribes, Managing Editors and Its Review by Their Contemporaries and Scholars* [Hebrew]. Tel Aviv: Hakibbutz Hameuchad, 1992.

―――. "Israel ben Shabbethai of Kozienice and His Interpretations of the Tractate of Avot" [Hebrew]. In *Hasidism in Poland* (127–165). Ed. I. Bartal, R. Elior, and C. Shmeruk. Jerusalem: Bialik Institute, 1994.

Grimm, J., and W. Grimm. *The Complete Fairy Tales of the Brothers Grimm*. Trans. and ed. J. Zipes. New York: Bantam, 1987. [Originally published 1812–1815.]

Griscom, A., ed. *The Historia Regum Britanni of Geoffrey of Monmouthe*. New York: Longmans, Green, 1929.

Groningen, G. Van. *Messianic Revelation in the Old Testament*. Grand Rapids, MI: Baker, 1990.

Gross, A., ed. *Gan Na'ul ve-ha-Igeret Sheva Netivot ha-Torah . . . of Abraham Abulafia* (The locked garden and the seven Torah paths). Jerusalem: Barazani, 1999.

Gross, M. D. *Otzar ha-Aggadah* (The treasure of the Aggadah). 3 vols. Jerusalem: Mossad Harav Kook, 1961.

Gross, N. *Maaselech un Mesholim: Tales and Parables* [Yiddish]. New York: Forewerts, 1955.

Grubmüller, K. *Meister Esopus: Untersuchungen zu Geschichte und Funktion der Fabel im Mittlealter*. Zürich and Munich: Artemis, 1977.

Grünbaum, M. *Neue Beiträge zur semitischen Sagenkunde*. Leiden: Brill, 1893.

Günzig, J. *Die "Wundermänner" im jüdischen Volke: Iher Leben und Treiben*. Antwerpen: Delplace, Koch, 1921.

Gupta, R. D. "Indian Parallels of the Fox Story." In *Aspects of the Medieval Animal Epic: Proceedings of the International Conference, May 15–17, 1972* (241–249). Eds. E. Rombauts and A. Welkenhuysen. Leuven, Belgium: University Press; The Hague: Martinus Nijhoff, 1975.

Gutenberg, G. "Animal Fables as a Historical-Cultural Source: Fables in Twelfth- and Thirteenth-Century Europe as Reflected in the Compilations of Marie de France, Berechiah Ha-Nakdan, Jacques de Vitry and Odo de Chertion" [Hebrew]. Unpublished thesis. Tel Aviv: Tel Aviv University, 1997.

Gutmann, J. "The Messiah at the Seder: A Fifteenth-Century Motif in Jewish Art" [Hebrew]. In *Studies in Jewish History: Presented to Professor Raphael Mahler on His Seventy-Fifth Birthday* (29–38). Ed. S. Yeivin. Merhavia, Israel: Sifriat Poalim, 1974.

Gutter, M. *Honor Your Mother: Twelve Folktales from Buczacz* [Hebrew]. IFAPS 23. Haifa: Haifa Municipality and Ethnological Museum and Folklore Archives, 1969.

Guttman, S. *Biographie des Gs. Berühmten Heiliger Grosrabiner Lewi Itzchac Oberrabiner zu Berditschew (Russland)*. Jassy, Romania: Progresul, 1909.

Haavio, M. *Kettenmärchen-Studien I*. FFC 88. Helsinki: Suomalainen Tiedeakatemia, 1929.

―――. *Kettenmärchen-Studien II*. FFC 99. Helsinki: Suomalainen Tiedeakatemia, 1932.

Habermann, A. M., ed. *Gezerot Ashkenaz ve-Zarfat: Divrei Zikhronot mi-Benei ha-Dorot sh-bi-Tekufot Masa'ei ha-Zelav u-Mivhar Piyutim* (German and French decrees: Memoirs and selected poems of writers from the Crusade periods). Jerusalem: Tarshish, 1946.

―――. *Me-Sippurei ha-Kara'im* (Karaite tales). Tel Aviv: Sifriat Poalim, 1947. [Reprinted in Pigit 1904.]

Haboucha, R. *Types and Motifs of the Judeo-Spanish Folktales*. The Garland Folklore Library 6. New York: Garland, 1992.

Hadas, M., trans. *The Book of Delight by Joseph Ben Meir Zabara*. Records of Civilization: Sources and Studies 16. New York: Columbia University Press, 1932.

Haddad, M. *Peki'in* [Hebrew]. Tel Aviv: Am Oved, 1987.

Haddawy, H., trans. *The Arabian Nights: Based on the Text of the Fourteenth-Century Syrian Manuscript Edited by Mushin Mahdi*. New York: Norton, 1990.

———. *The Arabian Nights II: Sindbad and Other Popular Stories*. New York: Norton, 1995.

Hahn, J. G. von. *Griechische und albanesische Märchen*. 2 vols. Leipzig: Engelmann, 1864. [Reprint ed. Munich and Berlin: Muller, 1918.]

Haidu, A., and Y. Mazor. "The Musical Tradition of Hasidism." *EJ* 7:1421–1432, 1971.

Haimovits, Z. M. *Faithful Guardians: Eighteen Folktales from Thirteen Narrators* [Hebrew]. Ed. D. Noy. IFAPS 34. Haifa: Ethnological Museum and Folklore Archives, 1976.

Hakim, K. A. *Islam and Communism*. Lahore, Pakistan: Institute of Islamic Culture, 1951.

Hakkarainen, H. J. *Studien zum Cambridge Codex T-S. 10.K.22*. Turku, Finland: Yliopsito, 1967–1973.

ha-Kohen, Rabbi Meir ben Judaha Loeb. *Or Zaddikim* (Righteous ones' light). Warsaw, 1889. [Written between 1640 and 1662.]

Haksar, A. N. D., trans. *Shuka Saptati: Seventy Tales of the Parrot*. New Delhi: HarperCollins, 2000.

Halberstam, H. Z. "*Toldot ha-Maggid of Kozienice*" (Biography of the preacher of Kozienice). Benei-Berak, Israel, 1973. [Bound with Israel ben Shabbethai of Kozienice, *Avodat Yisrael* (The service of Israel).]

Halevi, Y. [J.]. *Kitab al-radd wa-'l-dalil fi 'l-din al -dhalil (al-kitab al khazari)*. Ed. D. H. Baneth. Prep. H. Ben-Shammai. Jerusalem: Magnes Press, 1977.

———. *The Kuzari: In Defense of the Despised Faith*. Trans. N. D. Korobkin. Northvale, NJ: Aronson, 1998.

Hall, S. G. "Melito in the Light of the Passover Haggadah." *JThS* 32, pt. 1, n.s. (1971), 29–46.

Hallamish, M. *Kabbalah: In Liturgy, Halakhah and Customs* [Hebrew]. Ramat Gan, Israel: Bar-Ilan University Press, 2000.

———. "*Nusah shel Aleinu Le-Shabe'ah*" (An early version of *Aleinu Le-Shabe'ah*). *Sinai* 110 (1992), 262–265.

———. *Path to the Tanya* [Hebrew]. Tel Aviv: Papyrus, 1987.

Halliwell-Phillips, J. O. *Popular Rhymes and Nursery Tales: A Sequel to the Nursery Rhymes of England*. London: Smith, 1849.

Halperin, F. *Ḥakhmei Ḥelem* (The wise men of Chelm). Warsaw: Ahisefer, n.d.

———. *Ḥelem ve-Ḥkhameha* (Helem and its wise men). Tel Aviv: Israel, 1939.

Halpern, I. [Y.]. *East European Jewry: Historical Studies* [Hebrew]. Jerusalem: Magnes Press, 1968.

———. "The Jews in Eastern Europe (from Ancient Times until the Partitions of Poland, 1772–1795)." In *The Jews: Their History, Culture, and Religion* (1:287–320). Ed. L. Finkelstein. Philadelphia: Jewish Publication Society of America, 1960. [Reprinted in Halpern, *East European Jewry* (11–33); and I. Bartal and I. Gutman, eds., *The Broken Chain—Polish Jewry through the Ages* (17–47) (Hebrew). Jerusalem: Zalman Shazar Center for Jewish History, 2001.]

———, ed. *Sefer ha-Gevurah: Antologyah Historit-Sifrutit* (The book of heroism: A literary-historical anthology). 2 vols. Tel Aviv: Am Oved, 1950.

Halpert, H. "The Cante Fable in Decay." *SFQ* 5 (1941), 191–200. [Reprinted in P. Beck, ed., *Folklore in Action: Essays for Discussion in Honor of MacEdward Leach* (139–150; rev. ed.). AFSBSS 14. Philadelphia: American Folklore Society, 1962.]

Hamil, G. *Memoirs and Studies on the Jewish Literature* [Yiddish]. Ed. J. Bernfeld. Musterverk fun der Yidisher Literatur 26. Buenos Aires: Ateneo Literario en le Institute Cientifico Judio, 1967.

Hamilton, D. B. "Some Romance Sources for *King Lear:* Robert of Sicily and Robert the Devil." *SP* 71 (1974), 173–191.

Hamilton, R. F., and H. H. Herwig, eds. *The Origins of World War I.* Cambridge, UK: Cambridge University Press, 2003.

Hammer, J., ed. *Geoffrey of Monmouth Historia Regum Britanniae: A Variant Version Edited from Manuscripts.* Mediaeval Academy of America Publication 57. Cambridge, MA: Mediaeval Academy of America, 1951.

———. "Remarks on the Sources and Textual History of Geoffrey of Monmouth's *Historia Regum Brit Anniae* with an Excursus on the Chronica Polonorum of Wincenty Kadlubek (Magister Vincentius)." *BPASA* 2 (1944), 501–565.

———. "Some Additional Manuscripts of Geoffrey of Monmouth's *Historia Regum Britanniae.*" *Modern Language Quarterly* 3 (1942), 235–242.

Handlin, O. *The Uprooted: The Epic Story of the Great Migrations That Made the American People.* Boston: Little, Brown, 1951.

Handwerk, G. I. *Irony and Ethics in Narrative.* New Haven, CT: Yale University Press, 1985.

Haney, J. V., ed. and trans. *Russian Animal Tales: The Complete Russian Folktales.* Armonk, NY: Sharpe, 1999.

———. *Russian Wondertales. I. Tales of Heroes and Villains. II. Tales of Magic and the Supernatural. Complete Russian Folktale.* Armonk, NY: Sharpe, 2001.

Hannover, N. N. *Abyss of Despair (Yeven Metzulah): The Famous 17th-Century Chronicle Depicting Jewish Life in Russia and Poland during the Chmielnicki Massacres of 1648–1649.* Trans. A. J. Mesch. New York: Bloch, 1950. [Reprinted in I. Halpern and J. Fichman, eds., *Sefer Yeven Metsulah.* Tel Aviv: Hakibbutz Hameuchad, 1966.]

Hansen, W. F. *Ariadne's Thread: A Guide to International Tales Found in Classical Literature.* Myth and Poetics. Ithaca, NY: Cornell University Press, 2002.

Hanser, R. *Putsch! How Hitler Made Revolution.* New York: Wyden, 1970.

Harari, Y. "Early Jewish Magic: Methodological and Phenomenological Studies" [Hebrew]. Unpublished dissertation. Jerusalem: Hebrew University, 1998.

———, ed. *Ḥarva de Moses: Mahadurah Ḥadashah ve-Meḥkar* (The sword of Moses: A new edition and an analysis). Jerusalem: Akademon, 1997.

Harel-Hoshen, S., and Y. Avner, eds. *Beyond the Sambatyon: The Myth of the Ten Lost Tribes.* Tel Aviv: Beth Hatefutsoth, Nahum Goldmann Museum of the Jewish Diaspora, 1991.

Haring, L. "Framing in Oral Narrative." *MT* 18 (2004), 229–245.

Harris, D. A., and I. Rabinovich. *The Jokes of Oppression: The Humor of Soviet Jews.* Northvale, NJ: Aronson, 1988.

Hartland, E. S. "The Outcast Child." *The Folk-Lore Journal* 4 (1886), 308–349.

Hasan-Rokem, G., ed. *Midrash Aseret ha-Dibrot, Nusaḥ Verona 1647* (Midrash of the Ten Commandments, Verona edition, 1647). Jerusalem: Akademon, 1981.

———. *Proverbs in Israeli Folk Narratives: A Structural Semantic Analysis.* FFC 232. Helsinki: Suomalainen Tiedeakatemia, 1982.

———. *Web of Life: Folklore and Midrash in Rabbinic Literature*. Trans. B. Stein. Stanford, CA: Stanford University Press, 2000.

Haviv, Y. *Never Despair: Seven Folktales, Related by Aliza Anidjar from Tangiers* [Hebrew]. IFAPS 13. Haifa: Ethnological Museum and Folklore Archives, 1966.

———. *Taba'at ha-Kesem be-Golani* (The magic ring in Golani). Tel Aviv: Hakibbutz Hameuchad, 1990.

Hays, D. G., et al. "Color Terms Salience." *AA* 74 (1972), 1107–1121.

Hayyim, Y. *Nifla'im Ma'assekhah* (Wonderful are your acts). Jerusalem: Bakal, 1955. [Originally published 1912.]

Hecker, J. *Mystical Bodies, Mystical Meals: Eating and Embodiment in Medieval Kabbalah*. Raphael Patai Series in Jewish Folklore and Anthropology. Detroit: Wayne State University Press, 2005.

Heilman, C. *When a Jew Dies: The Ethnography of a Bereaved Son*. Berkeley: University of California Press, 2001.

Heinemann, J. [I.]. "Amidah." *EJ* 2:838–845, 1971.

———. *Darkhei Aggadah* (The methods of the Aggadah). Jerusalem: Magnes Press, 1954.

———. *Derashot ba-Tsibur bi-Tekufat ha-Talmud* (Sermon in public in the talmudic period). Jerusalem: Bialik Institute, 1970.

———. *Prayer in the Talmud: Forms and Patterns*. Studia Judaica: Forschungen zur Wissenschaft des Judentums 9. Berlin: de Gruyter, 1977.

———. "Prayers of the Beth Midrash Origin." *Journal of Semitic Studies* 5 (1960), 264–280.

Hellinga, W. G. *Van den vos Reynaerde: Diplomatisch uitg naar de bronnen vóór het jaar 1500*. Zwolle, The Netherlands: Tjeenk Willink, 1952.

Hendler, H. "The Jars of Honey" [Hebrew]. In *Encyclopedia of the Jewish Story: Sippur Okev Sippur* (297–305). Ed. Y. Elsetein, A. Lipsker, and R. Kushelevsky. Ramat-Gan, Israel: Bar-Ilan University Press, 2004.

Herceberg, I. *Hershele ha-Ostropoli. Melekh ha-Leitzanim. Sefer Hayav, Ta'alulav, ma'asav, u-Vdihotav* (Hershele of Ostropol. The king of the clowns. His biography, his pranks, acts, and jokes). Tel Aviv: Sreberk, 1959.

Hermes, E., trans. and ed. *The "Disciplina Clericalis" of Petrus Alfonsi*. Trans. P. R. Quarrie. Berkeley: University of California Press, 1977.

Herr, M. D. "Matters of Palestine Halakha during the Six and Seventh Centuries C.E." [Hebrew]. *Tarbiz* 49 (1980), 62–80.

Herrmann, S. "Die Königsnovelle in Ägypten und Israel." *WZKMU* ser. 3, no. 1 (1953–1954), 51–62.

Hertel, J. S. *Indische Märchen*. Die Märchen der Weltliteratur. Jena, Germany: Eugen Diederichs, 1921.

———, ed. *The Panchatantra: A Collection of Ancient Hindu Tales in the Recension Called Panchakh-yanaka and Dated 1199 A.D. of the Jaine Monk Purnabhadra*. Cambridge, MA: Harvard University Press, 1908.

———. *The Panchatantra—Text of Purnabhadra: Critical Introduction and List of Variants*. Harvard Oriental Series 12. Cambridge, MA: Harvard University Press, 1912.

Hervieux, L., ed. *Les Fabulistes Latines*. 2nd ed. Paris: Librairie de Firmin-Didot, 1894.

Heschel, A. J. "Rabbi Pinhas of Korzec." In *The Circle of the Baal Shem Tov: Studies in Hasidism* (1–43). Ed. S. H. Dresner. Chicago: University of Chicago Press, 1985.

———. "*Reb Pinkhes Koritser.*" *YIVO Bleter* 33 (1949), 9–48.

———. "*R. Pinḥas mi-Korits ve-ha-Maggid mi-Mezeritch*" (Rab Pinḥas of Korets and the Maggid of Mezeritch). In *Sefer ha-Yovel shel ha-Do'ar: Li-Melot lo sheloshim Shanah* (The *Do'ar* festschrift on its thirtieth anniversary) (279–285). Ed. M. Ribolov. New York: Ha-Histadrut ha-Ivrit be-Amerika, 1952.

———. "*Le-Toldot R. Pinḥas mi-Korits*" (Toward a biography of Rabbi Pinḥas of Korets). In *Ale Ayin: Minḥiat Devarim li-Shelomoh Zalman Shoken Aḥre Melot lo Shiv'im Shanah* (Upon seventy: A homage to Shelomoh Zalman Schocken on his seventieth birthday) (213–244). Tel Aviv: n.p., 1951 or 1952.

Hess, I. "Kaddish yatom." *Morashah* 2 (1972), 87–111.

Heuberger, G., ed. *The Rothschilds: Essays on the History of a European Family*. Frankfurt am Main: Thorbecke; and Suffolk, UK: Boydell & Brewer, 1994.

Hey, B., M. Rickling, and K. Stockhecke. *Kurt Gerstein (1905–1945): Widerstand in SS-Uniform*. Schriften des Landeskirchlichen Archives der Evangelischen Kirche von Westfalen 6. Bielefeld, Germany: Verlag für Regionalgeschichte, 2000.

Heynick, F. *Jews and Medicine: An Epic Saga*. Hoboken, NJ: Ktav, 2002.

Higger, M. *Halakhot ve-Aggadot* (Laws and legends). Newark, NJ: Devei Rabanan, 1933.

———, ed. "*Pirkei de Rabbi Eliezer*" [Hebrew]. *Ḥorev* 8 (1944), 82–119; 9 (1945), 95–166; 10 (1946), 185–294.

Hill, A. E. "Malachi, Book of." *ABD* 4:478–485, 1992.

Hillenbrand, F. K. M. *Underground Humour in Nazi Germany 1933–1945*. London and New York: Routledge, 1995.

Hillers, D. R. "Demons, Demonology." *EJ* 5:1521–1526, 1971.

Hinckley, H. B. "The Framing-Tale." *MLN* 49 (1934), 69–80.

Hingley, R., trans. and ed. *The Oxford Chekhov: Stories 1893–1895*. Oxford, UK: Oxford University Press, 1978.

Hirschberg, J. W. [H. Z.], trans. and ed. *Ḥibbur Yafe me-ha-Yeshu'ah* (An elegant composition concerning relief after adversity). Sifriat Mekorot 15. Jerusalem: Mossad Harav Kook, 1954.

Hitchins, K. *Rumania 1866–1947*. Oxford, UK: Clarendon Press, 1994.

Hobbes, T. *Leviathan*. Ed. R. Tuck. Cambridge, UK: Cambridge University Press, 1991. [Originally published in 1651.]

Hoffman, D., ed. *Midrash ha-gadol zum Buch Exodus* [Hebrew]. 2 vols. Berlin: Itzkowski/Mekizei Nirdamim, 1913.

Hoffman, L. A. *The Canonization of the Synagoguge Service*. University of Notre Dame Center for the Study of Judaism and Christianity in Antiquity 4. Notre Dame, IN: University of Notre Dame Press, 1979.

Hoffmann, D. L., ed. *Stalinism: The Essential Readings*. Malden, MA.: Blackwell, 2003.

Hoffmann-Krayer, E. "Neujahrsfeier im alten Basel und Verwandtes." *SAV* 7 (1903), 102–131, 187–209.

Holdes, A. *Bajki i anegdoty Herszla z Ostropola* [Yiddish]. Mala Biblioteka 6. Ed. D. Sfard. Warsaw: Idisz-Buch, 1960.

Holland, G. S. *Divine Irony*. Selinsgrove, PA: Susquehanna University Press, 2000.

Hollis, S. T. *The Ancient Egyptian Story "Tale of Two Brothers": The Oldest Fairy Tale in the World*. Norman: University of Oklahoma Press, 1990.

Holtz, A. *Mar'ot u-Mekorot: Mahadurah Mu'eret u-Me'uyert shel Hakhnasat Kallah le-Sha'y Agnon* (References and sources: An annotated and illustrated edition of Agnon's "Bridal Canopy"). Jerusalem and Tel Aviv: Schocken, 1995.

———. *The Tale of Reb Yudel Hasid: From a Yiddish Narrative in Nissim V'niflaot to S. Y. Agnon's Hakhnasat Kalla* [Hebrew and Yiddish]. New York: Jewish Theological Seminary of America, 1986.

Holzberg, N. *Die antike Fabel: Eine Einführung*. Darmstadt, Germany: Wissenschaftliche Buchgesellschaft, 1993.

Homolka, W., W. Jacob, and E. Seidel, eds. *Not by Birth Alone: Conversion to Judaism*. London and Washington, DC: Cassell, 1997.

Honemann, V. "*Unibos und Amis*." In *Kleinere Erzählformen im Mittelalter: Paderborner Colloquium 1987* (67–82). Schriften der Universität-Gesamthochschule-Paderborn 10. Ed. K. Grubmüller, L. P. Johnson, and H. H. Steinhoff. Paderborn, Germany: Ferdinand Schöningh, 1988.

Horálek, K. "Brüdermärchen: Das ägyptische B. (AaTh 318=590A. 516B, 870C*, 302B)." *EM* 2 (1979), 925–940.

———. "*Geist im Glas* (AaTh 331)." *EM* 5:922–928, 1987.

———. "Zur slavischen Überlieferung des Märchentyps AaTh 331 *(Der Geist im Glas).*" In *Festschrift für Margarete Woltner zum 70 Geburstag am 4. Dezember 1967* (83–90). Ed. P. Brang. Heidelberg: Winter, 1967.

Horodezky, S. A. *Ha-Ḥasidut ve-ha-Ḥasidim* (Hasidism and Hasidim). 4 vols. Berlin: Devir, 1922.

Horowitz, E. M. *Yad El'azar: . . . She'elot u-Teshuvot* (El'azar's hand . . . Responsa). Vienna: Schlossberg, 1870.

Horowitz, J. *The Kaddish: Its Origin and Significance Historically Considered* [Yiddish and English]. Hartford, CT: Author, 1938.

Horowitz, Rabbi Isaiah ben Abraham Ha-Levi. *Shenei Luḥt ha-berit*. Amsterdam, n.p., 1649. [Reprint ed. Warsaw, 1852.]

Horowitz, S. S. *Divrei Shemuel* (Samuel's words). L'viv, 1862.

———. *Nezir ha-Shem* (Godi hermit). L'viv, 1869.

Horwitz, R. G., and Y. [J.] Dan. "Shekhinah." *EJ* 14:1349–1354, 1971.

Howe, I., and E. Greenberg, eds. "Stories of Hershel Ostropolier." In *A Treasury of Yiddish Stories* (614–620). New York: Viking Press, 1965.

Howe, I., and R. R. Wisse, eds. *The Best of Sholom Aleichem*. Washington, DC: New Republic, 1979.

Hrushevsky, M. *History of Ukraine-Rus'*. Vol. 7: *The Cossack Age to 1625: The History of the Ukrainian Cossacks 1*. Hrushevsky Translation Project. Ed. S. Plokhy, F. E. Sysyn, and U. M. Pasicznyk. Trans. B. Struminski. Edmonton, AB: Canadian Institute of Ukrainian Studies Press, 1999.

———. *History of Ukraine-Rus'*. Vol. 8: *The Cossack Age, 1626–1650: The History of the Ukrainian Cossacks 2*. Hrushevsky Translation Project. Ed. F. E. Sysyn and M. Yurkevich. Trans. M. D. Olynyki. Edmonton, AB: Canadian Institute of Ukrainian Studies Press, 2002.

Hübscher, J. *The Kaddish Prayer: Its Meaning, Significance and Tendency*. Berlin: Author, 1929.

Hultkrantz, A., ed. *The Supernatural Owners of Nature: Nordic Symposium on the Religious Conceptions of Ruling Spirits (genii loci, genii speciei) and Allied Conceptions*. Stockholm Studies in Comparative Religion 1. Stockholm: Almqvist & Wiksell, 1961.

Hundert, G. D., ed. *Essential Papers on Hasidism: Origins to Present.* New York: New York University Press, 1991.

Hunt, R. *Popular Romances of the West of England; or, The Drolls, Traditions, and Superstitions of Old Cornwall.* London: Chatto & Windus, 1903. [Originally published 1881.]

Hurewitz, J. *The Care of Animals in Jewish Life and Lore.* New York: Union of Orthodox Jewish Congregations of America, 1926.

Hurwitz, S., ed. *Machsor Vitrynach der Handschrift im British Museum (Cod. Add. No. 27200 u. 27201)* [Hebrew]. Nurenberg: Bulka, 1923.

Huzin, S. B. *Ma'aseh Nissim* (Miracles). Baghdad, 1890.

Hyde, L. *Trickster Makes This World: Mischief, Myth, and Art.* New York: Farrar, Straus & Giroux, 1998.

Ibn Sahula, Isaac ben Solomon. *Meshal ha-kadmoni* (The ancient fable). Tel Aviv: Maḥbarot le-sifrut, 1953. [Originally composed 1281.]

———. *Meshal Haqadmoni: Fables from the Distant Past. A Parallel Hebrew-English Text.* Ed. and trans. R. Loewe. 2 vols. Oxford, UK; and Portland, OR: Littman Library of Jewish Civilization, 2004.

Idel, M. *Kabbalah: New Perspectives.* New Haven, CT: Yale University Press, 1988.

———. *Messianic Mystics.* New Haven, CT: Yale University Press, 1998.

Idelsohn, A. Z. "*Ha-Neginah ha-Ḥasidit*" (The Hasidic melody). *SHAHYB* 1 (1931), 74–87.

———. "The *Kol Nidre* Tune." *HUCA* 8–9 (1931–1932), 493–509.

Ikeda, H. *A Type and Motif Index of Japanese Folk-Literature.* FFC 209. Helsinki: Suomalainen Tiedeakatemia, 1971.

Indritch, M. "*Nigun Devekut shel ha-Rabi mi-Liadi*" (The Rabbi of Lyady's devotional melody). In *La-Ḥasidim Mizmor* (A hymn to Hasidim) (42–43). Ed. M. S. Geshuri. Jerusalem: Ḥever Ḥovevim shel Neginat ha-Ḥasidim, 1936.

Iraki, E. *Sefer ha-Ma'asiyyot* (A book of folktales). Bagdhad: Ḥuzin, 1892. [Originally published 1852.]

Irwin, B. D. "What's in a Frame? The Medieval Textualisation of Traditional Storytelling." *OT* 10 (1995), 27–53.

Izbits, Y. *Der lustiger hoyz-fraynd: A szamlung fun 450 fershiedene vittsen, satiren un frehlikhe ertsehlungen . . .* (The delightful family friend: A collection of 450 different witty and satirical anecdotes and delightful stories . . .). St. Louis, MO: Moinester Printing, 1919.

Jacob Joseph of Polonnoye. *Sefer Toldot Yaakov Yosef* (The generations of Jacob Joseph). Warsaw: Shkena, 1881.

Jacob, W., and M. Zemer, eds. *Conversion to Judaism in Jewish Law: Essays and Responsa.* Studies in Progressive Halakhah 3. Tel Aviv and Pittsburgh: Rodef Shalom Press, 1994.

Jacobs, J. C., ed. and trans. *The Fables of Odo of Cheriton.* Syracuse, NY: Syracuse University Press, 1985.

Jacobs, L. *Principles of the Jewish Faith: An Analytical Study.* New York: Basic Books, 1964.

Jakobsdottir, G. S. "The Luck-Bringing Shirt: Variations on Type 844." *AO* 45 (1984), 43–50.

Janekeviciene, A. *Vilniaus Didzioji Sinagoga: The Great Synagogue of Vilnius*. Vilnius, Lithuania: Savastis Vilnius, 1996.

Jason, H. "Elijah in the Israel Folktale Archives." In *Elijah the Prophet in Painting and Folk Art* (7–8). Ed. anonymous. Haifa: Haifa Municipality and the Ethnological Museum and Folktale Archives, 1961.

———. *Ethnopoetry: Form, Content, Function*. Forum Theologiae Linguistica 11. Bonn: Linguistica Biblica, 1977.

———. *Folktales of the Jews of Iraq: Tale-Types and Genres*. Studies in the History and Culture of Iraqi Jewry 5. Or Yehuda, Israel: Babylonian Jewry Heritage Center, Research Institute of Iraqi Jewry, 1988.

———. *Märchen aus Israel*. Trans. S. Gassmann. Die Märchen der Weltliteratur. Düsseldorf: Diederichs, 1976.

———. "Precursors of Propp: Formalist Theories of Narrative in Early Russian Ethnopoetics." *PTL* 2 (1977), 471–516.

———. "The Russian Criticism of the 'Finnish School' in Folktale Scholarship." *Norveg* 14 (1970), 285–294.

———. "Structural Analysis and the Concept of the 'Tale-Type.'" *Arv* 28 (1972), 36–54.

———. *Types of Indic Oral Tales: Supplement*. FFC 242. Helsinki: Suomalainen Tiedeakatemia, 1989.

———. "Types of Jewish-Oriental Oral Tales." *Fabula* 7 (1965), 115–224.

———. *Types of Oral Tales in Israel*. Part 2. Israel Ethnographic Society 2. Jerusalem: Israel Ethnographic Society, 1974.

Jedrzejewicz, W. *Pilsudski: A Life for Poland*. New York: Hippocrene, 1982.

Jellinek, A. *Bet ha-Midrasch: Sammlung kleiner Midraschim und vermischter Abhandlung aus der ältern jüdischen Literatur* [Hebrew]. 6 parts. Leipzig: Nies, 1853–1877. [Reprint ed. Jerusalem: Wahrmann, 1967.]

Jernudd, B. H. "The Concept of Basic Color Terms: Variability in For and Arabic." *ALing* 25 (1983), 61–81.

Jersch-Wenzel, S., F. Geusnet, G. Pickhan, A. Reinke, and D. Schwara, eds. *Juden und Armut in Mittle- und Osteuropa*. Simon-Dubnow-Instituts für Jüdische Geschichte und Kulture V. Cologne: Böhlau Verlag, 2000.

Jeshurin, E. H. *Sh. An-Ski Bibliografye*. Steven Spielberg Digital Yiddish Library 01908. Amherst, MA: National Yiddish Book Center, 1999.

———, ed. *Wilno: A Book Dedicated to the City of Wilno* [Yiddish]. New York: Wilner Branch 367 Workmen's Circle, 1935.

Jochnowitz, G. "Had Gadya in Judeo-Italian and Shuadit (Judeo-Provencal)." In *Readings in the Sociology of Jewish Languages* (241–245). Ed. J. A. Fishman. Leiden: Brill, 1985.

Joffe, J. A., ed. *Elia Bachur's Poetical Works* [Yiddish]. 3 vols. New York: Joffe Publication Committee, 1949.

Johnson, D. O., trans. *An English Translation of Claudius Aelianus' Varia Historia*. Studies in Classics 2. Lewiston, NY: Edwin Mellen Press, 1997.

Joll, J. *The Origins of the First World War*. New York: Longman, 1984.

Jolles, A. *Einfache Formen: Legende/Sage/Mythe/Rätsel/Spruch/Kasus/Memorabile/Märchen/Witz*. Tübingen, Germany: Max Niemeyer, 1958. [Originally published 1930.]

Jones, G., and T. Jones, trans. *The Mabinogion*. Everyman's Library. New York: Knopf, 2000. [Originally published 1949.]

Jones, S. S. *The Fairy Tale: The Magic Mirror of Imagination*. Studies in Literary Themes and Genres 5. New York: Twayne, 1995.

Kabarnit [Likvornick], S. *Sippurim ve-Zutoth* (Tales and anecdotes) [Hebrew]. Reḥovoth, Israel: Author, 1986.

Kabashnikau, K. P. *From Aggada to Modern Fiction in the Work of Berdichevsky* [Hebrew]. Tel Aviv: Hakibbutz Hameuchad, 1983.

———. *Kazki pra zhyviol i charadzeinyia kazki* (Fairy tales about animals, and magic fairy tales). Minsk: Navuka I Tekhnika, 1971.

Kahan, A. *Essays in Jewish Social and Economic History*. Ed. R. Weiss. Chicago: University of Chicago Press, 1986.

Kahana, A. *Rabbi Israel Baal Shem Tov (Besht): Ḥayav, shitato, u-Phe'ulato* (Rabbi Israel Baal Shem Tov: His life, method, and actions). Zhitomir, Ukraine: Author, 1900.

Kahana, D. *Perakim be-Toldot ha-Yehudim be-Polin* (Chapters in the history of the Jews of Poland). Jerusalem: Mossad Harav Kook, 1983.

Kahana, H. *Even Shtiyah: Toldotehem shel Zddikim u-Ma'asehem ha-Tovim ve-ha-Na'im ve-Sippurei Nora' im ve-Nifla'im ve-Ḥayei Torah shel Raboteinu ha-Kedushim* (A foundation stone: The biographies of righteous people and their good and pleasant deeds and awesome and wonderful stories and pious lives of our holy rabbis). Munkacs (Mukacevo), Czechoslovakia [now Ukraine], 1930. [Reprint ed. Ateret, 1975.]

Kahle, P. E. *The Cairo Geniza*. Oxford, UK: Blackwell, 1959.

Kalish, A. L. "Chelm." *EJ* 5:371–373, 1971.

Kann, R. A. "Assimilation and Antisemitism in the German French Orbit." *LBIYB* 14 (1969), 92–118.

Kantsedikas, A., and I. Serheyeva. *The Jewish Artistic Heritage Album by Semyon An-Sky* [Russian and English]. Moscow: Cultural Bridges, 2001.

Karl, Z. "Ha-Kaddish." *Ha-Shiloah* 35 (1918), 36–49, 426–430, 521–527.

Karpinowitz, A. *The Story of the Vilnian Righteous Proselyte Count Valentine Potocki* [Yiddish]. Tel Aviv: Vilner Pinkas, 1990.

Kasher, M. M. *Hagadah Shelemah: The Complete Passover Hagadah* [Hebrew]. Jerusalem: Torah Shelema Institute, 1967.

———. *Torah Shelemah (Complete Torah): Talmudic Midrashic Encyclopedia of the Pentateuch* [Hebrew]. 43 vols. Vols. 1–7, Jerusalem: Author, 1927–1938; vols. 8–29, New York: American Biblical Encyclopedia Society, 1944–1978; vols. 30–43, Jerusalem: Beth Torah Shelemah, 1979–1992.

Kasprzyk, K. "*L'homme et l'animal: Du* Roman de Renart *au Folklore Polonais.*" In *Et c'est la fin pour quoy sommes ensemble: Hommage à Jean Dufournet: Littérature, Histoire et Langue du Moyen Âge* (2:775–782). Ed. J. C. Aubailly. Paris: Honore Champion, 1993.

Katz, D., ed. *Dialects of the Yiddish Language: Papers from the Second Annual Oxford Winter Symposium in Yiddish Language and Literature, 14–16 December 1986*. Winter Studies in Yiddish 2. New York: Pergamon, 1988.

———. "The Mamzer and the Shifcha." *JHCS* 28 (1994), 73–104.

———. *Tenu'at ha-musar* (The Musar movement). 5 vols. Jerusalem: Tsiyoni, 1967–1974.

Katz, E. *Book of Fables: The Yiddish Fable Collection of Reb Moshe Wallich Frankfurt am Main, 1697*. Jewish Folklore and Anthropology Series. Detroit: Wayne State University Press, 1994.

———. "*Das 'Kuhbukh' und das 'Sefer Mešolim':* Die Überlieferung eines mitteljiddischen Textes." *BGDSL* 112 (1990), 81–95.
Katz, J. *Emancipation and Assimilation: Studies in Modern Jewish History.* Westmead, Australia: Gregg International, 1972.
———. *Tradition and Crisis: Jewish Society at the End of the Middle Ages.* New York: Schocken, 1961.
Katzoff, R. "*Donatio Ante Nuptias* and Jewish Dowry Additions." In *Papyrology* (231–244). YCS 28. Ed. N. Lewis. Cambridge, UK: Cambridge University Press, 1985.
Kaufmann, D., ed. *Die Memoiren der Glückel von Hameln 1645–1719.* Frankfurt am Main: Kaufmann, 1896.
Kaufmann, Y. *The Religion of Israel: From Its Beginnings to the Babylonian Exile.* Trans. M. Greenberg. Chicago: University of Chicago Press, 1960.
Kay, P. "Synchronic Variability and Diachronic Change in Basic Color Terms." *LiS* 4 (1975), 257–270.
———, and C. K. McDaniel. "The Linguistic Significance of the Meanings of Basic Color Terms." *Language* 54 (1978), 610–646.
Keep, J. L. H. *Soldiers of the Tsar: Army and Society in Russia 1462–1874.* Oxford, UK: Clarendon Press, 1985.
Kehimkar, H. S. *The History of the Bene-Israel of India.* Tel Aviv: Dayag Press, 1937.
Kellner, M. "Overcoming Chosenness." In *Covenant and Chosenness in Judaism and Mormonism* (147–172). Ed. R. Jospe, T. G. Madsen, and S. Ward. Madison, WI: Fairleigh Dickinson University Press, 2001.
Kenik, H. A. *Design for Kingship: The Deuteronomistic Narrative Technique in 1 Kings 3:4–15.* SBL Dissertation Series 69. Chico, CA: Scholars Press, 1983.
Kerbelyte, B. *Lietuviu Pasakojamosios Tautosakos Katalogas. I. Pasakos Apie Gyvunus. Pasakecios. Stebuklines Pasakos* (The catalog of Lithuanian narrative folklore. I. Animal tales, fables, fairy tales). Vilnius, Lithuania: Lietuvie Literaturos ir Tautosakos Institutas, 1999.
Keren, A. *Advice from the Rothschilds: 28 Humorous Stories from Poland.* IFAPS 43. Ed. O. Schnitzler. Jerusalem: Magnes Press, 1981.
Kiel, M. W. "A Twice Lost Legacy: Ideology, Culture and the Pursuit of Jewish Folklore in Russia until Stalinization (1930–1931)." Unpulished dissertation. New York: Jewish Theological Seminary of America, 1991.
———. "*Vox Populi Vox Dei:* The Centrality of Peretz in Jewish Folkloristics." *Polin* 7 (1992), 88–119.
Kierkegaard, S. *The Concept of Irony with Constant Reference to Socrates.* Trans. L. M. Capel. New York: Harper & Row, 1965.
Kieval, H. J. "The Curious Case of Kol Nidre." *Commentary* 46, no. 4 (1968), 53–58.
———. "Kol Nidrei." *EJ* 10:1167, 1971.
Kilgannon, C. "Miracle? Dream? Prank? Fish Talks, Town Buzzes." *New York Times,* March 15, 2003, A1, B5.
Kimmel, E. *The Adventures of Hershel of Ostropol.* New York: Holiday House, 1995.
———. *Hershel and the Hanukkah Goblins.* New York: Holiday House, 1989.
Kirshenblatt-Gimblett, B. "A Parable in Context: A Social Interactional Analysis of Storytelling Performance." In *Folklore: Performance and Communication* (105–130). Approaches to Semiotics 40. Ed. D. Ben-Amos and K. S. Goldstein. The Hague: Mouton, 1975.

———. "Traditional Storytelling in the Toronto Jewish Community: A Study in Performance and Creativity in an Immigrant Culture." Unpublished dissertation. Bloomington: Indiana University, 1972.

Kitov, E. Ḥassidim ve-Anshei Ma'aseh (Men of spirit, men of merit). Jerusalem: Yad Eliyahu Kitov, 1977.

Klaar, M. Christo und das verschenkte Brot: Neugriechische Volkslegenden und Legendenmärchen. Kassel, Israel: Röth-Verlag, 1963.

Klainman, H. M. Zikaron la-Rishonim (Commemoration for the early [righteous people]). Piotrkow, Poland: Rosenberg, 1912.

Klar, B. Megillat Ahimaaz: The Chronicle of Ahimaaz, with a Collection of Poems from Byzantine Southern Italy [Hebrew]. 2nd ed. Jerusalem: Tarshish, 1974. [Originally published 1944.]

Klausner, I. The Jewish Community of Vilno in the Days of the "Gaon" [Hebrew]. Jerusalem: Mass, 1942.

———. "Vilna" [Hebrew]. In Arim ve-Amahot be-Yisrael (Jewish cities and great communities) (141–175). Ed. Y. L. Ha-Cohen Fishman. Jerusalem: Mossad Harav Kook, 1946.

———. Vilna, "Jerusalem of Lithuania": Generations from 1495–1881 [Hebrew]. Ed. S. Barantchok. Loḥamei ha-Getta'ot and Tel Aviv: Ghetto Fighter's House and Hakibbutz Hameuchad, 1988.

Klausner, J. The Messianic Idea in Israel: From the Beginnings to the Completion of the Mishnah. Trans. W. F. Stinespring. New York: Macmillan, 1955.

Klein, E. "Alenu and the Censors." Jewish Spectator 63, no. 2 (1998), 27–28.

Kleinman, M. A. Sefer Zikaron la-Rishonim (A memorial book for the early tzaddikim). Piotrkow, Poland: Rosenberg, 1912.

Klier, J. D., and S. Lambroza, eds. Pogroms: Anti-Jewish Violence in Modern Russian History. Cambridge, UK: Cambridge University Press, 1992.

Klutz, T. E. "The Grammar of Exorcism in the Ancient Mediterranean World." In The Jewish Roots of Christological Monotheism: Papers from the St. Andrews Conference on the Historical Origins of the Worship of Jesus. Ed. C. C. Newman, J. R. Davila, and G. S. Lewis. JSJ Suppl. 63 (1999), 156–165.

Knaphais, M., ed. Elias Levita, Buovo d'Antona. Bove-Buj: Novela en versos. Buenos Aires: Farlag il'lit'bleter, 1970.

Knibb, M. A. "Martydom and Ascension of Isaiah (Second Century B.C.–Fourth Century A.D.)." In The Old Testament Pseudepigraphia (143–177). Ed. J. H. Charlesworth. Garden City, NY: Doubleday, 1985.

Knox, M. "Irony." Dictionary of the History of Ideas 2:626–634, 1973.

———. The Word Irony and Its Context, 1500–1750. Durham, NC: Duke University Press, 1961.

Kobler, F. Napoleon and the Jews. New York: Schocken, 1975.

Koch, H. J. Der 9. November in der deutschen Geschichte 1918–1923–1938–1989. Freiburg im Breisgau, Germany: Rombach, 1998.

Koenig, J. "Hospitality." ABD 3:299–301, 1992.

Koen-Sarano, M. Konsejas i konsejikas del mundo djudeo-espanyol [Hebrew and Judeo-Spanish]. Jerusalem: Kana, 1994.

———. Kuentos del folklor de la famiya Djudeo-Espanyola [Hebrew and Judeo-Spanish]. Jerusalem: Kana, 1982. [Reprint ed. 1986.]

Kohler, K. "The Origin and Composition of the Eighteen Benedictions with a Translation of the Corresponding Essene Prayers in the Apostolic Constitutions." *HUCA* 1 (1924), 387–425.

Köhler, R. "Zu dem Märchen von der Lebenszeit (Grimm KHM no. 176)." *Jarbuch für Literaturegeschichte* 1 (1865): 196–198. [Reprinted in J. Bolte, ed., *Kleinere Schriften zur Märchenforschung* (42–45). Weimar, Germany: Felber, 1898.]

Kohut, A., ed. *Aruch Completum*. 2nd ed. 9 vols. Vienna and Berlin: Menora, 1926.

Kohut, G. A. "Had Gadya." *JE* 6:127–128, 1904.

———. "Le Had Gadya et les chansons similaires." *RÉJ* 31 (1895), 240–246.

Koidonover [Kaidenover], Z. H. *Sefer Kav ha-Yashar* (The book of the straight line). Frankfurt [Frankfurt am Main], 1705–1706. [Multiple editions.]

Koppman, S., and L. Koppman. *A Treasury of American Jewish Folklore*. Northvale, NJ: Aronson, 1996.

Kort [Qort], Z. *Sippurei 'Am mi-Pi Yehudei Afghanistan* (Folktales of the Jews of Afghanistan). Ed. H. Schwarzbaum. Tel Aviv and Jerusalem: Dvir, 1983.

Kosko, M. "L'auberge de Jérusalem à Dantzig." *Fabula* 4 (1961), 81–98.

———. *Le fils assassiné (AT 939 A), étude d'un thème légendaire*. FFC 83. Helsinki: Suomalainen Tiedeakatemia, 1966.

———. "A propos du malentendu." *CL* 10 (1958), 376–377.

Koskoff, E. *Music in Lubavitcher Life*. Urbana: University of Illinois Press, 2001.

Kottek, S. S. *Medicine and Hygiene in the Works of Flavius Josephus*. Leiden: Brill, 1994.

———, S. M. Horstmanshoff, et al., eds. *From Athens to Jerusalem: Medicine in Hellenized Jewish Lore and in Early Christian Literature. Papers of the Symposium in Jerusalem, 9–11 September 1996*. Rotterdam: Erasmus, 2000.

Kovács, A., and B. Katalin. *Magyar Népmesekatalógus* (Hungarian folktale catalogue). 10 vols. Budapest: MTA Néprajzi Kutatócsoport, 1981–1992.

Kraemer, D. *The Meaning of Death in Rabbinic Judaism*. New York: Routledge, 2000.

Kramer, S. N. *History Begins at Sumer: Thirty-Nine Firsts in Man's Recorded History*. Philadelphia: University of Pennsylvania Press, 1981.

Krauss, S. "The Great Synod." *JQR* 10, o.s. (1898), 347–377.

———. "Mahut ha Kaddish, Mkorotav ve-Korotav" (The nature of the Kaddish, its sources, and its history). *Bitzaron* 1 (1939), 125–139.

———. "Das Problem Kol Nidrei." *JJLG* 19 (1928), 85–97.

Krejci, K. "Putování sujetu o 'synu, zavrazdeném rudici.' " *Slavia* 18 (1947–1948), 406–437.

Kremer, M. "Jewish Artisans in Poland in the XVI–XVII Centuries" [Hebrew]. *Zion* 3–4, n.s. (1937), 295–325.

Krikmann, A. "The Great Chain Metaphor: An Open Sesame for Proverb Semantics?" *Proverbium* 11 (1994), 117–124.

———. "On the Denotative Indefiniteness of Proverbs." *Proverbium* 1 (1984), 47–92.

———. "Some Additional Aspects of Semantic Indefiniteness of Proverbs." *Proverbium* 2 (1985), 58–86.

Krinsky, C. H. *Synagogues of Europe: Architecture, History, Meaning*. Cambridge Architectural History Foundation 9. Cambridge, MA: MIT Press, 1985.

Krohn, K. *Mann und Fuchs: Drei Vergleichende Märchenstudien*. Helsinki: Frenckell, 1891.

Krzyżanowski, J. *Polska bajka ludowa w ukladzie systematycznym* (A systemic classification of the Polish folk tale). 2 vols. Wroclaw, Poland: Zaklad Narodowy im. Ossolińskich, 1962–1963.

———. "Sprichtwort und Märchen in der polnischen Volkserzählung." In *Volksüberlieferung: Festschrift für Kurt Ranke zur Vollendung des 60. Lebensjahres* (151–158). Ed. F. Harkort, K. Peeters, and R. Wildhaber. Göttingen, Germany: Schwartz, 1968.

Kuemmerlin-McLean, J. K. "Demons." *ABD* 2:138–140, 1992.

Kugel, J. L. *In Potiphar's House: The Interpretive Life of Biblical Texts*. Cambridge, MA: Harvard University Press, 1990.

Kugelmass, J. "The Father of Jewish Ethnography." In *The Worlds of S. An-Sky: A Russian Jewish Intellectual at the Turn of the Century* (346–360). Ed. G. Safran and S. J. Zipperstein. Stanford, CA: Stanford University Press, 2006.

Kuhlmann, W., and L. Röhrich, eds. *Witz, Humor und Komik im Volksmärchen*. Veröffentlichungen Der Europäischen Märchengesellschaft 17. Regensburg, Germany: Röth, 1993.

Kushelevsky, R. "Some Remarks on the Date and Sources of '*Sefer ha-Ma'asiyyot*' " [Hebrew]. Ed. Y. Rosenberg. *Kiryat Sefer: Collected Essays, Articles and Book Reviews in Jewish Studies* Suppl. 68 (1998), 155–157.

———. "The *Tanna* and the Restless Dead" [Hebrew]. *Encyclopedia of the Jewish Story: Sippur Okev Sippur* (261–296). Ed. Y. Elsetein, A. Lipsker, and R. Kushelevsky. Ramat-Gan, Israel: Bar-Ilan University Press, 2004.

———. "The *Tanna* and the Restless Dead: Jewish or Non-Jewish Legend?" [Hebrew]. *Criticism and Interpretation* 30 (1994), 41–64.

Kuttner, B. *Jüdische Sagen und Legenden für jung und alt*. Frankfurt: Kauffmann, 1920.

Kuznitz, C. E. "The Origins of Yiddish Scholarship and the YIVO Institute for Jewish Research." Unpublished dissertation. Stanford, CA: Stanford University, 2000.

Laato, A., and J. C. de Moor, eds. *Theodicy in the World of the Bible*. Leiden: Brill, 2003.

Lachower, F., and I. Tishby. *The Wisdom of the Zohar: An Anthology of Texts*. Littman Library of Jewish Civilization. Trans. D. Goldstein. 3 vols. Oxford, UK: Oxford University Press for the Littman Library, 1989.

Lambert, W. G. *Babylonian Wisdom Literature*. Oxford, UK: Clarendon Press, 1960.

Lambroza, S. "Jewish Self-Defense during the Russian Pogroms of 1903–1906." *JJS* 23 (1981), 123–134.

Landau, B. "*Melavveh Malkah*" (Escorting the Sabbath Queen). *Mahanayyim* 85–86 (1964), 68–75.

Landau, L. *Arthurian Legends: Or the Hebrew-German Rhymed Version of the Legend of King Arthur*. Leipzig, Germany: Avenarius, 1912.

———. "Rashi's Tales in the Babylonian Talmud" [Hebrew]. *EBS* 3 (1986), 101–117.

Landau, M. "Zbitkower, (Joseph) Samuel." *EJ* 16:944–945, 1971.

Landis, J. C., ed. and trans. *The Dybbuk and Other Great Jewish Plays*. New York: Bantam, 1966.

Landman, L. *Messianism in the Talmudic Era*. New York: Ktav, 1979.

Landmann, S. *Jüdische Anekdoten und Sprichwörter*. Munich: Deutscher Taschenbuch Verlag, 1965.

———. *Jüdische Schwänke: Eine volkskundliche studie*. Wiesbaden, Germany: Rheinische Verlags-Anstalt, 1964.

———. *Der Jüdische Witz: Sozologie und Sammlung.* Olten and Freiburg im Breisgau, Germany: Walter-Verlag, 1962.
Lane, C. *Christian Religion in the Soviet Union: A Sociological Study.* Albany: State University of New York Press, 1978.
Lange, A. H. Lichtenberger, and K. F. D. Römheld, eds. *Die Dämonen/Demons: Die Dämonologie der israelitisch-jüdischen und frühchristlichen Literatur im Kontext ihrer Umwelt/The Demonology of Israelite-Jewish and Early Christian Literature in Context of Their Environment.* Tübingen, Germany: Mohr Siebeck, 2003.
Langosch, K. *Waltharius-Ruodlieb Märchenepen: Lateinische Epik des Mittelalters mit deutschen Versen.* Berlin: Rütten & Loening, 1956.
Langton, E. *Essential of Demonology: A Study of Jewish and Christian Doctorine, Its Origin and Development.* London: Epworth Press, 1949. [Reprint ed. New York: AMS Press, 1982.]
Larrea Palacin, A. de. *Cuentos populares de los Judios del Norte de Marrueccos.* 2 vols. Tetuán, Morocco: Marroqui, 1953.
Lasine, S. "The Riddle of Solomon's Judgment and the Riddle of Human Nature in the Hebrew Bible." *JSOT* 45 (1989), 61–86.
Lassri, Y. *Bimhitsat Hakhamim ve-Rabanim be-Marocco, Tunis ve-Algir* (In the company of rabbis in Morocco, Tunisia and Algiers). Beer-Sheva, Israel: Mor, 1978.
Latour, C. de [pseudonym of L. Cortambert?]. *Le langage des fleurs.* Paris: Audot, 1819.
Lauterbach, J. Z. "The Origin and Development of Two Sabbath Ceremonies." *HUCA* 15 (1940), 367–424. [Reprinted in B. J. Bamberger, ed., *Studies in Jewish Law, Custom and Folklore* (75–132). (New York): Ktav, 1970.]
Leach, M., ed. *Paris and Vienne: Translated from the French and Printed by William Caxton.* Early English Text Society. Original Series 234. London and New York: Early English Text Society and Oxford University Press, 1957.
Learsi, R. *The Book of Jewish Folk Humor: Stories of the Wise Men of Chelem and Other Tales.* New York: Bloch, 1941.
———. *Filled with Laughter: A Fiesta of Jewish Folk Humor.* New York: Yoseloff, 1961.
Lee, A. C. *The Decameron: Its Sources and Analogues.* London: Nutt, 1909.
Lehman, S. "*Folk-mayselekh un anekdoten mit nigunim*" (Folktales and anecdotes with melodies). In *Studies in Yiddish Philology, Literature and Ethnology* (1:355–432). Ed. [N. Prylucki] and S. Lehman. Warsaw: Najer Farlag, 1926–1933.
———. "*Ganeivim un gneiva*" (Stealers and stealing). In *Ba ync Jid'n: ksi̧cga zbiorowa folkloru i filologji*" (Among us Jews: An anthology of folklore and philology) (44–91). Ed. M. Wanwild. Warsaw: Graubard, 1923.
Lehnardt, A. "*Qaddish und Sifre Devarim 306-Anmerkungen zur Entwicklung eines rabbinischen Gebetes.*" *FJB* 28 (2001), 1–20.
———. *Qaddish: Untersuchungen zur Entstehung und Rezeption eines rabbinischen Gebetes.* Texts and Studies in Ancient Judaism 87. Tübingen, Germany: Mohr Siebeck, 2002.
Leib of Sasow, Moses. *Likkutei Ramal.* Lvov, Ukraine: Stand, 1864 or 1865.
Lieberman, S. *Tosefta Ki-Fshutah: A Comprehensive Commentary on the Tosefta.* 10 vols. New York: Jewish Theological Seminary of America, 1955–1988.
Lenaghan, R. T., ed. *Caxton's Aesop.* Cambridge, MA: Harvard University Press, 1967.
Lenowitz, H. *The Jewish Messiahs: From the Galilee to Crown Heights.* New York: Oxford University Press, 1998.

Lerner, D. "The Enduring Legend of the Jewish Pope." *Judaism* 40 (1991), 148–170.
Lerner, M. B. "*Ma'aseh ha-Tanna ve-ha-Met: Gilgulav ha-Sifrutiim ve-ha-Halakhatiim*" (The story of the Tanna and the dead man: Its literary and religious transformations). *Asufot* 2 (1988), 29–67.
Levi, B., and P. Wackers, eds. *The Fox and Other Animals (Selected Proceedings of the Spa Colloquium)*. Reinardus: Yearbook of the International Reynard Society [Special Volume]. Amsterdam and Philadelphia: Benjamin, 1993.
Levi, E. *The Habima—Israel's National Theater 1917–1977: A Study of Cultural Nationalism*. New York: Columbia University Press, 1979.
Levi Yitzhak of Berdichev. *Kedushat Levi* (Levi's "holiness") [Hebrew]. Slavuta, Ukraine, 1798.
———. *Sefer Kedushat Levi ha-Shalem* (The complete book of *Kedushat Levi*). Jerusalem: Mossad le-Hozaat Sifrei Musar ve-Hasidut, 1964.
Leviant, C. *King Artus: A Hebrew Arthurian Romance of 1279*. New York: Ktav, 1969.
Levin, Is. *Abraham ibn Ezra: His Life and His Poetry* [Hebrew]. Tel Aviv: Hakibutz Hameuchad, 1970.
———, ed. *Abraham ibn Ezra: Reader* [Hebrew]. New York and Tel Aviv: Israel Matz Hebrew Classics and I. Edward Kiev Library Foundation, 1985.
———, ed. *The Religious Poems of Abraham ibn Ezra* [Hebrew]. 2 vols. Jerusalem: Israel Academy of Science and Humanities, 1975–1980.
Levin, It. *Beyond the Tears: [Jewish Humor in the Nazi Regime]* [Hebrew]. Tel Aviv, Israel: Yedioth Ahronoth and Chemed Books, 2004.
Levin, Zevi Hirsch ben Aryeh Loeb. *Sefer Tsava Rav: Hidushim ve-Hagahot 'al Shishah Sidre Mishnah ve-'al Arba'ah Helke ha-Tur veha-Shulham 'Arukh* (The book of multitudes: New interpretations and amendations of the six orders of the Mishnah and the four parts of the *Tur* and the *Shulhian Arukh*). Jerusalem: Mekhon Yerushalayim, 2001. [Originally published Piotrkow, Poland: Kronenberg ve-Folman, 1907.]
Levine, B. A. "The Language of the Magical Bowls." In *A History of the Jews in Babylonia* (5:343–37). Ed. J. Neusner. Leiden: Brill, 1970.
Levitats, I. *The Jewish Community in Russia, 1772–1844*. Studies in History, Economics, and Public Law 505. New York: Columbia University Press, 1943.
Levitsky, J. "The Illegitimate Child (Mamzer) in Jewish Law." *JBQ* 18, no. 1 (1989), 6–12.
Lewin, A. *Kantonistn: Vegn der yiddisher rekrutshine in Rusland in di tsaytn fun Tsar Nikolay dem ershtn, 1827–1856* (Conscripts: About the Jewish recruits in Russia in the period of Tzar Nikolai the First, 1827–1856). Warsaw: Grafia, 1934.
Lewin, B. M. *Otsar ha-Ge'onim: Teshuvot Ge'one Bavel u-Ferushehem 'al pi Seder ha-Talmud* (The Gaonic treasure: The responses of the Babylonian Gaonim and their interpretations according to the sequence of the Talmud). 13 vols. Jerusalem: Vegshal, 1984. [Originally published 1928–1943.]
Lewinski, Y. T. *Encyclopedia of Folklore, Customs and Tradition in Judaism* [Hebrew]. 2 vols. Tel Aviv: Devir, 1970.
———, ed. *Sefer ha-Mo'adim* (The festivals book). 9 vols. Tel Aviv: Agudat 'Oneg Shabat 'al yad Devir, 1950–1964/1965. [Vols. 1 and 9, ed. Y. L. Barukh.]
Lewis, J. E. *The English Fable: Aesop and Literary Culture 1651–1740*. Cambridge, UK: Cambridge University Press, 1996.
Liber, M. "Structure and History of the *Tefilah*." *JQR* 40 (1949–1950), 331–357.

Liebes, Y. *Studies in Jewish Myth and Jewish Messianism.* Trans. B. Stein. Albany: State University of New York Press, 1993.

———. *Studies in the Zohar.* Trans. A. Schwartz, S. Nakache, and P. Peli. State University of New York Series in Judaica: Hermeneutics, Mysticism and Religion. Albany: State University of New York Press, 1993.

Liebreich, J. L. "The Intermediate Benedictions of the *Amidah.*" *JQR* 42 (1951–1952), 423–426.

Lieu, J. M. *Image and Reality: The Jews in the World of the Christians in the Second Century.* London and New York: Clark, 1996.

Lif, A. [Draitser, E. A.]. *Forbidden Laughter (Soviet Underground Jokes).* Trans. A. Ostash. Los Angeles: Almanac Press, 1979.

Lifshitz, Y. "*Badḥonim un leytsim bay Yidn*" (Jesters and jokers among the Jews). In *Archiwum Historji Teatru I Sztuki Dramatycznei Zydowskiej* (1:33–74). Ed. J. Szacki. Vilnius, Lithuania, and New York: Zydowski Instytut Naukowy, 1930.

Likhtenshtain [Lichtenstein], K., ed. *Pinkas Slonim: Record and Face of a Town, Ruin of the Community. In Memoriam* [Hebrew]. Tel Aviv: Irgun 'Olei Slonim be-Yisrael, 1961.

Lillo, G. *The London Merchant or the History of George Barnwell and Fatal Curiosity.* Ed. A. W. Ward. Boston: Heath, 1906.

Lincoln, W. B. "Nikolai Alekseevich Milyutin and Problems of State Reform in Nicholaevan Russia." Unpublished dissertation. Chicago: University of Chicago, 1966.

Lindeberg, B. "Rabbi Shneur Zalmans Anthropologi." *NJ* 16 (1995), 83–100.

Lipman, S. *Laughter in Hell: The Use of Humor During the Holocaust.* Northvale, NJ: Aronson, 1991.

Lipsker, A. " 'Light Is Sown for the Righteous'—Shifts in the Iconic Fashioning of the Zaddik's Halo—A Study of the Transformation of a Specific Configuration in Four Thematic Series" [Hebrew]. *Encyclopedia of the Jewish Story: Sippur Okev Sippur* (105–135). Ed. Y. Elsetein, A. Lipsker, and R. Kushelevsky. Ramat-Gan, Israel: Bar-Ilan University Press, 2004.

———. "The Unreflecting Mirror" [Hebrew]. *Chuliyot* 3 (1996), 33–57.

Lipson, M. *Di Velt Dertzeilt: Ma'asiyot, vertlakh, hanhagot un midot fun anshei-shem bay iden* (The world tells: Tales, idioms, customs and norms among famous Jewish people). New York: Dorot, 1928.

———. *Medor Dor* (From days of old). 4 vols. Tel Aviv: Achiasaf, 1968. [Originally published Tel Aviv: Dorot, 1929–1938.]

Litvak, O. "The Literary Response to Conscription: Individuality and Authority in the Russian-Jewish Enlightenment." Unpublished dissertation. New York: Columbia University, 1999.

Litvin, A. *Yudishe neshomes* (Jewish souls). 6 vols. New York: Ferlag Folksbildung, 1916.

Liungman, W. *Sagan om Bata och Anubis och den Orientalisk-europeiska undersagans ursprung.* Djursholm, Sweden: Förlags A. B. Vald Litteratur, 1946.

———. *Die Schwedischen Volksmärchen: Herkunft und Geschichte.* Veröffentlichungen des Instituts für deutsche Volkskunde 20. Berlin: Akademie-Verlag, 1961.

Lodge, A., and K. Varty, eds. *The Earliest Branches of the* Roman de Renar. Synthema 1. Louvain, Belgium, and Sterling, VA: Peeters, 2001.

Loewe, H. *Catalogue of the Manuscripts in the Hebrew Character: Collected and*

Bequeathed to Trinity College Library by the Late William Aldis Wright. Cambridge, UK: Cambridge University Press, 1926.

———. *Schelme und Narren mit jüdischen Kappen.* Berlin: Welt Verlag, 1920.

Loewenthal, N. *Communicating the Infinite: The Emergence of Habad School.* Chicago: University of Chicago Press, 1990.

———. "Rabbi Schneur Zalman of Liadi's Kitzur Likkutei Amarim British Library Or 10456." In *Studies in Jewish Manuscripts* (89–129). Ed. J. Dan and K. Herrmann, in collaboration with J. Hoornweg and M. Petzoldt. Tübingen, Germany: Mohr Siebeck, 1999.

———. "Women and the Dialectic of Spirituality in Hasidism." In *Within Hasidic Circles: Studies in Hasidism in Memory of Mordecai Wilensky* (7–65). Ed. I. Etkes, D. Assaf, I. Bartal, and E. Reiner. Jerusalem: Bialik Institute, 1999.

Lomax, J. A., and A. Lomax, eds. *Negro Folk Songs as Sung by Lead Belly.* New York: Macmillan, 1936.

Longworth, P. *The Cossacks.* New York: Holt, Rinehart & Winston, 1970.

Loukatos, D. "*Le proverbe dans le conte.*" *Laographia* 22 (1970), 229–233.

Lovlace, M. "Cante Fable." *Encyclopedia of Folklore and Literature,* 89–90, 1998.

Löw, A., K. Robusch, and S. Walter, eds. *Deutsche—Juden—Polen: Geschichte einer wechselvollen Bezeihung im 20. Jahrhunderet.* Frankfurt and New York: Campus Verlag, 2004.

Luckens, M. J. "The Life of Levi Yizhaq of Berdichev." In *Jewish Civilization: Essays and Studies* (141–159). Ed. R. A. Brauner. Philadelphia: Reconstructionist Rabbinical College, 1979.

Luncz, A. M. "*Yiḥus avot*" (Ancestral geneology). *Ha-Me'ammer* 3 (1920), 209–223.

Lurie, B. Z., ed. *Meggillath Ta'anith* [Hebrew]. Jerusalem: Bialik Institute, 1964.

Lustiger, A. *Stalin and the Jews: The Red Book. The Tragedy of the Jewish Anti-Fascist Committee and the Soviet Jews.* New York: Enigma Books, 2003.

Lüthi, M. "*Bruder, Brüder.*" *EM* 2:844–861, 1978.

———. *The European Folktale: Form and Nature.* Trans. J. D. Niles. Philadelphia: Institute for the Study of Human Issues, 1982.

———. *The Fairytale as Art Form and Portrait of Man.* Trans. J. Erickson. Bloomington: Indiana University Press, 1984.

———. *Once Upon a Time: On the Nature of Fairy Tales.* New York: Ungar, 1970.

———. *So leben sie noch heute: Betrachtungen zum Volksmärchen.* Göttingen, Germany: Vandenhoeck & Ruprecht, 1969.

———. *Volksmärchen und Volkssage.* Bern and Münich: Francke, 1961.

Luz, E. *Parallels Meet: Religion and Nationalism in Early Zionist Movement (1882–1904)* [Hebrew]. Tel Aviv: Am Oved, 1985.

Luzzatto, J. ben Isaac, *Kaftor va-feraḥ* (A bud and a flower). Basle, 1581.

Mader, M. *Die Dukus Horant Forschung: Bericht und Kritik.* Osnabrück, Germany: Biblio, 1979.

Mahdi, M., ed. *The Thousand and One Nights (alf layla wa-layla): From the Earliest Known Sources.* 3 vols. Leiden: Brill, 1984–1994.

Mahler, R. *Hasidism and the Jewish Enlightenment: Their Confrontation in Galicia and Poland in the First Half of the Nineteenth Century.* Trans. E. Orenstein, A. Klein, and J. Machlowitz Klein. Philadelphia: Jewish Publication Society of America, 1985.

———. *History of Jews in Poland* [Hebrew]. Merḥavyah: Sifriyat Po'alim, 1946.

Maimon, S. *The Autobiography of Solomon Maimon*. Trans. J. C. Murray. London: East and West Library, 1954.
Maitlis, J., ed. *The Book of Stories, Basel 1602*. Musterwerk fun der Yiddisher Literature. Buenos Aires: Ateneo Literario en el Instituto Cientifico Judio, 1969.
Malchow, B. V. *Social Justice in the Hebrew Bible: What Is New and What Is Old*. Collegeville, MN: Liturgical Press, 1996.
Manger, I. *Lid un Balade: Song and Ballade*. Tel Aviv: Peretz, 1976.
Mann, J. *Texts and Studies in Jewish History and Literature*. 2 vols. Cincinnati, OH: Hebrew Union College Press, 1931.
———, ed. and trans. *Ysengrimus*. Mittekkateinische Studien und Texte 12. Leiden: Brill, 1987.
Mann, K. "Die Mythen der Unterwelt—Horst Wessel." *FHL* 11 (1991), 101–116.
Mantel, H. "The Nature of the Great Synagogue." *HTR* 60 (1967), 69–91.
Maranda, P., ed. *Soviet Structural Folkloristics*. Approaches to Semiotics 42. The Hague: Mouton, 1974.
Marcus, E. "The Confrontation between Jews and Non-Jews in Folktales of the Jews of Islamic Countries" [Hebrew]. Unpublished dissertation. Jerusalem: Hebrew University, 1977.
———. *Jewish Festivities* [Hebrew]. Jerusalem: Keter, 1990.
———. *Min ha-Mabua (From the Fountainhead): Forty-four Folktales Collected by the "Mabuim" School Pupils* [Hebrew]. IFAPS 12. Haifa: Haifa Municipality Ethnological Museum and Folklore Archives, 1966.
Marcus, I. G. *The Jewish Life Cycle: Rites of Passage from Biblical to Modern Times*. Seattle: University of Washington Press, 2004.
Marcus, M. "Cross-Fertilizations: Folklore and Literature in Decameron 4,5." *Italica* 66 (1989), 383–398.
Margaliot, R. *Mal'akhei 'Elyon ha-Muzkarim be-Talmud Bavli ve-Yerushalmi, Bekhol ha-Midrashim, Zohar ve-Tikunim, Targumim ve-Likutim 'Im Tsiyunim Le-Sifre Kodesh Shel Kabalah* (Heavenly angels that are mentioned in the Babylonian and Jerusalemian Talmuds and in all the midrashic books, the Zohar, the translations with references to the books of mysticism). Jerusalem: Mossad Harav Kook, 1945.
Margalioth, M. *Halakhot Erez-Israel min ha-Geniza* (Land of Israel halokhot from the Geniza). Ed. I. Ta-Shema. Jerusalem: Mossad Harav Kook, 1973.
———. *Sepher Ha-Razim: A Newly Recovered Book of Magic from the Talmudic Period* [Hebrew]. Jerusalem: American Academy for Jewish Research, 1966.
Margalits, E. *Magyar közmondások és közmondászerû szólások* (Hungarian proverbs and proverb-like sayings). Budapest: Academy Publisher, 1990. [Originally published 1897.]
Margoliouth, G. *Catalogue of the Hebrew and Samaritan Manuscripts in the British Museum*. London: Trustees of the British Museum, 1965.
Margulies, M., ed. *Midrash Haggadol on the Pentateuch: Exodus* [Hebrew]. 2 vols. Jerusalem: Mossad Harav Kook, 1956.
———, ed. *Midrash Haggadol on the Pentateuch: Genesis* [Hebrew]. 2 vols. Jerusalem: Mossad Harav Kook, 1947.
Marinov, Y., and A. Vohliner [pseudonym], eds. *Humor un satire. Driter band: Visenshaft un folks humor*. (Humor and satire. Vol. 3: Science and folk humor). New York: Ramal, 1912.

Mark, N. *Le-Vedihut ha-Da'at: Bedihot, Havrakot, Divrei Ḥakhamim ve-Khayotse be-Eleh, Devarim she-Yesh ba-Hem le-Vadeah et ha-Da'at* (For entertainment: Jokes, brilliant ideas, wise words and other entertaining subjects). Tel Aviv: Izrael, 1978.

Marmorstein, A. "Das Motiv vom veruntreuten Depositum in der jüdischen Volkskunde." *MGWJ* 78 (1934), 183–195.

Marshall, G. J. *Angels: An Indexed and Partially Annotated Bibliography of Over 4300 Scholarly Books and Articles Since the 7th Century B.C.* Jefferson, NC: McFarland, 1999.

Martin, M. L., trans. *The Fables of Marie de France: An English Translation.* Birmingham, AL: Summa, 1984.

Martineau, W. H. "A Model for the Social Functions of Humor." In *The Psychology of Humor: Theoretical Perspectives and Empirical Issues* (101–125). Ed. J. H. Goldstein and P. H. McGhee. New York: Academic Press, 1972.

Marzolph, U. *Arabia Ridens: Die humoristische Kurzprosa der frühen adab-Literatur im internationalen Traditionsgeflecht.* 2 vols. Frankfurt am Main: Vittorio Klostermann, 1992.

———. *Nasreddin Hodscha: 666 wahre Geschichten.* Münich: Beck, 1996.

———. *Typologie des persischen Volksmärchens.* Beiruter Texts und Studien 31. Beirut, Lebanon: Orient-Institut der Deutschen Morgenländischen Gesellschaft, 1984.

———, and R. van Leeuwen, eds. *The Arabian Nights Encyclopedia.* 2 vols. Santa Barbara, CA: ABC Clio, 2004.

Matenko, P., and S. Sloan. "Aqedath Jishaq." In *Two Studies in Yiddish Culture* (3–70). Ed. P. Matenko. Leiden: Brill, 1968

Matt, D. C., trans. *The Zohar: Spitzker Edition.* Stanford, CA: Stanford University Press, 2004.

Matt, H. J. "Acknowledging the King: The You and He, the They and We, of Aleinu." *CJ* 30, no. 2 (1976), 68–77.

Maugham, W. S. *The Complete Short Stories of W. Somerset Maugham, II: The World Over.* Garden City, NY: Doubleday, 1952.

———. *Cosmopolitans.* New York: Sun Dial Press, 1938.

———. "The Man Who Made His Mark." *International* combined with *Cosmopolitan*, June 1929, 62–63. [Also published *Nash's Magazine,* August 1929, 20.]

McKenzie, K. "An Italian Fable, Its Sources, and Its History." *MP* 1 (1904), 497–523.

———, and W. A. Oldfather, eds. *Ysopet-Avionnet: The Latin and French Texts.* University of Illinois Studies in Language and Literature 5, no. 4. Urbana: University of Illinois, 1919.

McManus, I. C. "Basic Colour Terms in Literature." *LS* 26 (1983), 247–252.

Medvedev, R., and Z. Medvedev. *The Unknown Stalin: His Life, Death, and Legacy.* Woodstock and New York: Overlook Press, 2004.

Medvedev, Zh. *Stalin everīskaia problema: novī analiz* (Stalin and the Jewish problem: new analysis). Moscow: Izdvo AST, 2004.

Megas, G. A., ed. *Folktales of Greece.* Folktales of the World. Trans. H. Colaclides. Chicago: University of Chicago Press, 1970.

———. "Some Oral Greek Parallels to Aesop's Fables." In *Humaniora: Essays in Literature, Folklore, Bibliography, Honoring Archer Taylor on His Seventieth Birthday* (195–207). Ed. W. D. Hand and G. O. Arlt. Locust Valley, NY: Augustin, 1960.

Meier, J., et al., eds. *Deutsche Volkslieder: Balladen. Deutsche Volkslieder mit ihren Melodien.* 5 vols. Berlin and Leipzig: Gruyter, 1935–1967. [Vol. 4, ed. E. Seemann and W. Wiora; vol. 5 pub. Freiburg/Breisgau: Verlag des Deutschen Volksliedarchives.]

Meitlis, J. *The Book of Stories, Basel 1602, and Studies on the Jewish Literature.* Musterverk fun der Yidisher Literature 38. Buenos Aires: Ateneo Literario en el Instituto Cientifico Judio, 1969.

———. *Das Ma'assebuch: Seine Entstehung und Quellengeschichte zugleich ein Beitrag zur Einfu?hrung in die altjiddische Agada.* Berlin: Mass, 1933.

———. "Some Extant Folktales in Yiddish Mss." *Fabula* 12 (1971), 212–217.

Melchior-Bonnet, S. *The Mirror: A History.* Trans. K. H. Jewett. New York: Routledge, 2001.

Ménard, P. *Le rire et le sourire dans le roman courtois en France au moyan âge (1150–1250).* Geneva: Librairie Droz, 1969.

Mendelsohn, F. S. *The Jew Laughs.* Chicago: Stein, 1935.

———. *The Merry Heart: Wit and Wisdom from Jewish Folklore.* New York: Bookman Associates, 1951.

Mendelsohn, J. *The Holocaust: 3. The Crystal Night Pogrom.* New York: Garland, 1982.

Merhaviah, H. " 'Kol Nidrei'—Problem and Riddle." In *Jubilee Volume in Honor of Moreinu Hagaon Rabbi Joseph B. Soloveitchik Shlyt"a* (Our teacher, the genius Rabbi Joseph B. Soloveitchik) (1056–1096). Ed. S. Israeli, N. Lamm, and Y. Raphael. Jerusalem and New York: Mossad Harav Kook and Yeshiva University, 1984.

Metzger, M. *La Haggada enluminée.* Études sur le Judaïsme Medieval 2. Leiden: Brill, 1973.

Meyer, R. "*Geschichte eines orientalischen Märchenmotives in der rabbinischen Literatur.*" In *Festschrift, Alfred Bertholet zum 80. Geburtstag gewidmet von Kollegen und Freunden* (365–378). Ed. W. Baumgartner et al. Tübingen, Germany: Mohr, 1950.

Michalowska, A. "Charity and the Charity Society (*Khevra Kadisha*) in the Jewish Community of Swarzedz in the Eighteenth Century." *APH* 87 (2003), 77–88.

Mieder, W. *Proverbs: A Handbook.* Westport, CT: Greenwood Press, 2004.

———, S. K. Kingsbury, and K. B. Harder, eds. *A Dictionary of American Proverbs.* New York: Oxford University Press, 1992.

Mikhalzohn, A. H. S. B. *Ohel Avraham* (Abraham's tent). Piotrokow, Poland: Rosenfeld, 1911.

———. *Sefer Dover Shalom* (The book of the speaker of peace). Przemysl: Amokroiot and Fraind, 1910. [Reprint ed. Tel Aviv, 1965.]

———. *Sefer Shemen ha-Tov* (The book of oil of goodness). Piotrkow, Poland: Kronenberg, 1905. [Reprint ed. Jerusalem, 1963.]

Miller, S. *Fun'm Yiddishn Kval: The Gist of Jewish Humor* [Yiddish]. Winnipeg, Canada: Dos Yidishe Vort, 1937.

Millien, A., and P. Delarue. *Contes du Nivernais et du Morvan.* Contes Merveilleux des Proveinces de France. Paris: Éditions Érasme, 1953.

Milner, S. "*Le-Korot ha-Yehudim be-Helem*" (The history of the Jews in Chelm). *Ha-Me'asef* 1 (1902), 154–160.

Minczeles, H. *Vilna, Wilno, Vilnius: La Jérusalem de Lituanie.* Paris: Éditions la Découverte, 1993.

Mindel, N. *Rabbi Schneur Zalman*. 2 vols. Brooklyn: Chabad Research Center and Kehot Publication Society, 1969.

Minkoff, N. B. *Elye Bokher and His Bove-Bukh* [Yiddish]. New York: Vaxer, 1950.

Mintz, J. R. *Hasidic People: A Place in the New World*. Cambridge, MA: Harvard University Press, 1992.

———. *Legends of the Hasidim: An Introduction to Hasidic Culture and Oral Tradition in the New World*. Chicago: University of Chicago Press, 1968.

Mintz, L. E. "The Rabbi Versus the Priest and Other Jewish Stories." In *Jewish Humor* (125–134). Classics in Communication and Mass Culture Series. Ed. A. Ziv. New Brunswick, NJ: Transaction Publishers, 1998. [Originally published as "Humoristic Confrontations of Religious Figures: Rabbi-Priest Jokes" (Hebrew). In *Jewish Humor* (99–106). Ed. A. Ziv. Tel Aviv: Papyrus, 1986.]

Miranda, E. "Fortuna." *EM* 5:1–6, 1987.

Mirsky, A. *HA'PIYUT: The Development of Post-Biblical Poetry in Eretz Israel and the Diaspora* [Hebrew]. Jerusalem: Magnes Press, 1990.

———. "The Origin of the 'Eighteen Benedictions' of the Daily Prayer" [Hebrew]. *Tarbiz* 33, no. 2 (1963), 28–39.

Mizrahi, H. *With Elders Is Wisdom: Forty Jewish-Persian Folktales Collected in Israel*. IFAPS 16. Ed. D. Noy. Haifa: Ethnological Museum and Folklore Archives, 1967.

Molesworth, W., ed. *The English Works of Thomas Hobbes of Malmesbury*. Ed. W. Molesworth. 10 vols. London: Bohn, 1840.

Mondschein, Y. *Shivhei Ha-Baal Shem Tov: A Facsimile of a Unique Manuscript, Variant Versions and Appendices* [Hebrew]. Jerusalem: Author, 1982.

———. *Torat Ḥabad: Bibliografia*. Part I: *Sefer ha-Tanya*. Part II: *Hilkhot T[almud] T[orha] Shu[ulḥan] 'A[rukh] Teshuvut u-fiskei ha-siddur*. Kefar Ḥabad, Israel: Kehot Publishing Society, 1981–1984.

Montgomery, J. A. *Aramaic Incantation Texts from Nippur*. The Museum Publications of the Babylonian Section 3. Philadelphia: University Museum, 1913.

Moore, C. A., ed and trans. *Daniel, Esther and Jeremiah the Additions*. Anchor Bible Series 44. Garden City, NY: Doubleday, 1977.

Morgan, M. A., trans. *"Sepher ha-Razim": The Book of the Mysteries*. Texts and Translations 25. Pseudepigrapha Series 11. Chico, CA: Scholars Press, 1983.

Morgan, T. *Maugham*. New York: Simon & Schuster, 1980.

Morreall, J., ed. *The Philosophy of Laughter and Humor*. Albany: State University of New York Press, 1987.

Morton, F. *The Rothschilds: A Family Portrait*. New York: Atheneum, 1962.

Moser, G. M. "The Talking Skull Refuses to Talk: Addenda from Portuguese Sources." *RAL* (1978), 256–258.

Moser-Rath, E. "Fisch: Den grossen F. befragen (AaTh 1567C)." *EM* 4:1218–1221, 1984.

Moss, A. E. "Basic Colour Terms: Problems and Hypotheses." *Lingus* 78 (1989), 313–320.

Mosse, G. L. "Jewish Emancipation: Between *Bildung* and Respectability." In *The Jewish Response to German Culture* (1–16). Ed. J. Reinharz and W. Schatzberg. Hanover, NH: University Press of New England, 1985.

Mowinckel, S. *He That Cometh*. Trans. G. W. Anderson. New York: Abingdon Press, [1954].

Muecke, D. C. *The Compass of Irony*. London: Methuen, 1969.

———. *Irony and the Ironic*. London: Methuen, 1970.

Muir, S. *Yiddish in Helsinki: A Study of a Colonial Yiddish, Dialect and Culture.* Studia Orientalia 100. Helsinki: Finnish Oriental Society, 2004.
Mulkay, M. *On Humor: Its Nature and Its Place in Modern Society.* Cambridge, UK: Basil Blackwell, 1988.
Müller, B., ed. *Parody: Dimensions and Perspectives.* Rodopi Perspectives on Modern Literature 19. Amsterdam and Atlanta: Rodopi, 1997.
Müller, J. *Das Märchen vom Unibos.* Jena, Germany: Eugen Diederichs Verlag, 1934.
Murik, L. *Yiddishe Hochme* (Yiddish wisdom). Tel Aviv: Author, 1984.
Na'anah, R. *Ozar ha-Ma'asiyyot* (A treasury of tales). 3 vols. Jerusalem: Author, 1979.
Nachbush, N. *Noah Nachbushe's Gems of Yiddish Poetry and Folklore,* vinyl recording. Produced by the author. LP330.
Nadav, M. "The Jewish Community of Nemyriv in 1648: Their Massacre and Loyalty Oath to the Cossacks." *HUS* 8 (1984), 376–395.
Nagy, J. F. "Hierarchy, Heroes, and Heads: Indo-European Structures in Greek Myth." In *Approaches to Greek Myth* (199–238). Ed. L. Edmunds. Baltimore: Johns Hopkins University Press, 1990.
Nahmad, H. M. *A Portion in Paradise and Other Jewish Folktales.* B'nai B'rith Jewish Heritage Classics. New York: Norton, 1970.
Narkiss, M. "The Origin of the Spice Box Known as the 'Hadass' " [Hebrew]. *Eretz-Israel* 6 (1960), 189–198.
Nathans, B. *Beyond the Pale: The Jewish Encounter with Late Imperial Russia.* Berkeley: University of California Press, 2002.
Naveh, J., and S. Shaked. *Amulets and Magic Bowls: Aramaic Incantations of Late Antiquity.* Jerusalem: Magnes Press, 1985.
———. *Magic Spells and Formulae: Aramaic Incantations of Late Antiquity.* Jerusalem: Magnes Press, 1993.
Nelles, W. *Frameworks: Narrative Levels and Embedded Narrative.* New York: Lang, 1997.
Ness, L. *Written in the Stars: Ancient Zodiac Mosaics.* Marco Polo Monographs 1. Warren Center, PA: Shangri-La Publications, 1999. [Annotated bibliography (178–226) with special section on Jewish astrology (201–207).]
Neubauer, A. *Catalogue of Hebrew Manuscripts in the Bodleian Library and in the College Libraries of Oxford.* 2 vols. Oxford, UK: Clarendon Press, 1886–1906.
Neuburger, N. "The Russo-Turkish War and the 'Eastern Jewish Question': Encounters between Victims and Victors in Ottoman Bulgaria." *EEJA* 26 (1996), 53–66.
Neufeld, E. *Ancient Hebrew Marriage Laws, with Special References to General Semitic Laws and Customs.* London: Longmans, Green, 1944.
Neugroschel, J., ed. and trans. *The Dybbuk and the Yiddish Imagination: A Haunted Reader.* Syracuse, NY: Syracuse University Press, 2000.
Neusner, J. *A History of the Jews in Babylonia.* 5 vols. Studia Post-Biblica 9–15. Leiden: Brill, 1965–1970.
———. *Messiah in Context: Israel's History and Destiny in Formative Judaism.* Philadelphia: Fortress Press, 1984.
———, W. S. Green, and E. S. Frerichs, eds. *Judaisms and Their Messiahs at the Turn of the Christian Era.* Cambridge, UK: Cambridge University Press, 1987.
Nevins, M. *The Jewish Doctor: A Narrative History.* Northvale, NJ: Aronson, 1996.
Newman, L. I. *The Hasidic Anthology: Tales and Teaching of the Hasidim.* New York: Bloch, 1944.

Niedzielski, H., H. R. Runte, and W. L. Hendrickson, eds. *Studies on the Seven Sages of Rome and Other Essays in Medieval Literature*. Honolulu: Educational Research Associates, 1978.

Nielsen, K. *YAHWEH as Prosecutor and Judge: An Investigation of the Prophetic Lawsuit (Rîb-Pattern)*. *JSOTSS* 9 (1978).

Nigal, G., *The Hasidic Tale: Its History and Topics* [Hebrew]. Jerusalem: Marcus, 1981.

———. *Magic, Mysticism, and Hasidism: The Supernatural in Jewish Thought*. Trans. E. Levin. Northvale, NJ: Aronson, 1994.

———, ed. *Sefer Sippurei Kedoshim* (A book of saints' tales). Jerusalem: Ma'ayanot ha-Ḥasidut, 1977. [Originally published Leipzig (Warsaw), 1866.]

Nikiforov, A. I. "Towards a Morphological Study of the Folktale." In *The Study of Russian Folklore* (155–162). Ed. and trans. F. J. Oinas and S. Soudakoff. The Hague: Mouton, 1975. [Originally published 1928.]

Nilsen, D. L. F. *Humor Scholarship: A Research Bibliography*. Bibliographies and Indexes in Popular Culture 1. Westport, CT: Greenwood Press, 1993.

Nitzan, B. "Hymns from Qumran *le-faḥed u-le-bhahel* [to scare] Evil Ghosts" [Hebrew]. *Tarbiz* 55 (1985–1986), 19–46.

———. *Qumran Prayer and Religious Poetry*. Studies on the Texts of the Desert of Judah 12. Trans. J. Chipman. Leiden: Brill, 1994.

Nøjgaard, M. *La fable antique*. Vol. 1: *La fable grecque avant Phèder*. Copenhagen: NYT Nordisk Forlag, 1964.

Norrick, N. R. *How Proverbs Mean: Semantic Studies in English Proverbs*. Trends in Linguistics Studies and Monographs 27. New York: Mouton, 1985.

North, T. *The Moral Philosophy of Doni Popularly Known as the Fables of Bidpai*. Ed. D. Beecher, J. Butler, and C. Di Biase. Ottawa, ON: Dovehouse Editions, 2003. [Originally published 1570.]

Noy, D. *"Ba'alei Nissim be-Sippureinu ha-Amamiim"* (Miracle workers in our folktales). *Maḥanayyim* 63 (1961), 78–85.

———. *"Bein Yisrael le-'Amim be-Aggadot-Am Shel Yehudei Teiman* (Conflicts between the Jews and other peoples in the legends of the Yemenite Jews). In *Studies in Geniza and Sephardi Heritage: Presented to Shelomo Dov Goitein on the Occasion of His Eightieth Birthday by His Students, Colleagues and Friends* (229–295). Ed. S. Morag, I. Ben-ami, and N. A. Stillman. Jerusalem: Magnes Press, 1981.

———. *The Diaspora and the Land of Israel: Seventeen Folkstories Narrated in Israel* [Hebrew]. Sha'ar 10. Jerusalem: Sha'ar, 1959.

———. *"Eliyahu ha-Navi be-Leil ha-Seder"* (Elijha the Prophet on Passover eve). *Maḥanayyim* 44 (1960), 110–116.

———. "Folktales Including Songs and Melodies" [Hebrew]. *Tatzlil* 3 (1965), 47–50.

———, ed. *Folktales of Israel*. Trans. G. Baharav. Chicago: University of Chicago Press, 1963.

———. "General and Jewish Folktale Types in the Decalogue Midrash." *4th WCJS* 2 (1969), 353–355.

———. "The Hidden Zaddik in Theodicy Legends" [Hebrew]. *YA* 18, nos. 43–44 (1976), 32–40.

———. *"Histaklut ba-Zipornayim bi-Sh'at ha-Havdalah"* (Observation of fingernails during the *Havdalah*). *Maḥanayyim* 85–86 (1963), 166–173.

———. "Introduction: Eighty Years of Jewish Folkloristics: Achievements and Tasks." In *Studies in Jewish Folklore: Proceedings of a Regional Conference of the Association* for Jewish Studies Held at the Spertus College of Judaica, Chicago, May 1–3, 1977 (1–12). Ed. D. Noy and F. Talmage. Cambridge, MA: Association for Jewish Studies, 1980.

———. *Jefet Schwili Erzähalt: Hundertneunundsechzig jemenitische Volkserzählungen aufgezeichnet in Israel 1957–1960. Fabula* Suppl. 4 (1963).

———. *The Jewish Animal Tale of Oral Tradition* [Hebrew]. IFAPS 29. Haifa: Haifa Municipality and Ethnological Museum and Folklore Archives, 1976.

———, ed. *Jewish Folktales from Libya: Seventy-One Tales from Oral Tradition* [Hebrew]. Jerusalem: Bi-Tefutsot ha-Golah, 1967.

———, ed. *Jewish Folktales from Morocco* [Hebrew]. Jerusalem: Bi-Tefutsot ha-Golah, 1967.

———, ed. *Jewish Folktales from Tunisia* [Hebrew]. Jerusalem: Bi-Tefutsot ha-Golah, 1966.

———, ed. *Jewish-Iraqi Folktales* [Hebrew]. Tel Aviv: Am Oved, 1965.

———, ed. *Moroccan Jewish Folktales*. New York: Herzl, 1966.

———. "The Place of Sh. Ansky in Jewish Folkloristics" [Hebrew]. *JSJF* 2 (1982), 94–107.

———, ed. *Sippurim mi-Pi Yehudei Polin* (Tales told by Polish Jews). Yahad Shivtei Israel. Simple Hebrew Library. Jerusalem: Department of Culture and Education in the Diaspora of the World Zionist Organization, 1967.

———, ed. *A Tale for Each Month 1962: Twelve Selected and Annotated IFA Folktales*. IFAPS 3. Haifa: Haifa Municipality and Ethnological Museum and Folklore Archives, 1963.

———, ed. *A Tale for Each Month 1965: Twelve Selected and Annotated IFA Folktales*. IFAPS 11. Haifa: Haifa Municipality and Ethnological Museum and Folklore Archives, 1966.

———, ed. *A Tale for Each Month 1966: Twelve Selected and Annotated Tales*. IFAPS 18. Haifa: Haifa Municipality and Ethnological Museum and Folklore Archives, 1967.

———, ed. *A Tale for Each Month 1970: Twleve Selected and Annotated IFA Folktales*. IFAPS 27. Haifa: Haifa Municipality and Ethnological Museum and Folklore Archives, 1971.

———, ed. *A Tale for Each Month 1971: Twelve Selected and Annotated IFA Folktales*. IFAPS 28. Haifa: Haifa Municipality and Ethnological Museum and Folklore Archives, 1972.

———, and G. Hasan-Rokem, eds. *Midrash Aseret ha-Dibrot, Nusah Verona T"Z* (Midrash of the Ten Commandments, Verona 1647 Edition). Jerusalem: Hebrew University, Department of Hebrew Literature, 1986.

———, and M. Noy. "Introduction." In *East European Jewish Cante Fables* (5–12) [Hebrew]. IFAPS 20. Ed. M. Noy. Haifa: Haifa Municipality and Ethnological Museum and Folklore Archives, 1968.

Noy, M. "Bibliographical References to the Song of Rothschild's End" [Hebrew]. *YA* 16, nos. 39–40 (1972), 95.

———. *East European Jewish Cante Fables*. IFAPS 20. Haifa: Haifa Municipality and Ethnological Museum and Folklore Archives, 1968.

Obermeyer, J. *Modernes Judentum im Morgen- und Abendland*. Vienna and Leipzig, Germany: Fromme, 1907.

Oegema, G. S. *The Anointed and His People: Messianic Expectations from the Maccabees to Bar Kochba. JSP* Suppl. 27 (1998).

Ofek, A. "Cantonists: Jewish Children as Soldiers in Tsar Nicholas's Army." *MJ* 13 (1993), 277–308.

———, and R. Ben-Ner, eds. *Harpatka'otav shel Hershele* (Hershele's adventures). N.p.: Kor'im, 2001.

———. *Hershele: Kol sippurei Hershele* (Hershele: All his tales). N.p.: Alumot, n.d.

Ogilvy, J. D. A. " 'Mimi,' 'Scurrae,' 'Histriones': Entertainers of the Early Middle Ages." *Speculum* 38 (1963), 603–619.

O'Kane, B. *Early Persian Painting: Kalila and Dimna Manuscripts of the Late Fourteenth Century*. London: Tauris, 2003.

O'Keefe, D. L. *Stolen Lightning: The Social Theory of Magic*. New York: Continuum, 1982.

Olayemi, V. "Forms of the Song in Yoruba Folktales." *AN* 5 (1968–1969), 25–32.

Olsvanger, I. *L'Chayim!* New York: Schocken, 1949.

———. *Rosinkess mit Mandlen: Aus der Volksliteratur der Ostjuden. Schwänke, Erzählungen, Sprichwörter, Rätsel*. 2nd ed. Basel: Schweizerische Gesellschaft für Volkskunde, 1931. [Reprint ed. Zurich: Verlag der Arche, 1965.]

———. *Röyte Pomerantsen or How to Laugh in Yiddish*. New York: Schocken, 1965.

Oron, M. *Samuel Falk: The Baal Shem of London*. Jerusalem: Bialik Institute, 2002.

O'Rourke, S. *Warriors and Peasants: The Don Cossacks in Late Imperial Russia*. New York: St. Martin's Press, 2000.

Ortutay, G. "Principles of Oral Transmission in Folk Culture." *AE* 8 (1959), 175–221. [Reprinted in Ortutay, ed. *Hungarian Folklore: Essays* (132–173). Budapest: Akademiai Kiado, 1972.]

Osten-Sacken, P. von der. *Gott und Belial: Traditionsgeschichtliche Untersuchungen zum Dualismus in den Texten aus Qumran*. Studiesn zur Umwelt des Neuen Testaments 6. Göttingen, Germany: Vandenhoeck & Ruprecht, 1969.

Pape, W., ed. *Arnim und die Berliner Romantik: Kunst, Literatur, und Politik: Berliner Kolloquium der internationalen Arnim-Gesellschaft*. Tübingen, Germany: Niemeyer, 2001.

———. *Das "Wunderhorn" und die Heidelberger Romantik: Mündlichkeit, Schriftlichkeit, Performanz*. Heidelberger Kolloquium der Internationalen Arnim-Gesellschaft. Schriften der Internationalen Arnim-Gesellschaft 5. Tübingen, Germany: Niemeyer, 2005.

Pappenheim, B. *Allerlei Geschichten Maasse-Buch: Buch der Sagen und Legenden aus Talmud und Midrash nebst Volkserzählungen in jüdisch-deutscher Sprache. Nach der Ausgabe des Maasse-Buches Amsterdam 1723*. Frankfurt am Main: Kauffmann, 1929.

———, trans. *Die Memoiren der Glückel von Hameln* [Yiddish]. Weinheim, Germany: Belz Athenäum, 1994.

Paris, G. "*Le 'Chanson du Chevreau.*' " *Romania* 1 (1872), 218–225.

Passamaneck, S. T. "Some Medieval Problems in Mamzeruth." *HUCA* 37 (1966), 121–145.

Patai, R. *The Hebrew Goddess*. 3rd ed. Jewish Folklore and Anthropology. Detroit: Wayne State University Press, 1990.

———. *The Messiah Texts: Jewish Legends of Three Thousand Years*. Detroit: Wayne State University Press, 1979.

Patch, H. R. *The Goddess Fortuna in Mediaeval Literature*. Cambridge, MA: Harvard University Press, 1927.

———. "The Tradition of the Goddess Fortuna in Roman Literature and the Transitional Period." *Smith College Studies in Modern Languages* 3 (1921–1922), 131–235.
Paton, G. E. C., C. Powell, and S. Wagg, eds. *The Social Faces of Humor: Practices and Issues*. Popular Cultural Studies. Brookfield, VT: Ashgate, 1996.
Paucker, A. "*Das Deutsche Volksbuch bei den Juden*." *ZDP* 80 (1961), 302–317.
———. "*Das Volksbuch von der Seiben Weisen Meistern in der Jüddischen Literatu*." *ZfV* 57 (1961), 177–194.
———. "Yiddish Versions of Early German Prose Novels." *JJS* 10 (1959), 151–167.
———. "The Yiddish Versions of the *Shildburger Buch*" [Yiddish]. *YB* 44 (1973), 59–79.
Pauli, J. *Schimpf und Ernst*. Ed. J. Bolte. 2 vols. Berlin: Stubenrauch, 1924.
Pawlowski, A. "The Quantitative Approach in Cultural Anthropology: Application of Linguistic Corpora in the Analysis of Basic Colour Terms." *JQL* 6 (1999), 222–234.
Pedaya, H. "The Development of the Social-Religious-Economic Model in Hasidism: The *Pidyyon*, the Community and the Pilgrimage" [Hebrew]. *Zaddik and Devotees: Historical and Sociological Aspects of Hasidism* (343–397). Ed. D. Assaf. Jerusalem: Zalman Shazar Center for Jewish History, 2001.
Pedrosa, J. M. "*Pluriliüngismo y paneuropeismo en la canción tradicional de el buen Viejo*." *Romania* 113 (1992–1995), 530–536.
Pelton, R. D. *The Trickster in West Africa: A Study of Mythic Irony and Sacred Delight*. Berkeley: University of California Press, 1980.
Peretz, Y. L. [Perez, I. L]. "*Oyb nisht nokh hekher*" (If not higher). In *The Complete Works of Y. L. Peretz* (4:98–102). New York: Central Yiddish Cultural Organization, 1947. [Originally published in *Der Yid* 1 (1900).]
———. *Peretz*. Trans. S. Liptzin. New York: Yiddish Scientific Institute, 1947.
———. *Selected Stories*. Ed. I. Howe and E. Greenberg. New York: Schocken, 1975.
———. *Stories and Pictures*. Trans. H. Frank. Philadelphia: Jewish Publication Society of America, 1906.
Perkal, J. R. "The Dual Nature of Cumulative Tales." *Laographia* 22 (1965), 338–342.
Perkins, R. L., ed. *International Kierkegaard Commentary: The Concept of Irony*. Macon, GA: Mercer University Press, 2001.
Permyakov, G. L. *From Proverb to Folktale: Notes on the General Theory of Cliché*. Moscow: Nauka, 1979.
Perrett, W. *The Story of King Lear from Geoffrey of Monmouth to Shakespeare*. Weimar, Germany: Wagner Sohn, 1903.
Perry, B. E. *Aesopica*. Urbana: University of Illinois Press, 1952.
———, trans. and ed. *Babrius and Phaedrus*. Loeb Classical Library. Cambridge, MA: Harvard University Press, 1965.
———. "Demetrius of Phalerum and the Aesopic Fables." *TAPA* 93 (1962), 287–346.
———. "The Origin of the Book of Sindbad." *Fabula* 3 (1960), 1–94.
———, ed. *Secundus, the Silent Philosopher: The Greek Life of Secundus*. Philological Monographs 22. Ithaca, NY: Cornell University Press and American Philological Association, 1964.
Petzoldt, L. "*Mord-Herbergen*: *Zur Text-und Überlieferungsgeschichte einer Zeitungssage (AaTh 939A) und verwandter Erzählungen*." In *Sichtweisen der Volkskunde: Zur Geschichte und Forshungspraxis einer Disziplin* (367–380). Lebensformen 3. Ed. A. Lehmann and A. Kuntz. Berlin: Dietrich Reimer, 1988.
Piekarz, M. *The Beginning of Hasidism: Ideological Trends in Derush and Musar Literature*. Jerusalem: Bialik Institute, 1978.

———. *Between Ideology and Reality: Humility, Ayin, Self-Negation and Devekut in Hasidic Thought* [Hebrew]. Jerusalem: Bialik Institute, 1994.

———. *The Hasidic Leadership: Authority and Faith in Zadicim* [sic] *as Reflected in the Hasidic Literature* [Hebrew]. Jerusalem: Bialik Institute, 1999.

———. *Ideological Trends of Hasidim in Poland during the Interwar Period and the Holocaust* [Hebrew]. Jerusalem: Bialik Institute, 1990.

———. *Studies in Bratslav Hasidism* [Hebrew]. Jerusalem: Bialik Institute, 1972.

Pilsudski, J. *The Memories of a Polish Revolutionary and Soldier.* Trans. D. R. Gillie. London: Faber & Faber, 1931. [Reprint ed. New York: AMS Press, 1971.]

Pinkas Hakehillot: Encyclopaedia of Jewish Communities, Poland. Vol. 2: *Eastern Galicia.* Ed. D. Domrovska, A. Wein, and A. Vais. Jerusalem: Yad Vashem, 1980.

Pinkus, B. *The Jews of the Soviet Union: The History of a National Minority.* Cambridge, UK: Cambridge University Press, 1988.

Pipe, S. Z. " Napoleon in Jewish Folklore." *YAJSS* 1 (1946), 294–304.

———. *Twelve Folktales from Sanok.* IFAPS 15. Ed. D. Noy. Haifa: Ethnological Museum and Folklore Archives, and Haifa Municipality, 1967.

Pipes, R. "Reflections on the Nationality Problems in the Soviet Union." In *Ethnicity: Theory and Experience* (453–465). Ed. N. Glazer and D. P. Moynihan. Cambridge, MA: Harvard University Press, 1975.

Pleins, J. D. "Poor, Poverty." *ABD* 5:402–414, 1992.

———. "Poverty in the Social World of the Wise." *JSOT* 37 (1987), 61–87.

Plokhy, S. *The Cossacks and Religion in Early Modern Ukraine.* Oxford, UK: Oxford University Press, 2001.

Poliva, A. "*Ḥamishah Shirim mi-pi Abba*" (Five songs my late father sang). *YA* 16, nos. 37–38 (1971), 84–85 (83–86).

Pollak, H. *Jewish Folkways in Germanic Lands (1648–1806): Studies in Aspects of Daily Life.* Cambridge, MA: MIT Press, 1971.

Polonsky, A., ed. "The Shtetl: Myth and Reality." Special issue, *Polin* 17 (2004), 3–409.

Pool, D. de Sola. *The Kaddish.* New York: Bloch, 1929. [Originally published 1909.]

Porten, B. "The Ideology of Totality-Frontality: The Literary and Contextual Continuity from P'sukei d'Zimra through Aleinu." *JJS* 53 (2002), 324–336.

———. "The Structure and Theme of the Solomon Narrative (1 Kings 3–11)." *HUCA* 37 (1967), 93–128.

Portmann, A., and R. Ritsema, eds. *The Realms of Colour / Die Welt der Farben / Le monde des couleurs.* Eranos 41. Leiden: Brill, 1974.

Posner, A., ed. *Law and Literature: A Misunderstood Relation.* Cambridge, MA: Harvard University Press, 1988.

Potichnyj, P. J., and H. Aster, eds. *Ukrainian-Jewish Relations in Historical Perspectives.* Edmonton, AB: Canadian Institute of Ukrainian Studies, University of Alberta, 1988.

Powell, C., and G. E. C. Paton, eds. *Humor in Society: Resistance and Control.* New York: St. Martin's Press, 1988.

Pradelles de Latour, C. H. " '*Le crâne qui parle*' *ou la réversibilité de la parole.*" In *D'un conte . . . a l'autre: la variabilité dans la literature orale.* (From one tale . . . to another: Variability in oral literature) (563–572). Ed. V. Görög-Karady and M. Chiche. Paris: Editions du Centre National de la Recherche Scientifique, 1990.

Präger, M., and S. Schmitz. *Jüdische Schwänke: Eine volkskundliche studie.* Wiesbaden, Germany: Rheinische Verlags-Anstalt, 1964. [Based on I. Olsvanger, *Rosinkess mit Mandlen.* Basel: Schweizerischen Gesellschaft für Volkskunde, 1924 (reprint ed).]

The *Precise Melodies of the Chabad Rebbes,* compact disc. Information available via niggun@netivision.net.il.

Preuss, J. *Biblical and Talmudic Medicine.* Trans. F. Rosner. New York: Sanhedrin Press, 1978. [Reprint ed. Northvale, NJ: Aronson, 1994; originally published 1911.]

Prilutski [Prilutzki; Prylucki], N. *Yidishe folkslider.* 2 vols. Warsaw: Bikher far ale and Nayer Ferlag, 1911–1913.

———. *Zamelbicher far Yidisher folklor, filologie, und kulturgeshichte.* Vol. 2. Warsaw: Nayer Ferlag, 1917.

———, and S. Lehman, eds. *Studies in Yiddish Philology, Literature and Ethnology* [Yiddish]. Warsaw: Nayer Farlag, 1926–1933.

Prince, G. "Meursault and Narrrative." In *Resonant Themes: Literature, History, and the Arts in Nineteenth- and Twentieth-Century Europe, Essays in Honor of Victor Brombert* (175–182). Ed. S. Haig. North Carolina Studies in the Romance Languages and Literatures 263. Chapel Hill: University of North Carolina Department of Romance Languages, 1999.

Propp, V. *Morphology of the Folktale.* 2nd rev. ed. Trans. L. Scott. American Folklore Society Bibliographical and Special Series 9. Indiana University Research Center in Anthropology, Folklore, and Linguistics Publication 10. Austin: University of Texas Press, 1968. [Originally published 1928.]

Prouser, J. H. *Noble Soul: The Life and Legend of the Vilna Ger Tzedek Count Walenty Potocki.* Judaism in Context 1. Piscataway, NJ: Gorgias Press, 2005.

Raba, J. *Between Remembrance and Denial: The Fate of the Jews in the Wars of the Polish Commonwealth during the Mid-Seventeenth Century as Shown in Contemporary Writings and Historical Research.* Boulder, CO: East European Monographs, 1995.

Rabach, E. "Had Gadya in Polish." *YB* 36 (1952), 370.

Rabbi, M. *Avoteinu Sipru: Sippurim u-ma'Assiyyot she-Nirshemu mi-Ziknei ha-Dor* (Our fathers told: Tales and stories that were written down from the elders). 3 vols. Jerusalem: Bakal, 1970–1975.

Rabinovitch, A. Z. *Zikhronot Glikl* (Glikl's memoirs). Tel Aviv: Devir, 1929.

Rabinowicz, H. "Dietary Laws." *EJ* 6:26–45, 1971.

Rabinowitsch, W. Z. *Lithuanian Hasidism.* Trans. M. B. Dagut. New York: Schocken, 1971.

Rabinowitz, H. R. *Portraits of Jewish Preachers* [Hebrew]. Jerusalem: Mass, 1967.

Rabinowitz, L. I. "*Gemilut Hasadim.*" *EJ* 7:374–376, 1971.

———. "Onkelos and Aquila." *EJ* 12:1405–1406, 1971.

Rabinowitz, M. Z. *Ha-Maggid mi-Kozienice: Ḥayav ve-Torato* (The preacher of Kozienice: His life and his teaching). Tel Aviv: Irgun "Tevunah" with the assistance of Mossad Harav Kook, 1947.

———. "*Sepher Ha-Ma'asim Livnei Erez-Yisra'el*—New Fragments" [Hebrew]. *Tarbiz* 41 (1972), 275–305.

Radin, P. *The Trickster: A Study in American Indian Mythology.* New York: Philosophical Library, 1956.

Radzinsky, E. *Stalin: The First In-Depth Biography Based on Explosive New Documents from Russia's Secret Archives.* Trans. H. T. Willetts. New York: Doubleday, 1996.

Raisin, J. S. *The Haskalah Movement in Russia.* Philadelphia: Jewish Publication Society of America, 1913.

Ran, L., ed. *Jerusalem of Lithuania: Illustrated and Documented.* 2 vols. New York: Vilno Album Committee, 1974. [Tri-language edition.]

Randolph, V. "Bedtime Stories from Missouri." *WF* 10 (1951), 1–10.
———, ed. *Ozark Folksongs*. Ed. F. C. Shoemaker and F. G. Emberson. 4 vols. Columbia, MO: State Historical Society of Missouri, 1946–1950.
———. *Who Blowed Up the Church House and Other Ozark Folk Tales*. New York: Columbia University Press, 1952.
Ranke, K. "*Blutegelkur* (AaTh 1349N*)." *EM* 2:522–523, 1978.
———. "*Brot des Bettlers* (AaTh 837)." *EM* 2:813–816, 1978.
———. "*Brüder: Die behenden B* (AaTh 654)." *EM* 2:868–871, 1978.
———, ed. *European Anecdotes and Jests*. Trans. T. Buck. European Folklore Series 4. Copenhagen: Rosenkilde & Bagger, 1972.
———. *Die Zwei Brüder, eine Studie zur Vergleichenden Märchenforschung*. FFC 114. Helsinki: Suomalainen Tiedeakatemia, 1934.
Raphael [Werfel], Y. [I]. *Ha-Ḥasidut ve-Eretz-Israel* (Hasidism and the land of Israel). Jerusalem: Eretz-Israel Publishing, 1940.
———. *Al Ḥasidut ve-Ḥasidim* (On Hasidism and Hasidim). Jerusalem: Mossad Harav Kook, 1991.
———. *Sasov: Matzevah le-Ayyarati* (Sasov: A monument for my shtetl). Jerusalem: Bamishor, 1946.
———. *Sefer ha-Ḥasidut* (The book of Hasidism). Tel Aviv: Tziony, 1955.
Rapoport-Albert, A. "Hasidism after 1772: Structural Continuity and Change." In *Hasidism Reappraised* (76–140). Ed. A Rapoport-Albert. London: Littman Library of Jewish Civilization, 1996.
———. "On Women in Hasidism, S. A. Horodecky, and the Maid of Ludmir Tradition." In *Jewish History: Essays in Honour of Chimen Abramsky* (495–525). Ed. A. Rapoport-Albert and S. J. Zipperstein. London: Halban, 1988. [Reprinted in *Zaddik and Devotees: Historical and Sociological Aspects of Hasidism* (496–527). Ed. D. Assaf. Jerusalem: Zalman Shazar Center for Jewish History, 2001 (rev. ed.; Hebrew).]
Ratzaby, Y., ed. *R. Jehoshua Hannagid Responsa* [Hebrew]. Kiryat Ono, Israel: Makhont Mishnat ha-Rambam, 1988 or 1989.
Rawnitzki, J. C. *Yidishe Witzn* (Jewish wit) [Yiddish]. 2nd ed. 2 vols. New York: Sklarsky, 1950.
Rayfield, D. *Stalin and His Hangmen: An Authoritative Portrait of a Tyrant and Those Who Served Him*. New York: Viking, 2004.
Read, C., ed. *The Stalin Years: A Reader*. New York: Palgrave Macmillan, 2003.
Rechtman, A. *Jewish Ethnography and Folklore* [Yiddish]. Buenos Aires: Yiddish Scientific Institute—IWO in Argentina, 1958.
Reder, R. *Belzec*. Trans. M. Jacobs. 2nd ed. Krakow: Fundacja Judaica, Panstwowe Muzeum Oswiecim-Brzezinka, 1999.
Reicher, M. M. *Shaʻarei Yerushalyim* (The gates of Jerusalem). Warsaw, 1879.
Reik, T. *Ritual: Four Psychoanalytical Studies*. Trans. D. Bryan. New York: Grove Press, 1946.
Reimer, A. M. "Rescuing the Fallen Angels: The Case of the Disappearing Angels of Qumran." *DSD* 7 (2000), 334–353.
Reinhard, J. R. "The Literary Background of the Chantefable." *Speculum* 1 (1926), 157–169.
Reventlow, H. G., and Y. Hoffman, eds. *Justice and Righteousness: Biblical Themes and Their Influence*. *JSOTSS* 137 (1992).

Rheinheimer, M. *Arme, Bettler und Vavanten: Überleben in der Not 1450–1850. Europäische Geschichte.* Frankfurt am Main: Fischer, 2000.

Riccardi, T., Jr., ed. and trans. *A Nepali Version of the Vetâlapañcavimsati.* American Oriental Series 54. New Haven, CT: American Oriental Society, 1971.

Richman, J. *Jewish Wit and Wisdom: Examples of Jewish Anecdotes, Folk Tales, Bon Mots, Magic, Riddles and Enigmas Since the Canonization of the Bible.* New York: Pardes, 1952.

———. *Laughs from Jewish Lore.* New York: Funk & Wagnalls, 1926.

Ringelblum, E. "Samuel Zbitkower: An Economic and Social Leader in Poland at the Time of the Partition" [Hebrew]. *Zion* 3 (1938), 246–266, 337–355.

Rivkind, I. *The Fight against Gambling among the Jews: A Study of Five Centuries of Jewish Poetry and Cultural History* [Yiddish]. New York: Yiddish Scientific Institute—YIVO, 1946.

Robeson, P. *Songs of Free Men: A Paul Robeson Recital*, compact disc. Sony Classical and Masterwords Heritage MHK 63223.

Rockett, R. L. *Ethnic Minorities in the Soviet Union: Sociological Perspectives on a Historical Problem.* New York: Praeger, 1981.

Rodkinson, M. L. *Sefer 'Adat Tsadikim: Ve-hu Sipurei Nora'ot ve-Nifla'ot me-Adon 'Uzenu . . . ha-Besht ha-Kadosh asher lo Huv'u be-Shivhe ha-Besht . . . ve-'Od Nosfu la-Zeh Sipurim Amitim* (The congregation of the holy people: It is the telling of the awesome wonders of our powerful master, the Holy Besht, which were not included in *In Praise of the Baal Shem Tov*, to which other true stories were added). Lemberg, Ukraine: Stand, 1964. [Originally published 1864.]

Rogal, S. J. *A William Somerset Maugham Encyclopedia.* Westport, CT: Greenwood Press, 1997.

Rohrbacher-Sticker, C. "From Sense to Nonsense: From Incantation Prayer to Magical Spell." *JSQ* 3 (1996), 24–46.

Röhrich, L. "Dämon." *EM* 3:223–237, 1979.

———. *Erzählungen der späten Mittelalters und ihr Weiterleben in Literatur und Volksdichtung bis zur Gegenwart: Sagen, Märchen, Exempel und Schwänke.* Bern and Munich: Franke Verlag, 1962–1967.

———, and R. W. Brednich, eds. *Deutsche Volkslieder: Texte und Melodien.* 4. vols. Düsseldorf: Pädagogischer Verlag Schwann, 1965.

Roitman, E. "*Der tokh fun der khelemer mayseh*" (The essence of the tales of Chelm). In *Yizkor Book in Memory of Chelem* (571–576). Ed. S. Kanc and M. Grinberg. N.p.: Irgun Yots'ei Ḥelem be-Yisrael uve-Artson ha-Brit, 1980 or 1981.

Roke'aḥ, M. *Ma'aseh Roke'aḥ.* Venice, 1734.

Rölleke, H. "Das Exempel vom undankbaren Sohn (KHM78/AT980B) in einer Fassung Moscheroschs von 1643." *Fabula* 14 (1973), 237–242.

———. *Grimms Märchen und ihre Quellen: Die literarischen Vorlagen der Grimmschen Märchen synoptisch vorgestellt und kommentiert.* Schriftenrehihe Literaturwissenschaft 35. Trier, Germany: WVT Wissenschaftlicher Verlag Trier, 1998.

———. "Die Volksballade von der Wiedervergeltung (DVldr Nr. 123) bei Hans Michael Moscherosch." *JVL* 18 (1973), 71–76.

Rombauts, E., and A. Welkenhusen A., eds. *Aspects of the Medieval Animal Epic: Proceedings of the International Conference, Louvain, May 15–17, 1972.* Louvain, Belgium: University Press; The Hague: Martinus Nijhoff, 1975.

Roques, M. *Aucassin et Nicolette: Chantefable du XIII siècle.* Paris: Champion, 1954.

———. *Le Roman de Renart: Branche X Renart et le Vilain Lietard.* Trans. J. Dufournet. Paris: Champion, 1989.
Rosenberg, R. "The Concept of Biblical 'Belial.' " *8th WCJS* 1 (1982), 35–40.
Rosenfeld, M. N. *The Book of Cows: A Facsimile Edition of the Famed Kuhbukh Verona 1595.* London: Hebraica, 1984.
Rosenson, I. "The *Aleinu* Prayer—Legends about Its Early Composer" [Hebrew]. *MH* 20 (2001), 74–86.
Rosenthal, F. *Humor in Early Islam.* Philadelphia: University of Pennsylvania Press, 1956.
Roskies, D. G. "Ansky Lives!" *JFER* 14, 1–2 (1992), 66–69.
———. *A Bridge of Longing: The Lost Art of Yiddish Storytelling.* Cambridge, MA: Harvard University Press, 1995.
———. "S. Ansky and the Paradigm of Return." In *The Uses of Tradition: Jewish Continuity in the Modern Era* (243–260). Ed. J. Wertheimer. New York: Jewish Theological Seminary of America, 1992.
Rosman, M. J. *Founder of Hasidism: A Quest for the Historical Ba'al Shem Tov.* Berkeley: University of California Press, 1996.
———. *The Lord's Jews: Magnet-Jewish Relations in the Polish-Lithuanian Commonwealth during the Eighteenth Century.* Harvard Judaic Texts and Studies 7. Harvard Ukrainian Research Institute Monograph Series. Cambridge, MA: Harvard University Press, 1990.
———. "In Praise of the Ba'al Shem Tov: A User's Guide to the Editions of *Shivḥei ha Besht.*" *Polin* 10 (1997), 183–199.
———. "The Relationship between the Jewish Lessee (*Arendarz*) and the Polish Nobleman: The Other Side" [Hebrew]. In *Jews in Economic Life: Collected Essays in Memory of Arkadius Kahan (1920–1982)* (237–244). Ed. N. Gross. Jerusalem: Zalman Shazar Center, 1985.
Rosten, L. *The Joys of Yiddish.* New York: McGraw-Hill, 1968.
Rostworowski, K. H. "*Niespodzianka*" (Surprise). In *Dramaty Wybrane* (2:5–100). Krakow, Poland: Wydawnictwo Literckie, 1967.
Roth, A. N. T. "*Sanegoria al Hakhmei Ḥelem*" (A defense for the wiseacres of Chelm). *Yeda 'Am* 2 (1954), 164.
Roth, A. Z. N. "*Azkarah, Haftarah ve-Kaddish Yatom*" (Memorial prayer, haftarah and an orphan's Kaddish). *Talpioth* 7 (1961), 369–381.
Roth, E. "*Das Wormser Machsor.*" In *Die alte Synagoge zu Worms* (217–228). Ed. E. Ro?th, G. Illert, and Ro?th H. Lamm. Frankfurt am Main: Ner Tamid, 1961.
Rothert, O. A. *The Outlaws of Cave-in-Rock: Historical Accounts of the Famous Highwayman and River Pirates Who Operated in Pioneer Days upon the Ohio and Mississippi Rivers and over the Old Natchez Trace.* Cleveland, OH: Clark, 1924. [Reprint ed. Carbondale: Southern Illinois University Press, 1996.]
Rothschild, J. *Pilsudski's Coup d'Etat.* New York: Columbia University Press, 1966.
Rubenstein, J. L. *The History of Sukkot in the Second Temple and Rabbinic Periods.* Brown Judaic Studies 302. Atlanta: Scholars Press, 1995.
Rubin, N. *The End of Life*: *Rites of Burial and Mourning in the Talmud and Midrash* [Hebrew]. Tel Aviv: Hakkibutz Hameuchad, 1997.
Rubin, R. "Y. L. Cahan and Jewish Folklore." *NYFQ* 11 (1955), 34–45.
Rubinstein, A., ed. *In Praise of the Ba'al Shem Tov [Shivhei ha-Besht]* [Hebrew]. Jerusalem: Rubin Mass, 1991.
———. "Kozienice, Israel ben Shabbetai Hapstein." *EJ* 10:1234–1235, 1971.

———. "Levi Isaac ben Meir of Berdichev." *EJ* 11:102–104, 1971.

———. "Notes on a Collection of Testimonies against Hasidism" [Hebrew]. *Tarbiz* 32 (1963), 80–97.

Rucker, L. *Staline, Israël et les Juifs*. Paris: Presses Universitaires de France, 2001.

Rugoff, M. *A Harvest of World Folk Tales*. New York: Viking Press, 1968. [Originally published 1949.]

Runte, H. R., J. K. Wikeley, and A. J. Farrell, eds. *The Seven Sages of Rome and the Book of Sindbad: An Annotated Bibliography*. Garland Reference Library of the Humanities 387. New York: Garland, 1984.

Rush, B. *The Book of Jewish Women's Tales*. Northvale, NJ: Aronson, 1994.

———, and E. Marcus, eds. *Seventy and One Tales for the Jewish Year: Folk Tales for the Festivals*. New York: A.Z.Y.F., 1980.

Russell, D. S. *The Method and Message of Jewish Apocalyptic, 200 BC–AD 100*. The Old Testament Library. Philadelphia: Westminster Press, 1974. [Originally published SCM Press, 1964.]

Russell, I. " 'My Dear, Dear Friends': The Parodic Sermon in Oral Tradition." In *Spoken in Jest* (237–256). Ed. G. Bennett. Sheffield, UK: Sheffield Academic Press, 1991.

Sacchetti, F. *Il Trecentonovelle*. Florence: Sansoni, 1984. [Written 1392–c. 1397.]

Sacks, M. P., and J. G. Pankhurst, eds. *Understanding Soviet Society*. Boston: Unwin Hyman, 1988.

Sadan, D. "*Aggadut Ḥuldah ve-Bor*" (The legend of the weasel and the well). *Molad* 15 (1957–1958), 367–381, 467–476.

———. *Ka'arat Egozim o Elef Bediḥah u-Bhdiḥah: Asufat Homor be-Israel* (A bowl of nuts or a thousand and one jokes: An anthology of Jewish humor). Tel Aviv: Neuman, 1953.

———. *Ka'arat Tsimmukim o Elef Bediḥah u-Bhdiḥah: Asufat Homor be-Israel* (A bowl of raisins or a thousand and one jokes: An anthology of Jewish humor). Tel Aviv: Neuman, 1952.

———. "The Midrashic Background of 'The Paradise' and Its Implications for the Evaluation of the Cambridge Yiddish Codex (1382)." In *The Field of Yiddish II* (253–262). Ed. U. Weinreich. The Hague: Mouton, 1965.

Safrai, S. R. *Akiva ben Yosef: Ḥayav u-Mishnato* (Rabbi Akiba ben Joseph: His life and his teaching). Jerusalem: Bialik Institute, 1970.

———, M. Stern, D. Flusser, and W. C. van Unnik, eds. *The Jewish People in the First Century: Historical Geography, Political History, Social, Cultural and Religious Life and Institutions*. Compendia Rerum Iudaicarum ad Novum Testamentum Assen. 2 vols. Amsterdam: Van Gorcum, 1976.

Safran, G. "Timeline: Semyon Akimovich An-Sky / Shloyme-Zanvel Rappoport." In *The Worlds of S. An-Sky: A Russian Jewish Intellectual at the Turn of the Century* (xv–xxix). Ed. G. Safran and S. J. Zipperstein. Stanford, CA: Stanford University Press, 2006.

———, and S. J. Zipperstein, eds. *The Worlds of S. An-Sky: A Russian Jewish Intellectual at the Turn of the Century*. Stanford, CA.: Stanford University Press, 2006.

Safrin, H. *Przy Szabasowych Świecach Wieczór Drugi Anegdoty i Przysłowia Żydowskie* (By the light of the Sabbath candles: A second evening. Jewish anecdotes and proverbs). Lodz, Poland: Wydawnictwo Lodzkie, 1988.

Samuel, E. "Dowry and Dowry Harassment in India: An Assessment Based on Modified Capitalist Patriarchy." *A&AS* 1, no. 3 (2002), 187–229.

Sand, I. Z. "A Linguistic Comparison of Five Versions of the Mayse Bukh (16th–18th Centuries)." In *The Field of Yiddish II* (24–48). Ed. U. Weinreich. The Hague: Mouton, 1965.

Sanderson, W. *A Compleat History of the Lives and Reigns of Mary Queen of Scotland, and of Her Son and Successor, James the Sixth, King of Scotland*. London: Printed for Humphrey Moseley, Richard Tomlins, and George Sawbridge, 1656.

Sandrow, N. *Vagabond Stars: A World History of Yiddish Theater*. New York: Harper & Row, 1977.

Saperstein, M. *Jewish Preaching 1200–1800: An Anthology*. Yale Judaica Series 26. New Haven, CT: Yale University Press, 1989.

———. *"Your Voice Like a Ram's Horn": Themes and Texts in Traditional Jewish Preaching*. Monographs of the Hebrew Union College 18. Cincinnati: Hebrew Union College Press, 1996.

Sapir-Abulafia, A. "Twelfth-Century Christian Expectations of Jewish Conversion: A Case Study of Peter of Blois." *Aschkenas* 8 (1998), 45–70.

Sarna, J. D. "The Myth of No Return: Jewish Return Migration to Eastern Europe, 1881–1914." *AJH* 71 (1981), 256–268. [Reprinted in *East European Jews in America, 1880–1920: Immigration and Adaptation* (3:169–181). Ed. J. S. Gurock. New York: Routledge, 1998.]

Sarnowski, J. "Things Exist in You without Your Knowing It: Robert Penn Warren's 'The Ballad of Billie Potts' as a Conglomeration of Myth and Folklore." *KR* 14 (1998), 28–37.

Satlow, M. L. *Jewish Marriage in Antiquity*. Princeton, NJ, and Oxford, UK: Princeton University Press, 2001.

Savran, G. W. *Telling and Retelling: Quotation in Biblical Narrative*. Indiana Studies in Biblical Literature. Bloomington: Indiana University Press, 1988.

Schäfer, J. *Kurt Gerstein—Zeuge des Holocaust: Ein Leben zwischen Bibelkreisen und SS*. Beiträge zur Westfälischen Kirchengeschichte 16. Bielefeld: Luther-Verlag, 1999.

Schatz-Uffenheimer, R. *Maggid Devarav Le-Ya'akov or The Maggid Dov Baer of Mezhirech* [Hebrew]. Jerusalem: Magnes Press, 1990.

———. *Quietistic Elements in 18th-Century Hasidic Thought* [Hebrew]. Jerusalem: Magnes Press, 1968.

Scheiber, A. *Essays on Jewish Folklore and Comparative Literature*. Budapest: Akadémiai Kiadó, 1985.

Schenda, R. "*Philippe le Picard und seine Nouvelle Fabrique, eine Studie zur französische Wunderliterature des 16. Jahrhunderts*." *Zeitschrift für französische Sprache und Literatur* 68 (1958), 43–61.

Scheppele, K. L., ed. "Legal Storytelling." *MLR* 87 (1989), 2073–2496.

Scherf, W. *Das Märchenlexikon*. 2 vols. Munich: Beck, 1995.

Scherman, N. *The Kaddish Prayer*. Brooklyn: Mesorah, 1980.

Schiffman, L. H. "The Conversion of the Royal House of Adiabene in Josephus and Rabbinic Sources." In *Josephus, Judaism, and Christianity* (293–312). Ed. L. H. Feldman and G. Hata. Detroit: Wayne State University Press, 1987.

———. *Reclaiming the Dead Sea Scrolls: The History of Judaism, the Background of Christianity, the Lost Library of Qumran*. Philadelphia: Jewish Publication Society, 1994.

Schirmann, J., ed. *Ha-Shirah ha-'Ivrit bi-Sefarad uvi-Provans: Mivhar shirim ve-sipurim mehorazim* (Hebrew poetry in Spain and in Provence: A selection of poems and rhymed narratives). 2 vols. Jerusalem: Bialik Institute, 1954–1956.

Schleifer, R., and R. Markley, eds. *Kierkegaard and Literature: Irony, Repetition, and Criticism*. Norman: University of Oklahoma, 1984.

Schmidl, E. A. *Juden in der K. (und) K. Armee 1788–1918: Jews in the Hubsburg Armed Forces*. Studia Judaica Austriaca 11. Eisenstadt, Austria: Österreichisches Jüdisches Museum, 1989.

Schmidt, H., and P. Kahle, eds. *Volkserzählungen aus Palästina: Gesammelt bei den Bauern von Bir-Zet und in Verbindung. Forschungen zur Religion und Literatur des Alten und Neuen Testaments*. Göttingen, Germany: Vandenhoeck und Ruprecht, 1918–1930.

Schmidt, L. *"Zu der Ballade 'die Mordeletern.'" DV* 34 (1932), 116–117.

Schmitt, C. *"Lieb wie das Salz* (AaTh 923)." *EM* 8:1038–1042, 1996.

Schmitt, J. C. *Ghosts in the Middle Ages: The Living and the Dead in Medieval Society*. Trans. T. L. Fagan. Chicago: University of Chicago Press, 1998.

Schneur Zalman of Liadi. *Likkutei Amarim First Versions (Based on Earliest Manuscripts)*. 2nd ed. Brooklyn: "Kehot," 1981.

———. *Likutei Amarim (Tanya)*. Trans. N. Mindel. 4th ed. Brooklyn: "Kehot" Publication Society, 1972. [Bilingual ed. London: "Kehot" and Soncino, 1973.]

Schoentjes, P. *Poétique de l'ironie*. Paris: Éditions du Seuil, 2001.

Schoeps, J. H. *Deutsch-Jüdische Symbiose Oder die Mißglückte Emanzipation*. Berlin: Philo, 1996.

Scholem [Shalom], G. "Ba'al Shem." *EJ* 4:5–7, 1971.

———. "Bilar (Bilad, Bilid, BEIAR) the King of the Demons." *Mada'ei ha-Yahadut* 1 (1926), 112–127.

———. "Colors and Their Symbolism in Jewish Tradition and Mysticism." *Diogenes* 108 (1979), 84–111. [Originally published as "Farben und ihre Symbolik in der jüdischen Überlieferung und Mystik." In *The Realms of Colour / Die Welt der Farben / Le monde des couleurs*. Eranos (41:1–49). Ed. A. Portmann and R. Ritsema. Leiden: Brill, 1974.]

———. "*Demuto ha-Historit Shel R. Yisrael Ba'al Shem Tov*" (The historical image of Israel Ba'al Shem Tov). *Molad* 18 (1960), 335–356.

———. "Gematria." *EJ* 7:369–374, 1971.

———. "*Havdala De-Rabbi 'Aqiva*—A Source for the Tradition of Jewish Magic during the Geonic Period" [Hebrew]. *Tarbiz* 50 (1980–1981), 243–281.

———. *The Messianic Idea in Judaism and Other Essays on Jewish Spirituality*. New York: Schocken, 1971.

———. *Origins of the Kabbalah*. Ed. R. J. Z. Werblowsky. Trans. A. Arkush. Philadelphia: Jewish Publication Society, 1987.

———. "*Shekhinah*: The Feminine Element in Divinity." In *On the Mystical Shape of the Godhead: Basic Concepts in the Kabbalah* (140–196). Ed. J. Chipman. Trans. J. Neugroschel. New York: Schocken, 1991.

Schöne, A. "*Lebenszeiten des Menschen* (AaTh173, 828)." *EM* 8:842–846, 1996.

Schram, P. *Jewish Stories One Generation Tells Another*. Northvale, NJ: Aronson, 1987.

———. *Stories within Stories: From the Jewish Oral Tradition*. Northvale, NJ: Aronson, 2000.

———. *Tales of Elijah the Prophet*. Northvale, NJ: Aronson, 1991.

Schrire, T. *Hebrew Magical Amulets: Their Decipherment and Interpretation*. London: Routledge & Paul, 1966. [Reprint ed. New York: Behrman, 1982.]

Schullerus, A. *Verzeichnis der Rumanischen Marchen und Marchenvarianten, nach dem System der Marchentypen Antti Aarne*. FFC 78. Helsinki: Suomalainen Tiedeakatemia, 1928.

Schumacher, A. *D'Ganshiadarin*. Vienna, 1833.

Schussman, A. "Abraham's Visits to Ishmael—The Jewish Origins and Orientation" [Hebrew]. *Tarbiz* 49 (1980), 325–345.

Schwadron, A. A. "*Un Cavritico*: The Sephardic Tradition." *JJML* 5 (1982), 24–39.

———. *Chad Gadya [One Kid]*, vinyl recording. Smithsonian Folkways Recordings FR8920.

———. " 'Khad Gadya'—The Italian Traditions." In *9th WCJS* 2 (1986), 257–264.

Schwartz, D. *Studies on Astral Magic in Medieval Jewish Thought*. Trans. D. Louvish and B. Stein. Brill Reference Library of Judaism. Leiden: Brill, 2005.

Schwartz, H. *Lilith's Cave: Jewish Tales of the Supernatural*. San Francisco: Harper & Row, 1988.

———. *Tree of Souls: The Mythology of Judaism*. Oxford, UK: Oxford University Press, 2004.

Schwartzfuchs, S. *Napoleon, the Jews and the Sanhedrin*. London: Routledge & Kegan Paul, 1979.

———. "Rothschild." *EJ* 14:334–340, 1971.

Schwarzbaum, H. "Aesopic Fables in the Talmudic Midrashic Folk-Literature" [Hebrew]. *Yeda-'Am* 8, no. 26 (1962), 54–56.

———. "*Badḥanim ve-Leitzim Mefursamim be-Yisrael*" (Famous Jewish jokers and pranksters). *Maḥanayim* 67 (1962), 57–63.

———. "International Folklore Motifs in Petrus Alfonsi's '*Disciplina Clericalis*.' " *Sefarad* 21 (1961), 267–99; 22 (1962), 17–59, 321–344; 23 (1963), 54–73. [Reprinted in Schwarzbaum, *Jewish Folklore between East and West* (239–358).]

———. *Jewish Folklore between East and West: Collected Papers*. Ed. E. Yassif. Beersheva, Israel: Ben-Gurion University of the Negev Press, 1989.

———. "Jewish and Moslem Versions of Some Theodicy Legends." *Fabula* 3 (1959), 119–169. [Reprinted in Schwarzbaum, *Jewish Folklore between East and West* (75–125).]

———. *The Mishle Shu'alim (Fox Fables) of Rabbi Berechiah ha-Nakdan: A Study in Comparative Folklore and Fable Lore*. Kiron, Israel: Institute for Jewish and Arab Folklore Research, 1979.

———. "Review of 'Aarne, Anti and Thompson, Stith, *The Types of the Folktale: A Classification and Bibliography*.' " 2nd ed. FFC 184. Helsinki: Academia Scientiarum Fennica, 1963.

———. *Studies in Jewish and World Folklore*. *Fabula* Suppl. B, 3 (1968).

———. "The Zoological Tinged Stages of Man's Existence (AT 173 & 828)." In *Folklore Research Center Studies* (267–290). Vol. 3. Ed. I. Ben-Ami. Jerusalem: Magnes, 1972. [Reprinted in Schwarzbaum, *Jewish Folklore between East and West* (215–238).]

Schweig, B. "Mirror." *Antiquity* 15 (1941), 257–268.

Scott, R. B. Y. "The Expectation of Elija." *CJRT* 3 (1926), 490–502.

Seaton, A. *The Horsemen of the Steppes: The Story of the Cossacks*. New York: Hippocrene, 1985.

Seaton, B. "Considering the Lilies: Ruskin's 'Proserpina' and Other Victorian Flower Books." *VS* 28 (1985), 256–282.
———. "The Flower Language Books of the Nineteenth Century." *MAQ* 16 (1980), 1–11.
———. "French Flower Books of the Early Nineteenth Century." *NCFS* 11 (1982), 60–71.
———. *The Language of Flowers: A History.* Charlottesville: University Press of Virginia, 1995.
———. "A Nineteenth-Century Metalanguage: La Langage des Fleurs." *Semiotica* 57 (1985), 73–56.
Segal, B. V. "Abderiten von Heute unter den Juden." *Am Urquell* 3 (1892), 28–29.
———. "Der König und seine vier Söhne." *ZÖV* 9 (1903), 243–245.
———. "Materialy do etnografii Żydów." *Zbiór wiadomosci do antropologii Krajowej* 17 (1893), 261–332.
——— [Bar Ami]. "Eliah der Prophet: Eine Studie zur jüdischen Volks-und Sagenkunde." *Ost und West* (1904), 477–488, 675–680, 807–812.
———. "Aus der jüdischen Sagen u. Märchen Welt." *Ost und West* (1905), 353–355.
Seki, K. *Folktales of Japan.* Trans. R. J. Adams. Folktales of the World. Chicago: University of Chicago Press, 1963.
Sela, M. "Ḥelem ve-Ḥakhameha" (The wise men of Chelm). In *Yizkor Book in Memory of Chelem* (567–570). Ed. S. Kanc and M. Grinberg. N.p.: Irgun Yots'ei Ḥelem be-Yisrael uve-Artson ha-Brit, 1980 or 1981.
Sela, S. *Abraham ibn Ezra and the Rise of Medieval Hebrew Science.* Brill's Series in Jewish Studies 32. Leiden: Brill, 2003.
———. *Astrology and Biblical Exegesis in Abraham ibn Ezra's Thought* [Hebrew]. Ramat Gan, Israel: Bar-Ilan University Press, 1999.
Seri, R. *The Holy Amulet: Twelve Jewish-Yemenite Folktales.* IFAPS 21. Ed. A. Shenhar. Haifa: Ethnological Museum and Folklore Archives, 1968.
Seymour, St. John D. *Tales of King Solomon.* London: Oxford University Press, 1924.
Sfard, D. *Studia i szkice* (Studies and notes). Warsaw: Idisz Buch, 1955.
Shapira, A. *Midrash Aseret ha-Dibrot (A Midrash on the Ten Commandments): Text, Sources and Interpretation* [Hebrew]. Jerusalem: Bialik Institute, 2005.
Shapiro, Z. R. "Fables in Jewish Writings: A Perspective on the Social, Moral and Ethical Lessons of Animals in Literature." Unpublished thesis. Cinncinati, OH: Hebrew Union College, 1997.
Sharot, S. *Messianism, Mysticism, and Magic: A Sociological Analysis of Jewish Religious Movements.* Chapel Hill: University of North Carolina Press, 1982.
Sharvit, U. *Chassidic Tunes from Galicia* [English and Hebrew]. Jerusalem: Renanot, 1995.
Shatzki, J. "S. Ansky, der folklorist." In *Vitbesk Amol: Geshikhte, zikhroynes, ḥurban* (Vitbesk yesterday: History, memories, and destruction) (263–274). Ed. G. Aronson, Y. Leshtsinki, and A. Kihn. New York: n.p., 1956.
———. "S. Ansky, der Meshulah fun folklore" (S. An-Sky, the emissary of folklore). *JBA* 9 (1950–1951), 113–119.
Shazar, S. Z. "Defenders of the City." In *The Golden Tradition: Jewish Life and Thought in Eastern Europe* (383–388). Ed. L. S. Dawidowicz. New York: Holt Reinhart & Winston, 1967.
Shenhar, A. "The Jewish Oicotype of the *Predestined Marriage* Folktale: AaTh 930*E (IFA)." *Fabula* 24 (1983), 43–55.

Shenhar, A., ed. *A Tale for Each Month: 1973*. IFAPS 32. Haifa: Ethnological Museum and Folklore Archives, 1974.

Shenhar, A., and H. Bar-Itzhak. *Sippurei 'Am me-Bet-She'an* (Folktales from Bet She'an). Haifa: Haifa University Press, 1981.

Sherman, E. *Hershele Ostropoler: Amza'otav ve-Ta'alulav, Bediḥotav ve-Halatsotav, Toldotav ve-Harpatka'otav* (Hershele Ostropoler: His tricks and pranks, his jokes and wits, his biography and his adventures). Trans. M. Harizman. Tel Aviv: "Le-ma'an ha-sefer," 1930.

Sherwin, B. L. "Original Sin: Is It Sufficient for Us?" *Mo'ed* 13 (2003), 22–32.

———. "Theodicy." In *Contemporary Jewish Religious Thought: Original Essays on Critical Concepts, Movements and Beliefs* (959–970). Ed. A. A. Cohen and P. Mendes-Flohr. New York: Scribner's, 1987.

Shields, K., Jr. "Indo-European Basic Colour Terms." *CJL* 24 (1979), 142–146.

Shinan, A. " 'The Chronicle of Moses'—The Genre, Time, Sources and Literary Nature of a Medieval Hebrew Story" [Hebrew]. *S/L* 24 (1977), 100–116.

Shmeruk [Szmeruk], C. [K.] "Can the Cambridge Manuscript Support the Spielman Theory of Yiddish Literature?" In *Studies in Yiddish Literature and Folklore* (1–36). Research Project of the Institute of Jewish Studies, Monograph Series 7. Ed. C. Turniansky. Jerusalem: Hebrew University, 1986.

———. "The Hasidic Movement and the 'Arendars' " [Hebrew]. *Zion* 35 (1970), 182–192.

———. "Tales about R' Adam Ba'al Shem in the Versions of *Shibkhei Ha'Besht*" [Hebrew]. *Zion* 28 (1963), 86–105.

———. *Yiddish Literature: Aspects of Its History* [Hebrew]. Literature, Meaning, Culture 5. Tel Aviv: The Porter Institute for Poetics & Semiotics, Tel Aviv University, 1978.

———. *Yiddish Literature in Poland: Historical Studies and Perspectives* [Hebrew]. Jerusalem: The Magnes Press, 1981.

———. "Yiddish Prints in Italy" [Hebrew]. *Italya* 3 (1982), 112–175.

———, and E. Timm, eds. *Paris un' Viena* [Hebrew and Yiddish]. Publications of the Israel Academy of Sciences and Humanities, Section of Humanities. Jerusalem: Israel Academy of Sciences and Humanities, 1996.

Shojaei Kawan, C. "Contemporary Legend Research in German-Speaking Countries." *Folklore* 106 (1995), 103–110.

Sholem Aleichem. *Ale verk fun Sholem Aleykhem* (Collected works of Sholem Aleykhem). 28 vols. New York: Moryn-Fraheyt, 1937. [Author is also known as Sholem-Aleykhem and Shalom Rabinovitz.]

———. *"Ven ikh bin Roytshild"* (If I were Rothschild). Odessa: Ferlag M. Kaplan, 1919.

Shtern, M. *Hershele Ostropoler un Motke Habad: Zeyere anekdoten, vitzen, stzenes un shtukes naye-be'abeytet* (Hershele Ostropoler and Motke Habad: Their anecdotes, jokes, scenes and pranks, newly worked-out). N.p.: Star Hebrew., n.d.

Shulman, E. " *'Ikesh u-ptaltol*" (Stubborn and twisted). *Ha-Shaḥar* 4 (1873), 281–293.

Shulvass, M. A. *From East to West: The Westward Migration of Jews from Eastern Europe during the Seventeenth and Eighteenth Centuries*. Detroit: Wayne State University Press, 1971.

S[human], A. M. *Dos Freylikhe Hershele Ostropolier: Oder der volveler teater shtik. Do verd dertzehlt azelkhe sheyne ertzehlungen fun dem beruhmten Hershele Ostropolier, velkhe zenen biz yetzt nokh nisht gedrukt un di lezer fun dem bikhel velen groys fergnigen hoben, azoy az zay velen nisht darfen afilu in keyn teater gehn* (The merry

Hershele Ostropoler: Or the cheap theatrical piece. Here are told such nice tales of the famous Hershele Ostropoler, which were not printed until now, and the reader of the booklet will have such a pleasure, that he will not even have to go to any theater). Warsaw, 1893.

Silberstein, J. L., and R. L. Cohn, eds. *The Other in Jewish Thought and History: Construction of Jewish Culture and Identity.* New York: New York University Press, 1994.

Silverstone, A. E. *Aquila and Onkelos.* Semitic Language Series 1. Manchester, UK: University Press of Manchester, 1931.

Simar, M. A., trans. *Tales of Parrot by Ziya' U'D-Din Nakhshabi: The Cleveland Museum of Art's Tuti-Nama.* Cleveland, OH: Cleveland Museum of Art, 1978.

Simon, S. *The Wise Men of Helm and Their Merry Tales.* Trans. B. Bengal and D. Simon. New York: Behrman House, 1945.

Simpson, J. R. *Animal Body, Literary Corpus: The Old French* Roman de Renart. Études de langue et littérature Françaises 110. Niederdeutsche Studien 27. Amsterdam and Atlanta: Rodopi, 1996.

Singerman, R. *Antisemitic Propaganda: An Annotated Bibliography and Research Guide.* New York: Garland, 1982.

Sirkin, Y. B. Y. "*Partzufim*" (Portraits). *Reshumot* 1 (1915), 195–198.

Sladvonik, M. T. *Sefer Ma'aseh Ha-Gedolim He-Ḥadash* (The new gests of the prominent men). Piotrkow, Poland: n.p., 1925.

Slavitt, D. R., trans. *The Fables of Avianus.* Baltimore: Johns Hopkins University Press, 1993.

Slutsky, Y. "Cantonists." *EJ* 5:130–133, 1971.

Smith, J. C. "Elia Levita's Bovo Buch: A Yiddish Romance of the Early 16th Century." Unpublished dissertation. Ithaca, NY: Cornell University Press, 1968.

Smith, R. E. "A Study of the Correspondence between the Roman de Renard, Jamaican Anansi Stories, and West African Animal Tales Collected in Cultural-Area V." Unpublished dissertation. Columbus: Ohio State University, 1971.

Smoliar, L. " 'In Every Generation': A Historical Perspective of the Kishinev Pogrom" [Hebrew]. Unpublished thesis. Tel Aviv University, 2003.

Sofer, Z. "*40 Jahre 'YIVO.'* " *Fabula* 8 (1966), 260–261.

Sokolow, N. *Ishim* (Personalities). Jerusalem: Ha-Sifriyah ha-Tsiyonit, 1958.

Solinas, G. *"Da Firenza a Verona e Vicenza sul filo di una novella del 'Decameron.' "* In *La letteratura popolare nella valle padana* (501–507). Florence: Olschki, 1972.

Soriano, M., ed. *Charles Perrault: Contes.* Paris: Flammarion, 1989.

Sorieri, L. *Boccaccio's Story of Tito e Gisippo in European Literature.* New York: Institute of French Studies, 1937.

Sorkin, D. "Emancipation and Assimilation—Two Concepts and Their Application to German-Jewish History." *LBIYB* 35 (1990), 17–33.

———. "The Genesis of the Ideology of Emancipation." *LBIYB* 32 (1987), 11–40.

———. "The Rediscovery of the Eastern Jews: German Jews in the East, 1890–1918." In *Jews and Germans from 1860 to 1933* (338–361). Ed. D. Bronsen. Heidelberg: Winter, 1979.

———. *The Transformation of German Jewry 1780–1840.* New York: Oxford University Press, 1987.

Spalding, H. D., ed. *Encyclopedia of Jewish Humor from Biblical Times to the Modern Age.* New York: David, 1969.

Spector, N. B., trans. and ed. *The Complete Fables of Jean de la Fontaine*. Evanston, IL: Northwestern University Press, 1988.

Sperber, D. *Magic and Folklore in Rabbinic Literature*. Bar-Ilan Studies in Near Eastern Languages and Culture. Ramat-Gan, Israel: Bar-Ilan University Press, 1994.

———. *Minhagei Yisrael: Mekorot ve-Toldot* (Jewish customs: Sources and history). 6 vols. Jerusalem: Mossad Harav Kook, 1990–1998.

Spiegel, S. "*In Monte Dominus Videbitur:* The Martyrs of Blois and the Early Accusations of Ritual Murder" [Hebrew]. In *Mordecai M. Kaplan Jubilee Volume on the Occasion of His Seventieth Birthday* (267–287). New York: Jewish Theological Seminary of America, 1953.

Spies, O. "*Das Grimmsche Märchen Bruder 'Lustig' in arabischer Uberlieferung.*" *RJV* 2 (1951): 48–60.

———. *Orientalische Stoffe in den* Kinder und Hausmärchen *der Bruder Grimm*. Beiträge zur Sprachund Kulturgeschichte des Orients 6. Walldorf-Hessen, Germany: Vorndran, 1952.

Spraycar, R. S. "Genre and Convention in *Aucassin et Nicolette*." *RR* 76 (1985), 94–115.

Stahl, A. *Edot Mesaprot: Leket Sippurim, Ma'asiyot Am u-Phitgamim mi-Mekorot she-bi-Khtav ve-she-be-Al Pe* (Tales of ethnic groups: A collection of stories, folktales, and proverbs from written and oral sources). Tel Aviv: Am Oved, 1976.

———, ed. *Stories of Faith and Morals: 36 Jewish Folktales* [Hebrew]. IFAPS 17. Haifa: Ethnological Museum and Folklore Archives, 1976.

Staiman, M. *Niggun: Stories behind the Chasidic Songs That Inspire Jews*. Northvale, NJ: Aronson, 1994.

Stanislawski, M. "Jewish Apostasy in Russia: A Tentative Typology." In *Jewish Apostasy in the Modern World* (189–205). Ed. T. M. Endelman. New York: Holmes & Meier, 1987.

———. *Tsar Nicholas I and the Jews: The Transformation of Jewish Society in Russia 1825–1855*. Philadelphia: Jewish Publication Society, 1983.

Starck, H., and P. Billerbeck. "*Kommentar zum neuen Testament aus Talmud und Midrasch.*" 5 vols. Munich: Beck, 1922–1956.

Steinmaetz, R. H. *Exemple und Auslegung: Studien zu den Sieben Weisen Meistern*. Scrinum Friburgense 14. Freiburg: Universitätsverlag Freiburg Schweiz, 2000.

Steinsaltz, A. *A Guide to Jewish Prayer*. Trans. R. Toueg. New York: Schocken, 2000.

———. *Opening the Tanya: Discovering the Moral and Mystical Teaching of a Classic Work of Kabbalah*. San Francisco: Jossey-Bass, 2003.

Steinschneider, M. "*Purim und Parodie*." *MGWJ* 46 (1902), 176–187, 275–280, 372–376, 473–478, 567–582; 47 (1903), 84–89, 169–180, 279–286, 360–370, 468–474; 48 (1904), 242–247, 504–509.

Stephani, C., ed. and trans. *Ostjüdische Märchen*. Die Märchen der Weltliteratur. Munich: Diederichs, 1998.

Stephenson, R. M. "Conflict and Control Functions of Humor." *AJS* 56 (1951), 569–574.

Sternbach, L. *The Kavya-Portions in the Katha-Literature (Pañcatantra, Hitopadesa, Vikramacarita, Vetalapancavimsatika and Sukasaptati): An Analysis*. Vol. 1: Pancatantra. Delhi: Meharchand Lachhmandas, 1971.

Steudel, A. "God and Belial." In *The Dead Sea Scrolls Fifty Years after Their Discovery, Proceedings of the Jerusalem Congress, July 20–25, 1997* (332–340). Ed. L. H. Schiffman, E. Tov, and J. C. VanderKam. Jerusalem: Israel Exploration Society, 2000.

Stewart, A. M. "The Tale of King Lear in Scots." *AUR* 46 (1975–1976), 205–210.
Stewart, P. J., and A. Strathern. *Witchcraft, Sorcery, Rumor, and Gossip*. Cambridge, UK: Cambridge University Press, 2004.
Stokker, K. *Folklore Fights the Nazis: Humor in Occupied Norway, 1940–1945*. Madison: University of Wisconsin Press, 1995.
Stökl Ben Ezra, D. *The Impact of Yom Kippur on Early Christianity: The Day of Atonement from Second Temple Judaism to the Fifth Century*. Wissenschaftliche Untersuchungen zum Neuen Testament 163. Tübingen, Germany: Mohr Siebeck, 2003.
Strauch, G. L. *Dukus Horant: Wanderer zwischen zwei Welten*. Amsterdam and Atlanta: Rodopi, 1990.
Strauss, H. A., ed. *A Bibliography on Antisemitism: The Library of the Zentrum für Antisemitismusforschung at the Technical University of Berlin*. 4 vols. Munich: Saur, 1989.
Stuart, K., and Limusishiden. *China's Monguor Minority: Ethnography and Folktales*. Sino-Platonic Papers 59. Philadelphia: Department of Middle East and Asian Studies, University of Pennsylvania, 1994.
Stuckenbruck, L. T. "The 'Angels' and 'Giants' of Genesis 6:1–4 in Second and Third Century BCE Jewish Interpretation: Reflections on the Posture of Early Apocalyptic Traditions." *DSD* 7 (2000), 354–377.
Stuckrad, K. von. *Frömmigkeit und Wissenschaft: Astrologie in Tanach, Qumran und frührabbinischer Literatur*. Europäische Hochschulschriften Series 22. Theology 572. Frankfurt am Main: Lang, 1996.
Stutchkoff, N. *Thesaurus of the Yiddish Languague* [Yiddish]. Ed. M. Weinreich. New York: Yiddish Scientific Institute, 1950.
Suchomski, J. *"Delectaio" und "Utilitas": Ein Beitrag zum Verständnis mittleaterlicher komischer Literatur*. Bern and München: Francke, 1975.
Sühling, F. *Die Taube als Religiöses Symbol im Christlichen Altertum*. Römische Quartalschrift für christliche Altertumskunde und für Kirchengeschichte Suppl. 24 (1930).
Swan, C., and W. Hooper, eds. and trans. *Gesta Romanorum: Or, Entertaining Moral Stories*. New York: Dover, 1959. [Originally published 1876.]
Sysyn, F. E. "The Khmelnytsky Uprising and Ukrainian Nation-Building." *JUS* 17 (1992), 141–169.
Szmeruk [Shmeruk], C. "The Earliest Aramaic and Yiddish Version of the 'Song of the Kid' (*Khad Gadye*)." In *The Field of Yiddish: Studies in Yiddish Language, Folklore, and Literature* (214–218). Ed. U. Weinreich. New York: Linguistic Circle of New York, Columbia University, 1954.
Tabory, J. *Jewish Prayer and the Yearly Cycle: A List of Articles. Kiryat Sefer: Collected Essays. Articles and Book Reviews in Jewish Studies* Suppl. 64 (1992–1993).
———. *Mekorot le-Toldot ha-Tefilah* (Sources for the history of the prayer). Jerusalem: Author, 1993.
Talmon, S. "Waiting for the Messiah: The Spiritual Universe of the Qumran Covenanters." In *Judaisms and Their Messiahs at the Turn of the Christian Era* (111–137). Ed. J. Neusner, W. S. Green, and E. S. Frerichs. Cambridge, UK: Cambridge University Press, 1987.
Ta-Shema, I. M. "Havdalah." *EJ* 7:1481–1482, 1971.

———. "Miriam's Well—French Customs Relating to the Sabbath Third Meal." *JSJT* 4 (1984–1985), 251–270. [Reprinted in Ta-Shema, *Early Franco-German Ritual and Custom* (201–220) (Hebrew). Jerusalem: Magnes Press, 1992.]

———. "Notes to 'Hymns from Qumran'" [Hebrew]. *Tarbiz* 55 (1985–1986), 440–442.

———. "Some Notes on the Origins of the '*Kaddish Yatom*' (Orphan's Kaddish)" [Hebrew]. *Tarbiz* 53 (1984), 559–568. [Reprinted in Ta-Shema, *Early Franco-German Ritual and Custom* (220–310) (Hebrew). Jerusalem: Magnes Press, 1992.]

Tauscher, R. *Volksmärchen aus dem Jeyporeland*. Supplement—Serie zu Fabula Zeitschrift für Erzählforschung Reihe A, Text, Band 2. Berlin: de Gruyter, 1959.

Taylor, A. "A Classification of Formula Tales." *JAF* 46 (1933), 77–88.

———. "The Predestined Wife." *Fabula* 2 (1958), 45–82.

———. *The Proverb and an Index to the Proverb*. Hatboro, PA: Folklore Associates, 1962. [Originally published 1931.]

———. "Review of *Varifrån Kommer Våra Sagor*. By Waldemar Liungman (Djursholm: Förlagsaktiebolaget Vald Literatur, 1952)." *JAF* 67 (1954), 92–94.

Tcherikover, E. *Antisemitism un pogromen in Ukraine, 1917–1918: Tsu der geshikhte fun Ukrainish-Yidishe batsihungen* (Anti-Semitism and pogroms in the Ukraine, 1917–1918: Toward a history of the Ukrainian-Jewish Relations). Berlin: Mizreh-Yidishn Historishn Arkhiv, 1923.

———. *Yehudim be-'Itot Mahapekhah* (Jews in periods of revolution). Tel Aviv: Am Oved, 1957.

Tcherikower [Tcherikover], E. *The Pogroms in the Ukraine in 1919* [Yiddish]. New York: YIVO Institute for Jewish Research, 1965.

Teitelbaum, E. *An Anthology of Jewish Humor and Maxims: A Compilation of Anecdotes, Parables, Fables, and Proverbs*. Ed. A. Burstein. New York: Pardes, 1945.

Teitelbaum, M. *Der Rabh von Ladi: Sein Leben, Werke und System sowie die Geschichte der Sekte Chabad* [Hebrew]. 2 vols. Warsaw: Tuschijah, 1910–1913.

Telsner, D. *The Kaddish: Its History and Significance*. Ed. G. A. Sivan. Jerusalem: Tal Orot Institute, 1995.

Tendlau, A. M. *Das der Sagen und Legenden jüdisher Vorzeit*. Frankfurt am Main: Kauffmann, 1873.

———. *Fellmeiers Abende: Märchen und Geschichte*. Frankfurt am Main: Literarische Ansalt, 1856.

———. *Sprichwörter und Redensarten deutsch-jüdischer Vorzeit*. Hildesheim, Germany: Georg Olms, 1980. [Originally published 1860.]

Testen, D. "Semitic Terms for 'Myrtle': A Study in Covert Cognates." *JNES* 57 (1998), 281–290.

Teugels, I. "The Creation of the Human in Rabbinic Interpretation." In *The Creation of Man and Woman: Interpretations of the Biblical Narratives in Jewish and Christian Traditions* (107–127). Ed. G. P. Luttikhuizen. Leiden: Brill, 2000.

Thalmann, R. and E. Feinermann. *Crystal Night: 9–10 November 1938*. Trans. G. Cremonesi. New York: Coward, McCann, & Geoghegan, 1974.

Theodor, J., and C. Albeck, eds. *Bereschit Rabba mit kritischen Apparat und Kommentar* [Hebrew]. 3 vols. Jerusalem: Wahrmann, 1965.

Thomas, D. W. "*Beliya 'al* in the Old Testament." In *Biblical and Patristic Studies in Memory of Robert Pierce Casey* (11–19). Ed. J. N. Birdsall and R. W. Thomson. Freiburg, Germany: Herder, 1963.

Thomas, G. *The Tall Tale and Philippe d'Alcripe: An Analysis of the Tall Tale Genre with Particular Reference to Philippe d'Alcripe's La Nouvelle Fabrique des Excellents Traits de Vérité, Together with an Annotated Translation of the Work.* St. John's, NL: Department of Folklore, Memorial University of Newfoundland, 1977.

Thompson, R. C. *Semitic Magic: Its Origins and Development.* Luzac's Oriental Religious Series 3. London: Luzac, 1908.

Thompson, S. *The Folktale.* New York: Holt, Rinehart & Winston, 1946.

———. *Motif-Index of Folk-Literature: A Classification of Narrative Elements in Folktales, Ballads, Myths, Fables, Mediaeval Romances, Exempla, Fabliaux, Jest-Books and Local Legends.* Rev. ed. 6 vols. Bloomington: Indiana University Press, 1955–1958.

———. "Type." *The Funk & Wagnalls Standard Dictonary of Folklore Mythology and Legend* (2:1137–1138). New York: Funk & Wagnalls, 1950.

———, and J. Balys. *The Oral Tales of India.* Indiana University Publications Folklore Series 10. Bloomington: Indiana University Press, 1958.

———, and W. E. Roberts. *Types of Indic Oral Tales: India, Pakistan, and Ceylon.* FFC 180. Helsinki: Suomalainen Tiedeakatemia, 1960.

Thomson, J. A. *Irony: An Historical Introduction.* Cambridge, MA: Harvard University Press, 1927.

Thorson-Collins, K. H. "Color Terms in British Folk Tales and Legends: A Computerized Analysis of Their Grammatical Functions and Symbolic Attributions." Unpublished dissertation. Philadelphia: University of Pennsylvania, 1979.

Thrower, J. *Marxist-Leninist "Scientific Atheism" and the Study of Religion and Atheism in the USSR.* Religion and Reason 25. New York: Mouton, 1983.

Timm, E. *Paris un Wiene: Ein jiddischer Stanzeroman des 16.* Jahrhunderts von (oder aus dem Umkreis von) Elia Levita. Tübingen, Germany: Niemeyer, 1996.

Ting, N. T. *A Type Index of Chinese Folktales in the Oral Tradition and Major Works of Non-Religious Classical Literature.* FFC 223. Helsinki: Suomalainen Tiedeakatemia, 1978.

Tomkowiak, I. *"Fuchs und Glieder (AaTh 154)." EM* 5:489–494, 1987.

Tomson, P. J., ed. *Abraham ibn Ezra savant universel: Conférences données au colloque de l'Institutum Iudaicum Namur, 25 November 1999.* Brussels: Institutum Iudaicum, 2000.

Torijano, P. A. *Solomon the Esoteric King: From King to Magus, Development of a Tradition.* Supplements to the JSJ Suppl. 73 (2002).

Touati, C. *"Le mamzer, la zona et le statut des enfants issus d'un mariage mixte en droit rabbinique; étude d'un développement historique."* In *Le Juifs au regard de l'histoire: Mélanges en l'honneur de Bernhard Blumenkranz* (37–47). Ed. G. Dahan. Paris: Picard, 1985.

———. *"Le problème du Kol Nidrey et le responsum inédit de Gersonide" (Lévi ben Gershom). REJ* 154 (1995), 327–341.

Trachtenberg, J. *The Devil and the Jews: The Medieval Conception of the Jews and Its Relation to Modern Antisemitism.* New Haven, CT: Yale University Press, 1943.

———. *Jewish Magic and Superstition: A Study in Folk Religion.* New York: Behrman's Jewish Book House, 1939.

Traxler, J. P. "Hide and Get Lost: Tristan in the Labyrinth of Incognito." *Tristiana* 20 (2000), 1–15.

Trotin, J. *"Vers et prose dans* Aucassin et Nicolette." *Romania* 97 (1976), 481–508.
Trunk, I. *Der Freilechster id in der velt (el Juido mas alegre del mundo)* (The happiest Jew in the world). Buenos Aires: "Idbuj," de la Associación Pro-Escuelas Laicas Israelitas en la Argentina, 1953.

———. *Ghetto Lodz* [Yiddish]. Yad Vashem Martyrs and Heroes Memorial Authority, Jerusalem, and YIVO Institute for Jewish Research, New York, Joint Documentary Project Monograph Series 1. New York: YIVO, 1962.

———. *Judenrat: The Jewish Councils in Eastern Europe under Nazi Occupation.* New York: Macmillan, 1972. [Reprint ed. Lincoln: University of Nebraska Press, 1996.]

Tsitron, S. L. *Meshumadim: Tipn un siluetn funm neontn over* (Apostates: Types and silhouettes from the recent past). 4 parts. 2 vols. Warsaw: Tsentral Farlag, 1923.

Tubach, F. C. *Index Exemplorum: A Handbook of Medieval Religious Tales.* FFC 204. Helsinki: Suomalainen Tiedeaktemia, 1969.

Turner, V. "Betwixt and Between: The Liminal Period in *Rites de Passage.*" In *The Forest of Symbols: Aspects of Ndembu Ritual* (93–111). Ithaca, NY: Cornell University Press, 1967.

———. "Color Classification in Ndembu Ritual: A Problem in Primitive Classification." In *The Forest of Symbols: Aspects of Ndembu Ritual* (59–92). Ithaca, NY: Cornell University Press, 1967.

———. *From Ritual to Theatre: The Human Seriousness of Play.* New York: PAJ, 1982.

———. *The Ritual Process: Structure and Anti-Structure.* Chicago: Aldine, 1969.

Turniansky, C., ed. and trans. *Glikl: Memoirs 1691–1719* [Hebrew and Yiddish]. Jerusalem: Zalman Shazar Center for Jewish History; The Ben-Zion Dinur Center for Research in Jewish History, The Hebrew University of Jerusalem, 2006.

———. "Literary Sources in the Memoirs of Glikl Hamel" [Yiddish]. In *Studies in Jewish Culture in Honour of Chone Shmeruk* (153–177). Ed. I. Bartal, E. Mendelsohn, and C. Turniansky. Jerusalem: Zalman Shazar Center for Jewish History, 1993.

Twersky, J. *Be-Ḥatsar ha-Zaddik* (In the zaddik's court). Tel Aviv: Zion, 1979.

Tyrrell, G. N. M. *Apparitions.* London: Duckworth, 1953.

Ulfgard, H. *The Story of Sukkot: The Setting, Shaping, and Sequel of the Biblical Feast of Tabernacles.* Beiträge zur Geschichte dere Biblischen Exegese 34. Tübingen, Germany: Mohr Siebeck, 1998.

Ulmer, R. *A Synoptic Edition of Pesiqta Rabbati Based upon Extant Manuscripts and the Editio Princeps.* 2 vols. South Florida Studies in the History of Judaism. Atlanta: Scholars Press, 1997.

Unger, M. "The Internal Life in the Lodz Ghetto 1940–1944." Unpublished dissertation. Jerusalem: Hebrew University, 1997.

———. *The Last Ghetto: Life in the Lodz Getto 1940–1944.* Jerusalem: Yad Vashem, 1995.

———. "Religion and Religious Institutions in the Lodz Ghetto." In *Remembering for the Future: The Holocaust in an Age of Genocide* (335–385). Ed. J. K. Roth, E. Maxwell, and M. Levy. New York: Palgrave, 2001.

Upadhyaya, H. S. "Indic Background of *The Book of Sindibad.*" *AFS* 27–28 (1968), 101–129.

Urbach, E. E. "Political and Social Tendencies in Talmudic Concepts of Charity" [Hebrew]. *Zion* 16 (1951), 1–27.

———. *The Sages: Their Concepts and Beliefs.* Trans. I. Abrahams. 2 vols. Jerusalem: Magnes Press, 1975.

———, ed. *Sefer Arugat Habosem: Auctore A Abraham b. R. Azriel (saec. XIII)*. 4 vols. Jerusalem: Mekize Nirdamim, 1939–1967.

Uther, H. J. *"Fuchs." EM* 5:447–486, 1987.

———, ed. *Grimms Kinder- und Hausmärchen*. 4 vols. Die Märchen der Weltliteratur. Munich: Diederichs, 1996.

———. *The Types of International Folktales: A Classification and Bibliography, Based on the System of Antti Aarne and Stith Thompson*. FFC 284–286. 3 parts. Helsinki: Suomalainen Tiedeakatemia, 2004.

Uziel, B. *"Ha-Folklor Shel ha-Yehudim ha-Sefardim"* (The folklore of the Sephardic Jews). *Reshumot* 5 (1927), 324–337.

Vail, Y. T., *Haggadah shel Pesah: Ha-Marbe le-Saper* (Passover Haggadah: The more one tells [the better]). Karlsrue, 1791. [Reprint ed. Jerusalem: Feldhaim, 2002.]

Varty, K. "Animal Fable and Fabulous Animal: The Evolution of the Species with Specific Reference to the Foxy Kind." *BYBFS* 3 (1991), 5–14.

———. "Back to the Beginning of the *Romans de Renart*." *NMS* 29 (1985): 44–72.

———. "The Death and Resurrection of Reynard in Medieval Literature and Art." *NMS* 10 (1966), 70–93.

———. "The Earliest Illustrated English Editions of 'Reynard the Fox' and Their Links with the Earliest Illustrated Continental Editions." In *Reynaert, Reynard, Reynke: Studien zu einem mittelalterlichen Tierepos* (160–195). Niederdeutsche Studien 27. Ed. J. Goossens and T. Sodmann. Cologne and Vienna: Böhlau, 1980.

———. *Reynard, Renart, Reinaert and Other Foxes in Medieval England: The Iconographic Evidence. A Study of the Illustrating of Fox Lore and Reynard the Fox Stories in England during the Middle Ages*. Amsterdam: Amsterdam University, 1999.

———, ed. *Reynard the Fox: Social Engagement and Cultural Metamorphoses in the Beast Epic from the Middle Ages to the Present*. New York: Berghahm, 2000.

———. *Reynard the Fox, a Study of the Fox in Medieval English Art*. Leicester, UK: Leicester University Press, 1967.

———. *The* Roman de Renart: *A Guide to Scholarly Work*. Lenham, MD: Scarecrow Press, 1998.

Vedder, R. *"Die Illustrationen in den frühen Drucken des Reynke de Vos."* In *Reynaert, Reynard, Reynke: Studien zu einem mittelalterlichen Tierepos* (196–248). Niederdeutsche Studien 27. Ed. J. Goossens and T. Sodmann. Cologne and Vienna: Böhlau, 1980.

Veining, N. *"Dos Poylishe Folkslid 'Wojna zydowska.'" FS* 3 (1929), 412–465.

Velikovsky, I. *Worlds in Collision*. Garden City, NY: Doubleday, 1950.

Vidar, N. *"Be'etyah shel Gimatria Anti-Nozrit ve-Anti-Islamit"* (An anti-Christian and anti-Islamic *Gematria*). *Sinai* 76 (1975), 1–14.

Vinaver, C. *Anthology of Hassidic Music*. Ed. E. Schleifer. Jerusalem: Music Research Center, Hebrew University of Jerusalem, 1985.

Virtanen, R. "Camus' *Le Malentendu* and Some Analogues." *CL* 10 (1958), 232–240.

Volkov, S. "The Dynamics of Dissimilation." In *The Jewish Response to German Culture* (195–211). Ed. J. Reinharz and W. Schatzberg. Hanover, NH: University Press of New England, 1985.

———. *Jüdisches Leben und Antisemitismus im 19. und 20. Jahrhundert*. Munich: Beck, 1990.

Vollmann, B. K. "Unibos." *DLMV* 10 (1999), 80–86.
Wachs, S. P. "Aleinu: Rabbinic Theology in Biblical Language." *CJ* 42, no. 1 (1989), 46–49.
Wagenaar-Nolthenius, H. *"Der Planctus Iudei und der Gesang jüdischer Märtyrer in Blois anno 1171."* In *Mélsnges offerts à René Crozet à l'occasion de son soixante-dixième anniversaire* (2:881–885). Ed. P. Gallais and Y. J. Riou. Poitiers, France: Société d'Etudes Médiévales, 1966.
Wahrmann, N. *The Holidays and Festivals of the Jewish People (Their Customs and Symbols)* [Hebrew]. Jerusalem: Achiasaf, 1959.
Walker, W. S., and A. E. Uysal. "An Ancient God in Modern Turkey: Some Aspects of the Cult of Hizir." *JAF* 86 (1973), 286–289.
Wander, K. F. W. *Deutsches Sprichwörter-Lexikon: Ein Hausschatz für das deutsche Volk.* Leipzig, Germany: Brockhaus, 1873.
Wanwild, M., ed. *Ba ync Jid'n: księga zbiorowa folkloru i filologji* (Among us Jews: An anthology of folklore and philology) [Yiddish]. Warsaw: Graubard, 1923.
Warnbud, N. *Neḥemyah Ba'a Guf: Sippuro shel 'Eglon* (Nehemyah the Heavy-Set: The story of a wagon driver). Ed. Z. Baharav. Tel Aviv: Alef, 1976.
Warren, R. P. *Selected Poems: 1923–1943.* New York: Harcourt, Brace, 1944.
Waters, W. G., trans. *The Nights of Straparola.* 2 vols. London: Lawrence & Bullen, 1894.
Wattenwyl, A. von, and H. Zollinger. "Color Terms Salience and Neurophysiology of Color Vision." *AA* 81 (1979), 279–288.
Waxman, M. *A History of Jewish Literature.* 5 vols. New York: Yoseloff, 1933.
Weber, M. *The Theory of Social and Economic Organization.* Trans. A. M. Henderson and T. Parsons. New York: Oxford University Press, 1947.
Weinberg, D. H. *Between Tradition and Modernity: Haim Zhitlowski, Simon Dubnow, Ahad Ha-Am, and the Shaping of Modern Jewish Identity.* New York: Holmes & Meier, 1996.
Weinberg, R. "Anti-Jewish Violence and Revolution in the Late Imperial Russia: Odessa, 1905." In *Riots and Pogroms* (56–88). Ed. P. R. Brass. New York: New York University Press, 1996.
Weinberger, L. J., ed. *Twilight of a Golden Age: Selected Poems of Abraham Ibn Ezra.* Judaic Studies Series. Tuscaloosa: University of Alabama Press, 1997.
Weinert, W. *Die Typen der griechisch-römischen Fabel mit einer Einleitung über das Wesen der Fabel.* FFC 56. Helsinki: Suomalainen Tiedeakatemia, 1925.
Weinfeld, M. *Social Justice in Ancient Israel and in the Ancient Near East.* Jerusalem: Magnes Press; and Minneapolis: Fortress Press, 1995.
Weinig, N. "B. W. Segel's Folkloristic Papers: A Bibliography" [Yiddish]. *JB* 3 (1932), 92–93.
———. "Necrology—Benjamin Wolf Segel" [Yiddish]. *JB* 3 (1932), 91.
Weinreich, B. S. "Four Yiddish Variants of the Master Thief Tale." In *The Field of Yiddish* (1:199–213). Ed. U. Weinreich. New York: Linguistic Circle of New York, 1954.
———. "Modern Yiddish Folktales." *JFER* 14 nos. 1–2 (1992), 14–15.
———. "The Prophet Elijah in Modern Yiddish Folktales." Unpublished masters' thesis. New York: Columbia University, 1957.
———. "Toward a Structural Analysis of Yiddish Proverbs." *YAJSS* 17 (1978), 1–20. [Reprinted in *The Wisdom of the Many* (65–85). Ed W. Meider and A. Dundes. New York: Garland, 1981.]

―――, ed. *Yiddish Folktales*. Trans. L. Wolf. Pantheon Fairy Tale and Folklore Library. New York: Pantheon Books and Yivo Institute for Jewish Research, 1998.

Weinreich, M. *Bilder fun der yiddisher literaturgeshikhte: Fun di onhevbn biz Mendele Mekher-Seforim* (Snapshots from the history of Yiddish literature from its beginnings until Mendele Mokher-Sefarim).Vilnius, Lithuania: "Tomor," 1928.

―――. *History of the Yiddish Language*. Trans. S. Noble, with the assistance of J. A. Fishman. Chicago: University of Chicago Press, 1980.

[Weinreich, U., and K. G. Mlotek.] *"Lider"* (Songs). *YF* 1 (1954), 4–10.

―――. *"Lider." YF* 1, no 2. (1955), 27–32.

Weinreich, U., and B. Weinreich. *Yiddish Language and Folklore: A Selected Bibliography for Research*. Janua Linguarum 10. The Hague: Mouton, 1959.

Weinryb, B. D. "The Beginnings of East-European Jewry in Legend and Historiography." In *Studies and Essays in Honor of Abraham A. Neuman* (445–502). Ed. M. Ben-Horin, B. D. Weinryb, and S. Zeitlin. Leiden: Brill; Philadelphia: Dropsie College, 1962.

―――. "East European Immigration to the United States." *JQR* 45 (1955), 497–528.

―――. "The Hebrew Chronicles on Bohdan Khmel'nyts'ki and the Cossack-Polish War." *HUS* 1 (1977), 153–177.

―――. *The Jews of Poland: A Social and Economic History of the Jewish Community in Poland from 1100 to 1800*. Philadelphia: Jewish Publication Society, 1972.

Weinstein, E. *Grandma Esther Relates. . . .* Ed. Z. Kagan. IFAPS 4. Haifa: Ethnological Museum and Folklore Archives and Haifa Municipality, 1964.

Weiss, J. "Beginning of Hasidism" [Hebrew]. *Zion* 16 (1951), 46–105.

―――. *Studies in East European Jewish Mysticism and Hasidism*. Ed. D. Goldstein. London: Littman Library of Jewish Civilization, 1997.

Weiss, Y. *Citizenship and Ethnicity: German Jews and Polish Jews* [Hebrew]. Jerusalem: Hebrew University Magnes Press, 2000.

―――. *Deutsche und Polnische Juden vor dem Holocaust: Jüdische Identität zwischen Staatsbürgerschaft und Ethnizität 1933–1940*. Schriftrnreihe der Vierteljahrshefte für Zeitgeschichte 81. Munich: Oldenbourg, 2000.

―――. "The 'Emigration Effort' or 'Repatriation': The Issue of the Relationship between Jewish-Polish Emigrants and the Jewish-German Establishment." In *Probing the Depths of German Antisemitism: German Society and the Persecution of the Jews, 1933–1941* (360–370). Ed. D. Bankier. New York: Berghahn; Jerusalem: Yad Vashem, Leo Baeck Institute, 2000.

―――. "Polish and German Jews between Hitler's Rise to Power and the Outbreak of the Second World War." *LBIYB* 44 (1999), 205–223.

Weisweiler, M. *Von Kalifen Spassmachern und klugen Haremsdamen: Arabischer Humor, aus altararabischen Quellen*. Düsseldorf and Cologne: Diederichs, 1963.

Weitzman, M. *"The Origin of the Qaddish."* In *Hebrew Scholarship and the Medieval World* (131–137). Ed. M. de Lange. Cambridge, UK: Cambridge University Press, 2001.

Wells, D. A. "Die biblischen Wörter im 'Unibos': Ein Beitrag zur Bedeutungsforschung und zum Verständnis des Antiklerikalismus im Frümittelalter." In *Kleinere Erzählformen im Mittelalter: Paderborner Colloquium 1987* (83–88). Schriften der Universität-Gesamthochschule-Paderborn 10. Ed. K. Grubmüller, L. P. Johnson, and H. H. Steinhoff. Paderborn, Germany: Schöningh, 1988.

Werner, E. "Melito of Sardes, First Poet of Deicide." *HUCA* 37 (1966), 191–210.

———. "Zur Textgeschichte der Improperia." In *Festschrift Bruno Stäblein zum 70. Geburtstag* (274–286). Ed. M. Ruhnke. Kassel, Germany: Bärenreiter-Verlag, 1967.

Werses, S. "*S. An-Ski's 'Tsvishn Tsvey Veltn' (Der Dybbuk / 'Beyn Shney Olamot')*" (Hadybbuk / Between two worlds: A Textual History) (99–185). In *Studies in Yiddish Literature and Folklore, Research Projects of the Institute of Jewish Studies Monograph Series* 7. Jerusalem: Hebrew University, 1986.

Werthheimer, J. *Unwelcome Strangers: East European Jews in Imperial Germany*. New York: Oxford University Press, 1987.

Wesselski, A. "Das Geschenk der Lebensjahre." *AO* 10 (1938), 79–114.

———. *Der Hodscha Nasreddin: Türkische, arabische, berberische, maltesische, sizilianische, kalabrische, kroatische, serbische und griechische Märlein und Schwänke*. 2 vols. Weimer, Germany: Duncker, 1911.

West, R. *Narrative, Authority, and Law*. Ann Arbor: University of Michigan Press, 1993.

Whiting, B. J. *Modern Proverbs and Proverbial Sayings*. Cambridge, MA: Harvard University Press, 1989.

Whitney, B. L. *Theodicy: An Annotated Bibliography on the Problem of Evil 1960–1990*. New York: Garland, 1993.

Wieder, N. " 'Kol Nidre': The Retroactive and Prospective Formulas." In *Michtam leDavid: Rabbi David Ochs Memorial Volume (1905–1975)* [Hebrew] (189–209). Ed. Y. Gilat and E. Stern. Ramat Gan, Israel: Bar-Ilan University, 1978.

———. "The Old Palestinian Ritual—New Sources." *JJS* 4 (1953), 30–37, 65–73.

Wienert, W. *Die Typen der griechischen-römischen Fabel, mit einer Einleitung über das Wesen der Fabel*. FFC 56. Helsinki: Suomalainen Tiedeakatemia, 1925.

Wienker-Piepho, S. "*Kettenmärchen*." *EM* 7:1194–1201, 1993.

Wieseltier, L. *Kaddish*. New York: Knopf, 1998.

Williams, C., and T. D. Sfikas, eds. *Ethnicity and Nationalism in Russia, the CIS and the Baltic States*. Brookfield, VT: Ashgate, 1999.

Wills, L. M. *The Jewish Novel in the Ancient World*. Ithaca, NY: Cornell University Press, 1995.

Wilson, D. *Rothschild: The Wealth and Power of a Dynasty*. New York: Scribner's, 1988.

Winsted, E. O. "The Self-Sacrificing Child." *Folk-Lore* 57 (1946), 139–150.

Wischnitzer, R. *The Architecture of the European Synagogue*. Philadelphia: Jewish Publication Society of America, 1964.

Wise, D. S. *Kaddish: Its Meaning and Practice*. Jerusalem: Author, 1997.

Wisse, R. S., ed. *The I. L. Peretz Reader*. New York: Schocken, 1990.

Wistinetzki, J., ed. *Das Buch der Frommen nach der Rezension in Cod. de Rossi No. 1133*. 2nd ed. Frankfurt am Main: Wahrmann, 1924.

Wistrich, R. S., ed. *Demonizing the Other: Antisemitism, Racism, and Xenophobia*. Studies in Antisemitism 4. Amsterdam: Hardwood Academic, 1999.

Wolfson, E. R. "Hai Gaon's Letter and Commentary on 'Aleynu': Further Evidence of Moses de Leon's Pseudepigraphic Activity." *JQR* 81 (1991), 365–410.

Wolterbeek, M. *Comic Tales of the Middle Ages: An Anthology and Commentary*. Contribution to the Study of World Literature 39. New York: Greenwood Press, 1991.

———, ed. and trans. "'Unibos': The Earliest Full-Length Fabliau (Text and Translation)." *Comitatus* 16 (1985), 46–76.

Wright, C. S., and J. B. Holloway, eds. *Tales within Tales: Apuleius through Time*. New York: AMS Press, 2000.
Wygodzki, S. "Nathanson, Joseph Saul." *EJ* 12:866–868, 1971.
Wyler, S. "Old English Colour Terms and Berlin and Kay's Theory of Basic Colour Terms." In *Modes of Interpretation: Essays Presented to Ernst Leisi on the Occasion of His 65th Birthday* (41–55). Ed. R. J. Watts and U. Weidmann. Tübingen, Germany: Gunter Narr, 1984.
Wyrozumski, J. "Jews in Medieval Poland." In *The Jews of Old Poland, 1000–1795* (13–22). Ed. A. Polonsky, J. Basista, and A. Link-Lenczowski. London: Tauris, in association with the Institute for Polish-Jewish Studies (Oxford), 1993.
Yaari, A. "Berdichev." *EJ* 4:589–591, 1971.
———. *Passover Haggadah: From the Earliest Printed Edition to 1960*. Jerusalem: Berger & Wahrman, 1960.
———. "R. Eliezer Paver, Life and Works" [Hebrew]. *KS* 35 (1960), 499–520.
Yahuda, I. B. S. E. *Proverbia Arabica e libris et populi sermone* [Hebrew]. 2 vols. Jerusalem: Society for Palestinian History and Ethnography, 1932–1934. [Reprint ed. Jerusalem: H. Bra'un, 1989 or 1990.]
Yamamoto, D. *The Boundaries of the Human in Medieval English Literature*. Oxford, UK: Oxford University Press, 2000.
Yarimi, Y. *Me'Aggadot Teiman: Mi-Sippurei Rabbi Yehudah ben Rabbi Aharon Yarimi z"l* (From the legends of Yemen: Some of the tales of the late Rabbi Yehudah ben Rabbi Aharon Yarimi). Ed. A. Yarimi. Ramat Gan, Israel: Editor, 1978.
Yassif, E. "Analysis of the Narrative Art of 'Megillat Ahimaaz," [Hebrew]. *JSHL* 4 (1984), 18–42.
———, ed. *The Book of Memory That Is the Chronicles of Jerahme'el* [Hebrew]. Tel Aviv: Chaim Rosenberg School of Jewish Studies, Tel Aviv University, 2001.
———. "Folktales in 'Megillat Ahimaaz' and Their Transformation in Medieval Oral Tradition" [Hebrew]. In *The A. M. Habermann Memorial Volume* (40–56). Ed. Z. Malachi. Lod, Israel: Habermann Institute for Literary Research, 1983.
———. *The Hebrew Folktale: History, Genre, Meaning* [Hebrew]. Jerusalem: Bialik Institute, 1994. [Also published as *The Hebrew Folktale: History, Genre, Meaning*. Trans. J. S. Teitelbaum. Folklore Studies in Translation. Bloomington: Indiana University Press, 1999.]
———. "Parables of Solomon" [Hebrew]. *JSHL* 9 (1986), 357–373.
Yehoshua, B. Z. *The Father's Will: Thirteen Folktales from Afghanistan, Related by Rafael Yehoshua-Raz* [Hebrew]. IFAPS 24. Ed. Z. Kagan. Haifa: Ethnological Museum and Folklore Archives and Haifa Municipality, 1969.
Yehuda, Z. A. "The Ritual and the Concept *Havdalah*." *Judaism* 43 (1994), 78–86.
Yenesovitch, I. "*Sippurei Helem ve-ha-Sifrut ha-Yehudit*" (Chelm tales and Jewish literature). In *Yizkor Book in Memory of Chelem* (563–568). Ed. S. Kanc and M. Grinberg. N.p.: Irgun Yots'ei Helem be-Yisrael uve-Artson ha-Brit, 1980 or 1981.
Yoffie, L. R. C. "Songs of the 'Twelve Numbers' and the Hebrew Chant of 'Echod Mi Yodea.'" *JAF* 62 (1949), 382–411.
Yohannan, J. D. *Joseph and Potiphar's Wife in World Literature: An Anthology of the Story of the Chaste Youth and the Lustful Stepmother*. New York: New Direction, 1968.
Yudlov, I. *The Haggadah Thesaurus: Bibliography of Passover Haggadot from the Beginning of Hebrew Printing until 1960*. Jerusalem: Magnes, 1997.

Yuval, I. *"Two Nations in Your Womb": Perceptions of Jews and Christians* [Hebrew]. Tel Aviv: Am Oved, 2000.

Zafiropoulos, C. A. *Ethics in Aesop's Fables: The Augustana Collection.* Mnemosyne: Bibliotheca Classica Batava Suppl. 216. Leiden: Brill, 2001.

Zalevsky, S. "The Revelation of God to Solomon in Gibeon" [Hebrew]. *Tarbiz* 42 (1973), 224–227.

Zalkin, M. *A New Dawn: The Jewish Enlightenment in the Russian Empire—Social Aspects* [Hebrew]. Jerusalem: Hebrew University Magnes Press, 2000.

Zalmanoff, S., ed. *Sefer Hanigunim: Book of Chasidic Songs* [Hebrew and Yiddish]. 2nd ed. Brooklyn: Nichoach, 1957.

Zborowski, M., and E. Herzog. *Life Is with People: The Culture of the Shtetl.* New York: Schocken, 1962. [Originally published 1952.]

Zeltser, F. R. *Hershele Ostropoler: Beshriben alle zayne ḥokhmes un alle zayne vertlekh, vos er hat iber gilozt. Men darf nit geyen in teriater fun gilekhter, yeder zol loyfen zayne ḥokhmes kofin far azoy vayne gelt vet er vissen vie zikh tsu firen oyf der velt* (R. Hershele Ostropoler: All his pranks and all his jokes that he uttered are written down. There is no need to go to comic theater. Each person can run and buy his own [book of] wit, for much less money, and would know how to handle himself among people). Warsaw: [Morgenstern], 1884.

Zevin, S. Y., ed. *Sippurei Ḥasidim: Mekhunasim mi-Pi Sefarim umi-Pi Sofrim* (Hasidic tales: Collected from books and authors). 3rd and 4th eds. 2 vols. Tel Aviv: Tsiyoni, 1959.

Zeydel, E. H. *Ecbasis cuiusdam captivi per tropologiam. Escape of a Certain Captive Told in a Figurative Manner.* University of North Carolina Studies in the Germanic Languages and Literatures 46. Chapel Hill: University of North Carolina Press, 1964.

Zfatman, S., ed. *Ma'asiyyot kesem mi-pi yehudei mizraḥ Eiropa/Yidishe vunder-ma'asiyyot fun mizrakh-eirope* (Yiddish wonder tales from East Europe). Trans. Y. Birstein and I. Basok. Tel Aviv: Hakibbutz Hameuchad, 1998.

———. *Ma'asiyyot kesem / vunder-ma'asiyyot* (Magical tales) [Hebrew and Yiddish]. Trans. Y. Birstein and I. Basok. Tel Aviv: Hakibbutz Hameuchad, 1998.

———. *The Marriage of a Mortal Man and a She-Demon: The Transformation of a Motif in the Folk Narrative of Ashkenazi Jewry in the Sixteenth–Nineteenth Centuries* [Hebrew]. Jerusalem: Akademon Press, 1987.

———. "The Mayse-Bukh: An Old Yiddish Literary Genre" [Hebrew]. *S/L* 28 (1979), 126–52.

———. *Yiddish Narrative Prose from Its Beginnings to "Shivhei ha-Besht" (1504–1814): An Annotated Bibliography.* Research Projects of the Institute of Jewish Studies Monograph 6. Jerusalem: Hebrew University, 1985.

Zfatman-Biller, S. "Yiddish Narrative Prose from Its Beginning to 'Shivhei Habesht' (1504–1814)." 2 vols. Unpublished dissertation. Jerusalem: Hebrew University, 1983.

Zibrt, C. *Ohlas obradnich pisni velikonocnich* (Haggadah: Chad Gadja, Echad mi Iodea). Prague: Nakladem Akademickeho Spolku "Kapper," 1928.

Zimmels, H. J. *Magicians, Theologians, and Doctors.* London: Goldston, 1952.

Zinberg, I. *A History of Jewish Literature.* 12 vols. Trans. and ed. B. Martin. Cincinnati, OH: Hebrew Union College; New York: Ktav, 1974–1978.

Ziolkowski, J. M. "A Medieval 'Little Claus and Big Claus': A *Fabliau* from before

Fabliaux?" The World and Its Rival: Essays on Literary Imagination in Honor of Per Nykrog (1–37). Études de Langue et Littéraqture Française Publiées 172. Ed. K. Karczewska and T. Conley. Amsterdam and Atlanta: Rodopi, 1999.

Zipes, J. *Why Fairy Tales Stick: The Evolution and Relevance of a Genre*. New York: Routledge, 2006.

Zlotnik [Avida], Y. L. [Zlothnik, J. L.]. *"Me-aggadot ha-Shabat u-Minhageah"* (Sabbath legends and customs). *Sinai* 13, nos. 1–2 (1950), 75–89.

Zobel, M. *Gottes Gesalbter: Der Messias und die messianische Zeit in Talmud und Midrasch*. Berlin: Schocken, 1938.

Zohary, M. *Plants of the Bible: A Complete Handbook to All the Plants with 200 Full Color Plates Taken in the Natural Habitat*. Cambridge, UK: Cambridge University Press, 1982.

Zuckermandel, M. S. *Tosephta. Based on the Erfurt and Vienna Codices*. With S. Lieberman, "Supplement to the Tosephta." New edition. Jerusalem: Wahrmann Books, 1970.

Zuckerman, M., G. Stillman, and M. Herbst, eds. *The Three Great Classic Writers of Modern Yiddish Literature: Selected Works of Mendele Moykher-Sforim*. N.p.: Pangloss Press, 1991.

Zulay, M. *"Le-ḥeker ha-Sidur ve-ha-Minhagim"* (Toward the study of the prayer book and customs). In *Sefer Assaf: Kovetz Ma'amarei Meḥkar* (The Assaf book: A collection of studies) (302–315). Ed. M. D. Cassuto, J. Klausner, and Y. Gutman. Jerusalem: Mossad Harav Kook, 1953.

Zunz, L. *Die gottesdienstlichen Vorträge der Juden: Historisch Entwickelt* [Hebrew]. Ed. C. Albek. Jerusalem: Bialik Institute, 1954. [Originally published 1832; reprint ed. 1892.]

Motif Indexes

A. Mythological Motifs

Number	Motif	IFA Tale(s)
A101	"Supreme god"	7755, 8794, 14026
A154	"Drink of the gods"	960
A165.2.2	"Birds as messengers of gods"	11165
*A183.2	"Messiah invoked"	14460
A187.1	"God as judge of men"	14026
*A582	"Messiah: cultural hero (divinity) who is expected to come"	6306, 14460
A661	"Heaven"	14026, 21022
A661.0.1	"Gate of heaven"	19585, 21022
*A661.0.6	"Angel as porter of heaven"	19585
*A661.0.1.3.1	"Angels measure on a heavenly scale the good and the bad deeds"	19585
A671	"Hell"	19585, 21022
A671.1	"Doorkeeper of hell"	19585, 21022
*A694.2	"Jewish paradise"	5377, 14264, 19585, 19892
*A694.3	"Selling one's share in paradise"	19892
A1321	"Men and animals readjust span of life"	6655
A1674	"Tribal characteristics—stealing"	4541
A1674.1	"Why it is not a sin for a gypsy to steal"	4541

B. Animals

Number	Motif	IFA Tale(s)
B103.0.4	"Gold-producing snake"	8004n
B103.0.4.1	"Grateful snake gives gold piece daily"	8004n
B184.6	"Magic sheep"	8915
B211.1.5	"Speaking cow"	8021
B211.2.3	"Speaking bear"	5361
B211.5	"Speaking fish"	8889
B274	"Animal as judge"	8004
B279	"Covenant with animals"	8004

Number	Motif	IFA Tale(s)
B336	"Helpful animal killed (threatened) by ungrateful hero"	8004
*B339.2	"Death of a pet animal (bird) from eating gold coins and precious stones"	18130
B412	"Helpful sheep"	8915
B435.4	"Helpful bear"	5361
B450	"Helpful birds"	11165
B457.1	"Helpful dove"	11165
B491.1	"Helpful serpent"	8004n
B592	"Animals bequeath characteristics to man"	6655
B765.6.1	"Snake drinks milk"	8004n

C. Tabu

Number	Motif	IFA Tale(s)
*C51.1.16	"Tabu: stopping a prayer before its completion"	9797
C58	"Tabu: profaning sacred day"	5609
C115	"Tabu: adultery"	7755
C220	"Tabu: eating certain things"	18140
C221.1.1.5	"Tabu: eating pork"	18140
C300	"Looking tabu"	4024
*C416	"Tabu: harboring suspicion"	18601
C423.1	"Tabu: disclosing source of magic power"	4024
C428	"Tabu: revealing time of Messiah's advent"	14460
C560	"Tabu: things not to be done by certain class"	7755
C575	"Tabus of bastards"	8794
C611	"Forbidden chamber"	779
C631	"Tabu: breaking the Sabbath"	5609, 13908
C631.1	"Tabu: journeying on Sabbath"	13908
*C631.7	"Carrying money on person on Sabbath"	13908
C786	"Tabu: stealing"	7755
C897.3	"Calculating time of Messiah's advent"	14460

D. Magic

Number	Motif	IFA Tale(s)
D42.2	"Spirit takes shape of man"	8792
D133.1	"Transformation: man to cow"	5361n, 8792
D133.2	"Transformation: man to bull"	8021
D313.3	"Transformation: bear to person"	5361
D333	"Transformation: bovine animal to a person"	8972
D475.4.5	"Tears become jewels"	7202
D672	"Obstacle flight"	8021

D771	"Disenchantment by use of magic object"	8792
D812.12	"Magic object received from dwarf"	7202
D817	"Magic object received from a grateful person"	7202
*D849.6.1	"Magic object under skull's tongue"	779
D1030.1	"Food supplied by magic"	4024
D1040	"Magic drink"	960
D1046	"Magic wine"	960
D1133	"Magic house"	7290
D1133.1	"House created by magic"	7290
D1162	"Magic light"	8915
D1171.8	"Magic bottle"	960, 4024
D1174	"Magic box"	7202
D1242.4	"Magic oil"	4024
D1252.3	"Magic gold"	8256
D1271	"Magic fire"	6098
*D1273.7	"Magic script"	7912
D1472	"Food and drink from magic object"	4024
D1472.1.17	"Magic bottle supplies drink"	960
D1482	"Magic object produces oil"	4024
D1500.1.2.2	"Magic healing ashes"	6098
D1502.1.1	"Charm for headache"	7912
D1652.1	"Inexhaustible food"	4024
D1652.1.0.1	"Miraculously increasing of small quantity of victuals or drinks to feed a great number of people"	4024
D1652.2	"Inexhaustible drink"	960
D1652.5	"Inexhaustible vessel"	960, 4024
D1711	"Magicians"	779
D1713	"Magic power of hermit (saint, yogi)"	4024, 8792
*D1739.3	"Magic power maintained by holding a third-generation rabbi in captivity"	779
D1792	"Magic results from curse"	8257
D1810.0.3	"Magic knowledge of saints and holy men"	708
D1810.8	"Magic knowledge from dream"	4032
D1810.8.2	"Information received through dream"	3892, 4032
D1810.8.3	"Warning in dreams"	4032, 8255
D1810.8.4	"Solution to problem discovered in dream"	18132
D1812.5.1.12.1	"Howling of dog as bad omen"	11165
D1814.2	"Advice from dream"	4032, 8255, 8257
D1817.2	"Saints magically detect crime"	708
D1820.1	"Magic sight of saints"	708
D1825.1	"Second sight"	708
D1840	"Magic invulnerability"	3892n
D1840.1	"Magic invulnerability of saints"	3892n

D1841.3.3	"Sacred book or manuscript does not burn in fire"	11165
D1925.3	"Barrenness removed by prayer"	18132
D2071	"Evil eye"	3892
D2072	"Magic paralysis"	8257
*D2082.3	"Magic glance reduces estate to ashes"	6098
*D2082.4	"Magic glance reduces flour mill to ashes"	6098
D2105	"Provisions magically furnished"	4024
D2176	"Exorcising by magic"	8792
D2176.3	"Evil spirit exorcised"	8792
D2176.3.2	"Evil spirit exorcised by religious ceremony"	8792
D2188	"Magic disappearance"	7290
*D2188.4	"House vanishes"	7290
D2601.2.4	"Death by cursing"	8257

E. The Dead

Number	Motif	IFA Tale(s)
E261.1.2	"Speaking skull tells about previous life, reveals future events"	779
*E286	"Souls haunt synagogue"	18159
E323.2	"Dead mother returns to aid persecuted children"	8915
*E323.8	"Dead mother prays for her children"	8256
E327	"Dead father's friendly return"	18159
*E327.6	"Dead father returns to ask someone to pray for his soul"	18159
E334.3	"Ghost of a person abandoned by faithless lover"	708
*E338.4	"Non-malevolent ghosts haunt synagogue"	18159
E341.3	"Dead grateful for prayers"	18159
*E351.1	"Dead returns and writes a check"	18159
E363	"Ghost returns to aid living"	708
E365.1	"Return from the dead to grant forgiveness"	708
*E365.2	"Return from the dead to request anniversary prayer"	18159
E402	"Mysterious ghostlike noises heard"	8256
E402.1.1	"Vocal sounds of ghost of human being"	8915
E411	"Dead cannot rest because of sin"	18159
E411.0.6	"Earth rejects buried body"	21021
*E411.0.6.1	"Water rejects corpse"	21021
*E411.0.6.2	"Fire does not consume corpse"	21021
E421.3	"Luminous ghosts"	8915
E422.4.5	"Revenant in male dress"	18159
E425.1	"Revenant as woman"	708
E425.2	"Revenant as man"	18159

E544.1.1	"Ghost leaves behind a crucifix"	3222
E545	"The dead speak"	4032, 8915, 18159
*E545.12.1	"The dead directs man to a hidden treasure"	4032
*E599.4.1	"Ghost asks for payment to be given to a living person (from one who does not know that asker has died)"	708
*E606.3	"Reincarnation for restoration of soul (*tikkun*)"	2634, 2644, 5361
E612.8	"Reincarnation as bear"	5361
E731.8	"Soul in form of bear"	5361
E754	"Saved souls"	18159
E755	"Destination of the soul"	19585, 21022
E755.1	"Souls in Heaven"	4541, 18159, 19585
*E755.1.5	"Souls of the pious accompany Moses to Mt. Sinai"	7755
E755.2	"Souls in Hell (Hades)"	19585
E783.5	"Vital head speaks"	779n

F. Marvels

Number	Motif	IFA Tale(s)
F111.2	"Voyage to Land of Promise"	18592, 19949
F172	"No time, no birth, no death in other world"	708
F177.1	"Court in other world"	19585
F183	"Foods in other world"	237
F321.0.1	"Child sold to fairies"	4813
F400	"Spirits and demons (general)"	8792
F401.2	"Luminous spirits"	8915
F402	"Evil spirits"	8792
F402.1.4	"Demons assume human forms in order to deceive"	8792
F403.2	"Spirits help mortal"	708
F451	"Dwarf"	7202
F451.3.4	"Dwarfs as workmen"	7202
F470	"Night-spirits"	8792
F480.2	"Serpent as house-spirit"	8004n
F541.1.1	"Eyes flash fire"	6098
F574	"Luminous person"	2361
F585	"Phantoms"	8915
F610	"Remarkably strong man"	3892
F701	"Land of plenty"	18592, 19949
*F701.3	"America, the land of gold"	18592, 19949
F731.1	"Island covered with gold"	19949
F761.5.1	"City paved with seeds of gold"	19949
F771.1.1.1	"Castles paved with gold and gems"	19949
F851	"Extraordinary food"	237

F883.1	"Extraordinary book"	11165
F883.1.4	"Books unscathed by water and fire"	11165
F900	"Extraordinary occurrences"	2361, 11165
F900.1.2	"Miracles on first night of Passover"	7290
*F900.1.4	"Miracles during Purim"	3892
F932	"Extraordinary occurrences connected with rivers"	3892
F964	"Extraordinary behavior of fire"	11165
F966	"Voices from Heaven (or from the air)"	8915
F969.3	"Marvelous light"	2361, 5609, 8915
F979.5.1	"Unconsumed burning bush"	11165
F989.14	"Birds hover over battlefield"	11165
F989.16	"Extraordinary swarms of birds"	11165
*F1041.1.3.7.1	"Woman dies of broken heart when deserted by fiancé"	708
F1041.1.13	"Death from shame"	708
F1068	"Realistic dream"	4032
*F1068.2.3	"Two individuals have the same dream"	4032, 8256

G. Ogres

Number	Motif	IFA Tale(s)
G200	"Witch"	38929
G302	"Demons"	8792
G303.9.9.20	"Satan entangles ram horns on altar"	4813

H. Tests

Number	Motif	IFA Tale(s)
H96.1	"Identification by tefillin"	18140
H580	"Enigmatic statements"	551
H588	"Enigmatic counsels of a father"	14962
H592	"Enigmatic statement made clear by experience"	551
H592.1	" 'Love like salt' "	7202
*H921.2	"Task set by king to daughters to determine heir to kingdom"	7202
H961	"Tasks performed by cleverness"	14264, 18601
H1210.1	"Quest assigned by father"	8021
H1242	"Youngest brother alone succeeds on quest"	8021n
*H1258	"Quest for the identity of neighbor in paradise"	5377
H1552	"Tests of generosity"	6098
*H1556.0.3	"Test of fidelity (loyalty) of citizen"	14263
H1564	"Test of hospitality"	6098

J. The Wise and the Foolish

Number	Motif	IFA Tale(s)
*J20	"Counsels proved wrong by experience"	13498
J21	"Counsels proved wise by experience"	14962, 19892
J21.2	" 'Do not act when angry' "	18140
J21.18	" 'Do not trust the over-holy' "	14962
*J21.26.1	"Buy the first thing you are offered"	19892
*J21.37.1	"Do not take a poor man's advice"	13498
*J21.53	"Judge not thy fellow until thou art come to his place [Avoth 2:4(5)]"	7612
J80	"Wisdom (knowledge) taught by parable"	7755
J121	"Ungrateful son reproved by naive action of his own son"	3364
J121.1	"Ungrateful son reproved by naive action of his own son"	3364
J151	"Wisdom from old person"	6098
J154	"Wise words of dying father"	14962
J191	"Wise men"	14962
J191.1	"Solomon as wise man"	13498
J227	"Death preferred to other evils"	14263
J260	"Choice between worth and appearance"	13498n
*J328	"People prefer their own respective troubles to those of others"	14460
J414	"Marriage with equal or with unequal"	7202, 8255
J706	"Acquisition of wealth"	18601
J751.1	"Truth the best policy"	6098
J1113	"Clever boy"	18601
J1115.2	"Clever physician"	18140
J1124	"Clever court jester"	7755
J1140	"Cleverness in detection of truth"	18136
J1141	"Confession obtained by a ruse"	18136
J1172.3	"Ungrateful animal returned to captivity"	8004
J1176.3	"Gold pieces in the honey-pot"	4032n
J1230	"Clever dividing"	13498
J1341.2	"Asking the large fish"	8889
*J1559.2.1	"God as surety"	7612
J1655.3	"Coins concealed in jar of oil (pickles)"	4032n
J1700	"Fools"	2826
J1703	"Town (country) of fools"	2826
*J1705.5	"Foolish rabbi"	13909
J1795.2*	"Man finds mirror, thinks it is a picture of his grandfather . . ."	20439n

J1820	"Inappropriate action from misunderstanding"	18156
J1832	"Jumping into the river after their comrade"	7127
J1853.1.1	"Money from the broken statue"	8256
J2076	"Absurdly modest wish"	4815
J2093	"Valuables given away or sold for trifle"	4541
J2102.3	"Bold man aims at fly: hurts his head"	21022
J2326	"The student from paradise"	2826
J2333	"The sledges turned in the direction of the journey"	6814
J2469.2	"Taking the prescription"	7912

K. Deceptions

Number	Motif	IFA Tale(s)
K113	"Pseudo-magic resuscitating object sold"	7127
K231.1	"Refusal to perform part in mutual agreement"	8004
*K231.16	"Banker refuses to return deposit, claiming it was never made"	13908
K235.1	"Fox is promised chickens: is driven off by dogs"	8004
K310	"Thief in disguise"	779, 3955
*K311.2 (Weinreich)	"Thief disguises as Elijah on Passover eve"	3955
K331.2	"Owner put to sleep and goods stolen"	3955
K420	"Thief loses his goods or is detected"	3955, 7812
K713.1	"Deception into allowing oneself to be tied"	8004
K842	"Dupe persuaded to take prisoner's place in a sack: killed"	7127
K1546	"Woman warns lover of husband by parody incantation"	6976
K1561	"The husband meets the paramour in the wife's place"	14962
K1600	"Deceiver falls into own trap"	551
K1667	"Unjust banker deceived into delivering deposits by making him expect even larger"	4032n, 13908
K1667.1.1	"Retrieving the buried treasure"	4032n
K1700	"Deception through bluffing"	3955, 6976
K1800	"Deception by disguise"	3955, 7211
K1810.1	"Disguise by putting on clothes (carrying accoutrements) of certain person"	3955
K1812	"King in disguise"	7812
K1812.1	"Incognito king helped by humble man"	4815
K1816.0.4	"Scholar disguised as a rustic along road answers questions of school inspector in Greek, Latin, and Hebrew"	13498n

K1816.9	"Disguise as peasant"	3892
K1816.9.1	"Wise men disguised as peasants"	6098
K1817.1	"Disguise as beggar"	4541, 6098, 8256, 13498n
K1817.4	"Disguise as merchant"	779, 5361
*K1817.6	"A Jew disguises as a gentile"	3892
K1821.8	"Disguise as old man"	3955
K1827.1	"Disguise as saint"	3955
*K1827.3	"Disguise as Elijah the Prophet"	3955
*K1827.4	"A Jew disguises as a gentile"	4541
K1860	"Deception by feigned death (sleep)"	7127
K1865	"Death feigned to establish reputation of false relic"	7127
K1900	"Impostures"	2826
*K1915.4	"Lover tricks an unloved bridegroom out of the marriage ceremony"	18132
K1930	"Treacherous impostors"	3955
K1965	"Sham wise man"	7812
K1961.1.5	"Sham holy man"	3955
*K1961.6	"Sham cantor"	6976
K2058	"Pretended piety"	3955
K2058.1	"Apparently pious man (sadhu) a thief"	3955
*K2059	"Pretended villainy"	13908
K2100	"False accusation"	18136
K2127	"False accusation of theft"	7812
K2248	"Treacherous minister"	7812

L. Reversal of Fortune

Number	Motif	IFA Tale(s)
L10	"Victorious youngest son"	8021n
L50	"Victorious youngest daughter"	7202
L111.1	"Exile returns and succeeds"	8915
L111.2	"Foundling hero"	8915
L111.3	"Widow's son as hero"	8915
L111.4	"Orphan hero"	5793, 8915, 18601
L111.4.2	"Orphan heroine"	8256
L162	"Lowly heroine marries prince (king)"	18132
*L212.5	"Choice of charitable life over prosperity"	19949
L217.1	"Former poverty chosen over new riches"	19949
L300	"Triumph of the weak"	8794
L400	"Pride brought low"	8794

M. Ordaining the Future

Number	Motif	IFA Tale(s)
M21	"King Lear judgment"	7202
M200	"Bargain and promises"	6976
M205	"Breaking of bargains or promises"	8004, 18132
*M241.3	"Dividing the winnings: between the clever person and the visitor who is about to discover his bluff"	6976
M363.2	"Prophecy: coming of Messiah"	14460
M410	"Pronouncement of curses"	8257
*M411. 24	"Curse by a rabbi"	8257
M444	"Curse of childlessness"	708, 18132, 18140

N. Chance and Fate

Number	Motif	IFA Tale(s)
*N103	"The peak of good luck"	12214
*N104	"The bottom of misfortune"	12214
N111.3	"Fortune's wheel"	12214
N112	"Bad luck personified"	14260
N127.1	"Tuesday as auspicious day"	19892
N131.5	"Luck changing after change of place"	7612, 14260
N135.2.1	"Discovery of treasure brings luck"	6306, 8021
*N135.2.2	"Discovery of lost treasure as omen for loss of good luck"	12214
N203	"Lucky person"	12214, 14351
N211	"Lost object returns to its owner"	12214
N250	"Persistent bad luck"	12214, 14260
*N250.5	"Bad luck welcomes man in his new place"	14260
N275	"Criminal confesses because he thinks himself accused"	7812
N300	"Unlucky accidents"	551
N320	"Person unwittingly killed"	551
N321	"Son returning home after long absence unwittingly killed by parents"	18140
N330	"Accidental killing or death"	551
N332	"Accidental poisoning"	551
N332.1	"Man accidentally fed bread which his father has poisoned"	551
N350	"Accidental loss of property"	12214
N410	"Lucky business venture"	14351
*N427	"Man cannot hold a lowly job because of illiteracy, pursues his own business and becomes rich"	14351
*N430	"Man buys melody"	5794

N440	"Valuable secrets learned"	18601
*N445	"Valuable melody learned"	5793, 5794
N511	"Treasure in ground"	4032, 8021
N511.1.1	"Treasure buried in graves"	4032
*N511.1.14	"Treasure buried in scrap iron"	6306
N517.2	"Treasure hidden within wall (under floor) of house"	18132
N524.1	"Money is found in the dead beggar's coat"	4541
*N529.3	"Treasure found in a carcass of an animal (bird)"	18130
N530	"Discovery of treasure"	6306, 8021, 18130
N531	"Treasure discovered through dream"	4032
N531.1	"Dream of treasure on the bridge"	4032
N534	"Treasure discovered by accident"	6306, 8021, 18601
*N534.7.2	"Man plows his field and discovers treasure"	18601
N538	"Treasure pointed out by supernatural creature (fairy, etc.)"	8256, 18132
*N538.3	"Discovery of treasure as a result of a holy man's blessing"	6306
N543	"Certain person to find treasure"	8256
N550	"Unearthing hidden treasure"	4032, 8021, 18601
N610	"Accidental discovery of crime"	7812
N611.1	"Criminal accidentally detected: 'that is the first'—sham wise man"	7812
N688	"What is in the dish: 'poor crab'"	7812
*N747	"Accidental meeting of childhood friends"	3222, 18132
*N768.1	"Abandoned children accidentally discovered by good people"	8915
N774.2	"Adventures from seeking (lost) domestic beast (bull) [sheep]"	8915
*N793	"Adventure from pursuing moving light at night"	8915
N819.3.1	"Helpful speaking skull"	779
N825.2	"Old man helper"	6098, 8256
N825.3.1	"Help from old beggar woman"	551
N826	"Help from beggar"	551
*N842.2	"Shoemaker as helper"	4813, 19949
N854	"Peasant as helper"	8915
N854.1	"Peasant as foster father"	8915

P. Society

Number	Motif	IFA Tale(s)
P10	"Kings"	7202, 7211, 7812
P60	"Noble (gentle) ladies"	551

P110	"Royal ministers"	7812
*P125	"Priest is left in the cold in revenge for his mistreatment of Jews"	3892
P150	"Rich men"	779, 4815, 6306, 7612, 8021, 7755, 8257, 13498, 18132, 18601, 19892
*P150.1	"Rich women"	551
P160	"Beggars"	551, 4541, 8255, 8256
*P165	"Poor men"	779, 4541, 6306, 7290, 7612, 8021, 8794, 13498, 18592, 19892, 19949
*P165.1	"Poor women"	551, 5609, 7290, 8255, 18132, 19949
P200	"The family"	8915
P210	"Husband and wife"	3364, 8021, 8255, 8915, 14962, 18140
P230	"Parents and children"	8021, 8915
P231	"Mother and son"	551, 8915, 18140
P232	"Mother and daughter"	5609, 8256, 18132
P233	"Father and son"	3364, 8021, 8792, 14962, 18132, 18140
P233.2	"Young hero rebuked by his father"	18132
*P233.12	"Like father like son(s)"	8257
P234	"Father and daughter"	7202, 19892
P236	"Undutiful children"	3364
P251	"Brothers"	4541, 8021
P251.5.4	"Two brothers as contrasts"	8021n
P251.6.1	"Three brothers"	8021, 8257
P251.6.2	"Four brothers"	8021n
P251.6.3	"Six or seven brothers"	8921n
P251.6.4	"Eight brothers"	8021n
P251.6.5	"Nine brothers"	8021n
*P251.6.5.1	"Ten brothers"	8021n
P251.6.6	"Eleven brothers"	8021n
P251.6.7	"Twelve brothers"	8021n
P252.2	"Three sisters"	7202, 8256, 19892
*P252.2.1	"Four sisters"	8972
P253.0.3	"One sister and three (four) brothers"	8257
P291	"Grandfather"	3364
*P299	"Grandson"	3364
P310	"Friendship"	3222, 13909, 17068, 18132, 18156, 18592
*P313.2	"Separate paths of childhood friends: one rich, the other poor"	3222, 18132
P320	"Hospitality"	4815, 6098, 7290, 8256, 13909
P336	"Poor person makes great effort to entertain guests"	6098
P411	"Peasant"	8257, 8792, 8915, 18136
P412	"Shepherd"	3892, 8915

*P412.4	"Geese herder"	8915
P414	"Hunter"	4815
*P416	"Wagon driver"	5793, 7912
*P417	"Water carrier"	3892, 5377
P421	"Judge"	13909, 14026, 18136
P422	"Lawyer"	18136
*P423	"Teacher"	7612
P424	"Physician"	3364, 6306, 8021, 18140
P426.1	"Parson (priest)"	3222, 3892, 14264, 14962, 18136
*P426.4	"Rabbi"	779, 960, 3892, 4541, 5377, 5609, 5793, 7612, 7755, 7912, 8021, 8256, 8792, 9797, 14264, 14460, 18601, 19892
*P426.5	"Preacher"	8794
P427.7	"Poet"	13498
P428	"Musician"	8021
P431	"Merchant"	4441, 5361, 7612, 12214, 13908
*P436	"Junk dealer"	6814
P440	"Artisans"	3892
P441	"Tailor"	4541, 8255, 19892
P443	"Miller"	6306, 6471
P445	"Weaver"	5609
P447	"Smith"	6306
*P449	"Innkeeper"	960, 4815, 7755, 18130, 18136
P453	"Shoemaker"	4813, 8592, 19949
P456	"Carpenter"	3364
P461	"Soldiers"	7920, 8915, 12214
P475	"Robber"	5361
*P476	"Thief"	779, 3892, 3955, 4815, 7812
*P486	"Scholar"	779, 18592
P510	"Law courts"	7612
P551	"Army"	7290
P623	"Fasting (as means of distrait)"	3892, 8257
P711	"Patriotism"	7211
P715.1	"Jews"	3892, 6306, 7812, 8915
*P715.2	"A hater of Jews"	3892, 6306, 7812
*P715.3	"Jews in denial of their own culture"	6306

Q. Rewards and Punishments

Number	Motif	IFA Tale(s)
Q1	"Hospitality rewarded—opposite punished"	9797
Q1.1	"Gods (saints) in disguise reward hospitality and punish inhospitality"	6098

Q2	"Kind and unkind"	6098
Q20	"Piety rewarded"	18601
Q22	"Reward for faith"	18130
Q33	"Reward for saying prayers"	18159
*Q38.1	"Reward for helping a holy man to avoid a sinful act"	18601
Q40	"Kindness rewarded"	6098, 7202
Q42	"Generosity rewarded"	6098, 7612, 19585
*Q42.8.1	"Angel gives a man all his credit for good deeds so that the man may go to heaven"	19585
Q45	"Hospitality rewarded"	4815, 6098, 8256
Q53	"Reward for rescue"	5377, 21022
Q68.2	"Honesty rewarded"	7612
Q72	"Loyalty rewarded"	14263
Q111	"Riches as reward"	6306, 8256, 18601
Q111.2	"Riches as reward (for hospitality)"	4815, 6098
Q114	"Gifts as reward"	7812
*Q115.4	"Reward: any boon that may be asked—man asks for the removal of a competitor"	4815
Q172	"Reward: admission to heaven"	4541, 19585
Q172.2	"Man admitted to heaven for a single act of charity"	5377, 19585, 21022
Q211.8	"Punishment for desire to murder"	551
Q212	"Theft punishment"	3955
Q222.2	"Punishment for heaping indignities upon crucifix"	3222
Q223.6	"Failure to observe holiness of Sabbath punished"	5609
Q252	"Punishment for breaking betrothal"	708
Q261.1	"Intended treachery punished"	551
Q281	"Ingratitude punished"	8004
Q286	"Uncharitableness punished"	19585
Q292	"Inhospitality punished"	6098, 9797
Q292.1	"Inhospitality to saint (god) punished"	6098
Q325	"Disobedience punished"	708
Q393.2	"Gossiping punished"	5609
Q402	"Punishment of children for parents' offense"	551
Q411	"Death as punishment"	551, 7812
Q411.3	"Death of father (son, etc.) as punishment"	551
Q551.6	"Magic sickness as punishment"	708
*Q551.6.8	"Infertility as punishment"	708
Q551.7	"Magic paralysis as punishment"	8257
Q572	"Magic sickness as punishment remitted"	708
Q588	"Ungrateful son punished by having a son equally ungrateful"	3364

R. Captives and Fugitives

Number	Motif	IFA Tale(s)
R10	"Abduction"	779
R10.3	"Children abducted"	4541, 18140
R10.3.1	"Children abducted by Gypsies"	4541
R11.2.2	"Abduction by demon"	8792
*R11.2.3	"Abduction by sorcerers"	779
R130	"Rescue of abandoned or lost persons"	5377
R130.10.2	"Water carrier rescues abandoned children"	5377
R210	"Escapes"	799
R122	"Miraculous rescue"	11165
R131	"Exposed or abandoned child rescued"	5377
*R131.21	"Shoemaker rescues abandoned or sold child"	4813
R131.6	"Peasant rescues abandoned child"	8915
*R132	"Jew rescues a Jewish child from Christians"	4813
R153.4	"Mother rescues son"	8915
R168	"Angels as rescuers"	11165

S. Unnatural Cruelty

Number	Motif	IFA Tale(s)
S21	"Cruel son"	3364
S110	"Murders"	8915, 11165
S111	"Murder by poisoning"	551
S111.1	"Murder with poisoned bread"	551
S140.1	"Abandonment of aged"	3364
S268	"Child sacrificed to provide blood for cure of friend"	6098n
S301	"Children abandoned (exposed)"	5377
S321	"Destitute parents abandon children"	4813
*S351.2.2	"Abandoned child reared by peasants"	8915
S431.2	"Wife and children exposed in forest"	5377

T. Sex

Number	Motif	IFA Tale(s)
T10	"Falling in love"	18132, 18156
T22	"Predestined lovers"	18132
T22.1	"Lovers mated before birth"	18132
T22.2	"Predestined wife"	18132
T22.3	"Predestined husband"	18132
T24.1	"Love-sickness"	18132, 18156
T53	"Matchmakers"	19892

Number	Motif	IFA Tale(s)
T52.4	"Dowry given at marriage of daughter"	708, 8256, 18132, 18601
*T52.4.2	"Bride, or bride's family does not have dowry money"	708, 8256, 18132, 19892
T61.5.3	"Unborn children promised in marriage to each other"	18132
T61.4	"Betrothal ceremony"	19892
T91	"Unequals in love"	18132
T91.6	"Noble and lowly in love"	18132
T91.6.2	"King (prince) in love with a lowly girl"	18132
*T98	"Father opposed to son's marriage"	18132
T100	"Marriage"	7202, 8255, 8256, 18132, 18592, 19892
*T104.3	"Foreign prince marries princess instead of waging war"	7202
T121	"Unequal marriage"	8255
T135	"Wedding ceremony"	19892
T471	"Rape"	11165
T481	"Adultery"	7755, 14962
T640	"Illegitimate children"	8794
T670	"Adoption of children"	18140

U. The Nature of Life

Number	Motif	IFA Tale(s)
U60	"Wealth and poverty"	4541, 18592, 19949
U110	"Appearances deceive"	4541

V. Religion

Number	Motif	IFA Tale(s)
*V28	"False confession: a person confesses to a sin not committed to help a wronged person"	18601, 7612
V50	"Prayer"	4813, 6306, 8792, 8794, 9797, 14460, 18140, 18159
*V54	"Public prayer requires a quorum of ten (minyan)"	4936, 8257
*V54.1.1	"Elijah serves as a sandek"	960
*V54.3	"Apostate completes a minyan for the Yom Kippur service"	4936
*V56	"Kaddish: mourners prayer said after the death of a close relative"	8792, 18159
V60	"Funeral rites"	4541, 7612
V71	"Sabbath"	5361, 5609, 5793, 7755, 8792, 8794, 8915, 13908, 19892, 19949, 21022

Motif Indexes 605

*V71.4	"Eating the rabbi's leftovers at the third Sabbath meal"	7755
*V71.5	"Escorting the Sabbath ritual"	5361, 5793
V75.1	"Passover"	237, 7211, 7812, 7290, 7612, 7912, 8792, 18130
*V75.1.1	"Seder, the Passover eve ceremonial dinner"	7211, 7290, 7812, 8792, 18130
*V75.2	"Day of Atonement"	960, 6306, 6976, 9606, 9797
*V75.4	"Rosh Hashanah (New Year)"	9797
*V75.5	"Purim"	3892
*V75.6	"Hanukkah"	12214
*V76	"Pentecost"	960, 7755
V82	"Circumcision"	960
V85	"Religious pilgrimages"	237, 960
V97	"Studying of Torah as religious service"	9797
V112.3	"Synagogues"	4813, 6814, 8794, 11165, 18159, 19892
*V112.3.1	"Miracles at synagogue"	11165
*V119	"Shofar (a ram's horn trumpet)"	4813, 6306
*V119.1	"Shofar is blown in the synagogue on the high Holy Days"	4813
*V119.2	"Satan blocks the shofar's sound"	4813
*V119.3	"Shofar's sound is blocked: a more meritorious person deserves the honor of blowing it"	4813
*V131.3	"Phylacteries (tefillin)"	5377, 8792, 18140
*V131.4	"Prayer showl (tallit)"	5377, 8792
*V131.5	"Mezuzah"	5361, 7290
*V131.6	"Prayer book (siddur)"	5377
*V151.2	"Sacred writings: the Torah"	8257, 11165
*V151.2.1	"Desecration of the Torah"	8257, 11165
*V222.1.5	"Supernatural light rests above a righteous person"	5609
V222.3	"Saint can perceive the thoughts of another man and reveal hidden sins"	708
V223	"Saints have miraculous knowledge"	708
V223.1	"Saint gives advice"	708
V226	"Saints as hermits"	9797
V227	"Saints have divine visitors"	9797
V228	"Immunities of saints (holy men)"	3892n
V229.5	"Saint banishes demons"	8792
*V229.15.1	"Thirty-six incognito saints preserve the integrity of the world"	2361, 4541, 5609
V230	"Angel"	11165, 14026, 19585
V231.1	"Angel in bird shape"	11165
V232.1	"Angel as helper in battle"	11165

V235	"Mortal visited by angel"	9797n, 14026
*V235.4	"Mortal visited by patriarchs"	9797
*V235.5	"Mortal visited by the 'Seven Visitors' (ushpizin)"	9797
*V295	"Elijah the Prophet"	960, 7290, 8792, 18132
V315	"Belief in the atonement"	8257
V331	"Conversion to Christianity"	4936
V336	"Conversion to Judaism"	4936, 8257
*V336.1	"Jewish apostate returns to Judaism"	4936
V340	"Miracles manifested to non-believers"	11165
V350	"Conflicts between religions"	3222, 11165
V365	"Jewish traditions concerning non-Jews"	3892
V400	"Charity"	237, 4541, 5377, 7202, 7612, 14351, 19949
V410	"Charity rewarded"	4541, 7202
*V412.3	"Replaced devotional bread that was given in charity to the poor has heavenly taste"	237
*V417	"Secret charity is superior to public donation"	7612
*V439	"A charitable poor"	19949
V530	"Pilgrimages"	237
*V536	"Pilgrimage to a holy man"	960

W. Traits of Character

Number	Motif	IFA Tale(s)
W10	"Kindness"	551
W11	"Generosity"	6098, 7290, 7612
W12	"Hospitality as a virtue"	8256, 9797
W34	"Loyalty"	14263
W126	"Disobedience"	708
W154	"Ingratitude"	3364, 8004
W154.2.1	"Rescued animal threatens rescuer"	8004
W154.2.2	"Man ungrateful for rescue by animal"	8004
W158	"Inhospitality"	4815, 9797

X. Humor

Number	Motif	IFA Tale(s)
X370	"Jokes on scholars"	21022
X410	"Jokes on parsons"	3222
X441	"Parson and sexton at mass"	6976
*X501	"Jokes about community leaders"	8794

Z. Miscellaneous Groups of Motifs

Number	Motif	IFA Tale(s)
Z64	"Proverbs"	551, 6814
*Z71.0.3	"Formulistic number: two"	3222, 18529
Z71.1	"Formulistic number: three"	6098, 7202, 7612, 8256, 8255, 8257, 8792
Z71.2	"Formulistic number: four"	8792
Z71.5	"Formulistic number: seven"	779, 9797
Z71.9	"Formulistic number: thirteen"	8915
Z71.16.2	"Formulistic number: ten"	7755
Z100	"Symbolism"	18156
Z141	"Symbolic color: red"	18156
Z141.4	"Red rose as symbol of love"	18156
Z142	"Symbolic color: white"	11165, 18156
*Z142.3	"White rose as symbol of friendship"	18156

Tale Type Indexes

Sources: A. Aarne and S. Thompson, *The Types of the Folktale*; and H. J. Uther, *The Types of International Folktales* [new edition].

Number	Tale Type	IFA Tale(s)
50	"The Sick Lion"	8004n
91	"Monkey (Cat) Who Left His Heart at Home"	8004n
154	"Bear Food"	8004
154	"The Fox and His Members" (new ed.)	8004
155	"The Ungrateful Serpent Returned to Captivity"	8004
173	"Men and Animals Readjust Span of Life"	6655
173	"Human and Animal Life Spans Are Readjusted" (new ed.)	6655
285D	"Serpent (Bird) Refuses Reconciliation"	8004n
303	"The Twins or Blood Brothers"	8021n
318	"The Faithless Wife"	8021
331	"The Spirit in the Bottle"	8004
461	"Three Hairs from the Devil's Beard, III; The Questions"	8021n
480	"The Spinning-Woman by the Spring. The Kind and Unkind Girls"	8021n
503	"The Gifts of the Little People"	8021n
510	"Cinderella and Cap o' Rushes"	7202
550A	"Only One Brother Grateful"	6098
610	"The Healing Fruit"	8021n
613	"The Two Travelers (Truth and Falsehood)"	8021n
653	"The Four Skillful Brothers"	8021n
653A	"The Rarest Thing in the World"	8021n
654	"The Three Brothers"	8021
654	"The Three Agile Brothers" (new ed.)	8021
655	"The Wise Brothers"	8021n
676	"Open Sesame"	8021n
735	"The Rich Man's and the Poor Man's Fortune"	8021n
735A	"Bad Luck Imprisoned"	8021n, 14260
745A	"The Predestined Treasure"	14260n

Tale Type Indexes

750D	"Three Brothers Each Granted a Wish by an Angel Visitor"	6098, 8021
750D	"God (St. Peter) and the Three Brothers" (new ed.)	8021
760*	"The Condemned Soul"	5361
796*	"Angels on the Widow's Roof" (old ed. only)	5609
809*	"Rich Man Allowed to Stay in Heaven for a Single Deed of Charity"	21022
809**	"Old Man Repaid for Good Deeds"	21022
828	"Men and Animals Readjust Span of Life"	6655
837	"How the Wicked Lord Was Punished"	551
837	"The Beggar's Bread (new ed.)"	551
842	"The Man Who Kicked aside Riches"	14260n
842B*	"The Serpent at the Wedding"	708n
844	"The Luck-Bringing Shirt"	12214n
849*	"The Cross as Security"	7612
891A	"The Princess from the Tower Recovers Her Husband"	8021n
910	"Precepts Bought or Given Prove Correct"	8021n
910–919	"Good Precepts" [cluster]	14962n
920C	"Shooting at the Father's Corpse Test of Paternity"	8021n
923	"Love Like Salt"	7202
926	"Judgment of Solomon"	18136n
926C	"Cases Solved in a Manner Worthy of Solomon"	18136
930	"The Prophecy"	18132n
930A	"The Predestined Wife"	18132
930*E	"Predestined Marriage"	18132n
930*F	"The Well and the Weasel as Witnesses"	18132n
930*H	"An Unsuccessful Human Trial in Match-Making"	18132n
903*J	"Taming the Father-in-Law"	18132n
931	"Oedipus"	18132n
931*A	"The Legend of Judas Iscariot"	18132n
931*B	"The Legend of Saint Andeas"	18132n
931*C	"The Legend of Patricide"	18132n
933	"Gregory on the Stone"	18132n
934	"The Prince and the Storm"	18132n
939A	"Killing the Returned Soldier"	18140
940*	"The Forgiven Debt"	7612
947A	"Bad Luck Cannot Be Arrested"	14260

947A*	"Bad Luck Refuses to Desert a Man" (old ed. only)	14260
950	"Rhampsinitus"	8021n
980	"The Ungrateful Son (Previously Ungrateful Son Reproved by Naive Actions of Own Son)" (new ed.)	3364
980A	"The Half-Carpet"	3364
980B	"Wooden Drinking Cup for Old Man"	3364
1009	"Guarding the Store-Room Door"	2826n
1225	"The Man without a Head in the Bear's Den"	2826n
1242A	"Carrying Part of the Load"	13498
1242A	"Relief for the Donkey" (new ed.)	13498
1242B	"Balancing the Mealsack"	13498
1243	"The Wood Is Carried down the Hill"	2826n
1275	"The Sledges Turned"	2826n, 6814
1275	"Sledges Turned" (new ed.)	6814
1281	"Getting Rid of Unknown Animal"	2826n
1284	"Person Does Not Know Himself"	20439
1291D	"Other Objects Sent to Go by Themselves"	2826n
1296A	"Fools Go to Buy Good Weather"	2826n
1297*	"Jumping into the River after Their Comrade"	7127
1310	"Drowning the Crayfish as Punishment"	2826n
1326	"Moving the Church"	2826n
1335	"Rescuing the Moon"	2826n
1336A	"Man Does Not Recognize His Own Reflection in the Water (Mirror)"	20439
1336A	"Not Recognizing Own Reflection" (new ed.)	20439
1336B	"The Peasant, His Relatives, and the Mirror"	20439n
1337	"Peasant Visits the City"	20439
1337	"A Farmer Visits the City" (new ed.)	20439
1349N*	"Leeches Prescribed by Doctor Eaten by Patient"	7912
1349N*	"The Mistaken Prescription" (new ed.)	7912
1384	"The Husband Hunts Three Persons as Stupid as His Wife"	2826n
1525	"The Master Thief"	8021n
1530	"Holding up the Rock"	2826n
1535	"The Rich and the Poor Peasant (Unibos)" (new ed.)	7127
1540	"The Student from Paradise (Paris)"	2826
1567C	"Asking the Large Fish"	8889
1617	"Unjust Banker Deceived into Delivering Deposits"	4032n, 13908
1641	"Doctor Know-All"	7812n

Tale Type Indexes

1645	"Treasure at Home"	14260n
1645A*	"Priest Points Out Treasure"	8256
1685A	"The Stupid Son-in-Law"	5794
1696	"What Should I Have Said (Done)?"	8021n
1824	"Parody Sermon"	21021
1862	"Jokes on Doctors (Physicians)"	2826n
2010	"Ehod Mi Yodea (One; Who Knows?)"	7211n
2030	"The Old Woman and Her Pig"	7211n
2031	"Stronger and Strongest"	7211n
2031A	"The Esdras Chain"	7211n
2031A*	"Wall in Construction Collapses"	7211n
2031B	"Abraham Learns to Worship God"	7211n
2031B*	"The Most Powerful Idol"	7211n
2031C	"The Man Seeks the Greatest Being as a Husband for His Daughter"	7211n

Israel Folktale Archives

Designated by "(IFA)" after the tale type number in the text.

Number	Tale Type	IFA Tale(s)
178*C	"The Slaughtered She-Goat"	8915
*730B	"Jewish Community Miraculously Saved from Mob's Attack"	3892, 11165
736*B	"The Peak of Good Luck, the Bottom of Misfortune"	12214
745*B	"The Predestined Treasure"	14260n
750*K	"Granted Any Wish, the Jew Who Saved the King Chooses a Trifle"	4815
759*D	"Three Cases of Generosity"	7612
*771	"Desecration (Sacrilege) Punished"	8257
*776	"Divine Reward"	19892
809*–*A	"The Companion in Paradise"	5377, 7612
839*C	"Miraculous Rescue of a Person"	5361, 8915
841*B	"Treasure in a Dead Monkey"	18130
*857	"Wooer Wins Girl by Performing Tasks"	8255
910*M	"Do Not Trust a Gentile, Even Forty Years after His Death"	4032
910*N	"Do Not Trust the Over Pious"	14962
920*E	"Children's Judgment"	4032
926*E–D	"The Counterfeited Money"	18136
960*C	"Crime Punished"	8257
960*E	"The Convert"	8257
1383*A	"Foolish Woman Sold New Name by Trickster"	2826n

1565*B	"Poor Jew Steals from the Statue of the Virgin Mary"	3222
1641*D	"*Dayenu*"	7812
*1768	"Jokes about Apostates"	4936n
*1799A	"A Shammes Becomes a Millionaire"	14351
1831*C	"Ignorance of Holidays"	6976
1870*A	"Jokes on Dictators"	14263, 14264

N. P. Andreev

Source: N. P. Andreev, *Ukazatel' skazochnykh siuzhetov po sisteme aarne*.
Designated by "(Andreev)" after the tale type number in the text.

Number	Tale Type	IFA Tale(s)
154	"Peasant, Bear and Fox"	8004
155	"Old [Custom] of Bread Sale Is Being Forgotten"	8004
331	"The Spirit in the Bottle"	8004
550	"Tsarevich Ivan and the Gray Wolf"	6098
654	"Three Skillful Brothers"	8021
796*	"Angel on the Widow's Roof"	5609
923	"Like Salt"	7202
1275	"People from Poshekhon Leave Their Sledges with the Runners Pointed toward Their Destination"	6814
1535	"The Expensive Leather"	7127
1540	"A Person from the Other World"	2826

R. T. Christiansen

Source: R. T. Christiansen, *The Migratory Legend*.
Designated by "(Christiansen)" after the tale type number in the text.

Number	Tale Type	IFA Tale
6025	"Calling the Dairymaid"	8256

W. Eberhard and P. N. Boratav

Source: W. Eberhard and P. N. Boratav, *Typen Türkischer Volksmärchen*.
Designated by "(Eberhard and Boratav)" after the tale type number in the text.

Number	Tale Type	IFA Tale(s)
48	"Die Schlange und der Mann" (The Snake and the Man)	8004
110	"Hizir und die Drei Brüdere" (Hizir and the Three Brothers)	6098

311	"Der Oberastrologe" (The Serious Astrologer)	7812
256	"Der Faule Mehmet" (The Lazy Mehmet)	7202
329	"Der Spiegel" (The Mirror)	20439

H. El-Shamy

Source: H. El-Shamy, *Types of the Folktales in the Arab World*.
Designated by "(El-Shamy)" after the tale type number in the text.

Number	Tale Type	IFA Tale(s)
809*	"Rich Man Allowed to Stay in Heaven"	21022
837	"How the Wicked Lord Was Punished [Poisoner's Son Unwittingly Poisoned]"	551
930A	"The Predestined Wife"	19132
947A	"Bad Luck Cannot Be Arrested"	14260
947A*	"Bad Luck Refuses to Desert a Man"	14260
980	"The Ungrateful Son"	3364
980A	"The Half-Carpet"	3364
980B	"Wooden Drinking Cup for Old Man"	3364
1242B	"Balancing the Mealsack [with a Rock]"	13498
1535	"The Rich and the Poor Peasant (Unibos)"	7127
1540	"The Student from Paradise (Paris)"	2826
1567C	"Asking for the Large Fish"	8889
1617	"Unjust Banker Deceived into Delivering Deposits"	13908
1824	"Parody Sermon [Fabricated Holy Text]"	21021

R. Haboucha

Source: R. Haboucha, *Types and Motifs of the Judeo-Spanish Folktales*.
Designated by "(Haboucha)" after the tale type number in the text.

Number	Tale Type	IFA Tale(s)
155	"The Ungrateful Serpent Returned to Captivity"	8004
750D	"Three Brothers Each Granted a Wish by an Angel Visitor"	6098
809*	"Rich Man Allowed to Stay in Heaven"	21022
**809A	"The Two Souls on Judgment Day"	21022
837	"How the Wicked Lord Was Punished"	551
910*Q(IFA)	"Father's Counsel"	14962
926C–*A	"The Lost Purse"	18136
926*E–E	"The Thief's Gesture"	18136
930A	"The Predestined Wife"	18132
980A	"The Half-Carpet"	3364
1641*D	"*Dayenu*"	7812

H. Jason

Sources: H. Jason, "Types of Jewish-Oriental Oral Tales," *Types of Oral Tales in Israel*, and *Folktales of the Jews of Iraq*.
Designated by "(Jason)" after the tale type number in the text.

Number	Tale Type	IFA Tales(s)
155	"The Ungrateful Serpent Returned to Captivity"	8004
331	"The Spirit in the Bottle"	8004
736*B(IFA)	"The Peak of Good Luck"	12214
750D	"Three Brothers Each Granted a Wish by an Angel Visitor"	6098
754	"The Happy Friar"	12214
796*	"Angels on the Widow's Roof"	5609
809*	"Rich Man Allowed to Stay in Heaven"	21022
809*–A(IFA)	"The Companion in Paradise"	7612
828	"Men and Animals Readjust Span of Life"	6655
837	"How the Wicked Lord Was Punished"	551
*857(IFA)	"Wooer Wins Girl by Performing Tasks"	8255
*857A	"Beggar Suitor"	8255
*857A(IFA)	"Realistic Suitor's Tasks"	8255
910*M(IFA)	"Do Not Believe a Gentile, Even Forty Years after His Death"	4032
910*N	"Do Not Believe in the Over Pious"	14962
923	"Love Like Salt"	7202
926*E–D	"The Counterfeited Money"	18136
930A	"The Predestined Wife"	18132
940*	"The Forgiven Debt"	7612
947A	"Bad Luck Cannot Be Arrested"	14260
947A*	"Bad Luck Refuses to Desert a Man"	14260
980A	"The Half-Carpet"	3364
980B	"Wooden Drinking Cup for Old Man"	3364
1275*	"Travelers Lose Way and Get Turned Around"	6814
1349N*	"Leeches Prescribed by Doctor Eaten by Patient [Prescription Treated as Charm]"	7912
1540	"The Student from Paradise (Paris)"	2826
1535	"The Rich Man and the Poor Peasant"	7127
1567C	"Asking the Large Fish"	8889
1617	"Unjust Banker Deceived into Delivering Deposits"	13908
1641*D	"*Dayenu*"	7812
1824	"Parody Sermon"	21021
1831*C(IFA)	"Ignorance of Holidays"	6976

Tale Type Indexes   ❧ **615** ❧

B. Kerbelyte

Source: B. Kerbelyte, *Lietuviu Pasakojamosios Tautosakos Katalogas*.
Designated by "(Kerbelyte)" after the tale type number in the text.

Number	Tale Type	IFA Tale(s)
155	"Už Gera Piktu Užmokama" (Return Evil for Good)	8004
331	"Dvasia Butelyje" (The Bottle's Spirit)	8004

A. Kovács and B. Katalin

Source: A. Kovács and B. Katalin, *Magyar Népmesekatalógua*.
Designated by "(Kovács and Katalin)" after the tale type number in the text.

Number	Tale Type	IFA Tale
MNK1275/I*	"*A Megaforditott Kocsi*" (The Reversed Wagon)	6814

J. Krzyžanowski

Source: J. Krzyžanowski, *Polska bajka ludowa*.
Designated by "(Krzyžanowski)" after the tale type number in the text.

Number	Tale Type	IFA Tale(s)
155	"*Waż, czlowiek I Lis*" (Snake, Man and Fox)	8004
331	"*Duch w Butelce*" (Spirit in the Bottle)	8004
550	"*Ptak Zlotopióry*" (The Golden Bird)	6098
750D	"*Pan bóg gościem*" (The Lord [Is] a Visitor)	6098
796*		5609
837	"*Kara za Otrucie*" (Punishment with Poison)	551
923	"*Drogi Jak Sól*" (Dear Like Salt)	7202
930A	"*Żona z przeznaczenia*" (The Destined Wife)	18132
939A	"*Niespodzianka*" (The Surprise)	18140
1275	"*Odwrócone wozy*" (The Reversed Wagon)	6814
1535	"*Sprytny Oszuzt (Unibos)*" (The Clever Cheat)	7127
1540	"*Wyslaniec z raju*" (The Messenger from Paradise)	2826
1824	"*Parodia Kazania*" (Parody Sermon)	21021
2462	"*Wiek Ludzki*" (Human Age)	6655

U. Marzolph

Source: U. Marzolph, *Typologie des persischen Volksmärchens* and *Arabia Ridens*.
Designated by "(Marzolph)" after the tale type number in the text.

Number	Tale Type	IFA Tale(s)
155	"*Die Undankbare Schlange*" (The Ungrateful Snake)	8004
401	"*Der Gierrige*" (The Greedy)	8889
*841	"*Das Schicksal Liegt Allein Bei Gott*" (Fate Is with God Alone)	6098
1540	"*Der Bote aus der Hölle*" (The Messenger from Hell)	2826

A. Schullerus

Source: A. Schullerus, *Verzeichnis der Rumanischen Marchen und Marchenvarianten.*
Designated by "(Schullerus)" after the tale type number in the text.

Number	Tale Type	IFA Tale(s)
923	"*Wie das Salz Lieben*" (Loving Like Salt)	6098

R. E. Smith

Source: R. E. Smith, "A Study of the Correspondence."
Designated by "(Smith)" after the tale type number in the text.

Number	Tale Type	IFA Tale(s)
154	"Bear-Food"	8004

N. T. Ting

Source: N. T. Ting, *A Type Index of Chinese Folktales*
Designated by "(Ting)" after the tale type number in the text.

Number	Tale Type	IFA Tale(s)
654*	"The Smart Brothers"	8021n

F. C. Tubach

Source: F. C. Tubach, *Index Exemplorum.*
Designated by "(Tubach)" after the tale type number in the text.

Number	Tale Type	IFA Tale(s)
1501	"Deeds Weighed (King Coenred's Knight)"	19585
2001	"Father in Stable"	3364
2157	"Fortune, Wheel of"	12214
2318	"God as Security"	7612
2944	"Knight, Dead, Return of (d)"	18159
3006	"Lear, and Daughters"	7202

3367	"Money Sack Recovered from Burgher"	4032n, 13908
3388	"Monk Returns from Dead"	18159
3469	"Nicholas, St. as Security"	7612
3738	"Philip, King, Godfather of"	4032n, 13908
3914	"Prayer Asked by Dead"	18159
4006	"Purgatory, Vision of, Seen by Monk"	18159
4180	"Scale of Judgment"	19585
4198	"Scholar Saved by Alms"	19585
4256	"Serpent, Frozen"	8004

B. S. Weinreich

Source: B. S. Weinreich, "The Prophet Elijah in Modern Yiddish Folktales."
Designated by "(Weinreich)" after the tale type number in the text.

Number	Tale Type	IFA Tale(s)
46	"Thief Disguises as Elijah on Passover Eve"	3955

A. Wesselski

Source: A. Wesselski, *Der Hodscha Nasreddin*.
Designated by "(Wesselski)" after the tale type number in the text.

Number		IFA Tale
305		2826

W. Wienert

Source: W. Wienert, *Die Typen der griechischen-römischen Fabel*.
Designated by "(Wienert)" after the tale type number in the text.

Number	Tale Type	IFA Tale(s)
ET293	"Der Bauer von der Undankbaren Schlange" (The Farmer of the Ungrateful Snake)	8004
ET347	"Pferd, Rind und Hund vom Menschen Beherbergt" (Horse, Cattle and Dog Sheltered by Man)	665

Index

Note: An f *following a page number indicates an illustration. This general index covers the folktales in this volume; the commentaries and notes to the tales are indexed in volume V. Consult the motif and tale types indexes in this volume for motifs and tale types.*

abduction/kidnapping, 26–28, 207–9, 214–15
Aktionen (Nazi roundups of Jews), 141, 141n
Aleinu prayer, 422, 422n
America, immigration to, 313–14, 480–81
anecdotes. *See* humor
animal dealer, 33–35
Anshel (Amschel), 81–83, 81n
anti-Semitism, 168–70, 221–23
apostate as minyan tenth, 133–34
arrack (brandy), 236, 236n
atonement, 230

Ba'al Shem blessing, 168
bad luck, 273
bad vs. good, 338–39, 473–74
Balta fair, 2–5, 3f
bank note, counterfeit, 236–37
Barukh the carpenter, 244–46
beggars, 263–64
beggar's secret, Gentile, 207–9
beit din (Jewish court of law), 473–74, 473n
beit midrash (religious school), 144–45, 144n
bekeshe (long coat), 162, 162n
Bendzin (Poland), 192
boots made from a Torah scroll, 229–31

boy and girl who were destined for each other, 356–58, 358n
boy who was kidnapped and brought to Russia, 214–15
bundles of troubles, 306–7
burial, 28

cantor, elderly, 427
cantors (half is mine and half is yours), 437–40
captives' redemption, 186–88
catch the thief, 398–400
cemetery, 29*f*
change of place/luck, 273
charity, 92–94, 186–88, 313–14, 338, 348–51
charms, 118–19
Chelem, town of fools, 452, 455*f*
cholent (slow-cooked stew), 313, 313n
Christianity, converts from, 230
colors of flowers, meaning of, 342
Communism vs. religion, 486
complaints against God, 422
congregants, 431–32
converts to Judaism, 230, 387–88
Cossacks, 221–23
counterfeit bank note, 236–37
coveting, 326–28
curse of a short life, 229

Dayenu the minister, 381
dead, reviving of, 459–60
demons and spirits under the fingernails, 33–35
destiny in marriage, 356–58, 358n
Dniester River, 221, 223
ducats (coins), 4, 4n

619

elderly cantor, 427
elderly's wooden dishes, 245–46
Eliezer the water carrier, 334–36
Elijah the Prophet
   blessings of, 102–4
   and the vanishing house, 21–23
   visits a family, 446–47
   wine of, 102–4
emissaries from the World to Come, 452
emissaries of the Holy One, 140
Ephraim, Yosef, 21
exodus from Yampol on Purim, 152–56

face answers to face in water, 317–20
father who has lived a full life, 33, 33n
fingernails, demons and spirits under, 33–35
fireflies on Rosh Hashanah, 140–41
First World War, 76, 162–63
Fischmann, David, 192–95
flower colors, meaning of, 342
frankincense, 404

Galician Hasidism, 76, 76n
Gan Eden (Garden of Eden), 473, 473n
Gehenna (Hell), 473, 473n
Gemara (in the Babylonian and Jerusalem Talmuds), 64, 64n
Gentile beggar's secret, 207–9
Gentile who wanted to screw the Jew, 236–37
German vs. Polish Jews, 162–63
God
   complaints against, 422
   help from, 278–79
   messenger of, 365
   secret name of, 27n
   gold ingot, 168
   good deeds, 282–83
   good vs. bad, 338–39, 473–74
   gossip as worse than profaning the Sabbath, 255–57
goy (non-Jew), 214, 214n
Greidinger, Froyim (or Greidinger or Greiding), 459–60

Ḥad Gadya (Ḥtital), 192–95, 194n

haggadah (book of Passover rituals), 34, 34n, 58, 58n
halakhah (Jewish law), 162, 162n
half mine and half yours, 437–40
   Isaac, 153, 154, 155
Halperin, Yosef, 92–94
Haman, 152
hamantashen, 152, 152n
hametz (forbidden food at Passover), 58, 58n
happy man, 76–77
Hasidism, 76, 76n
Havdalah, 70, 70n, 123
Hayyim, Reb, 64–67, 437–38
ḥazzan (cantor), 140, 140n
Heaven, trial in, 338–39
Heaven, who has it better in, 473–74
heretic's death, 466
Hershele the jester, 326–28
   as a cantor, 437–38
High Holy Days, 109
historical tales
   exodus from Yampol on Purim, 152–56
   what really caused World War I, 162–63
Holocaust miracles
   fireflies on Rosh Hashanah, 140–41
   white doves, 144–45
Holy Land, and the bottle of oil, 53
house that vanished with all inhabitants, 21–23
humor
   cantors, 427, 437–40
   complaints against God, 422
   congregants, 431–32
   Elijah the Prophet, 446–47
   good vs. bad, 473–74
   half mine and half yours, 437–40
   heretics, 466
   illiteracy, 477
   immigration to America, 480–81
   Jew from Mád, 404–6
   Jewish innkeeper, 410, 412
   little fish, big fish, 418
   rabbis, 434–35
   reviving the dead, 459–60
   Stalin, 483, 486
   thievery, 446–47

town of fools, 452
Yom Kippur, 437–40
huppah (wedding canopy), 358, 358n

Ibn-Ezra, Abraham, 269–70
illiteracy, 477
immigration to America, 313–14, 480–81
impurity, name of, 27, 27n
ingot of gold, 168
innkeeper, Jewish, 410, 412
Ivan the beggar, 207–9

Jacob, 110
jesters' pew, 404, 404n, 406
Jew from Mád, 398–400
Jewish innkeeper, 410, 412
Jews, German vs. Polish, 162–63
Jews vs. non-Jews
   anti-Semitism, 168–70, 221–23
   charity, 186–88
   converts, 229–31, 387–88
   Cossacks, 221–23
   and the counterfeit bank note, 236–37
   kidnapping, 207–9, 214–15
   redemption of captives, 186–88
   righteous men, 208
   sinning, 229–31
Jew who returned to his people, 221–23
Judaism, converts to, 230, 387–88
Judenrat (Jewish council in the ghetto), 140

Kaddish prayer, 12–13, 12n, 33, 33n
kapote (long coat), 162, 162n
kapparos (chicken) ritual, 103, 103n
Karliner rebbe's prescription, 118–19
kashrut (kosher law), 319, 319n
keri' at Shema prayer, 34
Kiddush (blessing over wine), 110, 110n
kidnapping/abduction, 26–28, 207–9, 214–15
king's three daughters, 348–51
kittel (special white gown), 193–94, 193n, 195*f*
kloyz (Hasidic house of prayer), 250, 250n
knaidlach (matzah ball), 194, 194n
Kol Nidrei prayer, 133, 133n, 170, 170n

kopeck (small coin), 65, 65n
Korets, Russia, 109
Kos Eliyahu (Cup of Elijah the Prophet), 446
Kozienitz (Poland), 2, 2n
   Rebbe of, 2, 2n

lamed-vav tzadikim (one of thirty-six righteous men), 141, 208
lamed-vovnik (one of thirty-six righteous men), 255, 255n
Leib, Moses (Moshe), 58–60
little fish, big fish, 418
Lodz Ghetto, 140–41
luck, change of, 273

Mád, Jew from (Hungary), 404–6
maggid (itinerant preacher), 422
magical box, 350
magnate and *rebbetzin*, 326–28
mahzor (special prayer book), 133, 133n
maim (water), 319–20, 319n
mamaliga (cornmeal mush), 222, 222n
mamzer (misbegotten), 422
marriage, destiny in, 356–58, 358n
Master of the Universe, 27, 28
matchmaking, 250–52, 356
matzos of Rebbe Shmelke, 58–60
matzot shemurot (special matzo), 58–59
meals of the Sabbath, 123–25
melavah malkah (Sabbath end ceremony), 123, 123n
melody, 192–95
   power of, 70–71
   unforgotten, 64–67
merchant, 405*f*
messenger of God, 365
Messiah, 306–7
Messiah's shofar, 168–70, 169n
mezuzah (container of Torah passages) and wool, 21, 21n
Mielnice, 144–45
minyan (quorum of ten for prayer group), 133–34, 229, 229n
miracles
   fireflies on Rosh Hashanah, 140–41
   by rabbis, 250–52

Index

miracles *(continued)*
   white doves, 144–45
mirror reflection, 317–20
Mishnah, 64, 64n
mit der puter a rop (buttered side down), 273
mitzvah (fulfilling of a commandment), 59, 59n, 92, 215, 215n
Modeh Ani prayer, 387, 387n
mohel (circumciser), 103, 103n
money hidden in the cemetery, 387–88
Monish the cobbler, 186–88
moral tales
   Barukh the carpenter, 244–46
   beggars, 263–64
   charity, 313–14, 338
   coveting, 326–28
   flower colors, 342
   God's help, 278–79
   good deeds, 282–83
   good vs. bad, 338–39
   gossip, 255–57
   matchmaking, 250–52
   Messiah, 306–7
   mirror reflection, 317–20
   old age, 244–46
   poor man's wisdom, 269–70
   profaning the Sabbath, 255–57
   rich vs. poor, 326–28
   Ten Commandments, 326–28
   troubles, 306–7
   truth vs. trickery, 288–90
Moses, divine protection by, 156

name of impurity, 27, 27n
Nazis, 140–41, 141n, 144–45
neighbor in Paradise, 334–36
nigun (melody), 64–67, 65n, 70–71
no place to rest, 480–81
no truth in the world, 288–90

oil bottle from the Holy Land, 53
old couple and their children, 244–46
Ostropoler, Hershele, 326–28

Paradise, neighbor in, 334–36
Passover, 58, 58n, 59

See also haggadah
Pinḥas'l of Korets, Rebbe, 109–12
pious people, trust in, 398–400
place, change of, 273
poisoned cake, 282–83
Polish radicals, 192–95
Polish town, 411*f*
Polish vs. German Jews, 162–63
poor man's wisdom scorned, 269–70
poor man who became rich, 372–73
poor vs. rich, 326–28
poritz (Polish landlord), 278–79, 278n
power of the rabbi, 250–52
prayers
   Aleinu, 422, 422n
   Kaddish, 12–13, 12n, 33, 33n
   keri' at Shema, 34
   Kol Nidrei, 133, 133n, 170, 170n
   Modeh Ani, 387, 387n
   Shema, 154, 154n
prescriptions, 118–19
Pripshila (abandoned child), 221–23
profaning the Sabbath, 255–57
property, 244–46
Purim exodus from Yampol, 152–56

rabbi(s) (rebbes)
   humorous tales, 434–35
   power of, 250–52
   prescriptions by, 118–19
   who was tricked, 26–28
rebbe's kloyz (house of prayer), 250
rebbe's nigun, 70–71
rebbetzin and magnate, 326–28
redemption of captives, 186–88
reflection in a mirror, 317–20
repentance, 134
reviving the dead, 459–60
rich vs. poor, 269–70, 326–28, 372–73
righteous men, 141, 208
ring, stolen, 381
Roitbart, Melekh, 140
Rothschild, Amschel (Anshel), 81–83, 81n
Romanian War of Independence, 21
Rosh Hashanah, 109, 140–41
rosh yeshivah (head of the yeshivah), 64
Rothschild's wealth, 81–83

Index

Sabbath, 123–25, 255–57
sandak (circumciser's assistant), 103, 103n
Sanderl, Reb, 154, 155
scorned wisdom, 269–70
seder. *See* Passover
shalosh se'udos (third Sabbath meal), 123
shammes (synagogue caretaker), 2, 2n, 477
Shavuot (celebrating Moses' receiving the Ten Commandments), 102, 102n
Shema prayer, 154, 154n
shiksa (non-Jewish woman), 473–74, 473n
Shlomo and Yitzhak, 434–35
Shmelke, Rebbe, 58–60
Shmelke's matzos, 58–60
shofar of the Messiah, 168–70, 169n
shofarot (rams' horns), 169n, 171*f*, 186–88, 186n
shohet (one who slaughters animals per kosher law), 103, 103n
shtetl house, 23*f*
shtreimel (special-occasion hat), 318–19, 318n
shul (synagogue), 230, 230n
shuster (shoemaker), 313, 313n
siddur (prayer book), 334, 334n
sin(s)
    atonement for, 230
    broken engagements, 2
    disrespect for parents, 2
    forgiveness for, 2–5
    and money, 26–28
    punishment for, 2–5, 26–28
sinners, 162–63, 466
sorcery, 26–28
spirits and demons under the fingernails, 33–35
Stalin, Joseph, 483, 486
stolen ring, 381
Stoller, Henokh, 250–52
Stretyn, rabbi of, 334–36
sukkah, 109–10, 110n, 111*f*
Sukkot festival, 110–12, 110n
supernatural tales
    Balta fair, 2–5, 3*f*

demons and spirits under the fingernails, 33–35
Kaddish, 12–13, 12n, 33, 33n
oil from the Holy Land, 53
rabbi who was tricked, 26–28
of treasure, 48–49
vanishing house, 21–23

tailor who was content with his lot, 263–64
tallitot (prayer shawls), 33, 33n, 257*f*
Talmud, 64, 64n
tavern owner, 236–37
tefillin (prayer boxes), 33, 33n
Ten Commandments, 102, 102n, 326–28
thievery by pious people, 398–400
third Sabbath meal, 123–25
three complaints, 422
three young men, 363–65
Tomek, 193–94
Torah scrolls, 229–31, 231*f*
town of fools, 452
treasure, 48–49
treif (nonkosher) food, 466, 466n
trial in Heaven, 338–39
troubles, everyone prefers own, 306–7
truth vs. falsehood, 363–65
truth vs. trickery, 288–90
tzedakah (charity), 92, 92n, 338, 338n

untergeboyt (resoling shoes), 313
ushpizin (holiday guests of Sukkot), 110

vanishing house, 21–23
Vilna, synagogue of, 186, 187*f*

war
    Romanian War of Independence, 21
    World War I, 76, 162–63
water reflection, 317–20
Weilącza, 33
white flowers, red flowers, 342
wisdom of the poor man, 269–70
Wiśniowieki, Kazimierz, 398
Wlodek and Avrum, 202–4
wooden dishes for the elderly, 245–46
World War I, 76, 162–63

yahrzeit (anniversary of death), 12–13, 12n
Yampol, Purim exodus from, 152–56
Yankel, Hayyim, 207–9
yeshivah (school of higher learning), 21n, 64, 64n, 357*f*
Yitzhak, Levi, 92–94
Yitzhak and Shlomo, 434–35
Yoel, Reb, 141
Yom Kippur, 102–4, 109–10, 133–34, 133n, 170, 437–40

Yossel, Hayyim, 398–400
young men, three, 363–65

Zalman, Rabbi Shneur , 70–71
zhids (Jews), 155, 155n
zloty (Polish coin), 77, 77n
Zusha the shoemaker, 313–14

LANDS OF THE ASHKENAZIC JEWS

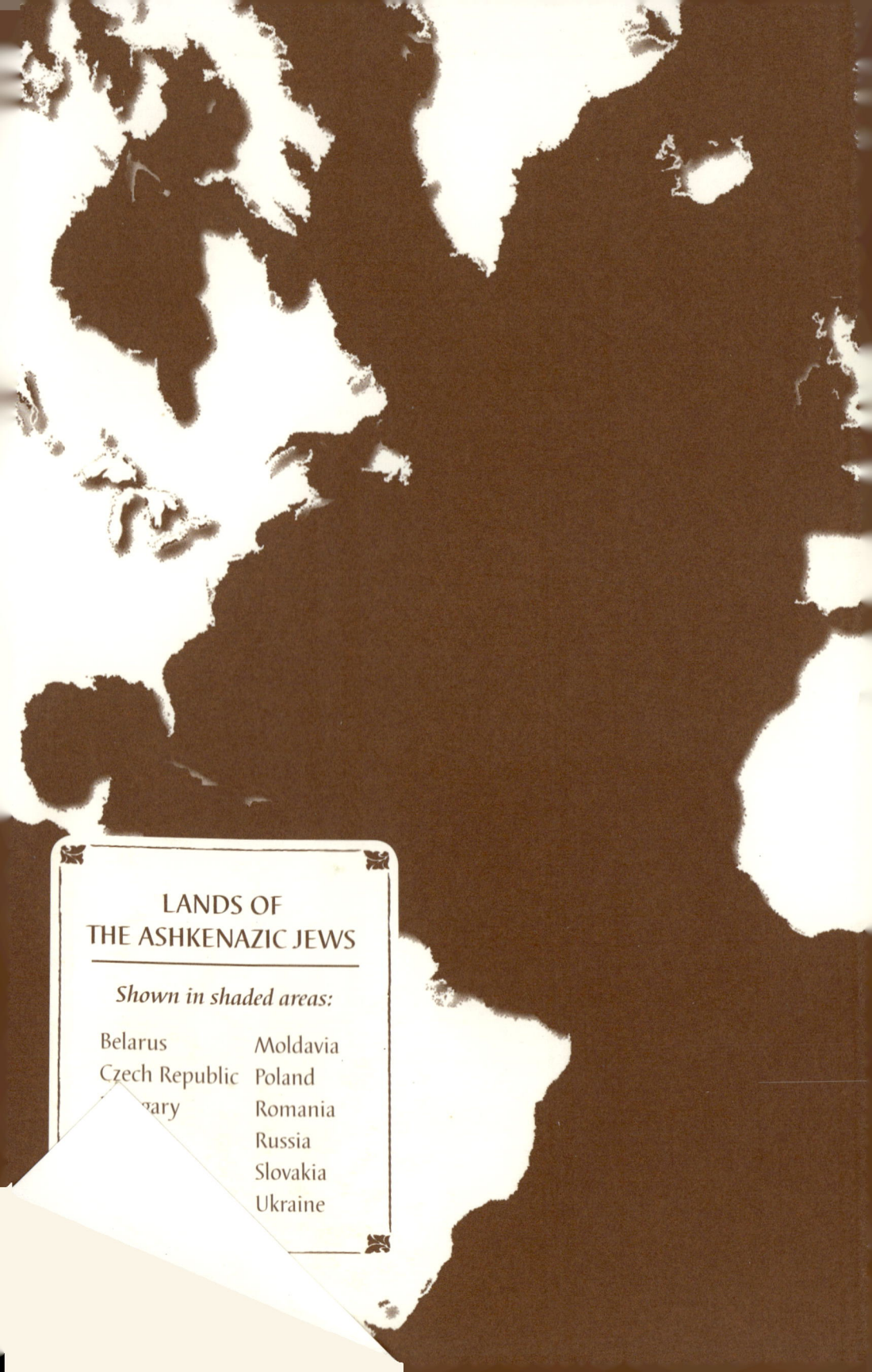

Shown in shaded areas:

Belarus
Czech Republic
Hungary
Moldavia
Poland
Romania
Russia
Slovakia
Ukraine